CONTENTS

CONTENTS

INTRODUCTION

It would probably be advisable to read the text of the novel before reading this Introduction, since inevitably, in discussing the novel, I indirectly reveal much of the plot.

True; if you look at it in one way, it had been only a summer in the country. But, considered in a profounder relation, it was part of another age, a different state of society, a segment of an existence peculiar in its aims and methods, a leaf of some mysterious volume, interpolated into the current history which Time was writing off. At one moment, the very circumstances now surrounding me—my coal-fire, and the dingy room in the bustling hotel—appeared far off and intangible. The next instant, Blithedale looked vague, as if it were at a distance both in time and space, and so shadowy, that a question might be raised whether the whole affair had been anything more than the thoughts of a speculative man. I had never before experienced a mood that so robbed the actual world of its solidity. It nevertheless involved a charm, on which—a devoted epicure of my own emotions—I resolved to pause, and enjoy the moral sillabub until quite dissolved away. (p. 146)

BY the end of this passage it is not entirely clear whether the 'dissolving away' refers to the sillabub or the writer himself. Certainly in a text in which the word 'melt' endlessly recurs and where dematerialization, attenuation, liquidation, vaporization, and other modes of desubstantiation seem variously to dominate the changing atmosphere, the facility with which a sweet dessert or a sentimental author might come to share in the prevailing tendency to fade, no matter how stickily, away could well come to seem about equal. We are certainly invited to consider what kind of writer, and what kind of writing, are here involved. Yes, it is, from one point of view, all based on 'a summer in the country'—the summer of 1841, to be precise, which Hawthorne himself spent at or in the experimental socialist (Utopian? perhaps Fourierist)[1] community at Brook Farm. But, looked at another way, and thus written another way, it might become 'a leaf of some mysterious volume, interpolated into the current history which Time was

---

[1] See explanatory note to p. 52, Charles Fourier.

writing off'. It is a somewhat curious formulation and one might wonder—who is doing the writing here? Does Time both write current history and write it off at the same time? Is history somehow at once inscribed and erased? But Time only writes by a metaphor (though I suppose we would have to say that it erases in good earnest). The writing here is being done by the narrator, Miles Coverdale, and, in likening his summer experiences to 'a leaf of some mysterious volume' interpolated into the, presumably, unmysterious history being written, and written off, by Time, he must be suggesting that, whatever it is he is now writing, it is not history—or not history as currently conceived. And indeed he calls his non-historical history of that summer in the country a Romance. Hawthorne and Romance is a subject to drown in, but for the moment I want to make only a restricted point. Why is Miles Coverdale *not* writing history? Why does he, gesturally, leave that to Time or whatever? Or perhaps it is a more mysterious kind of history he is writing—devious, surreptitious, interpolatory? The matter is important because, as I shall try to suggest, problems involved in writing American history, the history of America (and in *not* writing it—writing off, writing out), are central to this novel. And whatever his relationship—non-relationship, sly-relationship—to history might be, the narrator has here reached a state of extreme reality-deprivation in which the 'actual world' has lost its solidity and he is collapsing into a state of solipsism—not to say infantilism—in which he has unashamed recourse to a kind of primal orality in which he sucks contentedly away on the (moral!) sillabub of the dissolving self.

What *is* Hawthorne doing?

When he returns to Blithedale after his sojourn in the city, Coverdale confessedly indulges in 'odd and extravagant conjectures' (p. 206). The conjectures are 'spectral' and are all concerned with the evacuation of the real.

Either there was no such place as Blithedale, nor ever had been, nor any brotherhood of thoughtful laborers ... or else it was all changed, during my absence. It had been nothing but dream-work and enchantment. I should seek in vain for the old farm-house ... and for all that configuration of the land which I had imagined. It would be another spot, and an utter strangeness. (p. 206)

There is a peculiarly American nightmare or dread summed up in that last sentence—a sudden sense of the *complete* defamiliarization of a site or terrain thought to be known and amenable. Coverdale looks for something to anchor him and finds it in the farm. 'That, surely, was something real' (p. 206). (On another occasion he describes his determination to force Zenobia out of what he takes to be her continual acting. 'She should be compelled to give me a glimpse of something true; some nature, some passion, no matter whether right or wrong, provided it were real' (p. 405). It is that same urgent need and desire for 'something real'. As in Frost's famous poem 'For once, then, something' (1923) which ends: 'What was that whiteness? | Truth? A pebble of quartz? For once, then, something.') The reality he finds is the very earth of the farm where, for a while, he had worked. 'I could have knelt down, and have laid my breast against that soil' (p. 206). I am prompted to invoke Robert Frost again, and his powerful poem 'To Earthward' (1923), which ends:

> When stiff and sore and scarred
> I take away my hand
> From leaning on it hard
> In grass and sand,
>
> The hurt is not enough:
> I long for weight and strength
> To feel the earth as rough
> To all my length.

—though it would have to be said that this longing stems from more powerful feelings than animate the always potentially dilettante Coverdale. Nor could the sybaritic Coverdale declare with the same authority as the austerely ascetic Thoreau—'Be it life or death, we crave only Reality.'[2] But it is an important aspect of him that he should at least intermittently experience this hunger for the real, undeveloped and undernourished an appetite as it may be. What might

[2] H. D. Thoreau, *Walden* (1854; New York: Library of America edn.), 400.

constitute the real or the Real are questions hardly to be addressed in this book, where reality, whatever and wherever it may be, is—it would appear—mainly to be known by the conviction that you have not got it.

What Coverdale does get, as he prowls around Blithedale looking for something real, is a 'concourse of strange figures' (p. 209) appearing and vanishing 'confusedly', consisting of, among others, an Indian chief, the goddess Diana, a Bavarian broom girl, a negro 'of the Jim Crow order', a Kentucky woodsman, a Shaker, Shepherds of Arcadia, grim Puritans, gay Cavaliers, Revolutionary officers, a gypsy, a witch, and so on—a disorderly medley of mythical and literary figures, national types, or stereotypes, and historical representatives. The chapter is called 'The Masqueraders' and that is what they are. The atmosphere of Blithedale has been saturated with artifice of all kinds from the start, as when Coverdale feels that the presence of Zenobia 'caused our heroic enter-prise to show like an illusion, a masquerade, a pastoral, a counterfeit Arcadia, in which we grown-up men and women were making a play-day of the years that were given us to live in' (p. 21). Noting the word 'counterfeit' we may just observe that all this pseudo-'masquerading' reveals itself to be piti-fully self-conscious, juvenile, and fragile. Is *this* what has become of the deeply resonant pastoral and Arcadian images and visions of old Europe, when transplanted to the New World? It is a sort of ultimate trivialization, and here the simple presence of the Yankee farmer Silas Foster, with his 'shrewd, acrid observation', is enough to 'disenchant the scene' (p. 210). And yet there was a strong line of thought, or a persistent dream, that America might be the last best chance of, if not literalizing Arcadia, then realizing—Real-izing—Utopia. And that, surely, is not a trivial aspiration. I shall return to these matters.

Fleeing from 'the whole fantastic rabble' (p. 211) of mas-queraders—'like a mad poet hunted by chimaeras', he rather extravagantly puts it, given that it seems more like a romp at a picnic—Coverdale finally finds himself alone and effectively lost deep in the woods where

I stumbled over a heap of logs and sticks that had been cut for firewood, a great while ago, by some former possessor of the soil, and piled up square, in order to be carted or sledded away to the farm-house. But, being forgotten, they had lain there, perhaps fifty years, and possibly much longer; until, by the accumulation of moss, and leaves falling over them and decaying there, from autumn to autumn, a green mound was formed, in which the softened outline of the wood-pile was still perceptible. In the fitful mood that then swayed my mind, I found something strangely affecting in this simple circumstance. I imagined the long-dead woodman, and his long-dead wife and children, coming out of their chill graves, and essaying to make a fire with this heap of mossy fuel. (p. 212)

This is, for me, one of the key moments of the book and to explain why I think so I want, once again, to invoke some lines by Frost from a poem called, indeed, 'The Wood-Pile' (1914). Frost describes going out for a walk in the woods and deciding at a certain point that, rather than turning back for home, he will 'go on farther'—a very Frostian moment. Soon he finds himself unable to 'mark or name a place' or 'say for certain I was here | Or somewhere else'. He is not exactly lost—'I was just far from home.' And then he comes upon a pile of wood.

> It was a cord of maple, cut and split
> And piled—and measured, four by four by eight.
> And not another like it could I see.
> No runner tracks in this year's snow looped near it.
> And it was older sure than this year's cutting,
> Or even last year's or the year's before.
> The wood was grey and the bark warping off it
> And the pile somewhat sunken. . . .
>
> . . . .
>   I thought that only
> Someone who lived in turning to fresh tasks
> Could so forget his handiwork on which
> He spent himself, the labour of his axe,
> And leave it there far from a useful fireplace
> To warm the frozen swamp as best it could
> With the slow smokeless burning of decay.

The two American poets—Coverdale is a poet, albeit a minor one—both find something almost namelessly pregnant and suggestive when they come across an abandoned wood-pile. Their somewhat disoriented, non-orientated state recapitulates in little—echoes if you like—the ontological situation of the original settlers of the land who would have found themselves, not lost exactly, but, with names and markers not yet affixed, definitely and definitively 'far from home', perhaps having to develop a sense of where they were from the knowledge of where they were not. The wood-pile, marked in both cases by 'decay', serves as both a sort of commemorial mound to 'some former possessor of the soil', and a reminder of the labour, the 'tasks', involved in the settling and domesticating (fuel essential for the 'useful fireplace'—the home) of the land. The 'axe' is the prime symbol of the pioneer and the advancing frontier. As an intentional object—in both cases the wood has been 'cut' and 'piled up square'—the wood-pile is a sign of culture in the wilderness; but a sign already mouldering away and being reclaimed by, reabsorbed into, nature, suggesting, a little, the pathos, transience, and ephemerality of the residual testimonies to the presence of human effort and constructive work. The wood-piles are inexplicably abandoned, suggesting that death—or distraction—always comes too soon; that man is everywhere outlasted by the poignant traces of his labour, leaving sundry edifices which he can no longer either tend or use. And with the 'softened outline' of the 'green mound', the pile is beginning—more specifically in Hawthorne—to resemble a grave. And it is this and all that it implies—call it mortality, call it mutability—which Coverdale has to face and his text, if it can, absorb. ET IN ARCADIA EGO.

In a much earlier scene, talking, somewhat banteringly, to Hollingworth about the future of their new Community, Coverdale says:

I shall never feel as if this were a real, practical, as well as poetical system of human life, until someone has sanctified it by death. . . . Let us choose the rudest, roughest, most uncultivatable spot, for Death's garden-ground; and Death shall teach us to beautify it, grave by grave. By our sweet, calm way of dying, and the airy elegance out of which we will shape our funeral rites, and the cheerful allegories which we will model into tombstones, the final scene shall lose its terrors . . . (p. 130) and more in the same vein. His tone as always tends uncontrollably towards the facetious, so that, even if he wants to take something seriously, by the time he has finished talking about it he has either undermined, ridiculed, banalized, or vaporized it. In this scene, it is quite understandable that the grim, humourless Hollingsworth is irritated by what he feels is Coverdale's 'nonsense'. I will come to Coverdale and his hapless, or worse, errancies of tone. Here I just want to stress that, although the tone of this speech is all wrong, the content is half right. What he touches on banteringly, another American poet, Louis Simpson, formulates with more appropriate seriousness in the last stanza of his poem 'To the Western World' (1955):

> The treasures of Cathay were never found.
> In this America, this wilderness
> Where the axe echoes with a lonely sound,
> The generations labor to possess
> And grave by grave we civilize the ground.

The treasures of Cathay, the fields of Arcadia, the phalansteries[3] of Utopia—alike, never found—or founded. Though some people may have been the better for the searching. Maybe better, and then again maybe worse. That is a part of what this book is about. What Coverdale has to confront— and not as a matter for banter, or light literary conceits, or the pale, etiolated images of a Puvis de Chavannes—is that, yes it *is* 'grave by grave' (his phrase as well as Simpson's) that we civilize the ground; that *death* is 'the real'; and that only by properly assimilating that will he—will we—find the real in anything else. By the end, of course, Blithedale has its grave. It contains the body of Zenobia, the figure accorded most physical, sexual, reality by Coverdale's account. Judging by the concluding chapter which follows her burial, she effectively, for Coverdale, takes 'the real' into the grave with her.

In Coverdale's story his primary involvement—if that is the word for his self-retentive, self-protective proximities to other people—is with Hollingsworth, Zenobia, and Priscilla. But he has a crucial conversation with the shadowy figure of

---

[3] See explanatory note to p. 19.

Old Moodie, who is indeed the first person who speaks to Coverdale (with a request which Coverdale characteristically shrinks from complying with). The shadowy Moodie turns out to be the father, by different mothers (one brilliant and voluptuous, the other a 'poor phantom') of the allegorically opposed half-sisters, Zenobia and Priscilla. Late in the book, in a saloon (and I shall return to this setting), Moodie tells Coverdale his life story, which Coverdale then reconstitutes and writes down, with his customary speculative largesse ('my pen has perhaps allowed itself a trifle of romantic and legendary license' (p. 181)). For the purposes of his story—one might, following Melville's use of the phrase, term it an 'inside narrative'—Coverdale rebaptizes Moodie and mystifies his origin. 'Five-and-twenty years ago . . . there dwelt, in one of the middle states, a man whom we shall call Fauntleroy . . .' (p. 182). Coverdale has a rather coy way with names which I shall look at later, but here I want to pause on the pseudonym—or is it the true name *behind* the name (but then what *is* a *true* name?)—he has chosen.

And first I want to point to an important word he deploys on just two occasions. After recounting Zenobia's passionate words spoken at Eliot's Pulpit, Coverdale wonders if they amounted to no more than a 'stage declamation'. 'Were they formed of a material lighter than common air? Or, supposing them to bear *sterling* weight, was it not a perilous and dreadful wrong, which she was meditating towards herself and Hollingsworth?' (p. 127; my italics). After they have recovered the corpse of Zenobia, rigid in an attitude of prayer but now disfigured and mutilated, Coverdale writes: 'A reflection occurs to me, that will show ludicrously, I doubt not, on my page, but must come in, for its *sterling* truth' (p. 236; my italics). The reflection is that if she could have foreseen what a horrid spectacle she would present when recovered from the river, she would no more have done it than she would have appeared in public wearing a badly fitting garment—that is to say, that she was 'not quite simple in her death', that it contained 'some tint of Arcadian affectation' (p. 237); acting, or counterfeiting, to the end we might say. 'Sterling' is of course the legal tender of what Hawthorne referred to as 'Our

Old Home' (1863), and by extension came to be an epithet meaning 'authentic'. In using the word in these two contexts, Coverdale implicitly raises the question of the problem of authenticity of both spoken and written words. How can we know if *any* words are, as it were, good currency, reliable 'scrip(t)'?

Now, 'Fauntleroy', it appeared, committed a crime which led him to flee to New England and live the shady, shadowy life of Old Moodie. And this crime 'was just the sort of crime, growing out of its artificial state, which society (unless it should change its entire constitution for this man's unworthy state) neither could nor ought to pardon. More safely might it pardon murder' (p. 183). This heinous crime would seem to be literally unspeakable, or unwritable, since Coverdale never names it. But, since the appearance of an article by Charles Swann,[4] there can be no doubt that the crime was forgery. Henry Fauntleroy (1785–1824), a London banker who was also a spendthrift forger, became what one writer described as 'the prototypal forger for his contemporaries'. He was caught and executed, though there was a rumour that he had mysteriously escaped death (by inserting a silver tube in his throat to avoid strangulation) and gone abroad, where he lived for many years. All this was reported at length in the *Gentleman's Magazine*, which we know Hawthorne read (he was in any case an avid reader of newspaper accounts of criminal cases), and it is marvellously to his purpose. By seeming to pluck a pseudonym out of the air at random and actually fastening on the—at the time well-known—name of a notorious English forger, Coverdale releases suggestive resonances which permeate the whole book he is writing.

The worryingly close similarity between writing fiction (or coining images) and counterfeiting the currency on which society depends (which is why the crime was regarded as more socially undermining than murder since it abuses the trust—ruins by falsifying and thus depreciating the 'value'—which enables social exchange and coherence) has often occurred to artists. What is a 'true' copy? How can you tell

[4] C. Swann, 'A Note on *The Blithedale Romance* or "Call him Fauntleroy"', *Journal of American Studies*, 10 (1976), 103–4.

the difference between 'forging' the uncreated conscience of your race, and the kind of forgery the police hunt down? You can, of course, but to a certain kind of writer it can seem that, at a certain level, both 'forgers' work by putting falsities/fictions into circulation. The matter has certainly worried more than one American writer (cf. *The Recognitions* by William Gaddis). But Hawthorne is effectively doing more than throw ironic light on the possible dubiety of his own writerly activity. Fauntleroy is a quintessentially European name, literally containing a recognition of that royalty (*le roi*) which America had violently repudiated in the process of asserting its own identity. Perhaps if Henry Fauntleroy *had* somehow escaped and come to live abroad—and where more obvious than America for his long declining years (he was thirty-nine when he was 'executed' and would have been fifty-six when the Blithedalers were forgathering)?—he would indeed be indistinguishable from Old Moodie. And *that* might suggest that, in addition to all the obvious beliefs and practices—in religion, law, literature—which America had inherited, or transplanted, from Our Old Home, it had latterly received a more sinister and unforeseen bequest—fakery. Dissimulation on an unknowably large scale. Or perhaps America replicated the English Fauntleroy with its own version engendered in those vague 'middle states'. Either way, Mr Fauntleroy has bequeathed to society, in the form of his children, not the customary patriarchal law and authority, but something catastrophically opposite—the seeds of paternal inauthenticity. Priscilla is more a void than a value (victim, too, perhaps): that she should 'triumph' or at least be the main survivor of the Blithedale experiment is by no means an unequivocally felicitous conclusion. While Zenobia, with her 'uncomfortable surplus of vitality' (p. 96), seemed to be the force which helped to drive Blithedale, Lady of the Revels, Queen of Arcadia. Was she all counterfeit? Was there *no* 'sterling' there? If so, the implications do not bear too much pondering—for that way lies the sort of scepticism, or distrust, which terminates in the nihilism of Billy Budd's posthumous rhetorical question—'aren't it all a sham?'[5] This is

[5] H. Melville, *Billy Budd, Foretopman* (1924; New York: Library of America, 1989), 1435.

INTRODUCTION

the other end—or is it the other side?—of the quest for the
Real.

All this goes some way to explaining Coverdale's, and the
book's, obsession with veils and veilings of all kinds. But
before addressing that, I want to revert to Coverdale's
slightly teasing, slightly uncomfortable, way with 'names'.
We may start with a short, jocular exchange between Coverdale and Old Moodie before he settles down to hear the life
story or confessional reminiscences of the great forger—not
that he is going to name *that*—to be recounted by, call him
Fauntleroy, in the local saloon. A bottle of claret arrives. '"It
should be good wine," I remarked, "if it have any right to its
label." "You cannot suppose, sir," said Moodie, with a sigh,
"that a poor old fellow, like me, knows any difference in
wines"' (p. 180). Nor any differencies in currencies, in view
of the story he is about to tell. More interesting is Coverdale's, perhaps habitual, suspicion. Does anything—
anyone—have a 'right to its label'? What is it—what could it
be—to have a *right* to a label? Take 'Zenobia'. What is the
relationship between that 'label' and the intoxicatingly full-
bodied wine of a woman who pours through these pages?

In Chapter II Coverdale says, or writes, to us, concerning
'Zenobia':

This (as the reader, if at all acquainted with our literary biography,
need scarcely be told) was not her real name. She had assumed it, in
the first instance, as her magazine signature; and as it accorded well
with something imperial which her friends attributed to this lady's
figure and deportment, they, half-laughingly, adopted it in their
familiar intercourse with her. She took the appellation in good part,
and even encouraged its constant use . . . (p. 13)

Real name? Where might we find that? Not in this book,
certainly. When Westervelt comes to Blithedale seeking information concerning 'Zenobia', Coverdale somewhat inef-
fectually hedges by replying: '"That is her name in literature
. . . a name, too, which possibly she may permit her private
friends to know and address her by;—but not one which they
feel at liberty to recognize, when used of her, personally, by a
stranger or casual acquaintance."' As it transpires, Westervelt is no stranger or casual acquaintance—though whether
he is/was Zenobia's lover or husband is never named, or,

perhaps we should say, spelled out—and here he replies, '"I am willing to know her by any cognomen that you may suggest."' Appellation, cognomen—what is the real name for a 'name'? Disliking Westervelt and wishing to get rid of him, Coverdale writes: 'I mentioned Zenobia's real name' (p. 93). Mentions it to Westervelt, but never to us. You could say that Zenobia's real name in real life was Margaret Fuller[6] and that Hawthorne, in his characteristically enigmatic way, is effectively saying: he who runs may read. But in terms of the novel as novel, that simply will not do. Coverdale as narrator is showing us that he is keeping something back—cover-ing it indeed—leaving us with a very uncertain sense of the relationship, in his story, between labels and bottles, people and names. Call him Fauntleroy: call her Zenobia. This, after a famous neighbour had started a great novel: 'Call me Ishmael'. Westervelt admits to Coverdale that '"my business is private, personal, and somewhat peculiar"' (p. 93). I think Coverdale, as writer, could say the same.

But the most interesting play with names occurs when a committee is formed 'for providing our infant Community with an appropriate name'. It is a more revealing moment than covering Coverdale lets on.

Blithedale was neither good nor bad. We should have resumed the old Indian name of the premises, had it possessed the oil-and-honey flow which the aborigines were so often happy in communicating to their local appellations; but it chanced to be a harsh, ill-connected, and interminable word, which seemed to fill the mouth with a mixture of very stiff clay and very crumbly pebbles. Zenobia suggested 'Sunny Glimpse' . . . too fine and sentimental a name . . . I ventured to whisper 'Utopia', which, however, was unanimously scouted down . . . Some were for calling our institution 'The Oasis,' . . . others insited on a proviso for reconsidering the matter, at a twelvemonth's end; when a final decision might be had, whether to name it 'The Oasis,' or 'Saharah.' So, at last, finding it impracticable to hammer out anything better, we resolved that the spot should still be Blithedale, as being of good augury enough. (p. 37)

The alternatives are anodyne and cosy enough—the sort of names you could doubtless see on some middle-class homes

---

[6] See explanatory note to p. 52, Miss Margaret Fuller.

and, in due course, on motels. But I wonder what that harsh and interminable 'old Indian name' was, the name given to the place by the, after all, ab-original inhabitants? That surely might be a label which, as it were, had a right to its bottle. Here we must 'go behind' a little, an activity particularly justified by this book, as I hope to show.

John Eliot, the famous apostle to the Indians and a leading founding Puritan, is a very important name in the book; more of that later. Crucially, he undertook to learn the language of the Indians, the better to preach to them. In *Magnalia Christi Americana*—almost a founding volume for America and one which not only Hawthorne but many of his readers would have known—Cotton Mather wrote the 'Life of John Eliot' and in particular animadverted on the great difficulties involved in mastering the Indian language:

> but if their *Alphabet* be *short*, I am sure the *Words* composed of it are long enough to trie the Patience of any Scholar in the World; they are *Sesquidipedalia Verba*, of which their *Lingua* is composed; one would think, they had been growing ever since *Babel*, unto the Dimensions to which they are now extended. For instance, if my reader will count how many Letters there are in this one Word, *Nummatchekod-tantamooonganunnonash*, when he has done, for his Reward I'll tell him, it signifies no more in *English*, than our *lusts*, and if I were to translate, *our Loves*; it must be nothing shorter than *Noowomantam-mooonkanunonnash*. Or, to give my Reader a longer Word than either of these, *Kummogkodonattoottummooetiteaongannunnonash*, is, in English, *Our Question*: But I pray, Sir, count the Letters! ... This tedious Language, our *Eliot* (the anagram of whose name was TOILE) quickly became a master of...[7]

Hellish difficult: why, says Mather, I tried it out on the *Daemons* of a possessed woman, and, although they had no trouble with Greek and Hebrew, they just could not cope with Indian. (Another justification, perhaps, for eliminating these tedious Lewis Carrolls of the forest.) Now perhaps the 'real name' of Blithedale was just such an 'ill-connected and interminable word' as the ones cited by Cotton Mather. Somewhat too harsh for the genteel New Englanders. Better

[7] C. Mather, *The Puritans*, ed. P. Miller and T. H. Johnson (New York, 1939), ii. 506.

change the label—something more soft and sweet. Something, too, which gets rid of the grating (and potentially embarrassing—whose Utopia was this?) otherness and Indianness of the original name. As a result, somehow the wrong book is being written. As a matter of fact, 'Our Lusts, Our Loves, Our Question' would have been no bad name for the site of this story, no bad title for the novel itself. I am suggesting, quite improperly, that the book we *should* have would have been *The History of Nummatchekodtantamooonganunnonash, Noowomantammooonkanunonnash, and Kummogkodonattoottummooetiteaongannunnonash* by Nathaniel Hawthorne. Instead we have *The Blithedale Romance* by Miles Coverdale—a sentimental over-writing of an earlier, uglier and harsher reality which is unpronounceable, unhandlable, unwritable. The Devil himself would not understand it. 'Blithedale' is a cover: indeed it is a 'Coverdale'—the narrator is peculiarly well named.

Names then, or names as Coverdale and some of his characters use them, are veils (and I have added the suggestion that the book itself is a kind of veil). An article by Frank Davidson[8] scrupulously notes the prolific references to veils and veilings throughout the novel. It has to be said, it would be hard *not* to notice them. The novel opens with a description of 'the wonderful exhibition of the Veiled Lady' (p. 5), and, in one way or another, the whole novel is a 'veiled exhibition'. In Frank Davidson's words, 'Almost everything in the romance except "the naked exposure" in Westervelt "of something that ought not to be left prominent" is partially hidden or totally obscured by a veiling medium or mask.'[9] Literal veils, false names, mysterious and mystified life histories (the whole Old Moodie/Fauntleroy family has an unpenetrated and perhaps impenetrable past—perhaps, in this, like America itself), and a general disposition towards 'screening' of all kinds—these are the hallmarks of the book. Old Moodie himself is, fittingly enough, particularly and literally self-effacing, as one might say—'He had a queer

[8] F. Davidson, 'Toward a Revaluation of *The Blithedale Romance*', *New England Quarterly*, 25/3 (1952), 374–83.
[9] Ibid. 376.

appearance of hiding himself behind the patch on his left eye'
(p. 82); 'his upper part was mostly hidden behind the shrubbery' (p. 83); in the tavern Coverdale 'recognized his hand
and arm, protruding from behind a screen' (p. 178)—but his
is only the most extreme case of a general tendency to lead a
masked life.

The case of Westervelt is interesting. One should note that
the characters seem to have differing ontological statuses—
more real and less real in differing ways—and he is at once the
most masked and the most exposed. Like his teeth, the man is
manifestly 'a sham'—he is all 'humbug'; his face might be
'removeable like a mask'; there is 'nothing genuine about
him', his visage is like 'polished steel' (pp. 95, 173) (remind-
ing me of a Faulkner character whose face has 'the depthless
brutality of stamped tin'). He leaves the tale as he enters it—
mysteriously, independently, his power unassailed. Coverdale, in one of his frequent less than charitable moods,
dismisses him, hoping that Heaven will 'annihilate him. He
was altogether earthy, worldly, made for time and its gross
objects, and incapable . . . of so much as one spiritual idea'
(p. 241). That is all very well, except that there is precious
little 'idealism' in the book that is not badly compromised by
the end. In all his fakery and falsity there is, nevertheless, that
'naked exposure of something that ought not to be left
prominent' (p. 92)—unlike the river with its 'broad, black
inscrutable depth, keeping its secrets from the eye of man'
(p. 232).

Coverdale does not attempt to put a name to that naked
something Westervelt leaves indecently showing (he would
rather cover than name), but we can perhaps suggest it is his
shameless appetite and will-to-power. Although Hollingsworth rescues Priscilla from him, Westervelt—on his own
terms—is the most powerful figure in the book. Of the male
figures, it is only he, so we are allowed to gather, who has
possessed Zenobia sexually. Man of mask he may be, but,
looked at from one point of view, there is more *to* him than to
the narrator. Coverdale's description of Christ as 'One, who
merely veiled himself in mortal and masculine shape, but
was, in truth, divine' (p. 121) suggests that corporeality, sheer

or mere physicality, is the unreal for Coverdale, an orthodox enough Transcendentalist tenet. Yet he is strangely drawn to the farm's pigs, 'involved, and almost stifled, and buried alive, in their own corporeal substance', and ponders 'the ponderous and fat satisfaction of their existence' (p. 144). Hawthorne particularly disliked fat on women (you should be allowed to cut it off, he, let us hope jocularly, maintained), and perhaps some of his ambivalence to flesh and fleshliness has got into Coverdale, but it is hard to find in the book any very deep conviction of the existence of any divine, spiritual, or ideal realm of Reality. Perhaps the corporeal veil is all we have got—not a thought for Coverdale, or even Hawthorne, to be easy with. Zenobia's farewell declaration concludes: '"When you next hear of Zenobia, her face will be behind the black veil . . ."' (p. 228). In the event it will be the black veil of the river, which now has another secret to keep.

More than anything else, veils ask to be looked behind, and Coverdale, who takes a 'back-room' in the hotel in town, makes a speciality of looking behind. Literally.

Bewitching to my fancy are all those nooks and crannies, where Nature, like a stray partridge, hides her head among the long-established haunts of men! It is likewise to be remarked, as a general rule, that there is far more of the picturesque, more truth to native and characteristic tendencies, and vastly greater suggestiveness, in the back view of a residence, whether in town or country, than in its front. The latter is always artificial; it is meant for the world's eye, and is therefore a veil and a concealment. Realities keep in the rear, and put forward an advance-guard of show and humbug. (p. 149)

Realities keep in the rear. Coverdale is interested (and excited by) 'posterior aspects' (p. 149)—in every sense, we may say. He announces his predilection—unambiguously enough we might feel—for getting acquainted with 'the backside of the universe' (p. 148). His curiosity, not least his sexual curiosity, is high and easily inflamed. In his last recorded comment on Hawthorne (in a letter of 1904) Henry James summed up what he admired about Hawthorne with apt words: he saw 'the interest *behind* the interest'.[10] In an essay of 1896 he had spelt it out at greater length.

[10] H. James, *Essays on Literature, American Writers, English Writers* (New York, 1984), 471.

It was a question of looking behind and beneath for the suggestive idea, the artistic motive . . . This ingenuity grew alert and irrepressible as it manoeuvred for the back view and turned up the under side of common aspects,—the laws secretly broken, the impulses secretly felt, the hidden passions, the double lives, the dark corners, the closed rooms, the skeletons in the cupboard and at the feast.[11]

'Behind and beneath' became one of James's favourite phrases as he grew more and more fascinated with 'the things *behind*', and one of the things behind was, awesomely and sometimes seemingly ubiquitously, the sexual.

Realities keep in the rear. All Coverdale's compulsive 'looking behind'—literally of houses, speculatively of people, their motives, their pasts, their relationships—suggests that, effete voyeur though he himself is, he has more than half a notion that he might find 'the real' in the sexual. Though, being the man he is, he is certainly not going to write like D. H. Lawrence! But he likes to imagine Zenobia naked and brood lasciviously on her past: '"Zenobia is a wife! Zenobia has lived, and loved! There is no folded petal, no latent dewdrop, in this perfectly developed rose"' (p. 47). And, talking of petals and roses, what is one to make of such a passage as the following, describing Priscilla's silk purses:

Their peculiar excellence, besides the great delicacy and beauty of the manufacture, lay in the almost impossibility that any uninitiated person should discover the aperture; although, to a practised touch, they would open as wide as charity or prodigality might wish. I wondered if it were not a symbol of Priscilla's own mystery. (p. 35)

One can only wonder at the sort of tacit cultural collusion which could maintain that no possibility of any *double entendre* and thus nothing remotely lubricious should attach to such writing, while being constantly ready to recoil in real or simulated horror if matters pertaining to sexual actualities were explicitly named. Coverdale, self-cosseting bachelor that he is, is not a passionate man, but he is a mighty prurient one; he is also a shameless fetishist: after Zenobia's corpse is recovered, he eagerly takes one of her shoes and has 'kept it ever since' (p. 232). The original Coverdale was the first translator of the Bible, in a version reputedly pretty inaccurate

---

[11] Ibid. 459.

but with some sudden arresting felicities. The same could be said of this Coverdale book, though what he translates is Fourier (likewise inaccurately if the one example we are given is anything to go by). Fourierism at that time was a code-word for free love and a byword for promiscuity—such as Coverdale more than hints obtained at Blithedale. (More than fifty Fourierist communities sprang up in America between 1840 and 1860, not all, of course, emphasizing the need for the multiple sexual servicing of their members.)[12] He admits to a certain male grossness of imagination, and, while we may choose not to place much credence on the concluding line of the book in which he claims that he was in love with Priscilla all along (a line opportunistically added by Hawthorne the day he dispatched the manuscript), we can feel fairly sure that he would not be above fantasizing about fingering and opening the aperture to Priscilla's purse, running more to prodigality than to charity perhaps.

When he is outlining what they hoped to erect and achieve at Blithedale, Coverdale undermines the formulaic and pro-grammatic optimism of their original intentions and ex-pectations with an unusual metaphor.

Altogether, by projecting our minds outward, we had imparted a show of novelty to existence, and contemplated it as hopefully as if the soil, beneath our feet, had not been fathom-deep with the dust of deluded generations, on every one of which, as on ourselves, the world had imposed itself as a hitherto unwedded bride. (p. 128)

It is, characteristically, an erotic image; but it reveals much more than that. In an important essay Lauren Berlant glosses the passage as follows:

This 'people', according to Coverdale, sees the present moment as a hopeful fore-gleam of a future luminescence. But the scene of utopian fantasy is founded on the repression of histories that would, presumably, challenge the 'fact' of our present existence: Coverdale notes that his follow workers act as if they are the land's first tillers and, by association, the nation's first utopians. But the community's historical amnesia with respect to the utopian projects that have preceded it reveals that American history has never been written or

[12] See explanatory note to p. 52, Charles Fourier.

even thought. It has only been repressed, buried by new 'dirt,' new stories. America, in this view, is always distinctively post-Utopian, but has never 'known' it.[13]

The image of the 'unwedded bride' suggests that Utopian dreams, hopes, and desires are dependent on, perhaps a function of, 'virginity' in every sense.

But when historical and sexual knowledge comes, when 'the world had imposed itself' upon us, we lose the clarity of utopian, libidinal perfection. The postvirginal bride who weds her demystifying knowledge to us is simultaneously the source of our historical consciousness, our historical amnesia, and our personal nostalgia for those moments before her 'knowledge' atomized our whole bodies and destroyed our utopian collective dreams.[14]

A striking example of such historical amnesia is given by Coverdale himself when Hollingsworth, describing his 'visionary edifice' for the reform of criminals, says: ' "But I offer my edifice as a spectacle to the world . . . that it may take example and build many another like it. Therefore I mean to set it on the open hill-side" ' (p. 80). The echo of John Winthrop's 'city on a hill' speech—a sort of foundational American declaration—could hardly be clearer. But it is lost on Coverdale. 'Twist these words how I might, they offered no very satisfactory import' (p. 80). If he can forget *that*, what may not an American writer forget? And yet Coverdale sees the Blithedale venture as both a recapitulation and an extension of the first Puritan errand into the wilderness, and he and his friends as 'the descendants of the Pilgrims, whose high enterprise, as we sometimes flattered ourselves, we had taken up, and were carrying it onward and aloft, to a point which they never dreamed of attaining' (p. 117). One may wonder if he has that original 'high enterprise' very clearly in his mind—and what it entailed for the original inhabitants.

This is the point of one of the slyest barbs, which Hawthorne releases through Coverdale when he describes the site of Eliot's Pulpit: 'as wild a tract of woodland as the great-

[13] L. Berlant, 'Fantasies of Utopia in *The Blithedale Romance*', *American Literary History*, I/I (1989), 30–62; pp. 31–2

[14] Ibid. 32.

great-great-great grandson of one of Eliot's Indians (had any such posterity been in existence) could have desired, for the site and shelter of his wigwam' (p. 118). As here quite literally, the Indians have everywhere been 'bracketed out' of American history. This is why the name of John Eliot is important in the book. He was a figure who, as it were, tried to bracket the Indians *in*—even while his contemporaries continued the work of dispossession. He set up 'praying towns' for numbers of Indians, and there is no reason to doubt the sincerity of his desire to transform, reclaim by converting, the manifestly un-Elect Indians. Coverdale 'romanticizes' Eliot—that, after all, is what he is writing: 'I used to see the holy Apostle of the Indians, with the sunlight flickering down upon him through the leaves, and glorifying his figure as with the half-perceptible glow of a transfiguration' (p. 119). If he had historicized Eliot, Coverdale might have brought to mind, and written in, the fact that Eliot created in his Christianized Indians vulnerable hybrids who could never survive. They were wiped out in King Philip's War (1673–5), not least because they were not yet fully trusted by the whites, and no longer trusted by the Indians. This must be marked up as another Utopian project which ended in disastrous failure. Or rather, not marked up but left out. Coverdale takes (makes) the Romance—the saint in the wilderness;—and forgets the history—the subsequent victims. Eliot trying to convert his Indians is clearly replicated in some way by Hollingsworth dedicated to reforming his criminals, another too fanatical attempt to assimilate the marginalized, or—to use a phrase of Bernard Schlurick—'le verrouillage de l'autre dans le même' (the locking up of the other in the same).[15] It is another massive failure. No criminals are reclaimed; instead Hollingsworth feels he has been criminalized by causing Zenobia's suicide.

I am not, in this introduction, going to discuss the characters and characterization. Henry James's summary in the essay of 1896 can hardly be bettered.

---

[15] Personal communication.

The idea that he most tangibly presents is that of the unconscious way in which the search for the common good may cover a hundred interested impulses and personal motives; the suggestion that such a company could only be bound together more by its delusions, its mutual suspicions and frictions, than by any successful surrender of the self.[16]

Psychologically, Hawthorne was clearly still interested in how relationships could in fact be power struggles, contests of adverse wills, as he dramatized most clearly in Chapter XIII of *The House of the Seven Gables*, 'Alice Pyncheon', in which Matthew Maule literally mesmerizes the proud Alice in an agonistic contest of the eyes. 'She instinctively knew, it may be, that some sinister or evil potency was now striving to pass her barriers; nor would she decline the contest. So Alice put woman's might against man's might; a match not often equal on the part of the woman.'[17] Indeed not. Matthew achieves total dominion, domination, saying to himself, '"She is mine! ... Mine, by the right of the strongest spirit."'[18] Hawthorne had a strikingly adversarial and appropriative sense of human relationships—'sharkish', Melville might have said—and this is again in evidence in the struggles between Hollingsworth and Zenobia, Hollingsworth and Coverdale, and the struggles over Priscilla. All this is clear enough in the book. But a word should be said about one of its central concerns—Reform.

'In the history of the world the doctrine of Reform had never such scope as at the present hour'—thus Emerson in 1841 in 'Man the Reformer'.[19] There was an extraordinary proliferation, explosion indeed, of reform literature and movements in antebellum America. In his very interesting work, *Beneath the American Renaissance*, David Reynolds describes this vast literature and suggests very plausibly how it affected the now-regarded major writers. Initially this reform literature was conventional.

[16] James, *Essays*, p. 464.
[17] N. Hawthorne, *The House of the Seven Gables* (1851; New York: Library of America, 1983), 527.
[18] Ibid. 529.
[19] *Emerson* (New York: Library of America, 1983), 135.

As time passed, however, there arose a strong subversive element, seen in a succession of vociferous reformers whose loudly announced goal was to stamp out various behavioral sins or social iniquities—intemperance, licentiousness, urban poverty, chattel and wage slavery, poor prison conditions, and so forth—but who described vice in such lurid detail that they were branded as dangerously immoral and sacrilegious. The *immoral* or *dark reformers*, as I call them, used didactic rhetoric as a protective shield for highly unconventional explorations of tabooed psychological and spiritual areas. . . . for both Hawthorne and Melville contemporary reform devices and themes provided an inroad toward literary ambiguity.[20]

'The dark reformers are largely responsible for transforming a culture of morality into a culture of ambiguity.'[21] The flood of this literature would seem to have had a destabilizing effect on the old certainties, even the old ontologies. Reynolds quotes from *The Quaker City* by George Lippard (1845), in which a character, bewildered by the instabilities and amoralities surrounding him, complains: '"Every thing fleeting and nothing stable, everything shifting and changing, and nothing substantial!"'[22] Reynolds comments: 'each of the major authors at one time or another expressed puzzlement and terror over the relativism implied by this fluid reform environment'.[23]

As we have seen at the start, this is certainly true of Coverdale, and he, of course, is surrounded by—up to his neck (though not his heart) in—reform movements of all kinds: prison reform, Associationism, temperance, feminism, spiritualism, mesmerism. Perhaps he does not directly confront the implication of his own writing (and non-writing)—namely that you cannot hope, and perhaps should hardly seek, to build a Utopia on a land stained by genocide and already replete with the dust of earlier failures. There is much talk of 'systems' in the book—throwing off old systems, devising new ones—but Coverdale finally finds that this talk is moving him towards a kind of vertigo of unreality.

[20] D. Reynolds, *Beneath the American Renaissance* (Cambridge, Mass., 1988), 55–6.
[21] Ibid. 59.
[22] Quoted in ibid. 84.
[23] Ibid. 85.

I was beginning to lose the sense of what kind of world it was, among innumerable schemes of what it might or ought to be. It was impossible, situated as we were, not to imbibe the idea that everything in nature and human existence was fluid, or fast becoming so; that the crust of the Earth, in many places, was broken, and its whole surface portentously upheaving; that it was a day of crisis, and that we ourselves were in the critical vortex. Our great globe floated in the atmosphere of infinite space like an unsubstantial bubble. No sagacious man will long retain his sagacity, if he lives exclusively among reformers and progressive people, without periodically returning into a settled system of things, to correct himself by a new observation from that old stand-point. (pp. 140–1)

After a quick good-bye to the pigs, he heads for town and some restabilizing talk with a few Cambridge conservatives. So we may return to our opening question. What *is* Hawthorne doing with—through—Miles Coverdale?

From the start, commentators on the book have noted and stressed that, whatever else he is, Coverdale is pre-eminently an observer.

Coverdale is a picture of the contemplative, observant, analytic nature, nursing its fancies, and yet, thanks to an element of strong good sense, not bringing them up to be spoiled children; having little at stake in life, at any given moment, and yet indulging, in imagination, in a good many adventures; a portrait of a man, in a word, whose passions are slender, whose imagination is active, and whose happiness lies, not in doing, but in perceiving—half a poet, half a critic, and all a spectator.[24]

Thus Henry James, seeing Coverdale, we might think, in the most generous possible light. Not, perhaps, surprisingly, since his own subsequent work would turn out to be well-populated with just such slender-passioned imaginative spectators as he here describes. Writing nearly one hundred years later, Richard Poirier is more diagnostic and critical:

one consequence of an idealism gone sour can be the self-absorbed fastidiousness of a character like Coverdale . . . A somewhat sickly, somewhat even masturbatory quality in Coverdale's self-regarding retreat is evident even in the images describing it. It is as if he were retreating into a state not of heightened consciousness but of death

[24] James, *Essays*, p. 419.

... Hawthorne is here showing us the transformations of a sort of Emersonian man into a Dandy. ... a man incapable of human fellowship.[25]

James thought that Hawthorne had put himself into Coverdale ('Miles Coverdale is evidently as much Hawthorne as he is any one else in particular'), but that is necessarily imponderable. What is clear is that Hawthorne is attempting a kind of self-revelatory portrait of an American artist at a particular, and particularly problematic, moment of time—rather, artist *manqué*, just as Coverdale is also a lover *manqué*, idealist *manqué*, Utopianist *manqué*, communalist *manqué*, farmer *manqué*, citizen both of country and world *manqué*, arguably human *manqué* who comes to rest in metaphorical sillabubs and actual sherry-cobblers. After diaries of nobodies and confessions of superfluous men, not to mention notes from underground and men without qualities, we are quite familiar with self-marginalizing, self-deprecating, even self-immolating narrators. But there is no narrator like him in earlier American literature (or in English, come to that) and I just want to ponder some of the possible implications of Hawthorne's handing over the telling of his novel to such a figure.

He is, we may say, bricked-in, bricked-up, from the start: 'a lodger—like myself—in one of the midmost houses of a brick-block; each house partaking of the warmth of all the rest' (p. 10). Since he is a 'frosty bachelor' (p. 9), this generalized, anonymous communal warmth is no doubt welcome to him, and I shall return to his ambiguous need for heat. Here I want to note that Coverdale is in fact a generic 'lodger'. He is most at home in apartments, hotel rooms, taverns—places of transience. Even at Blithedale, for all his simulated commitment, he was only ever, really, passing through. He has a cat-like knack of making himself comfortable, particularly in his own apartment, but he is truly at home nowhere. Taking the word with its broadest implications, the 'lodger' as failed artist, or the failed artist as 'lodger', was a new figure for Hawthorne to have introduced into American literature. And I think it has something to do with the spread of the 'brick-

[25] R. Poirier, *A World Elsewhere* (London, 1967), 116–22.

block'—let us call it the suburbanization of America. I take the word from a very important sentence in the novel. It concerns the audience at the village Lyceum-hall where the (melo-)drama of the 'Veiled Lady' is to be enacted. Coverdale lists the varied occupations of this audience—farmers, shop-keepers, lawyers, students, and so on—and comments: 'all looking rather suburban than rural. In these days, there is absolutely no rusticity, except when the actual labor of the soil leaves its earth-mould on the person' (p. 197). It was in quest of some such absolute 'rusticity' that Coverdale went to Blithedale, even to the extent of indeed getting 'earth-mould' on his person. And what he discovered is that it cannot be done. The attempt is *bound* to seem affected, factitious. The suburban lodger can never, despite or perhaps because of his sentimental pastoral nostalgia, reachieve or rediscover any absolute 'rusticity'—always supposing, of course, that there ever was such a thing. Suburban, not urban—suburbia as that indeterminate, homogenizing area between the true town and the real country, which seeks to combine the comforts and amenities of the one with the beauties and felicities of the other, arguably, in the process, losing contact with the differing, dynamic energies of both. Hawthorne was astute enough to see that it was becoming increasingly difficult to avoid—ontologically, let us say—some variant of the sub-urban condition. Lodgers—in a sense—all, or most, of us.

This is why Coverdale's tone is so uncertain, veering always towards self-defeating facetiousness. He says he might join an Exploring Expedition up the Nile, or go and fight for Kossuth in Hungary, but just to formulate the notional possibilities is to become aware of their absurd unrealizabil-ity. 'Suburbanized' self-consciousness seems to corrode in advance any possibility of significant action and commitment. (In this, Coverdale is remarkably similar to the narrator figures of the poetry of Arthur Hugh Clough.) He tries to throw himself into Blithedale, and even seems to undergo some temporary re-birth there, but very soon he finds that he has, as it were, come out on the other side, floundering among failed hyperboles, bitter scepticism, and bathetic self-ridi-cule. But *is* there a right tone for Blithedale? Is it not from the

start an impossible and doomed project? Economically—
'I very soon became sensible, that, as regarded society at
large, we stood in a position of new hostility, rather than new
brotherhood' (p. 20)—and socially; it seems soon to disin-
tegrate into the centrifugality of unaligned power-plays—it is
something of a disaster. Everybody is, more or less, posing
(leaving aside Priscilla, who has something of an object
status) and at least Coverdale *knows* he is posing. The motives
of some of the other leading figures at Blithedale would not
stand much scrutiny—particularly Hollingsworth's—and we
may want to look again at Coverdale's motives, for at least he
seems to have the virtue, even if it has curiously deleterious
effects, of refusing to succumb to the lures of self-deception.
At Blithedale and after, he is, indeed, the less—the least—
deceived.

One thing he is not is an 'unreliable narrator', if by that we
mean a narrator who, we somehow gather, is seeking to
deceive the reader and probably him or her self, by dis-
ingenuousness, editing out, reformulation, or whatever (there
are distinct traces of this in the narrative account of Gatsby
by Nick Carraway, who otherwise is the American narrator
who bears the greatest resemblance to Coverdale). Coverdale
readily admits, when he does not positively flaunt the fact,
that he has endless recourse to supplementation, speculation,
fabrication, imagination, fantasy—the lot, you might say.
'I hardly could make out an intelligible sentence, on either
side. What I seem to remember, I yet suspect may have been
patched together by my fancy, in brooding over the matter,
afterwards' (p. 104)—this is a characteristic admission. He is
usually too far away in some sense or another—up the tree of
his 'hermitage', in a distant hotel room looking through
windows over which curtains are suddenly drawn—out of
earshot and eyeshot. When he returns to Blithedale, he says:
'Had it been evening, I would have stolen to some lighted
window of the old farm-house, and peeped darkling in . . .'
(p. 207)—a dark peeper, and a peeper usually in the dark.
Such is the darkling voyeur who nevertheless writes—fabric-
ates, forges—a narrative of some considerable length concerning matters of some considerable importance. Of himself,

he writes in the last chapter: 'But what, after all, have I to tell? Nothing, nothing, nothing!' (p. 245). But, though there is a feeling of vacancy, vacuity, at the end, Coverdale has in fact told us a great deal about himself—not only his unreconstructible bachelorhood predilections, but the motivations behind his enquiry, his narrative.

That these motivations are deeply ambiguous he is well aware. The start of Chapter IX is a long meditation on the unhealthiness of devoting oneself 'too exclusively to the study of individual men and women' (p. 69). He makes the acute observation that, if we 'put a friend under our microscope, we thereby insulate him from many of his true relations, magnify his peculiarities, inevitably tear him into parts' (p. 69) and Coverdale knows that he may be doing Hollingsworth 'a great wrong by prying into his character . . . *But I could not help it*' (p. 69; my italics). Blithedale and its inhabitants comprise both a 'problem' which it is his 'business', his 'vocation' (p. 97), to solve and also 'my private theatre' (p. 70), at once an obligation and a pastime. He often makes statements such as 'making my prey of peoples' individualities, as my custom was' (p. 84), and he can recognize that 'That cold tendency, between instinct and intellect, which made me pry with a speculative interest into people's passions and impulses, appeared to have gone far towards unhumanizing my heart' (p. 154). Peep, pry, prey—these are not very pleasant words, and it becomes something of a question whether Coverdale can justify his uncontrollable speculative curiosity—he cannot help it, and will not—even to himself. When he talks about his 'experiments' on people, and collecting them as 'specimens' (p. 160), he is, morally speaking, in the most dangerous of areas as far as Hawthorne is concerned. Zenobia is quite certain of the culpability of his pursuits. '"You know not what you do! It is dangerous, sir, believe me, to tamper thus with earnest human passions, out of your own mere idleness, and for your sport"' (p. 170). She says she will hold him 'responsible' for any future 'mischief' that may follow, on account of his 'interference'. Since the main mischief will be her suicide, the charge is, in effect, a capital one. Again, when he spies on her in town, she indicts him for '"following up your game, groping for human emotions in the dark corners of the heart"' (p. 214). But what she calls his 'game', he also claims is his 'duty'. His main defence of his uncontrollable curiosity and obsessive observation is as follows:

For, was mine a mere vulgar curiosity? Zenobia should have known me better than to suppose it. She should have been able to appreciate that quality of the intellect and the heart, which impelled me (often against my own will, and to the detriment of my own comfort) to live in other lives, and to endeavour—by generous sympathies, by delicate intuitions, by taking note of things too slight for record, and by bringing my human spirit into manifold accordance with the companions whom God assigned me—to learn the secret which was hidden even from themselves. (p. 160)

This, we may think, is to make the best possible case for his compulsions—though there is a bit of a sting in the tail with the last words raising the matter of prying and preying. More generally, it reads like an artist's defence or apologia. The key claim is that the inquisitive spectatorial compulsion derives from, or crucially involves, 'generous sympathy'. It is Hawthorne's achievement, through Coverdale, to suggest just how many other derivations may be involved, what an inextricable cluster of motives may be determining the compulsion to watch, speculate, and 'narrativize'—or peep, pry, and prey.

An obvious comparison with Coverdale is the unnamed first-person narrator (*very* rare in Henry James) of *The Sacred Fount*, who is indeed James's Coverdale. To remind you, this narrator is a weekend guest at a country house party and he spends the time quite frantically speculating about the possible sexual relations—and their effects—among the guests. He may be right and he may be, as some think him, 'mad'. Whatever else, he is undoubtedly obsessive. I will run together some of his statements or claims.

My extraordinary interest in my fellow-creatures. I have more than most men. I've never really seen anyone with half so much. That breeds observation, and observation breeds ideas....

the best example I can give of the intensity of amusement I had at last enabled my private madness to yield me....

the common fault of minds for which the vision of life is an obsession. The obsession pays, if one will; but to pay it has to borrow....

it justified my indiscreet curiosity; it crowned my underhand process with beauty....

I alone was magnificently and absurdly aware—everyone else was benightedly out of it....

I struck myself as knowing again the joy of the intellectual mastery of things unamenable, that joy of determining, almost of creating results....

Light or darkness, my imagination rides me....

The satisfaction of my curiosity is the pacification of my mind....

I couldn't save Mrs. Server, and I couldn't save poor Briss; I *could*, however, guard to the last grain of gold, my precious sense of their loss, their disintegration and their doom.[26]

The key notion here is that of *guardianship*—not of the people involved, since they may be on their unarrestable way to doom and disintegration, but of the observer's *sense* of their experience, which is, by comparison, pure gold. It is, in Jamesian translation, the translator Coverdale's claim. It is somewhat akin to the Conradian notion of art as a constant act of salvage from the perpetual wreckage of life. To this extent, Coverdale, in all his ambiguity, hesitations, mixed motives, and uncertainties of tone, embodies a flawed stance and articulates an equivocal defence which would become increasingly discernible and audible in the art, and among the artists, of the next hundred years. He also reveals some of the dangers which attach to the observer–speculator–empathizer stance.

I had given up my heart and soul to interests that were not mine. What had I ever had to do with them? And why, being now free, should I take this thraldom on me, once again? It was both sad and dangerous ... to be in too close affinity with the passions, the errors, and misfortunes, of individuals who stood within a circle of their own, into which, if I stept at all, it must be as an intruder, and at a peril that I could not estimate. (p. 206)

[26] H. James, *The Sacred Fount* (1901; New York: Grove Press, 1953), 147, 162, 23, 128, 177, 214, 276, 287, 273.

The artist as 'intruder' is another fine adumbration on Hawthorne's part. And, while the figures he watches have 'absorbed my life into themselves' (p. 194), he has also vaporized reality by too much thinking about it. 'I spent painful hours in recalling these trifles, and rendering them more misty and unsubstantial than at first, by the quality of speculative musing, thus kneaded in with them' (p. 194). Why do it? Why all this kneading and losing? Why incur such pain and sadness? Why risk such danger? Because he cannot help it. No wonder James spoke of 'the madness of art'.[27]

In his self-confessed 'frostiness', Coverdale clearly needs something to warm him up. There are many grateful references to actual domestic fires—his own apartment, we may infer, was warm even to fugginess—though even here a note of wariness enters, as when, at Blithedale, he speaks of enjoying 'the warm and radiant luxury of a *somewhat too abundant* fire' (p. 23; my italics). Sex, not to put too fine a point upon it, would also seem to offer the possibility of thermal consolation, but here again a note of caution enters, as when, in reference to Zenobia, even Westervelt speaks of 'her *uncomfortable surplus* of vitality' (p. 96; my italics). Just as Coverdale is drawn to, he draws back from, any heat which threatens to lead to excess, to involve him in a surplus abundance. At a, perhaps, higher level, the Transcendentalist excitations and Utopian warmth of Blithedale seem to hold out 'delectable visions of the spiritualization of labor' (p. 65). But materiality remains coldly resistant. 'The clods of earth, which we so constantly belabored and turned over and over, were never etherealized into thought. Our thoughts, on the contrary, were fast becoming cloddish. Our labor symbolized nothing . . .' (p. 66). This is only a disillusioning deflation if you feel it must symbolize *something* or else, in Melville's words, be of little worth. In an admittedly very diluted and attenuated way, Coverdale is still a late product of that Puritan–Transcendentalist line of American thought which requires a second order of justifying meaning behind the merely materially visible and palpable. If earth is only

[27] *The Complete Tales of Henry James*, ix (London, 1964), 75.

'cloddish', if pigs in the 'fat satisfaction of their existence' (p. 144), have, as it were, got it right—well, says this kind of mentality, what really is it all about? Blithedale might turn out to be a cold comfort farm indeed.

But there is one thing which is guaranteed, and can be relied on, to afford an instant warmth, without involving the difficulties of engaging with other people or bothering about proto-religious convictions—'a sherry-cobbler'. And, away from Blithedale, Coverdale seldom enters his apartment, or a hotel or tavern, without procuring one. Which makes his reference to himself, in the tavern scene, as 'we temperance people' a singular piece of effrontery. That scene (Chapter XXI) again marks an innovation, for I can think of no earlier serious work of American fiction which situates one of its most important scenes in a tavern (temperance tracts with sensationalist accounts of the results of drink already abounded, as David Reynolds has documented,[28] but that is not quite the same thing; and T. S. Arthur's influential *Ten Nights in a Barroom* (1854) was still three years away). Coverdale's mild—let us assume—solitary tippling perhaps only tells us something about his somewhat regressive, oral, narcissistic character—sucking on sillabubs, various. But references to alcohol play an important part in this novel. This is no place to attempt a brief history of alcohol. Suffice it here to remind ourselves that the word itself is Arabic and refers to the paint used to cover the eyelids of the dead—thus having connections with the 'spirit' world—and that in the early years of distilling alcohol in Europe (the fifteenth and sixteenth centuries) it was often closely associated with alchemy, which was involved in the attempts to distil other 'essences', and thus the attempt to produce what we call 'spirits' in some vague way carried overtones of a quest for higher 'spirit-ual' things, even when the searches set themselves in direct opposition.

It is these overtones which Hawthorne exploits. He will deliberately mix realms, as when, for instance, Coverdale imagines Zenobia's death-moment—'her soul, bubbling out

[28] See Reynolds, *Beneath the American Renaissance*.

through her lips, may be' (p. 235). Since we have had not a few references to the bubbles of sparkling wine previously, it is hard to say whether she died a Christian penitent, or went out like a bottle of opened champagne. Quite so, Hawthorne might say: not hard—*impossible*. Twice Coverdale comes across strangely—strangely in New England—luxuriant grape vines. There are grapes in his hermitage 'in abundant clusters of the deepest purple' (p. 228), and they provoke him to almost Dionysiac reveries.

Methinks a wine might be pressed out of them, possessing a passionate zest, and endowed with a new kind of intoxicating quality, attended with such bacchanalian ecstasies as the tamer grapes of Madeira, France, and the Rhine, are inadequate to produce. And I longed to quaff a great goblet of it, at that moment. (p. 228)

Methinks, if he was actually offered any such goblet, he would demur and settle for a sherry-cobbler, not being one actually to capitulate to bacchanalian ecstasies—as opposed to fantasizing about them. In the tavern scene Coverdale attempts a cautious and measured defence of wine, if not of spirits: 'Human nature, in my opinion, has a naughty instinct that approves of wine, if not of stronger liquor' (p. 175). (This sentence was crossed out, possibly by Sophia Hawthorne, so you can see what he was up against, and, in his sly Hawthorne way, writing against.)[29]

There are various paintings on the walls of the tavern, all concerned with representations of food and drink, or drinking, and this permits Coverdale, and doubtless Hawthorne, to meditate on varying modes of representation, from low mimetic realism to a more etherealizing kind of art. By situating the book's main discussion of *art* in a *tavern* Hawthorne is again doing something rather novel, or, rather, raising an old problem in a new way. Since the paintings concern food, drink, and 'revelling' (wenching?), we may say that in their varying ways—gross, life-like, noble, ideal, *too real*—they engage with our basic hungers and desires. Which implicitly points to the larger problem: what is, what can be, what should be, the relationship between art and appetite?

[29] See explanatory notes to pp. 10, 17, and 175.

Do such representations pander to our lowest, most basic and most powerful, wants and desires, courting and inflaming them? Or, by transposing such appetites and objects of desire into another medium, can such representations ideal-ize and spirit-ualize them? Hawthorne would not be one to resolve such a potentially infinite debate: characteristically, inasmuch as he hopes the latter, he fears the former—and vice versa. And, anyway, it is all just 'painted canvas'. But on this occasion, and in this setting, meditations about why men paint lead on to a discussion of why men drink. Art shades into alcohol. And Coverdale has a most interesting subversive thought. There is a fountain in the tavern and the basin or 'lakelet' in which it stands contains several 'gold-fishes'. Coverdale indulges a fancy.

Never before, I imagine, did a company of water-drinkers remain so entirely uncontaminated by the bad example around them, nor could I help wondering that it had not occurred to any freakish inebriate, to empty a glass of liquor into their lakelet. What a delightful idea! Who would not be a fish, if he could inhale jollity with the essential element of his existence! (p. 178)

Is the artist, perhaps, just such a 'freakish inebriate', subtly introducing his potent stimulants into the very cultural air his unsuspecting compatriots breathe? Is it a beneficence ('bringing warmth and cheer'), or a treachery ('intoxicating' people secretly and against their will)? Inasmuch as alcohol is known temporarily to raise the 'spirits', it may, with an ironic turn, be said to 'spiritualize' the consumer. But, despite its undoubted properties of bringing temporary consolation, short-lived feelings of gladness and hope, a brief illusion of restored 'youth and vigour' (p. 178), alcohol is far more likely to bestialize the one who turns to it too often. What clearly worried or preoccupied Hawthorne was the extent to which the questions and considerations raised in those last two sentences might exactly be applied to art.

Very near the end, Coverdale draws a 'moral' from what Hollingsworth's 'ruling passion' has done to him.

It ruins, or is fearfully apt to ruin, the heart; the rich juices of which God never meant should be pressed violently out, and distilled into alcoholic liquor, by an unnatural process; but should render life sweet, bland, and gently beneficent, and sensibly influence other hearts and other lives to the same blessed end. (p. 243)

A nice distinction, particularly in view of all the references to alcoholic drinks which have preceded it. Our heart's juices were not meant to be 'distilled' into strong liquor—certainly an unnatural and, if you will, a violent process; rather they should simply render life 'sweet' and 'bland'—a sherry-cobbler of a life (sherry is fortified but not distilled—a suitably equivocal potion), a sillabub existence. Coverdale is truly not a man of, or for, strong spirit(s)—in *every* sense of the word. But the most crucial play with this word occurs in the closing words of the narrative (excluding here the last short chapter which is a sort of postscript). Coverdale muses that, while Zenobia was alive, 'Nature was proud of her'. Now she is dead, will not 'Nature shed a tear?' (p. 244).

Ah, no! She adopts the calamity at once into her system, and is just as well pleased, for aught we can see, with the tuft of ranker vegetation that grew out of Zenobia's heart, as with all the beauty which has bequeathed us no earthly representative, except in this crop of weeds. It is because the spirit is inestimable, that the lifeless body is so little valued. (p. 244)

Nature is the system which absorbs *all* the other systems, the provisional, partial, and ephemeral structures and social orderings which man attempts to erect. Nature simply waits for all human signs to fail, and Zenobia, like Conrad's Decoud, is 'swallowed up in the immense indifference of things'.[30] That being so, 'the spirit is inestimable'—but by this end-point of the book what on earth, literally on that cloddish earth, can 'spirit' signify? Throughout, Coverdale has revealed himself to be adrift in a lexicon of failed transcendence; a 'strayed reveller' (in Matthew Arnold's phrase) who has indeed lost his way, his home, his sense of history, his grasp of the real, any access to any ideal realm. That last appearance of the word 'spirit' gestures both pathetically to the final vagueness of a fading religious sense, and bathetically to those always available sherry-cobblers. Inasmuch as he sees him as a true product of America, in his

[30] J. Conrad, *Nostromo* (London, 1904), 501.

disorientation, amnesia, and general sense of loss—*that* is what Hawthorne is doing with Coverdale. Saying to American society, American history, American religion and culture: *this* is the artist you have produced—intruder, lodger, spy.

As Michael Colacurcio[31] and Richard Brodhead[32] have very well demonstrated, Hawthorne could use his fiction brilliantly to reinsert aspects of the American past which had been, or were being, assiduously left out and erased in the official versions—writing back *on*, as it were, what triumphalist American historiography was busy 'writing *off*'. But in *The Blithedale Romance*, though he does make his point about the occlusion and elimination of the Indians, he shows us an artist forgetting the American past, while being disablingly sceptical about the American present. Always dubious, undecided, ambiguous, about the ultimate validity or value of 'fiction' and art in general, Hawthorne has written that uncertainty all through this book. Indeed one could say that he has taken that uncertainty, and a very far-reaching anatomy of it, and made it *into* a book. A curious dividend of this enterprise is that the book has more of the American nineteenth century in it than any other novel I know, and contains innumerable unforeseen and unforeseeable profundities and insights. In all its idiosyncratic inconsistencies of tone, its narrative vacillations and swerves, its inconclusiveness and loose ends, its unpredictable ranging through incongruously contiguous settings and scenes, its collocation of wildly dissimilar characters—in all these features, and indeed because of them, it is, almost despite itself, undoubtedly one of the great American novels. And, in its way, one of the saddest and most pessimistic. For by the end clearly America itself has become for Coverdale 'another spot, and an utter strangeness' (p. 206). Perhaps for Hawthorne, too. For it was one of Henry James's late and considered characterizations of him that 'He is outside of everything, and an alien everywhere.'[33]

[31] M. Colacurcio, *The Province of Piety: Moral History in Hawthorne's Early Tales* (London and Cambridge, Mass., 1984).

[32] R. Brodhead, *The School of Hawthorne* (Oxford and New York, 1986).

[33] James, *Essays*, p. 467.

NOTE ON THE TEXT

The text of this volume is that of *The Blithedale Romance*, Volume III of the *Centenary Edition of the Works of Nathaniel Hawthorne*, published in 1964 by the Ohio State University Press for the Ohio State University Center for Textual Studies. The Centenary text was established by the application of bibliographical and analytical criticism to the evidence of the various documentary forms in which the text had appeared. It is a critical, unmodernized reconstruction of Hawthorne's text, and is approved by the Center for Editions of the Modern Language Association of America.

SELECT BIBLIOGRAPHY

LETTERS AND NOTEBOOKS

The Letters 1813–1843 (Centenary Edition of the Works of Nathaniel Hawthorne, 25; Columbus, Ohio, 1984).

The American Notebooks (Centenary Edition, 8; Columbus, Ohio, 1972).

Love Letters of Nathaniel Hawthorne (2 vols., Chicago, 1907).

BIOGRAPHY

Hawthorne, Julian, *Nathaniel Hawthorne and his Wife* (2 vols., Boston, 1884).

Mellow, James, *Nathaniel Hawthorne in his Times* (Boston, 1980).

Stewart, Randall, *Nathaniel Hawthorne: A Biography* (New Haven, 1948).

Turner, Arlin, *Nathaniel Hawthorne: A Biography* (New York and Oxford, 1980).

CRITICISM: GENERAL

Baym, Nina, 'Thwarted Nature: Hawthorne as Feminist', in Fritz Fleischmann (ed.), *American Novelists Revisited: Essays in Feminist Criticism* (Boston, 1982), 55–77.

—— *The Shape of Hawthorne's Career* (Ithaca and London, 1976).

—— 'The Significance of Plot in Hawthorne's Romances', in G. R. Thompson and V. L. Lokke (eds.), *Ruined Eden of the Present* (West Lafayette, Ind., 1981), 49–70.

Bloom, Harold (ed.), *Nathaniel Hawthorne* (New York, 1986).

Brodhead, Richard, *Hawthorne, Melville, and the Novel* (Chicago, 1976).

—— *The School of Hawthorne* (Oxford and New York, 1986).

Cameron, Sharon, *The Corporeal Self: Allegories of the Body in Melville and Hawthorne* (Baltimore and London, 1979).

Cohen, Bernard (ed.), *The Recognition of Nathaniel Hawthorne: Selected Criticism Since 1828* (Ann Arbor, Mich., 1969).

Colacurcio, M., *The Province of Piety: Moral History in Hawthorne's Early Tales* (London and Cambridge, Mass., 1984).

Crane, Teresa, *The Hawthorne Heritage* (London, 1988).

Crews, Frederick, *The Sins of the Fathers: Hawthorne's Psychological Themes* (New York, 1966).

Crowley, J. Donald (ed.), *Hawthorne: The Critical Heritage* (London, 1970).

DeSalvo, Louise, *Nathaniel Hawthorne* (Brighton, 1987).

Dryden, Edgar, *Nathaniel Hawthorne: The Poetics of Enchantment* (Ithaca, NY, 1977).

James, Henry, *Hawthorne* (1879; repr. Ithaca, New York, 1956).

Lee, A. R. (ed.), *Nathaniel Hawthorne: New Critical Essays* (London, 1982).

Lloyd Smith, Allan Gardner, *Eve Tempted: Writing and Sexuality in Hawthorne's Fiction* (Sydney and London, 1984).

Martin, Terence, *Nathaniel Hawthorne* (rev. edn., New York, 1983).

Pearce, Roy Harvey (ed.), *Hawthorne: Centenary Essays* (Columbus, Ohio, 1964).

Poirier, Richard, *A World Elsewhere* (London, 1967).

CRITICISM: 'THE BLITHEDALE ROMANCE'

Berlant, L., 'Fantasies of Utopia in *The Blithedale Romance*'. *American Literary History*, 1/1 (1989), 30–62.

Carabine, Keith, '"Bitter Honey": Miles Coverdale as Narrator in *The Blithedale Romance*', in A. R. Lee (ed.), *Nathaniel Hawthorne: New Critical Essays* (London, 1982), 110–130.

Crews, Frederick, 'A New Reading of *The Blithedale Romance*', *American Literature*, 29 (May 1957), 147–70.

Davidson, F., 'Toward a Revaluation of *The Blithedale Romance*', *New England Quarterly*, 25/3 (1952), 374–83.

Eliot, George, review in *Westminster Review*, 58 (1852), 592–8; repr. in J. Donald Crowley (ed.), *Hawthorne: The Critical Heritage* (London, 1970), 259–64.

Elliott, Robert C., '*The Blithedale Romance*', in Roy Harvey Pearce (ed.), *Hawthorne: Centenary Essays* (Columbus, Ohio, 1964), 103–17.

Fryer, Judith, *The Faces of Eve: Women in the Nineteenth Century American Novel* (New York, 1976).

Garrett, J. C., *Hope or Disillusion: Three Versions of Utopia: Nathaniel Hawthorne, Samuel Butler, George Orwell* (Christchurch, New Zealand, 1984).

Griffith, Kelley, Jr., 'Form in *The Blithedale Romance*', *American Literature*, 40 (1968), 15–26.

Gross, Seymour, and Murphy, Rosalie (eds.), *The Blithedale Romance* (Norton Critical Edition; New York, 1978).

Howe, Irving, 'Hawthorne—Pastoral and Politics', in *Politics and the Novel* (New York, 1957), 163–75.

Justin, James, 'Hawthorne's Coverdale: Character and Art in *The Blithedale Romance*', *American Literature*, 47 (1975), 21–36.

Kolodny, Annette, Introduction to Penguin edition (Harmondsworth, 1983).

Lefcowitz, A., and Lefcowitz, B., 'Some Rents in the Veil: New Light on Priscilla and Zenobia in *The Blithedale Romance*', *Nineteenth Century Fiction*, 21/3 (1966), 263–75.

Stoehr, T., 'Art vs. Utopia: The Case of Nathaniel Hawthorne and Brook Farm', *Antioch Review*, 36/1 (1978), 89–102.

Swann, C., 'A Note on *The Blithedale Romance* or "Call him Fauntleroy"', *Journal of American Studies*, 10 (1976), 103–4.

Turner, Arlin, Introduction to Norton edition (New York, 1958).

Winslow, Joan, 'New Light on Hawthorne's Miles Coverdale', *Journal of Narrative Technique*, 7 (1977), 189–99.

ON RELATED SUBJECTS

Flaxner, E., *Century of Struggle: The Women's Rights Movement in the USA* (Cambridge, Mass., 1975).

Fuller, Margaret, *Memories of Margaret Fuller* (Boston, 1852).

—— *Women in the Nineteenth Century*, ed. A. D. Fuller (1864; repr. Greenwood, New York, 1968).

—— *Writings of Margaret Fuller*, ed. M. Wade (Clifton, 1973).

Goldfarb, Clare, and Goldfarb, Russell, *Spiritualism and Nineteenth Century Letters* (London, 1978).

Miller, Perry (ed.), *The Transcendentalists* (Cambridge, Mass., 1971).

Reynolds, D., *Beneath the American Renaissance* (Cambridge, Mass., 1988).

Tatar, Maria, *Spellbound: Studies on Mesmerism and Literature* (Princeton, 1978).

Tharp, L. H., *The Peabody Sisters of Salem* (Boston, 1950).

Wilson, Edmund, *To The Finland Station* [sections on nineteenth-century Utopian communities] (1942; London, 1974).

BIBLIOGRAPHIES

Boswell, Jeanetta, *Nathaniel Hawthorne and the Critics: A Checklist of Criticism, 1900–1978* (Methuchen, NJ, and London, 1982).

Browne, Nina, *A Bibliography of Nathaniel Hawthorne* (1905; New York, 1968).

Frazer Clark, C. E., Jr., *Nathaniel Hawthorne: A Descriptive Bibliography* (Pittsburgh, 1978); 'limited to writings by Hawthorne'.

Ricks, Beatrice, Adams, Joseph D., and Hazelrig, Jack O., *Nathaniel Hawthorne: A Reference Bibliography, 1900–1971* (Boston, 1972).

For more recent criticism, see the annual MLA Bibliographies, and the periodical *Nathaniel Hawthorne Review*.

A CHRONOLOGY OF
NATHANIEL HAWTHORNE

1804   4 July: born in Salem, Massachusetts, second of three children of Elizabeth (*née* Manning) and Nathaniel Hathorne.

1808   Father, a ship's captain, dies of yellow fever at Surinam (Dutch Guiana). The Hathornes move to the Manning family home in Salem.

1813   November: a foot injury causes lameness and keeps Nathaniel from school for fourteen months.

1818   October: the Hathorne family moves to Raymond, Maine, which is still a wilderness area. Nathaniel hunts, fishes, and runs wild.

1819   July: Nathaniel returns to Salem to live with his mother's family, under the guardianship of his uncle Robert Manning. His mother stays in Maine.

1820   Prepares for college under Benjamin L. Oliver in Salem.

1821   October: enters Bowdoin College, Brunswick, Maine. College friendships with Horatio Bridge, Franklin Pierce, Jonathan Cilley.

1822   H. W. Longfellow enters Bowdoin. He and Hawthorne meet.

1825   September: graduates from Bowdoin. Returns to live with family in Salem. According to his sister Elizabeth, Nathaniel has completed 'Seven Tales of My Native Land' by the time he graduates from Bowdoin.

1828   October: *Fanshawe* published anonymously and at the author's expense. By now Nathaniel has added the 'w' to his family name.

1829   Plans a second collection of stories, to be called 'Provincial Tales', and submits manuscript to S. G. Goodrich, editor of *The Token*, an annual.

1830   12 November and 21 December: 'The Hollow of the Three Hills' and 'An Old Woman's Tale'—Hawthorne's first known tales to appear in print—published in *Salem Gazette*.

1831   Releases some tales intended for 'Provincial Tales' for publication in *The Token*, dated 1832: 'The Gentle Boy', 'The Wives of the Dead', 'Roger Malvin's Burial', 'My Kinsman, Major Molineux'.

1832   Plans a third collection, to be called 'The Story Teller'. September–October: makes extensive journeys in Vermont and New York State, gathering literary materials.

1834   November and December: 'The Story Teller, Nos I and II' published in *New England Magazine*.

1835   'The Minister's Black Veil', 'The Maypole of Merry Mount', and 'The Wedding-Knell' published in *The Token* for 1836.

1836   January: moves to Boston to edit *American Magazine of Useful and Entertaining Knowledge*. March: first issue with Nathaniel Hawthorne as editor. His salary is not paid. Magazine goes bankrupt in May. May to September: writes—with the help of Elizabeth—*Peter Parley's Universal History, on the Basis of Geography*.

1837   March: *Twice-told Tales* published. Unknown to Hawthorne, Horatio Bridge has given financial guarantee to publisher. July: Longfellow's highly favourable review of *Twice-told Tales* appears in the *North American Review*. November: meets Sophia Amelia Peabody. October: begins his association with John L. O'Sullivan's *Democratic Review*. Eight Hawthorne pieces appear there in fifteen months.

1838   July–September: begins three months of seclusion in North Adams, Massachusetts, with trips to the Berkshires, upstate New York, Vermont, Connecticut.

1839   January: takes up appointment as measurer in the Boston Custom House. 6 March: writes first surviving love-letter to Sophia Peabody.

1840   November: resigns from Custom House with effect from 1 January 1841. December: *Grandfather's Chair* published, dated 1841, a children's history of New England.

1841   January: returns to Salem. *Famous Old People* published. March: *The Liberty Tree* published. April: joins the Brook Farm Associationist experiment at West Roxbury, near Boston, as working member. Becomes a paying boarder at the Farm, with no work commitments, in the autumn.

September: buys two shares in the Brook Farm project, planning to bring Sophia to live there when they are married. October: leaves the Farm for Boston.

1842 January: second edition of *Twice-told Tales* published, with additional volume containing sixteen recent tales and sketches together with five that antedate the 1837 collection. 9 July: Hawthorne and Sophia Peabody married. They move to Concord, Mass., where they rent the Old Manse. October: withdraws from the Brook Farm project and requests return of his stock.

1844 3 March: daughter (Una) born.

1845 January–April: edits Horatio Bridge's *Journal of an African Cruiser*. October: the Hawthornes move to Herbert Street, Salem, as the owner wants Old Manse.

1846 9 April: sworn in a surveyor at Salem Custom House, having been nominated by President Polk, the new Democratic President. June: *Mosses from an Old Manse* published in two volumes. A critical, but not a financial, success. 22 June: Julian Hawthorne born. August: Hawthornes move to Salem.

1848 November: becomes manager and corresponding secretary of Salem Lyceum. Invites Emerson, Thoreau, Theodore Parker, Horace Mann, Louis Agassiz to lecture.

1849 7 June: removed from office in Custom House, following election of Whig President, Zachary Taylor, in 1848. 31 July: Mother dies. September: begins writing *The Scarlet Letter* and 'The Custom-House'.

1850 16 March: *The Scarlet Letter* published in edition of 2,500 copies. April: second edition published. May: Hawthornes move to 'Red Cottage', Lenox, Massachusetts. 5 August: Hawthorne meets Melville at a literary picnic. August: begins *The House of the Seven Gables*. 17 and 24 August: Melville's 'Hawthorne and His Mosses' appears anonymously in *The Literary World*. November: *True Stories* (reissue of *Grandfather's Chair* and *Biographical Stories*) published, dated 1851.

1851 April: *The House of the Seven Gables* published. March: third edition of *Twice-told Tales* published, with preface. 20 May: Rose Hawthorne born. November: *A Wonder Book for Girls and Boys* published, dated 1852. December: *The Snow-Image* published, dated 1852.

1852   April: buys the Alcott House in Concord, naming it 'The Wayside'. July: *The Blithedale Romance* published. September: *Life of Franklin Pierce*—a campaign biography of the Presidential candidate—published.

1853   March: nominated to consulship at Liverpool and Manchester by President Pierce. Appointment confirmed by US Senate. July: sails for England with family. September: *Tanglewood Tales* published.

1853–7 While working as consul, Hawthorne keeps notebooks in which he records his English experiences and impressions.

1854   Revised edition of *Mosses* published.

1856   November: Melville visits Hawthorne in Liverpool on way to the Holy Land. He also meets Hawthorne briefly on return journey in May 1857.

1857   October: gives up consulship.

1858   January: travels to Italy by way of France. Takes up residence in Rome. Keeps notebooks on his Italian experiences and begins work on an English romance, never to be completed, but published posthumously as *The Ancestral Footstep*. May to October: the Hawthornes live in Florence. He begins work on romance with an Italian theme.

1859   June: returns to England, where he rewrites the Italian romance.

1860   February: *The Transformation* published in England; in March the romance is published in America with the title *The Marble Faun*. June: returns to America and settles at 'The Wayside', Concord, where he begins work on a second version of his English romance.

1861   Abandons the romance, after making seven studies for the story. The fragment is published posthumously as *Dr Grimshaw's Secret*. Autumn: begins work on series of English essays. Begins a new romance on theme of the elixir of life but abandons this in 1862. Set at the time of the Revolution, the fragment is published posthumously as *Septimius Felton*.

1863   September: *Our Old Home* published—the collected essays on England—most of which had appeared separately in the *Atlantic Monthly*.

1864   19 May: dies at Plymouth, New Hampshire, having written
        three chapters of another romance about the elixir of life,
        which is posthumously published as *The Dolliver Romance*.

THE BLITHEDALE ROMANCE

PREFACE

I N THE 'BLITHEDALE' of this volume, many readers will
probably suspect a faint and not very faithful shadowing
of BROOK FARM,* in Roxbury, which (now a little more
than ten years ago) was occupied and cultivated by a company
of socialists. The Author does not wish to deny, that he had
this Community in his mind, and that (having had the good
fortune, for a time, to be personally connected with it) he
has occasionally availed himself of his actual reminiscences,
in the hope of giving a more lifelike tint to the fancy-sketch*
in the following pages. He begs it to be understood, however,
that he has considered the Institution itself as not less fairly
the subject of fictitious handling, than the imaginary personages whom he has introduced there. His whole treatment of
the affair is altogether incidental to the main purpose of the
Romance; nor does he put forward the slightest pretensions
to illustrate a theory, or elicit a conclusion, favorable or otherwise, in respect to Socialism.

In short, his present concern with the Socialist Community
is merely to establish a theatre, a little removed from the
highway of ordinary travel, where the creatures of his brain
may play their phantasmagorical antics, without exposing
them to too close a comparison with the actual events of real
lives. In the old countries, with which Fiction has long been

conversant, a certain conventional privilege seems to be awarded to the romancer; his work is not put exactly side by side with nature; and he is allowed a license with regard to every-day Probability, in view of the improved effects which he is bound to produce thereby. Among ourselves, on the contrary, there is as yet no such Faery Land, so like the real world, that, in a suitable remoteness, one cannot well tell the difference, but with an atmosphere of strange enchantment, beheld through which the inhabitants have a propriety of their own. This atmosphere is what the American romancer* needs. In its absence, the beings of imagination are compelled to show themselves in the same category as actually living mortals; a necessity that generally renders the paint and pasteboard of their composition but too painfully discernible. With the idea of partially obviating this difficulty, (the sense of which has always pressed very heavily upon him,) the Author has ventured to make free with his old, and affectionately remembered home, at BROOK FARM, as being, certainly, the most romantic episode of his own life—essentially a daydream, and yet a fact—and thus offering an available foothold between fiction and reality. Furthermore, the scene was in good keeping with the personages whom he desired to introduce.

These characters, he feels it right to say, are entirely fictitious. It would, indeed, (considering how few amiable qualities he distributes among his imaginary progeny,) be a most grievous wrong to his former excellent associates, were the Author to allow it to be supposed that he has been sketching any of their likenesses. Had he attempted it, they would at least have recognized the touches of a friendly pencil. But he has done nothing of the kind. The self-concentrated Philanthropist; the high-spirited Woman, bruising herself against the narrow limitations of her sex; the weakly Maiden, whose tremulous nerves endow her with Sibylline* attributes; the Minor Poet, beginning life with strenuous aspirations, which die out with his youthful fervor —all these might have been looked for, at BROOK FARM, but, by some accident, never made their appearance there.

The Author cannot close his reference to this subject, without expressing a most earnest wish that some one of the many cultivated and philosophic minds, which took an interest in that enterprise, might now give the world its history. Ripley, with whom rests the honorable paternity of the Institution, Dana, Dwight, Channing, Burton, Parker,* for instance—with others, whom he dares not name, because they veil themselves from the public eye—among these is the ability to convey both the outward narrative and the inner truth and spirit of the whole affair, together with the lessons which those years of thought and toil must have elaborated, for the behoof of future experimentalists. Even the brilliant Howadji* might find as rich a theme in his youthful reminiscenses of BROOK FARM, and a more novel one—close at hand as it lies—than those which he has since made so distant a pilgrimage to seek, in Syria, and along the current of the Nile.

CONCORD (Mass.), May, 1852.

THE BLITHEDALE ROMANCE

I

OLD MOODIE

THE EVENING before my departure for Blithedale, I was returning to my bachelor-apartments, after attending the wonderful exhibition of the Veiled Lady, when an elderly-man of rather shabby appearance met me in an obscure part of the street.

"Mr. Coverdale,"*said he, softly, "can I speak with you a moment?"

As I have casually alluded to the Veiled Lady, it may not be amiss to mention, for the benefit of such of my readers as are unacquainted with her now forgotten celebrity, that she was a phenomenon in the mesmeric line;* one of the earliest that had indicated the birth of a new science, or the revival of an old humbug. Since those times, her sisterhood have grown too numerous to attract much individual notice; nor, in fact, has any one of them ever come before the public under such skilfully contrived circumstances of stage-effect, as those which at once mystified and illuminated the remarkable performances of the lady in question. Now-a-days, in the management of his 'subject,' 'clairvoyant,' or 'medium,' the exhibitor affects the simplicity and openness of scientific experiment; and even if he profess to tread a step or two across the boundaries of the spiritual world, yet carries with him the laws of our actual life, and extends them over his preternatural conquests. Twelve or fifteen years ago, on the contrary, all the arts of mysterious arrangement, of picturesque disposition, and artistically contrasted light and shade, were made available in order to set the apparent miracle in the strongest attitude of opposition to ordinary facts. In the case of the Veiled Lady, moreover, the interest of the spectator was further wrought up by the enigma of her identity, and an absurd rumor (probably set afloat by the exhibitor, and at one time very prevalent) that a beautiful young lady, of family and fortune, was enshrouded within the misty drapery of the veil. It was white, with somewhat of a subdued silver sheen, like the sunny side of a cloud; and falling over the wearer, from head to foot, was supposed to insulate her from the material world, from time and space, and to endow her with many of the privileges of a disembodied spirit.

Her pretensions, however, whether miraculous or otherwise, have little to do with the present narrative; except, indeed, that I had propounded, for the Veiled Lady's prophetic solution, a query as to the success of our Blithedale enterprise. The response, by-the-by, was of the true Sibylline stamp, nonsensical in its first aspect, yet, on closer study, unfolding a variety of interpretations, one of which has certainly accorded with the event. I was turning over this riddle in my mind, and trying to catch its slippery purport by the tail, when the old man, above-mentioned, interrupted me.

"Mr. Coverdale!—Mr. Coverdale!" said he, repeating my name twice, in order to make up for the hesitating and ineffectual way in which he uttered it—"I ask your pardon, sir—but I hear you are going to Blithedale tomorrow?"

I knew the pale, elderly face, with the red-tipt nose, and the patch over one eye, and likewise saw something characteristic in the old fellow's way of standing under the arch of a gate, only revealing enough of himself to make me recognize him as an acquaintance. He was a very shy personage, this Mr. Moodie; and the trait was the more singular, as his mode of getting his bread necessarily brought him into the stir and hubbub of the world, more than the generality of men.

"Yes, Mr. Moodie," I answered, wondering what interest he could take in the fact, "it is my intention to go to Blithedale tomorrow. Can I be of any service to you, before my departure?"

"If you pleased, Mr. Coverdale," said he, "you might do me a very great favor."

"A very great one!" repeated I, in a tone that must have expressed but little alacrity of beneficence, although I was ready to do the old man any amount of kindness involving no special trouble to myself. "A very great favor, do you say? My time is brief, Mr. Moodie, and I have a good many preparations to make. But be good enough to tell me what you wish."

"Ah, sir," replied old Moodie, "I don't quite like to do that; and, on further thoughts, Mr. Coverdale, perhaps I had better apply to some older gentleman, or to some lady, if you would have the kindness to make me known to one, who may happen to be going to Blithedale. You are a young man, sir!"

"Does that fact lessen my availability for your purpose?" asked I. "However, if an older man will suit you better, there is Mr. Hollingsworth, who has three or four years the advantage of me in age, and is a much more solid character, and a philanthropist to boot. I am only a poet, and, so the critics tell me, no great affair at that! But what can this business be, Mr. Moodie? It begins to interest me; especially since your hint that a lady's influence might be found desirable. Come; I am really anxious to be of service to you."

But the old fellow, in his civil and demure manner, was both freakish and obstinate; and he had now taken some notion or other into his head that made him hesitate in his former design.

"I wonder, sir," said he, "whether you know a lady whom they call Zenobia?"*

"Not personally," I answered, "although I expect that pleasure tomorrow, as she has got the start of the rest of us, and is already a resident at Blithedale. But have you a literary turn, Mr. Moodie?—or have you taken up the advocacy of women's rights?—or what else can have interested you in this lady? Zenobia, by-the-by, as I suppose you know, is merely her public name; a sort of mask in which she comes before the world, retaining all the privileges of privacy—a contrivance, in short, like the white drapery of the Veiled Lady, only a little more transparent. But it is late! Will you tell me what I can do for you?"

"Please to excuse me to-night, Mr. Coverdale," said Moodie. "You are very kind; but I am afraid I have troubled you, when, after all, there may be no need. Perhaps, with your good leave, I will come to your lodgings tomorrow-morning, before you set out for Blithedale. I wish you a good-night, sir, and beg pardon for stopping you."

And so he slipt away; and, as he did not show himself, the next morning, it was only through subsequent events that I ever arrived at a plausible conjecture as to what his business could have been. Arriving at my room, I threw a lump of cannel coal*upon the grate, lighted a cigar, and spent an hour in musings of every hue, from the brightest to the most sombre; being, in truth, not so very confident as at some former periods, that this final step, which would mix me up irrevocably with the Blithedale affair, was the wisest that could possibly be taken. It was nothing short of midnight when I went to bed, after drinking a glass of particularly fine Sherry, on which I used to pride myself, in those days. It was the very last bottle; and I finished it, with a friend, the next forenoon, before setting out for Blithedale.

II

BLITHEDALE

THERE can hardly remain for me, (who am really getting to be a frosty bachelor, with another white hair, every week or so, in my moustache,) there can hardly flicker up again so cheery a blaze upon the hearth, as that which I remember, the next day, at Blithedale. It was a wood-fire, in the parlor of an old farm-house, on an April afternoon, but with the fitful gusts of a wintry snow-storm roaring in the chimney. Vividly does that fireside re-create itself, as I rake away the ashes from the embers in my memory, and blow them up with a sigh, for lack of more inspiring breath. Vividly, for an instant, but, anon, with the dimmest gleam, and with just as little fervency for my heart as for my finger-ends! The staunch oaken-logs were long ago burnt out. Their genial glow must be represented, if at all, by the merest phosphoric glimmer, like that which exudes, rather than shines, from damp fragments of decayed trees, deluding the benighted wanderer through a forest. Around such chill mockery of a fire, some few of us might sit on the withered leaves, spreading out each a palm towards the imaginary warmth, and talk over our exploded scheme for beginning the life of Paradise anew.

Paradise, indeed! Nobody else in the world, I am bold to affirm—nobody, at least, in our bleak little world of New

England—had dreamed of Paradise, that day, except as the pole suggests the tropic. Nor, with such materials as were at hand, could the most skilful architect have constructed any better imitation of Eve's bower, than might be seen in the snow-hut of an Esquimaux.* But we made a summer of it, in spite of the wild drifts.

It was an April day, as already hinted, and well towards the middle of the month. When morning dawned upon me, in town, its temperature was mild enough to be pronounced even balmy, by a lodger—like myself—in one of the midmost houses of a brick-block; each house partaking of the warmth of all the rest, besides the sultriness of its individual furnace-heat. But, towards noon, there had come snow, driven along the street by a north-easterly blast, and whitening the roofs and sidewalks with a business-like perseverance that would have done credit to our severest January tempest. It set about its task, apparently as much in earnest as if it had been guaranteed from a thaw, for months to come. The greater, surely, was my heroism, when, puffing out a final whiff of cigar-smoke, I quitted my cosey pair of bachelor-rooms—with a good fire burning in the grate, and a closet right at hand, where there was still a bottle or two in the champagne-basket, and a residuum of claret in a box, and somewhat of proof in the concavity of a big demijohn*—quitted, I say, these comfortable quarters, and plunged into the heart of the pitiless snow-storm, in quest of a better life.

The better life! Possibly, it would hardly look so, now; it is enough if it looked so, then. The greatest obstacle to being heroic, is the doubt whether one may not be going to prove one's self a fool; the truest heroism is, to resist the doubt—and the profoundest wisdom, to know when it ought to be resisted, and when to be obeyed.

Yet, after all, let us acknowledge it wiser, if not more sagacious, to follow out one's day-dream to its natural consummation, although, if the vision have been worth the having, it is certain never to be consummated otherwise than by a failure. And what of that! Its airiest fragments, impalpable as they may be, will possess a value that lurks not in the most ponderous realities of any practicable scheme. They are not the rubbish of the mind. Whatever else I may repent of, therefore, let it be reckoned neither among my sins nor follies, that I once had faith and force enough to form generous hopes of the world's destiny—yes!—and to do what in me lay for their accomplishment; even to the extent of quitting a warm fireside, flinging away a freshly lighted cigar, and travelling far beyond the strike of city-clocks, through a drifting snow-storm.

There were four of us who rode together through the storm; and Hollingsworth, who had agreed to be of the number, was accidentally delayed, and set forth at a later hour, alone. As we threaded the streets, I remember how the buildings, on either side, seemed to press too closely upon us, insomuch that our mighty hearts found barely room enough to throb between them. The snow-fall, too, looked inexpressibly dreary, (I had almost called it dingy,) coming down through an atmosphere of city-smoke, and alighting on the sidewalk, only to be moulded into the impress of somebody's patched boot or over-shoe. Thus, the track of an old conventionalism was visible on what was freshest from the sky. But—when we left the pavements, and our muffled hoof-tramps beat upon a desolate extent of country-road, and were effaced by the unfettered blast, as soon as stamped—then, there was better air to breathe. Air, that had not been breathed, once and again! Air, that had not been spoken into words of falsehood, formality, and error, like all the air of the dusky city!

"How pleasant it is!" remarked I, while the snow-flakes flew into my mouth, the moment it was opened. "How very mild and balmy is this country-air!"

"Ah, Coverdale, don't laugh at what little enthusiasm you

have left," said one of my companions. "I maintain that this nitrous atmosphere is really exhilarating; and, at any rate, we can never call ourselves regenerated men, till a February north-easter shall be as grateful to us as the softest breeze of June."

So we all of us took courage, riding fleetly and merrily along, by stone-fences that were half-buried in the wave-like drifts; and through patches of woodland, where the tree-trunks opposed a snow-encrusted side towards the north-east; and within ken of deserted villas, with no foot-prints in their avenues; and past scattered dwellings, whence puffed the smoke of country fires, strongly impregnated with the pungent aroma of burning peat. Sometimes, encountering a traveller, we shouted a friendly greeting; and he, unmuffling his ears to the bluster and the snow-spray, and listening eagerly, appeared to think our courtesy worth less than the trouble which it cost him. The churl! He understood the shrill whistle of the blast, but had no intelligence for our blithe tones of brotherhood. This lack of faith in our cordial sympathy, on the traveller's part, was one among the innumerable tokens how difficult a task we had in hand, for the reformation of the world. We rode on, however, with still unflagging spirits, and made such good companionship with the tempest, that, at our journey's end, we professed ourselves almost loth to bid the rude blusterer good bye. But, to own the truth, I was little better than an icicle, and began to be suspicious that I had caught a fearful cold.

And, now, we were seated by the brisk fireside of the old farm-house; the same fire that glimmers so faintly among my reminiscences, at the beginning of this chapter. There we sat, with the snow melting out of our hair and beards, and our faces all a-blaze, what with the past inclemency and present warmth. It was, indeed, a right good fire that we found awaiting us, built up of great, rough logs, and knotty limbs, and splintered fragments of an oak-tree, such as farmers are wont to keep for their own hearths; since these crooked and unmanageable boughs could never be measured into merchantable cords for the market. A family of the old Pilgrims might have swung their kettle over precisely such a fire as this, only, no doubt, a bigger one; and, contrasting it with my coal-grate, I felt, so much the more, that we had transported ourselves a world-wide distance from the system of society that shackled us at breakfast-time.

Good, comfortable Mrs. Foster (the wife of stout Silas Foster, who was to manage the farm, at a fair stipend, and be our tutor in the art of husbandry) bade us a hearty welcome. At her back—a back of generous breadth—appeared two young women, smiling most hospitably, but looking rather awkward withal, as not well knowing what was to be their position in our new arrangement of the world. We shook hands affectionately, all round, and congratulated ourselves that the blessed state of brotherhood and sisterhood, at which we aimed, might fairly be dated from this moment. Our greetings were hardly concluded, when the door opened, and Zenobia—whom I had never before seen, important as was her place in our enterprise—Zenobia entered the parlor.

This (as the reader, if at all acquainted with our literary biography, need scarcely be told) was not her real name. She had assumed it, in the first instance, as her magazine-signature; and as it accorded well with something imperial which her friends attributed to this lady's figure and deportment, they, half-laughingly, adopted it in their familiar intercourse with her. She took the appellation in good part, and even encouraged its constant use, which, in fact, was thus far appropriate, that our Zenobia—however humble looked her new philosophy—had as much native pride as any queen would have known what to do with.

III

A KNOT OF DREAMERS

ZENOBIA bade us welcome, in a fine, frank, mellow voice, and gave each of us her hand, which was very soft and warm. She had something appropriate, I recollect, to say to every individual; and what she said to myself was this:—

"I have long wished to know you, Mr. Coverdale, and to thank you for your beautiful poetry, some of which I have learned by heart;—or, rather, it has stolen into my memory, without my exercising any choice or volition about the matter. Of course—permit me to say—you do not think of relinquishing an occupation in which you have done yourself so much credit. I would almost rather give you up, as an associate, than that the world should lose one of its true poets!"

"Ah, no; there will not be the slightest danger of that, especially after this inestimable praise from Zenobia!" said I, smiling and blushing, no doubt, with excess of pleasure. "I hope, on the contrary, now, to produce something that shall really deserve to be called poetry—true, strong, natural, and sweet, as is the life which we are going to lead—something that shall have the notes of wild-birds twittering through it, or a strain like the wind-anthems in the woods, as the case may be!"

"Is it irksome to you to hear your own verses sung?" asked

Zenobia, with a gracious smile. "If so, I am very sorry; for you will certainly hear me singing them, sometimes, in the summer evenings."

"Of all things," answered I, "that is what will delight me most."

While this passed, and while she spoke to my companions, I was taking note of Zenobia's aspect; and it impressed itself on me so distinctly, that I can now summon her up like a ghost, a little wanner than the life, but otherwise identical with it. She was dressed as simply as possible, in an American print, (I think the dry-goods people*call it so,) but with a silken kerchief, between which and her gown there was one glimpse of a white shoulder. It struck me as a great piece of good-fortune that there should be just that glimpse. Her hair —which was dark, glossy, and of singular abundance—was put up rather soberly and primly, without curls, or other ornament, except a single flower. It was an exotic, of rare beauty, and as fresh as if the hot-house gardener had just clipt it from the stem. That flower has struck deep root into my memory. I can both see it and smell it, at this moment. So brilliant, so rare, so costly as it must have been, and yet endur-ing only for a day, it was more indicative of the pride and pomp, which had a luxuriant growth in Zenobia's character, than if a great diamond had sparkled among her hair.

Her hand, though very soft, was larger than most women would like to have—or than they could afford to have—though not a whit too large in proportion with the spacious plan of Zenobia's entire development. It did one good to see a fine intellect (as hers really was, although its natural tendency lay in another direction than towards literature) so fitly cased. She was, indeed, an admirable figure of a woman, just on the hither verge of her richest maturity, with a combination of features which it is safe to call remarkably beautiful, even if some fastidious persons might pronounce them a little defi-cient in softness and delicacy. But we find enough of those

attributes, everywhere. Preferable—by way of variety, at least
—was Zenobia's bloom, health, and vigor, which she possessed
in such overflow that a man might well have fallen in love
with her for their sake only. In her quiet moods, she seemed
rather indolent; but when really in earnest, particularly if
there were a spice of bitter feeling, she grew all alive, to her
finger-tips.

"I am the first-comer," Zenobia went on to say, while her
smile beamed warmth upon us all; "so I take the part of
hostess, for to-day, and welcome you as if to my own fireside.
You shall be my guests, too, at supper. Tomorrow, if you
please, we will be brethren and sisters, and begin our new
life from day-break."

"Have we our various parts assigned?" asked some one.

"Oh, we of the softer sex," responded Zenobia, with her
mellow, almost broad laugh—most delectable to hear, but not
in the least like an ordinary woman's laugh—"we women
(there are four of us here, already) will take the domestic
and indoor part of the business, as a matter of course. To
bake, to boil, to roast, to fry, to stew—to wash, and iron, and
scrub, and sweep, and, at our idler intervals, to repose ourselves on knitting and sewing—these, I suppose, must be feminine occupations for the present. By-and-by, perhaps, when
our individual adaptations begin to develop themselves, it
may be that some of us, who wear the petticoat, will go
afield, and leave the weaker brethren to take our places in
the kitchen!"

"What a pity," I remarked, "that the kitchen, and the
house-work generally, cannot be left out of our system altogether! It is odd enough, that the kind of labor which falls
to the lot of women is just that which chiefly distinguishes
artificial life—the life of degenerated mortals—from the life
of Paradise. Eve had no dinner-pot, and no clothes to mend,
and no washing-day."

"I am afraid," said Zenobia, with mirth gleaming out of

her eyes, "we shall find some difficulty in adopting the Paradisiacal system, for at least a month to come. Look at that snow-drift sweeping past the window! Are there any figs ripe, do you think? Have the pine-apples been gathered, to-day? Would you like a bread-fruit, or a cocoa-nut? Shall I run out and pluck you some roses? No, no, Mr. Coverdale, the only flower hereabouts is the one in my hair, which I got out of a green-house, this morning. As for the garb of Eden," added she, shivering playfully, "I shall not assume it till after May-day!"

Assuredly, Zenobia could not have intended it—the fault must have been entirely in my imagination—but these last words, together with something in her manner, irresistibly brought up a picture of that fine, perfectly developed figure, in Eve's earliest garment. I almost fancied myself actually beholding it.* Her free, careless, generous modes of expression often had this effect of creating images which, though pure, are hardly felt to be quite decorous, when born of a thought that passes between man and woman. I imputed it, at that time, to Zenobia's noble courage, conscious of no harm, and scorning the petty restraints which take the life and color out of other women's conversation. There was another peculiarity about her. We seldom meet with women, now-a-days, and in this country, who impress us as being women at all; their sex fades away and goes for nothing, in ordinary intercourse. Not so with Zenobia. One felt an influence breathing out of her, such as we might suppose to come from Eve, when she was just made, and her Creator brought her to Adam, saying— 'Behold, here is a woman!' Not that I would convey the idea of especial gentleness, grace, modesty, and shyness, but of a certain warm and rich characteristic, which seems, for the most part, to have been refined away out of the feminine system.

"And now," continued Zenobia, "I must go and help get supper. Do you think you can be content—instead of figs, pine-apples, and all the other delicacies of Adam's supper-table—with tea and toast, and a certain modest supply of ham and tongue, which, with the instinct of a housewife, I brought hither in a basket? And there shall be bread-and-milk, too, if the innocence of your taste demands it."

The whole sisterhood now went about their domestic avocations, utterly declining our offers to assist, farther than by bringing wood, for the kitchen-fire, from a huge pile in the back-yard. After heaping up more than a sufficient quantity, we returned to the sitting-room, drew our chairs closer to the hearth, and began to talk over our prospects. Soon, with a tremendous stamping in the entry, appeared Silas Foster, lank, stalwart, uncouth, and grisly-bearded. He came from foddering the cattle, in the barn, and from the field, where he had been ploughing, until the depth of the snow rendered it impossible to draw a furrow. He greeted us in pretty much the same tone as if he were speaking to his oxen, took a quid from his iron tobacco-box, pulled off his wet cow-hide boots, and sat down before the fire in his stocking-feet. The steam arose from his soaked garments, so that the stout yeoman looked vaporous and spectre-like.

"Well, folks," remarked Silas, "you'll be wishing yourselves back to town again, if this weather holds!"

And, true enough, there was a look of gloom, as the twilight fell silently and sadly out of the sky, its gray or sable flakes intermingling themselves with the fast descending snow. The storm, in its evening aspect, was decidedly dreary. It seemed to have arisen for our especial behoof; a symbol of the cold, desolate, distrustful phantoms that invariably haunt the mind, on the eve of adventurous enterprises, to warn us back within the boundaries of ordinary life.

But our courage did not quail. We would not allow ourselves to be depressed by the snow-drift, trailing past the window, any more than if it had been the sigh of a summer wind among rustling boughs. There have been few brighter seasons for us, than that. If ever men might lawfully dream awake, and give utterance to their wildest visions, without dread of laughter or scorn on the part of the audience—yes, and speak of earthly happiness, for themselves and mankind, as an object to be hopefully striven for, and probably attained —we, who made that little semi-circle round the blazing fire, were those very men. We had left the rusty iron frame-work of society behind us. We had broken through many hindrances that are powerful enough to keep most people on the weary tread-mill of the established system, even while they feel its irksomeness almost as intolerable as we did. We had stept down from the pulpit; we had flung aside the pen; we had shut up the ledger; we had thrown off that sweet, bewitching, enervating indolence, which is better, after all, than most of the enjoyments within mortal grasp. It was our purpose—a generous one, certainly, and absurd, no doubt, in full proportion with its generosity—to give up whatever we had heretofore attained, for the sake of showing mankind the example of a life governed by other than the false and cruel principles, on which human society has all along been based.

And, first of all, we had divorced ourselves from Pride, and were striving to supply its place with familiar love. We meant to lessen the laboring man's great burthen of toil, by performing our due share of it at the cost of our own thews and sinews. We sought our profit by mutual aid, instead of wresting it by the strong hand from an enemy, or filching it craftily from those less shrewd than ourselves, (if, indeed, there were any such, in New England,) or winning it by selfish competition with a neighbor; in one or another of which fashions, every son of woman both perpetrates and suffers his share of the common evil, whether he chooses it or no. And, as the basis of our institution, we purposed to offer up the earnest toil of our bodies, as a prayer, no less than an effort, for the advancement of our race.

Therefore, if we built splendid castles (phalansteries,*

perhaps, they might be more fitly called,) and pictured beautiful scenes, among the fervid coals of the hearth around which we were clustering—and if all went to rack with the crumbling embers, and have never since arisen out of the ashes—let us take to ourselves no shame. In my own behalf, I rejoice that I could once think better of the world's improvability than it deserved. It is a mistake into which men seldom fall twice, in a lifetime; or, if so, the rarer and higher is the nature that can thus magnanimously persist in error.

Stout Silas Foster mingled little in our conversation; but when he did speak, it was very much to some practical purpose. For instance:—

"Which man among you," quoth he, "is the best judge of swine? Some of us must go to the next Brighton fair, and buy half-a-dozen pigs!"

Pigs! Good heavens, had we come out from among the swinish multitude, for this? And again, in reference to some discussion about raising early vegetables for the market:—

"We shall never make any hand at market-gardening," said Silas Foster, "unless the women-folks will undertake to do all the weeding. We haven't team enough for that and the regular farm-work, reckoning three of you city-folks as worth one common field-hand. No, no, I tell you, we should have to get up a little too early in the morning, to compete with the market-gardeners round Boston!"

It struck me as rather odd, that one of the first questions raised, after our separation from the greedy, struggling, self-seeking world, should relate to the possibility of getting the advantage over the outside barbarians, in their own field of labor. But, to own the truth, I very soon became sensible, that, as regarded society at large, we stood in a position of new hostility, rather than new brotherhood. Nor could this fail to be the case, in some degree, until the bigger and better half of society should range itself on our side. Constituting so pitiful a minority as now, we were inevitably estranged from the rest of mankind, in pretty fair proportion with the strictness of our mutual bond among ourselves.

This dawning idea, however, was driven back into my inner consciousness by the entrance of Zenobia. She came with the welcome intelligence that supper was on the table. Looking at herself in the glass, and perceiving that her one magnificent flower had grown rather languid, (probably by being exposed to the fervency of the kitchen-fire,) she flung it on the floor, as unconcernedly as a village-girl would throw away a faded violet. The action seemed proper to her character; although, methought, it would still more have befitted the bounteous nature of this beautiful woman to scatter fresh flowers from her hand, and to revive faded ones by her touch. Nevertheless—it was a singular, but irresistible effect—the presence of Zenobia caused our heroic enterprise to show like an illusion, a masquerade, a pastoral, a counterfeit Arcadia,* in which we grown-up men and women were making a play-day of the years that were given us to live in. I tried to analyze this impression, but not with much success.

"It really vexes me," observed Zenobia, as we left the room, "that Mr. Hollingsworth should be such a laggard. I should not have thought him at all the sort of person to be turned back by a puff of contrary wind, or a few snow-flakes drifting into his face."

"Do you know Hollingsworth personally?" I inquired.

"No; only as an auditor—auditress, I mean—of some of his lectures," said she. "What a voice he has! And what a man he is! Yet not so much an intellectual man, I should say, as a great heart; at least, he moved me more deeply than I think myself capable of being moved, except by the stroke of a true, strong heart against my own. It is a sad pity that he should have devoted his glorious powers to such a grimy, unbeautiful, and positively hopeless object as this reformation of criminals, about which he makes himself and his wretchedly small audiences so very miserable. To tell you a secret, I never could tolerate a philanthropist, before. Could you?"

"By no means," I answered; "neither can I now!"

"They are, indeed, an odiously disagreeable set of mortals," continued Zenobia. "I should like Mr. Hollingsworth a great deal better, if the philanthropy had been left out. At all events, as a mere matter of taste, I wish he would let the bad people alone, and try to benefit those who are not already past his help. Do you suppose he will be content to spend his life— or even a few months of it—among tolerably virtuous and comfortable individuals, like ourselves?"

"Upon my word, I doubt it," said I. "If we wish to keep him with us, we must systematically commit at least one crime apiece! Mere peccadillos will not satisfy him."

Zenobia turned, sidelong, a strange kind of a glance upon me; but, before I could make out what it meant, we had entered the kitchen, where, in accordance with the rustic simplicity of our new life, the supper-table was spread.

IV

THE SUPPER-TABLE

THE PLEASANT firelight! I must still keep harping on it.

The kitchen-hearth had an old-fashioned breadth, depth, and spaciousness, far within which lay what seemed the butt of a good-sized oak-tree, with the moisture bubbling merrily out of both ends. It was now half-an-hour beyond dusk. The blaze from an armfull of substantial sticks, rendered more combustible by brush-wood and pine, flickered powerfully on the smoke-blackened walls, and so cheered our spirits that we cared not what inclemency might rage and roar, on the other side of our illuminated windows. A yet sultrier warmth was bestowed by a goodly quantity of peat, which was crumbling to white ashes among the burning brands, and incensed the kitchen with its not ungrateful fragrance. The exuberance of this household fire would alone have sufficed to bespeak us no true farmers; for the New England yeoman, if he have the misfortune to dwell within practicable distance of a wood-market, is as niggardly of each stick as if it were a bar of California gold.*

But it was fortunate for us, on that wintry eve of our untried life, to enjoy the warm and radiant luxury of a somewhat too abundant fire. If it served no other purpose, it made the men look so full of youth, warm blood, and hope, and the women—

such of them, at least, as were anywise convertible by its magic —so very beautiful, that I would cheerfully have spent my last dollar to prolong the blaze. As for Zenobia, there was a glow in her cheeks that made me think of Pandora,* fresh from Vulcan's workshop, and full of the celestial warmth by dint of which he had tempered and moulded her.

"Take your places, my dear friends all," cried she; "seat yourselves without ceremony—and you shall be made happy with such tea as not many of the world's working-people, except yourselves, will find in their cups to-night. After this one supper, you may drink butter-milk, if you please. To-night, we will quaff this nectar, which, I assure you, could not be bought with gold."

We all sat down—grisly Silas Foster, his rotund helpmate, and the two bouncing handmaidens, included—and looked at one another in a friendly, but rather awkward way. It was the first practical trial of our theories of equal brotherhood and sisterhood; and we people of superior cultivation and refine-ment (for as such, I presume, we unhesitatingly reckoned ourselves) felt as if something were already accomplished towards the millennium of love.* The truth is, however, that the laboring oar was with our unpolished companions; it being far easier to condescend, than to accept of condescension. Neither did I refrain from questioning, in secret, whether some of us—and Zenobia among the rest—would so quietly have taken our places among these good people, save for the cherished consciousness that it was not by necessity, but choice. Though we saw fit to drink our tea out of earthen cups to-night, and in earthen company, it was at our own option to use pictured porcelain and handle silver forks again, tomorrow. This same salvo, as to the power of regaining our former position, contributed much, I fear, to the equanimity with which we subsequently bore many of the hardships and humiliations of a life of toil. If ever I have deserved—(which has not often been the case, and, I think, never)—but if ever

I did deserve to be soundly cuffed by a fellow-mortal, for secretly putting weight upon some imaginary social advantage, it must have been while I was striving to prove myself ostentatiously his equal, and no more. It was while I sat beside him on his cobbler's bench, or clinked my hoe against his own, in the cornfield, or broke the same crust of bread, my earth-grimed hand to his, at our noontide lunch. The poor, proud man should look at both sides of sympathy like this.

The silence, which followed upon our sitting down to table, grew rather oppressive; indeed, it was hardly broken by a word, during the first round of Zenobia's fragrant tea.

"I hope," said I, at last, "that our blazing windows will be visible a great way off. There is nothing so pleasant and encouraging to a solitary traveller, on a stormy night, as a flood of firelight, seen amid the gloom. These ruddy window-panes cannot fail to cheer the hearts of all that look at them. Are they not warm and bright with the beacon-fire which we have kindled for humanity?"

"The blaze of that brush-wood will only last a minute or two longer," observed Silas Foster; but whether he meant to insinuate that our moral illumination would have as brief a term, I cannot say.

"Meantime," said Zenobia, "it may serve to guide some wayfarer to a shelter."

And, just as she said this, there came a knock at the house-door.

"There is one of the world's wayfarers!" said I.

"Aye, aye, just so!" quoth Silas Foster. "Our firelight will draw stragglers, just as a candle draws dor-bugs, on a summer night."

Whether to enjoy a dramatic suspense, or that we were selfishly contrasting our own comfort with the chill and dreary situation of the unknown person at the threshold—or that some of us city-folk felt a little startled at the knock which came so unseasonably, through night and storm, to the door of the lonely farm-house—so it happened, that nobody, for an instant or two, arose to answer the summons. Pretty soon, there came another knock. The first had been moderately loud; the second was smitten so forcibly that the knuckles of the applicant must have left their mark in the door-panel.

"He knocks as if he had a right to come in," said Zenobia, laughing. "And what are we thinking of? It must be Mr. Hollingsworth!"

Hereupon, I went to the door, unbolted, and flung it wide open. There, sure enough, stood Hollingsworth, his shaggy great-coat all covered with snow; so that he looked quite as much like a polar bear as a modern philanthropist.

"Sluggish hospitality, this!" said he, in those deep tones of his, which seemed to come out of a chest as capacious as a barrel. "It would have served you right if I had lain down and spent the night on the door-step, just for the sake of putting you to shame. But here is a guest, who will need a warmer and softer bed."

And stepping back to the wagon, in which he had journeyed hither, Hollingsworth received into his arms, and deposited on the door-step, a figure enveloped in a cloak. It was evidently a woman; or rather—judging from the ease with which he lifted her, and the little space which she seemed to fill in his arms—a slim and unsubstantial girl. As she showed some hesitation about entering the door, Hollingsworth, with his usual directness and lack of ceremony, urged her forward, not merely within the entry, but into the warm and strongly lighted kitchen.

"Who is this?" whispered I, remaining behind with him, while he was taking off his great-coat.

"Who? Really, I don't know," answered Hollingsworth, looking at me with some surprise. "It is a young person who belongs here, however; and, no doubt, she has been expected. Zenobia, or some of the women-folks, can tell you all about it."

"I think not," said I, glancing towards the new-comer and

the other occupants of the kitchen. "Nobody seems to welcome her. I should hardly judge that she was an expected
guest."

"Well, well," said Hollingsworth, quietly. "We'll make
it right."

The stranger, or whatever she were, remained standing
precisely on that spot of the kitchen-floor, to which Hollingsworth's kindly hand had impelled her. The cloak falling partly
off, she was seen to be a very young woman, dressed in a
poor, but decent gown, made high in the neck, and without
any regard to fashion or smartness. Her brown hair fell down
from beneath a hood, not in curls, but with only a slight
wave; her face was of a wan, almost sickly hue, betokening
habitual seclusion from the sun and free atmosphere, like a
flower-shrub that had done its best to blossom in too scanty
light. To complete the pitiableness of her aspect, she shivered either with cold, or fear, or nervous excitement, so that
you might have beheld her shadow vibrating on the fire-
lighted wall. In short, there has seldom been seen so depressed
and sad a figure as this young girl's; and it was hardly possible
to help being angry with her, from mere despair of doing
anything for her comfort. The fantasy occurred to me, that
she was some desolate kind of a creature, doomed to wander
about in snow-storms, and that, though the ruddiness of our
window-panes had tempted her into a human dwelling, she
would not remain long enough to melt the icicles out of
her hair.

Another conjecture likewise came into my mind. Recollecting Hollingsworth's sphere of philanthropic action, I deemed
it possible that he might have brought one of his guilty
patients, to be wrought upon, and restored to spiritual health,
by the pure influences which our mode of life would create.

As yet, the girl had not stirred. She stood near the door,
fixing a pair of large, brown, melancholy eyes upon Zenobia—
only upon Zenobia!—she evidently saw nothing else in the

room, save that bright, fair, rosy, beautiful woman. It was the strangest look I ever witnessed; long a mystery to me, and forever a memory. Once, she seemed about to move forward and greet her—I know not with what warmth, or with what words;—but, finally, instead of doing so, she drooped down upon her knees, clasped her hands, and gazed piteously into Zenobia's face. Meeting no kindly reception, her head fell on her bosom.

I never thoroughly forgave Zenobia for her conduct on this occasion. But women are always more cautious, in their casual hospitalities, than men.

"What does the girl mean?" cried she, in rather a sharp tone. "Is she crazy? Has she no tongue?"

And here Hollingsworth stept forward.

"No wonder if the poor child's tongue is frozen in her mouth," said he—and I think he positively frowned at Zenobia —"The very heart will be frozen in her bosom, unless you women can warm it, among you, with the warmth that ought to be in your own!"

Hollingsworth's appearance was very striking, at this moment. He was then about thirty years old, but looked several years older, with his great shaggy head, his heavy brow, his dark complexion, his abundant beard, and the rude strength with which his features seemed to have been hammered out of iron, rather than chiselled or moulded from any finer or softer material. His figure was not tall, but massive and brawny, and well befitting his original occupation, which —as the reader probably knows—was that of a blacksmith. As for external polish, or mere courtesy of manner, he never possessed more than a tolerably educated bear; although, in his gentler moods, there was a tenderness in his voice, eyes, mouth, in his gesture, and in every indescribable manifestation, which few men could resist, and no woman. But he now looked stern and reproachful; and it was with that inauspicious meaning in his glance, that Hollingsworth first met Zenobia's eyes, and began his influence upon her life.

To my surprise, Zenobia—of whose haughty spirit I had been told so many examples—absolutely changed color, and seemed mortified and confused.

"You do not quite do me justice, Mr. Hollingsworth," said she, almost humbly. "I am willing to be kind to the poor girl. Is she a protégée of yours? What can I do for her?"

"Have you anything to ask of this lady?" said Hollingsworth, kindly, to the girl. "I remember you mentioned her name, before we left town."

"Only that she will shelter me," replied the girl, tremulously. "Only that she will let me be always near her!"

"Well, indeed," exclaimed Zenobia, recovering herself, and laughing, "this is an adventure, and well worthy to be the first incident in our life of love and free-heartedness! But I accept it, for the present, without further question—only," added she, "it would be a convenience if we knew your name!"

"Priscilla," said the girl; and it appeared to me that she hesitated whether to add anything more, and decided in the negative. "Pray do not ask me my other name—at least, not yet—if you will be so kind to a forlorn creature."

Priscilla! Priscilla! I repeated the name to myself, three or four times; and, in that little space, this quaint and prim cognomen had so amalgamated itself with my idea of the girl, that it seemed as if no other name could have adhered to her for a moment. Heretofore, the poor thing had not shed any tears; but now that she found herself received, and at least temporarily established, the big drops began to ooze out from beneath her eyelids, as if she were full of them. Perhaps it showed the iron substance of my heart, that I could not help smiling at this odd scene of unknown and unaccountable calamity, into which our cheerful party had been entrapped, without the liberty of choosing whether to sympathize or no.

Hollingsworth's behavior was certainly a great deal more creditable than mine.

"Let us not pry farther into her secrets," he said to Zenobia and the rest of us, apart—and his dark, shaggy· face looked really beautiful with its expression of thoughtful benevolence —"Let us conclude that Providence has sent her to us, as the first fruits of the world, which we have undertaken to make happier than we find it. Let us warm her poor, shivering body with this good fire, and her poor, shivering heart with our best kindness. Let us feed her, and make her one of us. As we do by this friendless girl, so shall we prosper! And, in good time, whatever is desirable for us to know will be melted out of her, as inevitably as those tears which we see now."

"At least," remarked I, "you may tell us how and where you met with her."

"An old man brought her to my lodgings," answered Hollingsworth, "and begged me to convey her to Blithedale, where—so I understood him—she had friends. And this is positively all I know about the matter."

Grim Silas Foster, all this while, had been busy at the supper-table, pouring out his own tea, and gulping it down with no more sense of its exquisiteness than if it were a decoction of catnip; helping himself to pieces of dipt toast on the flat of his knife-blade, and dropping half of it on the table-cloth; using the same serviceable implement to cut slice after slice of ham; perpetrating terrible enormities with the butter-plate; and, in all other respects, behaving less like a civilized Christian than the worst kind of an ogre. Being, by this time, fully gorged, he crowned his amiable exploits with a draught from the water-pitcher, and then favored us with his opinion about the business in hand. And, certainly, though they proceeded out of an unwiped mouth, his expressions did him honor.

"Give the girl a hot cup of tea, and a thick slice of this first-rate bacon," said Silas, like a sensible man as he was. "That's what she wants. Let her stay with us as long as she likes, and help in the kitchen, and take the cow-breath at milking-time; and, in a week or two, she'll begin to look like a creature of this world!"

So we sat down again to supper, and Priscilla along with us.

V

UNTIL BEDTIME

SILAS FOSTER, by the time we concluded our meal, had stript off his coat and planted himself on a low chair by the kitchen-fire, with a lap-stone, a hammer, a piece of sole-leather, and some waxed ends, in order to cobble an old pair of cow-hide boots; he being, in his own phrase, 'something of a dab' (whatever degree of skill that may imply) at the shoemaking-business. We heard the tap of his hammer, at intervals, for the rest of the evening. The remainder of the party adjourned to the sitting-room. Good Mrs. Foster took her knitting-work, and soon fell fast asleep, still keeping her needles in brisk movement, and, to the best of my observation, absolutely footing a stocking out of the texture of a dream. And a very substantial stocking it seemed to be. One of the two handmaidens hemmed a towel, and the other appeared to be making a ruffle, for her Sunday's wear, out of a little bit of embroidered muslin, which Zenobia had probably given her.

It was curious to observe how trustingly, and yet how timidly, our poor Priscilla betook herself into the shadow of Zenobia's protection. She sat beside her on a stool, looking up, every now and then, with an expression of humble delight at her new friend's beauty. A brilliant woman is often an object of the devoted admiration—it might almost be termed worship, or idolatry—of some young girl, who perhaps beholds the cynosure only at an awful distance, and has as little hope of personal intercourse as of climbing among the stars of heaven. We men are too gross to comprehend it. Even a woman, of mature age, despises or laughs at such a passion. There occurred to me no mode of accounting for Priscilla's behavior, except by supposing that she had read some of Zenobia's stories, (as such literature goes everywhere,) or her tracts in defence of the sex, and had come hither with the one purpose of being her slave. There is nothing parallel to this, I believe—nothing so foolishly disinterested, and hardly anything so beautiful—in the masculine nature, at whatever epoch of life; or, if there be, a fine and rare development of character might reasonably be looked for, from the youth who should prove himself capable of such self-forgetful affection.

Zenobia happening to change her seat, I took the opportunity, in an under tone, to suggest some such notion as the above.

"Since you see the young woman in so poetical a light," replied she, in the same tone, "you had better turn the affair into a ballad. It is a grand subject, and worthy of supernatural machinery. The storm, the startling knock at the door, the entrance of the sable knight Hollingsworth and this shadowy snow-maiden, who, precisely at the stroke of midnight, shall melt away at my feet, in a pool of ice-cold water, and give me my death with a pair of wet slippers! And when the verses are written, and polished quite to your mind, I will favor you with my idea as to what the girl really is."

"Pray let me have it now," said I. "It shall be woven into the ballad."

"She is neither more nor less," answered Zenobia, "than a seamstress from the city,* and she has probably no more transcendental purpose than to do my miscellaneous sewing; for I suppose she will hardly expect to make my dresses."

"How can you decide upon her so easily?" I inquired.

"Oh, we women judge one another by tokens that escape the obtuseness of masculine perceptions," said Zenobia. "There is no proof, which you would be likely to appreciate, except the needle marks on the tip of her forefinger. Then, my supposition perfectly accounts for her paleness, her nervousness, and her wretched fragility. Poor thing! She has been stifled with the heat of a salamander-stove,* in a small, close room, and has drunk coffee, and fed upon dough-nuts, raisins, candy, and all such trash, till she is scarcely half-alive; and so, as she has hardly any physique, a poet, like Mr. Miles Coverdale, may be allowed to think her spiritual!"

"Look at her now!" whispered I.

Priscilla was gazing towards us, with an inexpressible sorrow in her wan face, and great tears running down her cheeks. It was difficult to resist the impression, that, cautiously as we had lowered our voices, she must have overheard and been wounded by Zenobia's scornful estimate of her character and purposes.

"What ears the girl must have!" whispered Zenobia, with a look of vexation, partly comic and partly real. "I will confess to you that I cannot quite make her out. However, I am positively not an ill-natured person, unless when very grievously provoked; and as you, and especially Mr. Hollingsworth, take so much interest in this odd creature—and as she knocks, with a very slight tap, against my own heart, likewise—why, I mean to let her in! From this moment, I will be reasonably kind to her. There is no pleasure in tormenting a person of one's own sex, even if she do favor one with a little more love than one can conveniently dispose of;— and that, let me say, Mr. Coverdale, is the most troublesome offence you can offer to a woman."

"Thank you!" said I, smiling. "I don't mean to be guilty of it."

She went towards Priscilla, took her hand, and passed her own rosy finger-tips, with a pretty, caressing movement, over the girl's hair. The touch had a magical effect. So vivid a look of joy flushed up beneath those fingers, that it seemed as if the sad and wan Priscilla had been snatched away, and another kind of creature substituted in her place. This one caress, bestowed voluntarily by Zenobia, was evidently received as a pledge of all that the stranger sought from her, whatever the unuttered boon might be. From that instant, too, she melted in quietly amongst us, and was no longer a foreign element. Though always an object of peculiar interest, a riddle, and a theme of frequent discussion, her tenure at Blithedale was thenceforth fixed; we no more thought of questioning it, than if Priscilla had been recognized as a domestic sprite, who had haunted the rustic fireside, of old, before we had ever been warmed by its blaze.

She now produced, out of a work-bag that she had with her, some little wooden instruments, (what they are called, I never knew,) and proceeded to knit, or net, an article which ultimately took the shape of a silk purse. As the work went on, I remembered to have seen just such purses, before. Indeed, I was the possessor of one. Their peculiar excellence, besides the great delicacy and beauty of the manufacture, lay in the almost impossibility that any uninitiated person should discover the aperture; although, to a practised touch, they would open as wide as charity or prodigality might wish. I wondered if it were not a symbol of Priscilla's own mystery.

Notwithstanding the new confidence with which Zenobia had inspired her, our guest showed herself disquieted by the storm. When the strong puffs of wind spattered the snow against the windows, and made the oaken frame of the farm-house creak, she looked at us apprehensively, as if to inquire whether these tempestuous outbreaks did not betoken some unusual mischief in the shrieking blast. She had been bred up, no doubt, in some close nook, some inauspiciously sheltered court of the city, where the uttermost rage of a tempest, though it might scatter down the slates of the roof into the bricked area, could not shake the casement of her little room. The sense of vast, undefined space, pressing from the outside against the black panes of our uncurtained windows, was fearful to the poor girl, heretofore accustomed to the narrowness of human limits, with the lamps of neighboring tenements glimmering across the street. The house probably seemed to her adrift on the great ocean of the night. A little parallelogram of sky was all that she had hitherto known of nature; so that she felt the awfulness that really exists in its limitless extent. Once, while the blast was bellowing, she caught hold of Zenobia's robe, with precisely the air of one who hears her own name spoken, at a distance, but is unutterably reluctant to obey the call.

We spent rather an incommunicative evening. Hollingsworth hardly said a word, unless when repeatedly and pertinaciously addressed. Then, indeed, he would glare upon us from the thick shrubbery of his meditations, like a tiger out of a jungle, make the briefest reply possible, and betake himself back into the solitude of his heart and mind. The poor fellow had contracted this ungracious habit from the intensity with which he contemplated his own ideas, and the infrequent sympathy which they met with from his auditors; a circumstance that seemed only to strengthen the implicit confidence that he awarded to them. His heart, I imagine, was never really interested in our socialist scheme, but was forever busy with his strange, and, as most people thought it, impracticable plan for the reformation of criminals, through an appeal to their higher instincts. Much as I liked Hollingsworth, it cost me many a groan to tolerate him on this point. He ought to have commenced his investigation of the subject by perpetrating some huge sin, in his proper person, and examining the condition of his higher instincts, afterwards.

The rest of us formed ourselves into a committee for providing our infant Community with an appropriate name; a matter of greatly more difficulty than the uninitiated reader would suppose. Blithedale*was neither good nor bad. We should have resumed the old Indian name of the premises, had it possessed the oil-and-honey flow which the aborigines were so often happy in communicating to their local appellations; but it chanced to be a harsh, ill-connected, and interminable word, which seemed to fill the mouth with a mixture of very stiff clay and very crumbly pebbles. Zenobia suggested 'Sunny Glimpse,' as expressive of a vista into a better system of society. This we turned over and over, for awhile, acknowledging its prettiness, but concluded it to be rather too fine and sentimental a name (a fault inevitable by literary ladies, in such attempts) for sun-burnt men to work under. I ventured to whisper 'Utopia,' which, however, was unanimously scouted down, and the proposer very harshly maltreated, as if he had intended a latent satire. Some were for calling our institution 'The Oasis,' in view of its being the one green spot in the moral sand-waste of the world; but others insisted on a proviso for reconsidering the matter, at a twelvemonth's end; when a final decision might be had, whether to name it 'The Oasis,' or 'Saharah.' So, at last, finding it impracticable to hammer out anything better, we resolved that the spot should still be Blithedale, as being of good augury enough.

The evening wore on, and the outer solitude looked in upon us through the windows, gloomy, wild, and vague, like another state of existence, close beside the littler sphere of warmth and light in which we were the prattlers and bustlers of a moment. By-and-by, the door was opened by Silas Foster, with a cotton handkerchief about his head, and a tallow candle in his hand.

"Take my advice, brother-farmers," said he, with a great, broad, bottomless yawn, "and get to bed as soon as you can. I shall sound the horn at day-break; and we've got the cattle to fodder, and nine cows to milk, and a dozen other things to do, before breakfast."

Thus ended the first evening at Blithedale. I went shivering to my fireless chamber, with the miserable consciousness (which had been growing upon me for several hours past) that I had caught a tremendous cold, and should probably awaken, at the blast of the horn, a fit subject for a hospital. The night proved a feverish one. During the greater part of it, I was in that vilest of states when a fixed idea remains in the mind, like the nail in Sisera's brain,* while innumerable other ideas go and come, and flutter to-and-fro, combining constant transition with intolerable sameness. Had I made a record of that night's half-waking dreams, it is my belief that it would have anticipated several of the chief incidents of this narrative, including a dim shadow of its catastrophe. Starting up in bed, at length, I saw that the storm was past, and the moon was shining on the snowy landscape, which looked like a lifeless copy of the world in marble.

From the bank of the distant river, which was shimmering in the moonlight, came the black shadow of the only cloud in heaven, driven swiftly by the wind, and passing over meadow and hillock—vanishing amid tufts of leafless trees, but reappearing on the hither side—until it swept across our door-step.

How cold an Arcadia* was this!

VI

COVERDALE'S SICK-CHAMBER

THE HORN sounded at day-break, as Silas Foster had
forewarned us, harsh, uproarious, inexorably drawn
out, and as sleep-dispelling as if this hard-hearted old
yeoman had got hold of the trump of doom.

On all sides, I could hear the creaking of the bedsteads,
as the brethren of Blithedale started from slumber, and thrust
themselves into their habiliments, all awry, no doubt, in
their haste to begin the reformation of the world. Zenobia
put her head into the entry, and besought Silas Foster to
cease his clamor, and to be kind enough to leave an armful
of firewood and a pail of water at her chamber-door. Of the
whole household—unless, indeed, it were Priscilla, for whose
habits, in this particular, I cannot vouch—of all our apostolic
society, whose mission was to bless mankind, Hollingsworth,
I apprehend, was the only one who began the enterprise with
prayer. My sleeping-room being but thinly partitioned from
his, the solemn murmur of his voice made its way to my ears,
compelling me to be an auditor of his awful privacy with
the Creator. It affected me with a deep reverence for Hollingsworth, which no familiarity then existing, or that afterwards
grew more intimate between us—no, nor my subsequent perception of his own great errors—ever quite effaced. It is so
rare, in these times, to meet with a man of prayerful habits,

(except, of course, in the pulpit,) that such an one is decidedly marked out by a light of transfiguration, shed upon him in the divine interview from which he passes into his daily life.

As for me, I lay abed, and, if I said my prayers, it was backward, cursing my day as bitterly as patient Job himself. The truth was, the hot-house warmth of a town-residence, and the luxurious life in which I indulged myself, had taken much of the pith out of my physical system; and the wintry blast of the preceding day, together with the general chill of our airy old farm-house, had got fairly into my heart and the marrow of my bones. In this predicament, I seriously wished—selfish as it may appear—that the reformation of society had been postponed about half-a-century, or at all events, to such a date as should have put my intermeddling with it entirely out of the question.

What, in the name of common-sense, had I to do with any better society than I had always lived in! It had satisfied me well enough. My pleasant bachelor-parlor, sunny and shadowy, curtained and carpeted, with the bed-chamber adjoining; my centre-table, strewn with books and periodicals; my writing-desk, with a half-finished poem in a stanza of my own contrivance; my morning lounge at the reading-room or picture-gallery; my noontide walk along the cheery pavement, with the suggestive succession of human faces, and the brisk throb of human life, in which I shared; my dinner at the Albion, where I had a hundred dishes at command, and could banquet as delicately as the wizard Michael Scott,* when the devil fed him from the King of France's kitchen; my evening at the billiard-club, the concert, the theatre, or at somebody's party, if I pleased:—what could be better than all this? Was it better to hoe, to mow, to toil and moil amidst the accumulations of a barn-yard, to be the chambermaid of two yoke of oxen and a dozen cows, to eat salt-beef and earn it with the sweat of my brow, and thereby take the tough morsel out of some wretch's mouth, into whose vocation I had thrust myself? Above all, was it better to have a fever, and die blaspheming, as I was like to do?

In this wretched plight, with a furnace in my heart, and another in my head, by the heat of which I was kept constantly at the boiling point—yet shivering at the bare idea of extruding so much as a finger into the icy atmosphere of the room—I kept my bed until breakfast-time, when Hollingsworth knocked at the door, and entered.

"Well, Coverdale," cried he, "you bid fair to make an admirable farmer! Don't you mean to get up to-day?"

"Neither to-day nor tomorrow," said I, hopelessly. "I doubt if I ever rise again!"

"What is the matter now?" he asked.

I told him my piteous case, and besought him to send me back to town, in a close carriage.

"No, no!" said Hollingsworth, with kindly seriousness. "If you are really sick, we must take care of you."

Accordingly, he built a fire in my chamber, and having little else to do while the snow lay on the ground, established himself as my nurse. A doctor was sent for, who, being homeopathic,* gave me as much medicine, in the course of a fortnight's attendance, as would have lain on the point of a needle. They fed me on water-gruel, and I speedily became a skeleton above ground. But, after all, I have many precious recollections connected with that fit of sickness.

Hollingsworth's more than brotherly attendance gave me inexpressible comfort. Most men—and, certainly, I could not always claim to be one of the exceptions—have a natural indifference, if not an absolutely hostile feeling, towards those whom disease, or weakness, or calamity of any kind, causes to faulter and faint amid the rude jostle of our selfish existence. The education of Christianity, it is true, the sympathy of a like experience, and the example of women, may soften, and possibly subvert, this ugly characteristic of our sex. But it is originally there, and has likewise its analogy in the practice of our brute brethren, who hunt the sick or disabled member of the herd from among them, as an enemy. It is for this reason that the stricken deer goes apart, and the sick lion grimly withdraws himself into his den. Except in love, or the attachments of kindred, or other very long and habitual affection, we really have no tenderness. But there was something of the woman moulded into the great, stalwart frame of Hollingsworth; nor was he ashamed of it, as men often are of what is best in them, nor seemed ever to know that there was such a soft place in his heart. I knew it well, however, at that time; although, afterwards, it came nigh to be forgotten. Methought there could not be two such men alive, as Hollingsworth. There never was any blaze of a fireside that warmed and cheered me, in the down-sinkings and shiverings of my spirit, so effectually as did the light out of those eyes, which lay so deep and dark under his shaggy brows.

· Happy the man that has such a friend beside him, when he comes to die! And unless a friend like Hollingsworth be at hand, as most probably there will not, he had better make up his mind to die alone. How many men, I wonder, does one meet with, in a lifetime, whom he would choose for his death-bed companions! At the crisis of my fever, I besought Hollingsworth to let nobody else enter the room, but continually to make me sensible of his own presence by a grasp of the hand, a word—a prayer, if he thought good to utter it—and that then he should be the witness how courageously I would encounter the worst. It still impresses me as almost a matter of regret, that I did not die, then, when I had tolerably made up my mind to it; for Hollingsworth would have gone with me to the hither verge of life, and have sent his friendly and hopeful accents far over on the other side, while I should be treading the unknown path. Now, were I to send for him, he would hardly come to my bedside; nor should I depart the easier, for his presence.

"You are not going to die, this time," said he, gravely smiling. "You know nothing about sickness, and think your case a great deal more desperate than it is."

"Death should take me while I am in the mood," replied I, with a little of my customary levity.

"Have you nothing to do in life," asked Hollingsworth, "that you fancy yourself so ready to leave it?"

"Nothing," answered I—"nothing, that I know of, unless to make pretty verses, and play a part, with Zenobia and the rest of the amateurs, in our pastoral. It seems but an unsubstantial sort of business, as viewed through a mist of fever. But, dear Hollingsworth, your own vocation is evidently to be a priest, and to spend your days and nights in helping your fellow-creatures to draw peaceful dying-breaths."

"And by which of my qualities," inquired he, "can you suppose me fitted for this awful ministry?"

"By your tenderness," I said. "It seems to me the reflection of God's own love."

"And you call me tender!" repeated Hollingsworth, thoughtfully. "I should rather say, that the most marked trait in my character is an inflexible severity of purpose. Mortal man has no right to be so inflexible, as it is my nature and necessity to be!"

"I do not believe it," I replied.

But, in due time, I remembered what he said.

Probably, as Hollingsworth suggested, my disorder was never so serious as, in my ignorance of such matters, I was inclined to consider it. After so much tragical preparation, it was positively rather mortifying to find myself on the mending hand.

All the other members of the Community showed me kindness, according to the full measure of their capacity. Zenobia brought me my gruel, every day, made by her own hands, (not very skilfully, if the truth must be told,) and, whenever I seemed inclined to converse, would sit by my bedside, and talk with so much vivacity as to add several gratuitous throbs to my pulse. Her poor little stories and tracts never half did justice to her intellect; it was only the lack of a fitter avenue that drove her to seek development in literature. She was made (among a thousand other things that she might have been) for a stump-oratress. I recognized no severe culture in Zenobia; her mind was full of weeds. It startled me, sometimes, in my state of moral, as well as bodily faint-heartedness, to observe the hardihood of her philosophy; she made no scruple of oversetting all human institutions, and scattering them as with a breeze from her fan. A female reformer, in her attacks upon society, has an instinctive sense of where the life lies, and is inclined to aim directly at that spot. Especially, the relation between the sexes is naturally among the earliest to attract her notice.

Zenobia was truly a magnificent woman. The homely simplicity of her dress could not conceal, nor scarcely diminish, the queenliness of her presence. The image of her form and face should have been multiplied all over the earth. It was wronging the rest of mankind, to retain her as the spectacle of only a few. The stage would have been her proper sphere. She should have made it a point of duty, moreover, to sit endlessly to painters and sculptors, and preferably to the latter; because the cold decorum of the marble would consist with the utmost scantiness of drapery, so that the eye might chastely be gladdened with her material perfection, in its entirety. I know not well how to express, that the native glow of coloring in her cheeks, and even the flesh-warmth over her round arms, and what was visible of her full bust—in a word, her womanliness incarnated—compelled me sometimes to close my eyes, as if it were not quite the privilege of modesty to gaze at her. Illness and exhaustion, no doubt, had made me morbidly sensitive.

I noticed—and wondered how Zenobia contrived it—that she had always a new flower in her hair. And still it was a hot-house flower—an outlandish flower—a flower of the tropics, such as appeared to have sprung passionately out of a soil, the very weeds of which would be fervid and spicy. Unlike as was the flower of each successive day to the preceding one, it yet so assimilated its richness to the rich beauty of the woman, that I thought it the only flower fit to be worn; so fit, indeed, that Nature had evidently created this floral gem, in a happy exuberance, for the one purpose of worthily adorning Zenobia's head. It might be, that my feverish fantasies clustered themselves about this peculiarity, and caused it to look more gorgeous and wonderful than if beheld with temperate eyes. In the height of my illness, as I well recollect, I went so far as to pronounce it preternatural.

"Zenobia is an enchantress!" whispered I once to Hollingsworth. "She is a sister of the Veiled Lady! That flower in her hair is a talisman. If you were to snatch it away, she would vanish; or be transformed into something else!"

"What does he say?" asked Zenobia.

"Nothing that has an atom of sense in it," answered Hollingsworth. "He is a little beside himself, I believe, and talks about your being a witch, and of some magical property in the flower that you wear in your hair."

"It is an idea worthy of a feverish poet," said she, laughing, rather compassionately, and taking out the flower. "I scorn to owe anything to magic. Here, Mr. Hollingsworth:—you may keep the spell, while it has any virtue in it; but I cannot promise you not to appear with a new one, tomorrow. It is the one relic of my more brilliant, my happier days!"

The most curious part of the matter was, that, long after my slight delirium had passed away—as long, indeed, as I continued to know this remarkable woman—her daily flower affected my imagination, though more slightly, yet in very much the same way. The reason must have been, that, whether intentionally on her part, or not, this favorite orna-ment was actually a subtile expression of Zenobia's character.

One subject, about which—very impertinently, moreover—I perplexed myself with a great many conjectures, was, whether Zenobia had ever been married. The idea, it must be understood, was unauthorized by any circumstance or suggestion that had made its way to my ears. So young as I beheld her, and the freshest and rosiest woman of a thousand, there was certainly no need of imputing to her a destiny already accomplished; the probability was far greater, that her coming years had all life's richest gifts to bring. If the great event of a woman's existence had been consummated, the world knew nothing of it, although the world seemed to know Zenobia well. It was a ridiculous piece of romance, undoubtedly, to imagine that this beautiful personage, wealthy as she was, and holding a position that might fairly enough be called distinguished, could have given herself away so privately, but that some whisper and suspicion, and, by degrees, a full understanding of the fact, would eventually be blown abroad. But, then, as I failed not to consider, her original home was at a distance of many hundred miles. Rumors might fill the social atmosphere, or might once have filled it, there, which would travel but slowly, against the wind, towards our north-eastern metropolis, and perhaps melt into thin air before reaching it.

There was not, and I distinctly repeat it, the slightest foundation in my knowledge for any surmise of the kind. But there is a species of intuition—either a spiritual lie, or the subtle recognition of a fact—which comes to us in a reduced state of the corporeal system. The soul gets the better of the body, after wasting illness, or when a vegetable diet* may have mingled too much ether in the blood. Vapors then rise up to the brain, and take shapes that often image falsehood, but sometimes truth. The spheres of our companions have, at such periods, a vastly greater influence upon our own, than when robust health gives us a repellent and self-defensive energy. Zenobia's sphere, I imagine, impressed itself powerfully on mine, and transformed me, during this period of my weakness, into something like a mesmerical clairvoyant.

Then, also, as anybody could observe, the freedom of her deportment (though, to some tastes, it might commend itself as the utmost perfection of manner, in a youthful widow, or a blooming matron) was not exactly maidenlike. What girl had ever laughed as Zenobia did! What girl had ever spoken in her mellow tones! Her unconstrained and inevitable manifestation, I said often to myself, was that of a woman to whom wedlock had thrown wide the gates of mystery. Yet, sometimes, I strove to be ashamed of these conjectures. I acknowledged it as a masculine grossness—a sin of wicked interpretation, of which man is often guilty towards the other sex—thus to mistake the sweet, liberal, but womanly frankness of a noble and generous disposition. Still, it was of no avail to reason with myself, nor to upbraid myself. Pertinaciously the thought—'Zenobia is a wife! Zenobia has lived, and loved! There is no folded petal, no latent dew-drop, in this perfectly developed rose!'—irresistibly that thought drove out all other conclusions, as often as my mind reverted to the subject.

Zenobia was conscious of my observation, though not, I presume, of the point to which it led me.

"Mr. Coverdale," said she, one day, as she saw me watching her, while she arranged my gruel on the table, "I have been exposed to a great deal of eye-shot in the few years of my mixing in the world, but never, I think, to precisely such glances as you are in the habit of favoring me with. I seem to interest you very much; and yet—or else a woman's instinct is for once deceived—I cannot reckon you as an admirer. What are you seeking to discover in me?"

"The mystery of your life," answered I, surprised into the truth by the unexpectedness of her attack. "And you will never tell me."

She bent her head towards me, and let me look into her

eyes, as if challenging me to drop a plummet-line down into the depths of her consciousness.

"I see nothing now," said I, closing my own eyes, "unless it be the face of a sprite, laughing at me from the bottom of a deep well."

A bachelor always feels himself defrauded, when he knows, or suspects, that any woman of his acquaintance has given herself away. Otherwise, the matter could have been no concern of mine. It was purely speculative; for I should not, under any circumstances, have fallen in love with Zenobia. The riddle made me so nervous, however, in my sensitive condition of mind and body, that I most ungratefully began to wish that she would let me alone. Then, too, her gruel was very wretched stuff, with almost invariably the smell of pine-smoke upon it, like the evil taste that is said to mix itself up with a witch's best concocted dainties. Why could not she have allowed one of the other women to take the gruel in charge? Whatever else might be her gifts, Nature certainly never intended Zenobia for a cook. Or, if so, she should have meddled only with the richest and spiciest dishes, and such as are to be tasted at banquets, between draughts of intoxicating wine.

VII

THE CONVALESCENT

A S SOON as my incommodities allowed me to think of past occurrences, I failed not to inquire what had become of the odd little guest, whom Hollingsworth had been the medium of introducing among us. It now appeared, that poor Priscilla had not so literally fallen out of the clouds, as we were at first inclined to suppose. A letter, which should have introduced her, had since been received from one of the city-missionaries, containing a certificate of character, and an allusion to circumstances which, in the writer's judgment, made it especially desirable that she should find shelter in our Community. There was a hint, not very intelligible, implying either that Priscilla had recently escaped from some particular peril, or irksomeness of position, or else that she was still liable to this danger or difficulty, whatever it might be. We should ill have deserved the reputation of a benevolent fraternity, had we hesitated to entertain a petitioner in such need, and so strongly recommended to our kindness; not to mention, moreover, that the strange maiden had set herself diligently to work, and was doing good service with her needle. But a slight mist of uncertainty still floated about Priscilla, and kept her, as yet, from taking a very decided place among creatures of flesh and blood.

The mysterious attraction, which, from her first entrance

on our scene, she evinced for Zenobia, had lost nothing of its force. I often heard her footsteps, soft and low, accompanying the light, but decided tread of the latter, up the staircase, stealing along the passage-way by her new friend's side, and pausing while Zenobia entered my chamber. Occasionally, Zenobia would be a little annoyed by Priscilla's too close attendance. In an authoritative and not very kindly tone, she would advise her to breathe the pleasant air in a walk, or to go with her work into the barn, holding out half a promise to come and sit on the hay with her, when at leisure. Evidently, Priscilla found but scanty requital for her love. Hollingsworth was likewise a great favorite with her. For several minutes together, sometimes, while my auditory nerves retained the susceptibility of delicate health, I used to hear a low, pleasant murmur, ascending from the room below, and at last ascertained it to be Priscilla's voice, babbling like a little brook to Hollingsworth. She talked more largely and freely with him than with Zenobia, towards whom, indeed, her feelings seemed not so much to be confidence, as involuntary affection. I should have thought all the better of my own qualities, had Priscilla marked me out for the third place in her regards. But, though she appeared to like me tolerably well, I could never flatter myself with being distinguished by her, as Hollingsworth and Zenobia were.

One forenoon, during my convalescence, there came a gentle tap at my chamber-door. I immediately said—"Come in, Priscilla!"—with an acute sense of the applicant's identity. Nor was I deceived. It was really Priscilla, a pale, large-eyed little woman, (for she had gone far enough into her teens to be, at least, on the outer limit of girlhood,) but much less wan than at my previous view of her, and far better conditioned both as to health and spirits. As I first saw her, she had reminded me of plants that one sometimes observes doing their best to vegetate among the bricks of an enclosed court, where there is scanty soil, and never any sunshine. At present, though with no approach to bloom, there were indications that the girl had human blood in her veins.

Priscilla came softly to my bedside, and held out an article of snow-white linen, very carefully and smoothly ironed. She did not seem bashful, nor anywise embarrassed. My weakly condition, I suppose, supplied a medium in which she could approach me.

"Do not you need this?" asked she. "I have made it for you."

It was a night-cap!

"My dear Priscilla," said I, smiling, "I never had on a night-cap in my life! But perhaps it will be better for me to wear one, now that I am a miserable invalid. How admirably you have done it! No, no; I never can think of wearing such an exquisitely wrought night-cap as this, unless it be in the day-time, when I sit up to receive company!"

"It is for use, not beauty," answered Priscilla. "I could have embroidered it and made it much prettier, if I pleased."

While holding up the night-cap, and admiring the fine needle-work, I perceived that Priscilla had a sealed letter, which she was waiting for me to take. It had arrived from the village post-office, that morning. As I did not immediately offer to receive the letter, she drew it back, and held it against her bosom, with both hands clasped over it, in a way that had probably grown habitual to her. Now, on turning my eyes from the night-cap to Priscilla, it forcibly struck me that her air, though not her figure, and the expression of her face, but not its features, had a resemblance to what I had often seen in a friend of mine, one of the most gifted women of the age. I cannot describe it. The points, easiest to convey to the reader, were, a certain curve of the shoulders, and a partial closing of the eyes, which seemed to look more penetratingly into my own eyes, through the narrowed apertures, than if they had been open at full width. It was a singular anomaly of likeness co-existing with perfect dissimilitude.

"Will you give me the letter, Priscilla?" said I.

She started, put the letter into my hand, and quite lost the look that had drawn my notice.

"Priscilla," I inquired, "did you ever see Miss Margaret Fuller?"*

"No," she answered.

"Because," said I, "you reminded me of her, just now, and it happens, strangely enough, that this very letter is from her!"

Priscilla, for whatever reason, looked very much discomposed.

"I wish people would not fancy such odd things in me!" she said, rather petulantly. "How could I possibly make myself resemble this lady, merely by holding her letter in my hand?"

"Certainly, Priscilla, it would puzzle me to explain it," I replied. "Nor do I suppose that the letter had anything to do with it. It was just a coincidence—nothing more."

She hastened out of the room; and this was the last that I saw of Priscilla, until I ceased to be an invalid.

Being much alone, during my recovery, I read interminably in Mr. Emerson's Essays, the Dial, Carlyle's works, George Sand's romances,* (lent me by Zenobia,) and other books which one or another of the brethren or sisterhood had brought with them. Agreeing in little else, most of these utterances were like the cry of some solitary sentinel, whose station was on the outposts of the advance-guard of human progression; or, sometimes, the voice came sadly from among the shattered ruins of the past, but yet had a hopeful echo in the future. They were well adapted (better, at least, than any other intellectual products, the volatile essence of which had heretofore tinctured a printed page) to pilgrims like ourselves, whose present bivouâc was considerably farther into the waste of chaos than any mortal army of crusaders had ever marched before. Fourier's* works, also, in a series of horribly tedious volumes, attracted a good deal of my attention, from the analogy which I could not but recognize between his system and our own. There was far less resemblance, it is true, than the world chose to imagine; inasmuch as the two theories differed, as widely as the zenith from the nadir, in their main principles.

I talked about Fourier to Hollingsworth, and translated, for his benefit, some of the passages that chiefly impressed me.

"When, as a consequence of human improvement," said I, "the globe shall arrive at its final perfection, the great ocean is to be converted into a particular kind of lemonade, such as was fashionable at Paris in Fourier's time. He calls it *limonade à cèdre.** It is positively a fact! Just imagine the city-docks filled, every day, with a flood-tide of this delectable beverage!"

"Why did not the Frenchman make punch of it, at once?" asked Hollingsworth. "The jack-tars would be delighted to go down in ships, and do business in such an element."

I further proceeded to explain, as well as I modestly could, several points of Fourier's system, illustrating them with here and there a page or two, and asking Hollingsworth's opinion as to the expediency of introducing these beautiful peculiarities into our own practice.

"Let me hear no more of it!" cried he, in utter disgust. "I never will forgive this fellow! He has committed the Unpardonable Sin! For what more monstrous iniquity could the Devil himself contrive, than to choose the selfish principle* —the principle of all human wrong, the very blackness of man's heart, the portion of ourselves which we shudder at, and which it is the whole aim of spiritual discipline to eradicate—to choose it as the master-workman of his system? To seize upon and foster whatever vile, petty, sordid, filthy, bestial, and abominable corruptions have cankered into our nature, to be the efficient instruments of his infernal regeneration! And his consummated Paradise, as he pictures it, would be worthy of the agency which he counts upon for establishing it. The nauseous villain!"

"Nevertheless," remarked I, "in consideration of the promised delights of his system—so very proper, as they certainly are, to be appreciated by Fourier's countrymen—I cannot but wonder that universal France did not adopt his theory, at a moment's warning. But is there not something very characteristic of his nation in Fourier's manner of putting forth his views? He makes no claim to inspiration. He has not persuaded himself—as Swedenborg* did, and as any other than a Frenchman would, with a mission of like importance to communicate—that he speaks with authority from above. He promulgates his system, so far as I can perceive, entirely on his own responsibility. He has searched out and discovered the whole counsel of the Almighty, in respect to mankind, past, present, and for exactly seventy thousand years to come, by the mere force and cunning of his individual intellect!"

"Take the book out of my sight!" said Hollingsworth, with great virulence of expression, "or, I tell you fairly, I shall fling it in the fire! And as for Fourier, let him make a Paradise, if he can, of Gehenna,* where, as I conscientiously believe, he is floundering at this moment!"

"And bellowing, I suppose," said I—not that I felt any ill-will towards Fourier, but merely wanted to give the finishing touch to Hollingsworth's image—"bellowing for the least drop of his beloved *limonade à cèdre!*"

There is but little profit to be expected in attempting to argue with a man who allows himself to declaim in this manner; so I dropt the subject, and never took it up again.

But had the system, at which he was so enraged, combined almost any amount of human wisdom, spiritual insight, and imaginative beauty, I question whether Hollingsworth's mind was in a fit condition to receive it. I began to discern that he had come among us, actuated by no real sympathy with our feelings and our hopes, but chiefly because we were estranging ourselves from the world, with which his lonely and exclusive object in life had already put him at odds. Hollingsworth must have been originally endowed with a great spirit of benevolence, deep enough, and warm enough, to be the source of as much disinterested good, as Providence often allows a human being the privilege of conferring upon his fellows. This native instinct yet lived within him. I myself had profited by it, in my necessity. It was seen, too, in his treatment of Priscilla. Such casual circumstances, as were here involved, would quicken his divine power of sympathy, and make him seem, while their influence lasted, the tenderest man and the truest friend on earth. But, by-and-by, you missed the tenderness of yesterday, and grew drearily conscious that Hollingsworth had a closer friend than ever you could be. And this friend was the cold, spectral monster which he had himself conjured up, and on which he was wasting all the warmth of his heart, and of which, at last—as these men of a mighty purpose so invariably do—he had grown to be the bond-slave. It was his philanthropic theory!

This was a result exceedingly sad to contemplate, considering that it had been mainly brought about by the very ardor and exuberance of his philanthropy. Sad, indeed, but by no means unusual. He had taught his benevolence to pour its warm tide exclusively through one channel; so that there was nothing to spare for other great manifestations of love to man, nor scarcely for the nutriment of individual attachments, unless they could minister, in some way, to the terrible egotism which he mistook for an angel of God. Had Hollingsworth's education been more enlarged, he might not so inevitably have stumbled into this pit-fall. But this identical pursuit had educated him. He knew absolutely nothing, except in a single direction, where he had thought so energetically, and felt to such a depth, that, no doubt, the entire reason and

justice of the universe appeared to be concentrated thitherward.

It is my private opinion, that, at this period of his life,
Hollingsworth was fast going mad; and, as with other crazy
people, (among whom I include humorists of every degree,)
it required all the constancy of friendship to restrain his
associates from pronouncing him an intolerable bore. Such
prolonged fiddling upon one string; such multiform presenta-
tion of one idea! His specific object (of which he made the
public more than sufficiently aware, through the medium of
lectures and pamphlets) was to obtain funds for the construction of an edifice, with a sort of collegiate endowment.
On this foundation, he purposed to devote himself and a
few disciples to the reform and mental culture of our criminal
brethren. His visionary edifice was Hollingsworth's one castle
in the air; it was the material type, in which his philanthropic
dream strove to embody itself; and he made the scheme more
definite, and caught hold of it the more strongly, and kept his
clutch the more pertinaciously, by rendering it visible to the
bodily eye. I have seen him, a hundred times, with a pencil
and sheet of paper, sketching the façade, the side-view, or
the rear of the structure, or planning the internal arrangements, as lovingly as another man might plan those of the
projected home, where he meant to be happy with his wife
and children. I have known him to begin a model of the
building with little stones, gathered at the brookside, whither
we had gone to cool ourselves in the sultry noon of haying-
time. Unlike all other ghosts, his spirit haunted an edifice
which, instead of being time-worn, and full of storied love,
and joy, and sorrow, had never yet come into existence.

"Dear friend," said I, once, to Hollingsworth, before leaving
my sick-chamber, "I heartily wish that I could make your
schemes my schemes, because it would be so great a happiness
to find myself treading the same path with you. But I am
afraid there is not stuff in me stern enough for a philanthropist

—or not in this peculiar direction—or, at all events, not solely in this. Can you bear with me, if such should prove to be the case?"

"I will, at least, wait awhile," answered Hollingsworth, gazing at me sternly and gloomily. "But how can you be my life-long friend, except you strive with me towards the great object of my life?"

Heaven forgive me! A horrible suspicion crept into my heart, and stung the very core of it as with the fangs of an adder. I wondered whether it were possible that Hollingsworth could have watched by my bedside, with all that devoted care, only for the ulterior purpose of making me a proselyte to his views!

VIII

A MODERN ARCADIA

MAY-DAY—I forget whether by Zenobia's sole decree, or by the unanimous vote of our Community—had been declared a moveable festival. It was deferred until the sun should have had a reasonable time to clear away the snow-drifts, along the lee of the stone-walls, and bring out a few of the readiest wild-flowers. On the forenoon of the substituted day, after admitting some of the balmy air into my chamber, I decided that it was nonsense and effeminacy to keep myself a prisoner any longer. So I descended to the sitting-room, and finding nobody there, proceeded to the barn, whence I had already heard Zenobia's voice, and along with it a girlish laugh, which was not so certainly recognizable. Arriving at the spot, it a little surprised me to discover that these merry outbreaks came from Priscilla.

The two had been a-maying together. They had found anemones in abundance, houstonias* by the handfull, some columbines, a few long-stalked violets, and a quantity of white everlasting-flowers, and had filled up their basket with the delicate spray of shrubs and trees. None were prettier than the maple-twigs, the leaf of which looks like a scarlet-bud, in May, and like a plate of vegetable gold in October. Zenobia—who showed no conscience in such matters—had also rifled a cherry-tree of one of its blossomed boughs; and, with all this variety of sylvan ornament, had been decking out Priscilla. Being done with a good deal of taste, it made her look more charming than I should have thought possible, with my recollection of the wan, frost-nipt girl, as heretofore described. Nevertheless, among those fragrant blossoms, and conspicuously, too, had been stuck a weed of evil odor and ugly aspect, which, as soon as I detected it, destroyed the effect of all the rest. There was a gleam of latent mischief— not to call it deviltry—in Zenobia's eye, which seemed to indicate a slightly malicious purpose in the arrangement.

As for herself, she scorned the rural buds and leaflets, and wore nothing but her invariable flower of the tropics.

"What do you think of Priscilla now, Mr. Coverdale?" asked she, surveying her as a child does its doll. "Is not she worth a verse or two?"

"There is only one thing amiss," answered I.

Zenobia laughed, and flung the malignant weed away.

"Yes; she deserves some verses now," said I, "and from a better poet than myself. She is the very picture of the New England spring, subdued in tint, and rather cool, but with a capacity of sunshine, and bringing us a few alpine blossoms, as earnest of something richer, though hardly more beautiful, hereafter. The best type of her is one of those anemones."

"What I find most singular in Priscilla, as her health improves," observed Zenobia, "is her wildness. Such a quiet little body as she seemed, one would not have expected that! Why, as we strolled the woods together, I could hardly keep her from scrambling up the trees like a squirrel! She has never before known what it is to live in the free air, and so it intoxicates her as if she were sipping wine. And she thinks it such a Paradise here, and all of us, particularly Mr. Hollingsworth and myself, such angels! It is quite ridiculous, and provokes one's malice, almost, to see a creature so happy— especially a feminine creature."

"They are always happier than male creatures," said I.

"You must correct that opinion, Mr. Coverdale," replied Zenobia, contemptuously, "or I shall think you lack the poetic insight. Did you ever see a happy woman in your life? Of course, I do not mean a girl—like Priscilla, and a thousand others, for they are all alike, while on the sunny side of experience—but a grown woman. How can she be happy, after discovering that fate has assigned her but one single event, which she must contrive to make the substance of her whole life? A man has his choice of innumerable events."

"A woman, I suppose," answered I, "by constant repetition of her one event, may compensate for the lack of variety."

"Indeed!" said Zenobia.

While we were talking, Priscilla caught sight of Hollingsworth, at a distance, in a blue frock* and with a hoe over his shoulder, returning from the field. She immediately set out to meet him, running and skipping, with spirits as light as the breeze of the May-morning, but with limbs too little exercised to be quite responsive; she clapt her hands, too, with great exuberance of gesture, as is the custom of young girls, when their electricity overcharges them. But, all at once, midway to Hollingsworth, she paused, looked round about her, towards the river, the road, the woods, and back towards us, appearing to listen, as if she heard some one calling her name, and knew not precisely in what direction.

"Have you bewitched her?" I exclaimed.

"It is no sorcery of mine," said Zenobia. "But I have seen the girl do that identical thing, once or twice before. Can you imagine what is the matter with her?"

"No; unless," said I, "she has the gift of hearing those 'airy tongues that syllable men's names'*—which Milton tells about."

From whatever cause, Priscilla's animation seemed entirely to have deserted her. She seated herself on a rock, and remained there until Hollingsworth came up; and when he took her hand and led her back to us, she rather resembled my original image of the wan and spiritless Priscilla, than the flowery May Queen of a few moments ago. These sudden transformations, only to be accounted for by an extreme nervous susceptibility, always continued to characterize the girl, though with diminished frequency, as her health progressively grew more robust.

I was now on my legs again. My fit of illness had been an avenue between two existences; the low-arched and darksome doorway, through which I crept out of a life of old conventionalisms, on my hands and knees, as it were, and gained admittance into the freer region that lay beyond. In this respect, it was like death. And, as with death, too, it was good to have gone through it. No otherwise could I have rid myself of a thousand follies, fripperies, prejudices, habits, and other such worldly dust as inevitably settles upon the crowd along the broad highway, giving them all one sordid aspect, before noontime, however freshly they may have begun their pilgrimage, in the dewy morning. The very substance upon my bones had not been fit to live with, in any better, truer, or more energetic mode than that to which I was accustomed. So it was taken off me and flung aside, like any other worn out or unseasonable garment; and, after shivering a little while in my skeleton, I began to be clothed anew, and much more satisfactorily than in my previous suit. In literal and physical truth, I was quite another man. I had a lively sense of the exultation with which the spirit will enter on the next stage of its eternal progress, after leaving the heavy burthen of its mortality in an earthly grave, with as little concern for what may become of it, as now affected me for the flesh which I had lost.

Emerging into the genial sunshine, I half fancied that the labors of the brotherhood had already realized some of Fourier's predictions. Their enlightened culture of the soil, and the virtues with which they sanctified their life, had begun to produce an effect upon the material world and its climate. In my new enthusiasm, man looked strong and stately!—and woman, oh, how beautiful!—and the earth, a green garden, blossoming with many-colored delights! Thus Nature, whose laws I had broken in various artificial ways, comported herself towards me as a strict, but loving mother, who uses the rod upon her little boy for his naughtiness, and then gives him a smile, a kiss, and some pretty playthings, to console the urchin for her severity.

In the interval of my seclusion, there had been a number of recruits to our little army of saints and martyrs. They were mostly individuals who had gone through such an experience as to disgust them with ordinary pursuits, but who were not yet so old, nor had suffered so deeply, as to lose their faith in the better time to come. On comparing their minds, one with another, they often discovered that this idea of a Community had been growing up, in silent and unknown sympathy, for years. Thoughtful, strongly-lined faces were among them, sombre brows, but eyes that did not require spectacles, unless prematurely dimmed by the student's lamplight, and hair that seldom showed a thread of silver. Age, wedded to the past, incrusted over with a stony layer of habits, and retaining nothing fluid in its possibilities, would have been absurdly out of place in an enterprise like this. Youth, too, in its early dawn, was hardly more adapted to our purpose; for it would behold the morning radiance of its own spirit beaming over the very same spots of withered grass and barren sand, whence most of us had seen it vanish. We had very young people with us, it is true—downy lads, rosy girls in their first teens, and children of all heights above one's knee;—but these had chiefly been sent hither for education, which it was one of the objects and methods of our institution to supply. Then we had boarders, from town and elsewhere, who lived with us in a familiar way, sympathized more or less in our theories, and sometimes shared in our labors.

On the whole, it was a society such as has seldom met

together; nor, perhaps, could it reasonably be expected to hold together long. Persons of marked individuality—crooked sticks, as some of us might be called—are not exactly the easiest to bind up into a faggot. But, so long as our union should subsist, a man of intellect and feeling, with a free nature in him, might have sought far and near, without finding so many points of attraction as would allure him hitherward. We were of all creeds and opinions, and generally tolerant of all, on every imaginable subject. Our bond, it seems to me, was not affirmative, but negative. We had individually found one thing or another to quarrel with, in our past life, and were pretty well agreed as to the inexpediency of lumbering along with the old system any farther. As to what should be substituted, there was much less unanimity. We did not greatly care—at least, I never did— for the written constitution under which our millennium had commenced. My hope was, that, between theory and practice, a true and available mode of life might be struck out, and that, even should we ultimately fail, the months or years spent in the trial would not have been wasted, either as regarded passing enjoyment, or the experience which makes men wise.

Arcadians though we were, our costume bore no resemblance to the be-ribboned doublets, silk breeches and stockings, and slippers fastened with artificial roses, that distinguish the pastoral people of poetry and the stage. In outward show, I humbly conceive, we looked rather like a gang of beggars or banditti, than either a company of honest laboring men or a conclave of philosophers. Whatever might be our points of difference, we all of us seemed to have come to Blithedale with the one thrifty and laudable idea of wearing out our old clothes. Such garments as had an airing, whenever we strode afield! Coats with high collars, and with no collars, broadskirted or swallow-tailed, and with the waist at every point between the hip and armpit; pantaloons of a dozen successive epochs, and greatly defaced at the knees by the humiliations of the wearer before his lady-love;—in short, we were a living epitome of defunct fashions, and the very raggedest present-ment of men who had seen better days. It was gentility in tatters. Often retaining a scholarlike or clerical air, you might have taken us for the denizens of Grub-street,* intent on getting a comfortable livelihood by agricultural labor; or Coleridge's projected Pantisocracy,* in full experiment; or Candide* and his motley associates, at work in their cabbage-garden; or anything else that was miserably out at elbows, and most clumsily patched in the rear. We might have been sworn comrades to Falstaff's* ragged regiment. Little skill as we boasted in other points of husbandry, every mother's son of us would have served admirably to stick up for a scarecrow. And the worst of the matter was, that the first energetic move-ment, essential to one downright stroke of real labor, was sure to put a finish to these poor habiliments. So we gradually flung them all aside, and took to honest homespun and linsey-woolsey,* as preferable, on the whole, to the plan recom-mended, I think, by Virgil—'*Ara nudus; sere nudus*'*—which, as Silas Foster remarked when I translated the maxim, would be apt to astonish the women-folks.

After a reasonable training, the yeoman-life throve well with us. Our faces took the sunburn kindly; our chests gained in compass, and our shoulders in breadth and squareness; our great brown fists looked as if they had never been capable of kid gloves. The plough, the hoe, the scythe, and the hay-fork, grew familiar to our grasp. The oxen responded to our voices. We could do almost as fair a day's work as Silas Foster himself, sleep dreamlessly after it, and awake at daybreak with only a little stiffness of the joints, which was usually quite gone by breakfast-time.

To be sure, our next neighbors pretended to be incredulous as to our real proficiency in the business which we had taken in hand. They told slanderous fables about our inability to yoke our own oxen, or to drive them afield, when yoked, or to release the poor brutes from their conjugal bond at nightfall. They had the face to say, too, that the cows laughed at our awkwardness at milking-time, and invariably kicked over the pails; partly in consequence of our putting the stool on the wrong side, and partly because, taking offence at the whisking of their tails, we were in the habit of holding these natural flyflappers with one hand, and milking with the other. They further averred, that we hoed up whole acres of Indian corn and other crops, and drew the earth carefully about the weeds; and that we raised five hundred tufts of burdock, mistaking them for cabbages; and that, by dint of unskilful planting, few of our seeds ever came up at all, or if they did come up, it was stern foremost, and that we spent the better part of the month of June in reversing a field of beans, which had thrust themselves out of the ground in this unseemly way. They quoted it as nothing more than an ordinary occurrence for one or other of us to crop off two or three fingers, of a morning, by our clumsy use of the hay-cutter. Finally, and as an ultimate catastrophe, these mendacious rogues circulated a report that we Communitarians were exterminated, to the last man, by severing ourselves asunder with the sweep of our own scythes!—and that the world had lost nothing by this little accident.

But this was pure envy and malice on the part of the neighboring farmers. The peril of our new way of life was not lest we should fail in becoming practical agriculturalists, but that we should probably cease to be anything else. While our enterprise lay all in theory, we had pleased ourselves with delectable visions of the spiritualization of labor. It was to be our form of prayer, and ceremonial of worship. Each stroke of the hoe was to uncover some aromatic root of wisdom, heretofore hidden from the sun. Pausing in the field, to let the wind exhale the moisture from our foreheads, we were to look upward, and catch glimpses into the far-off soul of

truth. In this point of view, matters did not turn out quite
so well as we anticipated. It is very true, that, sometimes,
gazing casually around me, out of the midst of my toil, I used
to discern a richer picturesqueness in the visible scene of earth
and sky. There was, at such moments, a novelty, an unwonted
aspect on the face of Nature, as if she had been taken by surprise and seen at unawares, with no opportunity to put off her
real look, and assume the mask with which she mysteriously
hides herself from mortals. But this was all. The clods of
earth, which we so constantly belabored and turned over and
over, were never etherealized into thought. Our thoughts, on
the contrary, were fast becoming cloddish. Our labor symbolized nothing, and left us mentally sluggish in the dusk of
the evening. Intellectual activity is incompatible with any
large amount of bodily exercise. The yeoman and the scholar—
the yeoman and the man of finest moral culture, though not
the man of sturdiest sense and integrity—are two distinct
individuals, and can never be melted or welded into one
substance.

Zenobia soon saw this truth, and gibed me about it, one
evening, as Hollingsworth and I lay on the grass, after a
hard day's work.

"I am afraid you did not make a song, to-day, while
loading the hay-cart," said she, "as Burns did, when he was
reaping barley."

"Burns never made a song in haying-time," I answered,
very positively. "He was no poet while a farmer, and no
farmer while a poet."

"And, on the whole, which of the two characters do you
like best?" asked Zenobia. "For I have an idea that you
cannot combine them, any better than Burns*did. Ah, I see,
in my mind's eye, what sort of an individual you are to be,
two or three years hence! Grim Silas Foster is your prototype,
with his palm of sole-leather, and his joints of rusty iron,
(which, all through summer, keep the stiffness of what he

calls his winter's rheumatize,) and his brain of—I don't know
what his brain is made of, unless it be a Savoy cabbage; but
yours may be cauliflower, as a rather more delicate variety.
Your physical man will be transmuted into salt-beef and fried
pork, at the rate, I should imagine, of a pound and a half a
day; that being about the average which we find necessary in
the kitchen. You will make your toilet for the day (still like
this delightful Silas Foster) by rinsing your fingers and the
front part of your face in a little tin-pan of water, at the
door-step, and teasing your hair with a wooden pocket-comb,
before a seven-by-nine-inch looking-glass. Your only pastime
will be, to smoke some very vile tobacco in the black stump
of a pipe!"

"Pray spare me!" cried I. "But the pipe is not Silas's only
mode of solacing himself with the weed."

"Your literature," continued Zenobia, apparently delighted
with her description, "will be the Farmer's Almanac; for, I
observe, our friend Foster never gets so far as the newspaper.
When you happen to sit down, at odd moments, you will fall
asleep, and make nasal proclamation of the fact, as he does;
and invariably you must be jogged out of a nap, after supper,
by the future Mrs. Coverdale, and persuaded to go regularly
to bed. And on Sundays; when you put on a blue coat with
brass buttons, you will think of nothing else to do, but to go
and lounge over the stone-walls and rail-fences, and stare at
the corn growing. And you will look with a knowing eye at
oxen, and will have a tendency to clamber over into pig-sties,
and feel of the hogs, and give a guess how much they will
weigh, after you shall have stuck and dressed them. Already,
I have noticed, you begin to speak through your nose, and
with a drawl. Pray, if you really did make any poetry to-day,
let us hear it in that kind of utterance!"

"Coverdale has given up making verses, now," said Hollingsworth, who never had the slightest appreciation of my
poetry. "Just think of him penning a sonnet, with a fist like

that! There is at least this good in a life of toil, that it takes the nonsense and fancy-work out of a man, and leaves nothing but what truly belongs to him. If a farmer can make poetry at the plough-tail, it must be because his nature insists on it; and if that be the case, let him make it, in Heaven's name!"

"And how is it with you?" asked Zenobia, in a different voice; for she never laughed at Hollingsworth, as she often did at me.—"You, I think, cannot have ceased to live a life of thought and feeling."

"I have always been in earnest," answered Hollingsworth. "I have hammered thought out of iron, after heating the iron in my heart! It matters little what my outward toil may be. Were I a slave at the bottom of a mine, I should keep the same purpose—the same faith in its ultimate accomplishment— that I do now. Miles Coverdale is not in earnest, either as a poet or a laborer."

"You give me hard measure, Hollingsworth," said I, a little hurt. "I have kept pace with you in the field; and my bones feel as if I had been in earnest, whatever may be the case with my brain!"

"I cannot conceive," observed Zenobia, with great emphasis—and, no doubt, she spoke fairly the feeling of the moment—"I cannot conceive of being, so continually as Mr. Coverdale is, within the sphere of a strong and noble nature, without being strengthened and enobled by its influence!"

This amiable remark of the fair Zenobia confirmed me in what I had already begun to suspect—that Hollingsworth, like many other illustrious prophets, reformers, and philanthropists, was likely to make at least two proselytes, among the women, to one among the men. Zenobia and Priscilla! These, I believe, (unless my unworthy self might be reckoned for a third,) were the only disciples of his mission; and I spent a great deal of time, uselessly, in trying to conjecture what Hollingsworth meant to do with them—and they with him!

IX

HOLLINGSWORTH, ZENOBIA, PRISCILLA

I T IS not, I apprehend, a healthy kind of mental occupation, to devote ourselves too exclusively to the study of individual men and women. If the person under examination be one's self, the result is pretty certain to be diseased action of the heart, almost before we can snatch a second glance. Or, if we take the freedom to put a friend under our microscope, we thereby insulate him from many of his true relations, magnify his peculiarities, inevitably tear him into parts, and, of course, patch him very clumsily together again. What wonder, then, should we be frightened by the aspect of a monster, which, after all—though we can point to every feature of his deformity in the real personage— may be said to have been created mainly by ourselves!

Thus, as my conscience has often whispered me, I did Hollingsworth a great wrong by prying into his character, and am perhaps doing him as great a one, at this moment, by putting faith in the discoveries which I seemed to make. But I could not help it. Had I loved him less, I might have used him better. He—and Zenobia and Priscilla, both for their own sakes and as connected with him—were separated from the rest of the Community, to my imagination, and stood forth as the indices of a problem which it was my business to solve. Other associates had a portion of my time; other matters amused me; passing occurrences carried me along with them, while they lasted. But here was the vortex of my meditations around which they revolved, and whitherward they too continually tended. In the midst of cheerful society, I had often a feeling of loneliness. For it was impossible not to be sensible, that, while these three characters figured so largely on my private theatre, I—though probably reckoned as a friend by all—was at best but a secondary or tertiary personage with either of them.

I loved Hollingsworth, as has already been enough expressed. But it impressed me, more and more, that there was a stern and dreadful peculiarity in this man, such as could not prove otherwise than pernicious to the happiness of those who should be drawn into too intimate a connection with him. He was not altogether human. There was something else in Hollingsworth, besides flesh and blood, and sympathies and affections, and celestial spirit.

This is always true of those men who have surrendered themselves to an over-ruling purpose. It does not so much impel them from without, nor even operate as a motive power within, but grows incorporate with all that they think and feel, and finally converts them into little else save that one principle. When such begins to be the predicament, it is not cowardice, but wisdom, to avoid these victims. They have no heart, no sympathy, no reason, no conscience. They will keep no friend, unless he make himself the mirror of their purpose; they will smite and slay you, and trample your dead corpse under foot, all the more readily, if you take the first step with them, and cannot take the second, and the third, and every other step of their terribly straight path. They have an idol, to which they consecrate themselves high-priest, and deem it holy work to offer sacrifices of whatever is most precious, and never once seem to suspect—so cunning has the Devil been with them—that this false deity, in whose iron features, immitigable to all the rest of mankind, they see only benignity and love, is but a spectrum of the very priest himself, projected upon the surrounding darkness. And the higher and purer the original object, and the more unselfishly it may have been taken up, the slighter is the probability that they can be led to recognize the process, by which godlike benevolence has been debased into all-devouring egotism.

Of course, I am perfectly aware that the above statement is exaggerated, in the attempt to make it adequate. Professed philanthropists have gone far; but no originally good man, I presume, ever went quite so far as this. Let the reader abate whatever he deems fit. The paragraph may remain, however, both for its truth and its exaggeration, as strongly expressive of the tendencies which were really operative in Hollingsworth, and as exemplifying the kind of error into which my mode of observation was calculated to lead me. The issue was, that, in solitude, I often shuddered at my friend. In my recollection of his dark and impressive countenance, the features grew more sternly prominent than the reality, duskier in their depth and shadow, and more lurid in their light; the frown, that had merely flitted across his brow, seemed to have contorted it with an adamantine wrinkle. On meeting him again, I was often filled with remorse, when his deep eyes beamed kindly upon me, as with the glow of a household fire that was burning in a cave.—"He is a man, after all!" thought I—"his Maker's own truest image, a philanthropic man!—not that steel engine of the Devil's contrivance, a philanthropist!"—But, in my wood-walks, and in my silent chamber, the dark face frowned at me again.

When a young girl comes within the sphere of such a man, she is as perilously situated as the maiden whom, in the old classical myths, the people used to expose to a dragon. If I had any duty whatever, in reference to Hollingsworth, it was, to endeavor to save Priscilla from that kind of personal worship which her sex is generally prone to lavish upon saints and heroes. It often requires but one smile, out of the hero's

eyes into the girl's or woman's heart, to transform this devotion, from a sentiment of the highest approval and confidence,
into passionate love. Now, Hollingsworth smiled much upon
Priscilla; more than upon any other person. If she thought
him beautiful, it was no wonder. I often thought him so,
with the expression of tender, human care, and gentlest sympathy, which she alone seemed to have power to call out upon
his features. Zenobia, I suspect, would have given her eyes,
bright as they were, for such a look; it was the least that our
poor Priscilla could do, to give her heart for a great many of
them. There was the more danger of this, inasmuch as the
footing, on which we all associated at Blithedale, was widely
different from that of conventional society. While inclining
us to the soft affections of the Golden Age,* it seemed to
authorize any individual, of either sex, to fall in love with any
other, regardless of what would elsewhere be judged suitable
and prudent. Accordingly, the tender passion was very rife
among us, in various degrees of mildness or virulence, but
mostly passing away with the state of things that had given
it origin. This was all well enough; but, for a girl like Priscilla,
and a woman like Zenobia, to jostle one another in their love
of a man like Hollingsworth, was likely to be no child's play.

Had I been as cold-hearted as I sometimes thought myself,
nothing would have interested me more than to witness the
play of passions that must thus have been evolved. But, in
honest truth, I would really have gone far to save Priscilla, at
least, from the catastrophe in which such a drama would be
apt to terminate.

Priscilla had now grown to be a very pretty girl, and still
kept budding and blossoming, and daily putting on some new
charm, which you no sooner became sensible of, than you
thought it worth all that she had previously possessed. So
unformed, vague, and without substance, as she had come to
us, it seemed as if we could see Nature shaping out a woman
before our very eyes, and yet had only a more reverential sense

of the mystery of a woman's soul and frame. Yesterday, her cheek was pale; to-day, it had a bloom. Priscilla's smile, like a baby's first one, was a wondrous novelty. Her imperfections and short-comings affected me with a kind of playful pathos, which was as absolutely bewitching a sensation as ever I experienced. After she had been a month or two at Blithedale, her animal spirits waxed high, and kept her pretty constantly in a state of bubble and ferment, impelling her to far more bodily activity than she had yet strength to endure. She was very fond of playing with the other girls, out-of-doors. There is hardly another sight in the world so pretty, as that of a company of young girls, almost women grown, at play, and so giving themselves up to their airy impulse that their tiptoes barely touch the ground.

Girls are incomparably wilder and more effervescent than boys, more untameable, and regardless of rule and limit, with an ever-shifting variety, breaking continually into new modes of fun, yet with a harmonious propriety through all. Their steps, their voices, appear free as the wind, but keep consonance with a strain of music, inaudible to us. Young men and boys, on the other hand, play according to recognized law, old, traditionary games, permitting no caprioles* of fancy, but with scope enough for the outbreak of savage instincts. For, young or old, in play or in earnest, man is prone to be a brute.

Especially is it delightful to see a vigorous young girl run a race, with her head thrown back, her limbs moving more friskily than they need, and an air between that of a bird and a young colt. But Priscilla's peculiar charm, in a foot-race, was the weakness and irregularity with which she ran. Growing up without exercise, except to her poor little fingers, she had never yet acquired the perfect use of her legs. Setting buoyantly forth, therefore, as if no rival less swift than Atalanta* could compete with her, she ran faulteringly, and often tumbled on the grass. Such an incident—though it seems too slight to think of—was a thing to laugh at, but which brought the water into one's eyes, and lingered in the memory after far greater joys and sorrows were swept out of it, as antiquated trash. Priscilla's life, as I beheld it, was full of trifles that affected me in just this way.

When she had come to be quite at home among us, I used to fancy that Priscilla played more pranks, and perpetrated more mischief, than any other girl in the Community. For example, I once heard Silas Foster, in a very gruff voice, threatening to rivet three horse-shoes round Priscilla's neck and chain her to a post, because she, with some other young people, had clambered upon a load of hay and caused it to slide off the cart. How she made her peace, I never knew; but very soon afterwards, I saw old Silas, with his brawny hands round Priscilla's waist, swinging her to-and-fro and finally depositing her on one of the oxen, to take her first lesson in riding. She met with terrible mishaps in her efforts to milk a cow; she let the poultry into the garden; she generally spoilt whatever part of the dinner she took in charge; she broke crockery; she dropt our biggest pitcher into the well; and—except with her needle, and those little wooden instruments for purse-making—was as unserviceable a member of society as any young lady in the land. There was no other sort of efficiency about her. Yet everybody was kind to Priscilla; everybody loved her, and laughed at her, to her face, and did not laugh, behind her back; everybody would have given her half of his last crust, or the bigger share of his plum-cake. These were pretty certain indications that we were all conscious of a pleasant weakness in the girl, and considered her not quite able to look after her own interests, or fight her battle with the world. And Hollingsworth—perhaps because he had been the means of introducing Priscilla to her new abode—appeared to recognize her as his own especial charge.

Her simple, careless, childish flow of spirits often made me sad. She seemed to me like a butterfly, at play in a flickering bit of sunshine, and mistaking it for a broad and eternal summer. We sometimes hold mirth to a stricter accountability than sorrow; it must show good cause, or the echo of its laughter comes back drearily. Priscilla's gaiety, moreover, was of a nature that showed me how delicate an instrument she was, and what fragile harp-strings were her nerves. As they made sweet music at the airiest touch, it would require but a stronger one to burst them all asunder. Absurd as it might be, I tried to reason with her, and persuade her not to be so joyous, thinking that, if she would draw less lavishly upon her fund of happiness, it would last the longer. I remember doing so, one summer evening, when we tired laborers sat looking on, like Goldsmith's old folks* under the village thorn-tree, while the young people were at their sports.

"What is the use or sense of being so very gay?" I said to Priscilla, while she was taking breath after a great frolic. "I love to see a sufficient cause for everything; and I can see none for this. Pray tell me, now, what kind of a world you imagine this to be, which you are so merry in?"

"I never think about it at all," answered Priscilla, laughing. "But this I am sure of—that it is a world where everybody is kind to me, and where I love everybody. My heart keeps dancing within me; and all the foolish things, which you see me do, are only the motions of my heart. How can I be dismal, if my heart will not let me?"

"Have you nothing dismal to remember?" I suggested. "If not, then, indeed, you are very fortunate!"

"Ah!" said Priscilla, slowly.

And then came that unintelligible gesture, when she seemed to be listening to a distant voice.

"For my part," I continued, beneficently seeking to overshadow her with my own sombre humor, "my past life has been a tiresome one enough; yet I would rather look backward ten times, than forward once. For, little as we know of our life to come, we may be very sure, for one thing, that the good we aim at will not be attained. People never do get just the good they seek. If it come at all, it is something else, which they never dreamed of, and did not particularly want. Then, again, we may rest certain that our friends of to-day will not be our friends of a few years hence; but, if we keep one of them, it will be at the expense of the others—and, most probably, we shall keep none. To be sure, there are more to be had! But who cares about making a new set of friends, even should they be better than those around us?"

"Not I!" said Priscilla. "I will live and die with these!"

"Well; but let the future go!" resumed I. "As for the present moment, if we could look into the hearts where we wish to be most valued, what should you expect to see? One's own likeness, in the innermost, holiest niche? Ah, I don't know! It may not be there at all. It may be a dusty image, thrust aside into a corner, and by-and-by to be flung out-of-doors, where any foot may trample upon it. If not to-day, then tomorrow! And so, Priscilla, I do not see much wisdom in being so very merry in this kind of a world!"

It had taken me nearly seven years of worldly life, to hive up the bitter honey which I here offered to Priscilla. And she rejected it!

"I don't believe one word of what you say!" she replied, laughing anew. "You made me sad, for a minute, by talking about the past. But the past never comes back again. Do we dream the same dream twice? There is nothing else that I am afraid of."

So away she ran, and fell down on the green grass, as it was often her luck to do, but got up again without any harm.

"Priscilla, Priscilla!" cried Hollingsworth, who was sitting on the door-step. "You had better not run any more to-night. You will weary yourself too much. And do not sit down out of doors; for there is a heavy dew beginning to fall!"

At his first word, she went and sat down under the porch, at Hollingsworth's feet, entirely contented and happy. What charm was there, in his rude massiveness, that so attracted and soothed this shadowlike girl? It appeared to me—who have always been curious in such matters—that Priscilla's vague and seemingly causeless flow of felicitous feeling was that with which love blesses inexperienced hearts, before they begin to suspect what is going on within them. It transports them to the seventh heaven; and if you ask what brought them thither, they neither can tell nor care to learn, but cherish an ecstatic faith that there they shall abide forever.

Zenobia was in the door-way, not far from Hollingsworth. She gazed at Priscilla, in a very singular way. Indeed, it was a sight worth gazing at, and a beautiful sight too, as the fair girl sat at the feet of that dark, powerful figure. Her air, while perfectly modest, delicate, and virginlike, denoted her as swayed by Hollingsworth, attracted to him, and unconsciously seeking to rest upon his strength. I could not turn away my own eyes, but hoped that nobody, save Zenobia and myself, were witnessing this picture. It is before me now, with the evening twilight a little deepened by the dusk of memory.

"Come hither, Priscilla!" said Zenobia. "I have something to say to you!"

She spoke in little more than a whisper. But it is strange how expressive of moods a whisper may often be. Priscilla felt at once that something had gone wrong.

"Are you angry with me?" she asked, rising slowly and standing before Zenobia in a drooping attitude. "What have I done? I hope you are not angry!"

"No, no, Priscilla!" said Hollingsworth, smiling. "I will answer for it, she is not. You are the one little person in the world, with whom nobody can be angry!"

"Angry with you, child? What a silly idea!" exclaimed Zenobia, laughing. "No, indeed! But, my dear Priscilla, you are getting to be so very pretty that you absolutely need a duenna; and as I am older than you, and have had my own little experience of life, and think myself exceedingly sage, I intend to fill the place of a maiden-aunt. Every day, I shall give you a lecture, a quarter-of-an-hour in length, on the morals, manners, and proprieties of social life. When our pastoral shall be quite played out, Priscilla, my worldly wisdom may stand you in good stead!"

"I am afraid you are angry with me," repeated Priscilla, sadly; for, while she seemed as impressible as wax, the girl often showed a persistency in her own ideas, as stubborn as it was gentle.

"Dear me, what can I say to the child!" cried Zenobia, in a tone of humorous vexation. "Well, well; since you insist on my being angry, come to my room, this moment, and let me beat you!"

Zenobia bade Hollingsworth good night very sweetly, and nodded to me with a smile. But, just as she turned aside with Priscilla into the dimness of the porch, I caught another glance at her countenance. It would have made the fortune of a tragic actress, could she have borrowed it for the moment when she fumbles in her bosom for the concealed dagger, or the exceedingly sharp bodkin, or mingles the ratsbane in her lover's bowl of wine, or her rival's cup of tea. Not that I in the least anticipated any such catastrophe; it being a remarkable truth, that custom has in no one point a greater sway than over our modes of wreaking our wild passions. And, besides, had we been in Italy, instead of New England, it was hardly yet a crisis for the dagger or the bowl.

It often amazed me, however, that Hollingsworth should show himself so recklessly tender towards Priscilla, and never once seem to think of the effect which it might have upon her heart. But the man, as I have endeavored to explain, was thrown completely off his moral balance, and quite bewildered as to his personal relations, by his great excrescence of a philanthropic scheme. I used to see, or fancy, indications that he was not altogether obtuse to Zenobia's influence as a woman. No doubt, however, he had a still more exquisite enjoyment of Priscilla's silent sympathy with his purposes, so unalloyed with criticism, and therefore more grateful than any intellectual approbation, which always involves a possible reserve of latent censure. A man—poet, prophet, or whatever he may be—readily persuades himself of his right to all the worship that is voluntarily tendered. In requital of so rich benefits as he was to confer upon mankind, it would have been hard to deny Hollingsworth the simple solace of a young girl's heart, which he held in his hand, and smelled to, like a rosebud. But what if, while pressing out its fragrance, he should crush the tender rosebud in his grasp!

As for Zenobia, I saw no occasion to give myself any trouble. With her native strength, and her experience of the world, she could not be supposed to need any help of mine. Nevertheless, I was really generous enough to feel some little interest likewise for Zenobia. With all her faults, (which might have been a great many, besides the abundance that I knew of,) she possessed noble traits, and a heart which must at least have been valuable while new. And she seemed ready to fling it away, as uncalculatingly as Priscilla herself. I could not but suspect, that, if merely at play with Hollingsworth, she was sporting with a power which she did not fully estimate. Or, if in earnest, it might chance, between Zenobia's passionate force and his dark, self-delusive egotism, to turn out such earnest as would develop itself in some sufficiently tragic catastrophe, though the dagger and the bowl should go for nothing in it.

Meantime, the gossip of the Community set them down as a pair of lovers. They took walks together, and were not seldom encountered in the wood-paths; Hollingsworth deeply discoursing, in tones solemn and sternly pathetic. Zenobia, with a rich glow on her cheeks, and her eyes softened from their ordinary brightness, looked so beautiful, that, had her companion been ten times a philanthropist, it seemed impossible but that one glance should melt him back into a man. Oftener than anywhere else, they went to a certain point on the slope of a pasture, commanding nearly the whole of our own domain, besides a view of the river and an airy prospect of many distant hills. The bond of our Community was such, that the members had the privilege of building cottages for their own residence, within our precincts, thus laying a hearth-stone and fencing in a home, private and peculiar, to all desirable extent; while yet the inhabitants should continue to share the advantages of an associated life. It was inferred, that Hollingsworth and Zenobia intended to rear their dwelling on this favorite spot.

I mentioned these rumors to Hollingsworth in a playful way.

"Had you consulted me," I went on to observe, "I should have recommended a site further to the left, just a little withdrawn into the wood, with two or three peeps at the prospect, among the trees. You will be in the shady vale of years, long before you can raise any better kind of shade around your cottage, if you build it on this bare slope."

"But I offer my edifice as a spectacle to the world," said Hollingsworth, "that it may take example and build many another like it. Therefore I mean to set it on the open hill-side."

Twist these words how I might, they offered no very satisfactory import. It seemed hardly probable that Hollingsworth should care about educating the public taste in the department of cottage-architecture, desirable as such improvement certainly was.

X

A VISITOR FROM TOWN

HOLLINGSWORTH and I—we had been hoeing potatoes, that forenoon, while the rest of the fraternity were engaged in a distant quarter of the farm —sat· under a clump of maples, eating our eleven o'clock lunch, when we saw a stranger approaching along the edge of the field. He had admitted himself from the road-side, through a turnstile, and seemed to have a purpose of speaking with us.

And, by-the-by, we were favored with many visits at Blithedale; especially from people who sympathized with our theories, and perhaps held themselves ready to unite in our actual experiment, as soon as there should appear a reliable promise of its success. It was rather ludicrous, indeed, (to me, at least, whose enthusiasm had insensibly been exhaled, together with the perspiration of many a hard day's toil,) it was absolutely funny, therefore, to observe what a glory was shed about our life and labors, in the imagination of these longing proselytes. In their view, we were as poetical as Arcadians, besides being as practical as the hardest-fisted husbandmen in Massachusetts. We did not, it is true, spend much time in piping to our sheep, or warbling our innocent loves to the sisterhood. But they gave us credit for imbuing the ordinary rustic occupations with a kind of religious poetry, insomuch that our very cow-yards and pig-sties were as delightfully fragrant as a flower-garden. Nothing used to please me more than to see one of these lay enthusiasts snatch up a hoe, as they were very prone to do, and set to work with a vigor that perhaps carried him through about a dozen ill-directed strokes. Men are wonderfully soon satisfied, in this day of shameful bodily enervation, when, from one end of life to the other, such multitudes never taste the sweet weariness that follows accustomed toil. I seldom saw the new enthusiasm that did not grow as flimsy and flaccid as the proselyte's moistened shirt-collar, with a quarter-of-an-hour's active labor, under a July sun.

But the person, now at hand, had not at all the air of one of these amiable visionaries. He was an elderly man, dressed rather shabbily, yet decently enough, in a gray frock-coat, faded towards a brown hue, and wore a broad-brimmed white hat, of the fashion of several years gone by. His hair was perfect silver, without a dark thread in the whole of it; his nose, though it had a scarlet tip, by no means indicated the jollity of which a red nose is the generally admitted symbol. He was a subdued, undemonstrative old man, who would doubtless drink a glass of liquor, now and then, and probably more than was good for him; not, however, with a purpose of undue exhilaration, but in the hope of bringing his spirits up to the ordinary level of the world's cheerfulness. Drawing nearer, there was a shy look about him, as if he were ashamed of his poverty, or, at any rate, for some reason or other, would rather have us glance at him sidelong than take a full-front view. He had a queer appearance of hiding himself behind the patch on his left eye.

"I know this old gentleman," said I to Hollingsworth, as we sat observing him—"that is, I have met him a hundred times, in town, and have often amused my fancy with wondering what he was, before he came to be what he is. He haunts restaurants and such places, and has an odd way of

lurking in corners or getting behind a door, whenever practicable, and holding out his hand, with some little article in
it, which he wishes you to buy. The eye of the world seems
to trouble him, although he necessarily lives so much in it. I
never expected to see him in an open field."

"Have you learned anything of his history?" asked Hollingsworth.

"Not a circumstance," I answered. "But there must be
something curious in it. I take him to be a harmless sort of a
person, and a tolerably honest one; but his manners, being
so furtive, remind me of those of a rat—a rat without the
mischief, the fierce eye, the teeth to bite with, or the desire
to bite. See, now! He means to skulk along that fringe of
bushes, and approach us on the other side of our clump of
maples."

We soon heard the old man's velvet tread on the grass,
indicating that he had arrived within a few feet of where
we sat.

"Good morning, Mr. Moodie," said Hollingsworth, addressing the stranger as an acquaintance. "You must have had a
hot and tiresome walk from the city. Sit down, and take a
morsel of our bread and cheese!"

The visitor made a grateful little murmur of acquiescence,
and sat down in a spot somewhat removed; so that, glancing
round, I could see his gray pantaloons and dusty shoes, while
his upper part was mostly hidden behind the shrubbery. Nor
did he come forth from this retirement during the whole of
the interview that followed. We handed him such food as
we had, together with a brown jug of molasses-and-water,
(would that it had been brandy, or something better, for the
sake of his chill old heart!) like priests offering dainty sacrifice
to an enshrined and invisible idol. I have no idea that he
really lacked sustenance; but it was quite touching, nevertheless, to hear him nibbling away at our crusts.

"Mr. Moodie," said I, "do you remember selling me one

of those very pretty little silk purses, of which you seem to have a monopoly in the market? I keep it, to this day, I can assure you."

"Ah, thank you!" said our guest. "Yes, Mr. Coverdale, I used to sell a good many of those little purses."

He spoke languidly, and only those few words, like a watch with an inelastic spring, that just ticks, a moment or two, and stops again. He seemed a very forlorn old man. In the wantonness of youth, strength, and comfortable condition—making my prey of people's individualities, as my custom was—I tried to identify my mind with the old fellow's, and take his view of the world, as if looking through a smoke-blackened glass at the sun. It robbed the landscape of all its life. Those pleasantly swelling slopes of our farm, descending towards the wide meadows, through which sluggishly circled the brimfull tide of the Charles, bathing the long sedges on its hither and farther shores; the broad, sunny gleam over the winding water; that peculiar picturesqueness of the scene, where capes and headlands put themselves boldly forth upon the perfect level of the meadow, as into a green lake, with inlets between the promontories; the shadowy woodland, with twinkling showers of light falling into its depths; the sultry heat-vapor, which rose everywhere like incense, and in which my soul delighted, as indicating so rich a fervor in the passionate day, and in the earth that was burning with its love:—I beheld all these things as through old Moodie's eyes. When my eyes are dimmer than they have yet come to be, I will go thither again, and see if I did not catch the tone of his mind aright, and if the cold and lifeless tint of his perceptions be not then repeated in my own.

Yet it was unaccountable to myself, the interest that I felt in him.

"Have you any objection," said I, "to telling me who made those little purses?"

"Gentlemen have often asked me that," said Moodie,

slowly; "but I shake my head, and say little or nothing, and creep out of the way, as well as I can. I am a man of few words; and if gentlemen were to be told one thing, they would be very apt, I suppose, to ask me another. But it happens, just now, Mr. Coverdale, that you can tell me more about the maker of those little purses, than I can tell you."

"Why do you trouble him with needless questions, Coverdale?" interrupted Hollingsworth. "You must have known, long ago, that it was Priscilla. And so, my good friend, you have come to see her? Well, I am glad of it. You will find her altered very much for the better, since that wintry evening when you put her into my charge. Why, Priscilla has a bloom in her cheeks, now!"

"Has my pale little girl a bloom?" repeated Moodie, with a kind of slow wonder. "Priscilla with a bloom in her cheeks! Ah, I am afraid I shall not know my little girl. And is she happy?"

"Just as happy as a bird," answered Hollingsworth.

"Then, gentlemen," said our guest, apprehensively, "I don't think it well for me to go any further. I crept hitherward only to ask about Priscilla; and now that you have told me such good news, perhaps I can do no better than to creep back again. If she were to see this old face of mine, the child would remember some very sad times which we have spent together. Some very sad times indeed! She has forgotten them, I know—them and me—else she could not be so happy, nor have a bloom in her cheeks. Yes—yes—yes," continued he, still with the same torpid utterance; "with many thanks to you, Mr. Hollingsworth, I will creep back to town again."

"You shall do no such thing, Mr. Moodie!" said Hollingsworth, bluffly. "Priscilla often speaks of you; and if there lacks anything to make her cheeks bloom like two damask roses, I'll venture to say, it is just the sight of your face. Come; we will go and find her."

"Mr. Hollingsworth!" said the old man, in his hesitating way.

"Well!" answered Hollingsworth.

"Has there been any call for Priscilla?" asked Moodie; and though his face was hidden from us, his tone gave a sure indication of the mysterious nod and wink with which he put the question. "You know, I think, sir, what I mean."

"I have not the remotest suspicion what you mean, Mr. Moodie," replied Hollingsworth. "Nobody, to my knowledge, has called for Priscilla, except yourself. But, come; we are losing time, and I have several things to say to you, by the way."

"And, Mr. Hollingsworth!" repeated Moodie.

"Well, again!" cried my friend, rather impatiently. "What now?"

"There is a lady here," said the old man; and his voice lost some of its wearisome hesitation. "You will account it a very strange matter for me to talk about; but I chanced to know this lady, when she was but a little child. If I am rightly informed, she has grown to be a very fine woman, and makes a brilliant figure in the world, with her beauty, and her talents, and her noble way of spending her riches. I should recognize this lady, so people tell me, by a magnificent flower in her hair!"

"What a rich tinge it gives to his colorless ideas, when he speaks of Zenobia!" I whispered to Hollingsworth. "But how can there possibly be any interest or connecting link between him and her?"

"The old man, for years past," whispered Hollingsworth, "has been a little out of his right mind, as you probably see."

"What I would inquire," resumed Moodie, "is, whether this beautiful lady is kind to my poor Priscilla."

"Very kind," said Hollingsworth.

"Does she love her?" asked Moodie.

"It should seem so," answered my friend. "They are always together."

"Like a gentlewoman and her maid servant, I fancy?" suggested the old man.

There was something so singular in his way of saying this, that I could not resist the impulse to turn quite round, so as to catch a glimpse of his face; almost imagining that I should see another person than old Moodie. But there he sat, with the patched side of his face towards me.

"Like an elder and younger sister, rather," replied Hollingsworth.

"Ah," said Moodie, more complaisantly—for his latter tones had harshness and acidity in them—"it would gladden my old heart to witness that. If one thing would make me happier than another, Mr. Hollingsworth, it would be, to see that beautiful lady holding my little girl by the hand."

"Come along," said Hollingsworth, "and perhaps you may."

After a little more delay on the part of our freakish visitor, they set forth together; old Moodie keeping a step or two behind Hollingsworth, so that the latter could not very conveniently look him in the face. I remained under the tuft of maples, doing my utmost to draw an inference from the scene that had just passed. In spite of Hollingsworth's off-hand explanation, it did not strike me that our strange guest was really beside himself, but only that his mind needed screwing up, like an instrument long out of tune, the strings of which have ceased to vibrate smartly and sharply. Methought it would be profitable for us, projectors of a happy life, to welcome this old gray shadow, and cherish him as one of us, and let him creep about our domain, in order that he might be a little merrier for our sakes, and we, sometimes, a little sadder for his. Human destinies look ominous, without some perceptible intermixture of the sable or the gray. And then, too, should any of our fraternity grow feverish with an over-exulting sense of prosperity, it would be a sort of cooling regimen to slink off into the woods, and spend an hour, or a day, or as many days as might be requisite to the cure, in uninterrupted communion with this deplorable old Moodie!

Going homeward to dinner, I had a glimpse of him behind the trunk of a tree, gazing earnestly towards a particular window of the farm-house. And, by-and-by, Priscilla appeared at this window, playfully drawing along Zenobia, who looked as bright as the very day that was blazing down upon us, only not, by many degrees, so well advanced towards her noon. I was convinced that this pretty sight must have been purposely arranged by Priscilla, for the old man to see. But either the girl held her too long, or her fondness was resented as too great a freedom; for Zenobia suddenly put Priscilla decidedly away, and gave her a haughty look, as from a mistress to a dependant. Old Moodie shook his head—and again, and again, I saw him shake it, as he withdrew along the road—and, at the last point whence the farm-house was visible, he turned, and shook his uplifted staff.

XI

THE WOOD-PATH

NOT LONG after the preceding incident, in order to get the ache of too constant labor out of my bones, and to relieve my spirit of the irksomeness of a settled routine, I took a holiday. It was my purpose to spend it, all alone, from breakfast-time till twilight, in the deepest wood-seclusion that lay anywhere around us. Though fond of society, I was so constituted as to need these occasional retirements, even in a life like that of Blithedale, which was itself characterized by a remoteness from the world. Unless renewed by a yet farther withdrawal towards the inner circle of self-communion, I lost the better part of my individuality. My thoughts became of little worth, and my sensibilities grew as arid as a tuft of moss, (a thing whose life is in the shade, the rain, or the noontide dew,) crumbling in the sunshine, after long expectance of a shower. So, with my heart full of a drowsy pleasure, and cautious not to dissipate my mood by previous intercourse with any one, I hurried away, and was soon pacing a wood-path, arched overhead with boughs, and dusky brown beneath my feet.

At first, I walked very swiftly, as if the heavy floodtide of social life were roaring at my heels, and would outstrip and overwhelm me, without all the better diligence in my escape. But, threading the more distant windings of the track, I abated my pace and looked about me for some side-aisle, that should admit me into the innermost sanctuary of this green cathedral; just as, in human acquaintanceship, a casual opening sometimes lets us, all of a sudden, into the long-sought intimacy of a mysterious heart. So much was I absorbed in my reflections—or rather, in my mood, the substance of which was as yet too shapeless to be called thought—that footsteps rustled on the leaves, and a figure passed me by, almost without impressing either the sound or sight upon my consciousness.

A moment afterwards, I heard a voice at a little distance behind me, speaking so sharply and impertinently that it made a complete discord with my spiritual state, and caused the latter to vanish, as abruptly as when you thrust a finger into a soap-bubble.

"Halloo, friend!" cried this most unseasonable voice. "Stop a moment, I say! I must have a word with you!"

I turned about, in a humor ludicrously irate. In the first place, the interruption, at any rate, was a grievous injury; then, the tone displeased me. And, finally, unless there be real affection in his heart, a man cannot—such is the bad state to which the world has brought itself—cannot more effectually show his contempt for a brother-mortal, nor more gallingly assume a position of superiority, than by addressing him as 'friend.' Especially does the misapplication of this phrase bring out that latent hostility, which is sure to animate peculiar sects, and those who, with however generous a purpose, have sequestered themselves from the crowd; a feeling, it is true, which may be hidden in some dog-kennel of the heart, grumbling there in the darkness, but is never quite extinct, until the dissenting party have gained power and scope enough to treat the world generously. For my part, I should have taken it as far less an insult to be styled 'fellow,' 'clown,' or 'bumpkin.' To either of these appellations, my rustic garb (it was a linen blouse, with checked shirt and striped pantaloons, a chip-hat on my head, and a rough hickory-stick in my hand) very fairly entitled me. As the case stood, my temper darted at once to the opposite pole; not friend, but enemy!

"What do you want with me?" said I, facing about.

"Come a little nearer, friend!" said the stranger, beckoning.

"No," answered I. "If I can do anything for you, without too much trouble to myself, say so. But recollect, if you please, that you are not speaking to an acquaintance, much less a friend!"

"Upon my word, I believe not!" retorted he, looking at me with some curiosity; and lifting his hat, he made me a salute, which had enough of sarcasm to be offensive, and just enough of doubtful courtesy to render any resentment of it absurd.— "But I ask your pardon! I recognize a little mistake. If I may take the liberty to suppose it, you, sir, are probably one of the Æsthetic—or shall I rather say ecstatic?—laborers, who have planted themselves hereabouts. This is your forest of Arden,* and you are either the banished Duke, in person, or one of the chief nobles in his train. The melancholy Jacques, perhaps? Be it so! In that case, you can probably do me a favor."

I never, in my life, felt less inclined to confer a favor on any man.

"I am busy!" said I.

So unexpectedly had the stranger made me sensible of his presence, that he had almost the effect of an apparition, and certainly a less appropriate one (taking into view the dim woodland solitude about us) than if the salvage man* of antiquity, hirsute and cinctured with a leafy girdle, had started out of a thicket. He was still young, seemingly a little under thirty, of a tall and well-developed figure, and as handsome a man as ever I beheld. The style of his beauty, however, though a masculine style, did not at all commend itself to my taste. His countenance—I hardly know how to describe the peculiarity—had an indecorum in it, a kind of rudeness, a hard, coarse, forth-putting freedom of expression, which no degree of external polish could have abated, one single jot. Not that it was vulgar. But he had no fineness of nature; there was in his eyes (although they might have artifice enough of another sort) the naked exposure of something that ought not to be left prominent. With these vague allusions to what I have seen in other faces, as well as his, I leave the quality to be comprehended best—because with an intuitive repugnance—by those who possess least of it.

His hair, as well as his beard and moustache, was coal-black; his eyes, too, were black and sparkling, and his teeth remarkably brilliant. He was rather carelessly, but well and fashionably dressed, in a summer-morning costume. There was a gold chain, exquisitely wrought, across his vest. I never saw a smoother or whiter gloss than that upon his shirt-bosom, which had a pin in it, set with a gem that glimmered, in the leafy shadow where he stood, like a living tip of fire. He carried a stick with a wooden head, carved in vivid imitation of that of a serpent. I hated him, partly, I do believe, from a comparison of my own homely garb with his well-ordered foppishness.

"Well, sir," said I, a little ashamed of my first irritation, but still with no waste of civility, "be pleased to speak at once, as I have my own business in hand."

"I regret that my mode of addressing you was a little unfortunate," said the stranger, smiling; for he seemed a very acute sort of person, and saw, in some degree, how I stood affected towards him. "I intended no offence, and shall certainly comport myself with due ceremony hereafter. I merely wish to make a few inquiries respecting a lady, formerly of my acquaintance, who is now resident in your Community, and, I believe, largely concerned in your social enterprise. You call her, I think, Zenobia."

"That is her name in literature," observed I—"a name, too, which possibly she may permit her private friends to know and address her by;—but not one which they feel at liberty to recognize, when used of her, personally, by a stranger or casual acquaintance."

"Indeed!" answered this disagreeable person; and he turned aside his face, for an instant, with a brief laugh, which struck me as a noteworthy expression of his character. "Perhaps I might put forward a claim, on your own grounds, to call the lady by a name so appropriate to her splendid qualities. But I am willing to know her by any cognomen that you may suggest."

Heartily wishing that he would be either a little more offensive, or a good deal less so, or break off our intercourse altogether, I mentioned Zenobia's real name.

"True," said he; "and, in general society, I have never heard her called otherwise. And, after all, our discussion of the point has been gratuitous. My object is only to inquire when, where, and how, this lady may most conveniently be seen?"

"At her present residence, of course," I replied. "You have but to go thither and ask for her. This very path will lead you within sight of the house;—so I wish you good morning."

"One moment, if you please," said the stranger. "The course you indicate would certainly be the proper one, in an ordinary morning-call. But my business is private, personal, and somewhat peculiar. Now, in a Community like this, I should judge that any little occurrence is likely to be discussed rather more minutely than would quite suit my views. I refer solely to myself, you understand, and without intimating that it would be other than a matter of entire indifference to the lady. In short, I especially desire to see her in private. If her habits are such as I have known them, she is probably often to be met with in the woods, or by the river-side; and I think you could do me the favor to point out some favorite walk, where, about this hour, I might be fortunate enough to gain an interview."

I reflected, that it would be quite a super-erogatory piece of quixotism,* in me, to undertake the guardianship of Zeno-bia, who, for my pains, would only make me the butt of endless ridicule, should the fact ever come to her knowledge. I therefore described a spot which, as often as any other, was Zenobia's resort, at this period of the day; nor was it so remote from the farm-house as to leave her in much peril, whatever might be the stranger's character.

"A single word more!" said he; and his black eyes sparkled at me, whether with fun or malice I knew not, but certainly as if the Devil were peeping out of them. "Among your fra-ternity, I understand, there is a certain holy and benevolent blacksmith; a man of iron, in more senses than one; a rough, cross-grained, well-meaning individual, rather boorish in his manners—as might be expected—and by no means of the highest intellectual cultivation. He is a philanthropical lec-turer, with two or three disciples, and a scheme of his own, the preliminary step in which involves a large purchase of land, and the erection of a spacious edifice, at an expense considerably beyond his means; inasmuch as these are to be reckoned in copper or old iron, much more conveniently than in gold or silver. He hammers away upon his one topic, as lustily as ever he did upon a horse-shoe! Do you know such a person?"

I shook my head, and was turning away.

"Our friend," he continued, "is described to me as a brawny, shaggy, grim, and ill-favored personage, not particu-larly well-calculated, one would say, to insinuate himself with the softer sex. Yet, so far has this honest fellow succeeded with one lady, whom we wot of, that he anticipates, from her abundant resources, the necessary funds for realizing his plan in brick and mortar!"

Here the stranger seemed to be so much amused with his sketch of Hollingsworth's character and purposes, that he burst into a fit of merriment, of the same nature as the brief, metallic laugh already alluded to, but immensely prolonged and enlarged. In the excess of his delight, he opened his mouth wide, and disclosed a gold band around the upper part of his teeth; thereby making it apparent that every one of his brilliant grinders and incisors was a sham. This discovery affected me very oddly. I felt as if the whole man were a moral and physical humbug; his wonderful beauty of face, for aught I knew, might be removeable like a mask; and, tall and comely as his figure looked, he was perhaps but a wizened little elf, gray and decrepit, with nothing genuine about him, save the wicked expression of his grin. The fantasy of his spectral character so wrought upon me, together with the contagion of his strange mirth on my sympathies, that I soon began to laugh as loudly as himself.

By-and-by, he paused, all at once; so suddenly, indeed, that my own cachinnation lasted a moment longer.

"Ah, excuse me!" said he. "Our interview seems to proceed more merrily than it began."

"It ends here," answered I. "And I take shame to myself, that my folly has lost me the right of resenting your ridicule of a friend."

"Pray allow me," said the stranger, approaching a step nearer, and laying his gloved hand on my sleeve. "One other favor I must ask of you. You have a young person, here at Blithedale, of whom I have heard—whom, perhaps, I have known—and in whom, at all events, I take a peculiar interest. She is one of those delicate, nervous young creatures, not un-common in New England, and whom I suppose to have become what we find them by the gradual refining away of the physical system, among your women. Some philosophers choose to glorify this habit of body by terming it spiritual; but, in my opinion, it is rather the effect of unwholesome food, bad air, lack of out-door exercise, and neglect of bathing, on the part of these damsels and their female progenitors; all resulting in a kind of hereditary dyspepsia. Zenobia, even with her uncomfortable surplus of vitality, is far the better model of womanhood. But—to revert again to this young person—she goes among you by the name of Priscilla. Could you possibly afford me the means of speaking with her?"

"You have made so many inquiries of me," I observed, "that I may at least trouble you with one. What is your name?"

He offered me a card, with 'Professor Westervelt' engraved on it. At the same time, as if to vindicate his claim to the professorial dignity, so often assumed on very questionable grounds, he put on a pair of spectacles, which so altered the character of his face that I hardly knew him again. But I liked the present aspect no better than the former one.

"I must decline any further connection with your affairs," said I, drawing back. "I have told you where to find Zenobia. As for Priscilla, she has closer friends than myself, through whom, if they see fit, you can gain access to her."

"In that case," returned the Professor, ceremoniously raising his hat, "good morning to you."

He took his departure, and was soon out of sight among the windings of the wood-path. But, after a little reflection, I could not help regretting that I had so peremptorily broken off the interview, while the stranger seemed inclined to continue it. His evident knowledge of matters, affecting my three friends, might have led to disclosures, or inferences, that would perhaps have been serviceable. I was particularly struck with the fact, that, ever since the appearance of Priscilla, it had been the tendency of events to suggest and establish a connection between Zenobia and her. She had come, in the first instance, as if with the sole purpose of claiming Zenobia's protection. Old Moodie's visit, it appeared, was chiefly to ascertain whether this object had been accomplished. And here, to-day, was the questionable Professor, linking one with the other in his inquiries, and seeking communication with both.

Meanwhile, my inclination for a ramble having been baulked, I lingered in the vicinity of the farm, with perhaps a vague idea that some new event would grow out of Westervelt's proposed interview with Zenobia. My own part, in these transactions, was singularly subordinate. It resembled that of the Chorus* in a classic play, which seems to be set aloof from the possibility of personal concernment, and bestows the whole measure of its hope or fear, its exultation or sorrow, on the fortunes of others, between whom and itself this sympathy is the only bond. Destiny, it may be—the most skilful of stage-managers—seldom chooses to arrange its scenes, and carry forward its drama, without securing the presence of at least one calm observer. It is his office to give applause, when due, and sometimes an inevitable tear, to detect the final fitness of incident to character, and distil, in his long-brooding thought, the whole morality of the performance.

Not to be out of the way, in case there were need of me in my vocation, and, at the same time, to avoid thrusting myself where neither Destiny nor mortals might desire my presence, I remained pretty near the verge of the woodlands. My position was off the track of Zenobia's customary walk, yet not so remote but that a recognized occasion might speedily have brought me thither.

XII

COVERDALE'S HERMITAGE

LONG since, in this part of our circumjacent wood, I had found out for myself a little hermitage. It was a kind of leafy cave, high upward into the air, among the midmost branches of a white-pine tree. A wild grape-vine, of unusual size and luxuriance, had twined and twisted itself up into the tree, and, after wreathing the entanglement of its tendrils around almost every bough, had caught hold of three or four neighboring trees, and married the whole clump with a perfectly inextricable knot of polygamy. Once, while sheltering myself from a summer shower, the fancy had taken me to clamber up into this seemingly impervious mass of foliage. The branches yielded me a passage, and closed again, beneath, as if only a squirrel or a bird had passed. Far aloft, around the stem of the central pine, behold, a perfect nest for Robinson Crusoe*or King Charles!* A hollow chamber, of rare seclusion, had been formed by the decay of some of the pine-branches, which the vine had lovingly strangled with its embrace, burying them from the light of day in an aerial sepulchre of its own leaves. It cost me but little ingenuity to enlarge the interior, and open loop-holes through the verdant walls. Had it ever been my fortune to spend a honey-moon, I should have thought seriously of inviting my bride up thither, where our next neighbors would have been two orioles in another part of the clump.

It was an admirable place to make verses, tuning the rhythm to the breezy symphony that so often stirred among the vine-leaves; or to meditate an essay for the Dial, in which the many tongues of Nature whispered mysteries, and seemed to ask only a little stronger puff of wind, to speak out the solution of its riddle. Being so pervious to air-currents, it was just the nook, too, for the enjoyment of a cigar. This hermitage was my one exclusive possession, while I counted myself a brother of the socialists. It symbolized my individuality, and aided me in keeping it inviolate. None ever found me out in it, except, once, a squirrel. I brought thither no guest, because, after Hollingsworth failed me, there was no longer the man alive with whom I could think of sharing all. So there I used to sit, owl-like, yet not without liberal and hospitable thoughts. I counted the innumerable clusters of my vine, and fore-reckoned the abundance of my vintage. It gladdened me to anticipate the surprise of the Community, when, like an allegorical figure of rich October,* I should make my appearance, with shoulders bent beneath the burthen of ripe grapes, and some of the crushed ones crimsoning my brow as with a blood-stain.

Ascending into this natural turret, I peeped, in turn, out of several of its small windows. The pine-tree, being ancient, rose high above the rest of the wood, which was of comparatively recent growth. Even where I sat, about midway between the root and the topmost bough, my position was lofty enough to serve as an observatory, not for starry investigations, but for those sublunary matters in which lay a lore as infinite as that of the planets. Through one loop-hole, I saw the river lapsing calmly onward, while, in the meadow near its brink, a few of the brethren were digging peat for our winter's fuel. On the interior cart-road of our farm, I discerned Hollingsworth, with a yoke of oxen hitched to a drag of stones, that were to be piled into a fence, on which we employed ourselves at the odd intervals of other labor. The harsh tones of his voice, shouting to the sluggish steers, made me sensible, even at such a distance, that he was ill at ease, and that the baulked philanthropist had the battle-spirit in his heart.

"Haw Buck!" quoth he. "Come along there, ye lazy ones! What are ye about now? Gee!"

"Mankind, in Hollingsworth's opinion," thought I, "is but another yoke of oxen, as stubborn, stupid, and sluggish, as our old Brown and Bright. He vituperates us aloud, and curses us in his heart, and will begin to prick us with the goad stick, by-and-by. But, are we his oxen? And what right has he to be the driver? And why, when there is enough else to do, should we waste our strength in dragging home the ponderous load of his philanthropic absurdities? At my height above the earth, the whole matter looks ridiculous!"

Turning towards the farm-house, I saw Priscilla (for, though a great way off, the eye of faith assured me that it was she) sitting at Zenobia's window, and making little purses, I suppose, or perhaps mending the Community's old linen. A bird flew past my tree; and as it clove its way onward into the sunny atmosphere, I flung it a message for Priscilla.

"Tell her," said I, "that her fragile thread of life has inextricably knotted itself with other and tougher threads, and most likely it will be broken. Tell her that Zenobia will not be long her friend. Say that Hollingsworth's heart is on fire with his own purpose, but icy for all human affection, and that, if she has given him her love, it is like casting a flower into a sepulchre. And say, that, if any mortal really cares for her, it is myself, and not even I, for her realities—poor little seamstress, as Zenobia rightly called her!—but for the fancy-work*with which I have idly decked her out!"

The pleasant scent of the wood, evolved by the hot sun, stole up to my nostrils, as if I had been an idol in its niche. Many trees mingled their fragrance into a thousand-fold odor. Possibly, there was a sensual influence in the broad light of noon that lay beneath me. It may have been the cause, in part, that I suddenly found myself possessed by a mood of disbelief in moral beauty or heroism, and a conviction of the folly of attempting to benefit the world. Our especial scheme of reform, which, from my observatory, I could take in with the bodily eye, looked so ridiculous that it was impossible not to laugh aloud.

"But the joke is a little too heavy," thought I. "If I were wise, I should get out of the scrape, with all diligence, and then laugh at my companions for remaining in it!"

While thus musing, I heard, with perfect distinctness, somewhere in the wood beneath, the peculiar laugh, which I have described as one of the disagreeable characteristics of Professor Westervelt. It brought my thoughts back to our recent interview. I recognized, as chiefly due to this man's influence, the sceptical and sneering view which, just now, had filled my mental vision in regard to all life's better purposes. And it was through his eyes, more than my own, that I was looking at Hollingsworth, with his glorious, if impracticable dream, and at the noble earthliness of Zenobia's character, and even at Priscilla, whose impalpable grace lay so singularly between disease and beauty. The essential charm of each had vanished. There are some spheres, the contact with which inevitably degrades the high, debases the pure, deforms the beautiful. It must be a mind of uncommon strength, and little impressibility, that can permit itself the habit of such intercourse, and not be permanently deteriorated; and yet the Professor's tone represented that of worldly society at large, where a cold scepticism smothers what it can of our spiritual aspirations, and makes the rest ridiculous.

I detested this kind of man, and all the more, because a part of my own nature showed itself responsive to him.

Voices were now approaching, through the region of the wood which lay in the vicinity of my tree. Soon, I caught glimpses of two figures—a woman and a man—Zenobia and the stranger—earnestly talking together as they advanced.

Zenobia had a rich, though varying color. It was, most of the while, a flame, and anon a sudden paleness. Her eyes glowed, so that their light sometimes flashed upward to me, as when the sun throws a dazzle from some bright object on the ground. Her gestures were free, and strikingly impressive. The whole woman was alive with a passionate intensity, which I now perceived to be the phase in which her beauty culminated. Any passion would have become her well, and passionate love, perhaps, the best of all. This was not love, but anger, largely intermixed with scorn. Yet the idea strangely forced itself upon me, that there was a sort of familiarity between these two companions, necessarily the result of an intimate love—on Zenobia's part, at least—in days gone by, but which had prolonged itself into as intimate a hatred, for all futurity. As they passed among the trees, reckless as her movement was, she took good heed that even the hem of her garment should not brush against the stranger's person. I wondered whether there had always been a chasm, guarded so religiously, betwixt these two.

As for Westervelt, he was not a whit more warmed by Zenobia's passion, than a salamander by the heat of its native furnace. He would have been absolutely statuesque, save for a look of slight perplexity tinctured strongly with derision. It was a crisis in which his intellectual perceptions could not altogether help him out. He failed to comprehend, and cared but little for comprehending, why Zenobia should put herself into such a fume; but satisfied his mind that it was all folly, and only another shape of a woman's manifold absurdity, which men can never understand. How many a woman's evil fate has yoked her with a man like this! Nature thrusts some of us into the world miserably incomplete, on the emotional side, with hardly any sensibilities except what pertain to us as animals. No passion, save of the senses; no holy tenderness, nor the delicacy that results from this. Externally, they bear a close resemblance to other men, and have perhaps all save the finest grace; but when a woman wrecks herself on such a being, she ultimately finds that the real womanhood, within her, has no corresponding part in him. Her deepest voice lacks a response; the deeper her cry, the more dead his silence. The fault may be none of his; he cannot give her what never lived within his soul. But the wretchedness, on her side, and the moral deterioration attendant on a false and shallow life, without strength enough to keep itself sweet, are among the most pitiable wrongs that mortals suffer.

Now, as I looked down from my upper region at this man and woman—outwardly so fair a sight, and wandering like two lovers in the wood—I imagined that Zenobia, at an earlier period of youth, might have fallen into the misfortune above indicated. And when her passionate womanhood, as was inevitable, had discovered its mistake, there had ensued the character of eccentricity and defiance, which distinguished the more public portion of her life.

Seeing how aptly matters had chanced, thus far, I began to think it the design of fate to let me into all Zenobia's secrets, and that therefore the couple would sit down beneath my tree, and carry on a conversation which would leave me nothing to inquire. No doubt, however, had it so happened, I should have deemed myself honorably bound to warn them of a listener's presence by flinging down a handful of unripe grapes; or by sending an unearthly groan out of my hiding-place, as if this were one of the trees of Dante's ghostly forest.*

But real life never arranges itself exactly like a romance. In the first place, they did not sit down at all. Secondly, even while they passed beneath the tree, Zenobia's utterance was so hasty and broken, and Westervelt's so cool and low, that I hardly could make out an intelligible sentence, on either side. What I seem to remember, I yet suspect may have been patched together by my fancy, in brooding over the matter, afterwards.

"Why not fling the girl off," said Westervelt, "and let her go?"

"She clung to me from the first," replied Zenobia. "I neither know nor care what it is in me that so attaches her. But she loves me, and I will not fail her."

"She will plague you, then," said he, "in more ways than one."

"The poor child!" exclaimed Zenobia. "She can do me neither good nor harm. How should she?"

I know not what reply Westervelt whispered; nor did Zenobia's subsequent exclamation give me any clue, except that it evidently inspired her with horror and disgust.

"With what kind of a being am I linked!" cried she. "If my Creator cares aught for my soul, let him release me from this miserable bond!"

"I did not think it weighed so heavily," said her companion.

"Nevertheless," answered Zenobia, "it will strangle me at last!"

And then I heard her utter a helpless sort of moan; a sound which, struggling out of the heart of a person of her pride and strength, affected me more than if she had made the wood dolorously vocal with a thousand shrieks and wails.

Other mysterious words, besides what are above-written, they spoke together; but I understood no more, and even question whether I fairly understood so much as this. By long brooding over our recollections, we subtilize them into something akin to imaginary stuff, and hardly capable of being distinguished from it. In a few moments, they were completely beyond ear-shot. A breeze stirred after them, and awoke the leafy tongues of the surrounding trees, which forthwith began to babble, as if innumerable gossips had all at once got wind of Zenobia's secret. But, as the breeze grew stronger, its voice among the branches was as if it said— 'Hush! Hush!'—and I resolved that to no mortal would I disclose what I had heard. And, though there might be room for casuistry, such, I conceive, is the most equitable rule in all similar conjunctures.

XIII

ZENOBIA'S LEGEND

THE illustrious Society of Blithedale, though it toiled in downright earnest for the good of mankind, yet not unfrequently illuminated its laborious life with an afternoon or evening of pastime. Pic-nics under the trees were considerably in vogue; and, within doors, fragmentary bits of theatrical performance, such as single acts of tragedy or comedy, or dramatic proverbs and charades. Zenobia, besides, was fond of giving us readings from Shakspeare, and often with a depth of tragic power, or breadth of comic effect, that made one feel it an intolerable wrong to the world, that she did not at once go upon the stage. *Tableaux vivants**were another of our occasional modes of amusement, in which scarlet shawls, old silken robes, ruffs, velvets, furs, and all kinds of miscellaneous trumpery, converted our familiar companions into the people of a pictorial world. We had been thus engaged, on the evening after the incident narrated in the last chapter. Several splendid works of art—either arranged after engravings from the Old Masters, or original illustrations of scenes in history or romance—had been presented, and we were earnestly entreating Zenobia for more.

She stood, with a meditative air, holding a large piece of gauze, or some such ethereal stuff, as if considering what picture should next occupy the frame; while at her feet lay a heap of many-colored garments, which her quick fancy and magic skill could so easily convert into gorgeous draperies for heroes and princesses.

"I am getting weary of this," said she, after a moment's thought. "Our own features, and our own figures and airs, show a little too intrusively through all the characters we assume. We have so much familiarity with one another's realities, that we cannot remove ourselves, at pleasure, into an imaginary sphere. Let us have no more pictures, to-night; but, to make you what poor amends I can, how would you like to have me trump up a wild, spectral legend, on the spur of the moment?"

Zenobia had the gift of telling a fanciful little story, off hand, in a way that made it greatly more effective, than it was usually found to be, when she afterwards elaborated the same production with her pen. Her proposal, therefore, was greeted with acclamation.

"Oh, a story, a story, by all means!" cried the young girls. "No matter how marvellous, we will believe it, every word! And let it be a ghost-story, if you please!"

"No; not exactly a ghost-story," answered Zenobia; "but something so nearly like it that you shall hardly tell the difference. And, Priscilla, stand you before me, where I may look at you, and get my inspiration out of your eyes. They are very deep and dreamy, to-night!"

I know not whether the following version of her story will retain any portion of its pristine character. But, as Zenobia told it, wildly and rapidly, hesitating at no extravagance, and dashing at absurdities which I am too timorous to repeat— giving it the varied emphasis of her inimitable voice, and the pictorial illustration of her mobile face, while, through it all, we caught the freshest aroma of the thoughts, as they came bubbling out of her mind—thus narrated, and thus heard, the legend seemed quite a remarkable affair. I scarcely knew, at the time, whether she intended us to laugh, or be more seriously impressed. From beginning to end it was undeniable nonsense, but not necessarily the worse for that.

THE SILVERY VEIL

You have heard, my dear friends, of the Veiled Lady, who grew suddenly so very famous, a few months ago. And have you never thought how remarkable it was, that this marvellous creature should vanish, all at once, while her renown was on the increase, before the public had grown weary of her, and when the enigma of her character, instead of being solved, presented itself more mystically at every exhibition? Her last appearance, as you know, was before a crowded audience. The next evening—although the bills had announced her, at the corner of every street, in red letters of a gigantic size—there was no Veiled Lady to be seen! Now, listen to my simple little tale; and you shall hear the very latest incident in the known life—(if life it may be called, which seemed to have no more reality than the candlelight image of one's self, which peeps at us outside of a dark window-pane)—the life of this shadowy phenomenon.

A party of young gentlemen, you are to understand, were enjoying themselves, one afternoon, as young gentlemen are sometimes fond of doing, over a bottle or two of champagne; and—among other ladies less mysterious—the subject of the Veiled Lady, as was very natural, happened to come up before them for discussion. She rose, as it were, with the sparkling effervescence of their wine, and appeared in a more airy and fantastic light, on account of the medium through which they saw her. They repeated to one another, between jest and earnest, all the wild stories that were in vogue; nor, I presume, did they hesitate to add any small circumstance that the inventive whim of the moment might suggest, to heighten the marvellousness of their theme.

"But what an audacious report was that," observed one, "which pretended to assert the identity of this strange creature with a young lady"—and here he mentioned her name—"the daughter of one of our most distinguished families!"

"Ah, there is more in that story than can well be accounted for!" remarked another. "I have it on good authority, that the young lady in question is invariably out of sight, and not to be traced, even by her own family, at the hours when the Veiled Lady is before the public; nor can any satisfactory explanation be given of her disappearance. And just look at the thing! Her brother is a young fellow of spirit. He cannot but be aware of these rumors in reference to his sister. Why, then, does he not come forward to defend her character, unless he is conscious that an investigation would only make the matter worse?"

It is essential to the purposes of my legend to distinguish one of these young gentlemen from his companions; so, for the sake of a soft and pretty name, (such as we, of the literary sisterhood, invariably bestow upon our heroes,) I deem it fit to call him 'Theodore.'

"Pshaw!" exclaimed Theodore. "Her brother is no such fool! Nobody, unless his brain be as full of bubbles as this wine, can seriously think of crediting that ridiculous rumor. Why, if my senses did not play me false, (which never was the case yet,) I affirm that I saw that very lady, last evening, at the exhibition, while this veiled phenomenon was playing off her juggling tricks! What can you say to that?"

"Oh, it was a spectral illusion that you saw!" replied his friends, with a general laugh. "The Veiled Lady is quite up to such a thing."

However, as the above-mentioned fable could not hold its ground against Theodore's downright refutation, they went on to speak of other stories, which the wild babble of the town had set afloat. Some upheld, that the veil covered the most beautiful countenance in the world; others—and certainly with more reason, considering the sex of the Veiled

Lady—that the face was the most hideous and horrible, and that this was her sole motive for hiding it. It was the face of a corpse; it was the head of a skeleton; it was a monstrous visage, with snaky locks, like Medusa's,* and one great red eye in the centre of the forehead. Again, it was affirmed, that there was no single and unchangeable set of features, beneath the veil, but that whosoever should be bold enough to lift it, would behold the features of that person, in all the world, who was destined to be his fate; perhaps he would be greeted by the tender smile of the woman whom he loved; or, quite as probably, the deadly scowl of his bitterest enemy would throw a blight over his life. They quoted, moreover, this startling explanation of the whole affair:—that the Magician (who exhibited the Veiled Lady, and who, by-the-by, was the handsomest man in the whole world) had bartered his own soul for seven years' possession of a familiar fiend, and that the last year of the contract was wearing towards its close.

If it were worth our while, I could keep you till an hour beyond midnight, listening to a thousand such absurdities as these. But, finally, our friend Theodore, who prided himself upon his common-sense, found the matter getting quite beyond his patience.

"I offer any wager you like," cried he, setting down his glass so forcibly as to break the stem of it, "that, this very evening, I find out the mystery of the Veiled Lady!"

Young men, I am told, boggle at nothing, over their wine. So, after a little more talk, a wager of considerable amount was actually laid, the money staked, and Theodore left to choose his own method of settling the dispute.

How he managed it, I know not, nor is it of any great importance to this veracious legend; the most natural way, to be sure, was by bribing the door-keeper, or, possibly, he preferred clambering in at the window. But, at any rate, that very evening, while the exhibition was going forward in the hall, Theodore contrived to gain admittance into the private withdrawing-room, whither the Veiled Lady was accustomed to retire, at the close of her performances. There he waited, listening, I suppose, to the stifled hum of the great audience; and, no doubt, he could distinguish the deep tones of the Magician, causing the wonders that he wrought to appear more dark and intricate, by his mystic pretence of an explanation; perhaps, too, in the intervals of the wild, breezy music which accompanied the exhibition, he might hear the low voice of the Veiled Lady, conveying her Sibylline responses. Firm as Theodore's nerves might be, and much as he prided himself on his sturdy perception of realities, I should not be surprised if his heart throbbed at a little more than its ordinary rate!

Theodore concealed himself behind a screen. In due time, the performance was brought to a close; and whether the door was softly opened, or whether her bodiless presence came through the wall, is more than I can say; but, all at once, without the young man's knowing how it happened, a veiled figure stood in the centre of the room. It was one thing to be in presence of this mystery, in the hall of exhibition, where the warm, dense life of hundreds of other mortals kept up the beholder's courage, and distributed her influence among so many; it was another thing to be quite alone with her, and that, too, with a hostile, or, at least, an unauthorized and unjustifiable purpose. I rather imagine that Theodore now began to be sensible of something more serious in his enterprise than he had been quite aware of, while he sat with his boon-companions over their sparkling wine.

Very strange, it must be confessed, was the movement with which the figure floated to-and-fro over the carpet, with the silvery veil covering her from head to foot; so impalpable, so ethereal, so without substance, as the texture seemed, yet hiding her every outline in an impenetrability like that of midnight. Surely, she did not walk! She floated, and flitted, and hovered about the room;—no sound of a footstep, no perceptible motion of a limb;—it was as if a wandering breeze wafted her before it, at its own wild and gentle pleasure. But, by-and-by, a purpose began to be discernible, throughout the seeming vagueness of her unrest. She was in quest of something! Could it be, that a subtile presentiment had informed her of the young man's presence? And, if so, did the Veiled Lady seek, or did she shun him? The doubt in Theodore's mind was speedily resolved; for, after a moment or two of these erratic flutterings, she advanced, more decidedly, and stood motionless before the screen.

"Thou art here!" said a soft, low voice. "Come forth, Theodore!"

Thus summoned by his name, Theodore, as a man of courage, had no choice. He emerged from his concealment, and presented himself before the Veiled Lady, with the wine-flush, it may be, quite gone out of his cheeks.

"What wouldst thou with me?" she inquired, with the same gentle composure that was in her former utterance.

"Mysterious creature," replied Theodore, "I would know who and what you are!"

"My lips are forbidden to betray the secret!" said the Veiled Lady.

"At whatever risk, I must discover it!" rejoined Theodore.

"Then," said the Mystery, "there is no way, save to lift my veil!"

And Theodore, partly recovering his audacity, stept forward, on the instant, to do as the Veiled Lady had suggested. But she floated backward to the opposite side of the room, as if the young man's breath had possessed power enough to waft her away.

"Pause, one little instant," said the soft, low voice, "and learn the conditions of what thou art so bold to undertake! Thou canst go hence, and think of me no more; or, at thy option, thou canst lift this mysterious veil, beneath which I am a sad and lonely prisoner, in a bondage which is worse to me than death. But, before raising it, I entreat thee, in all maiden modesty, to bend forward, and impress a kiss, where my breath stirs the veil; and my virgin lips shall come forward to meet thy lips; and from that instant, Theodore, thou shalt be mine, and I thine, with never more a veil between us! And all the felicity of earth and of the future world shall be thine and mine together. So much may a maiden say behind the veil! If thou shrinkest from this, there is yet another way."

"And what is that?" asked Theodore.

"Dost thou hesitate," said the Veiled Lady, "to pledge thyself to me, by meeting these lips of mine, while the veil yet hides my face? Has not thy heart recognized me? Dost thou come hither, not in holy faith, nor with a pure and generous purpose, but in scornful scepticism and idle curiosity? Still, thou mayst lift the veil! But from that instant, Theodore, I am doomed to be thy evil fate; nor wilt thou ever taste another breath of happiness!"

There was a shade of inexpressible sadness in the utterance of these last words. But Theodore, whose natural tendency was towards scepticism, felt himself almost injured and insulted by the Veiled Lady's proposal that he should pledge himself, for life and eternity, to so questionable a creature as herself; or even that she should suggest an inconsequential kiss, taking into view the probability that her face was none of the most bewitching. A delightful idea, truly, that he should salute the lips of a dead girl, or the jaws of a skeleton, or the grinning cavity of a monster's mouth! Even should she prove a comely maiden enough, in other respects, the odds were ten to one that her teeth were defective; a terrible drawback on the delectableness of a kiss!

"Excuse me, fair lady," said Theodore—and I think he nearly burst into a laugh—"if I prefer to lift the veil first; and for this affair of the kiss, we may decide upon it, afterwards!"

"Thou hast made thy choice," said the sweet, sad voice, behind the veil; and there seemed a tender, but unresentful sense of wrong done to womanhood by the young man's contemptuous interpretation of her offer. "I must not counsel thee to pause; although thy fate is still in thine own hand!"

Grasping at the veil, he flung it upward, and caught a glimpse of a pale, lovely face, beneath; just one momentary glimpse; and then the apparition vanished, and the silvery veil fluttered slowly down, and lay upon the floor. Theodore was alone. Our legend leaves him there. His retribution was, to pine, forever and ever, for another sight of that dim, mournful face—which might have been his life-long, household, fireside joy—to desire, and waste life in a feverish quest, and never meet it more!

But what, in good sooth, had become of the Veiled Lady? Had all her existence been comprehended within that mysterious veil, and was she now annihilated? Or was she a spirit, with a heavenly essence, but which might have been tamed down to human bliss, had Theodore been brave and true enough to claim her? Hearken, my sweet friends—and hearken, dear Priscilla—and you shall learn the little more that Zenobia can tell you!

Just at the moment, so far as can be ascertained, when the Veiled Lady vanished, a maiden, pale and shadowy, rose up amid a knot of visionary people, who were seeking for the better life. She was so gentle and so sad—a nameless melancholy gave her such hold upon their sympathies—that they never thought of questioning whence she came. She might have heretofore existed; or her thin substance might have been moulded out of air, at the very instant when they first beheld her. It was all one to them; they took her to their hearts. Among them was a lady, to whom, more than to all the rest, this pale, mysterious girl attached herself.

But, one morning, the lady was wandering in the woods, and there met her a figure in an Oriental robe, with a dark beard, and holding in his hand a silvery veil. He motioned her to stay. Being a woman of some nerve, she did not shriek, nor run away, nor faint, as many ladies would have been apt to do, but stood quietly, and bade him speak. The truth was, she had seen his face before, but had never feared it, although she knew him to be a terrible magician.

"Lady," said he, with a warning gesture, "you are in peril!"

"Peril!" she exclaimed. "And of what nature?"

"There is a certain maiden," replied the Magician, "who has come out of the realm of Mystery, and made herself your most intimate companion. Now, the fates have so ordained it, that, whether by her own will, or no, this stranger is your deadliest enemy. In love, in worldly fortune, in all your pursuit of happiness, she is doomed to fling a blight over your prospects. There is but one possibility of thwarting her disastrous influence."

"Then, tell me that one method," said the lady.

"Take this veil!" he answered, holding forth the silvery texture. "It is a spell; it is a powerful enchantment, which I wrought for her sake, and beneath which she was once my prisoner. Throw it, at unawares, over the head of this secret foe, stamp your foot, and cry—'Arise, Magician, here is the Veiled Lady'—and immediately I will rise up through the earth, and seize her. And from that moment, you are safe!"

So the lady took the silvery veil, which was like woven air, or like some substance airier than nothing, and that would float upward and be lost among the clouds, were she once to let it go. Returning homeward, she found the shadowy girl, amid the knot of visionary transcendentalists,* who were still seeking for the better life. She was joyous, now, and had a rose-bloom in her cheeks, and was one of the prettiest creatures, and seemed one of the happiest, that the world could show. But the lady stole noiselessly behind her, and threw the veil over her head. As the slight, ethereal texture sank inevitably down over her figure, the poor girl strove to raise it, and met her dear friend's eyes with one glance of mortal terror, and deep, deep reproach. It could not change her purpose.

"Arise, Magician!" she exclaimed, stamping her foot upon the earth. "Here is the Veiled Lady!"

At the word, uprose the bearded man in the Oriental robes—the beautiful!—the dark Magician, who had bartered away his soul! He threw his arms around the Veiled Lady; and she was his bond-slave, forever more!

———————

Zenobia, all this while, had been holding the piece of gauze, and so managed it as greatly to increase the dramatic effect of the legend, at those points where the magic veil was to be described. Arriving at the catastrophe, and uttering the fatal words, she flung the gauze over Priscilla's head; and, for an instant, her auditors held their breath, half expecting, I verily believe, that the Magician would start up through the floor, and carry off our poor little friend, before our eyes.

As for Priscilla, she stood, droopingly, in the midst of us, making no attempt to remove the veil.

"How do you find yourself, my love?" said Zenobia, lifting a corner of the gauze, and peeping beneath it, with a mischievous smile. "Ah, the dear little soul! Why, she is really going to faint! Mr. Coverdale, Mr. Coverdale, pray bring a glass of water!"

Her nerves being none of the strongest, Priscilla hardly recovered her equanimity during the rest of the evening. This, to be sure, was a great pity; but, nevertheless, we thought it a very bright idea of Zenobia's, to bring her legend to so effective a conclusion.

XIV

ELIOT'S PULPIT

OUR SUNDAYS, at Blithedale, were not ordinarily kept with such rigid observance as might have befitted the descendants of the Pilgrims, whose high enterprise, as we sometimes flattered ourselves, we had taken up, and were carrying it onward and aloft, to a point which they never dreamed of attaining.

On that hallowed day, it is true, we rested from our labors. Our oxen, relieved from their week-day yoke, roamed at large through the pasture; each yoke-fellow, however, keeping close beside his mate, and continuing to acknowledge, from the force of habit and sluggish sympathy, the union which the taskmaster had imposed for his own hard ends. As for us, human yoke-fellows, chosen companions of toil, whose hoes had clinked together throughout the week, we wandered off, in various directions, to enjoy our interval of repose. Some, I believe, went devoutly to the village-church. Others, it may be, ascended a city or a country-pulpit, wearing the clerical robe with so much dignity that you would scarcely have suspected the yeoman's frock to have been flung off, only since milking-time. Others took long rambles among the rustic lanes and by-paths, pausing to look at black, old farm-houses, with their sloping roofs; and at the modern cottage, so like a plaything that it seemed as if real joy or sorrow could have no scope within; and at the more pretending villa, with its range of wooden columns, supporting the needless insolence of a great portico. Some betook themselves into the wide, dusky barn, and lay there, for hours together, on the odorous hay; while the sunstreaks and the shadows strove together— these to make the barn solemn, those to make it cheerful—and both were conquerors; and the swallows twittered a cheery anthem, flashing into sight, or vanishing, as they darted to-and-fro among the golden rules of sunshine. And others went a little way into the woods, and threw themselves on Mother Earth, pillowing their heads on a heap of moss, the green decay of an old log; and dropping asleep, the humble-bees and musquitoes sung and buzzed about their ears, causing the slumberers to twitch and start, without awakening.

With Hollingsworth, Zenobia, Priscilla, and myself, it grew to be a custom to spend the Sabbath-afternoon at a certain rock. It was known to us under the name of Eliot's pulpit, from a tradition that the venerable Apostle Eliot* had preached there, two centuries gone by, to an Indian auditory. The old pine-forest, through which the Apostle's voice was wont to sound, had fallen, an immemorial time ago. But the soil, being of the rudest and most broken surface, had apparently never been brought under tillage; other growths, maple, and beech, and birch, had succeeded to the primeval trees; so that it was still as wild a tract of woodland as the great-great-great-great grandson of one of Eliot's Indians (had any such posterity been in existence) could have desired, for the site and shelter of his wigwam. These after-growths, indeed, lose the stately solemnity of the original forest. If left in due neglect, however, they run into an entanglement of softer wildness, among the rustling leaves of which the sun can scatter cheerfulness, as it never could among the dark-browed pines.

The rock itself rose some twenty or thirty feet, a shattered granite boulder, or heap of boulders, with an irregular outline and many fissures, out of which sprang shrubs, bushes, and even trees; as if the scanty soil, within those crevices, were sweeter to their roots than any other earth. At the base of the pulpit, the broken boulders inclined towards each other, so as to form a shallow cave, within which our little party had sometimes found protection from a summer shower. On the threshold, or just across it, grew a tuft of pale columbines, in their season, and violets, sad and shadowy recluses, such as Priscilla was, when we first knew her; children of the sun, who had never seen their father, but dwelt among damp mosses, though not akin to them. At the summit, the rock was overshadowed by the canopy of a birch-tree, which served as a sounding-board for the pulpit. Beneath this shade, (with my eyes of sense half shut, and those of the imagination widely opened,) I used to see the holy Apostle of the Indians, with the sunlight flickering down upon him through the leaves, and glorifying his figure as with the half-perceptible glow of a transfiguration.

I the more minutely describe the rock, and this little Sabbath solitude, because Hollingsworth, at our solicitation, often ascended Eliot's pulpit, and—not exactly preached—but talked to us, his few disciples, in a strain that rose and fell as naturally as the wind's breath among the leaves of the birch-tree. No other speech of man has ever moved me like some of those discourses. It seemed most pitiful—a positive calamity to the world—that a treasury of golden thoughts should thus be scattered, by the liberal handful, down among us three, when a thousand hearers might have been the richer for them; and Hollingsworth the richer, likewise, by the sympathy of multitudes. After speaking much or little, as might happen, he would descend from his gray pulpit, and generally fling himself at full length on the ground, face downward. Meanwhile, we talked around him, on such topics as were suggested by the discourse.

Since her interview with Westervelt, Zenobia's continual

inequalities of temper had been rather difficult for her friends to bear. On the first Sunday after that incident, when Hollingsworth had clambered down from Eliot's pulpit, she declaimed with great earnestness and passion, nothing short of anger, on the injustice which the world did to women, and equally to itself, by not allowing them, in freedom and honor, and with the fullest welcome, their natural utterance in public.

"It shall not always be so!" cried she. "If I live another year, I will lift up my own voice, in behalf of woman's wider liberty."

She, perhaps, saw me smile.

"What matter of ridicule do you find in this, Miles Coverdale?" exclaimed Zenobia, with a flash of anger in her eyes. "That smile, permit me to say, makes me suspicious of a low tone of feeling, and shallow thought. It is my belief—yes, and my prophecy, should I die before it happens—that, when my sex shall achieve its rights,* there will be ten eloquent women, where there is now one eloquent man. Thus far, no woman in the world has ever once spoken out her whole heart and her whole mind. The mistrust and disapproval of the vast bulk of society throttles us, as with two gigantic hands at our throats! We mumble a few weak words, and leave a thousand better ones unsaid. You let us write a little, it is true, on a limited range of subjects. But the pen is not for woman. Her power is too natural and immediate. It is with the living voice, alone, that she can compel the world to recognize the light of her intellect and the depth of her heart!"

Now—though I could not well say so to Zenobia—I had not smiled from any unworthy estimate of woman, or in denial of the claims which she is beginning to put forth. What amused and puzzled me, was the fact, that women, however intellectually superior, so seldom disquiet themselves about the rights or wrongs of their sex, unless their own individual affections chance to lie in idleness, or to be ill at ease. They are not natural reformers, but become such by the pressure of exceptional misfortune. I could measure Zenobia's inward trouble, by the animosity with which she now took up the general quarrel of woman against man.

"I will give you leave, Zenobia," replied I, "to fling your utmost scorn upon me, if you ever hear me utter a sentiment unfavorable to the widest liberty which woman has yet dreamed of. I would give her all she asks, and add a great deal more, which she will not be the party to demand, but which men, if they were generous and wise, would grant of their own free motion. For instance, I should love dearly—for the next thousand years, at least—to have all government devolve into the hands of women. I hate to be ruled by my own sex; it excites my jealousy and wounds my pride. It is the iron sway of bodily force, which abases us, in our compelled submission. But, how sweet the free, generous courtesy, with which I would kneel before a woman-ruler!"

"Yes; if she were young and beautiful," said Zenobia, laughing. "But how if she were sixty, and a fright?"

"Ah; it is you that rate womanhood low," said I. "But let me go on. I have never found it possible to suffer a bearded priest so near my heart and conscience, as to do me any spiritual good. I blush at the very thought! Oh, in the better order of things, Heaven grant that the ministry of souls may be left in charge of women! The gates of the Blessed City will be thronged with the multitude that enter in, when that day comes! The task belongs to woman. God meant it for her. He has endowed her with the religious sentiment in its utmost depth and purity, refined from that gross, intellectual alloy, with which every masculine theologist—save only One, who merely veiled Himself in mortal and masculine shape, but was, in truth, divine—has been prone to mingle it. I have always envied the Catholics their faith in that sweet, sacred Virgin Mother, who stands between them and the Deity, intercepting somewhat of His awful splendor, but permitting His love to stream upon the worshipper, more intelligibly to human comprehension, through the medium of a woman's tenderness. Have I not said enough, Zenobia?"

"I cannot think that this is true," observed Priscilla, who had been gazing at me with great, disapproving eyes. "And I am sure I do not wish it to be true!"

"Poor child!" exclaimed Zenobia, rather contemptuously. "She is the type of womanhood, such as man has spent centuries in making it. He is never content, unless he can degrade himself by stooping towards what he loves. In denying us our rights, he betrays even more blindness to his own interests, than profligate disregard of ours!"

"Is this true?" asked Priscilla, with simplicity, turning to Hollingsworth. "Is it all true that Mr. Coverdale and Zenobia have been saying?"

"No, Priscilla," answered Hollingsworth, with his customary bluntness. "They have neither of them spoken one true word yet."

"Do you despise woman?" said Zenobia. "Ah, Hollingsworth, that would be most ungrateful!"

"Despise her?—No!" cried Hollingsworth, lifting his great shaggy head and shaking it at us, while his eyes glowed almost fiercely. "She is the most admirable handiwork of God, in her true place and character. Her place is at man's side. Her office, that of the Sympathizer; the unreserved, unquestioning Believer; the Recognition, withheld in every other manner, but given, in pity, through woman's heart, lest man should utterly lose faith in himself; the Echo of God's own voice, pronouncing—'It is well done!' All the separate action of woman is, and ever has been, and always shall be, false, foolish, vain, destructive of her own best and holiest qualities, void of every good effect, and productive of intolerable mischiefs! Man is a wretch without woman; but woman is a monster—and, thank Heaven, an almost impossible and

hitherto imaginary monster—without man, as her acknowledged principal! As true as I had once a mother, whom I
loved, were there any possible prospect of woman's taking
the social stand which some of them—poor, miserable, abortive
creatures, who only dream of such things because they have
missed woman's peculiar happiness, or because Nature made
them really neither man nor woman!—if there were a chance
of their attaining the end which these petticoated monstrosities
have in view, I would call upon my own sex to use its physical
force, that unmistakeable evidence of sovereignty, to scourge
them back within their proper bounds! But it will not be
needful. The heart of true womanhood knows where its own
sphere is, and never seeks to stray beyond it!"

Never was mortal blessed—if blessing it were—with a glance
of such entire acquiescence and unquestioning faith, happy
in its completeness, as our little Priscilla unconsciously bestowed on Hollingsworth. She seemed to take the sentiment
from his lips into her heart, and brood over it in perfect
content. The very woman whom he pictured—the gentle
parasite, the soft reflection of a more powerful existence—sat
there at his feet.

I looked at Zenobia, however, fully expecting her to resent
—as I felt, by the indignant ebullition of my own blood, that
she ought—this outrageous affirmation of what struck me as
the intensity of masculine egotism. It centred everything in
itself, and deprived woman of her very soul, her inexpressible
and unfathomable all, to make it a mere incident in the great
sum of man. Hollingsworth had boldly uttered what he, and
millions of despots like him, really felt. Without intending
it, he had disclosed the well-spring of all these troubled
waters. Now, if ever, it surely behoved Zenobia to be the
champion of her sex.

But, to my surprise, and indignation too, she only looked
humbled. Some tears sparkled in her eyes, but they were
wholly of grief, not anger.

"Well; be it so," was all she said. "I, at least, have deep cause to think you right. Let man be but manly and godlike, and woman is only too ready to become to him what you say!"

I smiled—somewhat bitterly, it is true—in contemplation of my own ill-luck. How little did these two women care for me, who had freely conceded all their claims, and a great deal more, out of the fulness of my heart; while Hollingsworth, by some necromancy of his horrible injustice, seemed to have brought them both to his feet!

"Women almost invariably behave thus!" thought I. "What does the fact mean? Is it their nature? Or is it, at last, the result of ages of compelled degradation? And, in either case, will it be possible ever to redeem them?"

An intuition now appeared to possess all the party, that, for this time, at least, there was no more to be said. With one accord, we arose from the ground, and made our way through the tangled undergrowth towards one of those pleasant wood-paths, that wound among the over-arching trees. Some of the branches hung so low as partly to conceal the figures that went before, from those who followed. Priscilla had leaped up more lightly than the rest of us, and ran along in advance, with as much airy activity of spirit as was typified in the motion of a bird, which chanced to be flitting from tree to tree, in the same direction as herself. Never did she seem so happy as that afternoon. She skipt, and could not help it, from very playfulness of heart.

Zenobia and Hollingsworth went next, in close contiguity, but not with arm in arm. Now, just when they had passed the impending bough of a birch-tree, I plainly saw Zenobia take the hand of Hollingsworth in both her own, press it to her bosom, and let it fall again!

The gesture was sudden and full of passion; the impulse had evidently taken her by surprise; it expressed all! Had Zenobia knelt before him, or flung herself upon his breast, and gasped out—'I love you, Hollingsworth!'—I could not have been more certain of what it meant. They then walked onward, as before. But, methought, as the declining sun threw Zenobia's magnified shadow along the path, I beheld it tremulous; and the delicate stem of the flower, which she wore in her hair, was likewise responsive to her agitation.

Priscilla—through the medium of her eyes, at least—could not possibly have been aware of the gesture above-described. Yet, at that instant, I saw her droop. The buoyancy, which just before had been so birdlike, was utterly departed; the life seemed to pass out of her, and even the substance of her figure to grow thin and gray. I almost imagined her a shadow, fading gradually into the dimness of the wood. Her pace became so slow, that Hollingsworth and Zenobia passed by, and I, without hastening my footsteps, overtook her.

"Come, Priscilla," said I, looking her intently in the face, which was very pale and sorrowful, "we must make haste after our friends. Do you feel suddenly ill? A moment ago, you flitted along so lightly that I was comparing you to a bird. Now, on the contrary, it is as if you had a heavy heart, and very little strength to bear it with. Pray take my arm!"

"No," said Priscilla, "I do not think it would help me. It is my heart, as you say, that makes me heavy; and I know not why. Just now, I felt very happy."

No doubt, it was a kind of sacrilege in me to attempt to come within her maidenly mystery. But as she appeared to be tossed aside by her other friends, or carelessly let fall, like a flower which they had done with, I could not resist the impulse to take just one peep beneath her folded petals.

"Zenobia and yourself are dear friends, of late," I remarked. "At first—that first evening when you came to us—she did not receive you quite so warmly as might have been wished."

"I remember it," said Priscilla. "No wonder she hesitated to love me, who was then a stranger to her, and a girl of no grace or beauty; she being herself so beautiful!"

"But she loves you now, of course," suggested I. "And, at this very instant, you feel her to be your dearest friend?"

"Why do you ask me that question?" exclaimed Priscilla, as if frightened at the scrutiny into her feelings which I compelled her to make. "It somehow puts strange thoughts into my mind. But I do love Zenobia dearly! If she only loves me half as well, I shall be happy!"

"How is it possible to doubt that, Priscilla?" I rejoined. "But, observe how pleasantly and happily Zenobia and Hollingsworth are walking together! I call it a delightful spectacle. It truly rejoices me that Hollingsworth has found so fit and affectionate a friend! So many people in the world mistrust him—so many disbelieve and ridicule, while hardly any do him justice, or acknowledge him for the wonderful man he is—that it is really a blessed thing for him to have won the sympathy of such a woman as Zenobia. Any man might be proud of that. Any man, even if he be as great as Hollingsworth, might love so magnificent a woman. How very beautiful Zenobia is! And Hollingsworth knows it, too!"

There may have been some petty malice in what I said. Generosity is a very fine thing, at a proper time, and within due limits. But it is an insufferable bore, to see one man engrossing every thought of all the women, and leaving his friend to shiver in outer seclusion, without even the alternative of solacing himself with what the more fortunate individual has rejected. Yes; it was out of a foolish bitterness of heart that I had spoken.

"Go on before!" said Priscilla, abruptly, and with true feminine imperiousness, which heretofore I had never seen her exercise. "It pleases me best to loiter along by myself. I do not walk so fast as you."

With her hand, she made a little gesture of dismissal. It provoked me, yet, on the whole, was the most bewitching thing that Priscilla had ever done. I obeyed her, and strolled moodily homeward, wondering—as I had wondered a thousand times, already—how Hollingsworth meant to dispose of these two hearts, which (plainly to my perception, and, as I could not but now suppose, to his) he had engrossed into his own huge egotism.

There was likewise another subject, hardly less fruitful of speculation. In what attitude did Zenobia present herself to Hollingsworth? Was it in that of a free woman, with no mortgage on her affections nor claimant to her hand, but fully at liberty to surrender both, in exchange for the heart and hand which she apparently expected to receive? But, was it a vision that I had witnessed in the wood? Was Westervelt a goblin? Were those words of passion and agony, which Zenobia had uttered in my hearing, a mere stage-declamation? Were they formed of a material lighter than common air? Or, supposing them to bear sterling weight, was it not a perilous and dreadful wrong, which she was meditating towards herself and Hollingsworth?

Arriving nearly at the farm-house, I looked back over the long slope of pasture-land, and beheld them standing together, in the light of sunset, just on the spot where, according to the gossip of the Community, they meant to build their cottage. Priscilla, alone and forgotten, was lingering in the shadow of the wood.

XV

A CRISIS

T HUS the summer was passing away; a summer of
toil, of interest, of something that was not pleasure,
but which went deep into my heart, and there became
a rich experience. I found myself looking forward to years,
if not to a lifetime, to be spent on the same system. The
Community were now beginning to form their permanent
plans. One of our purposes was to erect a Phalanstery (as
I think we called it, after Fourier; but the phraseology of
those days is not very fresh in my remembrance) where the
great and general family should have its abiding-place. Individual members, too, who made it a point of religion to preserve the sanctity of an exclusive home, were selecting sites
for their cottages, by the wood-side, or on the breezy swells,
or in the sheltered nook of some little valley, according as
their taste might lean towards snugness or the picturesque.
Altogether, by projecting our minds outward, we had imparted a show of novelty to existence, and contemplated it
as hopefully as if the soil, beneath our feet, had not been
fathom-deep with the dust of deluded generations, on every
one of which, as on ourselves, the world had imposed itself
as a hitherto unwedded bride.

Hollingsworth and myself had often discussed these prospects. It was easy to perceive, however, that he spoke with

little or no fervor, but either as questioning the fulfilment of our anticipations, or, at any rate, with a quiet consciousness that it was no personal concern of his. Shortly after the scene at Eliot's pulpit, while he and I were repairing an old stone-fence, I amused myself with sallying forward into the future time.

"When we come to be old men," I said, "they will call us Uncles, or Fathers—Father Hollingsworth and Uncle Cover-dale—and we will look back cheerfully to these early days, and make a romantic story for the young people (and if a little more romantic than truth may warrant, it will be no harm) out of our severe trials and hardships. In a century or two, we shall every one of us be mythical personages, or exceedingly picturesque and poetical ones, at all events. They will have a great public hall, in which your portrait, and mine, and twenty other faces that are living now, shall be hung up; and as for me, I will be painted in my shirt-sleeves, and with the sleeves rolled up, to show my muscular development. What stories will be rife among them about our mighty strength," continued I, lifting a big stone and putting it into its place; "though our posterity will really be far stronger than ourselves, after several generations of a simple, natural, and active life! What legends of Zenobia's beauty, and Pris-cilla's slender and shadowy grace, and those mysterious quali-ties which make her seem diaphanous with spiritual light! In due course of ages, we must all figure heroically in an Epic Poem; and we will ourselves—at least, I will—bend unseen over the future poet, and lend him inspiration, while he writes it."

"You seem," said Hollingsworth, "to be trying how much nonsense you can pour out in a breath."

"I wish you would see fit to comprehend," retorted I, "that the profoundest wisdom must be mingled with nine-tenths of nonsense; else it is not worth the breath that utters it. But I do long for the cottages to be built, that the creeping plants may begin to run over them, and the moss to gather on the walls, and the trees—which we will set out—to cover them with a breadth of shadow. This spick-and-span novelty does not quite suit my taste. It is time, too, for children to be born among us. The first-born child is still to come! And I shall never feel as if this were a real, practical, as well as poetical, system of human life, until somebody has sanctified it by death."

"A pretty occasion for martyrdom, truly!" said Hollingsworth.

"As good as any other!" I replied. "I wonder, Hollingsworth, who, of all these strong men, and fair women and maidens, is doomed the first to die. Would it not be well, even before we have absolute need of it, to fix upon a spot for a cemetery? Let us choose the rudest, roughest, most uncultivable spot, for Death's garden-ground; and Death shall teach us to beautify it, grave by grave. By our sweet, calm way of dying, and the airy elegance out of which we will shape our funeral rites, and the cheerful allegories which we will model into tombstones, the final scene shall lose its terrors; so that, hereafter, it may be happiness to live, and bliss to die. None of us must die young. Yet, should Providence ordain it so, the event shall not be sorrowful, but affect us with a tender, delicious, only half-melancholy, and almost smiling pathos!"

"That is to say," muttered Hollingsworth, "you will die like a Heathen, as you certainly live like one! But, listen to me, Coverdale. Your fantastic anticipations make me discern, all the more forcibly, what a wretched, unsubstantial scheme is this, on which we have wasted a precious summer of our lives. Do you seriously imagine that any such realities as you, and many others here, have dreamed of, will ever be brought to pass?"

"Certainly, I do," said I. "Of course, when the reality comes, it will wear the every-day, common-place, dusty, and rather homely garb, that reality always does put on. But, setting aside the ideal charm, I hold, that our highest anticipations have a solid footing on common-sense."

"You only half believe what you say," rejoined Hollingsworth; "and as for me, I neither have faith in your dream, nor would care the value of this pebble for its realization, were that possible. And what more do you want of it? It has given you a theme for poetry. Let that content you. But, now, I ask you to be, at last, a man of sobriety and earnestness, and aid me in an enterprise which is worth all our strength, and the strength of a thousand mightier than we!"

There can be no need of giving, in detail, the conversation that ensued. It is enough to say, that Hollingsworth once more brought forward his rigid and unconquerable idea; a scheme for the reformation of the wicked by methods moral, intellectual, and industrial, by the sympathy of pure, humble, and yet exalted minds, and by opening to his pupils the possibility of a worthier life than that which had become their fate. It appeared, unless he over-estimated his own means, that Hollingsworth held it at his choice (and he did so choose) to obtain possession of the very ground on which we had planted our Community, and which had not yet been made irrevocably ours, by purchase. It was just the foundation that he desired. Our beginnings might readily be adapted to his great end. The arrangements, already completed, would work quietly into his system. So plausible looked his theory, and, more than that, so practical; such an air of reasonableness had he, by patient thought, thrown over it; each segment of it was contrived to dove-tail into all the rest, with such a complicated applicability; and so ready was he with a response for every objection—that, really, so far as logic and argument went, he had the matter all his own way.

"But," said I, "whence can you, having no means of your own, derive the enormous capital which is essential to this experiment? State-street,* I imagine, would not draw its purse-strings very liberally, in aid of such a speculation."

"I have the funds—as much, at least, as is needed for a commencement—at command," he answered. "They can be produced within a month, if necessary."

My thoughts reverted to Zenobia. It could only be her wealth which Hollingsworth was appropriating so lavishly. And on what conditions was it to be had? Did she fling it into the scheme, with the uncalculating generosity that characterizes a woman, when it is her impulse to be generous at all? And did she fling herself along with it? But Hollingsworth did not volunteer an explanation.

"And have you no regrets," I inquired, "in overthrowing this fair system of our new life, which has been planned so deeply, and is now beginning to flourish so hopefully around us? How beautiful it is, and, so far as we can yet see, how practicable! The Ages have waited for us, and here we are—the very first that have essayed to carry on our mortal existence, in love, and mutual help! Hollingsworth, I would be loth to take the ruin of this enterprise upon my conscience!"

"Then let it rest wholly upon mine!" he answered, knitting his black brows. "I see through the system. It is full of defects—irremediable and damning ones!—from first to last, there is nothing else! I grasp it in my hand, and find no substance whatever. There is not human nature in it!"

"Why are you so secret in your operations?" I asked. "God forbid that I should accuse you of intentional wrong; but the besetting sin of a philanthropist, it appears to me, is apt to be a moral obliquity. His sense of honor ceases to be the sense of other honorable men. At some point of his course—I know not exactly when nor where—he is tempted to palter with the right, and can scarcely forbear persuading himself that the importance of his public ends renders it allowable to throw aside his private conscience. Oh, my dear friend, beware this error! If you meditate the overthrow of this establishment,

call together our companions, state your design, support it
with all your eloquence, but allow them an opportunity of
defending themselves!"

"It does not suit me," said Hollingsworth. "Nor is it my
duty to do so."

"I think it is!" replied I.

Hollingsworth frowned; not in passion, but like Fate,
inexorably.

"I will not argue the point," said he. "What I desire to
know of you is—and you can tell me in one word—whether
I am to look for your co-operation in this great scheme of
good. Take it up with me! Be my brother in it! It offers you
(what you have told me, over and over again, that you most
need) a purpose in life, worthy of the extremest self-devotion
—worthy of martyrdom, should God so order it! In this view,
I present it to you. You can greatly benefit mankind. Your
peculiar faculties, as I shall direct them, are capable of being
so wrought into this enterprise, that not one of them need
lie idle. Strike hands with me; and, from this moment, you
shall never again feel the languor and vague wretchedness
of an indolent or half-occupied man! There may be no more
aimless beauty in your life; but, in its stead, there shall be
strength, courage, immitigable will—everything that a manly
and generous nature should desire! We shall succeed! We
shall have done our best for this miserable world; and happiness (which never comes but incidentally) will come to us
unawares!"

It seemed his intention to say no more. But, after he had
quite broken off, his deep eyes filled with tears, and he held
out both his hands to me.

"Coverdale," he murmured, "there is not the man in this
wide world, whom I can love as I could you. Do not for-
sake me!"

As I look back upon this scene, through the coldness and
dimness of so many years, there is still a sensation as if

Hollingsworth had caught hold of my heart, and were pulling it towards him with an almost irresistible force. It is a mystery to me, how I withstood it. But, in truth, I saw in his scheme of philanthropy nothing but what was odious. A loathsomeness that was to be forever in my daily work! A great, black ugliness of sin, which he proposed to collect out of a thousand human hearts, and that we should spend our lives in an experiment of transmuting it into virtue! Had I but touched his extended hand, Hollingsworth's magnetism would perhaps have penetrated me with his own conception of all these matters. But I stood aloof. I fortified myself with doubts whether his strength of purpose had not been too gigantic for his integrity, impelling him to trample on considerations that should have been paramount to every other.

"Is Zenobia to take a part in your enterprise?" I asked.

"She is," said Hollingsworth.

"She!—the beautiful!—the gorgeous!" I exclaimed. "And how have you prevailed with such a woman to work in this squalid element?"

"Through no base methods, as you seem to suspect," he answered, "but by addressing whatever is best and noblest in her."

Hollingsworth was looking on the ground. But, as he often did so—generally, indeed, in his habitual moods of thought—I could not judge whether it was from any special unwillingness now to meet my eyes. What it was that dictated my next question, I cannot precisely say. Nevertheless, it rose so inevitably into my mouth, and, as it were, asked itself, so involuntarily, that there must needs have been an aptness in it.

"What is to become of Priscilla?"

Hollingsworth looked at me fiercely, and with glowing eyes. He could not have shown any other kind of expression than that, had he meant to strike me with a sword.

"Why do you bring in the names of these women?" said he, after a moment of pregnant silence. "What have they to do with the proposal which I make you? I must have your answer! Will you devote yourself, and sacrifice all to this great end, and be my friend of friends, forever?"

"In Heaven's name, Hollingsworth," cried I, getting angry, and glad to be angry, because so only was it possible to oppose his tremendous concentrativeness and indomitable will, "cannot you conceive that a man may wish well to the world, and struggle for its good, on some other plan than precisely that which you have laid down? And will you cast off a friend, for no unworthiness, but merely because he stands upon his right, as an individual being, and looks at matters through his own optics, instead of yours?"

"Be with me," said Hollingsworth, "or be against me! There is no third choice for you."

"Take this, then, as my decision," I answered. "I doubt the wisdom of your scheme. Furthermore, I greatly fear that the methods, by which you allow yourself to pursue it, are such as cannot stand the scrutiny of an unbiassed conscience."

"And you will not join me?"

"No!"

I never said the word—and certainly can never have it to say, hereafter—that cost me a thousandth part so hard an effort as did that one syllable. The heart-pang was not merely figurative, but an absolute torture of the breast. I was gazing steadfastly at Hollingsworth. It seemed to me that it struck him, too, like a bullet. A ghastly paleness—always so terrific on a swarthy face—overspread his features. There was a convulsive movement of his throat, as if he were forcing down some words that struggled and fought for utterance. Whether words of anger, or words of grief, I cannot tell; although, many and many a time, I have vainly tormented myself with conjecturing which of the two they were. One other appeal to my friendship—such as once, already, Hollingsworth had made—taking me in the revulsion that followed a strenuous exercise of opposing will, would completely have subdued me. But he left the matter there.

"Well!" said he.

And that was all! I should have been thankful for one word more, even had it shot me through the heart, as mine did him. But he did not speak it; and, after a few moments, with one accord, we set to work again, repairing the stone-fence. Hollingsworth, I observed, wrought like a Titan;* and, for my own part, I lifted stones which, at this day—or, in a calmer mood, at that one—I should no more have thought it possible to stir, than to carry off the gates of Gaza* on my back.

XVI

LEAVE-TAKINGS

A FEW DAYS after the tragic passage-at-arms between Hollingsworth and me, I appeared at the dinner-table, actually dressed in a coat, instead of my customary blouse; with a satin cravat, too, a white vest, and several other things that made me seem strange and outlandish to myself. As for my companions, this unwonted spectacle caused a great stir upon the wooden benches, that bordered either side of our homely board.

"What's in the wind now, Miles?" asked one of them. "Are you deserting us?"

"Yes, for a week or two," said I. "It strikes me that my health demands a little relaxation of labor, and a short visit to the seaside, during the dog-days."

"You look like it!" grumbled Silas Foster, not greatly pleased with the idea of losing an efficient laborer, before the stress of the season was well over. "Now, here's a pretty fellow! His shoulders have broadened, a matter of six inches, since he came among us; he can do his day's work, if he likes, with any man or ox on the farm;—and yet he talks about going to the seashore for his health! Well, well, old woman," added he to his wife, "let me have a platefull of that pork and cabbage! I begin to feel in a very weakly way. When the others have had their turn, you and I will take a jaunt to Newport or Saratoga!"*

"Well, but, Mr. Foster," said I, "you must allow me to take a little breath."

"Breath!" retorted the old yeoman. "Your lungs have the play of a pair of blacksmith's bellows, already. What on earth do you want more? But go along! I understand the business. We shall never see your face here again. Here ends the reformation of the world, so far as Miles Coverdale has a hand in it!"

"By no means," I replied. "I am resolute to die in the last ditch, for the good of the cause."

"Die in a ditch!" muttered gruff Silas, with genuine Yankee intolerance of any intermission of toil, except on Sunday, the Fourth of July, the autumnal Cattle-show, Thanksgiving, or the annual Fast.* "Die in a ditch! I believe in my conscience you would, if there were no steadier means than your own labor to keep you out of it!"

The truth was, that an intolerable discontent and irksomeness had come over me. Blithedale was no longer what it had been. Everything was suddenly faded. The sun-burnt and arid aspect of our woods and pastures, beneath the August sky, did but imperfectly symbolize the lack of dew and moisture that, since yesterday, as it were, had blighted my fields of thought, and penetrated to the innermost and shadiest of my contemplative recesses. The change will be recognized by many, who, after a period of happiness, have endeavored to go on with the same kind of life, in the same scene, in spite of the alteration or withdrawal of some principal circumstance. They discover (what heretofore, perhaps, they had not known) that it was this which gave the bright color and vivid reality to the whole affair.

I stood on other terms than before, not only with Hollingsworth, but with Zenobia and Priscilla. As regarded the two latter, it was that dreamlike and miserable sort of change that denies you the privilege to complain, because you can assert no positive injury, nor lay your finger on anything tangible. It is a matter which you do not see, but feel, and which, when you try to analyze it, seems to lose its very existence, and resolve itself into a sickly humor of your own. Your understanding, possibly, may put faith in this denial. But your heart will not so easily rest satisfied. It incessantly remonstrates, though, most of the time, in a bass-note, which you do not separately distinguish; but, now-and-then, with a sharp cry, importunate to be heard, and resolute to claim belief. 'Things are not as they were!'—it keeps saying—'You shall not impose on me! I will never be quiet! I will throb painfully! I will be heavy, and desolate, and shiver with cold! For I, your deep heart, know when to be miserable, as once I knew when to be happy! All is changed for us! You are beloved no more!' And, were my life to be spent over again, I would invariably lend my ear to this Cassandra*of the inward depths, however clamorous the music and the merriment of a more superficial region.

My outbreak with Hollingsworth, though never definitely known to our associates, had really an effect upon the moral atmosphere of the Community. It was incidental to the closeness of relationship, into which we had brought ourselves, that an unfriendly state of feeling could not occur between any two members, without the whole society being more or less commoted*and made uncomfortable thereby. This species of nervous sympathy (though a pretty characteristic enough, sentimentally considered, and apparently betokening an actual bond of love among us) was yet found rather inconvenient in its practical operation; mortal tempers being so infirm and variable as they are. If one of us happened to give his neighbor a box on the ear, the tingle was immediately felt, on the same side of everybody's head. Thus, even on the supposition that we were far less quarrelsome than the rest of the world, a great deal of time was necessarily wasted in rubbing our ears.

Musing on all these matters, I felt an inexpressible longing for at least a temporary novelty. I thought of going across the Rocky Mountains, or to Europe, or up the Nile—of offering myself a volunteer on the Exploring Expedition—of taking a ramble of years, no matter in what direction, and coming back on the other side of the world. Then, should the colonists of Blithedale have established their enterprise on a permanent basis, I might fling aside my pilgrim-staff and dusty shoon, and rest as peacefully here as elsewhere. Or, in case Hollingsworth should occupy the ground with his School of Reform, as he now purposed, I might plead earthly guilt enough, by that time, to give me what I was inclined to think the only trustworthy hold on his affections. Meanwhile, before deciding on any ultimate plan, I determined to remove myself to a little distance, and take an exterior view of what we had all been about.

In truth, it was dizzy work, amid such fermentation of opinions as was going on in the general brain of the Community. It was a kind of Bedlam, for the time being; although, out of the very thoughts that were wildest and most destructive, might grow a wisdom, holy, calm, and pure, and that should incarnate itself with the substance of a noble and happy life. But, as matters now were, I felt myself (and having a decided tendency towards the actual, I never liked to feel it) getting quite out of my reckoning, with regard to the existing state of the world. I was beginning to lose the sense of what kind of a world it was, among innumerable schemes of what it might or ought to be. It was impossible, situated as we were, not to imbibe the idea that everything in nature and human existence was fluid, or fast becoming so; that the crust of the Earth, in many places, was broken, and its whole surface portentously upheaving; that it was a day of crisis, and that we ourselves were in the critical vortex. Our great globe floated in the atmosphere of infinite space like an unsubstantial bubble. No sagacious man will long retain his sagacity, if he live exclusively among reformers and progressive people, without periodically returning into the settled system of things, to correct himself by a new observation from that old stand-point.

It was now time for me, therefore, to go and hold a little talk with the conservatives, the writers of the North American Review,* the merchants, the politicians, the Cambridge men,* and all those respectable old blockheads, who still, in this intangibility and mistiness of affairs, kept a death-grip on one or two ideas which had not come into vogue since yesterday-morning.

The brethren took leave of me with cordial kindness; and as for the sisterhood, I had serious thoughts of kissing them all round, but forbore to do so, because, in all such general salutations, the penance is fully equal to the pleasure. So I kissed none of them, and nobody, to say the truth, seemed to expect it.

"Do you wish me," I said to Zenobia, "to announce, in town, and at the watering-places, your purpose to deliver a course of lectures on the rights of women?"

"Women possess no rights," said Zenobia, with a half-melancholy smile; "or, at all events, only little girls and grandmothers would have the force to exercise them."

She gave me her hand, freely and kindly, and looked at me, I thought, with a pitying expression in her eyes; nor was there any settled light of joy in them, on her own behalf, but a troubled and passionate flame, flickering and fitful.

"I regret, on the whole, that you are leaving us," she said; "and all the more, since I feel that this phase of our life is finished, and can never be lived over again. Do you know, Mr. Coverdale, that I have been several times on the point of making you my confidant, for lack of a better and wiser one? But you are too young to be my Father Confessor; and you would not thank me for treating you like one of those good little handmaidens, who share the bosom-secrets of a tragedy-queen!"

"I would at least be loyal and faithful," answered I, "and would counsel you with an honest purpose, if not wisely."

"Yes," said Zenobia, "you would be only too wise—too honest. Honesty and wisdom are such a delightful pastime, at another person's expense!"

"Ah, Zenobia," I exclaimed, "if you would but let me speak!"

"By no means," she replied; "especially when you have just resumed the whole series of social conventionalisms, together with that straight-bodied coat. I would as lief open my heart to a lawyer or a clergyman! No, no, Mr. Coverdale; if I choose a counsellor, in the present aspect of my affairs, it must be either an angel or a madman; and I rather apprehend that the latter would be likeliest of the two to speak the fitting word. It needs a wild steersman when we voyage through Chaos! The anchor is up! Farewell!"

Priscilla, as soon as dinner was over, had betaken herself into a corner, and set to work on a little purse. As I approached her, she let her eyes rest on me, with a calm, serious look; for, with all her delicacy of nerves, there was a singular self-possession in Priscilla, and her sensibilities seemed to lie sheltered from ordinary commotion, like the water in a deep well.

"Will you give me that purse, Priscilla," said I, "as a parting keepsake?"

"Yes," she answered; "if you will wait till it is finished."

"I must not wait, even for that," I replied. "Shall I find you here, on my return?"

"I never wish to go away," said she.

"I have sometimes thought," observed I, smiling, "that you, Priscilla, are a little prophetess; or, at least, that you have spiritual intimations respecting matters which are dark to us grosser people. If that be the case, I should like to ask you what is about to happen. For I am tormented with a strong foreboding, that, were I to return even so soon as tomorrow morning, I should find everything changed. Have you any impressions of this nature?"

"Ah, no!" said Priscilla, looking at me apprehensively. "If any such misfortune is coming, the shadow has not reached me yet. Heaven forbid! I should be glad if there might never be any change, but one summer follow another, and all just like this!"

"No summer ever came back, and no two summers ever were alike," said I, with a degree of Orphic wisdom* that astonished myself. "Times change, and people change; and if our hearts do not change as readily, so much the worse for us! Good bye, Priscilla!"

I gave her hand a pressure, which, I think, she neither resisted nor returned. Priscilla's heart was deep, but of small compass; it had room but for a very few dearest ones, among whom she never reckoned me.

On the door-step, I met Hollingsworth. I had a momentary impulse to hold out my hand, or, at least, to give a parting nod, but resisted both. When a real and strong affection has come to an end, it is not well to mock the sacred past with any show of those common-place civilities that belong to ordinary intercourse. Being dead henceforth to him, and he to me, there could be no propriety in our chilling one another with the touch of two corpse-like hands, or playing at looks of courtesy with eyes that were impenetrable beneath the glaze and the film. We passed, therefore, as if mutually invisible.

I can nowise explain what sort of whim, prank, or perversity it was, that, after all these leave-takings, induced me to go to the pig-stye and take leave of the swine! There they lay, buried as deeply among the straw as they could burrow, four huge black grunters, the very symbols of slothful ease and sensual comfort. They were asleep, drawing short and heavy breaths, which heaved their big sides up and down. Unclosing their eyes, however, at my approach, they looked dimly forth at the outer world, and simultaneously uttered a gentle grunt; not putting themselves to the trouble of an additional breath for that particular purpose, but grunting with their ordinary inhalation. They were involved, and almost stifled, and buried alive, in their own corporeal substance. The very unreadiness and oppression, wherewith these greasy citizens gained breath enough to keep their life-machinery in sluggish movement, appeared to make them only the more sensible of the ponderous and fat satisfaction of their existence. Peeping at me, an instant, out of their small, red, hardly perceptible eyes, they dropt asleep again; yet not so far asleep but that their unctuous bliss was still present to them, betwixt dream and reality.

"You must come back in season to eat part of a spare-rib," said Silas Foster, giving my hand a mighty squeeze. "I shall have these fat fellows hanging up by the heels, heads downward, pretty soon, I tell you!"

"Oh, cruel Silas, what a horrible idea!" cried I. "All the rest of us, men, women, and live-stock, save only these four porkers, are bedevilled with one grief or another; they alone are happy—and you mean to cut their throats, and eat them! It would be more for the general comfort to let them eat us; and bitter and sour morsels we should be!"

XVII

THE HOTEL

ARRIVING in town, (where my bachelor-rooms, long before this time, had received some other occupant,) I established myself, for a day or two, in a certain respectable hotel. It was situated somewhat aloof from my former track in life; my present mood inclining me to avoid most of my old companions, from whom I was now sundered by other interests, and who would have been likely enough to amuse themselves at the expense of the amateur working-man. The hotel-keeper put me into a back-room of the third story of his spacious establishment. The day was lowering, with occasional gusts of rain, and an ugly-tempered east-wind, which seemed to come right off the chill and melancholy sea, hardly mitigated by sweeping over the roofs, and amalgamating itself with the dusky element of city-smoke. All the effeminacy of past days had returned upon me at once. Summer as it still was, I ordered a coal-fire in the rusty grate, and was glad to find myself growing a little too warm with an artificial temperature.

My sensations were those of a traveller, long sojourning in remote regions, and at length sitting down again amid customs once familiar. There was a newness and an oldness, oddly combining themselves into one impression. It made me acutely sensible how strange a piece of mosaic-work had lately been wrought into my life. True; if you look at it in one way, it had been only a summer in the country. But, considered in a profounder relation, it was part of another age, a different state of society, a segment of an existence peculiar in its aims and methods, a leaf of some mysterious volume, interpolated into the current history which Time was writing off. At one moment, the very circumstances now surrounding me—my coal-fire, and the dingy room in the bustling hotel—appeared far off and intangible. The next instant, Blithedale looked vague, as if it were at a distance both in time and space, and so shadowy, that a question might be raised whether the whole affair had been anything more than the thoughts of a speculative man. I had never before experienced a mood that so robbed the actual world of its solidity. It nevertheless involved a charm, on which—a devoted epicure of my own emotions—I resolved to pause, and enjoy the moral sillabub* until quite dissolved away.

Whatever had been my taste for solitude and natural scenery, yet the thick, foggy, stifled element of cities, the entangled life of many men together, sordid as it was, and empty of the beautiful, took quite as strenuous a hold upon my mind. I felt as if there could never be enough of it. Each characteristic sound was too suggestive to be passed over, unnoticed. Beneath and around me, I heard the stir of the hotel; the loud voices of guests, landlord, or barkeeper; steps echoing on the staircase; the ringing of a bell, announcing arrivals or departures; the porter lumbering past my door with baggage, which he thumped down upon the floors of neighboring chambers; the lighter feet of chamber-maids scudding along the passages;—it is ridiculous to think what an interest they had for me. From the street, came the tumult of the pavements, pervading the whole house with a continual uproar, so broad and deep that only an unaccustomed ear would dwell upon it. A company of the city-soldiery, with a full military band, marched in front of the hotel, invisible to me, but stirringly audible both by its foot-tramp and the clangor of its instruments. Once or twice, all the city-bells jangled together, announcing a fire, which brought out the engine-men and their machines, like an army with its artillery rushing to battle. Hour by hour, the clocks in many steeples responded one to another. In some public hall, not a great way off, there seemed to be an exhibition of a mechanical diorama;*for, three times during the day, occurred a repetition of obstreperous music, winding up with the rattle of imitative cannon and musketry, and a huge final explosion. Then ensued the applause of the spectators, with clap of hands, and thump of sticks, and the energetic pounding of their heels. All this was just as valuable, in its way, as the sighing of the breeze among the birch-trees, that overshadowed Eliot's pulpit.

Yet I felt a hesitation about plunging into this muddy tide of human activity and pastime. It suited me better, for the present, to linger on the brink, or hover in the air above it. So I spent the first day, and the greater part of the second, in the laziest manner possible, in a rocking-chair, inhaling the fragrance of a series of cigars, with my legs and slippered feet horizontally disposed, and in my hand a novel, purchased of a railroad bibliopolist.* The gradual waste of my cigar accomplished itself with an easy and gentle expenditure of breath. My book was of the dullest, yet had a sort of sluggish flow, like that of a stream in which your boat is as often aground as afloat. Had there been a more impetuous rush, a more absorbing passion of the narrative, I should the sooner have struggled out of its uneasy current, and have given myself up to the swell and subsidence of my thoughts. But, as it was, the torpid life of the book served as an unobtrusive accompaniment to the life within me and about me. At intervals, however, when its effect grew a little too soporific—not for my patience, but for the possibility of keeping my eyes open—I bestirred myself, started from the rocking-chair, and looked out of the window.

A gray sky; the weathercock of a steeple, that rose beyond the opposite range of buildings, pointing from the eastward; a sprinkle of small, spiteful-looking raindrops on the window-pane! In that ebb-tide of my energies, had I thought of venturing abroad, these tokens would have checked the abortive purpose.

After several such visits to the window, I found myself getting pretty well acquainted with that little portion of the backside of the universe which it presented to my view. Over against the hotel and its adjacent houses, at the distance of forty or fifty yards, was the rear of a range of buildings, which appeared to be spacious, modern, and calculated for fashionable residences. The interval between was apportioned into grass-plots, and here and there an apology for a garden, pertaining severally to these dwellings. There were apple-trees, and pear and peach-trees, too, the fruit on which looked singularly large, luxuriant, and abundant; as well it might, in a situation so warm and sheltered, and where the soil had doubtless been enriched to a more than natural fertility. In two or three places, grape-vines clambered upon trellises, and bore clusters already purple, and promising the richness of Malta or Madeira*in their ripened juice. The blighting winds of our rigid climate could not molest these trees and vines; the sunshine, though descending late into this area, and too early intercepted by the height of the surrounding houses, yet lay tropically there, even when less than temperate in every other region. Dreary as was the day, the scene was illuminated by not a few sparrows and other birds, which spread their wings, and flitted and fluttered, and alighted now here, now there, and busily scratched their food out of the wormy earth. Most of these winged people seemed to have their domicile in a robust and healthy buttonwood-tree.* It aspired upward, high above the roof of the houses, and spread a dense head of foliage half across the area.

There was a cat—as there invariably is, in such places—who evidently thought herself entitled to all the privileges of forest-life, in this close heart of city-conventionalisms. I watched her creeping along the low, flat roofs of the offices, descending a flight of wooden steps, gliding among the grass, and besieging the buttonwood-tree, with murderous purpose against its feathered citizens. But, after all, they were birds of city-breeding, and doubtless knew how to guard themselves against the peculiar perils of their position.

Bewitching to my fancy are all those nooks and crannies, where Nature, like a stray partridge, hides her head among the long-established haunts of men! It is likewise to be remarked, as a general rule, that there is far more of the picturesque, more truth to native and characteristic tendencies, and vastly greater suggestiveness, in the back view of a residence, whether in town or country, than in its front. The latter is always artificial; it is meant for the world's eye, and is therefore a veil and a concealment. Realities keep in the rear, and put forward an advance-guard of show and humbug. The posterior aspect of any old farm-house, behind which a railroad has unexpectedly been opened, is so different from that looking upon the immemorial highway, that the spectator gets new ideas of rural life and individuality, in the puff or two of steam-breath which shoots him past the premises. In a city, the distinction between what is offered to the public, and what is kept for the family, is certainly not less striking.

But, to return to my window, at the back of the hotel. Together with a due contemplation of the fruit-trees, the grape-vines, the buttonwood-tree, the cat, the birds, and many other particulars, I failed not to study the row of fashionable dwellings to which all these appertained. Here, it must be confessed, there was a general sameness. From the upper-story to the first floor, they were so much alike that I could only conceive of the inhabitants as cut out on one identical pattern, like little wooden toy-people of German manufacture.

One long, united roof, with its thousands of slates glittering in the rain, extended over the whole. After the distinctness of separate characters, to which I had recently been accustomed, it perplexed and annoyed me not to be able to resolve this combination of human interests into well-defined elements. It seemed hardly worth while for more than one of those families to be in existence; since they all had the same glimpse of the sky, all looked into the same area, all received just their equal share of sunshine through the front windows, and all listened to precisely the same noises of the street on which they bordered. Men are so much alike, in their nature, that they grow intolerable unless varied by their circumstances.

Just about this time, a waiter entered my room. The truth was, I had rung the bell and ordered a sherry-cobbler.*

"Can you tell me," I inquired, "what families reside in any of those houses opposite?"

"The one right opposite is a rather stylish boarding-house," said the waiter. "Two of the gentlemen-boarders keep horses at the stable of our establishment. They do things in very good style, sir, the people that live there."

I might have found out nearly as much for myself, on examining the house a little more closely. In one of the upper chambers, I saw a young man in a dressing-gown, standing before the glass and brushing his hair, for a quarter-of-an-hour together. He then spent an equal space of time in the elaborate arrangement of his cravat, and finally made his appearance in a dress-coat, which I suspected to be newly come from the tailor's, and now first put on for a dinner-party. At a window of the next story below, two children, prettily dressed, were looking out. By-and-by, a middle-aged gentleman came softly behind them, kissed the little girl, and playfully pulled the little boy's ear. It was a papa, no doubt, just come in from his counting-room or office; and anon appeared mamma, stealing as softly behind papa, as he had stolen behind the children, and laying her hand on his shoulder to surprise him. Then followed a kiss between papa and mamma, but a noiseless one; for the children did not turn their heads.

"I bless God for these good folks!" thought I to myself. "I have not seen a prettier bit of nature, in all my summer in the country, than they have shown me here in a rather stylish boarding-house. I will pay them a little more attention, by-and-by."

On the first floor, an iron balustrade ran along in front of the tall, and spacious windows, evidently belonging to a back drawing-room; and, far into the interior, through the arch of the sliding-doors, I could discern a gleam from the windows of the front apartment. There were no signs of present occupancy in this suite of rooms; the curtains being enveloped in a protective covering, which allowed but a small portion of their crimson material to be seen. But two housemaids were industriously at work; so that there was good prospect that the boarding-house might not long suffer from the absence of its most expensive and profitable guests. Meanwhile, until they should appear, I cast my eyes downward to the lower regions. There, in the dusk that so early settles into such places, I saw the red glow of the kitchen-range; the hot cook, or one of her subordinates, with a ladle in her hand, came to draw a cool breath at the back-door; as soon as she disappeared, an Irish man-servant, in a white jacket, crept slily forth and threw away the fragments of a china-dish, which unquestionably he had just broken. Soon afterwards, a lady, showily dressed, with a curling front of what must have been false hair, and reddish brown, I suppose, in hue—though my remoteness allowed me only to guess at such particulars—this respectable mistress of the boarding-house made a momentary transit across the kitchen-window, and appeared no more. It was her final, comprehensive glance, in order to make sure that soup, fish, and flesh, were in a proper state of readiness, before the serving up of dinner.

There was nothing else worth noticing about the house; unless it be, that, on the peak of one of the dormer-windows, which opened out of the roof, sat a dove, looking very dreary and forlorn; insomuch that I wondered why she chose to sit there, in the chilly rain, while her kindred were doubtless nestling in a warm and comfortable dove-cote. All at once, this dove spread her wings, and launching herself in the air, came flying so straight across the intervening space, that I fully expected her to alight directly on my window-sill. In the latter part of her course, however, she swerved aside, flew upward, and vanished, as did likewise the slight, fantastic pathos with which I had invested her.

XVIII

THE BOARDING-HOUSE

THE NEXT day, as soon as I thought of looking again towards the opposite house, there sat the dove again, on the peak of the same dormer-window!

It was by no means an early hour; for, the preceding evening, I had ultimately mustered enterprise enough to visit the theatre, had gone late to bed, and slept beyond all limit, in my remoteness from Silas Foster's awakening horn. Dreams had tormented me, throughout the night. The train of thoughts which, for months past, had worn a track through my mind, and to escape which was one of my chief objects in leaving Blithedale, kept treading remorselessly to-and-fro, in their old footsteps, while slumber left me impotent to regulate them. It was not till I had quitted my three friends that they first began to encroach upon my dreams. In those of the last night, Hollingsworth and Zenobia, standing on either side of my bed, had bent across it to exchange a kiss of passion. Priscilla, beholding this—for she seemed to be peeping in at the chamber-window—had melted gradually away, and left only the sadness of her expression in my heart. There it still lingered, after I awoke; one of those unreasonable sadnesses that you know not how to deal with, because it involves nothing for common-sense to clutch.

It was a gray and dripping forenoon; gloomy enough in town, and still gloomier in the haunts to which my recollections persisted in transporting me. For, in spite of my efforts to think of something else, I thought how the gusty rain was drifting over the slopes and valleys of our farm; how wet must be the foliage that overshadowed the pulpit-rock; how cheerless, in such a day, my hermitage—the tree-solitude of my owl-like humors—in the vine-encircled heart of the tall pine! It was a phase of home-sickness. I had wrenchéd myself too suddenly out of an accustomed sphere. There was no choice now, but to bear the pang of whatever heart-strings were snapt asunder, and that illusive torment (like the ache of a limb long ago cut off) by which a past mode of life prolongs itself into the succeeding one. I was full of idle and shapeless regrets. The thought impressed itself upon me, that I had left duties unperformed. With the power, perhaps, to act in the place of destiny, and avert misfortune from my friends, I had resigned them to their fate. That cold tendency, between instinct and intellect, which made me pry with a speculative interest into people's passions and impulses, appeared to have gone far towards unhumanizing my heart.

But a man cannot always decide for himself whether his own heart is cold or warm. It now impresses me, that, if I erred at all, in regard to Hollingsworth, Zenobia, and Priscilla, it was through too much sympathy, rather than too little.

To escape the irksomeness of these meditations, I resumed my post at the window. At first sight, there was nothing new to be noticed. The general aspect of affairs was the same as yesterday, except that the more decided inclemency of to-day had driven the sparrows to shelter, and kept the cat within doors, whence, however, she soon emerged, pursued by the cook, and with what looked like the better half of a roast chicken in her mouth. The young man in the dress-coat was invisible; the two children, in the story below, seemed to be romping about the room, under the superintendence of a nursery-maid. The damask curtains of the drawing-room, on the first floor, were now fully displayed, festooned gracefully from top to bottom of the windows, which extended from the ceiling to the carpet. A narrower window, at the left of the drawing-room, gave light to what was probably a small boudoir, within which I caught the faintest imaginable glimpse of a girl's figure, in airy drapery. Her arm was in regular movement, as if she were busy with her German worsted, or some other such pretty and unprofitable handiwork.

While intent upon making out this girlish shape, I became sensible that a figure had appeared at one of the windows of the drawing-room. There was a presentiment in my mind; or perhaps my first glance, imperfect and sidelong as it was, had sufficed to convey subtle information of the truth. At any rate, it was with no positive surprise, but as if I had all along expected the incident, that, directing my eyes thitherward, I beheld—like a full-length picture, in the space between the heavy festoons of the window-curtains—no other than Zenobia! At the same instant, my thoughts made sure of the identity of the figure in the boudoir. It could only be Priscilla.

Zenobia was attired, not in the almost rustic costume which she had heretofore worn, but in a fashionable morning-dress. There was, nevertheless, one familiar point. She had, as usual, a flower in her hair, brilliant, and of a rare variety, else it had not been Zenobia. After a brief pause at the window, she turned away, exemplifying, in the few steps that removed her out of sight, that noble and beautiful motion which characterized her as much as any other personal charm. Not one woman in a thousand could move so admirably as Zenobia. Many women can sit gracefully; some can stand gracefully; and a few, perhaps, can assume a series of graceful positions. But natural movement is the result and expression of the whole being, and cannot be well and nobly performed, unless responsive to something in the character. I often used to think that music—light and airy, wild and passionate, or the full harmony of stately marches, in accordance with her varying mood—should have attended Zenobia's footsteps.

I waited for her re-appearance. It was one peculiarity, distinguishing Zenobia from most of her sex, that she needed for her moral well-being, and never would forego, a large amount of physical exercise. At Blithedale, no inclemency of sky or muddiness of earth had ever impeded her daily walks. Here, in town, she probably preferred to tread the extent of the two drawing-rooms, and measure out the miles by spaces of forty feet, rather than bedraggle her skirts over the sloppy pavements. Accordingly, in about the time requisite to pass through the arch of the sliding-doors to the front window, and to return upon her steps, there she stood again, between the festoons of the crimson curtains. But another personage was now added to the scene. Behind Zenobia appeared that face which I had first encountered in the wood-path; the man who had passed, side by side with her, in such mysterious familiarity and estrangement, beneath my vine-curtained hermitage in the tall pine-tree. It was Westervelt. And though he was looking closely over her shoulder, it still seemed to me, as on the former occasion, that Zenobia repelled him—that, perchance, they mutually repelled each other—by some incompatibility of their spheres.

This impression, however, might have been altogether the result of fancy and prejudice, in me. The distance was so great as to obliterate any play of feature, by which I might otherwise have been made a partaker of their counsels.

There now needed only Hollingsworth and old Moodie to complete the knot of characters, whom a real intricacy of events, greatly assisted by my method of insulating them from other relations, had kept so long upon my mental stage, as actors in a drama. In itself, perhaps, it was no very remarkable event, that they should thus come across me, at the moment when I imagined myself free. Zenobia, as I well knew, had retained an establishment in town, and had not unfrequently withdrawn herself from Blithedale, during brief intervals, on one of which occasions she had taken Priscilla along with her. Nevertheless, there seemed something fatal in the coincidence that had borne me to this one spot, of all others in a great city, and transfixed me there, and compelled me again to waste my already wearied sympathies on affairs which were none of mine, and persons who cared little for me. It irritated my nerves; it affected me with a kind of heart-sickness. After the effort which it cost me to fling them off—after consummating my escape, as I thought, from these goblins of flesh and blood, and pausing to revive myself with a breath or two of an atmosphere in which they should have no share—it was a positive despair, to find the same figures arraying themselves before me, and presenting their old problem in a shape that made it more insoluble than ever.

I began to long for a catastrophe. If the noble temper of Hollingsworth's soul were doomed to be utterly corrupted by the too powerful purpose, which had grown out of what was noblest in him; if the rich and generous qualities of Zenobia's womanhood might not save her; if Priscilla must perish by her tenderness and faith, so simple and so devout;—then be it so! Let it all come! As for me, I would look on, as it seemed my part to do, understandingly, if my intellect could fathom the meaning and the moral, and, at all events, reverently and sadly. The curtain fallen, I would pass onward with my poor individual life, which was now attenuated of much of its proper substance, and diffused among many alien interests.

Meanwhile, Zenobia and her companion had retreated from the window. Then followed an interval, during which I directed my eyes towards the figure in the boudoir. Most certainly it was Priscilla, although dressed with a novel and fanciful elegance. The vague perception of it, as viewed so far off, impressed me as if she had suddenly passed out of a chrysalis state and put forth wings. Her hands were not now in motion. She had dropt her work, and sat with her head thrown back, in the same attitude that I had seen several times before, when she seemed to be listening to an imperfectly distinguished sound.

Again the two figures in the drawing-room became visible. They were now a little withdrawn from the window, face to face, and, as I could see by Zenobia's emphatic gestures, were discussing some subject in which she, at least, felt a passionate concern. By-and-by, she broke away, and vanished beyond my ken. Westervelt approached the window, and leaned his forehead against a pane of glass, displaying the sort of smile on his handsome features which, when I before met him, had let me into the secret of his gold-bordered teeth. Every human being, when given over to the Devil, is sure to have the wizard mark upon him, in one form or another. I fancied that this smile, with its peculiar revelation, was the Devil's signet on the Professor.

This man, as I had soon reason to know, was endowed with a cat-like circumspection; and though precisely the most unspiritual quality in the world, it was almost as effective as spiritual insight, in making him acquainted with whatever it suited him to discover. He now proved it, considerably to my discomfiture, by detecting and recognizing me, at my post of observation. Perhaps I ought to have blushed at being caught in such an evident scrutiny of Professor Westervelt and his affairs. Perhaps I did blush. Be that as it might, I retained presence of mind enough not to make my position yet more irksome, by the poltroonery of drawing back.

Westervelt looked into the depths of the drawing-room, and beckoned. Immediately afterwards, Zenobia appeared at the window, with color much heightened, and eyes which, as my conscience whispered me, were shooting bright arrows, barbed with scorn, across the intervening space, directed full at my sensibilities as a gentleman. If the truth must be told,

far as her flight-shot was, those arrows hit the mark. She signified her recognition of me by a gesture with her head and
hand, comprising at once a salutation and dismissal. The
next moment, she administered one of those pitiless rebukes
which a woman always has at hand, ready for an offence,
(and which she so seldom spares, on due occasion,) by letting
down a white linen curtain between the festoons of the
damask ones. It fell like the drop-curtain of a theatre, in the
interval between the acts.

Priscilla had disappeared from the boudoir. But the dove
still kept her desolate perch, on the peak of the attic-window.

XIX

ZENOBIA'S DRAWING-ROOM

THE REMAINDER of the day, so far as I was concerned, was spent in meditating on these recent incidents. I contrived, and alternately rejected, innumerable methods of accounting for the presence of Zenobia and Priscilla, and the connection of Westervelt with both. It must be owned, too, that I had a keen, revengeful sense of the insult inflicted by Zenobia's scornful recognition, and more particularly by her letting down the curtain; as if such were the proper barrier to be interposed between a character like hers, and a perceptive faculty like mine. For, was mine a mere vulgar curiosity? Zenobia should have known me better than to suppose it. She should have been able to appreciate that quality of the intellect and the heart, which impelled me (often against my own will, and to the detriment of my own comfort) to live in other lives, and to endeavor— by generous sympathies, by delicate intuitions, by taking note of things too slight for record, and by bringing my human spirit into manifold accordance with the companions whom God assigned me—to learn the secret which was hidden even from themselves.

Of all possible observers, methought, a woman, like Zenobia, and a man, like Hollingsworth, should have selected me. And, now, when the event has long been past, I retain the same opinion of my fitness for the office. True; I might have condemned them. Had I been judge, as well as witness, my sentence might have been stern as that of Destiny itself. But, still, no trait of original nobility of character; no struggle against temptation; no iron necessity of will, on the one hand, nor extenuating circumstance to be derived from passion and despair, on the other; no remorse that might co-exist with error, even if powerless to prevent it; no proud repentance, that should claim retribution as a meed—would go unappreciated. True, again, I might give my full assent to the punishment which was sure to follow. But it would be given mournfully, and with undiminished love. And, after all was finished, I would come, as if to gather up the white ashes of those who had perished at the stake, and to tell the world— the wrong being now atoned for—how much had perished there, which it had never yet known how to praise.

I sat in my rocking-chair, too far withdrawn from the window to expose myself to another rebuke, like that already inflicted. My eyes still wandered towards the opposite house, but without effecting any new discoveries. Late in the afternoon, the weathercock on the church-spire indicated a change of wind; the sun shone dimly out, as if the golden wine of its beams were mingled half-and-half with water. Nevertheless, they kindled up the whole range of edifices, threw a glow over the windows, glistened on the wet roofs, and, slowly withdrawing upward, perched upon the chimney-tops; thence they took a higher flight, and lingered an instant on the tip of the spire, making it the final point of more cheerful light in the whole sombre scene. The next moment, it was all gone. The twilight fell into the area like a shower of dusky snow; and before it was quite dark, the gong of the hotel summoned me to tea.

When I returned to my chamber, the glow of an astral lamp* was penetrating mistily through the white curtain of Zenobia's drawing-room. The shadow of a passing figure was now-and-then cast upon this medium, but with too vague an outline for even my adventurous conjectures to read the hieroglyphic that it presented.

All at once, it occurred to me how very absurd was my behavior, in thus tormenting myself with crazy hypotheses as to what was going on within that drawing-room, when it was at my option to be personally present there. My relations with Zenobia, as yet unchanged—as a familiar friend, and associated in the same life-long enterprise—gave me the right, and made it no more than kindly courtesy demanded, to call on her. Nothing, except our habitual independence of conventional rules, at Blithedale, could have kept me from sooner recognizing this duty. At all events, it should now be performed.

In compliance with this sudden impulse, I soon found myself actually within the house, the rear of which, for two days past, I had been so sedulously watching. A servant took my card, and immediately returning, ushered me up-stairs. On the way, I heard a rich, and, as it were, triumphant burst of music from a piano, in which I felt Zenobia's character, although heretofore I had known nothing of her skill upon the instrument. Two or three canary-birds, excited by this gush of sound, sang piercingly, and did their utmost to produce a kindred melody. A bright illumination streamed through the door of the front drawing-room; and I had barely stept across the threshold before Zenobia came forward to meet me, laughing, and with an extended hand.

"Ah, Mr. Coverdale," said she, still smiling, but, as I thought, with a good deal of scornful anger underneath, "it has gratified me to see the interest which you continue to take in my affairs! I have long recognized you as a sort of transcendental Yankee, with all the native propensity of your countrymen to investigate matters that come within their range, but rendered almost poetical, in your case, by the refined methods which you adopt for its gratification. After

all, it was an unjustifiable stroke, on my part—was it not?—
to let down the window-curtain!"

"I cannot call it a very wise one," returned I, with a secret
bitterness which, no doubt, Zenobia appreciated. "It is really
impossible to hide anything, in this world, to say nothing of
the next. All that we ought to ask, therefore, is, that the witnesses of our conduct, and the speculators on our motives,
should be capable of taking the highest view which the circumstances of the case may admit. So much being secured, I,
for one, would be most happy in feeling myself followed,
everywhere, by an indefatigable human sympathy."

"We must trust for intelligent sympathy to our guardian
angels, if any there be," said Zenobia. "As long as the only
spectator of my poor tragedy is a young man, at the window
of his hotel, I must still claim the liberty to drop the curtain."

While this passed, as Zenobia's hand was extended, I had
applied the very slightest touch of my fingers to her own. In
spite of an external freedom, her manner made me sensible
that we stood upon no real terms of confidence. The thought
came sadly across me, how great was the contrast betwixt this
interview and our first meeting. Then, in the warm light of
the country fireside, Zenobia had greeted me cheerily and
hopefully, with a full sisterly grasp of the hand, conveying
as much kindness in it as other women could have evinced by
the pressure of both arms around my neck, or by yielding a
cheek to the brotherly salute. The difference was as complete
as between her appearance, at that time—so simply attired,
and with only the one superb flower in her hair—and now,
when her beauty was set off by all that dress and ornament
could do for it. And they did much. Not, indeed, that they
created, or added anything to what Nature had lavishly done
for Zenobia. But, those costly robes which she had on, those
flaming jewels on her neck, served as lamps to display the
personal advantages which required nothing less than such
an illumination, to be fully seen. Even her characteristic

flower, though it seemed to be still there, had undergone a cold and bright transfiguration; it was a flower exquisitely imitated in jeweller's work, and imparting the last touch that transformed Zenobia into a work of art.

"I scarcely feel," I could not forbear saying, "as if we had ever met before. How many years ago it seems, since we last sat beneath Eliot's pulpit, with Hollingsworth extended on the fallen leaves, and Priscilla at his feet! Can it be, Zenobia, that you ever really numbered yourself with our little band of earnest, thoughtful, philanthropic laborers?"

"Those ideas have their time and place," she answered, coldly. "But, I fancy, it must be a very circumscribed mind that can find room for no others."

Her manner bewildered me. Literally, moreover, I was dazzled by the brilliancy of the room. A chandelier hung down in the centre, glowing with I know not how many lights; there were separate lamps, also, on two or three tables, and on marble brackets, adding their white radiance to that of the chandelier. The furniture was exceedingly rich. Fresh from our old farm-house, with its homely board and benches in the dining-room, and a few wicker-chairs in the best parlor, it struck me that here was the fulfilment of every fantasy of an imagination, revelling in various methods of costly self-indulgence and splendid ease. Pictures, marbles, vases; in brief, more shapes of luxury than there could be any object in enumerating, except for an auctioneer's advertisement—and the whole repeated and doubled by the reflection of a great mirror, which showed me Zenobia's proud figure, likewise, and my own. It cost me, I acknowledge, a bitter sense of shame, to perceive in myself a positive effort to bear up against the effect which Zenobia sought to impose on me. I reasoned against her, in my secret mind, and strove so to keep my footing. In the gorgeousness with which she had surrounded herself—in the redundance of personal ornament, which the largeness of her physical nature and the rich type of her beauty caused to seem so suitable—I malevolently beheld the true character of the woman, passionate, luxurious, lacking simplicity, not deeply refined, incapable of pure and perfect taste.

But, the next instant, she was too powerful for all my opposing struggles. I saw how fit it was that she should make herself as gorgeous as she pleased, and should do a thousand things that would have been ridiculous in the poor, thin, weakly characters of other women. To this day, however, I hardly know whether I then beheld Zenobia in her truest attitude, or whether that were the truer one in which she had presented herself at Blithedale. In both, there was something like the illusion which a great actress flings around her.

"Have you given up Blithedale forever?" I inquired.

"Why should you think so?" asked she.

"I cannot tell," answered I; "except that it appears all like a dream that we were ever there together."

"It is not so to me," said Zenobia. "I should think it a poor and meagre nature, that is capable of but one set of forms, and must convert all the past into a dream, merely because the present happens to be unlike it. Why should we be content with our homely life of a few months past, to the exclusion of all other modes? It was good; but there are other lives as good or better. Not, you will understand, that I condemn those who give themselves up to it more entirely than I, for myself, should deem it wise to do."

It irritated me, this self-complacent, condescending, qualified approval and criticism of a system to which many individuals—perhaps as highly endowed as our gorgeous Zenobia—had contributed their all of earthly endeavor, and their loftiest aspirations. I determined to make proof if there were any spell that would exorcise her out of the part which she seemed to be acting. She should be compelled to give me a glimpse of something true; some nature, some passion, no matter whether right or wrong, provided it were real.

"Your allusion to that class of circumscribed characters, who can live only in one mode of life," remarked I, coolly, "reminds me of our poor friend Hollingsworth. Possibly, he was in your thoughts, when you spoke thus. Poor fellow! It is a pity that, by the fault of a narrow education, he should have so completely immolated himself to that one idea of his; especially as the slightest modicum of common-sense would teach him its utter impracticability. Now that I have returned into the world, and can look at his project from a distance, it requires quite all my real regard for this respectable and well-intentioned man to prevent me laughing at him—as, I find, society at large does!"

Zenobia's eyes darted lightning; her cheeks flushed; the vividness of her expression was like the effect of a powerful light, flaming up suddenly within her. My experiment had fully succeeded. She had shown me the true flesh and blood of her heart, by thus involuntarily resenting my slight, pity-ing, half-kind, half-scornful mention of the man who was all in all with her. She herself, probably, felt this; for it was hardly a moment before she tranquillized her uneven breath, and seemed as proud and self-possessed as ever.

"I rather imagine," said she, quietly, "that your appreciation falls short of Mr. Hollingsworth's just claims. Blind enthusi-asm, absorption in one idea, I grant, is generally ridiculous, and must be fatal to the respectability of an ordinary man; it requires a very high and powerful character, to make it otherwise. But a great man—as, perhaps, you do not know—attains his normal condition only through the inspiration of one great idea. As a friend of Mr. Hollingsworth, and, at the same time, a calm observer, I must tell you that he seems to me such a man. But you are very pardonable for fancying him ridiculous. Doubtless, he is so—to you! There can be no truer test of the noble and heroic, in any individual, than the degree in which he possesses the faculty of distinguishing heroism from absurdity."

I dared make no retort to Zenobia's concluding apothegm. In truth, I admired her fidelity. It gave me a new sense of Hollingsworth's native power, to discover that his influence was no less potent with this beautiful woman, here, in the midst of artificial life, than it had been, at the foot of the gray rock, and among the wild birch-trees of the wood-path, when she so passionately pressed his hand against her heart. The great, rude, shaggy, swarthy man! And Zenobia loved him!

"Did you bring Priscilla with you?" I resumed. "Do you know, I have sometimes fancied it not quite safe, considering the susceptibility of her temperament, that she should be so constantly within the sphere of a man like Hollingsworth? Such tender and delicate natures, among your sex, have often, I believe, a very adequate appreciation of the heroic element in men. But, then, again, I should suppose them as likely as any other women to make a reciprocal impression. Hollingsworth could hardly give his affections to a person capable of taking an independent stand, but only to one whom he might absorb into himself. He has certainly shown great tenderness for Priscilla."

Zenobia had turned aside. But I caught the reflection of her face in the mirror, and saw that it was very pale;—as pale, in her rich attire, as if a shroud were round her.

"Priscilla is here," said she, her voice a little lower than usual. "Have not you learnt as much, from your chamber-window? Would you like to see her?"

She made a step or two into the back drawing-room, and called:—

"Priscilla! Dear Priscilla!"

XX

THEY VANISH

PRISCILLA immediately answered the summons, and made her appearance through the door of the boudoir.

I had conceived the idea—which I now recognized as a very foolish one—that Zenobia would have taken measures to debar me from an interview with this girl, between whom and herself there was so utter an opposition of their dearest interests, that, on one part or the other, a great grief, if not likewise a great wrong, seemed a matter of necessity. But, as Priscilla was only a leaf, floating on the dark current of events, without influencing them by her own choice or plan—as she probably guessed not whither the stream was bearing her, nor perhaps even felt its inevitable movement—there could be no peril of her communicating to me any intelligence with regard to Zenobia's purposes.

On perceiving me, she came forward with great quietude of manner; and when I held out my hand, her own moved slightly towards it, as if attracted by a feeble degree of magnetism.

"I am glad to see you, my dear Priscilla," said I, still holding her hand. "But everything that I meet with, now-a-days, makes me wonder whether I am awake. You, especially, have always seemed like a figure in a dream—and now more than ever."

"Oh, there is substance in these fingers of mine!" she answered, giving my hand the faintest possible pressure, and then taking away her own. "Why do you call me a dream? Zenobia is much more like one than I; she is so very, very beautiful! And, I suppose," added Priscilla, as if thinking aloud, "everybody sees it, as I do."

But, for my part, it was Priscilla's beauty, not Zenobia's, of which I was thinking, at that moment. She was a person who could be quite obliterated, so far as beauty went, by anything unsuitable in her attire; her charm was not positive and material enough to bear up against a mistaken choice of color, for instance, or fashion. It was safest, in her case, to attempt no art of dress; for it demanded the most perfect taste, or else the happiest accident in the world, to give her precisely the adornment which she needed. She was now dressed in pure white, set off with some kind of a gauzy fabric, which—as I bring up her figure in my memory, with a faint gleam on her shadowy hair, and her dark eyes bent shyly on mine, through all the vanished years—seems to be floating about her like a mist. I wondered what Zenobia meant by evolving so much loveliness out of this poor girl. It was what few women could afford to do; for, as I looked from one to the other, the sheen and splendor of Zenobia's presence took nothing from Priscilla's softer spell, if it might not rather be thought to add to it.

"What do you think of her?" asked Zenobia.

I could not understand the look of melancholy kindness with which Zenobia regarded her. She advanced a step, and beckoning Priscilla near her, kissed her cheek; then, with a slight gesture of repulse, she moved to the other side of the room. I followed.

"She is a wonderful creature," I said. "Ever since she came among us, I have been dimly sensible of just this charm which you have brought out. But it was never absolutely visible till now. She is as lovely as a flower!"

"Well; say so, if you like," answered Zenobia. "You are a poet—at least, as poets go, now-a-days—and must be allowed to make an opera-glass of your imagination, when you look at women. I wonder, in such Arcadian freedom of falling in love as we have lately enjoyed, it never occurred to you to fall in love with Priscilla! In society, indeed, a genuine American never dreams of stepping across the inappreciable air-line* which separates one class from another. But what was rank to the colonists of Blithedale?"

"There were other reasons," I replied, "why I should have demonstrated myself an ass, had I fallen in love with Priscilla. By-the-by, has Hollingsworth ever seen her in this dress?"

"Why do you bring up his name, at every turn?" asked Zenobia, in an undertone, and with a malign look which wandered from my face to Priscilla's. "You know not what you do! It is dangerous, sir, believe me, to tamper thus with earnest human passions, out of your own mere idleness, and for your sport. I will endure it no longer! Take care that it does not happen again! I warn you!"

"You partly wrong me, if not wholly," I responded. "It is an uncertain sense of some duty to perform, that brings my thoughts, and therefore my words, continually to that one point."

"Oh, this stale excuse of duty!" said Zenobia, in a whisper so full of scorn that it penetrated me like the hiss of a serpent. "I have often heard it before, from those who sought to interfere with me, and I know precisely what it signifies. Bigotry; self-conceit; an insolent curiosity; a meddlesome temper; a cold-blooded criticism, founded on a shallow interpretation of half-perceptions; a monstrous scepticism in regard to any conscience or any wisdom, except one's own; a most irreverent propensity to thrust Providence aside, and substitute one's self in its awful place—out of these, and other motives as miserable as these, comes your idea of duty!

But beware, sir! With all your fancied acuteness, you step blindfold into these affairs. For any mischief that may follow your interference, I hold you responsible!"

It was evident, that, with but a little further provocation, the lioness would turn to bay; if, indeed, such were not her attitude, already. I bowed, and, not very well knowing what else to do, was about to withdraw. But, glancing again towards Priscilla, who had retreated into a corner, there fell upon my heart an intolerable burthen of despondency, the purport of which I could not tell, but only felt it to bear reference to her. I approached her, and held out my hand; a gesture, however, to which she made no response. It was always one of her peculiarities that she seemed to shrink from even the most friendly touch, unless it were Zenobia's or Hollingsworth's. Zenobia, all this while, stood watching us, but with a careless expression, as if it mattered very little what might pass.

"Priscilla," I inquired, lowering my voice, "when do you go back to Blithedale?"

"Whenever they please to take me," said she.

"Did you come away of your own free-will?" I asked.

"I am blown about like a leaf," she replied. "I never have any free-will."

"Does Hollingsworth know that you are here?" said I.

"He bade me come," answered Priscilla.

She looked at me, I thought, with an air of surprise, as if the idea were incomprehensible, that she should have taken this step without his agency.

"What a gripe* this man has laid upon her whole being!" muttered I, between my teeth. "Well; as Zenobia so kindly intimates, I have no more business here. I wash my hands of it all. On Hollingsworth's head be the consequences! Priscilla," I added, aloud, "I know not that ever we may meet again. Farewell!"

As I spoke the word, a carriage had rumbled along the street, and stopt before the house. The door-bell rang, and steps were immediately afterwards heard on the staircase. Zenobia had thrown a shawl over her dress.

"Mr. Coverdale," said she, with cool courtesy, "you will perhaps excuse us. We have an engagement, and are going out."

"Whither?" I demanded.

"Is not that a little more than you are entitled to inquire?" said she, with a smile. "At all events, it does not suit me to tell you."

The door of the drawing-room opened, and Westervelt appeared. I observed that he was elaborately dressed, as if for some grand entertainment. My dislike for this man was infinite. At that moment, it amounted to nothing less than a creeping of the flesh, as when, feeling about in a dark place, one touches something cold and slimy, and questions what the secret hatefulness may be. And, still, I could not but acknowledge, that, for personal beauty, for polish of manner, for all that externally befits a gentleman, there was hardly another like him. After bowing to Zenobia, and graciously saluting Priscilla in her corner, he recognized me by a slight, but courteous inclination.

"Come, Priscilla," said Zenobia, "it is time. Mr. Coverdale, good evening!"

As Priscilla moved slowly forward, I met her in the middle of the drawing-room.

"Priscilla," said I, in the hearing of them all, "do you know whither you are going?"

"I do not know," she answered.

"Is it wise to go?—and is it your choice to go?" I asked. "If not—I am your friend, and Hollingsworth's friend—tell me. so, at once!"

"Possibly," observed Westervelt, smiling, "Priscilla sees in me an older friend than either Mr. Coverdale or Mr. Hollingsworth. I shall willingly leave the matter at her option."

While thus speaking, he made a gesture of kindly invitation; and Priscilla passed me, with the gliding movement of a sprite, and took his offered arm. He offered the other to Zenobia. But she turned her proud and beautiful face upon him, with a look which—judging from what I caught of it in profile—would undoubtedly have smitten the man dead, had he possessed any heart, or had this glance attained to it. It seemed to rebound, however, from his courteous visage, like an arrow from polished steel. They all three descended the stairs; and when I likewise reached the street-door, the carriage was already rolling away.

XXI

AN OLD ACQUAINTANCE

THUS excluded from everybody's confidence, and attaining no further, by my most earnest study, than to an uncertain sense of something hidden from me, it would appear reasonable that I should have flung off all these alien perplexities. Obviously, my best course was, to betake myself to new scenes. Here, I was only an intruder. Elsewhere, there might be circumstances in which I could establish a personal interest, and people who would respond, with a portion of their sympathies, for so much as I should bestow of mine.

Nevertheless, there occurred to me one other thing to be done. Remembering old Moodie, and his relationship with Priscilla, I determined to seek an interview, for the purpose of ascertaining whether the knot of affairs was as inextricable, on that side, as I found it on all others. Being tolerably well acquainted with the old man's haunts, I went, the next day, to the saloon of a certain establishment about which he often lurked. It was a reputable place enough, affording good entertainment in the way of meat, drink, and fumigation;* and there, in my young and idle days and nights, when I was neither nice nor wise, I had often amused myself with watching the staid humors and sober jollities of the thirsty souls around me.

At my first entrance, old Moodie was not there. The more patiently to await him, I lighted a cigar, and establishing myself in a corner, took a quiet, and, by sympathy, a boozy kind of pleasure in the customary life that was going forward. Human nature, in my opinion, has a naughty instinct that approves of wine, at least, if not of stronger liquor. The temperance-men may preach till doom's day; and still this cold and barren world will look warmer, kindlier, mellower, through the medium of a toper's glass; nor can they, with all their efforts, really spill his draught upon the floor, until some hitherto unthought-of discovery shall supply him with a truer element of joy. The general atmosphere of life must first be rendered so inspiriting that he will not need his delirious solace. The custom of tippling has its defensible side, as well as any other question. But these good people snatch at the old, time-honored demijohn, and offer nothing— either sensual or moral—nothing whatever to supply its place; and human life, as it goes with a multitude of men, will not endure so great a vacuum as would be left by the withdrawal of that big-bellied convexity. The space, which it now occupies, must somehow or other be filled up. As for the rich, it would be little matter if a blight fell upon their vineyards; but the poor man—whose only glimpse of a better state is through the muddy medium of his liquor—what is to be done for him? The reformers should make their efforts positive, instead of negative; they must do away with evil by substituting good.*

The saloon was fitted up with a good deal of taste. There were pictures on the walls, and among them an oil-painting of a beef-steak, with such an admirable show of juicy tenderness, that the beholder sighed to think it merely visionary, and incapable of ever being put upon a gridiron. Another work of high art was the lifelike representation of a noble sirloin; another, the hind-quarters of a deer, retaining the hoofs and tawny fur; another, the head and shoulders of a salmon; and, still more exquisitely finished, a brace of canvass-back ducks, in which the mottled feathers were depicted with the accuracy of a daguerreotype.* Some very hungry painter, I suppose, had wrought these subjects of still life, heightening his imagination with his appetite, and earning, it is to be hoped, the privilege of a daily dinner off whichever of his pictorial viands he liked best. Then there was a fine old cheese, in which you could almost discern the mites; and some sardines, on a small plate, very richly done, and looking as if oozy with the oil in which they had been smothered. All these things were so perfectly imitated, that you seemed to have the genuine article before you, and yet with an indescribable, ideal charm; it took away the grossness from what was fleshiest and fattest, and thus helped the life of man, even in its earthliest relations, to appear rich and noble, as well as warm, cheerful, and substantial. There were pictures, too, of gallant revellers, those of the old time, Flemish, apparently, with doublets and slashed sleeves, drinking their wine out of fantastic, long-stemmed glasses; quaffing joyously, quaffing forever, with inaudible laughter and song; while the champagne bubbled immortally against their moustaches, or the purple tide of Burgundy ran inexhaustibly down their throats.

But, in an obscure corner of the saloon, there was a little picture—excellently done, moreover—of a ragged, bloated, New England toper, stretched out on a bench, in the heavy, apoplectic sleep of drunkenness. The death-in-life was too well portrayed. You smelt the fumy liquor that had brought on this syncope.* Your only comfort lay in the forced reflection, that, real as he looked, the poor caitiff was but imaginary, a bit of painted canvass, whom no delirium tremens, nor so much as a retributive headache, awaited, on the morrow.

By this time, it being past eleven o'clock, the two bar-keepers of the saloon were in pretty constant activity. One of these young men had a rare faculty in the concoction of gin-cocktails. It was a spectacle to behold, how, with a tumbler in each hand, he tossed the contents from one to the other. Never conveying it awry, nor spilling the least drop, he compelled the frothy liquor, as it seemed to me, to spout forth from one glass and descend into the other, in a great parabolic curve, as well-defined and calculable as a planet's orbit. He had a good forehead, with a particularly large development just above the eyebrows; fine intellectual gifts, no doubt, which he had educated to this profitable end; being famous for nothing but gin-cocktails, and commanding a fair salary by his one accomplishment. These cocktails, and other artificial combinations of liquor, (of which there were at least a score, though mostly, I suspect, fantastic in their differences,) were much in favor with the younger class of customers, who, at farthest, had only reached the second stage of potatory life. The staunch, old soakers, on the other hand— men who, if put on tap, would have yielded a red alcoholic liquor, by way of blood—usually confined themselves to plain brandy-and-water, gin, or West India rum; and, oftentimes, they prefaced their dram with some medicinal remark as to the wholesomeness and stomachic qualities of that particular drink. Two or three appeared to have bottles of their own, behind the counter; and winking one red eye to the bar-keeper, he forthwith produced these choicest and peculiar cordials, which it was a matter of great interest and favor, among their acquaintances, to obtain a sip of.

Agreeably to the Yankee habit, under whatever circumstances, the deportment of all these good fellows, old or young, was decorous and thoroughly correct. They grew only the more sober in their cups; there was no confused babble, nor boisterous laughter. They sucked in the joyous fire of the decanters, and kept it smouldering in their inmost recesses, with a bliss known only to the heart which it warmed and comforted. Their eyes twinkled a little, to be sure; they hemmed vigorously, after each glass, and laid a hand upon the pit of the stomach, as if the pleasant titillation, there, was what constituted the tangible part of their enjoyment. In that spot, unquestionably, and not in the brain, was the acme of the whole affair. But the true purpose of their drinking—and one that will induce men to drink, or do something equivalent, as long as this weary world shall endure—was the renewed youth and vigor, the brisk, cheerful sense of things present and to come, with which, for about a quarter-of-an-hour, the dram permeated their systems. And when such quarters-of-an-hour can be obtained in some mode less baneful to the great sum of a man's life—but, nevertheless, with a little spice of impropriety, to give it a wild flavor—we temperance-people may ring out our bells for victory!

The prettiest object in the saloon was a tiny fountain, which threw up its feathery jet, through the counter, and sparkled down again into an oval basin, or lakelet, containing several gold-fishes. There was a bed of bright sand, at the bottom, strewn with coral and rock-work; and the fishes went gleaming about, now turning up the sheen of a golden side, and now vanishing into the shadows of the water, like the fanciful thoughts that coquet with a poet in his dream. Never before, I imagine, did a company of water-drinkers remain so entirely uncontaminated by the bad example around them; nor could I help wondering that it had not occurred to any freakish inebriate, to empty a glass of liquor into their lakelet. What a delightful idea! Who would not be a fish, if he could inhale jollity with the essential element of his existence!

I had begun to despair of meeting old Moodie, when, all at once, I recognized his hand and arm, protruding from behind a screen that was set up for the accommodation of bashful topers. As a matter of course, he had one of Priscilla's little purses, and was quietly insinuating it under the notice of a person who stood near. This was always old Moodie's way. You hardly ever saw him advancing towards you, but became aware of his proximity without being able to guess how he had come thither. He glided about like a spirit, assuming visibility close to your elbow, offering his petty trifles of merchandise, remaining long enough for you to purchase, if so disposed, and then taking himself off, between two breaths, while you happened to be thinking of something else.

By a sort of sympathetic impulse that often controlled me, in those more impressible days of my life, I was induced to approach this old man in a mode as undemonstrative as his own. Thus, when, according to his custom, he was probably just about to vanish, he found me at his elbow.

"Ah!" said he, with more emphasis than was usual with him. "It is Mr. Coverdale!"

"Yes, Mr. Moodie, your old acquaintance," answered I. "It is some time now since we ate our luncheon together, at Blithedale, and a good deal longer since our little talk together, at the street-corner."

"That was a good while ago," said the old man.

And he seemed inclined to say not a word more. His existence looked so colorless and torpid—so very faintly shadowed on the canvass of reality—that I was half afraid lest he should altogether disappear, even while my eyes were fixed full upon his figure. He was certainly the wretchedest old ghost in the world, with his crazy hat, the dingy handkerchief about his throat, his suit of threadbare gray, and especially that patch over his right eye,* behind which he always seemed to be hiding himself. There was one method, however, of bringing him out into somewhat stronger relief. A glass of brandy would effect it. Perhaps the gentler influence of a bottle of claret might do the same. Nor could I think it a matter for the recording angel to write down against me, if—with my painful consciousness of the frost in this old man's blood, and the positive ice that had congealed about his heart—I should thaw him out, were it only for an hour, with the summer warmth of a little wine. What else could possibly be done for him? How else could he be imbued with energy enough to hope for a happier state, hereafter? How else be inspirited to say his prayers? For there are states of our spiritual system, when the throb of the soul's life is too faint and weak to render us capable of religious aspiration.

"Mr. Moodie," said I, "shall we lunch together? And would you like to drink a glass of wine?"

His one eye gleamed. He bowed; and it impressed me that he grew to be more of a man at once, either in anticipation of the wine, or as a grateful response to my good-fellowship in offering it.

"With pleasure," he replied.

The barkeeper, at my request, showed us into a private room, and, soon afterwards, set some fried oysters and a bottle of claret on the table; and I saw the old man glance curiously at the label of the bottle, as if to learn the brand.

"It should be good wine," I remarked, "if it have any right to its label."

"You cannot suppose, sir," said Moodie, with a sigh, "that a poor old fellow, like me, knows any difference in wines."

And yet, in his way of handling the glass, in his preliminary snuff at the aroma, in his first cautious sip of the wine, and the gustatory skill with which he gave his palate the full advantage of it, it was impossible not to recognize the connoisseur.

"I fancy, Mr. Moodie," said I, "you are a much better judge of wines than I have yet learned to be. Tell me fairly—did you never drink it where the grape grows?"

"How should that have been, Mr. Coverdale?" answered old Moodie, shyly; but then he took courage, as it were, and uttered a feeble little laugh. "The flavor of this wine," added he, "and its perfume, still more than its taste, makes me remember that I was once a young man!"

"I wish, Mr. Moodie," suggested I—not that I greatly cared about it, however, but was only anxious to draw him into some talk about Priscilla and Zenobia—"I wish, while we sit over our wine, you would favor me with a few of those youthful reminiscences."

"Ah," said he, shaking his head, "they might interest you more than you suppose. But I had better be silent, Mr. Coverdale. If this good wine—though claret, I suppose, is not apt to play such a trick—but if it should make my tongue run too freely, I could never look you in the face again."

"You never did look me in the face, Mr. Moodie," I replied, "until this very moment."

‘ "Ah!" sighed old Moodie.

It was wonderful, however, what an effect the mild grape-juice wrought upon him. It was not in the wine, but in the associations which it seemed to bring up. Instead of the mean, slouching, furtive, painfully depressed air of an old city-vagabond, more like a gray kennel-rat* than any other living thing, he began to take the aspect of a decayed gentleman. Even his garments—especially after I had myself quaffed a glass or two—looked less shabby than when we first sat down. There was, by-and-by, a certain exuberance and elaborateness of gesture, and manner, oddly in contrast with all that I had hitherto seen of him. Anon, with hardly any impulse from me, old Moodie began to talk. His communications referred exclusively to a long past and more fortunate period of his life, with only a few unavoidable allusions to the circumstances that had reduced him to his present state. But, having once got the clue, my subsequent researches acquainted me with the main facts of the following narrative; although, in writing it out, my pen has perhaps allowed itself a trifle of romantic and legendary license, worthier of a small poet than of a grave biographer.

XXII

FAUNTLEROY

FIVE-AND-TWENTY years ago, at the epoch of this story, there dwelt, in one of the middle states, a man whom we shall call Fauntleroy;* a man of wealth, and magnificent tastes, and prodigal expenditure. His home might almost be styled a palace; his habits, in the ordinary sense, princely. His whole being seemed to have crystallized itself into an external splendor, wherewith he glittered in the eyes of the world, and had no other life than upon this gaudy surface. He had married a lovely woman, whose nature was deeper than his own. But his affection for her, though it showed largely, was superficial, like all his other manifestations and developments; he did not so truly keep this noble creature in his heart, as wear her beauty for the most brilliant ornament of his outward state. And there was born to him a child, a beautiful daughter, whom he took from the beneficent hand of God with no just sense of her immortal value, but as a man, already rich in gems, would receive another jewel. If he loved her, it was because she shone.

After Fauntleroy had thus spent a few empty years, corruscating continually an unnatural light, the source of it— which was merely his gold—began to grow more shallow, and finally became exhausted. He saw himself in imminent peril of losing all that had heretofore distinguished him; and, conscious of no innate worth to fall back upon, he recoiled from this calamity, with the instinct of a soul shrinking from annihilation. To avoid it—wretched man!—or, rather, to defer it, if but for a month, a day, or only to procure himself the life of a few breaths more, amid the false glitter which was now less his own than ever—he made himself guilty of a crime. It was just the sort of crime, growing out of its artificial state, which society (unless it should change its entire constitution for this man's unworthy sake) neither could nor ought to pardon. More safely might it pardon murder. Fauntleroy's guilt was discovered. He fled; his wife perished by the necessity of her innate nobleness, in its alliance with a being so ignoble; and betwixt her mother's death and her father's ignominy, his daughter was left worse than orphaned.

There was no pursuit after Fauntleroy. His family-connections, who had great wealth, made such arrangements with those whom he had attempted to wrong, as secured him from the retribution that would have overtaken an unfriended criminal. The wreck of his estate was divided among his creditors. His name, in a very brief space, was forgotten by the multitude who had passed it so diligently from mouth to mouth. Seldom, indeed, was it recalled, even by his closest former intimates. Nor could it have been otherwise. The man had laid no real touch on any mortal's heart. Being a mere image, an optical delusion, created by the sunshine of prosperity, it was his law to vanish into the shadow of the first intervening cloud. He seemed to leave no vacancy; a phenomenon which, like many others that attended his brief career, went far to prove the illusiveness of his existence.

Not, however, that the physical substance of Fauntleroy had literally melted into vapor. He had fled northward, to the New England metropolis,* and had taken up his abode, under another name, in a squalid street, or court, of the older portion of the city. There he dwelt among poverty-stricken wretches, sinners, and forlorn, good people, Irish, and whomsoever else were neediest. Many families were clustered in each house together, above stairs and below, in the little peaked garrets, and even in the dusky cellars. The house, where Fauntleroy paid weekly rent for a chamber and a closet, had been a stately habitation, in its day. An old colonial Governor had built it, and lived there, long ago, and held his levees in a great room where now slept twenty Irish bedfellows, and died in Fauntleroy's chamber, which his embroidered and white-wigged ghost still haunted. Tattered hangings, a marble hearth, traversed with many cracks and fissures, a richly-carved oaken mantel-piece, partly hacked-away for kindling-stuff, a stuccoed ceiling, defaced with great, unsightly patches of the naked laths;—such was the chamber's aspect, as if, with its splinters and rags of dirty splendor, it were a kind of practical gibe at this poor, ruined man of show.

At first, and at irregular intervals, his relatives allowed Fauntleroy a little pittance to sustain life; not from any love, perhaps, but lest poverty should compel him, by new offences, to add more shame to that with which he had already stained them. But he showed no tendency to further guilt. His character appeared to have been radically changed (as, indeed, from its shallowness, it well might) by his miserable fate; or, it may be, the traits now seen in him were portions of the same character, presenting itself in another phase. Instead of any longer seeking to live in the sight of the world, his impulse was to shrink into the nearest obscurity, and to be unseen of men, were it possible, even while standing before their eyes. He had no pride; it was all trodden in the dust. No ostentation; for how could it survive, when there was nothing left of Fauntleroy, save penury and shame! His very gait demonstrated that he would gladly have faded out of view, and have crept about invisibly, for the sake of sheltering himself from the irksomeness of a human glance. Hardly, it was averred, within the memory of those who knew him now, had he the hardihood to show his full front to the world. He skulked in corners, and crept about in a sort of noonday twilight, making himself gray and misty, at all hours, with his morbid intolerance of sunshine.

In his torpid despair, however, he had done an act which that condition of the spirit seems to prompt, almost as often as prosperity and hope. Fauntleroy was again married. He had taken to wife a forlorn, meek-spirited, feeble young woman, a seamstress, whom he found dwelling with her mother in a contiguous chamber of the old gubernatorial residence. This poor phantom—as the beautiful and noble companion of his former life had done—brought him a daughter. And sometimes, as from one dream into another, Fauntleroy looked forth out of his present grimy environment, into that past magnificence, and wondered whether the grandee of yesterday or the pauper of to-day were real. But, in my mind, the one and the other were alike impalpable. In truth, it was Fauntleroy's fatality to behold whatever he touched dissolve. After a few years, his second wife (dim shadow that she had always been) faded finally out of the world, and left Fauntleroy to deal as he might with their pale and nervous child. And, by this time, among his distant relatives—with whom he had grown a weary thought, linked with contagious infamy, and which they were only too willing to get rid of—he was himself supposed to be no more.

The younger child, like his elder one, might be considered as the true offspring of both parents, and as the reflection of their state. She was a tremulous little creature, shrinking involuntarily from all mankind, but in timidity, and no sour repugnance. There was a lack of human substance in her; it seemed as if, were she to stand up in a sunbeam, it would pass right through her figure, and trace out the cracked and dusty window-panes upon the naked floor. But, nevertheless, the poor child had a heart; and from her mother's gentle character, she had inherited a profound and still capacity of affection. And so her life was one of love. She bestowed it partly on her father, but, in greater part, on an idea.

For Fauntleroy, as they sat by their cheerless fireside—which was no fireside, in truth, but only a rusty stove—had often talked to the little girl about his former wealth, the noble loveliness of his first wife, and the beautiful child whom she had given him. Instead of the fairy tales, which other parents tell, he told Priscilla this. And, out of the loneliness of her sad little existence, Priscilla's love grew, and tended upward, and twined itself perseveringly around this unseen sister; as a grape-vine might strive to clamber out of a gloomy hollow among the rocks, and embrace a young tree, standing in the sunny warmth above. It was almost like worship, both in its earnestness and its humility; nor was it the less humble, though the more earnest, because Priscilla could claim human kindred with the being whom she so devoutly loved. As with worship, too, it gave her soul the refreshment of a purer atmosphere. Save for this singular, this melancholy, and yet beautiful affection, the child could hardly have lived; or, had she lived, with a heart shrunken for lack of any sentiment to fill it, she must have yielded to the barren miseries of her position, and have grown to womanhood, characterless and worthless. But, now, amid all the sombre coarseness of her father's outward life, and of her own, Priscilla had a higher and imaginative life within. Some faint gleam thereof was often visible upon her face. It was as if, in her spiritual visits to her brilliant sister, a portion of the latter's brightness had permeated our dim Priscilla, and still lingered, shedding a faint illumination through the cheerless chamber, after she came back.

As the child grew up, so pallid and so slender, and with much unaccountable nervousness, and all the weaknesses of neglected infancy still haunting her, the gross and simple neighbors whispered strange things about Priscilla. The big, red, Irish matrons, whose innumerable progeny swarmed out of the adjacent doors, used to mock at the pale Western child. They fancied—or, at least, affirmed it, between jest and 'earnest—that she was not so solid flesh and blood as other children, but mixed largely with a thinner element. They called her ghost-child, and said that she could indeed vanish, when she pleased, but could never, in her densest moments, make herself quite visible. The sun, at mid-day, would shine through her; in the first gray of the twilight, she lost all the distinctness of her outline; and, if you followed the dim thing into a dark corner, behold! she was not there. And it was true, that Priscilla had strange ways; strange ways, and stranger words, when she uttered any words at all. Never stirring out of the old Governor's dusky house, she sometimes talked of distant places and splendid rooms, as if she had just left them. Hidden things were visible to her, (at least, so the people inferred from obscure hints, escaping unawares out of her mouth,) and silence was audible. And, in all the world, there was nothing so difficult to be endured, by those who had any dark secret to conceal, as the glance of Priscilla's timid and melancholy eyes.

Her peculiarities were the theme of continual gossip among the other inhabitants of the gubernatorial mansion. The rumor spread thence into a wider circle. Those who knew old Moodie—as he was now called—used often to jeer him, at the very street-corners, about his daughter's gift of second-sight and prophecy. It was a period when science (though mostly through its empirical professors) was bringing forward, anew, a hoard of facts and imperfect theories, that had partially won credence, in elder times, but which modern scepticism had swept away as rubbish. These things were now tossed up again, out of the surging ocean of human thought and experience. The story of Priscilla's preternatural manifestations, therefore, attracted a kind of notice of which it would have been deemed wholly unworthy, a few years earlier. One day, a gentleman ascended the creaking staircase, and inquired which was old Moodie's chamber-door. And, several times, he came again. He was a marvellously handsome man, still youthful, too, and fashionably dressed. Except that Priscilla, in those days, had no beauty, and, in the languor of her existence, had not yet blossomed into womanhood, there would have been rich food for scandal in these visits; for the girl was unquestionably their sole object, although her father was supposed always to be present. But, it must likewise be added, there was something about Priscilla that calumny could not meddle with; and thus far was she privileged, either by the preponderance of what was spiritual, or the thin and watery blood that left her cheek so pallid.

Yet, if the busy tongues of the neighborhood spared Priscilla, in one way, they made themselves amends by renewed and wilder babble, on another score. They averred that the strange gentleman was a wizard, and that he had taken advantage of Priscilla's lack of earthly substance to subject her to himself, as his familiar spirit, through whose medium he gained cognizance of whatever happened, in regions near or remote. The boundaries of his power were defined by the verge of the pit of Tartarus, on the one hand, and the third sphere of the celestial world, on the other. Again, they declared their suspicion that the wizard, with all his show of manly beauty, was really an aged and wizened figure, or else that his semblance of a human body was only a necromantic, or perhaps a mechanical contrivance, in which a demon walked about. In proof of it, however, they could merely instance a gold band around his upper teeth, which had once been visible to several old women, when he smiled at them from the top of the Governor's staircase. Of course, this was all absurdity, or mostly so. But, after every possible deduction, there remained certain very mysterious points about the stranger's character, as well as the connection that he established with Priscilla. Its nature, at that period, was even less understood than now, when miracles of this kind have grown so absolutely stale, that I would gladly, if the truth allowed, dismiss the whole matter from my narrative.

We must now glance backward, in quest of the beautiful daughter of Fauntleroy's prosperity. What had become of her? Fauntleroy's only brother, a bachelor, and with no other relative so near, had adopted the forsaken child. She grew up in affluence, with native graces clustering luxuriantly about her. In her triumphant progress towards womanhood, she was adorned with every variety of feminine accomplishment. But she lacked a mother's care. With no adequate control, on any hand, (for a man, however stern, however wise, can never sway and guide a female child,) her character was left to shape itself. There was good in it, and evil. Passionate, self-willed, and imperious, she had a warm and generous nature; showing the richness of the soil, however, chiefly by the weeds that flourished in it, and choked up the herbs of grace. In her girlhood, her uncle died. As Fauntleroy was supposed to be likewise dead, and no other heir was known to exist, his wealth devolved on her, although, dying suddenly, the uncle left no will. After his death, there were obscure passages in Zenobia's history. There were whispers of an attachment, and even a secret marriage, with a fascinating and accomplished, but unprincipled young man. The incidents and appearances, however, which led to this surmise, soon passed away and were forgotten.

Nor was her reputation seriously affected by the report. In fact, so great was her native power and influence, and such seemed the careless purity of her nature, that whatever Zenobia did was generally acknowledged as right for her to do. The world never criticised her so harshly as it does most women who transcend its rules. It almost yielded its assent, when it beheld her stepping out of the common path, and asserting the more extensive privileges of her sex, both theoretically and by her practice. The sphere of ordinary womanhood was felt to be narrower than her development required.

A portion of Zenobia's more recent life is told in the foregoing pages. Partly in earnest—and, I imagine, as was her disposition, half in a proud jest, or in a kind of recklessness that had grown upon her, out of some hidden grief—she had given her countenance, and promised liberal pecuniary aid, to our experiment of a better social state. And Priscilla followed her to Blithedale. The sole bliss of her life had been a dream of this beautiful sister, who had never so much as known of her existence. By this time, too, the poor girl was enthralled in an intolerable bondage, from which she must either free herself or perish. She deemed herself safest near Zenobia, into whose large heart she hoped to nestle.

One evening, months after Priscilla's departure, when Moodie (or shall we call him Fauntleroy?) was sitting alone in the state-chamber of the old Governor, there came footsteps up the staircase. There was a pause on the landing-place. A lady's musical, yet haughty accents were heard making an inquiry from some denizen of the house, who had thrust a head out of a contiguous chamber. There was then a knock at Moodie's door.

"Come in!" said he.

And Zenobia entered. The details of the interview that followed, being unknown to me—while, notwithstanding, it would be a pity quite to lose the picturesqueness of the situation—I shall attempt to sketch it, mainly from fancy, although with some general grounds of surmise in regard to the old man's feelings.

She gazed, wonderingly, at the dismal chamber. Dismal to her, who beheld it only for an instant, and how much more so to him, into whose brain each bare spot on the ceiling, every tatter of the paper-hangings, and all the splintered carvings of the mantel-piece, seen wearily through long years, had worn their several prints! Inexpressibly miserable is this familiarity with objects that have been, from the first, disgustful.

"I have received a strange message," said Zenobia, after a moment's silence, "requesting, or rather enjoining it upon me, to come hither. Rather from curiosity than any other motive—and because, though a woman, I have not all the timidity of one—I have complied. Can it be you, sir, who thus summoned me?"

"It was," answered Moodie.

"And what was your purpose?" she continued. "You require charity, perhaps? In that case, the message might have been more fitly worded. But you are old and poor; and age and poverty should be allowed their privileges. Tell me, therefore, to what extent you need my aid."

"Put up your purse," said the supposed mendicant, with an inexplicable smile. "Keep it—keep all your wealth—until I demand it all, or none! My message had no such end in view. You are beautiful, they tell me; and I desired to look at you!"

He took the one lamp that showed the discomfort and sordidness of his abode, and approaching Zenobia, held it up, so as to gain the more perfect view of her, from top to toe. So obscure was the chamber, that you could see the reflection of her diamonds thrown upon the dingy wall, and flickering with the rise and fall of Zenobia's breath. It was the splendor of those jewels on her neck, like lamps that burn before some fair temple, and the jewelled flower in her hair, more than the murky yellow light, that helped him to see her beauty. But he beheld it, and grew proud at heart; his own figure, in spite of his mean habiliments, assumed an air of state and grandeur.

"It is well!" cried old Moodie. "Keep your wealth. You are right worthy of it. Keep it, therefore, but with one condition, only!"

Zenobia thought the old man beside himself, and was moved with pity.

"Have you none to care for you?" asked she. "No daughter? —no kind-hearted neighbor?—no means of procuring the attendance which you need? Tell me, once again, can I do nothing for you?"

"Nothing," he replied. "I have beheld what I wished. Now, leave me! Linger not a moment longer; or I may be tempted to say what would bring a cloud over that queenly brow. Keep all your wealth, but with only this one condition. Be kind—be no less kind than sisters are—to my poor Priscilla!"

And, it may be, after Zenobia withdrew, Fauntleroy paced his gloomy chamber, and communed with himself, as follows: —or, at all events, it is the only solution, which I can offer, of the enigma presented in his character.

"I am unchanged—the same man as of yore!" said he. "True; my brother's wealth, he dying intestate, is legally my own. I know it; yet, of my own choice, I live a beggar, and go meanly clad, and hide myself behind a forgotten ignominy. Looks this like ostentation? Ah, but, in Zenobia, I live again! Beholding her so beautiful—so fit to be adorned with all imaginable splendor of outward state—the cursed vanity, which, half-a-lifetime since, dropt off like tatters of once gaudy apparel from my debased and ruined person, is all renewed for her sake! Were I to re-appear, my shame would go with me from darkness into daylight. Zenobia has the splendor, and not the shame. Let the world admire her, and be dazzled by her, the brilliant child of my prosperity! It is Fauntleroy that still shines through her!"

But, then, perhaps, another thought occurred to him.

"My poor Priscilla! And am I just, to her, in surrendering all to this beautiful Zenobia? Priscilla! I love her best—I love her only!—but with shame, not pride. So dim, so pallid, so shrinking—the daughter of my long calamity! Wealth were but a mockery in Priscilla's hands. What is its use, except to fling a golden radiance around those who grasp it? Yet, let Zenobia take heed! Priscilla shall have no wrong!"

But, while the man of show thus meditated—that very evening, so far as I can adjust the dates of these strange incidents—Priscilla—poor, pallid flower!—was either snatched from Zenobia's hand, or flung wilfully away!

XXIII

A VILLAGE-HALL

WELL! I betook myself away, and wandered up and down, like an exorcised spirit that had been driven from its old haunts, after a mighty struggle. It takes down the solitary pride of man, beyond most other things, to find the impracticability of flinging aside affections that have grown irksome. The bands, that were silken once, are apt to become iron fetters, when we desire to shake them off. Our souls, after all, are not our own. We convey a property in them to those with whom we associate, but to what extent can never be known, until we feel the tug, the agony, of our abortive effort to resume an exclusive sway over ourselves. Thus, in all the weeks of my absence, my thoughts continually reverted back, brooding over the by-gone months, and bringing up incidents that seemed hardly to have left a trace of themselves, in their passage. I spent painful hours in recalling these trifles, and rendering them more misty and unsubstantial than at first, by the quantity of speculative musing, thus kneaded in with them. Hollingsworth, Zenobia, Priscilla! These three had absorbed my life into themselves. Together with an inexpressible longing to know their fortunes, there was likewise a morbid resentment of my own pain, and a stubborn reluctance to come again within their sphere.

All that I learned of them, therefore, was comprised in a few brief and pungent squibs, such as the newspapers were then in the habit of bestowing on our socialist enterprise. There was one paragraph which, if I rightly guessed its purport, bore reference to Zenobia, but was too darkly hinted to convey even thus much of certainty. Hollingsworth, too, with his philanthropic project, afforded the penny-a-liners*a theme for some savage and bloody-minded jokes; and, considerably to my surprise, they affected me with as much indignation as if we had still been friends.

Thus passed several weeks; time long enough for my brown and toil-hardened hands to re-accustom themselves to gloves. Old habits, such as were merely external, returned upon me with wonderful promptitude. My superficial talk, too, assumed altogether a worldly tone. Meeting former acquaintances, who showed themselves inclined to ridicule my heroic devotion to the cause of human welfare, I spoke of the recent phase of my life as indeed fair matter for a jest. But I also gave them to understand that it was, at most, only an experiment, on which I had staked no valuable amount of hope or fear; it had enabled me to pass the summer in a novel and agreeable way, had afforded me some grotesque specimens of artificial simplicity, and could not, therefore, so far as I was concerned, be reckoned a failure. In no one instance, however, did I voluntarily speak of my three friends. They dwelt in a profounder region. The more I consider myself, as I then was, the more do I recognize how deeply my connection with those three had affected all my being.

As it was already the epoch of annihilated space, I might, in the time I was away from Blithedale, have snatched a glimpse at England, and been back again. But my wanderings were confined within a very limited sphere. I hopped and fluttered, like a bird with a string about its leg, gyrating round a small circumference, and keeping up a restless activity to no purpose. Thus, it was still in our familiar Massachusetts—

in one of its white country-villages—that I must next particu-
larize an incident.

The scene was one of those Lyceum-halls,* of which almost
every village has now its own, dedicated to that sober and
pallid, or, rather, drab-colored, mode of winter-evening entertainment, the Lecture. Of late years, this has come strangely
into vogue, when the natural tendency of things would seem
to be, to substitute lettered for oral methods of addressing
the public. But, in halls like this, besides the winter course
of lectures, there is a rich and varied series of other exhibitions.
Hither comes the ventriloquist, with all his mysterious tongues;
the thaumaturgist,* too, with his miraculous transformations of
plates, doves, and rings, his pancakes smoking in your hat,
and his cellar of choice liquors, represented in one small bottle.
Here, also, the itinerant professor instructs separate classes
of ladies and gentlemen in physiology, and demonstrates his
lessons by the aid of real skeletons, and mannikins in wax,
from Paris. Here is to be heard the choir of Ethiopian melo-
dists, and to be seen, the diorama of Moscow or Bunker Hill,
or the moving panorama of the Chinese wall. Here is displayed the museum of wax figures, illustrating the wide
catholicism of earthly renown by mixing up heroes and
statesmen, the Pope and the Mormon Prophet,* kings, queens,
murderers, and beautiful ladies; every sort of person, in short,
except authors, of whom I never beheld even the most
famous, done in wax. And here, in this many-purposed hall,
(unless the selectmen of the village chance to have more
than their share of the puritanism, which, however diversified
with later patchwork, still gives its prevailing tint to New
England character,) here the company of strolling players
sets up its little stage, and claims patronage for the legitimate
drama.

But, on the autumnal evening which I speak of, a number
of printed handbills—stuck up in the bar-room and on the
sign-post of the hotel, and on the meeting-house porch, and

distributed largely through the village—had promised the inhabitants an interview with that celebrated and hitherto inexplicable phenomenon, the Veiled Lady!

The hall was fitted up with an amphitheatrical descent of seats towards a platform, on which stood a desk, two lights, a stool, and a capacious, antique chair. The audience was of a generally decent and respectable character; old farmers, in their Sunday black coats, with shrewd, hard, sun-dried faces, and a cynical humor, oftener than any other expression, in their eyes; pretty girls, in many-colored attire; pretty young men—the schoolmaster, the lawyer, or student-at-law, the shopkeeper—all looking rather suburban than rural. In these days, there is absolutely no rusticity, except when the actual labor of the soil leaves its earth-mould on the person. There was likewise a considerable proportion of young and middle-aged women, many of them stern in feature, with marked foreheads, and a very definite line of eyebrow; a type of womanhood in which a bold intellectual development seems to be keeping pace with the progressive delicacy of the physical constitution. Of all these people I took note, at first, according to my custom. But I ceased to do so, the moment that my eyes fell on an individual who sat two or three seats below me, immoveable, apparently deep in thought, with his back, of course, towards me, and his face turned stead-fastly upon the platform.

After sitting awhile, in contemplation of this person's familiar contour, I was irresistibly moved to step over the intervening benches, lay my hand on his shoulder, put my mouth close to his ear, and address him in a sepulchral, melo-dramatic whisper:—

"Hollingsworth! Where have you left Zenobia!"

His nerves, however, were proof against my attack. He turned half around, and looked me in the face, with great, sad eyes, in which there was neither kindness nor resentment, nor any perceptible surprise.

"Zenobia, when I last saw her," he answered, "was at Blithedale."

He said no more. But there was a great deal of talk going on, near me, among a knot of people who might be considered as representing the mysticism, or, rather, the mystic sensuality, of this singular age. The nature of the exhibition, that was about to take place, had probably given the turn to their conversation.

I heard, from a pale man in blue spectacles, some stranger stories than ever were written in a romance; told, too, with a simple, unimaginative steadfastness, which was terribly efficacious in compelling the auditor to receive them into the category of established facts. He cited instances of the miraculous power of one human being over the will and passions of another; insomuch that settled grief was but a shadow, beneath the influence of a man possessing this potency, and the strong love of years melted away like a vapor. At the bidding of one of these wizards, the maiden, with her lover's kiss still burning on her lips, would turn from him with icy indifference; the newly made widow would dig up her buried heart out of her young husband's grave, before the sods had taken root upon it; a mother, with her babe's milk in her bosom, would thrust away her child. Human character was but soft wax in his hands; and guilt, or virtue, only the forms into which he should see fit to mould it. The religious sentiment was a flame which he could blow up with his breath, or a spark that he could utterly extinguish. It is unutterable, the horror and disgust with which I listened, and saw, that, if these things were to be believed, the individual soul was virtually annihilated, and all that is sweet and pure, in our present life, debased, and that the idea of man's eternal responsibility was made ridiculous, and immortality rendered, at once, impossible, and not worth acceptance. But I would have perished on the spot, sooner than believe it.

The epoch of rapping spirits,* and all the wonders that

have followed in their train—such as tables, upset by invisible agencies, bells, self-tolled at funerals, and ghostly music, performed on jewsharps—had not yet arrived. Alas, my countrymen, methinks we have fallen on an evil age! If these phenomena have not humbug at the bottom, so much the worse for us. What can they indicate, in a spiritual way, except that the soul of man is descending to a lower point than it has ever before reached, while incarnate? We are pursuing a downward course, in the eternal march, and thus bring ourselves into the same range with beings whom death, in requital of their gross and evil lives, has degraded below humanity. To hold intercourse with spirits of this order, we must stoop, and grovel in some element more vile than earthly dust. These goblins, if they exist at all, are but the shadows of past mortality, outcasts, mere refuse-stuff, adjudged unworthy of the eternal world, and, on the most favorable supposition, dwindling gradually into nothingness. The less we have to say to them, the better; lest we share their fate!

The audience now began to be impatient; they signified their desire for the entertainment to commence, by thump of sticks and stamp of boot-heels. Nor was it a great while longer, before, in response to their call, there appeared a bearded personage in Oriental robes, looking like one of the enchanters of the Arabian Nights. He came upon the platform from a side-door—saluted the spectators, not with a salaam, but a bow—took his station at the desk—and first blowing his nose with a white handkerchief, prepared to speak. The environment of the homely village-hall, and the absence of many ingenious contrivances of stage-effect, with which the exhibition had heretofore been set off, seemed to bring the artifice of this character more openly upon the surface. No sooner did I behold the bearded enchanter, than laying my hand again on Hollingsworth's shoulder, I whispered in his ear:—

"Do you know him?"

"I never saw the man before," he muttered, without turning his head.

But I had seen him, three times, already. Once, on occasion of my first visit to the Veiled Lady; a second time, in the wood-path at Blithedale; and, lastly, in Zenobia's drawing-room. It was Westervelt. A quick association of ideas made me shudder, from head to foot; and, again, like an evil spirit, bringing up reminiscences of a man's sins, I whispered a question in Hollingsworth's ear.

"What have you done with Priscilla?"

He gave a convulsive start, as if I had thrust a knife into him, writhed himself round on his seat, glared fiercely into my eyes, but answered not a word.

The Professor began his discourse, explanatory of the psychological phenomena, as he termed them, which it was his purpose to exhibit to the spectators. There remains no very distinct impression of it on my memory. It was eloquent, ingenious, plausible, with a delusive show of spirituality, yet really imbued throughout with a cold and dead materialism. I shivered, as at a current of chill air, issuing out of a sepulchral vault and bringing the smell of corruption along with it. He spoke of a new era that was dawning upon the world; an era that would link soul to soul, and the present life to what we call futurity, with a closeness that should finally convert both worlds into one great, mutually conscious brotherhood. He described (in a strange, philosophical guise, with terms of art, as if it were a matter of chemical discovery) the agency by which this mighty result was to be effected; nor would it have surprised me, had he pretended to hold up a portion of his universally pervasive fluid, as he affirmed it to be, in a glass phial.

At the close of his exordium, the Professor beckoned with his hand—one, twice, thrice—and a figure came gliding upon the platform, enveloped in a long veil of silvery whiteness. It fell about her, like the texture of a summer cloud, with a kind of vagueness, so that the outline of the form, beneath it, could not be accurately discerned. But the movement of the Veiled Lady was graceful, free, and unembarrassed, like that of a person accustomed to be the spectacle of thousands. Or, possibly, a blindfold prisoner within the sphere with which this dark, earthly magician had surrounded her, she was wholly unconscious of being the central object to all those straining eyes.

Pliant to his gesture, (which had even an obsequious courtesy, but, at the same time, a remarkable decisiveness,) the figure placed itself in the great chair. Sitting there, in such visible obscurity, it was perhaps as much like the actual presence of a disembodied spirit as anything that stage-trickery could devise. The hushed breathing of the spectators proved how high-wrought were their anticipations of the wonders to be performed, through the medium of this incomprehensible creature. I, too, was in breathless suspense, but with a far different presentiment of some strange event at hand.

"You see before you the Veiled Lady," said the bearded Professor, advancing to the verge of the platform. "By the agency of which I have just spoken, she is, at this moment, in communion with the spiritual world. That silvery veil is, in one sense, an enchantment, having been dipt, as it were, and essentially imbued, through the potency of my art, with the fluid medium of spirits. Slight and ethereal as it seems, the limitations of time and space have no existence within its folds. This hall—these hundreds of faces, encompassing her within so narrow an amphitheatre—are of thinner substance, in her view, than the airiest vapor that the clouds are made of. She beholds the Absolute!"

As preliminary to other, and far more wonderful psychological experiments, the exhibitor suggested that some of his auditors should endeavor to make the Veiled Lady sensible of their presence by such methods—provided, only, no touch

were laid upon her person—as they might deem best adapted
to that end. Accordingly, several deep-lunged country-fellows,
who looked as if they might have blown the apparition away
with a breath, ascended the platform. Mutually encouraging
one another, they shouted so close to her ear, that the veil
stirred like a wreath of vanishing mist; they smote upon the
floor with bludgeons; they perpetrated so hideous a clamor,
that methought it might have reached, at least a little way,
into the eternal sphere. Finally, with the assent of the Professor, they laid hold of the great chair, and were startled,
apparently, to find it soar upward, as if lighter than the air
through which it rose. But the Veiled Lady remained seated
and motionless, with a composure that was hardly less than
awful, because implying so immeasurable a distance betwixt
her and these rude persecutors.

"These efforts are wholly without avail," observed the Professor, who had been looking on with an aspect of serene
indifference. "The roar of a battery of cannon would be
inaudible to the Veiled Lady. And yet, were I to will it,
sitting in this very hall, she could hear the desert-wind sweeping over the sands, as far off as Arabia; the ice-bergs grinding
one against the other, in the polar seas; the rustle of a leaf
in an East Indian forest; the lowest whispered breath of the
bashfullest maiden in the world, uttering the first confession
of her love! Nor does there exist the moral inducement, apart
from my own behest, that could persuade her to lift the
silvery veil, or arise out of that chair!"

Greatly to the Professor's discomposure, however, just as
he spoke these words, the Veiled Lady arose. There was a
mysterious tremor that shook the magic veil. The spectators,
it may be, imagined that she was about to take flight into that
invisible sphere, and to the society of those purely spiritual
beings, with whom they reckoned her so near akin. Hollingsworth, a moment ago, had mounted the platform, and now
stood gazing at the figure, with a sad intentness that brought

the whole power of his great, stern, yet tender soul, into his glance.

"Come!" said he, waving his hand towards her. "You are safe!"

She threw off the veil, and stood before that multitude of people, pale, tremulous, shrinking, as if only then had she discovered that a thousand eyes were gazing at her. Poor maiden! How strangely had she been betrayed! Blazoned abroad as a wonder of the world, and performing what were adjudged as miracles—in the faith of many, a seeress and a prophetess—in the harsher judgment of others, a mountebank —she had kept, as I religiously believe, her virgin reserve and sanctity of soul, throughout it all. Within that encircling veil, though an evil hand had flung it over her, there was as deep a seclusion as if this forsaken girl had, all the while, been sitting under the shadow of Eliot's pulpit, in the Blithedale woods, at the feet of him who now summoned her to the shelter of his arms. And the true heart-throb of a woman's affection was too powerful for the jugglery that had hitherto environed her. She uttered a shriek and fled to Hollingsworth, like one escaping from her deadliest enemy, and was safe forever!

XXIV

THE MASQUERADERS

TWO NIGHTS had passed since the foregoing occurrences, when, in a breezy September forenoon, I set forth from town, on foot, towards Blithedale.

It was the most delightful of all days for a walk, with a dash of invigorating ice-temper in the air, but a coolness that soon gave place to the brisk glow of exercise, while the vigor remained as elastic as before. The atmosphere had a spirit and sparkle in it., Each breath was like a sip of ethereal wine, tempered, as I said, with a crystal lump of ice. I had started on this expedition in an exceedingly sombre mood, as well befitted one who found himself tending towards home, but was conscious that nobody would be quite overjoyed to greet him there. My feet were hardly off the pavement, however, when this morbid sensation began to yield to the lively influences of air and motion. Nor had I gone far, with fields yet green on either side, before my step became as swift and light as if Hollingsworth were waiting to exchange a friendly hand-grip, and Zenobia's and Priscilla's open arms would welcome the wanderer's re-appearance. It has happened to me, on other occasions, as well as this, to prove how a state of physical well-being can create a kind of joy, in spite of the profoundest anxiety of mind.

The pathway of that walk still runs along, with sunny freshness, through my memory. I know not why it should be so. But my mental eye can even now discern the September grass, bordering the pleasant roadside with a brighter verdure than while the summer-heats were scorching it; the trees, too, mostly green, although, here and there, a branch or shrub has donned its vesture of crimson and gold, a week or two before its fellows. I see the tufted barberry bushes,* with their small clusters of scarlet fruit; the toadstools, likewise, some spotlessly white, others yellow or red—mysterious growths, springing suddenly from no root or seed, and growing nobody can tell how or wherefore. In this respect, they resembled many of the emotions in my breast. And I still see the little rivulets, chill, clear, and bright, that murmured beneath the road, through subterranean rocks, and deepened into mossy pools where tiny fish were darting to-and-fro, and within which lurked the hermit-frog. But, no—I never can account for it—that, with a yearning interest to learn the upshot of all my story, and returning to Blithedale for that sole purpose, I should examine these things so like a peaceful-bosomed naturalist. Nor why, amid all my sympathies and fears, there shot, at times, a wild exhilaration through my frame!

Thus I pursued my way, along the line of the ancient stone-wall that Paul Dudley*built, and through white villages, and past orchards of ruddy apples, and fields of ripening maize, and patches of woodland, and all such sweet rural scenery as looks the fairest, a little beyond the suburbs of a town. Hollingsworth, Zenobia, Priscilla! They glided mistily before me, as I walked. Sometimes, in my solitude, I laughed with the bitterness of self-scorn, remembering how unreservedly I had given up my heart and soul to interests that were not mine. What had I ever had to do with them? And why, being now free, should I take this thraldom on me, once again? It was both sad and dangerous, I whispered to myself, to be in too close affinity with the passions, the errors, and the misfortunes, of individuals who stood within a circle of their own, into which, if I stept at all, it must be as an intruder, and at a peril that I could not estimate.

Drawing nearer to Blithedale, a sickness of the spirits kept alternating with my flights of causeless buoyancy. I indulged in a hundred odd and extravagant conjectures. Either there was no such place as Blithedale, nor ever had been, nor any brotherhood of thoughtful laborers, like what I seemed to recollect there; or else it was all changed, during my absence. It had been nothing but dream-work and enchantment. I should seek in vain for the old farm-house, and for the greensward, the potatoe-fields, the root-crops, and acres of Indian corn, and for all that configuration of the land which I had imagined. It would be another spot, and an utter strangeness.

These vagaries were of the spectral throng, so apt to steal out of an unquiet heart. They partly ceased to haunt me, on my arriving at a point whence, through the trees, I began to catch glimpses of the Blithedale farm. That, surely, was something real. There was hardly a square foot of all those acres, on which I had not trodden heavily in one or another kind of toil. The curse of Adam's posterity—and, curse or blessing be it, it gives substance to the life around us—had first come upon me there. In the sweat of my brow, I had there earned bread and eaten it, and so established my claim to be on earth, and my fellowship with all the sons of labor. I could have knelt down, and have laid my breast against that soil. The red clay, of which my frame was moulded, seemed nearer akin to those crumbling furrows than to any other portion of the world's dust. There was my home; and there might be my grave.

I felt an invincible reluctance, nevertheless, at the idea of presenting myself before my old associates, without first ascertaining the state in which they were. A nameless foreboding weighed upon me. Perhaps, should I know all the circumstances that had occurred, I might find it my wisest course to turn back, unrecognized, unseen, and never look at Blithedale more. Had it been evening, I would have stolen softly to some lighted window of the old farm-house, and peeped darkling in, to see all their well-known faces round the supper-board. Then, were there a vacant seat, I might noiselessly unclose the door, glide in, and take my place among them, without a word. My entrance might be so quiet, my aspect so familiar, that they would forget how long I had been away, and suffer me to melt into the scene, as a wreath of vapor melts into a larger cloud. I dreaded a boisterous greeting. Beholding me at table, Zenobia, as a matter of course, would send me a cup of tea, and Hollingsworth fill my plate from the great dish of pan-dowdy, and Priscilla, in her quiet way, would hand the cream, and others help me to the bread and butter. Being one of them again, the knowledge of what had happened would come to me, without a shock. For, still, at every turn of my shifting fantasies, the thought stared me in the face, that some evil thing had befallen us, or was ready to befall.

Yielding to this ominous impression, I now turned aside into the woods, resolving to spy out the posture of the Community, as craftily as the wild Indian before he makes his onset. I would go wandering about the outskirts of the farm, and, perhaps catching sight of a solitary acquaintance, would approach him amid the brown shadows of the trees, (a kind of medium fit for spirits departed and revisitant, like myself,) and entreat him to tell me how all things were.

The first living creature that I met, was a partridge, which sprung up beneath my feet, and whirred away; the next was a squirrel, who chattered angrily at me, from an overhanging bough. I trod along by the dark, sluggish river, and remember pausing on the bank, above one of its blackest and most placid pools—(the very spot, with the barkless stump of a tree aslantwise over the water, is depicting itself to my fancy, at this instant)—and wondering how deep it was, and if any over-laden soul had ever flung its weight of mortality in thither, and if it thus escaped the burthen, or only made it heavier. And perhaps the skeleton of the drowned wretch still lay beneath the inscrutable depth, clinging to some sunken log at the bottom with the gripe of its old despair. So slight, however, was the track of these gloomy ideas, that I soon forgot them in the contemplation of a brood of wild ducks, which were floating on the river, and anon took flight, leaving each a bright streak over the black surface. By-and-by, I came to my hermitage, in the heart of the white-pine tree, and clambering up into it, sat down to rest. The grapes, which I had watched throughout the summer, now dangled around me in abundant clusters of the deepest purple, deliciously sweet to the taste, and though wild, yet free from that un-gentle flavor which distinguishes nearly all our native and uncultivated grapes. Methought a wine might be pressed out of them, possessing a passionate zest, and endowed with a new kind of intoxicating quality, attended with such bac-chanalian ecstasies as the tamer grapes of Madeira, France, and the Rhine, are inadequate to produce. And I longed to quaff a great goblet of it, at that moment!

While devouring the grapes, I looked on all sides out of the peep-holes of my hermitage, and saw the farm-house, the fields, and almost every part of our domain, but not a single human figure in the landscape. Some of the windows of the house were open, but with no more signs of life than in a dead man's unshut eyes. The barn-door was ajar, and swing-ing in the breeze. The big, old dog—he was a relic of the former dynasty of the farm—that hardly ever stirred out of the yard, was nowhere to be seen. What, then, had become of all the fraternity and sisterhood? Curious to ascertain this point, I let myself down out of the tree, and going to the edge of the wood, was glad to perceive our herd of cows, chewing the cud, or grazing, not far off. I fancied, by their manner, that two or three of them recognized me, (as, indeed, they ought, for I had milked them, and been their chamberlain, times without number;) but, after staring me in the face, a little while, they phlegmatically began grazing and chewing their cuds again. Then I grew foolishly angry at so cold a reception, and flung some rotten fragments of an old stump at these unsentimental cows.

Skirting farther round the pasture, I heard voices and much laughter proceeding from the interior of the wood. Voices, male and feminine; laughter, not only of fresh young throats, but the bass of grown people, as if solemn organ-pipes should pour out airs of merriment. Not a voice spoke, but I knew it better than my own; not a laugh, but its cadences were familiar. The wood, in this portion of it, seemed as full of jollity as if Comus*and his crew were holding their revels, in one of its usually lonesome glades. Stealing onward as far as I durst, without hazard of discovery, I saw a concourse of strange figures* beneath the overshadowing branches; they appeared, and vanished, and came again, confusedly, with the streaks of sunlight glimmering down upon them.

Among them was an Indian chief, with blanket, feathers and war-paint, and uplifted tomahawk; and near him, looking fit to be his woodland-bride, the goddess Diana, with the crescent on her head, and attended by our big, lazy dog, in lack of any fleeter hound. Drawing an arrow from her quiver, she let it fly, at a venture, and hit the very tree behind which I happened to be lurking. Another group consisted of a Bavarian broom-girl,* a negro of the Jim Crow*order, one or two foresters of the middle-ages, a Kentucky woodsman in his trimmed hunting-shirt and deerskin leggings, and a Shaker* elder, quaint, demure, broad-brimmed, and square-skirted. Shepherds of Arcadia, and allegoric figures from the Faerie Queen,* were oddly mixed up with these. Arm in arm, or otherwise huddled together, in strange discrepancy, stood grim Puritans, gay Cavaliers, and Revolutionary officers, with three-cornered cocked-hats, and queues longer than their swords. A bright-complexioned, dark-haired, vivacious little gipsy, with a red shawl over her head, went from one group to another, telling fortunes by palmistry; and Moll Pitcher,* the renowned old witch of Lynn, broomstick in hand, showed herself prominently in the midst, as if announcing all these apparitions to be the offspring of her necromantic art. But Silas Foster, who leaned against a tree near by, in his customary blue frock, and smoking a short pipe, did more to disenchant the scene, with his look of shrewd, acrid, Yankee observation, than twenty witches and necromancers could have done, in the way of rendering it weird and fantastic.

A little further off, some old-fashioned skinkers and drawers,* all with portentously red noses, were spreading a banquet on the leaf-strewn earth; while a horned and long-tailed gentleman (in whom I recognized the fiendish musician, erst seen by Tam O'Shanter)* tuned his fiddle, and summoned the whole motley rout to a dance, before partaking of the festal cheer. So they joined hands in a circle, whirling round so swiftly, so madly, and so merrily, in time and tune with the Satanic music, that their separate incongruities were blended all together; and they became a kind of entanglement that went nigh to turn one's brain, with merely looking at it. Anon, they stopt, all of a sudden, and staring at one another's figures, set up a roar of laughter; whereat, a shower of the September leaves (which, all day long, had been hesitating whether to fall or no) were shaken off by the movement of the air, and came eddying down upon the revellers.

Then, for lack of breath, ensued a silence; at the deepest point of which, tickled by the oddity of surprising my grave associates in this masquerading trim, I could not possibly refrain from a burst of laughter, on my own separate account.

"Hush!" I heard the pretty gipsy fortuneteller say. "Who is that laughing?"

"Some profane intruder!" said the goddess Diana. "I shall send an arrow through his heart, or change him into a stag, as I did Actaeon,* if he peeps from behind the trees!"

"Me take his scalp!" cried the Indian chief, brandishing his tomahawk, and cutting a great caper in the air.

"I'll root him in the earth, with a spell that I have at my tongue's end!" squeaked Moll Pitcher. "And the green moss shall grow all over him, before he gets free again!"

"The voice was Miles Coverdale's," said the fiendish fiddler, with a whisk of his tail and a toss of his horns. "My music has brought him hither. He is always ready to dance to the devil's tune!"

Thus put on the right track, they all recognized the voice at once, and set up a simultaneous shout.

"Miles! Miles! Miles Coverdale, where are you?" they cried. "Zenobia! Queen Zenobia! Here is one of your vassals lurking in the wood. Command him to approach, and pay his duty!"

The whole fantastic rabble forthwith streamed off in pursuit of me, so that I was like a mad poet hunted by chimaeras. Having fairly the start of them, however, I succeeded in making my escape, and soon left their merriment and riot at a good distance in the rear. Its fainter tones assumed a kind of mournfulness, and were finally lost in the hush and solemnity of the wood. In my haste, I stumbled over a heap of logs and sticks that had been cut for firewood, a great while ago, by some former possessor of the soil, and piled up square, in order to be carted or sledded away to the farm-house. But, being forgotten, they had lain there, perhaps fifty years, and possibly much longer; until, by the accumulation of moss, and the leaves falling over them and decaying there, from autumn to autumn, a green mound was formed, in which the softened outline of the wood-pile was still perceptible. In the fitful mood that then swayed my mind, I found something strangely affecting in this simple circumstance. I imagined the long-dead woodman, and his long-dead wife and children, coming out of their chill graves, and essaying to make a fire with this heap of mossy fuel!

From this spot I strayed onward, quite lost in reverie, and neither knew nor cared whither I was going, until a low, soft, well-remembered voice spoke, at a little distance.

"There is Mr. Coverdale!"

"Miles Coverdale!" said another voice—and its tones were very stern—"Let him come forward, then!"

"Yes, Mr. Coverdale," cried a woman's voice—clear and melodious, but, just then, with something unnatural in its chord—"You are welcome! But you come half-an-hour too late, and have missed a scene which you would have enjoyed!"

I looked up, and found myself nigh Eliot's pulpit, at the base of which sat Hollingsworth, with Priscilla at his feet, and Zenobia standing before them.

XXV

THE THREE TOGETHER

HOLLINGSWORTH was in his ordinary working-dress. Priscilla wore a pretty and simple gown, with a kerchief about her neck, and a calash,* which she had flung back from her head, leaving it suspended by the strings. But Zenobia (whose part among the masquers, as may be supposed, was no inferior one) appeared in a costume of fanciful magnificence, with her jewelled flower as the central ornament of what resembled a leafy crown, or coronet. She represented the Oriental princess, by whose name we were accustomed to know her. Her attitude was free and noble, yet, if a queen's, it was not that of a queen triumphant, but dethroned, on trial for her life, or perchance condemned, already. The spirit of the conflict seemed, nevertheless, to be alive in her. Her eyes were on fire; her cheeks had each a crimson spot, so exceedingly vivid, and marked with so definite an outline, that I at first doubted whether it were not artificial. In a very brief space, however, this idea was shamed by the paleness that ensued, as the blood sank suddenly away. Zenobia now looked like marble.

One always feels the fact, in an instant, when he has intruded on those who love, or those who hate, at some acme of their passion that puts them into a sphere of their own, where no other spirit can pretend to stand on equal ground with them. I was confused—affected even with a species of terror—and wished myself away. The intentness of their feelings gave them the exclusive property of the soil and atmosphere, and left me no right to be or breathe there.

"'Hollingsworth—Zenobia—I have just returned to Blithe-dale," said I, "and had no thought of finding you here. We shall meet again at the house. I will retire."

"This place is free to you," answered Hollingsworth.

"As free as to ourselves," added Zenobia. "This long while past, you have been following up your game, groping for human emotions in the dark corners of the heart. Had you been here a little sooner, you might have seen them dragged into the daylight. I could even wish to have my trial over again, with you standing by, to see fair-play! Do you know, Mr. Coverdale, I have been on trial for my life?"

She laughed, while speaking thus. But, in truth, as my eyes wandered from one of the group to another, I saw in Hollingsworth all that an artist could desire for the grim portrait of a Puritan magistrate, holding inquest of life and death in a case of witchcraft;—in Zenobia, the sorceress herself, not aged, wrinkled, and decrepit, but fair enough to tempt Satan with a force reciprocal to his own;—and, in Priscilla, the pale victim, whose soul and body had been wasted by her spells. Had a pile of faggots been heaped against the rock, this hint of impending doom would have completed the suggestive picture.

"It was too hard upon me," continued Zenobia, addressing Hollingsworth, "that judge, jury, and accuser, should all be comprehended in one man! I demur, as I think the lawyers say, to the jurisdiction. But let the learned Judge Coverdale seat himself on the top of the rock, and you and me stand at its base, side by side, pleading our cause before him! There might, at least, be two criminals, instead of one."

"You forced this on me," replied Hollingsworth, looking her sternly in the face. "Did I call you hither from among the masqueraders yonder? Do I assume to be your judge? No; except so far as I have an unquestionable right of judgment, in order to settle my own line of behavior towards those, with whom the events of life bring me in contact. True; I have already judged you, but not on the world's part—neither do I pretend to pass a sentence!"

"Ah, this is very good!" said Zenobia, with a smile. "What strange beings you men are, Mr. Coverdale!—is it not so? It is the simplest thing in the world, with you, to bring a woman before your secret tribunals, and judge and condemn her, unheard, and then tell her to go free without a sentence. The misfortune is, that this same secret tribunal chances to be the only judgment-seat that a true woman stands in awe of, and that any verdict short of acquittal is equivalent to a death-sentence!"

The more I looked at them, and the more I heard, the stronger grew my impression that a crisis had just come and gone. On Hollingsworth's brow, it had left a stamp like that of irrevocable doom, of which his own will was the instrument. In Zenobia's whole person, beholding her more closely, I saw a riotous agitation; the almost delirious disquietude of a great struggle, at the close of which, the vanquished one felt her strength and courage still mighty within her, and longed to renew the contest. My sensations were as if I had come upon a battle-field, before the smoke was as yet cleared away.

And what subjects had been discussed here? All, no doubt, that, for so many months past, had kept my heart and my imagination idly feverish. Zenobia's whole character and history; the true nature of her mysterious connection with Westervelt; her later purposes towards Hollingsworth, and, reciprocally, his in reference to her; and, finally, the degree in which Zenobia had been cognizant of the plot against Priscilla, and what, at last, had been the real object of that scheme. On these points, as before, I was left to my own conjectures. One thing, only, was certain. Zenobia and Hollingsworth were friends no longer. If their heart-strings were ever intertwined, the knot had been adjudged an entanglement, and was now violently broken.

But Zenobia seemed unable to rest content with the matter, in the posture which it had assumed.

"Ah! Do we part so?" exclaimed she, seeing Hollingsworth about to retire.

"And why not?" said he, with almost rude abruptness. "What is there further to be said between us?"

"Well; perhaps nothing!" answered Zenobia, looking him in the face, and smiling. "But we have come, many times before, to this gray rock, and we have talked very softly, among the whisperings of the birch-trees. They were pleasant hours! I love to make the latest of them, though not altogether so delightful, loiter away as slowly as may be. And, besides, you have put many queries to me, at this, which you design to be our last interview; and being driven, as I must acknowledge, into a corner, I have responded with reasonable frankness. But, now, with your free consent, I desire the privilege of asking a few questions in my turn."

"I have no concealments," said Hollingsworth.

"We shall see!" answered Zenobia. "I would first inquire, whether you have supposed me to be wealthy?"

"On that point," observed Hollingsworth, "I have had the opinion which the world holds."

"And I held it, likewise," said Zenobia. "Had I not, Heaven is my witness, the knowledge should have been as free to you as me. It is only three days since I knew the strange fact that threatens to make me poor; and your own acquaintance with it, I suspect, is of at least as old a date. I fancied myself affluent. You are aware, too, of the disposition which I purposed making of the larger portion of my imaginary opulence;—nay, were it all, I had not hesitated. Let me ask you further, did

I ever propose or intimate any terms of compact, on which depended this—as the world would consider it—so important sacrifice?"

"You certainly spoke of none," said Hollingsworth.

"Nor meant any," she responded. "I was willing to realize your dream, freely—generously, as some might think—but, at all events, fully—and heedless though it should prove the ruin of my fortune. If, in your own thoughts, you have imposed any conditions of this expenditure, it is you that must be held responsible for whatever is sordid and unworthy in them. And, now, one other question! Do you love this girl?"

"Oh, Zenobia!" exclaimed Priscilla, shrinking back, as if longing for the rock to topple over, and hide her.

"Do you love her?" repeated Zenobia.

"Had you asked me that question, a short time since," replied Hollingsworth, after a pause, during which, it seemed to me, even the birch-trees held their whispering breath, "I should have told you—'No!' My feelings for Priscilla differed little from those of an elder brother, watching tenderly over the gentle sister whom God has given him to protect."

"And what is your answer, now?" persisted Zenobia.

"I do love her!" said Hollingsworth, uttering the words with a deep, inward breath, instead of speaking them outright. "As well declare it thus, as in any other way. I do love her!"

"Now, God be judge between us," cried Zenobia, breaking into sudden passion, "which of us two has most mortally offended Him! At least, I am a woman—with every fault, it may be, that a woman ever had, weak, vain, unprincipled, (like most of my sex; for our virtues, when we have any, are merely impulsive and intuitive,) passionate, too, and pursuing my foolish and unattainable ends, by indirect and cunning, though absurdly chosen means, as an hereditary bond-slave must—false, moreover, to the whole circle of good, in my reckless truth to the little good I saw before me—but still a woman! A creature, whom only a little change of earthly fortune, a little kinder smile of Him who sent me hither, and one true heart to encourage and direct me, might have made all that a woman can be! But how is it with you? Are you a man? No; but a monster! A cold, heartless, self-beginning and self-ending piece of mechanism!"

"With what, then, do you charge me?" asked Hollingsworth, aghast, and greatly disturbed at this attack. "Show me one selfish end in all I ever aimed at, and you may cut it out of my bosom with a knife!"

"It is all self!" answered Zenobia, with still intenser bitterness. "Nothing else; nothing but self, self, self! The fiend, I doubt not, has made his choicest mirth of you, these seven years past, and especially in the mad summer which we have spent together. I see it now! I am awake, disenchanted, disenthralled! Self, self, self! You have embodied yourself in a project. You are a better masquerader than the witches and gipsies yonder; for your disguise is a self-deception. See whither it has brought you! First, you aimed a death-blow, and a treacherous one, at this scheme of a purer and higher life, which so many noble spirits had wrought out. Then, because Coverdale could not be quite your slave, you threw him ruthlessly away. And you took me, too, into your plan, as long as there was hope of my being available, and now fling me aside again, a broken tool! But, foremost, and blackest of your sins, you stifled down your inmost consciousness!— you did a deadly wrong to your own heart!—you were ready to sacrifice this girl, whom, if God ever visibly showed a purpose, He put into your charge, and through whom He was striving to redeem you!"

"This is a woman's view," said Hollingsworth, growing deadly pale—"a woman's, whose whole sphere of action is in the heart, and who can conceive of no higher nor wider one!"

"Be silent!" cried Zenobia, imperiously. "You know neither man nor woman! The utmost that can be said in your behalf—and because I would not be wholly despicable in my own eyes, but would fain excuse my wasted feelings, nor own it wholly a delusion, therefore I say it—is, that a great and rich heart has been ruined in your breast. Leave me, now! You have done with me, and I with you. Farewell!"

"Priscilla," said Hollingsworth, "come!"

Zenobia smiled; possibly, I did so too. Not often, in human life, has a gnawing sense of injury found a sweeter morsel of revenge, than was conveyed in the tone with which Hollingsworth spoke those two words. It was the abased and tremulous tone of a man, whose faith in himself was shaken, and who sought, at last, to lean on an affection. Yes; the strong man bowed himself, and rested on this poor Priscilla. Oh, could she have failed him, what a triumph for the lookers-on!

And, at first, I half imagined that she was about to fail him. She rose up, stood shivering, like the birch-leaves that trembled over her head, and then slowly tottered, rather than walked, towards Zenobia. Arriving at her feet, she sank down there, in the very same attitude which she had assumed on their first meeting, in the kitchen of the old farm-house. Zenobia remembered it.

"Ah, Priscilla," said she, shaking her head, "how much is changed since then! You kneel to a dethroned princess. You, the victorious one! But he is waiting for you. Say what you wish, and leave me."

"We are sisters!" gasped Priscilla.

I fancied that I understood the word and action; it meant the offering of herself, and all she had, to be at Zenobia's disposal. But the latter would not take it thus.

"True; we are sisters!" she replied; and, moved by the sweet word, she stooped down and kissed Priscilla—but not lovingly;

for a sense of fatal harm, received through her, seemed to be lurking in Zenobia's heart—"We had one father! You knew it from the first; I, but a little while—else some things, that have chanced, might have been spared you. But I never wished you harm. You stood between me and an end which I desired. I wanted a clear path. No matter what I meant. It is over now. Do you forgive me?"

"Oh, Zenobia," sobbed Priscilla, "it is I that feel like the guilty one!"

"No, no, poor little thing!" said Zenobia, with a sort of contempt. "You have been my evil fate; but there never was a babe with less strength or will to do an injury. Poor child! Methinks you have but a melancholy lot before you, sitting all alone in that wide, cheerless heart, where, for aught you know—and as I, alas! believe—the fire which you have kindled may soon go out. Ah, the thought makes me shiver for you! What will you do, Priscilla, when you find no spark among the ashes?"

"Die!" she answered.

"That was well said!" responded Zenobia, with an approving smile. "There is all a woman in your little compass, my poor sister. Meanwhile, go with him, and live!"

She waved her away, with a queenly gesture, and turned her own face to the rock. I watched Priscilla, wondering what judgment she would pass, between Zenobia and Hollingsworth; how interpret his behavior, so as to reconcile it with true faith both towards her sister and herself; how compel her love for him to keep any terms whatever with her sisterly affection! But, in truth, there was no such difficulty as I imagined. Her engrossing love made it all clear. Hollingsworth could have no fault. That was the one principle at the centre of the universe. And the doubtful guilt or possible integrity of other people, appearances, self-evident facts, the testimony of her own senses—even Hollingsworth's self-accusation, had he volunteered it—would have weighed not the value of a mote of thistle-down, on the other side. So secure was she of his right, that she never thought of comparing it with another's wrong, but left the latter to itself.

Hollingsworth drew her arm within his, and soon disappeared with her among the trees. I cannot imagine how Zenobia knew when they were out of sight; she never glanced again towards them. But, retaining a proud attitude, so long as they might have thrown back a retiring look, they were no sooner departed—utterly departed—than she began slowly to sink down. It was as if a great, invisible, irresistible weight were pressing her to the earth. Settling upon her knees, she leaned her forehead against the rock, and sobbed convulsively; dry sobs, they seemed to be, such as have nothing to do with tears.

XXVI

ZENOBIA AND COVERDALE

ZENOBIA had entirely forgotten me. She fancied herself alone with her great grief. And had it been only a common pity that I felt for her—the pity that her proud nature would have repelled, as the one worst wrong which the world yet held in reserve—the sacredness and awfulness of the crisis might have impelled me to steal away, silently, so that not a dry leaf should rustle under my feet. I would have left her to struggle, in that solitude, with only the eye of God upon her. But, so it happened, I never once dreamed of questioning my right to be there, now, as I had questioned it, just before, when I came so suddenly upon Hollingsworth and herself, in the passion of their recent debate. It suits me not to explain what was the analogy that I saw, or imagined, between Zenobia's situation and mine; nor, I believe, will the reader detect this one secret, hidden beneath many a revelation which perhaps concerned me less. In simple truth, however, as Zenobia leaned her forehead against the rock, shaken with that tearless agony, it seemed to me that the self-same pang, with hardly mitigated torment, leaped thrilling from her heart-strings to my own. Was it wrong, therefore, if I felt myself consecrated to the priesthood, by sympathy like this, and called upon to minister to this woman's affliction, so far as mortal could?

But, indeed, what could mortal do for her? Nothing! The attempt would be a mockery and an anguish. Time, it is true, would steal away her grief, and bury it, and the best of her heart in the same grave. But Destiny itself, methought, in its kindliest mood, could do no better for Zenobia, in the way of quick relief, than to cause the impending rock to impend a little further, and fall upon her head. So I leaned against a tree, and listened to her sobs, in unbroken silence. She was half prostrate, half kneeling, with her forehead still pressed against the rock. Her sobs were the only sound; she did not groan, nor give any other utterance to her distress. It was all involuntary.

At length, she sat up, put back her hair, and stared about her with a bewildered aspect, as if not distinctly recollecting the scene through which she had passed, nor cognizant of the situation in which it left her. Her face and brow were almost purple with the rush of blood. They whitened, however, by-and-by, and, for some time, retained this deathlike hue. She put her hand to her forehead, with a gesture that made me forcibly conscious of an intense and living pain there.

Her glance, wandering wildly to-and-fro, passed over me, several times, without appearing to inform her of my presence. But, finally, a look of recognition gleamed from her eyes into mine.

"Is it you, Miles Coverdale?" said she, smiling. "Ah, I perceive what you are about! You are turning this whole affair into a ballad. Pray let me hear as many stanzas as you happen to have ready!"

"Oh, hush, Zenobia!" I answered. "Heaven knows what an ache is in my soul!"

"It is genuine tragedy, is it not?" rejoined Zenobia, with a sharp, light laugh. "And you are willing to allow, perhaps, that I have had hard measure. But it is a woman's doom, and I have deserved it like a woman; so let there be no pity, as, on my part, there shall be no complaint. It is all right now, or will shortly be so. But, Mr. Coverdale, by all means, write this ballad, and put your soul's ache into it, and turn your sympathy to good account, as other poets do, and as poets must, unless they choose to give us glittering icicles instead of lines of fire. As for the moral, it shall be distilled into the final stanza, in a drop of bitter honey."

"What shall it be, Zenobia?" I inquired, endeavoring to fall in with her mood.

"Oh, a very old one will serve the purpose," she replied. "There are no new truths, much as we have prided ourselves on finding some. A moral? Why, this:—that, in the battle-field of life, the downright stroke, that would fall only on a man's steel head-piece, is sure to light on a woman's heart, over which she wears no breastplate, and whose wisdom it is, therefore, to keep out of the conflict. Or this:—that the whole universe, her own sex and yours, and Providence, or Destiny, to boot, make common cause against the woman who swerves one hair's breadth out of the beaten track. Yes; and add, (for I may as well own it, now,) that, with that one hair's breadth, she goes all astray, and never sees the world in its true aspect, afterwards!"

"This last is too stern a moral," I observed. "Cannot we soften it a little?"

"Do it, if you like, at your own peril, not on my responsi-bility," she answered; then, with a sudden change of subject, she went on:—"After all, he has flung away what would have served him better than the poor, pale flower he kept. What can Priscilla do for him? Put passionate warmth into his heart, when it shall be chilled with frozen hopes? Strengthen his hands, when they are weary with much doing and no per-formance? No; but only tend towards him with a blind, instinctive love, and hang her little, puny weakness for a clog upon his arm! She cannot even give him such sympathy as is worth the name. For will he never, in many an hour of darkness, need that proud, intellectual sympathy which he might have had from me?—the sympathy that would flash light along his course, and guide as well as cheer him? Poor Hollingsworth! Where will he find it now?"

"Hollingsworth has a heart of ice!" said I, bitterly. "He is a wretch!"

"Do him no wrong!" interrupted Zenobia, turning haughtily upon me. "Presume not to estimate a man like Hollingsworth! It was my fault, all along, and none of his. I see it now! He never sought me. Why should he seek me? What had I to offer him? A miserable, bruised, and battered heart, spoilt long before he met me! A life, too, hopelessly entangled with a villain's! He did well to cast me off. God be praised, he did it! And yet, had he trusted me, and borne with me a little longer, I would have saved him all this trouble."

She was silent, for a time, and stood with her eyes fixed on the ground. Again raising them, her look was more mild and calm.

"Miles Coverdale!" said she.

"Well, Zenobia!" I responded. "Can I do you any service?"

"Very little," she replied. "But it is my purpose, as you may well imagine, to remove from Blithedale; and, most likely, I may not see Hollingsworth again. A woman in my position, you understand, feels scarcely at her ease among former friends. New faces—unaccustomed looks—those only can she tolerate. She would pine, among familiar scenes; she would be apt to blush, too, under the eyes that knew her secret; her heart might throb uncomfortably; she would mortify herself, I suppose, with foolish notions of having sacrificed the honor of her sex, at the foot of proud, contumacious man. Poor womanhood, with its rights and wrongs! Here will be new matter for my course of lectures, at the idea of which you smiled, Mr. Coverdale, a month or two ago. But, as you have really a heart and sympathies, as far as they go, and as I shall depart without seeing Hollingsworth, I must entreat you to be a messenger between him and me."

"Willingly," said I, wondering at the strange way in which her mind seemed to vibrate from the deepest earnest to mere levity. "What is the message?"

"True;—what is it?" exclaimed Zenobia. "After all, I hardly know. On better consideration, I have no message. Tell him—tell him something pretty and pathetic, that will come nicely and sweetly into your ballad—anything you please, so it be tender and submissive enough. Tell him he has murdered me! Tell him that I'll haunt him!"—she spoke these words with the wildest energy—"And give him—no, give Priscilla—this!"

Thus saying, she took the jewelled flower out of her hair; and it struck me as the act of a queen, when worsted in a combat, discrowning herself, as if she found a sort of relief in abasing all her pride.

"Bid her wear this for Zenobia's sake," she continued. "She is a pretty little creature, and will make as soft and gentle a wife as the veriest Bluebeard could desire. Pity that she must fade so soon! These delicate and puny maidens always do. Ten years hence, let Hollingsworth look at my face and Priscilla's, and then choose betwixt them. Or, if he pleases, let him do it now!"

How magnificently Zenobia looked, as she said this! The effect of her beauty was even heightened by the over-consciousness and self-recognition of it, into which, I suppose, Hollingsworth's scorn had driven her. She understood the look of admiration in my face; and—Zenobia to the last—it gave her pleasure.

"It is an endless pity," said she, "that I had not bethought myself of winning your heart, Mr. Coverdale, instead of Hollingsworth's. I think I should have succeeded; and many women would have deemed you the worthier conquest of the two. You are certainly much the handsomest man. But there is a fate in these things. And beauty, in a man, has been of little account with me, since my earliest girlhood, when, for once, it turned my head. Now, farewell!"

"Zenobia, whither are you going?" I asked.

"No matter where," said she. "But I am weary of this place, and sick to death of playing at philanthropy and progress. Of all varieties of mock-life, we have surely blundered into the very emptiest mockery, in our effort to establish the one true system. I have done with it; and Blithedale must find another woman to superintend the laundry, and you, Mr. Coverdale, another nurse to make your gruel, the next time you fall ill. It was, indeed, a foolish dream! Yet it gave us some pleasant summer days, and bright hopes, while they lasted. It can do no more; nor will it avail us to shed tears over a broken bubble. Here is my hand! Adieu!"

She gave me her hand, with the same free, whole-souled gesture as on the first afternoon of our acquaintance; and being greatly moved, I bethought me of no better method of expressing my deep sympathy than to carry it to my lips. In so doing, I perceived that this white hand—so hospitably warm when I first touched it, five months since—was now cold as a veritable piece of snow.

"How very cold!" I exclaimed, holding it between both my own, with the vain idea of warming it. "What can be the reason? It is really deathlike!"

"The extremities die first, they say," answered Zenobia, laughing. "And so you kiss this poor, despised, rejected hand! Well, my dear friend, I thank you! You have reserved your homage for the fallen. Lip of man will never touch my hand again. I intend to become a Catholic, for the sake of going into a nunnery. When you next hear of Zenobia, her face will be behind the black-veil; so look your last at it now—for all is over! Once more, farewell!"

She withdrew her hand, yet left a lingering pressure, which I felt long afterwards. So intimately connected, as I had been, with perhaps the only man in whom she was ever truly interested, Zenobia looked on me as the representative of all the past, and was conscious that, in bidding me adieu, she likewise took final leave of Hollingsworth, and of this whole epoch of her life. Never did her beauty shine out more lustrously, than in the last glimpse that I had of her. She departed, and was soon hidden among the trees.

But, whether it was the strong impression of the foregoing scene, or whatever else the cause, I was affected with a fantasy that Zenobia had not actually gone, but was still hovering about the spot, and haunting it. I seemed to feel her eyes upon me. It was as if the vivid coloring of her character had left a brilliant stain upon the air. By degrees, however, the impression grew less distinct. I flung myself upon the fallen leaves, at the base of Eliot's pulpit. The sunshine withdrew up the tree-trunks, and flickered on the topmost boughs; gray twilight made the wood obscure; the stars brightened out; the pendent boughs became wet with chill autumnal dews. But I was listless, worn-out with emotion on my own behalf, and sympathy for others, and had no heart to leave my comfortless lair, beneath the rock.

I must have fallen asleep, and had a dream, all the circumstances of which utterly vanished at the moment when they converged to some tragical catastrophe, and thus grew too powerful for the thin sphere of slumber that enveloped them. Starting from the ground, I found the risen moon shining upon the rugged face of the rock, and myself all in a tremble.

XXVII

MIDNIGHT

I T COULD not have been far from midnight, when I came beneath Hollingsworth's window, and finding it open, flung in a tuft of grass, with earth at the roots, and heard it fall upon the floor. He was either awake, or sleeping very lightly; for scarcely a moment had gone by, before he looked out and discerned me standing in the moonlight.

"Is it you, Coverdale?" he asked. "What is the matter?"

"Come down to me, Hollingsworth!" I answered. "I am anxious to speak with you."

The strange tone of my own voice startled me, and him, probably, no less. He lost no time, and soon issued from the house-door, with his dress half-arranged.

"Again, what is the matter?" he asked, impatiently.

"Have you seen Zenobia," said I, "since you parted from her, at Eliot's pulpit?"

"No," answered Hollingsworth; "nor did I expect it."

His voice was deep, but had a tremor in it. Hardly had he spoken, when Silas Foster thrust his head, done up in a cotton handkerchief, out of another window, and took what he called—as it literally was—a squint at us.

"Well, folks, what are ye about here?" he demanded. "Aha, are you there, Miles Coverdale? You have been turning night into day, since you left us, I reckon; and so you find it quite natural to come prowling about the house, at this time o' night, frightening my old woman out of her wits, and making her disturb a tired man out of his best nap. In with you, you vagabond, and to bed!"

"Dress yourself quietly, Foster," said I. "We want your assistance."

I could not, for the life of me, keep that strange tone out of my voice. Silas Foster, obtuse as were his sensibilities, seemed to feel the ghastly earnestness that was conveyed in it, as well as Hollingsworth did. He immediately withdrew his head, and I heard him yawning, muttering to his wife, and again yawning heavily, while he hurried on his clothes. Meanwhile, I showed Hollingsworth a delicate handkerchief, marked with a well-known cypher, and told where I had found it, and other circumstances which had filled me with a suspicion so terrible, that I left him, if he dared, to shape it out for himself. By the time my brief explanation was finished, we were joined by Silas Foster, in his blue woollen frock.

"Well, boys," cried he, peevishly, "what is to pay now?"

"Tell him, Hollingsworth!" said I.

Hollingsworth shivered, perceptibly, and drew in a hard breath betwixt his teeth. He steadied himself, however, and looking the matter more firmly in the face than I had done, explained to Foster my suspicions and the grounds of them, with a distinctness from which, in spite of my utmost efforts, my words had swerved aside. The tough-nerved yeoman, in his comment, put a finish on the business, and brought out the hideous idea in its full terror, as if he were removing the napkin from the face of a corpse.

"And so you think she's drowned herself!"*he cried.

I turned away my face.

"What on earth should the young woman do that for?" exclaimed Silas, his eyes half out of his head with mere surprise. "Why, she has more means than she can use or waste, and lacks nothing to make her comfortable, but a husband—and that's an article she could have, any day! There's some mistake about this, I tell you!"

"Come," said I, shuddering. "Let us go and ascertain the truth."

"Well, well," answered Silas Foster, "just as you say. We'll take the long pole, with the hook at the end, that serves to get the bucket out of the draw-well, when the rope is broken. With that, and a couple of long-handled hay-rakes, I'll answer for finding her, if she's anywhere to be found. Strange enough! Zenobia drown herself! No, no, I don't believe it. She had too much sense, and too much means, and enjoyed life a great deal too well."

When our few preparations were completed, we hastened, by a shorter than the customary route, through fields and pastures, and across a portion of the meadow, to the particular spot, on the river-bank, which I had paused to contemplate, in the course of my afternoon's ramble. A nameless presentiment had again drawn me thither, after leaving Eliot's pulpit. I showed my companions where I had found the handkerchief, and pointed to two or three footsteps, impressed into the clayey margin, and tending towards the water. Beneath its shallow verge, among the water-weeds, there were further traces, as yet unobliterated by the sluggish current, which was there almost at a stand-still. Silas Foster thrust his face down close to these footsteps, and picked up a shoe, that had escaped my observation, being half imbedded in the mud.

"There's a kid-shoe that never was made on a Yankee last," observed he. "I know enough of shoemaker's craft to tell that. French manufacture; and see what a high instep!—and how evenly she trod in it! There never was a woman that stept handsomer in her shoes than Zenobia did. Here," he added, addressing Hollingsworth, "would you like to keep the shoe?"

Hollingsworth started back.

"Give it to me, Foster," said I.

I dabbled it in the water, to rinse off the mud, and have kept it ever since. Not far from this spot, lay an old, leaky punt, drawn up on the oozy river-side, and generally half-full of water. It served the angler to go in quest of pickerel, or the sportsman to pick up his wild-ducks. Setting this crazy barque afloat, I seated myself in the stern, with the paddle, while Hollingsworth sat in the bows, with the hooked pole, and Silas Foster amidships, with a hay-rake.

"It puts me in mind of my young days," remarked Silas, "when I used to steal out of bed to go bobbing for horn-pouts* and eels. Heigh-ho!—well!—life and death together make sad work for us all. Then, I was a boy, bobbing for fish; and now I am getting to be an old fellow, and here I be, groping for a dead body! I tell you what, lads, if I thought anything had really happened to Zenobia, I should feel kind o' sorrowful."

"I wish, at least, you would hold your tongue!" muttered I.

The moon, that night, though past the full, was still large and oval, and having risen between eight and nine o'clock, now shone aslantwise over the river, throwing the high, opposite bank, with its woods, into deep shadow, but lighting up the hither shore pretty effectually. Not a ray appeared to fall on the river itself. It lapsed imperceptibly away, a broad, black, inscrutable depth, keeping its own secrets from the eye of man, as impenetrably as mid-ocean could.

"Well, Miles Coverdale," said Foster, "you are the helmsman. How do you mean to manage this business?"

"I shall let the boat drift, broadside foremost, past that stump," I replied. "I know the bottom, having sounded it in fishing. The shore, on this side, after the first step or two, goes off very abruptly; and there is a pool, just by the stump, twelve or fifteen feet deep. The current could not have force enough to sweep any sunken object—even if partially buoyant —out of that hollow."

"Come, then," said Silas. "But I doubt whether I can touch bottom with this hay-rake, if it's as deep as you say.

Mr. Hollingsworth, I think you'll be the lucky man, to-night, such luck as it is!"

We floated past the stump. Silas Foster plied his rake manfully, poking it as far as he could into the water, and immersing the whole length of his arm besides. Hollingsworth at first sat motionless, with the hooked-pole elevated in the air. But, by-and-by, with a nervous and jerky movement, he began to plunge it into the blackness that upbore us, setting his teeth, and making precisely such thrusts, methought, as if he were stabbing at a deadly enemy. I bent over the side of the boat. So obscure, however, so awfully mysterious, was that dark stream, that—and the thought made me shiver like a leaf—I might as well have tried to look into the enigma of the eternal world, to discover what had become of Zenobia's soul, as into the river's depths, to find her body. And there, perhaps, she lay, with her face upward, while the shadow of the boat, and my own pale face peering downward, passed slowly betwixt her and the sky.

Once, twice, thrice, I paddled the boat up stream, and again suffered it to glide, with the river's slow, funereal motion, downward. Silas Foster had raked up a large mass of stuff, which, as it came towards the surface, looked somewhat like a flowing garment, but proved to be a monstrous tuft of water-weeds. Hollingsworth, with a gigantic effort, upheaved a sunken log. When once free of the bottom, it rose partly out of water—all weedy and slimy, a devilish-looking object, which the moon had not shone upon for half a hundred years —then plunged again, and sullenly returned to its old resting-place, for the remnant of the century.

"That looked ugly!" quoth Silas. "I half thought it was the Evil One on the same errand as ourselves—searching for Zenobia!"

"He shall never get her!" said I, giving the boat a strong impulse.

"That's not for you to say, my boy!" retorted the yeoman. "Pray God he never has, and never may! Slow work this, however! I should really be glad to find something. Pshaw! What a notion that is, when the only good-luck would be, to paddle, and drift and poke, and grope, hereabouts, till morning, and have our labor for our pains! For my part, I shouldn't wonder if the creature had only lost her shoe in the mud, and saved her soul alive, after all. My stars, how she will laugh at us, tomorrow morning!"

It is indescribable what an image of Zenobia—at the breakfast-table, full of warm and mirthful life—this surmise of Silas Foster's brought before my mind. The terrible phantasm of her death was thrown by it into the remotest and dimmest back-ground, where it seemed to grow as improbable as a myth.

"Yes, Silas; it may be as you say!" cried I.

The drift of the stream had again borne us a little below the stump, when I felt—yes, felt, for it was as if the iron hook had smote my breast—felt Hollingsworth's pole strike some object at the bottom of the river. He started up, and almost overset the boat.

"Hold on!" cried Foster. "You have her!"

Putting a fury of strength into the effort, Hollingsworth heaved amain, and up came a white swash to the surface of the river. It was the flow of a woman's garments. A little higher, and we saw her dark hair, streaming down the current. Black River of Death, thou hadst yielded up thy victim Zenobia was found!

Silas Foster laid hold of the body—Hollingsworth, likewise, grappled with it—and I steered towards the bank, gazing, all the while, at Zenobia, whose limbs were swaying in the current, close at the boat's side. Arriving near the shore, we all three stept into the water, bore her out, and laid her on the ground, beneath a tree.

"Poor child!" said Foster—and his dry old heart, I verily believe, vouchsafed a tear—"I'm sorry for her!"

Were I to describe the perfect horror of the spectacle, the reader might justly reckon it to me for a sin and shame. For more than twelve long years I have borne it in my memory, and could now reproduce it as freshly as if it were still before my eyes. Of all modes of death, methinks it is the ugliest. Her wet garments swathed limbs of terrible inflexibility. She was the marble image of a death-agony. Her arms had grown rigid in the act of struggling, and were bent before her, with clenched hands; her knees, too, were bent, and—thank God for it!—in the attitude of prayer. Ah, that rigidity! It is impossible to bear the terror of it. It seemed—I must needs impart so much of my own miserable idea—it seemed as if her body must keep the same position in the coffin, and that her skeleton would keep it in the grave, and that when Zenobia rose, at the Day of Judgment, it would be in just the same attitude as now!

One hope I had; and that, too, was mingled half with fear. She knelt, as if in prayer. With the last, choking consciousness, her soul, bubbling out through her lips, it may be, had given itself up to the Father, reconciled and penitent. But her arms! They were bent before her, as if she struggled against Providence in never-ending hostility. Her hands! They were clenched in immitigable defiance. Away with the hideous thought! The flitting moment, after Zenobia sank into the dark pool—when her breath was gone, and her soul at her lips—was as long, in its capacity of God's infinite forgiveness, as the lifetime of the world.

Foster bent over the body, and carefully examined it.

"You have wounded the poor thing's breast," said he to Hollingsworth. "Close by her heart, too!"

"Ha!" cried Hollingsworth, with a start.

And so he had, indeed, both before and after death.

"See!" said Foster. "That's the place where the iron struck her. It looks cruelly, but she never felt it!"

He endeavored to arrange the arms of the corpse decently by its side. His utmost strength, however, scarcely sufficed to bring them down; and rising again, the next instant, they bade him defiance, exactly as before. He made another effort, with the same result.

"In God's name, Silas Foster," cried I, with bitter indignation, "let that dead woman alone!"

"Why, man, it's not decent!" answered he, staring at me in amazement. "I can't bear to see her looking so! Well, well," added he, after a third effort, "'tis of no use, sure enough; and we must leave the women to do their best with her, after we get to the house. The sooner that's done, the better."

We took two rails from a neighboring fence, and formed a bier by laying across some boards from the bottom of the boat. And thus we bore Zenobia homeward. Six hours before, how beautiful! At midnight, what a horror! A reflection occurs to me, that will show ludicrously, I doubt not, on my page, but must come in, for its sterling truth. Being the woman that she was, could Zenobia have foreseen all these ugly circumstances of death, how ill it would become her, the altogether unseemly aspect which she must put on, and, especially, old Silas Foster's efforts to improve the matter, she would no more have committed the dreadful act, than have exhibited herself to a public assembly in a badly-fitting garment! Zenobia, I have often thought, was not quite simple in her death. She had seen pictures, I suppose, of drowned persons, in lithe and graceful attitudes. And she deemed it well and decorous to die as so many village-maidens have, wronged in their first-love, and seeking peace in the bosom of the old, familiar stream—so familiar that they could not dread it—where, in childhood, they used to bathe their little feet, wading mid-leg deep, unmindful of wet skirts. But, in Zenobia's case, there was some tint of the Arcadian affectation that had been visible enough in all our lives, for a few months past.

This, however, to my conception, takes nothing from the tragedy. For, has not the world come to an awfully sophisticated pass, when, after a certain degree of acquaintance with it, we cannot even put ourselves to death in whole-hearted simplicity?

Slowly, slowly, with many a dreary pause—resting the bier often on some rock, or balancing it across a mossy log, to take fresh hold—we bore our burthen onward, through the moonlight, and, at last, laid Zenobia on the floor of the old farm-house. By-and-by, came three or four withered women, and stood whispering around the corpse, peering at it through their spectacles, holding up their skinny hands, shaking their night-capt heads, and taking counsel of one another's experience what was to be done.

With those tire-women,* we left Zenobia!

XXVIII

BLITHEDALE-PASTURE

BLITHEDALE, thus far in its progress, had never found the necessity of a burial-ground. There was some consultation among us, in what spot Zenobia might most fitly be laid. It was my own wish, that she should sleep at the base of Eliot's pulpit, and that, on the rugged front of the rock, the name by which we familiarly knew her— ZENOBIA—and not another word, should be deeply cut, and left for the moss and lichens to fill up, at their long leisure. But Hollingsworth (to whose ideas, on this point, great deference was due) made it his request that her grave might be dug on the gently sloping hill-side, in the wide pasture, where, as we once supposed, Zenobia and he had planned to build their cottage. And thus it was done, accordingly.

She was buried very much as other people have been, for hundreds of years gone by. In anticipation of a death, we Blithedale colonists had sometimes set our fancies at work to arrange a funereal ceremony, which should be the proper symbolic expression of our spiritual faith and eternal hopes; and this we meant to substitute for those customary rites, which were moulded originally out of the Gothic gloom, and, by long use, like an old velvet-pall, have so much more than their first death-smell in them. But, when the occasion came, we found it the simplest and truest thing, after all, to content ourselves with the old fashion, taking away what we could, but interpolating no novelties, and particularly avoiding all frippery of flowers and cheerful emblems. The procession moved from the farm-house. Nearest the dead walked an old man in deep mourning, his face mostly concealed in a white handkerchief, and with Priscilla leaning on his arm. Hollingsworth and myself came next. We all stood around the narrow niche in the cold earth; all saw the coffin lowered in; all heard the rattle of the crumbly soil upon its lid—that final sound, which mortality awakens on the utmost verge of sense, as if in the vain hope of bringing an echo from the spiritual world.

I noticed a stranger—a stranger to most of those present, though known to me—who, after the coffin had descended, took up a handful of earth, and flung it first into the grave. I had given up Hollingsworth's arm, and now found myself near this man.

"It was an idle thing—a foolish thing—for Zenobia to do!" said he. "She was the last woman in the world to whom death could have been necessary. It was too absurd! I have no patience with her."

"Why so?" I inquired, smothering my horror at his cold comment in my eager curiosity to discover some tangible truth, as to his relation with Zenobia. "If any crisis could justify the sad wrong she offered to herself, it was surely that in which she stood. Everything had failed her—prosperity, in the world's sense, for her opulence was gone—the heart's prosperity, in love. And there was a secret burthen on her, the nature of which is best known to you. Young as she was, she had tried life fully, had no more to hope, and something, perhaps, to fear. Had Providence taken her away in its own holy hand, I should have thought it the kindest dispensation that could be awarded to one so wrecked."

"You mistake the matter completely," rejoined Westervelt.

"What, then, is your own view of it?" I asked.

"Her mind was active, and various in its powers," said he; "her heart had a. manifold adaptation; her constitution an infinite buoyancy, which (had she possessed only a little patience to await the reflux of her troubles) would have borne her upward, triumphantly, for twenty years to come. Her beauty would not have waned—or scarcely so, and surely not beyond the reach of art to restore it—in all that time. She had life's summer all before her, and a hundred varieties of brilliant success. What an actress Zenobia might have been! It was one of her least valuable capabilities. How forcibly she might have wrought upon the world, either directly in her own person, or by her influence upon some man, or a series of men, of controlling genius! Every prize that could be worth a woman's having—and many prizes which other women are too timid to desire—lay within Zenobia's reach."

"In all this," I observed, "there would have been nothing to satisfy her heart."

"Her heart!" answered Westervelt, contemptuously. "That troublesome organ (as she had hitherto found it) would have been kept in its due place and degree, and have had all the gratification it could fairly claim. She would soon have established a control over it. Love had failed her, you say! Had it never failed her before? Yet she survived it, and loved again—possibly, not once alone, nor twice either. And now to drown herself for yonder dreamy philanthropist!"

"Who are you," I exclaimed, indignantly, "that dare to speak thus of the dead? You seem to intend a eulogy, yet leave out whatever was noblest in her, and blacken, while you mean to praise. I have long considered you as Zenobia's evil fate. Your sentiments confirm me in the idea, but leave me still ignorant as to the mode in which you have influenced her life. The connection may have been indissoluble, except by death. Then, indeed—always in the hope of God's infinite mercy—I cannot deem it a misfortune that she sleeps in yonder grave!"

"No matter what I was to her," he answered, gloomily, yet without actual emotion. "She is now beyond my reach. Had she lived, and hearkened to my counsels, we might have served each other well. But there Zenobia lies, in yonder pit, with the dull earth over her. Twenty years of a brilliant lifetime thrown away for a mere woman's whim!"

Heaven deal with Westervelt according to his nature and deserts!—that is to say, annihilate him. He was altogether earthy, worldly, made for time and its gross objects, and incapable—except by a sort of dim reflection, caught from other minds—of so much as one spiritual idea. Whatever stain Zenobia had, was caught from him; nor does it seldom happen that a character of admirable qualities loses its better life, because the atmosphere, that should sustain it, is rendered poisonous by such breath as this man mingled with Zenobia's. Yet his reflections possessed their share of truth. It was a woful thought, that a woman of Zenobia's diversified capacity should have fancied herself irretrievably defeated on the broad battle-field of life, and with no refuge, save to fall on her own sword, merely because Love had gone against her. It is nonsense, and a miserable wrong—the result, like so many others, of masculine egotism—that the success or failure of woman's existence should be made to depend wholly on the affections, and on one species of affection; while man has such a multitude of other chances, that this seems but an incident. For its own sake, if it will do no more, the world should throw open all its avenues to the passport of a woman's bleeding heart.

As we stood around the grave, I looked often towards Priscilla, dreading to see her wholly overcome with grief. And deeply grieved, in truth, she was. But a character, so simply constituted as hers, has room only for a single predominant affection. No other feeling can touch the heart's inmost core, nor do it any deadly mischief. Thus, while we see that such a being responds to every breeze, with tremulous vibration, and imagine that she must be shattered by the first rude blast, we find her retaining her equilibrium amid shocks that might have overthrown many a sturdier frame. So with Priscilla! Her one possible misfortune was Hollingsworth's unkindness; and that was destined never to befall her—never yet, at least—for Priscilla has not died.

But, Hollingsworth! After all the evil that he did, are we to leave him thus, blest with the entire devotion of this one true heart, and with wealth at his disposal, to execute the long contemplated project that had led him so far astray? What retribution is there here? My mind being vexed with precisely this query, I made a journey, some years since, for the sole purpose of catching a last glimpse at Hollingsworth, and judging for myself whether he were a happy man or no. I learned that he inhabited a small cottage, that his way of life was exceedingly retired, and that my only chance of encountering him or Priscilla was, to meet them in a secluded lane, where, in the latter part of the afternoon, they were accustomed to walk. I did meet them, accordingly. As they approached me, I observed in Hollingsworth's face a depressed and melancholy look, that seemed habitual; the powerfully built man showed a self-distrustful weakness, and a childlike, or childish, tendency to press close, and closer still, to the side of the slender woman whose arm was within his. In Priscilla's manner, there was a protective and watchful quality, as if she felt herself the guardian of her companion, but, likewise, a deep, submissive, unquestioning reverence, and also a veiled happiness in her fair and quiet countenance.

Drawing nearer, Priscilla recognized me, and gave me a kind and friendly smile, but with a slight gesture which I could not help interpreting as an entreaty not to make myself known to Hollingsworth. Nevertheless, an impulse took possession of me, and compelled me to address him.

"I have come, Hollingsworth," said I, "to view your grand edifice for the reformation of criminals. Is it finished yet?"

"No—nor begun!" answered he, without raising his eyes. "A very small one answers all my purposes."

Priscilla threw me an upbraiding glance. But I spoke again, with a bitter and revengeful emotion, as if flinging a poisoned arrow at Hollingsworth's heart.

"Up to this moment," I inquired, "how many criminals have you reformed?"

"Not one!" said Hollingsworth, with his eyes still fixed on the ground. "Ever since we parted, I have been busy with a single murderer!"

Then the tears gushed into my eyes, and I forgave him. For I remembered the wild energy, the passionate shriek, with which Zenobia had spoken those words—'Tell him he has murdered me! Tell him that I'll haunt him!'—and I knew what murderer he meant, and whose vindictive shadow dogged the side where Priscilla was not.

The moral which presents itself to my reflections, as drawn from Hollingsworth's character and errors, is simply this:—that, admitting what is called Philanthropy, when adopted as a profession, to be often useful by its energetic impulse to society at large, it is perilous to the individual, whose ruling passion, in one exclusive channel, it thus becomes. It ruins, or is fearfully apt to ruin, the heart; the rich juices of which God never meant should be pressed violently out, and distilled into alcoholic liquor, by an unnatural process; but should render life sweet, bland, and gently beneficent, and insensibly influence other hearts and other lives to the same blessed end. I see in Hollingsworth an exemplification of the most awful truth in Bunyan's book* of such;—from the very gate of Heaven, there is a by-way to the pit!

But, all this while, we have been standing by Zenobia's grave. I have never since beheld it, but make no question that the grass grew all the better, on that little parallelogram of pasture-land, for the decay of the beautiful woman who slept beneath. How much Nature seems to love us! And how readily, nevertheless, without a sigh or a complaint, she converts us to a meaner purpose, when her highest one—that of conscious, intellectual life, and sensibility—has been untimely baulked! While Zenobia lived, Nature was proud of her, and directed all eyes upon that radiant presence, as her fairest handiwork. Zenobia perished. Will not Nature shed a tear? Ah, no! She adopts the calamity at once into her system, and is just as well pleased, for aught we can see, with the tuft of ranker vegetation that grew out of Zenobia's heart, as with all the beauty which has bequeathed us no earthly representative, except in this crop of weeds. It is because the spirit is inestimable, that the lifeless body is so little valued.

XXIX

MILES COVERDALE'S CONFESSION

IT REMAINS only to say a few words about myself. Not improbably, the reader might be willing to spare me the trouble; for I have made but a poor and dim figure in my own narrative, establishing no separate interest, and suffering my colorless life to take its hue from other lives. But one still retains some little consideration for one's self; so I keep these last two or three pages for my individual and sole behoof.

But what, after all, have I to tell? Nothing, nothing, nothing! I left Blithedale within the week after Zenobia's death, and went back thither no more. The whole soil of our farm, for a long time afterwards, seemed but the sodded earth over her grave. I could not toil there, nor live upon its products. Often, however, in these years that are darkening around me, I remember our beautiful scheme of a noble and unselfish life, and how fair, in that first summer, appeared the prospect that it might endure for generations, and be perfected, as the ages rolled away, into the system of a people, and a world. Were my former associates now there—were there only three or four of those true-hearted men, still laboring in the sun—I sometimes fancy that I should direct my world-weary footsteps thitherward, and entreat them to receive me, for old friendship's sake. More and more, I feel that we had struck upon what ought to be a truth. Posterity may dig it up, and profit by it. The experiment, so far as its original projectors were concerned, proved long ago a failure, first lapsing into Fourierism, and dying, as it well deserved, for this infidelity to its own higher spirit. Where once we toiled with our whole hopeful hearts, the town-paupers, aged, nerveless, and disconsolate, creep sluggishly afield. Alas, what faith is requisite to bear up against such results of generous effort!

My subsequent life has passed—I was going to say, happily —but, at all events, tolerably enough. I am now at middle-age—well, well, a step or two beyond the midmost point, and I care not a fig who knows it!—a bachelor, with no very decided purpose of ever being otherwise. I have been twice to Europe, and spent a year or two, rather agreeably, at each visit. Being well to do in the world, and having nobody but myself to care for, I live very much at my ease, and fare sumptuously every day. As for poetry, I have given it up, notwithstanding that Doctor Griswold*—as the reader, of course, knows—has placed me at a fair elevation among our minor minstrelsy, on the strength of my pretty little volume, published ten years ago. As regards human progress, (in spite of my irrepressible yearnings over the Blithedale reminiscences,) let them believe in it who can, and aid in it who choose! If I could earnestly do either, it might be all the better for my comfort. As Hollingsworth once told me, I lack a purpose. How strange! He was ruined, morally, by an overplus of the very same ingredient, the want of which, I occasionally suspect, has rendered my own life all an emptiness. I by no means wish to die. Yet, were there any cause, in this whole chaos of human struggle, worth a sane man's dying for, and which my death would benefit, then—provided, however, the effort did not involve an unreasonable amount of trouble—methinks I might be bold to offer up my life. If Kossuth,* for example, would pitch the battle-field of Hungarian rights within an easy ride of my abode, and choose a mild, sunny morning, after breakfast, for the conflict, Miles Coverdale would gladly be his man, for one brave rush upon the levelled bayonets. Farther than that, I should be loth to pledge myself.

I exaggerate my own defects. The reader must not take my own word for it, nor believe me altogether changed from the young man, who once hoped strenuously, and struggled, not so much amiss. Frostier heads than mine have gained honor in the world; frostier hearts have imbibed new warmth, and been newly happy. Life, however, it must be owned, has come to rather an idle pass with me. Would my friends like to know what brought it thither? There is one secret—I have concealed it all along, and never meant to let the least whisper of it escape—one foolish little secret, which possibly may have had something to do with these inactive years of meridian manhood, with my bachelorship, with the unsatisfied retrospect that I fling back on life, and my listless glance towards the future. Shall I reveal it? It is an absurd thing for a man in his afternoon—a man of the world, moreover, with these three white hairs in his brown moustache, and that deepening track of a crow's foot on each temple—an absurd thing ever to have happened, and quite the absurdest for an old bachelor, like me, to talk about. But it rises in my throat; so let it come.

I perceive, moreover, that the confession, brief as it shall be, will throw a gleam of light over my behavior throughout the foregoing incidents, and is, indeed, essential to the full understanding of my story. The reader, therefore, since I have disclosed so much, is entitled to this one word more. As I write it, he will charitably suppose me to blush, and turn away my face:—

I—I myself—was in love—with—PRISCILLA!

THE END.

EXPLANATORY NOTES

1   *Brook Farm*: co-operative community (1841–7), near West Roxbury, Mass., 9 miles from Boston. It was established by the Transcendentalist movement (see note to p. 115), but leading figures like Emerson, Channing, Alcott, and Margaret Fuller were regular visitors rather than members. Hawthorne was a founding member, residing at Brook Farm from April to November 1841.

fancy-sketch: whimsical picture.

2   *the American romancer*: Hawthorne makes similar pleas for the nature of his fiction in other prefaces, notably in *The House of the Seven Gables* (1851).

Sibylline: prophetic; from the sibyls of classical mythology.

3   *Ripley ... Dana, Dwight, Channing, Burton, Parker*: George Ripley (1802–80) was a religious thinker who founded Brook Farm on leaving his Unitarian ministry in 1841. Among the original members were Charles Dana (1819–97), later a newspaper editor; John Dwight (1813–93), a music critic, and Warren Burton (1800–60), a minister and teacher. The Channing associated with the community was the Christian socialist William Henry Channing (1810–84), rather than his uncle Ellery Channing. Theodore Parker (1810–60), another Transcendentalist, was an unorthodox Unitarian minister.

Howadji: George Curtis (1824–92), travel writer and later social reformer, attended the school at Brook Farm in the community's early years. Hawthorne refers to the pen-name used in his books *Nile Notes of a Howadji* (1851) and *The Howadji in Syria* (1852).

5   *Mr. Coverdale*: Hawthorne names his narrator after a historical figure, Miles Coverdale (1488–1568), a priest and biblical scholar who produced an important translation of the Bible into English during the reign of Henry VIII.

a phenomenon in the mesmeric line: Franz Mesmer (1734–1815), an Austrian physician, became an international celebrity after announcing his theory of 'animal magnetism' in Paris in 1778. His influence continued throughout the first half of the nineteenth century, and the word 'mesmerism' came to be used of all phenomena now identified as 'spiritualism', and of hypnotism (hence our word 'mesmerize'). In the 1830s the mesmerist Charles Poyen toured New England, lecturing on animal magnetism and giving demonstrations of hypnotism, using his 'trance-maidens' as subjects. Elizabeth Peabody, Hawthorne's future sister-in-law, was among the many who heard him speak.

8   *Zenobia*: the name of a famous Queen of Palmyra in the third century AD. She was defeated by the Roman Emperor Aurelian in 272, after extending the territories under her control, and led captive through Rome.

cannel coal: bright-burning candle coal.

10   *Esquimaux*: Eskimo.

and somewhat of proof . . . a big demijohn: these words were omitted in the first edition, apparently at the instigation of the author's wife, who was strongly opposed to drinking. A demijohn is a large bottle enclosed in wickerwork, probably containing whisky.

15   *dry-goods people*: drapers.

17   *I almost fancied myself actually beholding it*: also omitted from the first edition, probably at Sophia Hawthorne's request.

19   *phalansteries*: the phalanstery was the multiple-purpose central building in the ideal community envisaged by Charles Fourier; see below, note to p. 52.

21   *Arcadia*: region of Greece inhabited largely by shepherds; associated in poetic tradition with the pastoral ideal.

23   *California gold*: still a relatively new phenomenon when the novel was written. Gold was discovered in January 1848, and the first great wave of migrants (the 'forty-niners') arrived in the following year.

24   *Pandora*: the first mortal woman in Greek mythology, parallel to Eve. Created by the blacksmith god Vulcan at Zeus's request, she opened a box the latter had given her, and thereby released all the troubles of the world.

the millennium of love: the second golden age which Utopian socialism sought to create.

33   *a seamstress from the city*: in his *American Notebooks* (9 October 1841), Hawthorne describes the arrival at Brook Farm of 'a little sempstress from Boston'.

34   *salamander-stove*: small portable stove for heating rooms.

37   *Blithedale*: the name hints at the 'happy valley' of the hero in Samuel Johnson's long prose romance *Rasselas* (1759).

38   *Sisera's brain*: fleeing after defeat by the Israelite armies, the Canaanite general Sisera took refuge in the tent of a woman called Jael. As foretold, she drove a tent nail into his skull. Judges 4: 21.

   How cold an Arcadia: the Forest of Arden in Shakespeare's *As You Like It*, another modern Arcadia, is also cold; e.g. II. i. 6–9, II. v. 42. The play is referred to again in Ch. XI.

40   *Michael Scott*: Scottish scholar, astrologer, and reputed magician (c.1175–1230) with an international reputation. He was said to be able to conjure food for his dinner guests from the kitchens of the royal courts of Europe.

41   *homeopathic*: invented in the eighteenth century, homeopathic treatment prescribes small doses of curatives related in some way to the illness.

46   *vegetable diet*: such a diet was thought at the time to result in 'ether' entering the system, making the person more spiritual, less fleshly.

52   *Miss Margaret Fuller*: essayist, teacher, and pioneering feminist (1810–50) associated with the Transcendentalist movement, and a friend of the Hawthornes (her famous conversational classes for women took place between 1839 and 1844 at the Boston home of Sophia's sister Elizabeth Peabody). Zenobia is usually taken to be in part a portrait of her, although Hawthorne seeks to head off such an inference in this passage, and gives Priscilla her squinting gaze and hunched posture. Fuller died tragically in a shipwreck off the American coast as she returned to the country after several years in Europe.

   Mr. Emerson's essays, ... the Dial, Carlyle's works, George Sand's romances: the works read by Coverdale represent the progressive thinking of the 1840s. The *Essays* of Ralph Waldo Emerson (1803–82), the central figure of the Transcendentalist movement, were published in collections in 1841 and 1844. They reflect his belief in the supreme value of the individual soul, and its kinship with the divine spirit. He succeeded Margaret Fuller as editor of the *Dial*, a Transcendentalist quarterly which appeared between 1840 and 1844. Emerson met the Scottish essayist, historian, and translator Thomas

Carlyle (1795–1881) during his European tour of 1832–3, and admired his passionate individualism and hostility to materialism, the prophetic force of his writing, and the breadth of his intellectual interests. They corresponded, and supported one another's work. George Sand was the pen-name of the French authoress Amandine Dudevant (1804–76). Her novels of the early 1830s, such as *Lélia* (1833), are extravagant romances concerned with love, reflecting her hostile view of marriage. In the 1840s she turned to works looking towards a future egalitarian golden age, and to studies of rural life. The attractions for Zenobia of Sand—feminist, socialist, romantic—are obvious. Hawthorne gives his character a name which could belong to a Sand heroine.

Fourier: Charles Fourier (1772–1837), French social theorist who advanced ideas closer to anarchism than socialism. Starting with *Théorie des quatre mouvements et des destinées générales* (1808), he developed a vision of society moving towards harmony through self-sufficient co-operative units (phalanges) of 1,500 people. The members would all live in a single building (phalanstery), receiving an equal basic wage. Brook Farm became Fourierist in some respects after 1843, but was not so while Hawthorne belonged to the community.

53 *limonade à cèdre*: a slightly distorted version of a passage in Fourier's *Théorie*. See *American Notebooks* entry, 7 August 1851.

the selfish principle: Fourier believed that a harmonious society would emerge if personal needs and desires were no longer repressed.

54 *Swedenborg*: the Swedish theologian Emanuel Swedenborg (1688–1772), a mystic who taught that natural objects are symbols of higher realities. His ideas influenced Emerson and the other Transcendentalists, notably the concept of 'correspondence' between the natural, the human, and the divine.

Gehenna: a hellish region, from Jeremiah via Milton.

58 *houstonias*: the four-petalled flowers of the genus Rubiaceae; the bluet is the best-known variety.

60 *frock*: rough outer shirt.

'airy tongues that syllable men's names': quoting *Comus* (1634), l. 209. There are clear parallels between Priscilla and the virtuous heroine of Milton's masque, held fast in her seat by a sorcerer's magic.

64   *Grub-street*: London street associated with impoverished writers from the seventeenth century onwards.

     Pantisocracy: in the 1790s, in the aftermath of the French Revolution, Coleridge and his fellow-poet Southey planned to found a Utopian community in Pennsylvania. The Greek name means 'all to rule equally'.

     Candide: Voltaire's satirical novella (1759) attacking optimistic philosophy and religion. The protagonists return from their travels to cultivate their garden.

     Falstaff: in *1 Henry IV*, IV. ii, the fat knight musters some unlikely soldiers in Gloucestershire in order to aid the royal campaign against the rebels.

     linsey-woolsey: coarse fabric mixing linen and wool, or cotton and wool.

     '*Ara nudus; sere nudus*': Virgil, *Georgics*, I, l. 299: 'Plow naked; sow naked'.

66   *Burns*: the Scottish poet Robert Burns (1759–96) worked as an agricultural labourer before seeking fame in Edinburgh, and as a farmer after his failure. Although the poems present him as happy, he found the work harsh.

72   *Golden Age*: in classical myth, the period after the creation of the world, in which mankind lived in perfect happiness and harmony.

73   *caprioles*: leaps, capers.

     Atalanta: in Greek myth, a princess of Arcadia who was the swiftest of mortals. Suitors for her hand were required to race her, accepting the penalty of death if they lost.

75   *Goldsmith's old folks*: in Oliver Goldsmith's pastoral elegy 'The Deserted Village' (1770), ll. 13–24.

91   *forest of Arden*: the pastoral refuge of all those banished or estranged from the court in *As You Like It*.

     salvage man: savage man, exemplified by Caliban in *The Tempest*; traditionally depicted in antiquity and the Renaissance as hairy and covered in foliage.

94   *quixotism*: extravagant romanticism, like that of the hero of Cervantes's *Don Quixote*, who, *inter alia*, appoints himself guardian of Dulcinea.

97   *the Chorus*: in Greek tragedy a group of ordinary citizens who act as commentators on the dramatic action.

98   *Robinson Crusoe*: the hero of Daniel Defoe's novel (1719) has a look-out platform in a tree.

     King Charles: Charles II, fleeing from the Parliamentarian army after the Battle of Worcester (1851), reputedly hid in a tree.

99   *allegorical figure of rich October*: Spenser, *The Faerie Queene* (1590), VII. vii. 39.

100   *fancy-work*: ornamental needlework.

103   *Dante's ghostly forest*: at the start of the *Inferno*, in the *Divine Comedy*.

106   *Tableaux vivants*: Fr. living pictures; standing motionless and wearing appropriate costumes, the participants re-create famous paintings. Hawthorne describes a *tableaux vivants* evening at Brook Farm in a letter to Sophia (4 May 1841).

110   *Medusa*: in Greek myth, the snake-haired Gorgon, whose gaze was fatal; Perseus was able to kill her because he looked only at her reflection in his shield.

115   *transcendentalists*: a New England literary and philosophical movement which flourished in the period between the publication of Emerson's *Nature* (1836) and the outbreak of the Civil War. Besides Emerson, the leading figures included Thoreau, Fuller, Bronson Alcott, Ellery Channing, and George Ripley. German philosophy and English Romanticism were important influences; there was no common credo, but members of the group shared a suspicion of organized religion, and a belief that the divine could also be found in nature, or in great art and thought. Transcendentalists were frequently associated with progressive causes, such as the anti-slavery struggle, or the campaign for women's rights.

118   *Apostle Eliot*: John Eliot (1604–90), a missionary who emigrated from England to Boston in 1631, had some success in converting the Indians of Massachusetts, and translated the Bible into their language.

120   *when my sex shall achieve its rights*: Margaret Fuller, the partial model for the character of Zenobia, was the author of *Women in the Nineteenth Century* (1845), and played an important role in the movement for social, educational, and political equality. Elizabeth Peabody, Hawthorne's sister-in-law, was another leading figure.

132   *State-street*: the Boston equivalent of Wall Street.

136   *Titan*: a member of the gigantic race defeated by Zeus and his brothers in Greek myth. The mighty Atlas was their war leader.

carry off the gates of Gaza: as Samson does in Judges 16: 1–3, foiling the attempt by the Philistines to trap him in the city.

138   *Newport or Saratoga*: fashionable resorts in Rhode Island and upstate New York, respectively.

the annual Fast: a custom in Puritan New England; later the day became a public holiday in many states.

139   *Cassandra*: the wild prophetess, accurate but unheeded, of Homer's *Iliad*.

commoted: disturbed (cf. 'commotion').

141   *the North American Review*: a conservative Bostonian quarterly.

Cambridge men: members of Harvard University, situated in Cambridge, near Boston.

143   *Orphic wisdom*: oracular, esoteric, prophetic; from Orpheus, the inspired musician of Greek myth, who was said to have founded a mystery religion.

146   *sillabub*: frothy cream dessert.

147   *diorama*: a miniature scene on public display; here depicting a battle, as in Ch. XXIII ('the diorama of Moscow or Bunker Hill'). A successful diorama made the nineteenth-century spectator feel part of the spectacle.

bibliopolist: bookseller.

148   *Malta or Madeira*: both islands were famous for producing wine.

buttonwood-tree: plane.

150   *sherry-cobbler*: drink mixing sherry, lemon, sugar, and ice.

161   *astral lamp*: type of oil lamp.

170   *air-line*: imaginary line in the air.

171   *gripe*: grip.

174   *fumigation*: smoking.

175   *Human nature ... substituting good*: restored by the editors of the *Centenary Edition*, this whole passage was crossed out in manuscript, and absent from editions published in the author's lifetime. Sophia Hawthorne's strong disapproval of alcohol is again assumed to have been decisive.

176   *daguerreotype*: the earliest form of photograph, invented by Louis Daguerre (1789–1851) in the 1820s.

syncope: fainting fit, black-out.

179   *patch over his right eye*: previously over the left eye.

181   *kennel-rat*: gutter rat; cf. canal, channel.

182   *Fauntleroy*: a probable allusion to the well-known case of the English banker Henry Fauntleroy, hanged for forgery in 1824 (see Introduction, pp. xiv–xviii).

183   *the New England metropolis*: Boston.

195   *penny-a-liners*: journalists paid at this rate.

196   *Lyceum-halls*: founded in the 1820s, and flourishing by the 1840s, the lyceum movement established colleges for adult education, which also served as venues for visiting lecturers and the kinds of entertainment Hawthorne describes.

thaumaturgist: magician.

the Mormon Prophet: Joseph Smith (1805–44), who founded the Church of Latter-Day Saints and published the *Book of Mormon* in 1830.

198   *the epoch of rapping spirits*: American spiritualism only became a widespread phenomenon in the late 1840s, after the publication of Andrew Jackson Davis's book *The Principles of Nature* (1847).

205   *barberry bushes*: Berberis.

Paul Dudley: Massachusetts landowner, judge, and legislator (1675–1751), credited with erecting such walls throughout the colony.

209   *Comus*: the sorcerer in Milton's masque, already referred to in Ch. VIII.

a concourse of strange figures: the source of this passage was a masquerade party at Brook Farm, recorded in Hawthorne's *American Notebooks* (28 September 1841).

Bavarian broom-girl: witch.

Jim Crow: a dancing negro character in minstrel shows who made his first appearance in the song 'Jim Crow' (1830), performed by T. D. Rice, the father of minstrelsy. The body of racist laws brought in in the latter part of the nineteenth century became known as the 'Jim Crow laws'.

Shaker: the Shakers were a millenarian Protestant sect

founded in the eighteenth century; Ann Lee, the church's leader, emigrated from England to America in 1774.

the Faerie Queen: Edmund Spenser's long poem, left incomplete at his death in 1598. Six of the planned twelve books were published in 1596.

210 *Moll Pitcher*: a famous Massachusetts fortune-teller and reputed witch, who died in 1813.

skinkers and drawers: men serving drinks.

Tam O'Shanter: the hero of a Robert Burns poem (1791), who is pursued by the Devil when drunk.

211 *Actaeon*: in Greek myth, a hunter who watched Artemis (Diana) and her attendants bathing; she changed him into a stag, and he was killed by his own hounds.

213 *calash*: hooped sun-bonnet.

214 *a Puritan magistrate, holding inquest ... in a case of witchcraft*: as one of Hawthorne's ancestors had done in the Salem witch trials of 1692.

230 *so you think she's drowned herself!*: in the *American Notebooks* (9 July 1845) Hawthorne records taking part in 'a search for the body of a drowned girl'.

232 *horn-pouts*: catfish.

237 *tire-women*: those who prepare (attire) the body for burial.

243 *Bunyan's book*: *The Pilgrim's Progress* (1678); an allegorical work, like Spenser's *Faerie Queene*, referred to in Ch. XXIV.

246 *Doctor Griswold*: Rufus Griswold (1815–57), literary journalist best known as the biographer of Poe, and the editor of his poetry; Coverdale refers to his survey *The Poets and Poetry of America* (1842).

Kossuth: Lajos Kossuth (1802–94), leader of the Hungarian Revolution of 1848, and head of the republic he had proclaimed until defeat in 1849. Hawthorne heard him speak in Boston in 1851.

CHARLES DICKENS	**A Tale of Two Cities**
GEORGE DU MAURIER	**Trilby**
MARIA EDGEWORTH	**Castle Rackrent**
GEORGE ELIOT	**Daniel Deronda** **The Lifted Veil and Brother Jacob** **Middlemarch** **The Mill on the Floss** **Silas Marner**
SUSAN FERRIER	**Marriage**
ELIZABETH GASKELL	**Cranford** **The Life of Charlotte Brontë** **Mary Barton** **North and South** **Wives and Daughters**
GEORGE GISSING	**New Grub Street** **The Odd Women**
EDMUND GOSSE	**Father and Son**
THOMAS HARDY	**Far from the Madding Crowd** **Jude the Obscure** **The Mayor of Casterbridge** **The Return of the Native** **Tess of the d'Urbervilles** **The Woodlanders**
WILLIAM HAZLITT	**Selected Writings**
JAMES HOGG	**The Private Memoirs and Confessions of a Justified Sinner**
JOHN KEATS	**The Major Works** **Selected Letters**
CHARLES MATURIN	**Melmoth the Wanderer**
JOHN RUSKIN	**Selected Writings**
WALTER SCOTT	**The Antiquary** **Ivanhoe**

	Six French Poets of the Nineteenth Century
HONORÉ DE BALZAC	**Cousin Bette**
	Eugénie Grandet
	Père Goriot
CHARLES BAUDELAIRE	**The Flowers of Evil**
	The Prose Poems and **Fanfarlo**
BENJAMIN CONSTANT	**Adolphe**
DENIS DIDEROT	**Jacques the Fatalist**
	The Nun
ALEXANDRE DUMAS (PÈRE)	**The Black Tulip**
	The Count of Monte Cristo
	Louise de la Vallière
	The Man in the Iron Mask
	La Reine Margot
	The Three Musketeers
	Twenty Years After
	The Vicomte de Bragelonne
ALEXANDRE DUMAS (FILS)	**La Dame aux Camélias**
GUSTAVE FLAUBERT	**Madame Bovary**
	A Sentimental Education
	Three Tales
VICTOR HUGO	**The Essential Victor Hugo**
	Notre-Dame de Paris
J.-K. HUYSMANS	**Against Nature**
PIERRE CHODERLOS DE LACLOS	**Les Liaisons dangereuses**
MME DE LAFAYETTE	**The Princesse de Clèves**
GUILLAUME DU LORRIS and JEAN DE MEUN	**The Romance of the Rose**

ÉMILE ZOLA

L'Assommoir
The Attack on the Mill
La Bête humaine
La Débâcle
Germinal
The Kill
The Ladies' Paradise
The Masterpiece
Nana
Pot Luck
Thérèse Raquin

ANTON CHEKHOV

About Love and Other Stories
Early Stories
Five Plays
The Princess and Other Stories
The Russian Master and Other Stories
The Steppe and Other Stories
Twelve Plays
Ward Number Six and Other Stories

FYODOR DOSTOEVSKY

Crime and Punishment
Devils
A Gentle Creature and Other Stories
The Idiot
The Karamazov Brothers
Memoirs from the House of the Dead
Notes from the Underground and
    The Gambler

NIKOLAI GOGOL

Dead Souls
Plays and Petersburg Tales

ALEXANDER PUSHKIN

Eugene Onegin
The Queen of Spades and Other Stories

LEO TOLSTOY

Anna Karenina
The Kreutzer Sonata and Other Stories
The Raid and Other Stories
Resurrection
War and Peace

IVAN TURGENEV

Fathers and Sons
First Love and Other Stories
A Month in the Country

The Oxford World's Classics Website

www.oup.com/uk/worldsclassics

- Information about new titles
- Explore the full range of Oxford World's Classics
- Links to other literary sites and the main OUP webpage
- Imaginative competitions, with bookish prizes
- Articles by editors
- Extracts from Introductions
- Special information for teachers and lecturers

www.oup.com/uk/worldsclassics

American Literature

Authors in Context

British and Irish Literature

Children's Literature

Classics and Ancient Literature

Colonial Literature

Eastern Literature

European Literature

History

Medieval Literature

Oxford English Drama

Poetry

Philosophy

Politics

Religion

The Oxford Shakespeare

ANTHEMS OF DEFEAT

Crackdown in Hunan Province, 1989-92

W9-CUE-961

An Asia Watch Report

A Division of Human Rights Watch

485 Fifth Avenue
New York, NY 10017
Tel: (212) 974-8400
Fax: (212) 972-0905

1522 K Street, NW, Suite 910
Washington, DC 20005
Tel: (202) 371-6592
Tel: (202) 371-0124

Cover Design by Patti Lacobee

Photo: AP/Wide World Photos

The cover photograph shows the huge portrait of Mao Zedong which hangs
above Tiananmen Gate at the north end of Tiananmen Square, just after it had
been defaced on May 23, 1989 by three pro-democracy demonstrators from
Hunan Province. The three men, Yu Zhijian, Yu Dongyue and Lu Decheng,
threw ink and paint at the portrait as a protest against China's one-party
dictatorship and the Maoist system. They later received sentences of between 16
years and life imprisonment.

THE ASIA WATCH COMMITTEE

Introduction

Acknowledgements

This report was compiled and written by Tang Boqiao, former chairman of the Hunan Students Autonomous Federation. Robin Munro, Asia Watch's staff specialist on China, coordinated the research project and edited the report. Jeannine Guthrie, Asia Watch associate, provided production assistance.

Asia Watch would like to express its sincere debt of gratitude toward Tang Boqiao and all of his colleagues still inside China who made this report possible. Their courage and dedication has been a constant source of inspiration.

Introduction

The images of the June 4, 1989 repression in China may have faded from many people's memory, but the human toll continues to be exacted. This report recovers the lost history of the crackdown on the 1989 pro-democracy movement in Hunan Province, where some 1000 activists and demonstrators were detained after June 4 and around 500 are still behind bars today. A comprehensive profile of the repression in one medium-sized Chinese province, the report opens a window on to the previously hidden processes of arbitrary mass detention, wholesale torture and politically-engineered trials that ensued throughout China's vast hinterland following the massacre in Beijing, in areas beyond the purview of foreign journalists and camera crews based in the capital.

The report is the result of a lengthy collaboration between Asia Watch and Tang Boqiao, a leader of the 1989 student pro-democracy movement in Hunan Province who spent 18 months in prison after June 1989 and then escaped from China in July 1991 after being placed on the government's wanted list for a second time. Working in association with a large, underground pro-democracy network with members in many different provinces of China, Tang has provided us with what is probably the most comprehensive account of systematic human rights violations to have emerged from the People's Republic of China in the past 15 years. In order to preserve the immediacy of his account, we have kept it in the first person.

More than 200 cases of political imprisonment in Hunan, almost all of them previously unknown, appear in the report, together with vivid details of the wide range of torture and abuse to which many of those detained have been subjected. Drawing on extensive, first-hand archival sources, the report also includes documents from the 1989 Hunan pro-democracy movement; prosecution bills of indictment and court verdicts; a near-exhaustive list of the prisons, forced-labor camps and jails in the province; and numerous maps. It comprises, in short, the outcome of the most effective large-scale human rights monitoring exercise ever to have been conducted by a group of PRC nationals working from within the country. Asia Watch has independently corroborated and supplemented their account, using a network of other sources, wherever possible.

The wealth of information provided by Tang and his underground group -- the All-China People's Autonomous Federation (ACPAF)[*] -- provides many new insights into the post-June 1989 repression both in Hunan and in China more generally. It shows that the crackdown was far more severe and intense in the provinces, and much wider in scope, than had previously been thought. Whatever the "leniency" of the sentences handed down to activists in Beijing, it is clear that many pro-democracy participants in the provinces suffered the full brunt of the government's wrath. More than 40 prisoners detained in the province in connection with the 1989 movement, for example, are currently serving sentences of between 10 years and life imprisonment. (Some were charged with violent offenses such as arson and "smashing and looting," but there is every reason to believe, given the well-documented pattern of arbitrary arrests and unfair trials that ensued, that many of them were in fact only involved in peaceful political activities.) The average length of sentence passed on worker participants in the movement was more than eight years.

The report highlights a number of heroes of the democracy movement in Hunan who are virtually unknown outside of China. One of these, a worker named Zhang Jingsheng, became known as the "Wei Jingsheng of the South" - after China's most famous political prisoner and pro-democracy activist. (The two men share the same given name.) Like his Beijing counterpart, Zhang Jingsheng had been imprisoned for his involvement in the Democracy Wall movement in the late 1970s, and after his release he went on to play an active role in the Workers Autonomous Federation in Changsha during May 1989. He was re-arrested and given a 13-year sentence for being a "stubborn anti-Party element."

Other activists became models of courage as much for their behavior in prison as for their role in the 1989 movement. An elderly

---

[*] A more literal translation of the organization's Chinese name - *Zhongguo Minzhong Tuanti Zizhi Lianhehui* - is "Federation of Autonomous People's Organizations of China." On June 2, 1992, following a decision reached with ACPAF leaders still inside China, Tang held a press conference in Washington D.C. to announce publicly the federation's existence. The identities of the ACPAF leaders and membership remain secret.

retired professor at Hunan University, Peng Yuzhang, was arrested in mid-June 1989 and forced to endure unimaginable torments for his sheer defiance of the prison authorities. He was eventually placed in a psychiatric institution, but not before he had inspired fellow-inmates 40 years younger with his will to resist intimidation.

In a sense, this report on the crackdown in Hunan signals the gradual convergence of China's heavily repressed pro-democracy movement with the current global trend toward the effective monitoring and enforcement of internationally-recognized human rights. Many people in China have taken enormous risks to compile and transmit this material to the outside world, and some of them may well go to prison for their efforts. The task of keeping a close eye on their future fate becomes, with the publication of this report, an item of the greatest urgency in Asia Watch's work and one which is likely to tax our monitoring capabilities to the full.

A much broader task is to build international pressure upon the Chinese authorities to allow full and regular access by acknowledged humanitarian organizations to the vast prison and labor camp systems of Hunan and the other provinces of China. Only when the doors of the Chinese *gulag* have finally been thrown open to such inspection will effective remedies begin to be put in place by the Chinese authorities and the kinds of endemic, systematic violence recorded in this report begin to diminish.

Finally, Asia Watch calls upon the Chinese authorities immediately and unconditionally to release all those currently detained in Hunan Province for the peaceful exercise of their rights to freedom of expression and association. In view of the serious grounds for doubting whether due process of law was observed in the cases of those convicted of violent offenses after June 4, 1989, moreover, the authorities should promptly reexamine all such cases and make public the evidence underlying the convictions.

1. The 1989 Democracy Movement in Hunan Province

The province of Hunan, with a population of over 55 million - ten million more than South Korea with more than twice its area - has been the scene of countless major and often tragic episodes in recent Chinese history. These large-scale social and political upheavals have produced and then destroyed one group after another of outstanding patriots who rose to the challenge of the times. Partial to hot, spicy food and strong liquor, the Hunanese are well-known for their stubbornness, political militancy and general strength of character.

Probably Hunan's best-loved and most famous historical figure was Qu Yuan, a poet and official of the 3rd-4th century B.C. who drowned himself in the Miluo River, near the present-day provincial capital Changsha, in protest at the corruption and impotence of the government. Another much-revered native of the province is Tan Sitong, an intellectual who helped lead the "100 Days Reform" movement in 1898 against Manchu autocracy, and who was later executed by the imperial forces after refusing to flee the ensuing repression. Tan's words, "If I don't shed my blood, who then will?", have inspired generations of Hunanese patriots, including Huang Xing, a colleague of Sun Yatsen and renowned "father of the Chinese revolution."

But the province has also produced numerous great tyrants, ranging from Zeng Guofan, the "Butcher of Hunan" who in the mid-19th century suppressed the massive Taiping Rebellion at the cost of millions of peasant lives, to Mao Zedong, the so-called "People's Emperor" who first united the nation and then inflicted on it such wholesale disasters as the Cultural Revolution. Indeed, an unusual preponderance of Chinese Communist Party leaders have hailed from Hunan. They include such enlightened figures as Liu Shaoqi, Peng Dehuai and Hu Yaobang, and even today's Zhu Rongji (sometimes known as "China's Gorbachev"), but also such hardline ultra-leftist figures as Wang Zhen and Deng Liqun.

From 1949 onward, Hunan Province has stood in the vanguard of the various political campaigns, both benign and repressive, that have swept the country. During the 1989 Democracy Movement, Hunan province experienced the largest and best-organized student and worker-led campaign for democracy of any part of China outside Beijing. The death on April 15, 1989 of Hu Yaobang, the standard bearer of political reform in China, evoked a deep sense of loss among Hunanese - but also a strong patriotic urge to inherit and defend his legacy of reform. During the 1989 movement, there was no sizeable city or district in Hunan which did not have its own autonomous student organization or independent workers' group, and in all parts of the province local residents came out in their tens of thousands to publicly demonstrate, time and time again, their support for the unprecedented movement. This report tells the story, previously unknown, of the 1989 pro-democracy movement in Hunan.

Student activism: a Hunan tradition

During the 1979-89 decade of Deng Xiaoping's "reform and open door" policy, a series of student protest campaigns occurred in Changsha, the capital of Hunan Province, demanding a faster pace of political reform and seeking to promote democracy. The first, a campaign in the summer of 1980 to freely elect student representatives to the local People's Congress, formed part of the nationwide unofficial pro-reform drive which had begun at Beijing's Democracy Wall some two years earlier. It mainly involved students from my own school, Hunan Teacher Training College (now Hunan Normal University), and was led by Tao Sen, a student from the Chinese department's class of 1977, and Liang Heng, who later left China and co-authored the best-seller *Son of the Revolution*.

A vanguard component of the first and only nationwide movement since 1949 for the free election of people's representatives, the 1980 Hunan student campaign lasted for nearly one month and included mass demonstrations, sit-ins and hunger strikes. Tao Sen, who was imprisoned for five years after 1989, led a delegation of student leaders to Beijing to negotiate with the central government and won a number of significant concessions, but these were later revoked and student activists were subsequently purged by the local authorities. The influence and effects of the campaign, however, resonated across the country for several years afterwards.

The second major student movement in Hunan took place in

November 1986, when activists at Hunan Normal University again launched a student strike calling for the authorities to observe human rights and the rule of law and to show greater respect for teachers. This campaign, later dubbed the "November 5 Incident" by the central government, spread quickly to include most of the Changsha campuses and was far-reaching in its effects. Preceding the student protests of later that month at the Hefei University of Science and Technology (where Professor Fang Lizhi was then vice-chancellor), it provided the initial inspiration and impetus for the massive wave of student demonstrations in support of democracy which swept China's major cities during the winter of 1986-87. In a counter-offensive launched in January 1987 by hardline Party leaders to root out so-called "bourgeois liberalism," Hu Yaobang was driven from power and replaced as Party general secretary by Zhao Ziyang. Li Peng was appointed as premier, and a severe political chill descended on the country.

The pro-democracy movement in Hunan, however, did not let up. The flashpoint for a third surge of activism occurred in September 1987, when a Hunan University student was beaten to death by a group of People's Liberation Army (PLA) soldiers. This incident sparked off a province-wide protest movement in which students sent telegrams all over the country, and there were rallies on the campuses of Hunan University and other colleges. Local outrage at the student's killing became so great that Deng Xiaoping himself had personally to intervene to restore social order and quell the unrest. He instructed the Central Military Commission to disband the PLA independent division concerned and to dismiss all its officers from their posts, from division commander to platoon leaders. The soldiers directly involved in the murder of the student were all sentenced to death and executed.

The 1989 Democracy Movement

Each campaign for democracy during the decade of reforms had been larger and more influential than the last, and students activists in Hunan all knew that 1989 was likely to produce a major new upsurge of pro-democracy activity throughout the country. Several key anniversaries by chance all happened to fall in that year: the 200th anniversary of the

3

French revolution, the 70th anniversary of China's May 4th Movement[1] and the 40th anniversary of the founding of the People's Republic of China. The high-tide of Deng Xiaoping's political and economic reforms, reached in late 1986, had by early 1989 subsided drastically in the face of an economic austerity program that had generated widespread discontent among the populace, and graft and corruption among Party officials was rampant.

Democracy Salon

At the beginning of 1989, an underground student organization was formed by activists of the Hunan Normal University. It was originally called, variously, the "Arts and Literature Salon" and the "Current Affairs Forum", but eventually the name of "Democracy Salon" *(Minzhu Shalong)* was decided upon. There was no contact with similar salons in Beijing, such as that run by student leader Wang Dan. Besides acting as a general focus for student debate on the topics of reform and democratization, the organization's main role lay in planning and preparing commemorative activities to mark the coming series of anniversaries.

The Democracy Salon's plans for 1989 included, notably, a series of large-scale street demonstrations in Changsha and other cities to promote democracy, oppose corruption and call for accelerated political reforms and a more open system. We proposed a four-point maxim for China's future governance, namely: "Democracy - Rule of Law - Science - Civilization." Although the organization was originally based at Hunan Normal University and carried out most of its planning activities there, it spread quickly during early 1989 to include students from all the institutes of higher education in Changsha. Many of the Salon's members went on to become core leaders of the 1989 Hunan Democracy Movement. The Salon, which met once a week was very tightly organized with officers, members and membership dues.

---

[1] The May Fourth Movement commemorates the day in 1919 when Beijing students staged protest actions against Chinese leaders' acceptance of a decision made by the victorious allied powers at the Treaty of Versailles to give Shandong Province over to Japan as its "sphere of influence." The protest turned into a movement for democracy and national freedom and led eventually to the founding of the Chinese Communist Party.

4

The "April 22 Incident"

The real starting date of the 1989 Hunan student movement fell on April 22, one week after the death of Hu Yaobang, and several days after the first unauthorized mourning activities for Hu had been launched by students in Beijing. (There were several small-scale demonstrations in Hunan before April 22, but these had very little impact.) On that day, the graduate students' associations of both Hunan University and Central-South Industrial University organized a group of around 5,000 students to take to the streets of Changsha and demonstrate publicly in support of their call for "dialogue" between the student representatives and the provincial government. The demonstration went off smoothly, and by around 4:00 pm all the demonstrators had gradually dispersed.

The same evening, however, another group of students took to the streets, carrying floral wreaths and mourning banners and setting off firecrackers as they went. These students were reportedly all from Liuyang, the hometown of Hu Yaobang. It was the weekend, so many ordinary residents of Changsha were out on the streets and joined in the marching column. Soon the whole of May 1st Avenue had become a sea of people. All kinds of slogans, such as "We demand freedom and democracy" and "Smash official profiteering and corruption!", filled the air and gradually a state of considerable chaos began to emerge. I was present throughout the evening and witnessed the whole incident.

Eventually, the mood turned nasty, and some over-excited youths proceeded to completely smash up around 40 of the shops along either side of the street. Very little looting occurred, however, since the incident was essentially an outpouring of pent-up anger and frustration by the crowd against escalating government corruption in recent years. Most of the rioters confined themselves to breaking up and stamping on the objects from the shops (mainly food and items of clothing) that lay scattered around, and few if any really valuable items such as gold or silver ornaments were looted. During the entire incident, no officials from any of the government departments emerged to try to take control or deal with the situation. It was as if the government had simply evaporated.

Finally, after most of the rioting had ended and the crowd had already begun to disperse, more than 1,000 policemen (many of them

5

from newly established anti-riot units) and dozens of plainclothes security agents were sent into the city center to "restore order." By the end of the evening, the authorities had seized and arrested around 100 of the demonstrators - all of whom were later characterized as being mere "beating, smashing and looting elements." It was the same term used to describe student and worker Red Guards after the Cultural Revolution.

The arrests were largely indiscriminate, however, and many of those detained, including some of those later convicted as "ringleaders," had actually played no part in the rioting. Indeed, the person who received the heaviest punishment in connection with the incident, a young factory worker named Li Weihong, had done nothing more than shout slogans urging the crowd to take action. He himself had not engaged in any violence at all. He was eventually handed down a sentence of death with a two-year reprieve. In all, more than 40 of those detained that night were later tried and sentenced by the courts, although the figure officially given was only 27.

The local government immediately relayed this incident to the senior authorities in Beijing. Together with a similar incident which occurred the same day in Xi'an, the capital of Shaanxi Province, it was cited in the April 26 *People's Daily* editorial - "Resolutely Oppose the Turmoil" - as a major grounds for the central government's condemnation of the student movement as a whole. Moreover, the movement was denounced not simply as posing a threat to public order, but as being "a planned conspiracy and turmoil...by an extremely small number of people" with ulterior motives. "Their aim," said the editorial, "was to sow dissension among the people, plunge the whole country into chaos and sabotage the political situation of stability and unity." Concluded the article: "Bans should be placed on unlawful parades and demonstrations and on such acts as going to factories, rural areas and schools to establish ties." From this moment on, plans for the coming repression accelerated across the country.

Commemoration of the May 4th anniversary

After the "April 22 Incident," the Changsha student body felt deeply unsettled and for a time had no idea what to do next. Once the government announced that there had been no students among those arrested, however, everyone felt greatly relieved. After assessing the prevailing situation, a group of core student activists then decided to set up the "May 4 Joint Steering Committee," which was to serve as a guiding body for the Hunan student movement as a whole. The key members of the Steering Committee were myself, Zheng Yan, Xia Siqing, Liu Qiaohui, Long Jianhua and Zhu Jianwen, all from Hunan Normal University; Hao Mingzhao, Lu Siqing, and He Zhiqiang from Central-South Industrial University; and, from Hunan University, Li Zhiping, Shui Li and Shen Yong.[2] A large number of the Steering Committee's members had been very influential in their own institutions and other universities and colleges in Changsha even before the 1989 student movement began. Lu Siqing, Hao Mingzhao, Xia Siqing, Li Zhiping and others had all been cadres of the official student association, and they were all straight-A students.

The first action by the Steering Committee took place on April 27, when students from Hunan Normal University, Hunan University and Central-South Industrial University took to the streets and demonstrated once again. Between 6,000 and 8,000 students tried to march into the provincial administration building. Officials closed the main gate but the crowd pushed it open. Lu Siqing and other students entered the building and met with Wang Fei, the deputy director of the provincial office. The dialogue lasted about two hours and was cordial. The two sides discussed the students' complaints of government corruption, and the officials promised to investigate. When the students left the building, most of the demonstrators were still sitting outside waiting for them.

The following day, several student delegates headed by Lu Siqing were put forward to open a dialogue with Wang Xiangtian, deputy-governor of Hunan Province, and Long Yuxian, chairman of the Provincial Education Commission. The main thrust of the talks concerned discussions on the problem of profiteering and corruption among Hunan officials. The talks proceeded in a friendly and constructive atmosphere, and this marked a turning point in the entire Hunan democracy movement. Henceforth, right up until the time of the June 4 repression, no major state of conflict or antagonism arose between the students and the government. This was one important feature of the Hunan pro-

---

[2] Of these, Long Jianhua, Hao Mingzhao and I were arrested after June 4.

democracy movement which differentiated it quite sharply from that in Beijing.

Between April 27 and May 3, the *May 4 Joint Steering Committee* printed and distributed a large quantity of leaflets and publicity materials in preparation for the May 4 anniversary, including a "Letter to Compatriots", a "Letter to the Students" and a "Letter to the Teachers". At eight o'clock in the morning of May 4, firecrackers were let off in Hunan Normal University, Hunan University, Central-South Industrial University and the Finance and Economics College to inaugurate a "May 4 Joint Action" in Changsha consisting of city-wide demonstrations. The various school authorities ordered all the campus gates to be locked, however, and as a result of this concerted obstruction and interference, only the students from Hunan Normal University, Changsha Railway College and a few other institutions managed to break out and join the demonstration. The rest remained stuck on campus.

As the students gradually converged on Changsha's Martyrs Park, they were joined by large crowds of city residents. By noon, there were 100,000 people gathered together there. After many people from the crowd had been freely allowed to make speeches (each limited to three minutes in length) I made a speech on behalf of the Steering Committee and announced the setting up of the "Joint Action Provisional Committee of Hunan Province Institutions of Higher Education." Immediately after the rally, representatives from all the colleges convened in the same park to hold the inaugural meeting of the Provisional Committee.

Thereafter, the campuses gradually quietened down for a time and no further protest demonstrations took place. During this period, the Provisional Committee held several meetings at the Aiwan Pavilion (a favored recreational spot on Mt. Yuelu, on the banks of Changsha's Xiang River between the Hunan Normal and Central-South Industrial universities, where Mao Zedong held many student movement meetings in the late 1910s), and at the Changsha Youth Palace and other places. These meetings dealt mainly with the problem of how best to develop our activities on a long-term basis, for example by publishing newspapers, setting up study-groups and extending our organizational scale and membership.

During this period, however, the authorities were also busy

preparing their next move. From the time of the April 26 *People's Daily* editorial onward, an intensive official investigation known as the "fight-back and counter-reckoning exercise" *(fangong daosuan)* had been underway in Hunan Province. Dossiers were opened on student activists, and it was made known to us that our "performance" in the coming weeks could be crucial to our future job prospects. In addition, certain key figures who had been active in earlier pro-democracy or student movements were placed under close police surveillance. These included, notably, Zhang Jingsheng, a worker who had spent four years in prison as a "counterrevolutionary" after editing an unofficial journal in Changsha during the 1978-81 Democracy Wall movement, and the former students Tao Sen and Zhou Zhirong, both of whom had been leaders of the 1980 Hunan Normal College free election campaign and subsequently spent time in prison as a result.

On the afternoon of May 4, Zhang Jingsheng was arrested and taken to the Changsha No.1 Jail after making a speech at a students' rally voicing his strong opposition toward the government's attempts to suppress the patriotic students. But in the days that followed, policy lines among the upper echelons of the central government remained unclear, and certain high-ranking supporters of the student movement had not yet fallen from power. The Changsha municipal government, seeing that no large-scale repressive actions had ensued in other parts of the country, had Zhang Jingsheng released within a matter of days.

The Hunan Students Autonomous Federation

On May 13, news reached Changsha that the Beijing students had begun a mass hunger strike in Tiananmen Square. The following day, the Hunan students' Provisional Committee called a meeting in which it was decided that I should travel immediately to Beijing to make contact with the students and assess the situation there. On May 15, some students spontaneously took to the streets of Changsha once again. Several thousand students from different universities converged on the Provincial Administration Building carrying banners supporting the hunger strikers in Beijing, supporting reform, and calling for an end to corruption. The demonstration lasted from about noon to about 5 p.m.

On May 16, the Provisional Committee organized a large-scale joint protest demonstration involving all the Changsha institutions of

9

higher education. On this occasion, Changsha residents from all walks of life joined in, prominent among them being journalists from the news and media units and cadres from the Hunan People's Political Consultative Conference.[3] That evening, the Provisional Committee renamed itself the "Hunan Students Autonomous Federation" (SAF) and started a mass hunger strike of around 2000 students and 100 or so workers outside the provincial government offices. Fan Zhong, chairman of the student association of Central-South Industrial University, acted as general commander of the hunger strike.

During the period of the hunger strike, the SAF held numerous dialogue sessions with the provincial government, demanding that official corruption and profiteering be severely punished and the democratization process steadily continued. But the provincial government adopted a careful wait-and-see attitude; it was clear that the lives of the hunger-striking students were of only secondary importance to them. Essentially, the provincial government was confused and uncertain about how best to proceed. In the absence of a clear policy direction from Beijing, it preferred simply to do nothing. This at least gave us some room for maneuver in the week preceding martial law.

On May 17 and 18, the SAF organized and led further large-scale demonstrations in Changsha, the main purpose of which was to show support for the Beijing hunger strikers and also those on hunger strike outside the Hunan provincial government offices. On each day, several tens of thousands of local people joined the demonstrations.

The situation became increasingly tense. On May 19, one of the SAF leaders, Lu Siqing, tried to commit suicide by slashing his wrists, in a desperate attempt to spur the government to action and win over society. Fortunately, he was discovered just in time and was saved from bleeding to death. At around the same time, another SAF leader, Hao Mingzhao, poured petrol all over himself in the public toilets and was

---

[3] The HPPCC is a provincial body which is supposed to represent all non-communist groups and be the "alternate" representative of the people. In reality, it has acted as a rubber stamp for decisions made by the Communist Party. There is one such body in every province and a national Chinese People's Political Consultative Conference.

about to go the provincial government offices to immolate himself. Luckily, he too was discovered by his class-mates and a tragedy was thereby averted.

Hunan's response to martial law

On the evening of May 19, martial law was imposed in Beijing. That same evening, I returned to Changsha. In view of the rapidly deteriorating political situation, the SAF decided to call off the students' hunger strike and alter it to a peaceful sit-down protest (also in front of the provincial government offices), and in this way to continue the struggle. It was an extremely moving scene that night, with everyone singing "The Internationale" and many of the students crying bitterly. When the Changsha residents heard rumors that the army was approaching Changsha, large bands of them headed off immediately toward each of the main intersections into the city and gathered together to block the troops. In the ensuing confusion, a number of people were arrested by the police, but the SAF sent delegates to negotiate with the provincial public security department and the detainees were soon freed.

In response to the news of martial law, large numbers of students and local residents also took to the streets and demonstrated in many other cities of Hunan Province. In Xiangtan, Hengyang, Yueyang and Zhuzhou, for example, further sit-down protests and hunger strikes were quickly staged in front of the government offices.

In Shaoyang City, tens of thousands of students and local residents marched toward People's Square in the downtown area on the night of May 19 to protest martial law. A number of arrests were made on the spot, and the crowd became angry. Some young people rushed forward, dragging policemen out from their vehicles and setting the vehicles on fire. Several sedan cars belonging to government officials were also stopped and set on fire by the crowd. More policemen quickly arrived on the scene and began indiscriminately seizing the demonstrators. The clashes continued until the early hours of the morning, at which time a section of the crowd broke through the police cordon and forced its way into the offices of the municipal Party committee. As a result, scores of people were arrested that night.

Secret arrests were also made in Hengyang City on May 20, after a large demonstration there against martial law in Beijing in which students and citizens clashed with the police. Official reports claimed that about 100 policemen were injured; from this it was reasonable to assume that the number of civilian casualties was far higher. Many people were arrested in Hengyang over the next few days, though this was denied by the government. After my release from prison on February 13, 1991, I made an investigation into the May 20 incident in Hengyang. Even then, the local people all still expressed strong outrage at the incident. In their words, "The dogs raised up by the people suddenly saw yellow." (In Hunan slang, "seeing yellow" means being treacherous and ungrateful.)

On the night of May 20, the Changsha public security authorities secretly arrested four workers named Dong Qi, He Jianming, Dai Dingxiang and Liang Chao, who had been active in organizing citizens in support of the students. Upon hearing a rumor that the army was entering Changsha, the four hurried to a meeting with student leaders to discuss countermeasures, but were intercepted by the police and arrested on the pretext that they were all carrying small pen-knives (there was in fact nothing unusual about this.) After June 4, they were sentenced to prison terms of between three and five years.[4] The incident was a classic example of the authorities' attempts to find non-student scapegoats to blame for the student movement - so-called "outside agitators" who were supposedly trying to pervert the movement's orientation. In reality, what the government feared most was the growing trend toward collaboration between workers and students.

May 22 brought further serious clashes between demonstrators and the police, this time in Xiangtan City, the hometown of Mao Zedong. The incident was triggered off when officers of the city's Pingzheng Road Police Station indiscriminately arrested some demonstrators. When the local people learned of this, they marched to the police post and gathered outside the main gate, shouting out slogans and demanding the release of all those arrested. The chief of the police post and several other cadres then proceeded to abuse and insult the crowd, and in a fit of anger, some people in the crowd broke into the police station and smashed it to pieces, setting fire to it as they left. Police reinforcements were rushed to the scene and up to ten people were arrested on the spot. (A report in the

---

[4] Hunan Daily, 12 June 1989.

Hunan Daily on June 16 revealed that 23 other demonstrators were arrested in connection with the incident after the June 4 crackdown.)

The Workers Autonomous Federation

On May 20, also in response to martial law, a number of worker activists who had been participating in the pro-democracy movement over the previous few weeks took the major step of formally establishing their own organization: the Changsha Workers Autonomous Federation (WAF). The main WAF standing committee members were Zhang Xudong, Zhou Yong, He Zhaohui, Zhou Min, Wang Changhuai, Zhang Jingsheng and Liu Yi.

Nearly all of the group's members had been actively involved in the hunger strike outside the provincial government offices in Changsha, and had played an important role in helping the students to forge links with the general public. They were tireless in organizing the workers to show support and solidarity for the student movement, and they gave us vital assistance in arranging food and equipment supplies and other logistical backup. The WAF and other worker groups in Hunan never managed to develop organizationally to a scale comparable to that of the student movement, and their prestige and influence among the general public remained considerably less than that of the SAF. But all of the WAF leaders were extremely resolute and dedicated pro-democracy activists, and they subsequently paid dearly for their attempts to form independent labor unions. None of them escaped from China after June 4, and their own story must therefore remain largely untold for the meantime.

Late May: the movement deepens

On May 22, the Hunan SAF decided to reorganize itself. First, we reformed and restructured the student governing bodies of all the participating colleges. Then we had each college reselect their delegates to the SAF, and formed a new standing committee from among those delegates. Those elected to the new standing committee included myself, Fan Zhong, Lu Siqing, Zhu Jianwen, Xia Siqing, Hao Mingzhao, Liu Wei,

Yue Weipeng, Shui Li, Li Zheng, and Hu Hao.[6] Later on, Xia Siqing quit and was replaced by Zheng Yan, a Ph.D student at Hunan Normal University.

By now, the SAF had effectively established itself as the unified voice of the province-wide student movement. Student representatives came to Changsha to participate in the SAF from colleges and universities throughout the province, including Xiangtan University, Zhongnan Institute of Forestry, Hengyang Medical Institute and Jishou University. The SAF dispatched "democracy propaganda teams" to all areas of Hunan to carry out public educational work among local residents, and these were highly influential and effective. In addition, Hunan Normal University's democracy propaganda team (headed by a famous student from the Chinese department nicknamed "Egghead") published a regular newsletter which was widely distributed throughout the province. Contacts with the student movement in other provinces of China were also well developed. One delegation led by Zhang Lixin from Beijing Teachers' College came to Hunan at the end of May.

Fan Zhong and I held full and overall responsibility for the SAF's affairs at this time. Moreover, we organized the sending out of students from all the higher colleges to the various prefectures and cities of Hunan to carry on propaganda and liaison work. On May 24, the SAF organized a massive city-wide demonstration in conjunction with the Changsha Workers Autonomous Federation (WAF). The demonstration went off in a well-disciplined and orderly way, with many different work units taking part - the procession extended for over five kilometers - and it had a considerable social impact. All the drivers from Changsha city's private taxi companies took part in the demonstration, with more than forty taxis altogether taking part in the demonstration column.

---

[6] Fan Zhong and Hao Mingzhao were undergraduates at Central-South Industrial University; Zhu Jianwen was a Hunan Normal University undergraduate; Xia Siqing and Lu Siqing were postgraduates from Hunan Normal University and Central-South Industrial University respectively; Liu Wei was a Changsha Railway College undergraduate; Yue Weipeng was from Hunan Hydroelectric Industry Teachers' College; Shui Li was a Hunan University undergraduate; Li Zheng was a Hunan Finance and Economics College undergraduate; and Hu Hao was a Hunan Medical University student.

After the May 24 demonstration wound up, the SAF convened a plenary session and decided both to continue with the peaceful sit-down demonstration outside the provincial government offices, and, at the same time, to send a group of students to all parts of the province to canvass delegates to the national and provincial People's Congresses. The SAF representatives called upon the delegates to support the students' righteous protest actions and to propose and support a legislative motion to dismiss Li Peng from office. In addition, we installed a sit-down protest group in front of the offices of the standing committee of the Hunan Provincial People's Congress.

Another highly significant event which occurred around this time was the joint drafting and signing, by no less than 60 committee members of the Hunan People's Political Consultative Conference, of a "Manifesto of the HPPCC" in which the delegates to this prestigious official body expressed their clear support for the aims of the student protest movement. The chief signatory of this manifesto was Zou Naishan, a former mayor of Changsha. (In 1990, Zou was dismissed for this by the Provincial Peoples' Congress from his post on the standing committee of the HPPCC.) Many journalists and editors in Hunan also publicly voiced their opposition to Li Peng's declaration of martial law, raising the slogan: "The media must tell the truth!"

Moreover, the workers of Changsha and other cities continued to maintain firm solidarity with the student movement throughout this period. A city-wide strike, which had been planned by the Changsha workers in response to martial law, only failed to materialize because of extreme pressure and intimidation brought to bear by the authorities in the factories.

On May 27, two SAF representatives (myself and Liu Wei) negotiated with Su Qingyun, head of the Provincial Petitions Bureau, with a view to re-establishing a dialogue with the provincial government. Su agreed to engage in dialogue with the students on the government's behalf, on condition that we first of all returned to our colleges and universities and resumed classes. In the end, we reached an agreement whereby the students would return to campus so long as the government began to conduct the dialogue before May 30; otherwise, the SAF would continue to organize its peaceful sit-down protest.

On May 28, after a great deal of hard work, the SAF finally managed to persuade the students to temporarily call off the protest and return to their institutions. Before dispersing late that evening, the students held a bonfire-light ceremony in front of the provincial government offices in which we all swore an oath of allegiance. We knelt down, facing toward the five-star national emblem which hung high over the entrance to the government offices, and everyone solemnly took the pledge: "We vow to uphold the ideals of democracy to the end!" A member of the SAF standing committee, Lu Siqing, suddenly raised his head high and with tears streaming down his face cried out, "Emblem of our nation! We won't let you down!"

Many of the students began to cry bitterly at that point. One fine arts student from Hunan University even stood up and threw himself into the bonfire that was blazing away in the square. He was rescued by some fellow-students, his face badly burnt. People in the crowd all around started angrily shouting slogans such as "Down with Li Peng!", "Long Live the Students!" The medical staff from the Red Cross who were present that night wept at the scene. Even the People's Armed Police officers, who were there to uphold public order, couldn't hold back their tears.

When the students finally departed from the provincial government offices, the sound of firecrackers could be heard all along the length and breadth of Changsha's May 1st Avenue. A group of city residents spontaneously organized themselves into a picket squad and escorted members of the SAF back to Hunan Normal University, setting off more firecrackers along the way. That night, even the heavens were moved to tears. The rain fell in torrents until dawn.

Prelude to repression

Again, however, the government vented its anger on the workers. Late on the night of May 28, four leaders of the Changsha WAF who had been participating with the students in the peaceful sit-in protest - Zhou Yong, Li Jian, Zhang Jingsheng and one other - were secretly arrested. Upon hearing of this the following day, the SAF leadership organized a student march on May 30 to the Hunan government offices to protest the arrests and negotiate with the provincial public security department. The effort bore some fruit, for Li Jian and Zhou Yong were set free (only, however, to be rearrested after June 4); the other two were not freed,

16

and Zhang Jingsheng eventually received a 13-year sentence.

By May 29, there was still no news from the provincial government about when the dialogue process would begin. On the morning of May 30, the SAF called Su Qingyun, head of the Provincial Petitions Bureau, to request a final response on the deadline for commencing dialogue, which had expired the previous day. We were informed that Su, together with the provincial Party secretary, had already left Changsha for the Yueyang Lake district to supervise flood relief work. When SAF leaders later relayed this information to the students, they responded with extreme dissatisfaction and anger.

On May 31, several dozen students from Hunan Normal University and Central-South Industrial University went spontaneously to the provincial government offices, wrote out a collective "last will and testament" and started a new hunger strike. On June 1, the SAF organized and led a further city-wide demonstration march and recommenced the sit-down protest outside the provincial government offices. Moreover, we mobilized the entire student population to put into action the so-called "empty campus" strategy *(kong xiao ji)*, whereby the students all simply evacuated their dormitories and went home. (After the June 4 massacre, similar actions were undertaken by the students in Beijing and Shanghai.)

Also in protest at the government's failure to begin dialogue, a group of students from Hunan University, Hunan Normal University and Changsha Railway Institute hoisted their college banners and marched through the streets to Changsha Railway Station, where they laid down on the tracks in an attempt to block the trains. Shortly afterwards, there occurred an ugly incident in which an angry crowd of Changsha residents smashed up all the windows on a No.48 Guangzhou-Beijing express train. The SAF tried its utmost at this time, intervening by all available means, to try to prevent the overall situation from deteriorating any further. We were especially concerned to prevent any possible fatalities.

The final days

Late on the evening of June 3, while the SAF was busy holding a meeting, the news came over the *Voice of America* and other international radio stations that the troops had opened fire in Beijing and were killing students and workers. Realizing how desperate the situation had become, we immediately conducted an emergency review of our options. After an extremely heated debate, the SAF standing committee finally decided (with a small dissenting minority) that on the following day the students would be mobilized to take to the streets to block all traffic, and that we would call upon the entire citizenry of Changsha to boycott markets and stage a general strike.

The people of Changsha and other cities of Hunan were stunned by the news of the massacre in Beijing, and, in a spontaneous public outpouring of grief and anger at the bloody repression, huge protest demonstrations quickly ensued throughout the province. Crowds of students and residents surged through the streets of Changsha, Hengyang, Xiangtan, Shaoyang, Yueyang, Changde and Yiyang for almost a week after June 4, and road traffic in all major cities in the province was brought to a standstill. In Changsha, a mass rally was held outside the provincial government offices on June 6, while no fewer than 100,000 demonstrators congregated on the city's Xiangjiang Bridge alone, blocking all traffic for several days. In Yueyang, a large crowd of angry protesters stormed the offices of the municipal Party committee, government and people's congress, then pulled down all the door signs and smashed them to bits, Only on June 9 did the authorities regain control of the city. Meanwhile, students and workers in Xiangtan not only demonstrated but also held strikes and suspended normal business activities in the city for several days, effectively paralyzing the local government. In an extraordinary departure from normal practice, the Hunan provincial government at first did virtually nothing to prevent all this.

It was clear from the government news bulletins, however, that a nationwide search and arrest operation was about to be launched against leaders of the pro-democracy movement. When a number of violent clashes with the security forces inevitably arose, the government, using these incidents as a pretext, moved in and began the crackdown immediately. Within days, several hundred alleged "thugs and hooligans" (baotu) were behind bars.

From June 6 to 7, the standing committee of the SAF met in continuous session to discuss future strategy and decide upon its next course of action. Eventually, it was unanimously agreed that we would all

18

run the risk of arrest by holding a mass memorial meeting in Changsha Railway Station to mourn the victims of the Beijing massacre. The meeting would also serve as an oath-taking ceremony at which SAF members would pledge their loyalty to the pro-democracy cause and bid a temporary farewell to the people of Changsha.

At 2:00 pm on June 8, with a vast crowd of around 140,000 people in attendance, the mass memorial meeting formally opened. The stage was piled high with floral wreaths, and thin white banners inscribed with funeral couplets were strewn all around. Zhang Lixin (representing the Beijing SAF) and I presided over the memorial meeting. One after another, delegates of the Hunan SAF and WAF, representatives of the Changsha residents, teachers' delegates and spokespersons for pro-democracy groups from other provinces all rose to give speeches. The mood of the meeting was extremely sad and emotional, and when the time finally came for the main memorial oration to be read out, the sound of weeping and wailing drifted upward from the crowd below, filling the air on all sides.[6] Finally, on behalf of the SAF standing committee, I made a closing speech vowing that we would never, regardless of whatever repression might lie ahead, abandon our goal of democracy. "Compatriots, please trust us!", I said. "We of the Students Autonomous Federation love our nation deeply, and we will never waver in the struggle for democracy."

The following day, all the students who had previously remained on campus began to flee. A couple of days later, on June 11, after completing as best we could our contingency plans for dealing with the coming repression, the members of the SAF standing committee also went to ground. On June 12, the provincial government issued an urgent order for the "Two Autonomous federations" (the SAF and the WAF) to disband and for the leaders to turn themselves in to the authorities. On June 17, the public security forces formally began to arrest activists from both groups on a large scale. I myself headed for Guangdong Province, where I was arrested, just over one month later, at dawn on July 13.

---

[6] See Appendix V. below for full translated text of the oration.

2. Enemies of the People: the Crackdown in Hunan

Hunan Province, together with Beijing, Shanghai and Chengdu, stood in the front ranks of the 1989 Democracy Movement, and after June 4, the campaign of political repression and judicial retaliation it suffered was among the most severe of any part of China. The following account of the situation in Hunan may give us some idea of the still-untold stories of the repression in many other Chinese provinces, some of which were even less accessible to outside scrutiny in the aftermath of the June 4 crackdown.

On June 9, 1989 at a meeting of senior officers of the PLA martial law units, Deng Xiaoping gave the green light for wholesale repression and round-up operations against the pro-democracy movement to commence across the country. According to Deng:

> *What we face is not simply ordinary people who are unable to distinguish between right and wrong. We also face a rebellious clique and a large number of the dregs of society, who want to topple our country and overthrow our party. This is the essence of the problem....They want to establish a totally Western-dependent bourgeois republic.*[7]

One week later, at a June 16 session of the newly appointed CCP Politburo Standing Committee, Deng added:

> *We must carry the work of suppressing the rebellion through to the end. This is a good chance for us to ban illegal organizations at one go....We must not be soft on those who are*

---

[7] "June 9 Speech to Martial Law Units," by Deng Xiaoping, in *Beijing Spring, 1989: Confrontation and Conflict*, Oksenberg, Sullivan and Lambert (eds.), M.E. Sharpe 1990, pp.377-8.

guilty of the most heinous crimes.[8]

By then, the repression in Hunan was already in full swing. On June 7, at a meeting of senior provincial Party and government officials, Hong Dechuan, provincial Party secretary, called on all regions in the province to take swift measures to round up activists, subdue the disturbances and restore stability. He demanded that a crushing campaign be waged and a rapid, overwhelming victory won. The head of the provincial Politics and Law Committee went further, insisting, "The riotous elements must be uprooted like weeds, so as to eradicate the pestilence once and for all." At a subsequent meeting, a senior public security official instructed, "There must be no mercy whatsoever shown to the riotous elements. Arrests and sentences should be carried out wherever appropriate."

The initial arrests

Within days, Hunan Daily announced that 31 workers and unemployed persons had been arrested, all of whom were described as "criminal elements who participated in the turmoil," although none had yet had the benefit of a trial.[9] They were all later tried and sentenced, with prison terms ranging from three years for Bu Yunhui, a peasant who had lain on the tracks at Changsha Railway Station on June 6 to protest the crackdown, to ten years for Liao Zhijun, a worker at the Changsha Pump Factory who had served in the SAF picket squad.

---

[8] "Full Text of Gists of Deng Xiaoping's Speech to Members of New Politburo Standing Committee [June 16, 1989]," in *ibid*, p.387. In a clear case of giving with one hand and taking away with the other, Deng then went on to say: "Of course, [the rebels] must be treated in light of the seriousness of their crimes. Everything must be based on facts and law. There must be a limit for killing those criminals. We must stress the policy of lenience to those who confess and severity to those who resist." In practice, the latter policy means that anyone detained by the authorities must confess, regardless of whether or not they have committed any offense. To "resist" - i.e. assert one's innocence - is taken merely as proof of a "bad attitude" and results in an even heavier punishment being imposed.

[9] Many of the citations from Hunan Daily given here are taken from undated clippings of the newspaper, so precise reference dates cannot be given. Most of the reports appeared during the last three weeks of June 1989.

Similar mass arrests occurred throughout the province. In Yiyang City, for example, Hunan Daily reported on June 9 that 120 people, "all dregs of society who took advantage of the student demonstrations and sit-ins to incite disturbances, block traffic and create turmoil," had been seized by the public security forces.

In Yueyang City, also on June 9, "Nine bad elements were arrested for involvement in beating, smashing and looting activities." In fact, the nine, all of whom were workers or unemployed persons between the ages of 20 and 35 years, had marched through Yueyang just after June 4 and lain down on the railway tracks to protest the suppression in Beijing. They had then headed to the city government offices, torn down an official door sign and trampled it underfoot. The "ringleader," Guo Yunqiao, was later given a suspended death sentence for this, while the other eight received prison terms ranging from seven to 15 years.

Workers' leaders were among the first to be targeted by the authorities. At dawn on June 9, a young worker named Li Wangyang, the leader of the Shaoyang Workers Autonomous Federation, was arrested in Shaoyang City. Among the charges listed against Li and his colleagues in the *Hunan Daily* were that they had "posted up banners, issued leaflets, carried out liaison trips, spread rumors, uttered reactionary slogans, incited workers to go on strike and proclaimed the founding of a completely independent and autonomous [workers] organization." Li was later sentenced to 13 years' imprisonment.

Similarly, Zhu Fangming, a worker at the Hengyang Flour Mill and vice-chairman of the Hengyang Workers Autonomous Federation, was arrested around June 11 together with Ding Longhua, a standing committee member of the federation. Zhu was later sentenced to life imprisonment; Ding received a six-year sentence. In reporting their arrests, *Hunan Daily* noted that the city's public security bureau had set up a "denunciation telephone hotline" so that "the entire citizenry can be actively mobilized to report and expose criminal elements responsible for the turmoil."

In mid-June, 27 of those detained after the "April 22 Incident" were brought to trial and sentenced heavily. The most severe sentences went to Li Weihong, a young worker in the Hunan Fire-fighting Appliances Factory, who was handed down a death sentence with two years' stay of execution, and Xia Changchun, a worker at the Changsha Port Authority, who received a 15-year prison term.

Banning of "illegal organizations"

On June 12, the Hunan provincial government issued a formal proclamation outlawing the Hunan Students Autonomous Federation and the Changsha Workers Autonomous Federation, and ordering the groups' leaders and core members to report to the public security authorities within five days. Failure to comply with the order would be severely punished by law, said the order, but all those who reported would be dealt with leniently. (In reality, all those blacklisted by the government after June 4 were rounded up and sentenced anyway, regardless of whether or not they complied with the order to turn themselves in.)

By June 16, six leaders of the Changsha WAF had been arrested and four had turned themselves in. Those arrested included the group's founding chairman Li Jian, a later chairman named Zhou Yong, vice-chairmen He Chaohui and Zhang Xudong, and standing committee members Lu Zhaixing, Liu Xingqi and Yang Xiong. The four who reported to the police were vice-chairman and head of propaganda Wang Changhuai, deputy picket leader Cai Jinxuan, picket leader Li Jie and standing committee member Zhou Min. In addition, dozens of members of the Changsha Workers Picket Team were also arrested, although this was not reported by the authorities. The detainees were later sentenced to terms of three to six years' imprisonment. (Zhou Min, who received a six-year term for having made an impassioned speech at the June 8 mass mourning ceremony in Changsha, is now reported to have become mentally disturbed following repeated physical abuse by prison guards.)

By June 17, more than ten leaders of the Hunan SAF had been seized, including the co-chairman of the federation, Fan Zhong, standing committee member Yue Weipeng, and core members Liu Zhongtao (alias Chen Le), Yu Chaohui, Liu Jianhua, Yi Gai and others. They were subsequently held in prison for periods of up to 18 months and then released. Around June 28, the Hunan Daily reported that a total of 23 leaders of the SAF had turned themselves in to the authorities. Most of these were dealt with relatively leniently. (See *Appendix III.A* for details.)

The same article stated that an elderly retired professor of Hunan University, named Peng Yuzhang, had been taken into detention for having acted as a behind-the-scenes adviser to both the SAF and the WAF, and for having participated in the hunger strike outside the provincial government offices in Changsha. Absurdly, the article accused Peng of having "pretended to be a university professor," and said that he had publicly called for a general strike after the May 20 declaration of martial law in Beijing. (Peng suffered severe abuse while in prison and was released in 1990 only to be committed immediately and forcibly to a mental hospital, where he still remains.)

In other cities in Hunan around this time, including Changde, Yiyang, Huaihua, Meizhou, Lianyuan, Loudi and Yongzhou, many other students and citizens were also arrested. *Hunan Daily* reported, for example, that Xiong Gang, a student from Shanxi Province who had been provisional commander of the Autonomous Federation of Students from Outside Beijing, had been arrested after fleeing to his hometown in Hunan's Hanshou County, and that two core members of the Beijing SAF, named Wu Yun and Xu Yue, had also been seized in the province. The subsequent fate of the three students is not known.

The hunt intensifies

After the official banning of the SAF and WAF, the authorities soon began to spread the net more widely. On June 17, the Changsha Party committee established a "Changsha Municipal Leading Group for Investigating and Purging Illegal Organizations," and an extensive clean-up operation was carried out by the city's public security bureau. Scores of printing firms, cafes, restaurants and hair salons were searched and closed down, on suspicion of involvement in the pro-democracy movement, as were certain publishing units of the Hunan People's Press. All of these concerns had their assets seized by the authorities, and their owners and managers were either detained for investigation and interrogation in isolation, or placed under house arrest. In addition, a large number of government cadres were placed under close investigation, on suspicion of having pro-democracy sympathies.

Arrests continued apace elsewhere in the province. According to a June 18 report in the *Hunan Daily*, 31 people were arrested in Xiangtan City for having "pushed their way into public security offices and frantically assaulted the police." Twenty-three of the detainees were workers who had allegedly "burst into the Pingzheng Road Police Station" (a local public security office in Xiangtan) on May 22; the known sentences eventually passed on members of this group ranged four to six years' imprisonment. The other eight detainees, headed by a worker in an electrical machinery factory named Chen Gang, were accused of having burst into the home of the factory's public security chief, who had tried to prevent them from carrying out a protest blockade of part of the factory on June 9, and of having allegedly carted out and set fire to the officer's television set, washing machine and other personal goods. For this act of *lèse majesté*, the courts eventually handed Chen a suspended death sentence.

Similarly draconian punishment was dealt out to nine workers who had earlier been arrested in connection with a riot in Shaoyang City on May 19. According to the *Hunan Daily*, "On June 17, the Shaoyang municipal authorities held a mass public-arrest meeting in Shaoyang, at which Wu Hepeng, Zhu Zhengying, Liu Jiye and six other criminals were formally placed under arrest for such crimes as arson, hooliganism and counterrevolutionary incitement." Wu was later condemned to death with a two-year reprieve, Zhu received life imprisonment and Liu was given a five-year term. The other six received upwards of five year sentences. The report did not indicate, however, which - or how many - of the nine were accused of violent offenses, and which merely of "counter-revolutionary incitement."

For three successive evenings, between June 27 and 29, Hunan Television publicly broadcast a government arrest warrant for me. On July 13, I was arrested in Jiangmen City in Guangdong Province, and towards the end of the month I was taken back to Changsha and locked up in the Changsha No.1 Jail. It was just around then that the rounding up of pro-democracy activists in Hunan was reaching a climax. Almost every police cell in Changsha, including those in the main jails, shelter-investigation centers and detention centers in the city, contained several so-called "riotous elements," and every day, more and more people were being thrown into prison. Moreover, most of the new arrivals around that time were students, teachers, cadres and other pro-democracy supporters who had been arrested purely for opposing the crackdown and expressing views critical of the government. Others were ordinary citizens who had tried to hide students or help them escape after the crackdown.

25

Among the most noteworthy of these "riotous elements," however, was a group of people who were arrested merely for having viewed scenes of the Beijing massacre on video tapes smuggled in from outside China, long after the June 4 incident had passed. In Changsha, anyone found to have seen these tapes was thoroughly investigated by the authorities, and about 30 people were taken into detention and interrogated over and over again until they agreed to say that they had not, after all, ever seen the tapes and had given their solemn word that they would never again speak about them. Thereafter, in Changsha, people would often joke about the "riotous elements who had seen the riot videotapes".

In early July, the central government issued a confidential directive ordering the media across the country to refrain as much as possible from carrying any news items concerning the arrests of Democracy Movement activists. From then on, only the occasional "model report" on such matters, designed to give the general public a periodic warning and reminder, would ever appear in the official press. Repressive activities, however, were neither suspended nor reduced. According to the official *Changsha Yearbook, 1990*:

> *In mid-August, in accordance with the spirit of CCP Central Committee Document No.3, Hunan Provincial Party Committee Document No.10 and Changsha Party Committee Document No.27, the Changsha Municipal Committee established a Leadership Group for Carrying Out the Investigations and Purge. The Municipal Politics and Law Committee then took the lead in setting up an Investigations and Purge Office, and deployed 68 cadres to form a special, full-time group to carry out this work.[10]*

Similar special duty units were also set up in other cities across the province, at great cost in manpower and other resources.

In Hunan Province, the government's round-up operation against student and worker pro-democracy activists continued right through to the end of 1989, and in some cases even beyond. In particular, a

---

[10] *Changsha Yearbook, 1990*, Hunan Publishing House, December 1990.

campaign to investigate and exhaustively document the statements, activities and "political performance" of any citizens suspected of even minor involvement in the pro-democracy movement, with a view to rooting out the broader social bases of support for what had been the greatest challenge to CCP power since 1949, was pursued relentlessly throughout the province until mid-1990. Countless people were subjected to various "administrative punishments" (including several-year terms of "re-education through labor"), were fired from their jobs or demoted, or otherwise had their careers or personal lives ruined by the authorities in this way.

The trials: applying a judicial gloss

The first set of cases to be brought before the Hunan courts, on and around June 15, 1989, was that of 27 people charged with violent involvement in the April 22 Incident. According to an official source, however, a total of 41 persons were eventually tried in connection with the incident. Of these, one person (Li Weihong) was convicted of "hooliganism" and received a suspended sentence of death; seven persons (including Xia Changchun, also convicted of "hooliganism") were sentenced to terms of 10-15 years' imprisonment; 16 persons were handed 5-10 year prison terms; 16 others were given terms of five years or less; and only one was exempted from punishment.[11]

From the outset, all the leaders of the Hunan pro-democracy movement deplored the violent rioting of April 22, and we strove hard to prevent the occurrence of any further such incidents. Indeed, given the subsequent scale of the movement in Hunan, there was remarkably little violence seen throughout, even after June 4. Major questions arose over the court handling of those accused of violent activities during the movement. In the trials of the April 22 detainees, for example, the authorities claimed that 21 public security officers and armed policemen had been injured during the riot, but in a striking departure from the norm, official press reports failed to identify any of those responsible for the alleged assaults. No such charges were laid against either Li or Xia, whose savage punishments were imposed by the court purely on charges of alleged incitement and damage to property.

---

[11] *Ibid*, p.24.

27

More generally, given the extremely low standards of evidence and judicial process that were applied after June 4, there can be no assurance that those arrested and convicted of violent offenses had actually committed such acts. As the authorities freely admitted, the guiding judicial policy at the time was "rapid reporting of arrests, rapid approval of arrests, and rapid sentencing" *(baobu kuai, pibu kuai, panjue kuai).*[12] The accused's guilt was trumpeted in the official press well in advance of the trials, which were duly held under the firm grip of the Party, so that verdicts of guilty were a foregone conclusion regardless of the merits of the evidence.

From early July onward, a wave of trials of leading pro-democracy activists and demonstrators was carried out across the province. The most notable feature of the trials was that almost all the defendants were either workers or ordinary urban residents. This reflected a clear and deliberate policy by the central government to scapegoat non-students for their alleged "manipulation" of events, and had two main objectives. One was to provide supporting evidence for the official conspiracy theory of the 1989 pro-democracy movement, whereby "well-intentioned but misguided" students were said to have been led astray and exploited by "outside elements with ulterior motives." (This theory was necessitated by the overwhelming support shown to the movement by the general public, and determined also that the student leaders themselves had to be given relatively minor punishment.)

The other overriding objective of the government was to crush all signs of emergent unrest and independent labor organization among the urban workforce. The CCP has had long and rich experience in controlling China's students and intellectuals, but perhaps its greatest fear in May-June 1989 was that its crucial ability to keep the workers well in line had finally begun to slip.

Chen Gang

A clear example of the way in which workers were victimized by the courts is provided by the case of Chen Gang. In early July, the Xiangtan Intermediate People's Court tried Chen Gang and seven other

---

[12] Ibid, p.24.

workers from the Xiangtan Electrical Machinery Plant on charges relating to the incident on June 9, mentioned above, in which a police officer's home was broken into and some of his belongings burned. The incident had been sparked off by a group of students from the Changsha Railroad College, headed by Chen's younger brother, Chen Ding, who had come to the Xiangtan Electrical Machinery Factory to urge the workers to strike. Moreover, Chen Gang himself had not even been present at the scene of the subsequent break-in at the policeman's house.

At the time of the Chen brothers' initial detention, the charge brought against both of them was "counterrevolutionary propaganda and incitement." Shortly afterwards, Chen Gang was formally indicted by the procuracy and the charge was changed to one of "robbery." The following day, the court opened to try the case, but by then the charge had been changed again, this time to "hooliganism." Only one day had elapsed between issuance of the indictment and the trial itself, leaving no time at all for preparation of a defense, and Chen Gang was duly sentenced to death. (In April 1990, the judgment was altered to death with a two-year reprieve.) Chen's seven co-defendants received sentences ranging from five years to life imprisonment. Chen's younger brother, Chen Ding, the student who, if anyone, had initiated the confrontation, was tried separately on a charge of "counterrevolutionary propaganda and incitement" and sentenced to one year's imprisonment. In mid-1990, he was released and allowed to resume his studies at college.

Many of the other harsh sentences imposed by the Hunan courts on workers during July - for example, the suspended death sentence for Guo Yunqiao of the Yueyang WAF, and the life sentence passed on Zhu Zhengying of Shaoyang City - have already been mentioned. Between August and September, however, dozens of other democracy movement activists in Changsha City were also tried and given heavy sentences, bringing to well over 200 the total number of those convicted since the onset of the crackdown.

Perhaps the most shocking of these cases involved Yao Guisheng, a member of the Changsha WAF, and two others, one a resident of Guangzhou named Hu Nianyou and one a resident of Lian County in Guangdong surnamed Chen (given name not known.) All three were arrested in Zhuzhou City for attempting to help WAF leaders escape from Changsha after June 4. At their trials in the Changsha Intermediate

29

Court in September 1989, Yao Guisheng and Hu Nianyou were convicted on spurious charges of "robbery and assault" arising from an argument in which they had been involved with a taxi driver over the fare for the WAF leaders. They were sentenced to terms of 15 years' and life imprisonment respectively. Chen was condemned to death, however, and was duly executed on December 26, 1989.

From the October 1 National Day until early 1990, a further series of trials was carried out in Hunan. In these, many influential figures who had been active during previous phases of the pro-democracy movement were sternly dealt with by the authorities and heavily sentenced. They included people who had been previously convicted for "counterrevolutionary activities" or for various "political mistakes"; so-called "rightists" and others who had regularly borne the brunt of the CCP's periodic political score-settling campaigns; and others who had long suffered persecution simply on account of their "complicated" family or individual backgrounds. Most of these individuals were ones whom the authorities had branded as being especially stubborn and persistent "reactionaries." In addition, many more members and leaders of the various Hunan regional WAFs continued to be brought to trial.

Zhang Jingsheng

Among the best-known of the "stubborn and reactionary" cases tried around this time was that of Zhang Jingsheng, the veteran pro-democracy activist who had founded and edited the unofficial journal *Wanderer (Liulangzhe)* in Changsha during the 1978-81 Democracy Wall movement. After the crackdown on that movement in spring 1981, Zhang was convicted of counterrevolution and spent four years in jail, where he quickly became known as the "Wei Jingsheng of the south" (the characters for both men's given names are identical.) While in prison, he wrote many protest poems which were set to music and are now sung by political prisoners and others in jails and labor camps throughout China (see *Appendix IX*). After his release in 1985, he was kept under close surveillance by the authorities.

During the 1989 Democracy Movement, Zhang Jingsheng was active in the Changsha WAF, although not in any leadership capacity. On May 4, he gave a rousing speech in the Martyr's Park to a large crowd of demonstrators, citing from his own experiences to illustrate China's need

30

for greater political democratization and official tolerance. He was loudly cheered by the crowd, but later that evening he was detained by the public security authorities and held for several days. Zhang took no part in any of the more radical actions undertaken during the 1989 movement, such as the blocking of traffic or laying down on railway tracks. He merely gave a few speeches at public gatherings and wrote some influential, though moderate, articles for the movement.

To the authorities, however, these were details of scant importance. Zhang was rearrested on May 28, following his participation in the student oath-taking ceremony earlier that evening outside the provincial government offices, and in December 1989 he was finally put on trial at the Changsha Intermediate Court on a charge of "counter-revolutionary propaganda and incitement." One of the main accusations made against Zhang at his trial was that, "While serving a previous prison sentence, the accused composed a large quantity of songs about prison life, the content of which was extremely reactionary." Originally, the provincial government had planned to impose a three-year sentence on Zhang. When the Beijing authorities got word of the case, however, they branded Zhang a "stubborn anti-Party element" and ordered that a figure "1" be placed in front of the scheduled "3." The order had come directly from the senior political authorities, and the Hunan court had no option but to meekly carry it out, despite widespread opposition within the local bureaucracy. Zhang is currently serving his 13-year sentence in the Provincial No.1 Prison in Yuanjiang.

Overview of the trials

Common to all the political trials carried out in Hunan Province after June 4 was an almost complete lack of regard for due process. First, in nearly all the cases, guilt was predetermined by the Party's "politics and law committees," which exist at all levels of the judicial, procuratorial and police hierarchy for the sole purpose of exercising so-called "unified leadership" by the Party over law-enforcement matters. In some cases, instructions as to the disposition of cases and level of sentencing were issued directly by the central Party authorities in Beijing. Second, in no cases were defense lawyers allowed to enter pleas of not guilty on behalf of their clients. Third, no prosecution witnesses were summoned to appear in court, thus depriving both the accused and their lawyers of any opportunity to cross-examine the state's evidence. Instead, written

31

statements from these "witnesses" were produced in court and quoted from in piecemeal fashion by the prosecution, and any attempt to challenge their veracity was disallowed. And fourth, most of the cases were held *in camera*, and defense witnesses requested by the accused were not permitted to appear or give evidence.

In general, the harshest and most arbitrary sentences were imposed on pro-democracy activists who were brought to trial during the months immediately following the June 4 crackdown. The level of sentencing remained unconscionably high for the remainder of the year, however, and only began to return to (for China) somewhat more "normal" levels after the lifting of martial law in Beijing in January 1990. Several leading democracy activists were taken to court and tried each month during 1990, mostly on charges of "counterrevolutionary propaganda and incitement." These included university and college teachers, government cadres, students, workers, private businessmen and even some peasants, and the sentences handed down generally ranged from two to five years' imprisonment. An important factor behind this more lenient treatment was undoubtedly the increasing international pressure brought to bear upon the Chinese government in 1990 over human rights issues.

Another clear and consistent pattern in the trials was that detainees of low social status were dealt with much more harshly than those with status. Workers, and particularly unemployed people, faced harsher penalties as a matter of course, with average levels of sentencing starting at around five years and rising, in some cases, all the way to life imprisonment or even death, though usually with a two-year reprieve. Students, intellectuals and government cadres generally fared much better. I myself, for example, was tried by the Changsha Intermediate Court on July 17, 1990 on a charge of "counterrevolutionary propaganda and incitement." Despite having been branded as one of those chiefly responsible for the province-wide "turmoil and chaos," I received a mere three-year sentence. It was the highest passed on any student in Hunan. I was released on parole in February 1991. A small number of other students were sentenced to prison terms, mainly for "common criminal" offenses, but the leading members of the Hunan SAF were for the most part eventually acquitted and set free.

A final hallmark of the trials was that defendants who pleaded not guilty were branded as persons with a "bad attitude," and were invariably punished more severely than those who bowed to the inevitable and expressed contrition. In fact, the more convincing and powerful a defense case that such persons managed to put forward, the sterner and more vengeful, usually, was the response of the court.

The central government was well pleased with the performance of the Hunan judicial authorities in crushing dissent in the province. On November 27, 1989, the Supreme People's Procuracy in Beijing conferred upon the Changsha Municipal Procuracy a "National-Level Advanced Collective Merit Award for Curbing the Turmoil and Suppressing the Counterrevolutionary Rebellion." On January 5, 1990, the Supreme People's Court conferred the same honor upon the Changsha Intermediate Court.[13]

Statistical summary of arrests and convictions

By mid-1990, well over 1000 people had been detained or taken in for so-called "shelter and investigation" in Hunan Province on charges arising out of involvement in the 1989 pro-democracy movement.

Of these, about 25 per cent, or roughly 300 persons, were detained in Changsha alone. These included the nearly 100 persons held after the April 22 Incident (of whom at least 40, and probably many more, were tried and sentenced) and also 140 "major riotous elements" (i.e. pro-democracy leaders) detained in the city between June and late December 1989. According to an official source, 66 of those 140 had been placed under formal arrest, and 46 already tried and sentenced, by year's end; seven persons had been sent for several-year terms of re-education through labor; 53 had been "released after education"; six had been transferred to other jurisdictions for trial; and eight remained in investigative custody.[14] In fact, however, the actual trial and conviction rate in Changsha was considerably higher than that claimed by the authorities, and at least 80 persons remained in untried custody in the

---

[13] *Changsha Yearbook, 1990*, p.108.

[14] *Ibid*, p.105.

33

city by the end of 1989.[15] In addition, several dozen more pro-democracy activists were arrested in the Changsha region in the course of 1990.

As regards the rest of Hunan, over 100 people were arrested from each of the province's other four main cities, namely Xiangtan, Shaoyang, Yueyang and Hengyang, and only slighter lesser numbers from the cities of Changde, Yiyang, Zhuzhou, Loudi and Huaihua. In addition, several dozen were arrested in the towns of Chenzhou, Lingling and Xiangxi.

At a conservative estimate, well over 65 per cent of all those detained in the province, or around 750 persons, were eventually either tried and sentenced to terms of imprisonment or reform through labor, or else were sentenced by the public security authorities to 2-3 year terms of re-education through labor. (Confidential government figures cited below, however, suggest that this may well be a considerable underestimate.)

The present report contains details of 219 pro-democracy activists detained in Hunan Province after June 4, 1989, of whom 172 (or just under 25 per cent of the total estimated convictions for the province) were sentenced to terms of either labor reform or labor re-education. Of the 219 detainees, 150 reportedly remained in prison or in labor re-education camps as of May 1992, while only 67, or less than one-third, had been released. The overall disposition of these cases by prisoner category is shown in *Table I*.[16] (For individual case details, please refer to *Appendix I*, below.)

Applying this average one-third release rate to the total convicted

---

[15] In late 1989 I was still being held in Changsha No.1 Jail, and those in untried detention in that jail alone at the time included Zhang Xudong, He Zhaohui, Xie Changfa, Tang Changye, Zhong Hua, Zhang Jie, Li Shaojun, Yu Chaohui, Chen Le, Zhou Min, Long Jianhua and Fan Zhong. Many more untried pro-democracy activists were still being held in other jails and detention centers in Changsha at that time.

[16] See note at end of chapter for explanation of the table.

Table I: Treatment of 213 Pro-democracy Prisoners in Hunan Province

Statistics based on Appendix I		Sentenced Prisoners		Detained without trial then freed	Total
		No.	Average Sentence		
Workers	Excl. lifers + death w/rep.	(79)	(6 years)	7	97
	Incl. lifers + death w/rep.	90	8.1 years		
Students		19	2.2 years	16	35
Intellectuals		32	4.5 years	5	37
Journalists		7	4 years	3	10
Businessmen		9	3 years	4	13
Cadres		11	5 years	3	14
Peasants		7	3.3 years	0	7
TOTAL		173	4.3 years	38	213

population for Hunan, it can be inferred that around 500 of those detained since June 1989 in the province probably still remained in prisons, labor-reform camps or labor re-education centers as of May 1992.

Confidential report on political imprisonment in Hunan

Compiling detailed information on the repression in China, especially in the provinces, is a daunting task, and while every effort has been made to confirm the information on political prisoners set forth in this report, a small margin of error may still remain.

The following remarkable figures can, however, be cited with absolute certainty, for they come from a highly-classified report compiled by the Hunan judicial authorities themselves. The document in question is entitled "Outline Report on the Numbers of Turmoil Elements Committed to Prisons in Hunan Province by the End of 1990." The term "turmoil elements" *(dongluan fenzi)* refers solely to political prisoners detained after June 4, 1989 on account of their involvement in the pro-democracy movement. The scope of the report, moreover, is confined to those pro-democracy detainees who had already, as of December 31, 1990, been tried and sentenced in court. (In China, only convicted criminals are sent to prisons; those still awaiting trial are kept in jails and detention centers.)

According to the report, a total of no fewer than 594 "turmoil elements" had been committed to the seven main prisons in Hunan Province by the end of 1990.[17] Sixteen of those were women, since they were sent to Changsha Prison, the province's only jail for female prisoners. The report even noted the successive batches in which those sent to each of the main prisons had been organized to commence "political study." **Table II** shows the core information from the report.[18]

As mentioned, only convicted criminals are ever sent to actual prisons in China. Furthermore, only two classes of convicted prisoners are ever sent to prisons: so-called "common criminals" who have been sentenced, on average, to terms of seven to ten years and above, and also the majority of "counterrevolutionaries" or political prisoners. Non-political prisoners serving lesser sentences are usually sent to labor-reform camps instead to complete their sentences.

---

[17] All 145 of the pro-democracy prisoners noted in the government report as having been committed to two of these seven prisons - namely Chenzhou and Huaihua prisons - are excluded from the purview of *Appendix I*, below, since Asia Watch was unable to obtain information on any of the individuals held in those two places.

[18] The "one late arrival" listed in the report under Longxi Prison was Tang Boqiao.

Table II: Figures from secret government report

Name of Prison	No. of "Turmoil Elements" by end of 1990	Commenced "political study" in batches of
Provincial No.1 Prison (Yuanjiang Prison)	121	24, 49 and 45 (+ three late arrivals)
Provincial No.2 Prison (Hengyang Prison)	98	16, 54 and 27 (+ one late arrival)
Provincial No.3 Prison (Lingling Prison)	106	28, 50 and 25 (+ three late arrivals)
Provincial No.4 Prison (Huaihua Prison)	77	55 and 22
Provincial No.5 Prison (Chenzhou Prison)	68	40 and 28
Provincial No.6 Prison (Longxi Prison)	108	33, 51 and 23 (+ one late arrival)
Changsha Prison	16	6 and 10
TOTAL	594	594

Hence, the figure of 594 "turmoil elements" committed to prisons in Hunan after June 1989 probably only includes those who were convicted of "counterrevolution" and those who received heavy sentences for such alleged crimes as arson and assault. It would include neither those who received lesser terms of imprisonment for other "common" criminal offenses during the 1989 movement, nor the many peaceful protestors who were sentenced without trial to terms of "re-education through labor." Given that the average length of sentence in the case of those committed to prisons is considerably higher than that for all other penal institutions in China, moreover, it is reasonable to assume that the great majority of the 594 "turmoil elements" cited in the confidential Hunan government report are still behind bars in the province today.

Notes to Table I:

* Categories in the table refer to the following: "Workers" includes both factory and service-sector employees, and also unemployed persons. "Students" includes both undergraduate and graduate students. "Intellectuals" includes university, college and high-school professors, as well as scientists, doctors, technicians and musicians. "Journalists" includes newspaper reporters, editors and television journalists. "Businessmen" includes private entrepreneurs, managers and salespersons. "Cadres" includes state administrative personnel, Party functionaries and ranking officials.

* *Appendix I* lists details of 219 named prisoners or ex-prisoners; the six persons not covered in *Table I* include one who was executed, one who died in prison and four who remain in untried detention. In addition, *Appendix I* mentions 12 others reported to have been tried and sentenced but whose names are not known.

* Sentences of both life imprisonment and death with reprieve are taken, for purposes of the table, as being equivalent to 25 years' imprisonment. In China, the longest sentence of fixed-term imprisonment that the courts can impose is 20 years. Life sentences begin at that level, and often mean life. Those sentenced to death with a reprieve are either executed at the end of the two-year probationary period, or else are left to serve out at least the equivalent of an average life sentence; most will never be released.

* There were 12 sentences of known length passed on students, totalling 26 years; the average known sentence for students was thus 2.2 years. (No college student in Hunan is known to have received a sentence exceeding three years. However, one high-school student, a 15-year-old named Liu Xin, received a 15-year sentence; this was excluded from the averaging here, as it was so much higher than any of the other sentences on students.) In addition, there were six sentences of unknown length passed on students; they have been arbitrarily assigned the average term of 2.2 years here.

* There were 29 sentences of known length passed upon intellectuals, averaging 4.5 years each. In addition, there were two intellectuals whose sentences were not known. They were each assigned the average of 4.5 years here.

* One of the seven journalists, Yu Zhijian (an editor), received a sentence of 20 years' imprisonment. Since this was far higher than any of the other sentences on journalists, it was excluded from calculation of the average figure given here. When the sentence on Yu is included, the average sentence for journalists rises to 6.3 years.

* Six businessmen received known sentences averaging three years. A seventh, Li Zimin, received a 15 year sentence which greatly exceeded any other in the category and so was excluded from calculation of the average. Two other businessmen received unknown sentences, and they were assigned average three-year sentences for purposes of this chart.

38

* Ten cadres were sentenced to known terms averaging five years. One other was sentenced to an unknown term and was assigned the average for purposes of this chart.

* The average terms of detention for the various categories of those listed in the column headed "Detained without trial then freed" are not known. These were mostly students who were held for periods of several months to a year before being released. An unknown number of people remain in untried detention in Hunan Province in connection with the 1989 pro-democracy movement.

3. Some Prominent Cases of Abuse and Injustice

Behind the prison gates in China, one sees the regime's veneer of "socialist humanitarianism" stripped bare, revealing the underlying brutality of the system in its clearest form. After my arrest on July 13, 1989, I changed overnight from a university student into an imprisoned "counterrevolutionary criminal," and over the next 18 months I was detained in seven different jails and detention centers in Guangdong and Hunan provinces.[19] While there, I witnessed numerous flagrant violations of basic human rights being committed by the prison authorities.

The first place I was taken was the Jiangmen City No. 1 Jail, and it was there that I met my first case of unjust imprisonment. The person's name was Zhang Xinbiao, a young fellow of strong character. As soon as I entered the cell, I noticed that Zhang was wearing leg irons. Perplexed by this - he was the only one of over 20 prisoners who was wearing shackles - I asked him what on earth he had done to deserve such treatment. He answered, in a matter of fact way, that it was because he had sworn and spat at a cadre. He had been shackled continuously from the moment, more than four months earlier, when he was first admitted to the jail. I was shaken by this information: how was it possible that in our country a person could be thrown into chains simply for daring to argue with a government official? Frankly, at the time I only half believed what he was telling me. Until then, I had always naively believed that the kinds of people who ended up in jail - shackled or not - must have committed unforgivable crimes and were merely getting their just deserts. Surely, the People's Government would never allow such things to happen?

But this was just the beginning. I soon realized that such sights were an everyday part of the prison scene and my eyes were quickly opened to the ugly realities all around. My way of thinking began to

---

[19] These included detention centers in Jiangmen City and Xinhui County; Guangdong Province Detention Center No.1; Changsha No. 1 and No.2 Jails; Shaoyang Jail; and Longxi Prison. In all, I spent time in 16 different cells.

change, and I felt increasing anger and contempt for the callous hypocrisy shown by the Chinese Communist prison authorities towards those whom they branded, often quite arbitrarily, as criminals. In the name of so-called "thought reform" and "recreating useful members of society," they thought nothing of destroying a man's spirit. Particularly in the case of political prisoners, indeed, this was seen as a necessary part of the "reform through labor" process (although physically, so-called "common criminals" often received worse treatment.)

The following are only a few of the more egregious examples of the kinds of systematic degradation, punishment and indignity that have all too frequently been inflicted upon detained pro-democracy figures in Hunan since June 4, 1989. Some of these individuals have already been released, and their stories are thus readily available. At least one is now dead. The others remain behind bars, and the information on their cases has been obtainable only through secret channels.

The "Mao portrait" case

Perhaps the best-known group of political prisoners currently being held in Hunan Province are three men - Yu Zhijian, Yu Dongyue and Lu Decheng - who defaced the giant portrait of Mao Zedong which hangs in Tiananmen Square by throwing ink and paint-filled eggshells at it on May 23, 1989. This case was reported worldwide at the time, and the public desecration of the Great Helmsman's image in this way so infuriated the Party leadership that the case was labelled as one of the foremost "counterrevolutionary incidents" of the entire 1989 Chinese pro-democracy movement.

Yu Zhijian, aged 27, was formerly a teacher at the Tantou Wan primary school in Dahu Township, Liuyang County, and Yu Dongyue was a fine arts editor for the *Liuyang News*. Lu Decheng, 28, worked for the Liuyang branch of the Hunan Provincial Bus Company. (Other notable figures from Liuyang include Tan Sitong, the late 19th century reformer, and Hu Yaobang.) The three were tried by the Beijing Intermediate Court in September 1989 on charges of "counterrevolutionary sabotage" and "counterrevolutionary propaganda and incitement" and sentenced variously to life, 20 years and 16 years' imprisonment.

According to the authorities, the three men had travelled from

Hunan to Beijing on May 19, 1989, having already displayed "counter-revolutionary" banners and given "counterrevolutionary speeches" in Changsha. In addition, Lu was accused of having organized a Liuyang branch of a group called the Hunan Delegation in Support of the Beijing Students. (The three probably went to Beijing as representatives of that body.) Regardless of whether or not one endorses their provocative act of defacing the Mao portrait, the fact remains that under any more civilized judicial system the men would have received at most short-term prison sentences for "disturbing the peace."

After their secret trials, Lu and the two Yus were transferred under armed guard back to Hunan from Beijing to serve out their sentences at the Provincial No. 3 Prison in Lingling. Ever since their initial detention, the three have consistently refused to admit that their protest action had any "counterrevolutionary intent" (a necessary factor for determination of guilt by the courts in such cases.) Because of this evidence of "bad attitude" on their part, they were subjected to manifold forms of severe torture and ill-treatment from the outset. After the men were transferred back to Hunan, the Lingling Prison authorities were instructed by Beijing to incarcerate them in a "strict regime" unit.

Conditions in such units vary from place to place in China, but they are usually extremely grim. (I myself was held under "strict regime" at Longxi Prison for several months, but because I was a university student and did not make any conspicuous trouble, I was assigned to teach Chinese language classes to the other prisoners.) In the case of the three "portrait desecrators," whose crimes were compounded by their "refusal to confess and submit to the law," one of the harshest prison measures - solitary confinement - was imposed. The solitary confinement cells at Lingling Prison are just over two square meters each in area. They have no ventilation or heating, which makes them freezing cold in winter and unbearably hot in summer, and they are almost pitch-dark. In addition, the cells are damp and sanitation is extremely deficient. Prisoners are only allowed to leave these cells for brief, thrice-daily meal periods during which they must eat their food while walking around in a tiny exercise yard.

According to the regulations, prisoners may only be held in solitary confinement for a maximum period of two weeks, and Lu Decheng was returned to a shared-cell regime after six months. Yu

Zhijian and Yu Dongyue, however, have been kept in solitary confinement ever since late 1989. According to reliable inside sources, Teacher Yu Zhijian's health has deteriorated dramatically as a result of his ongoing 30-month ordeal. He has dramatically lost weight and now appears severely emaciated and skeletal. Yu Dongyue, the one-time fine arts editor, has become badly disturbed psychologically, to the extent even of having lost control of his excretory functions. On top of this, both men have been subjected to a range of overt physical tortures, ostensibly because they uttered "reactionary statements" about certain government officials.

According to the prison leadership, the two men have "completely failed to reform their reactionary nature." Other cadres at Lingling Prison, however, are reported to be greatly dissatisfied with the inhumane treatment still being meted out to the two Yus. International attention to the plight of Yu Zhijian and Yu Dongyue is now urgently required.

Peng Yuzhang

A retired professor of Hunan University now in his seventies, Peng Yuzhang showed active support for the students throughout the 1989 pro-democracy movement by participating in our various sit-ins and hunger strikes. He was arrested at his home in mid-June, 1989, and thrown into Changsha No. 1 Jail. Despite his advanced years, Professor Peng showed real spirit. Every day, he would shout out loudly from his cell, "Why are you detaining me!", and "I demand to be released!" This overt show of resistance did not go unpunished for long. Peng was eventually taken from his cell and placed on a device known as the "shackle board" - a horizontal plank roughly the size of a door, equipped with metal shackles at the four corners and a large hole at the lower end. The offending prisoner is laid upwards on the board, and his hands and feet are secured by the four shackles. The hole allows the prisoner to perform basic bodily functions. Although highly illegal, this inhuman instrument of torture can be found in most of the jails and prisons in Hunan Province. Its existence, of course, is a closely guarded secret.

After I was escorted back from Guangdong to the Changsha No. 1 Jail in July, every night I used to hear Professor Peng's distressed cries of protest from his punishment cell. "Let me out!", "I need to take a bath" and "We are not afraid!", he would shout out. He remained very sensible

43

and coherent, however, and took care to never utter extreme slogans. Sometimes he would even sing the old primary school anthem, "Learn from the Good Example of Lei Feng." At the last line ("Stand firm and never waver!"), his voice would rise to a crescendo, as he bravely sought to give heart and encouragement to the rest of us. We, in turn, would cry out in unison: "Professor Peng! A good example!"

At one point, I could bear it no longer and roared out a demand that he be released from the "shackle board" immediately. The only response I got from the jail warden, however, was that Peng was "psychiatrically ill," and that this, precisely, was why he had to be kept in shackles. Appalled and enraged by this, I argued with the cadre that under Chinese criminal law, far from being subject to such additional torments, the mentally ill are in fact meant to be "exempt from prosecution." He then replied that since there was as yet no concrete proof of his illness, Professor Peng did not qualify for this exemption and so could not be released. The truth of the matter, I discovered later, was that prison officials in Hunan deliberately use the "shackle board" punishment as a means of determining whether unruly prisoners who show signs of mental illness are genuinely disturbed or whether they are just feigning it. In Peng Yuzhang's case, the ordeal lasted for more than three months. When finally he was taken off the "shackle board," he was a mere shadow of his former self.

Some time later, while I was being taken down one of the jail corridors to an interrogation session, I happened to pass by Peng, who was just then being brought back from one himself. All shrivelled and dried up, he was barely conscious and was being carried out on a warden's back. I began to say, "Professor Peng, you've suffered so much...", but my voice became choked with sobs and I couldn't go on. Somehow, he managed to smile at me - just like before, in May 1989 when we held the sit-in protest together outside the Changsha government offices. "Don't worry, Little Tang," he said. "I'll be all right." That was the last time I ever saw him. Some days later, a pre-trial investigator told me that the hospital had given a clear diagnosis of psychiatric illness on Peng's part, and so the government had decided to release him and allow him to return home. I felt greatly relieved.

Much later, upon my own release in February 1991, I found out that Professor Pang had in fact been forcibly committed to a psychiatric

44

asylum immediately after his release from the Changsha No. 1 Jail. In effect, the authorities had contrived to pass a life sentence on him by other means. Since then, none of Professor Peng's friends or relatives have been allowed to visit him in the psychiatric asylum, and there are reports that he may have committed suicide soon after being admitted there.[20]

Zhou Zhirong

Zhou Zhirong, a graduate of the Hunan Normal College (which later became Hunan Normal University), was prior to the 1989 pro-democracy movement a geography teacher at the Xiangtan No. 2 Middle School. He entered college at the age of only 15, in the class of '77 - the first group of students to be enrolled since the Cultural Revolution on the basis of competitive examinations. During the 1980 student protest campaign at Hunan Normal College against official interference in that year's free elections to the local legislature, Zhou emerged as a dauntless activist and was one of the last to give up a collective hunger strike staged by the students.

During the 1989 pro-democracy movement, Zhou, 32 years old, gave numerous public speeches in Changsha, Xiangtan and elsewhere to promote democratic ideas. He did not, however, join in any of the student or worker organizations. After the June 4 crackdown - despite the brutal heat of the Hunan summer, he put on a black woollen coat bearing the Chinese character for "sadness" on the front and the character for "mourning" on the back, and staged a lone sit-in protest with his eyes closed outside the Xiangtan municipal government offices.

He then fled Xiangtan for several months, before eventually and

---

[20] Other sources speculate that the authorities may simply have disposed of Peng in the same way that they did Chen Guangdi, a well-known political activist who was imprisoned in Hunan toward the end of the Cultural Revolution for having served as an adviser to a radical Red Guard group called the "Hunan Provincial Proletarian League" *(Sheng-Wu-Lian.)* Chen's body was found in 1975 at a rubbish dump at the Pingtang Labor-Reform Farm, Changsha. According to the government, Chen had "committed suicide to escape punishment." By coincidence, Chen, like Peng Yuzhang, was also a teacher at Hunan University.

after much thought deciding in September to report voluntarily to the public security authorities. He was seized on the spot and carted away to be locked up in the Xiangtan Jail. From that time onward, his life became an unending round of gross torment and abuse. At first, the prison authorities treated him, if anything, somewhat more politely than the so-called "common criminals." But Zhou's character was such that he used to insist on having the few formal rights that were left him as a prisoner respected, and he would often complain when this did not happen. Soon, the prison cadres began to fear and resent him, and eventually to hate him.

At first they just used to scold and humiliate him, but then later they instructed his cellmates to begin tormenting him. From then on, the other prisoners would not allow him on to the sleeping platform at night, so he had to sleep on the concrete floor. During the daytime, they forced him to scrub the floor endlessly, hour after hour, long after it had become spotlessly clean. As he scrubbed, he was made to sing songs like the opening theme to "Clever Yi Xiu" (a popular Japanese animated film) - the lyrics having first been altered to include the line "Hurray! Let's scrub and clean this floor! Hurray! Let's polish it all the way into the cassia blossom room!" (In prison slang, "cassia blossom room" means the toilet cubicle at the end of the cell.) In the evenings, they even made him imitate bird and animal calls - in short, they tried in every way imaginable to demean and humiliate him.

"How do you like it now?", the prison cadres would ask him spitefully. Again, Zhou's character was such that while he would never clash with his fellow prisoners, he used to break into the most vehement curses when taunted by a prison guard or other official. He used to tell them that he was already being more than polite enough to them, simply by considering them as human. They couldn't believe their ears. He would never submit to them - this was his way of retaining his human dignity. Every time a cadre ordered him to kneel, for example, he would refuse. They would interpret this lack of subservience as a major challenge to their authority, even seeing it as a source of personal humiliation, and they would promptly beat the shit out of him. The other prisoners all came to regard him as a sheer madman.

In early 1990, Zhou was brought to trial and sentenced to seven years' imprisonment for "counterrevolutionary incitement," reduced after appeal to five years. His defense argument at the trial consisted of two points. First, he was not guilty, because none of the various speeches he had made during the 1989 movement were counterrevolutionary in nature. And second, he denied that he had, as claimed by the prosecution, "turned himself in" to the authorities, since that would have implied an admission of guilt on his part. A man of forthright and outspoken character, Zhou knew all along that by taking this principled stand he would surely be dooming himself. Ironically, the only part of his defense that the court accepted was that he had not, after all, "turned himself in." As a result, not only was he denied the reduced punishment accorded to those who were held to have done so - he was even sentenced more heavily.

Zhou was sent to Longxi Prison, in a remote mountainous part of Shaoyang, several months before me, and we spent time in the "strict regime" unit there together with other political prisoners. Latterly, he even tried to organize secret political discussions between us, and for this, seven or eight of us were put into solitary confinement for seven days in the prison's "black rooms" - windowless, pitch-dark boxes of less than two meters in area. Prior to that time, Zhou had still not properly recovered physically or psychologically from the ill-treatment he had suffered in Xiangtan Jail. He was prone to sudden outbursts of wild and erratic speech, alternating with periods of deep depression and silence.

On February 12, 1991, Zhou was transferred to a solitary-confinement punishment unit at the Provincial No. 3 Prison in Hunan's Lingling Prefecture. Once there, he was put on a "shackle board" and kept there, without respite, for a full three months. When he showed continued resistance by shouting at his jailers, a filthy rag was stuffed in his mouth, to be removed only at feeding times. According to an inside source, Zhou had become severely psychiatrically disturbed by the time of his eventual removal from the "shackle board" in May 1991.

What makes Zhou Zhirong's story all the more sad is that his father died early and his sick mother now lies paralyzed and bed-ridden at their home in a poor, remote village, with only Zhou's younger brother left to look after her. Zhou wrote to his friends from prison, begging them to help his mother out financially, so they started sending her small sums of money. But after a few months the authorities found out about it and the friends were interrogated by the police and told to stop "giving assistance to a counterrevolutionary family." One day, when Zhou's younger brother was on his way to visit Zhou at the Xiangtan Jail, he became involved in a traffic accident and his leg was crushed by a tractor. As they say, troubles never come singly in life.

Fan Zhong

Another political prisoner whom I saw with my own eyes being cruelly mistreated was Fan Zhong. A student in the class of '85 at Central-South Industrial University, Fan was at the time of the 1989 pro-democracy movement chairman of the official students union, vice-chairman of the provincial students federation and a member of the Chinese Communist Party. Although initially reluctant to involve himself in the movement, he eventually did so and soon rose to become a standing committee member of the SAF. When I travelled to Beijing in late May to assess the situation there, Fan acted as SAF chairman.

Arrested at the end of June 1989, he was first held in the Changsha No. 2 Jail, before being transferred in mid-July to Changsha No. 2 Jail where he was kept in Cell 6, just a few doors away from my cell. Whenever I was taken out for interrogation, I passed right by Fan's cell and had the chance to see him and exchange a few words. He would always flash me a quick V-for-victory sign, and initially he was full of optimism. As time passed by and hopes of an early release began to fade, however, his mood sank and his eyes took on a dark and lost expression. Shortly after the 1990 Spring Festival, he came close to mental collapse and began shouting out loudly and making big scenes. (On another level, this was actually a form of resistance).

The jail officials soon marked Fan down as a troublemaker, and before long they took to pulling him out of his cell and giving him what they used to refer to in jail slang as a "reaming." This is a form of punishment commonly found in Hunan jails, and involves being given repeated shocks by an electric baton to sensitive parts of the body. The somewhat obscure nickname "reaming" (*jiao*) derives from the fact that when the cadres torture prisoners in this way, they not only go for places like the neck, face and ears, but quite often even push the baton inside the victim's mouth and start twisting it around from one side to the other - as if reaming out a hole. Each time this happened to Fan and I would hear his agonized cries of pain, I felt my heart being pierced by a knife.

Finally, they put him on to the "shackle board" and then he really did start to go crazy. The first thing we would hear on returning to our cells after work in the evening would be Fan's shouts of "You bastards are going to die a bad death!", "Let me out of here!" and "I'm so angry I could die!" Sometimes he could be heard barking like a dog, quacking like a duck or crowing like a chicken. At other times he would just lie there talking to himself all night long, right through until daybreak. In the daytime, he would sometimes be carried out for another dose of electric "reaming" or handed over to a bunch of prisoners to be tormented by them, falling asleep when his body could eventually stand no more. On one occasion, unable to bear the loathsome spectacle any longer, I called one of the prison cadres and requested that Fan's punishment be halted. He told me that Fan had brought the whole thing on himself by pretending to be mad, when in fact he was perfectly sane. I asked how they could possibly justify treating prisoners like this. But I might as well have saved my breath. The cadre replied that Fan had violated prison rules and stirred up trouble, and so it was essential that he be punished.

Fan's condition deteriorated day by day. He lost all control over his bowel and urinary movements and even began to stop responding physically to the electrical assaults. In the end, when he could no longer differentiate between different people or objects, the cadres no longer doubted that Fan really did have psychiatric problems, and for a while they more or less stopped beating him with the electric batons. But by then Fan had lost all physical coordination, which often led to him being teased and tormented by the other prisoners. They would vent all their pent-up frustration and resentments against Fan, either by stuffing dirty socks or cloths into his mouth, pouring cold water over his body (this was during a bitterly cold winter) or just kicking him. All the while, Fan was just lying there, fixed to the "shackle board" and unable to move or do anything but endure the torment.

Three months went by before the higher authorities acknowledged the situation as being at all serious - and only then because they realized that if the facts became known outside the prison there would be widespread public discontent and strenuous criticisms would be raised. They then did an enormous amount of so-called "ideological work" on Fan, and he was only released from the "shackle board" after he had given an undertaking that he would stop all his protests and not make any more trouble. No one made any attempt to stop the bullying by his fellow prisoners, however, and it continued right up until his release in late 1990.

The next and last time I met Fan Zhong was in mid-July 1991, shortly before I escaped from China. We talked through the night, and he poured out all his feelings about the terrible experience he had been through. Thinking back on it all, I too felt overwhelmed with emotion. He and I were true friends in adversity. Fan told me that he was no longer in contact with anyone anymore, and that until the social system changed, he would not dare to re-enter society again. As I left his place, the thought occurred to me: if the government wouldn't even spare a youth like him, someone who had been raised in the teachings of the Party from earliest childhood, then the government must surely be blind. It was, to coin a phrase, creating its own grave-diggers.

Chen Gang

Immediately after his conviction in June 1989, Chen Gang (the Xiangtan worker who was sentenced to death in June 1989 on trumped-up charges) was put into handcuffs and leg-irons - the usual practice for condemned prisoners in China. He secretly wrote out a last will and testament and entrusted it to be passed on to his younger brother, Chen Ding. In the letter, Chen expressed the hope that his younger brother would never abandon his ideals or the pursuit of justice.

Chen's fellow workers at the Xiangtan Electrical Machinery Factory, however, refused to accept the court's verdict against him, and several tens of thousands of them prepared to stage a protest strike. The mood was extremely tense and explosive, and the case was referred upward through ever higher levels of the bureaucracy for resolution, and as a means of holding the strike at bay. On several occasions, Chen was taken from his cell by armed guards in preparation for execution, only to be sent back inside again later.

In early April 1990, workers at the Xiangtan Electrical Machinery Factory heard that Chen was to be executed on April 22 and spread the news all around. The following day, the entire factory workforce came out on strike. This incident alerted those at the most senior levels of government to the depth of popular local feeling over the issue, and showed the strength of the people. A series of official "studies" then followed, at the end of which, in May 1990, the judicial authorities altered the sentence on Chen Gang to one of death penalty with a two-year stay of execution.

Throughout this 10-month period, from initial imposition of the death penalty to the final review and reduction of sentence, Chen Gang had been kept shackled hand and foot. One can scarcely imagine the mental and physical suffering he must have gone through as a result of this brutal, and entirely unnecessary, punitive measure.

After my release from prison, I made a special trip to the Xiangtan Electrical Machine Factory, hoping to meet with Chen's parents. While having lunch at a local restaurant, I asked the proprietor if he knew their address. Upon hearing that I was Chen's friend, the restaurant owner became very excited and began telling me all the latest news. Apparently, the security section chief whose belongings had been burned in the original incident had since been transferred to a post elsewhere, because the local people used to stare at him angrily all the time and stones were often thrown at his home at night. Chen's mother, it turned out, was an old teacher at the factory kindergarten, and people all said that she was a good and kind woman. Chen Gang's younger brothers and sisters were all said to be coping well. But now, a once happy family had been plunged into tragedy. "The Chen brothers were indeed unfortunate!" said the restaurant owner, with mixed sadness and anger.

My friend then quietly told him that I was a student leader who had been jailed together with Chen Gang, and pointed to my head. (In prison, my head had been shaved, so I normally wore a hat to avoid attracting attention). The owner was surprised and delighted, and his family all came over and began asking me many questions, including all about Chen Gang's current condition and about our experiences in jail. They said that everyone in the area wanted to know if Chen Gang had any chance of being released in the near future. I comforted them as best I could, saying I believed that the day would not be too far off. Before I left, the restaurant owner and his family toasted me with a glass of wine and declined all attempts to pay my bill. My friend and I then went to the Chen family home, but the door was locked and nobody was there. We next went to the kindergarten where Chen's mother worked, but still there was nobody. So I had to return to Changsha without having seen Chen's mother. I had met many people who loved and cared about the family, however, and I was moved and comforted by this fact.

Li Maoqiu, Zhang Zhonghui and Liu Fuyuan

Three of my fellow prisoners in Cell 12 of the Changsha No. 1 Jail were pure cases of unjust imprisonment. The oldest was a man named Li Maoqiu, 53 years old, a senior engineer at the Changsha Non-Ferrous Metals Design Institute and latterly a millionaire. The youngest was a 16 year-old lad named Zhang Zhonghui, who had been falsely accused of theft. The other, a severely ill man named Liu Fuyuan, had been accused of economic crimes. (Although ostensibly unrelated to the 1989 pro-democracy movement, his arrest was a direct consequence of the indiscriminate "law and order" campaign which accompanied the movement's suppression.)

In 1986, Li Maoqiu went off the payroll[21] of the Nonferrous Metals Design Institute in order to set up a private business. By 1989, less than three years later, the business had expanded to include a chicken farm, a dog farm, a salted goods shop and a roasted snack shop.[22]

After the outbreak of the 1989 Democracy Movement, Li, who felt strongly about the escalating problem of official profiteering and government corruption in China, demonstrated his firm and unconditional support for the protesting students by donating over 10,000 *yuan* to our fighting fund.[23] This gesture of financial support was much appreciated by the student movement in Hunan.

---

[21] *Tingxin liuzhi*, a fairly common procedure whereby employees of state enterprises can sometimes seek other employment while retaining their original job-benefit package.

[22] Around this time, a friend of Li's named Zhou Zhenhua, a lecturer at the Central-South Industrial University, set up a technology development enterprise called the Central-South Materials Company. Li Maoqiu invested more than RMB 270,000 *yuan* in the company, but in early 1989 it went bankrupt and Li lost most of his money.

[23] One US dollar equals approximately 5.20 *yuan*.

At the end of June 1989, however, the public security authorities secretly arrested Li and threw him into the Changsha No. 1 Jail for interrogation and investigation. (Li was an obvious target for political scapegoating: both his maternal grandfather and his father-in-law had been students at the Whampoa Military Academy in the 1920s and went on to become high-ranking Guomindang generals.) For some time, the authorities' attempts failed to bear fruit, and they were at a loss as to what to charge him with. Finally, in mid-1990, the Changsha Procuracy brought formal charges of economic fraud and sealed up all his property, including even his home electrical appliances. His wife, a woman named Yu Ziyu, was distraught and made several unsuccessful suicide attempts.

In jail, Li Maoqiu always maintained a high level of self-composure and integrity, and he would often say to us: "A true gentleman can be killed, but cannot be shamed" *(shi ke sha, bu ke ru.)* Deep down, however, he was overwhelmed with feelings of sadness and anger at his situation. One evening in late 1990, he suddenly just died. The authorities later announced to the assembled prisoners that the cause of death had been "an explosion of the coronary arteries" *(xin xueguan baozha)* - an explanation which we all regarded as being nothing more than a cynical lie. Thereafter, whenever anyone else died in the prison we would be sure to refer to the event as an "explosion of the coronary arteries."

At least Li had done something wrong in the government's eyes by donating money to the students. The case of Zhang Zhonghui, however, was an utter miscarriage of justice. Zhang, who had just turned sixteen and was still legally a minor, had been arrested with several others in June, 1989 and accused of theft. In early 1990, the procuracy brought formal charges against him and in May of that year he had his first public trial. But because the evidence against him was insufficient, the trial was suspended and Zhang was returned to jail. (Elsewhere, of course, insufficient evidence would have been grounds for immediate release, but not in China.)

What with one delay after another, the case dragged on to the end of 1990, until finally Zhang's family petitioned the government and, at the same time, made public the results of fingerprint tests taken at the scene of the crime which demonstrated Zhang's innocence. On seeing the evidence, the workers at the factory where Zhang had worked rose up in arms, the accusation against Zhang was swiftly withdrawn and he was released as not guilty. Through a sheer injustice, he had spent a year and a half in prison. It later emerged that the real reason for Zhang and the others having been arrested in the first place was simply that they had offended the son of the factory security chief.[25]

As for Liu Fuyuan, his case was similar to that of Li Maoqiu - he had been slapped with a charge of economic crime for purely political reasons. In his youth, Liu had come under the influence of the Cultural Revolution pro-democracy activist, Chen Guangdi, and become involved in dissident activities. The government, however, had never been able to pin anything specific on him. With the crackdown on the 1989 pro-democracy movement, the authorities decided to sweep up all alleged "dangerous elements" without further distinction, and Liu Fuyuan was one of the many who were unjustly imprisoned as a result.

By the time of my departure from Changsha No. 1 Jail in October 1990, Liu had not eaten for more than a month. He suffered severely from kidney stones, and every night would roll around and scream in pain. His body weight had dropped from over 80 kilograms when he first arrived at the prison, to under 40 kilograms by the time I left. The doctors who were brought to examine him all recommended that he be released on bail pending trial, so that he could begin to receive proper treatment. But a leading official of the Changsha Municipal Public Security Bureau was resolutely opposed to the idea. "Let him die in jail," said the official in October 1990. I never managed to find out what later became of Liu.

---

[25] Security cadres at state enterprises are often appointed directly by and responsible to the local police. Thus, they are much more like policemen than like private security guards.

4. Widening the Purge

In the 1989 crackdown, the authorities did not confine themselves to carrying out only the more obvious repressive measures, such as large-scale arrests, expedited trials and heavy sentences. They also resorted to more subtle methods of persecuting and punishing pro-democracy activists, including job dismissal or demotion, exile to the remote countryside, various administrative punishments and marathon doses of "ideological re-education." Since tens of thousands of students and many times more workers and ordinary citizens had participated in the 1989 democracy movement in Hunan, it was clearly not feasible for the government to arrest all of them. Toward the rank-and-file supporters of the movement, therefore, the authorities adopted a policy of "attacking the few and educating the many."

In China, the law is only one instrument for maintaining the political and social order. It is also the least commonly used. Countless "directives," "documents" and "policies," all formulated by the Party, exist for this purpose, and they carry considerably more weight than the law. Of the estimated 100 million or so people in China who have fallen victim to the endless "political movements" waged by the authorities over the past 40 years and more, only a small minority were ever actually tried in court and sent to prison. The vast majority were simply branded with the Party's hate-term of the day: "landlords," rich peasants," bad elements" and "rightists" in the 1950s, "capitalist-roaders" and "revisionists" in the 1960s, "hangers-on of the Lin Biao/Gang of Four clique" in the 1970s, and "bourgeois liberals" and "turmoil elements" in the 1980s. Then they were subjected to a barrage of mental and physical persecution, professional ruin, public humiliation and social ostracism. Following the defeat of the 1989 pro-democracy movement, a similar tragic scenario was played out yet again throughout the country.

Province-wide investigations

Following the June 4 massacre, the Hunan authorities conducted a comprehensive investigation to identify all those in the province who had ever participated in any of the pro-democracy groups or demonstrations. Tens of thousands of students, workers, ordinary citizens and even government officials were "ferreted out" in this way, and many were branded as "major targets for re-education." Internal Party documents repeatedly stressed the need to pursue the investigations with the utmost thoroughness and severity, and each "battlefront" in society - that is, each different sector, department or profession - was instructed to draw up its own detailed plan of action for implementing the purge. The official score-settling was especially intense in Changsha, the provincial capital.

The lucky ones among those investigated were simply ordered to "perform introspection and repent their ways." A large number, however, were eventually subjected to so-called "administrative discipline" by their work-units. Such discipline included expulsion from college or university; dismissal from public employment; being placed on probation within the work-unit for a period of six months to two years; having "demerits" entered in personal dossiers; and being issued formal "disciplinary warnings." Most were forced to attend so-called "political study classes" so that they could be brainwashed into giving up their dissident ideas. Others were dragged before mass public rallies around the province and subjected to humiliating denunciation and criticism. (The Communist Party's methods of "re-educating" people are many and various.)

The combing-out operation continued right through until May 1990, by which time several tens of thousands of activists across the province had been identified and punished. The authorities stipulated that all those found to have committed "political errors" during the 1989 pro-democracy movement would be denied promotion until further notice and would under no circumstances be eligible for employment in key posts or positions of trust. In a more positive, self-congratulatory vein, it was required also that every locality had to muster a group of so-called "outstanding youth": students and other young people who had "taken a firm and clear-cut stand against the turmoil." These worthies were paraded in the media and rewarded with important government posts, and they even received cash bonuses.

The purge was pursued somewhat differently among the various sectors of society. The workers, as discussed above, bore the brunt of the arrests and sentencing·side of the crackdown, but in the wider investigation and purge they fared much the same as other sectors. A certain proportion of the workforce in a given factory would be singled out for public criticism, demotion or dismissal, but simply too many workers had joined in the demonstrations, and to amplify the purge would have been unnecessarily risky for the authorities. In the main, therefore, they relied upon exemplary criminal proceedings against selected workers in order to instil a deterrent effect among the workforce as a whole.

In the universities, colleges and scientific establishments, teaching staff who had "committed errors" during the democracy movement were treated more harshly than those of their students who did so. Minor punishments included being organized to take part in "study classes," having salary docked, or receiving a Party warning or some administrative-disciplinary sanction. More serious cases brought outright dismissal (a dire prospect for most academics in China, who often have nowhere else to go.)

After my release from prison, I visited a number of university teachers who had been pro-democracy activists during the 1989 movement. The great majority of them had, by way of punishment, been put through "study classes," a vague and nebulous concept which covers a multitude of sins. For some people, this involved actually being sent to a political study group to receive "ideological education." For less fortunate individuals, it meant being sent down to some work-unit at the grassroots to undergo "re-education by the masses." While for the really unlucky ones, it entailed being forcibly rusticated to some backward and impoverished part of the countryside to take part in the so-called "socialist education movement."

Forced rustication

The Hunan "socialist education movement", which began in the summer of 1989, was a highly significant event, for it turned out to be the prototype for a massive campaign of the same name which was launched throughout the country in 1990. The campaign's ostensible purpose was to mobilize urban resources to help "raise the political and cultural level" of the peasants. In reality, it served to a large extent as a means of punishing pro-democracy intellectuals and officials. In March 1990 in Changsha alone, a city with a population of just over 1 million people, at least 50,000 young government cadres and university teachers were sent down to villages throughout the province to perform agricultural labor.

According to the government, those sent down to the countryside were only supposed to remain there for three months. But a large number of them, those branded as being seriously "bourgeois liberal" or just plain "incorrigible" have still, almost three years later, not received their "certificates of reform" from the local authorities. They look set to remain in the countryside making "contributions to socialism" indefinitely. The majority of the young cadres sent down after June 1989 had only recently graduated from university and so tended to be the most enthusiastic about reform and democracy. In the countryside, however, little attempt was made to utilize their skills and training. As for the university and research institute staffers who were sent down at the same time, professors of mathematics are now having to teach elementary arithmetic to the peasants, and holders of doctoral degrees in philosophy are being forced to teach basic literacy classes.[25] Since March 1990, when the "socialist education movement" was launched nationally, several more armies of urban individuals, each over 10,000-strong, have been dumped into villages all over Hunan to "undergo reform." In each batch, there has been a certain group of people who will never be allowed to return. They themselves refer to their plight as "forced banishment."[26]

Bureaucratizing the purge: the students

University and college students suffered relatively less harassment in the wider purge. As everyone knows, the 1989 pro-democracy

---

[25] Among several dozen people I know personally who were sent down in the "socialist education movement" and have not yet been allowed back to the cities are: Jiang Caoxin, from the general office of the Hunan provincial government; Li Chuan, from Hunan provincial television; Li Manyu, from Central-South Industrial University; and Deng Chaohua, Jiang Jianwu and Wan Zhongxue from Hunan Normal University. Some of them have been married for many years, but now have to live separated from their spouses.

[26] In Chinese, *chong jun*, the term used in imperial times to describe the forced sending into exile by the emperor of out-of-favor officials. Such people were usually sent to the remote desert areas of the far northwest or to the malaria-infested swamplands of Yunnan.

movement began on the campuses, and students formed the highest proportion of activists throughout the entire movement. Faced with this fact, the authorities "ingeniously" decided to adopt a strategy of divide and rule to deal with the students afterwards. Soon after June 4, all the universities and colleges organized a one-month long "study course in political ideology." At Hunan Normal University, Hunan Agricultural College, Changsha Railway College and other places, they even set up "intensive training courses" in the subject. The purpose of these classes was not, however, to punish student activists immediately, but rather to establish an overall hierarchy of guilt and to assign each student to one of three categories.

The first category, known as "dangerous turmoil elements" *(dongluan weixian fenzi)*, were punished by means of administrative sanctions and restricted job assignments after graduation. Those placed in this category were the ones whom the authorities believed could not, in the short term, be "educated and persuaded" out of their beliefs. They therefore had to be actively punished, and the best way to do this was to assign them a job in some remote, rural area where the local people's low level of political awareness and the practical difficulty in maintaining contact with other student activists would effectively neutralize them and prevent them "stirring up trouble" again.

The second category, those known as "wavering radical elements" *(dongyao buding de jijin fenzi)*, were dealt with by a combination of threats and promises. Most students placed in this category proved unable to withstand the sheer force of government propaganda after June 4, and in the end were persuaded to renounce their ideas about democracy. Superficially, the authorities did not punish or discriminate against such students in any way, but their activities were all carefully noted down in their personal dossiers. Provided they stayed out of trouble, no further action was taken, although they had little chance of ever gaining a position of trust. But if they were caught engaging in pro-democracy activities again, then the old score would be settled along with the new one. (Many student activists of the 1989 movement who had also participated in the winter 1986-87 student movement were punished on the basis of this rule.) Those who didn't toe the line were penalized either by bad job placements or even, in some cases, by getting no job assignment at all. (This had been almost unheard of prior to 1989.)

The third category comprised "students who acted on impulse and made mistakes through a momentary lack of understanding" (*yi shi bu ming zhenxiang, ganqing chongdong fanyou cuowu de xuesheng*). Such students were not punished by the authorities, apart for being made to undergo "ideological education. They too, however, were barred from subsequent employment in Party or government organs, key enterprises or any of the other departments offering good working conditions.

The intense stress and anxiety caused among students by the post-June 4 settling of accounts resulted in a number of tragedies. A male student from Hunan University's forestry department (class of '87) and a female student from Hunan Normal University's history department were both so devastated by their protracted interrogation that they committed suicide. The male student, who lived in Room 411 of Dormitory 11, lay down on the railroad track and was run over by a train. The woman, who lived in Dormitory 7 of Hunan Normal University, wrote out her will and then jumped to her death from the twelfth floor of the Moshan Hotel, after loudly shouting some slogans. The government viewed this incident as being extremely sensitive and all information on it was strictly suppressed.

The net outcome of the campus investigations in Hunan was roughly as follows. By the end of 1990, more than 40 students from my own school, Hunan Normal University, had either been expelled, placed on probation, had a major or minor "demerit" marked in their personal dossier or been given a serious warning or a caution.[27] At the Changsha Railway College, 23 students were expelled and 37 received lesser punishments.[28] In addition, groups of between 10 and 50 students were similarly penalized at each of the following: Hunan University, Hunan Agricultural Institute, Central-South Industrial University, Hunan Water Conservancy and Electrical Power Normal College, Hunan College of

---

[27] These included Xia Siqing, Zheng Yan, Liu Chaohui, Zhu Jianwen, Qin Jianxin, Nie Qinglong, Nie Weihong, Li Wenjun, Bai Hua, Qu Zhaowu, Luo Weiguo, Chen Jianwei and He Zhongxia.

[28] The expelled students included Liu Wei, Li Lanlan, Li Chunyuan, Jia Jinfeng and He Guanghui. In early 1991, some of the 23 were readmitted to the college.

Finance and Economics, Changsha University, Hunan Communications College and Changsha Basic University.

Most of those punished had been members of either the Hunan SAF or the various autonomous campus federations. Indeed, out of all my friends who were active in these organizations, there was not one who managed to avoid some form of official discrimination or retaliation. Those expelled from college found life very difficult thereafter, since no one would employ them and they had to spend all their time and energy searching for ways to support themselves - which is just what the government intended. Many of my friends from the former SAF leadership remained destitute for a long time after June 1989, before eventually finding work outside the province in places like Shenzhen, Guangzhou, Hainan and Xiamen. Some of them are still unemployed and have to rely entirely on help from their families to support themselves.

Plight of released dissidents

The plight of pro-democracy activists who were sentenced to prison terms after June 1989 and have since been released, however, is still worse. For the most part, they have become a new class of highly-educated, unemployed vagrants, discriminated against by the authorities at every turn. Most firms and companies are afraid to hire them because of their "counterrevolutionary" records, and they are barred from employment in colleges and State-run enterprises. If they try to set up small private businesses, they are harassed by the public security authorities and usually denied the necessary operating permits. Those not originally from the cities have been stripped of their urban residency permits, and their only options are thus either to remain unlawfully as "black city-dwellers" or to return to their homes in the countryside and become "repairers of the planet" *(xiu diqiu)* - that is, farm laborers.

Zhou Liwu

The experiences of Zhou Liwu, formerly a teacher at the No.2 Light Industrial College in Changsha, typify those of many recently-released dissidents in Hunan. Zhou was sentenced to two years in prison on a charge of "counterrevolutionary propaganda and incitement" for his involvement in the 1989 movement. After being released in early 1991, he went back to his old college, only to be informed that he had been fired from his post there long ago. He then returned to his parents' home in the countryside to recuperate for a while, hoping that he would soon receive good news and believing that the government would be sure to find some use for a talented university graduate such as himself. (Zhou's graduation thesis in philosophy won widespread local academic acclaim.) But he remained in limbo for months. Eventually, not wishing to be a burden on his parents any longer, he headed for Changsha in search of work.

Several collective enterprises in Changsha were keen to hire him, but they finally all refused on the grounds that he had a "problematic personal history." Thinking that some of the coastal cities might be less concerned about enforcing the government's repressive policies, he then borrowed 300 yuan and went south to Guangzhou City, where he finally found employment with a Taiwanese joint venture company. His boss was so pleased with him that he quickly put him in charge of personnel matters. All went well until the end of the first month, when he was suddenly fired. According to the boss, he had come under such pressure from the government for hiring Zhou that in the end he had no choice but to fire him. Subsequently, Zhou found other positions in joint venture companies, but he was always fired within the first month following renewed government threats and pressure on the management. Finally, Zhou gave up and went back to his home village, where he now scrapes out a living as a peasant.

Other students I know who have encountered the same problem since being released from prison include Tan Liliang, formerly a teacher at Loudi Vocational Normal College; Zhang Xiaojun, formerly a teacher at Changde's Taoyuan Normal College; Zeng Ming, formerly a teacher at Central-South Industrial University; and Jiang Fengshan, formerly a teacher at Xiangtan University. Each time any of them found jobs, the government invariably found out about it and had them fired. During 1991, for example, Tan Liliang had to change jobs no fewer than 20 different times.

Mo Lihua

One of the most outstanding activists of the 1989 pro-democracy movement in Hunan was a woman named Mo Lihua (the name means simply "Jasmine"), formerly a teacher at the Shaoyang Vocational Normal college. She went to Beijing during the movement, returning to Hunan shortly before the June 4 massacre. She later made passionate public speeches denouncing the crackdown, including one at a mourning ceremony on June 5 in which she called it "a bloody repression of the people by a fascist government." Her husband resigned from the Party after June 4, and when Mo was eventually arrested he went to the Shaoyang public security bureau and demanded (unsuccessfully) that they arrest him too. Tried by the Shaoyang Intermediate Court on December 21, 1989 on charges of "counterrevolutionary propaganda and incitement," Mo was sentenced to three years' imprisonment and sent to the women-only Changsha Prison. (See *Appendix VIII.C* for full text of the court verdict.) In mid-1991, she was released early on parole - but only to find that a couple of months previously she had been fired from her college teaching post.

A gentle and sensitive intellectual, she nonetheless showed her strength of character by deciding to head south in search of work, leaving behind her husband and a seven-year old daughter. As she was about to leave, however, a government official arrived and laid down a set of "rules" for her parole. She was not allowed to leave the school where they were living, and she was especially forbidden to travel to other parts of the country; she even had to get the authorities' prior permission to visit friends and relatives in Shaoyang. She was, to all intents and purposes, under a form of house arrest. Since then, she has been stuck in a state of futile and enforced inactivity, with no job, no money and no future.

Pan Mingdong

One of the more inspirational stories of the post-June 1989 suppression in Hunan is that of Pan Mingdong, a former boxing coach in the provincial Commission for Physical Education. Pan is a big, kind-hearted man with a strong sense of justice. His father, although a veteran of the "Autumn Harvest Uprising,"[30] was executed in the 1950s as a

---

[30] The Autumn Harvest Uprising was a series of attacks carried out, on Stalin's orders, by the Communist Party forces against Guomindang-held cities in Hunan and other southern provinces in the summer of 1927. The failure of the uprising prompted Mao's retreat to the Jinggangshan mountains along the Hunan-Jiangxi border and led to the formation of the Red Army.

"counterrevolutionary" for allegedly opposing Mao's line (he was posthumously "rehabilitated"), leaving Pan's mother to bring up him and his younger sister all on her own. He knows life at the grassroots, having spent several years as a peasant and several as a worker.

In October 1989, Pan was arrested on suspicion of having drafted the "Declaration of Hunan Autonomy," a radical manifesto which was issued on June 8 by a group called the "Preparatory Committee for Patriotic Self-Governance by the People of Hunan," calling for a military rebellion against the Li Peng government. (Many PLA officers, among others, were investigated in connection with this startling document; see *Appendix VII* for full translation.) But the prosecution could produce no evidence, and Pan was administratively sentenced instead to two years' "re-education through labor." His mother was devastated and took to her bed for most of the next two years, surviving only thanks to the constant care and attention of her daughter and the generosity of neighbors.

When Pan was released in late 1991 from the Changsha Xinkaipu Labor Re-education Center (known outwardly as the Hunan Switchgear Factory), he went to the public security bureau to reclaim his possessions which had been confiscated at the time of his arrest. The police refused, however, and to this day he has still not been given them back. He cannot find a job, and he and his mother now rely on regular small donations from his many friends.

An incident I remember from one day soon after June 4, 1989 vividly illustrates the irony and injustice of Pan's treatment by the government. We were on the run together, sitting on a train headed south, when suddenly a gang of about 20 young thugs burst into the carriage and began systematically robbing the terrified passengers of all their valuables. (Such crimes are becoming increasingly common all over China nowadays.) No one dared confront or resist the robbers, and they made a clean sweep of the carriage. But then one of them began to fondle a pretty young woman sitting next to us. Having taken her last two *yuan*, he stroked her on the cheek and said, "Why, that's not even enough for my pack of cigarettes."

At this, Pan Mingdong leapt to his feet and took up a martial-arts combat stance in front of the man. "Okay, tough guy, let's see what you're made of now!", he hissed. The thug pulled out a huge knife, but began to back off nervously. Stopping what they were doing, the rest of the gang slowly started to close in on Pan, their weapons also drawn. But Pan just coolly stood his ground. "Fine," he said, "I can easily handle all you creeps at once!" Just then, one of the armed police guards on the train came into the carriage, his pistol at the ready. After sizing up the situation, he looked over at Pan and said, "What're you making trouble for? This has nothing to do with you." The members of the gang just laughed and put their weapons away, then drifted back toward the far door and moved on into the next carriage. But the police officer made no move to arrest or even challenge them - and it was then we realized that he must actually be in cahoots with them. (No doubt, he would be getting his share of the loot later on.) As he slipped quietly away, the passengers all stood up and applauded Pan. They never got their valuables back, but at least the young woman's honor had been defended.

Incidents like this revealed clearly the true character of pro-democracy activists like Pan, and gave the lie to the cynical government propaganda depicting us as being mere "thugs" and "hooligans." In this case, as in many others, it was a so-called "counterrevolutionary" who stood up for the common people - and a corrupt government functionary who let the real thugs and hooligans go scot free.

Purging dissent within the Party: the Yin Zhenggao Affair

With the onset of the June 4 crackdown, the Hunan authorities availed themselves of the opportunity to wreak vengeance upon a number of senior and mid-ranking provincial Party officials who had been rocking the boat by criticizing government corruption and promoting political reform. Foremost among these was Yin Zhenggao, until November 1988 the pioneering vice-mayor of Yueyang City and a man often referred to in Chinese pro-reform circles as "Hunan's Gorbachev." Soon after taking office in 1985, Yin initiated three major projects, all of which benefitted the city's quality of life and economy and greatly endeared him to the local people: improving environmental protection, building up the urban infrastructure and renovating major historical sites such as the Yueyang Tower.

He was also a model of moral rectitude, and demanded clean government on the part of his subordinates. For this, the residents of Yueyang gave him the affectionate nickname of "Clear Skies Yin" *(Yin*

Qing Tian).[30] Among his many pathbreaking political innovations was the setting up of a new government body called the "Office of Discussion and Criticism" *(Jiang-Ping-Ban)* which held regular open meetings at which members of the public were invited and encouraged to expose corrupt activities within the local Party and government administrations. People flocked to these meetings, and each session was extensively broadcast on Hunan Television the same evening. The effect was astonishing. For the first time in China since 1949, a measure of real, direct accountability had been introduced into the political process, and officials all over Yueyang City soon began to feel the pinch of public scrutiny. Corrupt local officials were weeded out and punished, and, under the threat of possible public exposure, others began to tone down or even dismantle their operations. Vice-mayor Yin, of course, who was only 45 years old at the time, made many enemies in high places as a result.

His downfall came in late 1988, after he had broken all known rules by denouncing at a municipal Party committee meeting his own superior, Mayor Tan Zhaohua, for flagrant graft and bribe-taking. The case was sent up to the provincial disciplinary commission for decision, but the latter bounced it right back down to the Yueyang authorities - all of whom were firmly under the patronage of Mayor Tan. In November 1988, Yin was suspended from all duties, accused of "conspiring to usurp power" and a major Party investigation was launched into him and his entire circle of associates. The Yueyang students and general public rose up in outrage, staging a series of large-scale protest demonstrations across the city over a several-week period. (These protests were, in effect, the first salvoes of the nationwide pro-democracy movement of the following year.) Other solidarity actions included a conference entitled "Symposium on the Yin Zhenggao Phenomenon," organized by Huang Yaru, professor of politics at the Yueyang Vocational Normal College, specially to provide a forum for critics of the attack on Yin. The central authorities in Beijing followed these events, which soon became known nationwide as the "Yin Zhenggao Affair," with the greatest concern.

The official investigation, during which time Yin and his circle

---

[30] *"Qing Tian"* was the term traditionally used in China to denote an upright and incorruptible local magistrate.

remained on ice, continued right up until the outbreak of the pro-democracy movement in May 1989. Some weeks prior to then, however, a journalist by the name of Mai Tianshu had arrived in Yueyang to prepare a long investigative article on the incident for publication in *Reportage Literature (Baogao Wenxue)*, the country's foremost political *exposé* news magazine. The editor in charge of this article, which was titled "Living Sacrifice" *(Huo Ji)* was Liu Xiaoyan, daughter of China's most famous investigative journalist, Liu Binyan. Moreover, the introduction to the article was written by Su Xiaokang, principle author of *River Elegy*, a controversial television series which had scathingly dismissed several millennia of Chinese culture and was screened in late 1988 and early 1989 to the consternation of the country's hardline elderly leaders.

Days before the article's scheduled publication in May 1989, the propaganda department of the Party central committee in Beijing issued an order banning all distribution of that entire issue of *Reportage Literature*. At great personal risk, however, some officials took a large number of copies of the magazine from Beijing to Hunan by car and secretly distributed it among the various government departments and the recently-formed autonomous student bodies - including the Hunan SAF. I myself sent a student from Hunan University to Yueyang to investigate the matter, and upon his return the SAF passed a resolution to begin lobbying the Hunan Provincial People's Congress with a view to winning their support for Yin Zhenggao and his cause. The majority of the congress delegates were right behind us, and they angrily denounced the local Party authorities' campaign of persecution against Yin.

After June 4, the retaliation began in earnest. Yin Zhenggao and several of his closest colleagues were placed under house arrest, and up to 50 other leading and middle-ranking Yueyang officials in his circle were formally arrested. Many of them were eventually tried and given heavy prison sentences. The most severe sentence went to Qin Hubao, a senior cadre in Yin's "Office of Discussion and Criticism" (ODC) and one of those who had secretly smuggled the banned copies of *Reportage Literature* down to Hunan from Beijing. Qin was convicted in the Yueyang Intermediate Court in December 1989 on a charge of "counter-revolutionary propaganda and incitement" and sentenced to ten years' imprisonment.

At least eight other officials from Yin's administration were also tried on the same charge and received sentences ranging from three to five years. They included Mei Shi, editor-in-chief of the *Yueyang Evening News*, who received a four-year sentence; Yang Shaoyue, former head of the ODC, sentenced to five years; Wu Weiguo, also a cadre in the ODC, five years; Xie Yang, first secretary of the Yueyang Communist Youth League, three years; He Aoqiu, assistant professor in Chinese at the Yueyang Normal College, three years; Zhang Jizhong, a reporter for the *Hunan Daily*, three years; Cheng Cun, reporter for the Yueyang bureau of *News Pictorial* magazine *(Xinwen Tupian Bao)*, five years; and Huang Yaru, the professor who had organized the solidarity conference for Yin Zhenggao at Yueyang Normal College, five years. All eight are currently being held in Hunan Provincial No.2 Prison in Hengyang City. Dozens of other journalists and state cadres were given a range of administrative punishments in connection with the Yin Zhenggao Affair. For the journalists, among the lightest of these was a ban on publication of their works for up to two years.

In keeping with Party tradition, the authorities neither arrested nor imprisoned Yin Zhenggao himself, preferring to victimize his colleagues instead. (They provided a softer target, and it is considered bad for "inner-Party unity" to destroy a senior comrade.) But Yin is now unemployed and near destitute, living in a tiny apartment with his wife at her work-unit, the Chongshan Metallurgy Plant. Perhaps the only source of comfort to him, however, is that the local people still refer to him as "Clear Skies Yin."

Suppression of renewed pro-democracy activism, 1989-92

The political changes that began to sweep through Eastern Europe less than six months after the onset of the crackdown in China only confirmed the Beijing leadership's fears about the emergence of "Gorbachev-style" figures at home. They also hardened the leadership's resolve to crush any future dissident trends in society at an early stage, and punishment for those who continued to organize underground for democracy after June 1989 has been correspondingly severe. In March, 1991, for example, 15 and 11-year prison terms were imposed on two graduate students at Beijing's Qinghua University, Chen Yanbin and Zhang Yafei, for producing a pro-democracy journal called *Iron Current (Tie Liu)*.

The authorities have dealt secretly with all such cases and made strenuous efforts to prevent them from becoming public knowledge. In Hunan, where the pro-democracy movement began to regroup relatively quickly after the body-blow of June 4, 1989, numerous isolated acts of repression have been carried out by the authorities over the past two years. The following are only a few such incidents on which firm information has become available.

In December 1989, news of the popular uprising in Romania and the fall and execution of Ceaucescu was greeted with exultation in Changsha, causing the local authorities to place the security forces on high alert. Students at the Central-South Industrial University planned to stage a celebratory demonstration, but large numbers of police were dispatched to block the main gate and seal off the campus. All the official banners and posters on campus proclaiming the glories of socialism were plastered with graffiti over the next few days, and a number of students, including Cai Feng of the physics department, were arrested and held for several months.

In the wake of the Romanian events, the central authorities issued an internal directive ordering the provinces to further boost the crackdown on dissent. In Hunan, several student and worker activists who had escaped arrest after June 4 were promptly hauled in. Zhong Hua, a 24-year old environmental planning student at Hunan University who had been head of the school's picket squad in May 1989 and had organized a lie-in on the railroad tracks at Changsha Station late that month, was arrested in March 1990. He went on trial in July, charged with "disrupting traffic order," and was sentenced to three years' imprisonment.

Around the same time, two scientific researchers named Ah Fang[31] and Zhang Jie, who in September 1989 had left their jobs at the Changsha Nonferrous Metals Design Academy in order to establish a private company, were arrested together with their entire company staff. The authorities branded the company as being a front organization for pro-democracy activities, and in mid-1990 both Zhang Jie and Ah Fang were convicted of "forming a counterrevolutionary organization" and

---

[31] This was the man's nickname; his actual name is not known.

sentenced to five years' imprisonment. It is not known what became of the other staff members.

In March 1990, a student in the foreign languages department of Hunan Normal University, named Long Jianhua, was detained and imprisoned for two months after the authorities discovered that he had decked out his bed to resemble a coffin and hung from it a poster of Hu Yaobang edged with black silk.

In April 1990, a group of workers were arrested in Changsha for having printed and distributed on the city's streets a large quantity of protest leaflets in advance of the first anniversary of the June 4 crackdown. The workers, all of whom had been detained and then released by the authorities the previous year for being members of the Changsha WAF, included three employees of the Hunan Electrical Battery Factory named Yang Rong, Wang Hong and Tang Yixin. The group's underground printing plant was uncovered by the authorities and destroyed, and the three men were charged with "forming a counter-revolutionary group." They have not yet been brought to trial, but the authorities have reportedly instructed that they be given long prison sentences.

In the early hours of May 1, 1990, dozens of big-character posters were pasted up on walls all around the Changsha Railroad Station, denouncing the June 1989 crackdown and raising criticisms on a range of issues including the sincerity of Deng Xiaoping's ten-year reform program and the wisdom of China's 1979 military incursion against Vietnam. The posters were swiftly torn down by the police, and from then on until after the first anniversary of the June 4 crackdown, the security forces throughout Hunan Province were placed on maximum alert. In August that year, several activists who had been detained the previous year and then released, including Liu Yi, the former treasurer of the Changsha WAF, were arrested once more and charged with the crime of "posting up counterrevolutionary slogans." They have not yet (so far as is known) been brought to trial.

In the summer of 1990, in the course of a nationwide "campaign to crack down on crime," more than 50 "common criminals" were executed in Changsha alone, ostensibly to "create a peaceful social atmosphere" in advance of China's hosting of the Asian Games. A number of private businessmen who had given financial support to the 1989 pro-democracy movement in Hunan are said to have been arrested on charges of economic corruption and severely punished during this campaign.

In February 1991, two brothers from Hengyang City named Li Lin and Li Zhi, both activists of the pro-democracy movement who had escaped to Hong Kong in July 1989, returned to Hunan after their families had been explicitly assured by local officials that they would not be punished if they did so. The brothers were arrested almost immediately. After being beaten and tortured in custody, the two were finally released and allowed to leave China following a major campaign of international pressure on their behalf. In May 1991, however, a young railway worker named Tang Zhijian was arrested for a second time on charges of having helped the Li brothers escape from China in July 1989. The authorities have secretly pressured Tang to confess to a false charge that he received money for helping in the escape, while at the same time publicly claiming that he is being held on charges of stealing a tape-recorder.

On June 4, 1991, students at Hunan Normal University, like those at Beijing University, let off firecrackers and smashed small bottles to commemorate the 1989 crackdown.[32] As a result of this incident, I myself was placed on a wanted list for a second time, having been released on parole only four months earlier, and so had to flee the country. In Guangzhou, also on June 4, a technician from a foreign joint venture company, a graduate of Qinghua University, wrote out a memorial banner bearing the words "The martyrs to democracy are not forgotten - the democratic movement will live forever." The man (name unknown) then took the banner to the Sun Yatsen Memorial Hall and placed it in front of Sun's statue, and was immediately arrested. There has been no further news on his fate since then.

With the collapse of the Soviet Communist Party in August 1991, the Chinese authorities again clamped down on dissident activities. In Hunan, one of the casualties of this was a 32-year old man from

---

[32] The Chinese for "small bottle," *xiao ping*, is evocative of Deng Xiaoping's given name, and smashing bottles thus represents a form of political protest.

71

Yongzhou City named Duan Ping, formerly a teacher in Qiyang No.1 Middle School. Duan had spent two years in Changsha's Xinkaipu Labor Re-education Center after June 1989 on account of his involvement in the pro-democracy movement. After his release in mid-1991, he opened an electronic games parlor. Following the failure of the coup in the Soviet Union, Duan was rearrested merely for expressing his support for those who had resisted the coup-plotters. In September 1991, he was sentenced without trial to a further three years' re-education through labor and sent back to Xinkaipu.

Li Shaojun, a physics student in the class of '88 at Hunan University, has been arrested no fewer than three times since June 1989. A founding member of the Democracy Salon and treasurer of the Hunan SAF, Li fled to Guangzhou after June 4 but returned to his hometown of Hengyang that August because he was penniless. He was arrested, held in Changsha No.1 Jail without trial until December 1989 and then released. In August 1990, he was again taken into detention after he telephoned a friend of his overseas who was a member of the Chinese exiled dissidents group, Federation for a Democratic China (FDC). He was freed again shortly after the end of the Asian Games. In early November 1991, Li was arrested for the third time, again in Guangzhou, and accused of "colluding with reactionary foreign powers" and "engaging in counterrevolutionary activities." He was sent back to Changsha No.1 Jail, and there has be no further word on his situation. (So capricious have the authorities been in his case that they may even release him yet again.) Li's father is a senior engineer in a car plant and his mother is a middle school teacher. He writes under the pen-name Li Aiju.

Finally, a 26-year-old man who was my personal bodyguard during the 1989 pro-democracy movement, Luo Ziren, was arrested for the second time in November 1991. Formerly a worker in the Changsha Cigarette Factory, Luo served during the 1989 movement as a SAF "special picket" and was responsible for guarding the organization's headquarters and protecting the SAF's main leaders. He was constantly by my side during the latter part of the movement. After June 4, 1989 he returned on our advice to his home province of Guizhou, but was arrested shortly thereafter and sent back to Changsha for interrogation. In November 1990, he was unexpectedly freed. Abandoning his job, however, he soon became involved once again in pro-democracy activities, and in November 1991 he was arrested again in Guiyang City,

72

the capital of Guizhou. The authorities have accused Luo of "organizing a group of social degenerates" to produce and distribute "large quantities of reactionary posters." No word has been heard of him since his arrest, but he is likely soon to be formally charged with "counterrevolutionary propaganda and incitement" and given a heavy sentence. Luo is a brave and dedicated pro-democracy activist, and his friends are now deeply concerned about him.

5. Torture and Ill-Treatment in Prison

During the year or so that I spent as a prisoner in Changsha No.1 and Changsha No.2 Jails, I witnessed and experienced many of the different kinds of torture and punishment that are commonly used nowadays within the Chinese Communist prison system. Reflecting on that experience now, after my escape from China, it feels to me almost like a year spent in an ancient Roman gladiator arena.

Torture and ill-treatment are rampant in Chinese jails, and the Changsha No.1 and No.2 Jails are certainly no exception. The cadres there know that so long as they don't actually beat a prisoner to death, they need have nothing to worry about, for there will be no repercussions. Prisoners transferred to those two jails from other prison facilities in Hunan, moreover, used to tell us that the problem was even worse elsewhere. Indeed, prison officials themselves boasted to us that Changsha No.1 and No.2 were "the most civilized and well-disciplined" jails in the whole province.

Prisoners in Changsha, like those held elsewhere in China, are routinely subjected to two broad categories of torment. The first is torture and ill-treatment inflicted directly by prison guards and other officials themselves. The second is that inflicted, usually at the instigation and direction of prison officials, by specially appointed prisoners known as "cell bosses" (*laotou yuba*). While both categories of abuse have the effect of turning a prisoner's life into a kind of living hell, the latter can often, if anything, be the more fearsome.

I. Abuses by prison officials

Few people in China would willingly work in prisons, and especially since the start of the economic reforms, the rewards and prestige of the job are low. Increasingly, only the most brutish and uneducated types of people end up working in the prison system. They torture and abuse for two main reasons: one is to vent their anger and frustration, while the other - slightly more subtle - purpose is to create an atmosphere of terror and intimidation among the prisoners. Simply put,

74

this makes it easier for the prison staff to "maintain order."

The following are the main types of torture and abuse commonly inflicted upon inmates by prison staff directly.

1) **Electrical assault** (*dian ji*). This is probably the most widespread form of torture used by officials - and also, according to some, the most "civilized." Electric batons, which first appeared on the Chinese law-enforcement scene in the mid-1980s, are now standard issue for police and prison officials, and the latter are liberally empowered to use them. Although the central authorities have drawn up detailed regulations governing the use of such implements, these are almost completely ignored.[33] In practice, prison staff regard their electric batons as being merely convenient tools for punishing and terrorizing the prisoners.

In Changsha No.1 and No.2, the scenario for such an assault is usually as follows. The prisoner is ordered to kneel down and face the wall, with his back straight and both hands raised high and pressed against the wall. The guard or other official then switches on the electric baton and touches it a few times against the metal cell-door or the lock, causing electric sparks to fly forth and giving out a sinister, crackling sound. Once the prisoner has been put into the required state of terror and anxiety, the guard then begins poking the back of his neck with the live electric baton. This makes him scream out in pain and turn his head around involuntarily, begging the guard for mercy. As a result, however,

---

[33] The gist of the regulations was summed up as follows in an article which appeared in *China Legal News (Zhongguo Fazhi Bao)* on February 15, 1985:

"The use of police batons is restricted to situations where an escaped criminal resists when being pursued in accordance with the law; where warnings have proven ineffectual when dealing with incidents of riotous assembly or gang fights among criminals; and where the need for self-defense arises following sudden attack by criminal elements. The use of police batons should be restricted to overpowering one's opponent and should cease as soon as the criminal acts of the felon have been curbed. In using a police baton for such purposes, the infliction of unwarranted mortal wounding should be avoided. We must strictly guard against and firmly rectify the continued use of police batons against criminals who have already been overpowered; the use of police batons against criminals guilty of everyday infringements of prison rules or discipline; indiscriminate poking or hitting; and random punishment."

he then suffers severe shocks to the face and mouth, making him whip his head back around again, at which time the guard will administer further electrical shocks to his ears. The cycle is usually repeated until the victim collapses from the pain or passes out.

Occasionally, prisoners become so inured to electrical assault that they never actually pass out. In such cases, the guard adopts the alternative method of holding the live electric baton steadily against a fixed point on the victim's body, until the flesh starts burning and smoke begins to rise. At that point, another part of the body will be selected and the punishment repeated. In prison jargon, this treatment is often sardonically referred to as "electro-curing therapy" *(dianliao)* - as if the flesh were actually being "cooked".

2) **Down-on-knees whipping** *(gui bian)*. This frequently encountered form of punishment in Changsha jails is, in some ways, sufficiently bizarre as to probably constitute a local invention. Far from reflecting the dignity of the "state," it reminds one superficially of the domestic chastisement of a young child by its irate parents. The procedure is as follows: the guard orders the prisoner to pull down his trousers and kneel down facing the wall, with back held straight and hands pressed against the wall well above head height. He then begins whipping the victim's exposed buttocks with a thin bamboo switch measuring around two feet long and half an inch wide.

In the course of the whipping, the following dialogue will typically occur. Guard: "Have you been well behaved lately?" Prisoner: "Yes, I have, sir!" Guard: "Oh yes? If you'd been well behaved, then why would I be whipping you right now?" (This forces the prisoner to backtrack.) Prisoner: "Perhaps it's true, sir, maybe I have been badly behaved!" Guard: "Badly behaved, eh! Well, in that case, I'll just have to whip you some more!" The performance continues until the prisoner breaks down (usually after about 30 to 50 strokes of the cane), starts to beg for mercy and promises henceforth to obey the guard's every word. The guard then admonishes the prisoner with a few final words, and one of the older inmates will often rise on cue and tell the prisoner to say: "Thank you kindly, Mr. Cadre."

This type of punishment serves the obvious purpose of inflicting intense physical pain on the prisoner, and the continuing discomfort he

76

experiences when sitting or lying down afterwards makes him "reflect on his errors" for some time to come. But it also serves the additional purpose of leaving scars on the buttocks. Such scars make the prisoner fearful of ever having to undergo the same treatment again, since any guard seeing them the next time will promptly identify him as being a "recidivist" and will whip him all the more severely.

3) **Chains and fetters**. In China, prison cadres are authorized by law to chain and fetter prisoners. According to the prison regulations, which all cadres and inmates are supposed to learn by heart, "Those who violate the regulations shall in minor cases be given education and criticism; in more serious cases, they shall be admonished and may be made to wear implements of restraint." The phrase "implements of restraint" (jieju) clearly refers to chains and fetters, while the word "admonished" means, in practice, corporal punishment. Only two types of restraint are officially permitted, namely handcuffs and ankle-fetters. In reality, however, a wide range of different implements are found in current use, some of which, such as chains, are explicitly banned by the government. Time limits are also supposed to apply, except in the case of condemned prisoners awaiting execution. (They are fettered hand and foot from the time of sentencing, and often from the time of initial arrest, right up until the moment of execution.)[34] In practice, such time limits are completely ignored.

---

[34] The article cited above gave the following summary of the rules:

"Handcuffs may be used on arrested escapees and on criminals in custodial transit. In the case of criminals sentenced to death and awaiting execution, both handcuffs and ankle-fetters may be applied simultaneously. Upon approval by the top leadership of the labor-reform unit in question, handcuffs or ankle fetters may also be applied to criminals who (in the course of undergoing prison control and reform) escape, commit arson or other violent acts, create disturbances in prison or seize weapons, or who sabotage the equipment, property or discipline of the labor-reform unit or camp. During the time in which such implements are applied, the criminal should be given intensive education, and once the dangerous behavior has ceased and been eliminated, the implements should be removed. Apart from the case of condemned criminals awaiting execution, a maximum period of 15 days for the use of handcuffs or ankle fetters applies. It is fundamentally incompatible with the civilized governance of China's labor-reform organs to regard handcuffs and ankle fetters as being instruments for the torture or punishment of criminals."

The following are the various kinds of handcuffs, chains and ankle-fetters that I personally saw being used in Changsha No.1 and No.2 Jails.

(i) *"Country cuffs" (tushoukao)*. Although this type of handcuff has long been banned by the authorities, it remains in widespread use. The handcuffs consist of one centrally-placed iron strip hinged at the top to two semi-circular strips. Each part has a small hole at its lower end, and the device is clamped shut by threading these together with a padlock. A range of different handcuff sizes is kept available, so that regardless of how narrow a prisoner's wrists may be, the guards will always be able to find a pair that clamps shut tightly. In fact, the main purpose of this type of handcuff is to cause the prisoner maximum discomfort, by obstructing circulation through the wrists and causing blood to well up painfully in the hands. ("Country cuffs" are also sometimes known as "tiger cuffs," since wearing them can give the sensation of being gnawed at by a wild animal.)

The handcuffs can be applied in three different ways: a) with the hands pointing to the front; b) with the hands pointing to either side, in opposite directions; and c) with the hands behind the back and pointing in opposite directions. Of the two frontward styles, the second is the worst, since it makes eating and other necessary tasks extremely difficult. Rearward handcuffing is the worst of all, since not only do all manual operations become virtually impossible, but also the blood flow is severely restricted and the pain is such that one cannot sleep at all.

(ii) *"Finger cuffs" (shouzhikao)*. As the name suggests, this type of handcuff is applied only to the fingers. Such cuffs are only ever used "internally" within the prison system and are never seen by members of the public. They consist of two pieces of rough metal wire crudely welded together, resembling a pair of finger rings set side by side, and are used exclusively for the purpose of punishing prisoners. To fix them in place, the prisoner's thumbs are inserted into the two holes and the open ends are then pinched shut using a pair of pliers. One word alone sums up these cuffs: tight. After a day or less of wearing them, the prisoner begins to experience intense pain, as the thumbs become ever more bloated and swollen.

(iii) *"Ankle fetters" (jiaolianliao)*. These are standard leg irons, used

78

to chain the prisoner's feet together in various different ways, and are available in a range of different weights and sizes. The lightest type weighs around eight kilograms, while the heaviest can extend to over 30 kilograms. All prisons and detention centers in China are obliged by law to be equipped with such fetters. In the standard variety, the chain connecting the two ankle-rings can be easily varied in length, depending upon how close the prisoner's feet are to be shackled together. Although this basic type of leg fetter can often be quite heavy, the prisoner can usually still move around without too much difficulty. It is most commonly applied to those prisoners condemned to death and awaiting execution. However, it may also be used as a form of punishment in the case of common criminals who have infringed some regulation or other.

(iv) *"Rod fetters" (zhiliao)*. This type of fetter differs from the standard variety in that, in place of a connecting chain allowing a certain degree of mobility, the ankle-rings are joined by a fixed iron bar of approximately one and a half feet in length. Again, it is most often used as a direct form of punishment. Prisoners shackled in this way experience extreme difficulty and discomfort in moving around, since the feet are always kept at a fixed distance apart. Sleeping is also difficult, for the slightest leg movements while lying down at night result in pain to the ankles and wake the prisoner up.

(v) *"Multiple fetters" (lianhuanliao)*. This device, consisting of several sets of ankle fetters chained together in a row, is used as a means of shackling several prisoners together by the legs simultaneously, usually as a form of collective punishment. The largest number of prisoners I ever saw being shackled together in this way in Changsha No.1 Jail was eight. An extremely inhumane form of punishment, it allows almost no individual movement by those being shackled. When one prisoner wants to go to the toilet, for example, all the others have to accompany him and stand next to him while he performs.

(vi) *"Shackle board" (menbanliao)*. This is the cruellest and most barbaric form of shackling that I saw used during my own term of imprisonment, and also among the worst that I have heard about from elsewhere. The device consists of a large wooden door laid flat and supported by four low legs, and equipped with a set of handcuffs secured to each corner. A hole situated toward the lower end allows the attached victim to perform (after a fashion) normal bodily functions.

79

Among those personally known to me who were subjected to such shackling are several pro-democracy prisoners arrested after June 1989 and also a number of common criminals with whom I subsequently shared cells. In addition, 26 condemned criminals who were executed in Changsha on June 9, 1990 were all fixed to "shackle boards" throughout the two days prior to their execution. The sufferings of those made to undergo this particular form of punishment are almost indescribable.

(vii) *"Full shackle set" (lianliaokao)*. This consists of standard handcuffs and standard ankle fetters, but with the two being joined together by either a steel chain or a fixed steel bar. The device comes in various shapes and sizes. The most common, the type with the connecting chain, is that applied to prisoners awaiting execution. Depending on the weight of the chains used, movement can be more or less difficult. Those prisoners able to move usually attach a strip of cloth to the chains that lie looped on the floor. This allows them to lift the chains up by their hands when moving around, which makes walking slightly easier.

Two other types of the "full shackle set," those having a steel bar placed between the handcuffs and ankle-fetters, are used solely and blatantly by prison officials as instruments of punishment and inflict severe physical and mental damage upon those subjected to them. They are known as the "standing up" and "sitting down" varieties. In the former, a steel bar of more than one meter in height is set vertically into the ground, with fetters at the base and cuffs attached to the top end. Prisoners attached to this device are physically unable to sit down and must remain standing at all times. Sleep is impossible because of the pain caused in the wrists and ankles if one slumps downwards. Most prisoners are unable to last more than two days on this device.

In the "sitting down" variant, the fixed vertical pole is only a few inches high, forcing the prisoner to remain in a crouched or seated position all the time. Some prisoners are shackled in this way for as long as a month. Typically, the legs and buttocks become all swollen with blood after a few days, and sores quickly appear. Sometimes, the flesh begins to fester and decay.

4) **"Martial arts practice"** *(liao quan jiao)*. During my time in Changsha No.1 and No.2 Detention Centers, there were several young prison guards whose greatest enjoyment in life seemed to come from

beating up the prisoners. They are Cadre Luo, Cadre Lu, Cadre Chen, Cadre Yao and Cadre Yang, and also another man named Yang who is one of the so-called "No.2 Cadres." (This is prisoners' jargon for those hired from outside to work as temporary prison guards. Many of these guards are local villagers who in fact have no legal authority to engage in such work.) All these cadres have been awarded the epithet "Killer" *(Sha)* by the prison inmates.

In the case of "Killer Luo" *(Luo Sha* - real name: Luo Jian), for example, physically tormenting prisoners had become second nature, and he used to beat people up on the slightest of pretexts. Quite often, he would summon a prisoner out of his cell and then suddenly and without warning attack him savagely. It usually went like this: Luo would call out the name of a certain prisoner and order him to step out of his cell into the corridor, kneel down and face the wall. Once the victim was in place, he would casually spin around and land a flying drop-kick to the man's back. After that, he would walk around for a while, and then repeat the same thing again, over and over. The performance would come to an end only when the prisoner had finally been battered senseless to the ground.

All the while, Killer Luo would be sure to maintain an air of complete coolness and nonchalance. His specialty, however, was that he never looked at his victim directly. Also, unlike the other guards, he never used his fists, only his feet. This was apparently because he feared dirtying his hands.

The "No.2 Cadre Yang," by contrast, appeared somewhat fairer and more conscientious, for at least he always used to "pick a fight" with the prisoners before beating them up. (Despite this courtesy, the prisoners would never, of course, dare to fight back.) Yang's belligerence was attributed by the prisoners to the fact of his lowly status as a mere "No.2" cadre.

5) **"Saochai descending from the mountain top."** The term *saochai*, meaning "those who sweep up the firewood," is prison slang for officers of the People's Armed Police (PAP), who are employed by the prison authorities to patrol the prison's safety perimeter and prevent any escapes. The phrase "descending from the mountain-top" refers to the periodic occasions on which PAP officers are ordered down from their watch-towers to conduct so-called "lightning raids" on the prisoners' cells.

81

These raids are ostensibly carried out for the purpose of inspecting the prisoners' cells and checking that no forbidden goods or objects are being concealed there. (According to regulations, however, checking the cells is the regular guards' responsibility. The PAP's sole duties are to prevent escapes and quell any prison riots or disturbances.) In Changsha No.1 Jail, these "saochai raids" took place on an average of once a month.

The real purpose of the raids was simply to allow the PAP into the cells for a so-called "contact session" with the prisoners - that is, an opportunity to beat up and terrorize them, in a display of crude military force. At each of these sessions, the PAP would suddenly arrive in the cell blocks brandishing special, military-issue leather belts in their hands. As soon as they threw open a cell door, they would immediately start lashing out at random at the terrified prisoners within, whipping and beating them with the belts. The ostensible reason for this violence was that they had to "drive back" anyone who might be hurriedly trying to conceal forbidden items. Some PAP officers would specifically pick out certain prisoners and start laying into them exclusively, shouting out things like, "Let's see if you dare challenge us now!" Since the PAP are mostly just powerfully-built and uneducated thugs, these "*saochai* raids" invariably used to leave the prisoners in a state of complete physical and psychological terror.

6) **Solitary confinement** *(jin bi)*. Previously, Changsha No.1 and No.2 Jails had no system of solitary confinement, although many other detention facilities in Hunan Province certainly did, and still do. In 1990, however, Changsha No.1 began building a solitary-confinement punishment block, and it was fully constructed by the time I left the prison. As a "cell delegate," I was once taken by cadres on a conducted tour of this special unit. The solitary cells resembled square metal boxes, measuring about 1.5 meters in height, width and depth, and without any window whatever. The door leading into the cell was less than one meter high. As the cadres explained to us, once inside, a prisoner could neither lie down properly nor stand up straight. I privately thanked heaven that I had never been consigned to one of these "black boxes," I'm not sure I could have withstood the experience. (The solitary confinement cells at Longxi Prison, in which I was placed for seven days in January 1991, were almost comfortable by comparison with those at Changsha No.1.)

II. Abuses by "Cell Bosses"

In addition to all these different types of punishment and abuse inflicted by the prison staff directly, Changsha No.1 and No.2 Jails, like all other prisons and labor camps in China, operate a complex and deeply-entrenched system of internal terror and control known as the "cell boss" system. This system is the scourge of prisoners' daily life, for it undermines all guarantees for even their most basic physical safety and security. Although strictly banned by the government, the cell boss system flourishes throughout the Hunan prison system. Moreover, the prisoner-thugs who act as the cell bosses are specifically appointed to play that role by prison officials themselves. These prisoners act as the latter's direct agents within the cells, and as a reward for this service they receive specially favorable treatment and conditions.

Prisoners are usually even more afraid of these cell bosses - the system's unofficial hit-men - than they are of the actual prison staff. Cell bosses have numerous specific ways and means of tormenting other prisoners and of making their lives intolerable. The twenty main varieties of such unofficial persecution and torture are described below, together with an outline of their officially-intended functions within the Chinese prison sub-culture.

(i) *"Paying respects to the cell god" (bai lao men)*. This is a technique commonly used to punish and intimidate new arrivals to the prison cells. Its purpose is to make the newly arrived prisoners submit symbolically to the cell boss's authority. The procedure is as follows. First, the new prisoner is ordered to kneel down in front the "cassia blossom vase" *(guihua tong*: prison jargon for the toilet bucket,) holding several rice-straws.

Second, just as if he were offering incense at a Buddhist altar, he has to offer forth the rice-straws in both hands and perform the so-called "three prostrations" before the "cassia blossom vase". These are: 1) a prostration to his mother *(yi bai qinniang)*; 2) a prostration to the prison cadres *(er bai ganbu)*; and 3) a prostration to the cell boss *(san bai laotou)*.

Third, the new prisoner has to insert one of the straws, the kind used to make the bedding quilts used in the cells, into the "cassia blossom vase" and blow forcefully through it, making bubbles froth up from the contents of the bucket and sending forth a foul smell. The cell boss will then ask the prisoner: "Is the cassia blossom fragrant?" The prisoner must immediately reply, "Yes, it smells lovely."

Finally, the prisoner has to suck some of the contents of the toilet bucket up through the straw. The cell boss again asks, "Does the cassia blossom taste sweet?", and the prisoner must reply "Yes, delicious." With this, the ceremony of "paying respects to the cell god" is formally concluded. If, however, the new arrival has failed in any way to perform as required, then new and still worse humiliations await him.

(ii) *"Electric shock treatment" (chu dian)*. Here, the cell inmate is ordered by the cell boss to go into the "cassia blossom chamber," that is, the toilet cubicle, located between the cell proper and the outside exercise yard, and to stretch his hand around the dividing wall into the cell and grope around for the "electric light switch." (Actually, there are no light switches or electric sockets in any of the cells.) The cell boss then gets one of the other prisoners, or sometimes he will do it himself, to crack some hard object like a wooden stool or the sole of a shoe down against the prisoner's fingers without warning. The prisoner will scream out in pain, just as if he'd received a sudden electric shock.

(iii) *"The sandwich filling" (jiaxin mianbao)*. This entails the prisoner being simultaneously struck on the back and chest. First, the victim is ordered to stand in front of the cell boss (or someone designated by him), facing toward the side. The cell boss then repeatedly strikes hard against the same spot on the prisoner's back and chest, until he develops an unbearable sensation of being unable to draw breath. This punishment can generate an intense feeling of fear and claustrophobia in the victim.

(iv) *"Jetplane ride" (zuo feiji)*.[35] The cell boss orders the prisoner to stand on the edge of the raised sleeping platform, of which there is one to each cell, facing across the side corridor toward the opposite wall. He

---

[35] This term, *zuo feiji*, is more commonly used in China to refer to another kind of punishment (often used by Red Guards during the Cultural Revolution) in which the victim's arms are pushed straight up behind the back, forcing him to bend down low at the waist. The backward-stretched arms make a "V" shape, rather like the outline of a jet plane.

then has to lean forward and support himself in a rigid, slanted posture against the wall, with a cup wedged firmly between his head and the wall. The cell boss then knocks the cup away with a stick or some other object, causing the victim to fall forward and strike his head against the wall, with the full force of his body-weight behind the impact. Repeated several times, this creates a sense of nausea and vertigo (thought to be reminiscent of being in an airplane at take-off), not to mention causing bruises to the head.

(v) "*Eating the golden carp*" *(chi jiyu)*. This is the easiest and most convenient method of inflicting punishment within the cells, and simply involves the cell boss repeatedly hitting the lower part of a prisoner's face with the sole of his shoe. In the process, small pieces of filth from the shoe usually drop into the victim's mouth. Also, the sole of the shoe somewhat resembles the shape of a golden carp - hence the name.

(vi) "*Heroic martyrdom*" *(yingyong jiuyi)*. This type of punishment, while not necessarily causing any serious physical damage to the victim, nonetheless often generates in him a considerable degree of psychological stress and anxiety. The name evokes the scenario of a condemned prisoner being dragged to the execution ground and shot. The process is this. First, the cell boss orders two of the other inmates to "apply the leg fetters" (actually, just a piece of cloth tied around the victim's feet.) The cell boss, pretending to be a judge, then declares that the death sentence has been imposed and orders that the prisoner be "dragged out and executed." The two stooges promptly drag him across the floor by his hands and make him stand near the cell wall.

At the sound of "gunfire" (in fact, just a "ping" sound emitted by the cell boss), the prisoner has immediately to fall directly backwards, landing flat on the cell floor. Prisoners who have experienced this punishment several times learn quite quickly how to fall backward without hurting themselves too much. But first-timers, especially if they are overly anxious, often crack the back of their heads hard against the stone floor, sometimes knocking themselves out.

(vii) "*Hammer clanging*" *(qiao xiang zhui)*. This is one of the more painful punishments commonly used within the cells, although it seldom leaves any permanent damage. It consists of the cell boss striking repeatedly at the victim's ankles with a wooden stick or some other hard

85

object. The name of the practice is derived from the percussive noise it creates, which is thought reminiscent of a particular style of folk-music performance known as the "Hebei Hammer" *(Hebei Zhuizi).*

(viii) *"Bouncy bouncy" (tan bengbeng).* This kind of punishment is meted out as a warning. The cell boss tucks his forefinger and middle-finger in firmly under the thumb, and then begins flicking the victim hard on a spot right in the center of his forehead, using each finger in turn. This is repeated over and over again, until eventually a large dark bruise appears over the spot.

(ix) *"Lotus-wrapped egg roll" (gun hebaodan).* A type of punishment clearly intended purely for the amusement of the cell boss, this one can nonetheless induce a protracted sense of nausea in the victim. It works like this. The cell boss selects a prisoner and tells him to kneel down, grasp his feet in both hands, and lean forward as far as possible, tucking his head in tightly so that his body assumes a ball-like shape. Another inmate is then ordered to push the victim forward and begin rolling him around all over the cell floor, until finally he becomes so dizzy that his body uncoils involuntarily and he comes to a halt. Someone else then forces the victim to his feet and orders him to stand still - something which he finds impossible to do, since he is swaying around uncontrollably. Eventually he collapses on the ground, and the whole process is then repeated all over again. If continued for long enough, the victim will be left feeling nauseous, giddy and extremely uncomfortable for the next several days.

(x) *"Staying upright thrice" (san bu dao).* This is a relatively straightforward type of abuse. The cell boss simply punches a prisoner on the chest as hard as he can three times in a row, and if the prisoner remains standing up, without having shifted his feet, then he passes the test. If he does not, on the other hand, the punishment will continue for as often as the cell boss feels inclined. (Many prison guards, especially younger ones, also like to perform this trick.)

(xi) *"Riding a donkey back to front" (dao qi maolü).* This is another of the many ways used by cell bosses to humiliate and demean their fellow inmates. The chosen prisoner is made to kneel down on all fours, on either the cell floor or the sleeping platform, and the cell boss then sits astride him facing to the rear and orders him to crawl around. As the prisoner does so, the cell boss beats him continuously on the buttocks with either his hand, a pair of chopsticks or some other hard implement.

(xii) "*Clubbing the dreamer*" *(pu meng gun)*. Cell bosses use this method to deal with any prisoners who will not readily submit to their authority or who fail to be subdued by a simple beating. The usual procedure is that late at night, when the defiant prisoner is soundly asleep, several other inmates will be directed by the cell to assault him. Some of them first wrap a cotton quilt tightly around his head and upper body, and the others then begin kicking him viciously, stamping on his body and battering him about the head. The victim, of course, is completely unable to fight back, and because of the quilt, his shouts and screams are completely inaudible outside the cell. All but the toughest of prisoners usually cannot withstand this treatment, and most will quickly begin begging the cell boss for mercy. The latter will only give the word for the beatings to stop once he is fully satisfied of the prisoner's submission.

(xiii) "*Cassia blossom perch*" *(guihua deng)*. This form of punishment is rife in virtually all the detention cells in China equipped with toilet buckets ("cassia blossom vases.") It entails the following. Usually around ten o'clock at night, after the guards have finished inspecting the cells and counting all the prisoners, the cell boss orders the prisoner slated for punishment to go to the toilet cubicle and squat on top of the "cassia blossom vase" for the entire night. (The cell boss has only to utter the words "Go perch!" and the victim will know what is in store for him.) The toilet buckets used in the cells are around two feet high and more than one foot in diameter around the top; the rim is a mere quarter of an inch wide. If the person perched on it loses concentration or falls asleep for even a moment, the "cassia blossom vase" will topple over and the muck will spill all over both the floor and himself. A terrible smell spreads throughout the cell, and the victim invariably gets punished for this with a severe beating.

(xiv) "*Playing the electric piano*" *(tan dianzi qin)*. This is a kind of game played by cell bosses as a way of passing the time. Although innocuous as compared to the other measures described here, it nonetheless serves to remind the prisoners of their depersonalized and subservient status within the cell. At the given order, at least eight inmates line up in a row and call out their numbers - "One, two, three..."

87

- in sequence. These numbers correspond to the standard notes of the musical scale: Do, Re, Me, etc., and the prisoners are ordered to remember their allotted notes. Another inmate, usually someone with a bit of musical knowledge - then stands in front of them brandishing a pair of chopsticks and proceeds to strike them smartly on the head in accordance with the notes of a particular tune. Whenever a member of the lineup feels the chopsticks landing, he must immediately sing out his own note. In this way, the tune takes shape and the cell boss gets his entertainment. The prisoners, of course, are reduced to mere piano keys - and any who miss their cue get punished for it later.

(xv) *"Learning to count" (xue shushu)*. This is a special type of punishment often favored by cell bosses as a means of sowing discord and antagonism among the other prisoners, thereby boosting their own dominant position. If used often enough, it leaves the prisoners incapable of uniting together in any form of resistance. It goes like this. Two inmates who are known to be close to each other are ordered to take turns counting backwards - "100, 99, 98..." etc., all the way to "3, 2, 1." If the person doing the counting happens to make a mistake, then the other one has to slap him across the ear, and then start counting backwards himself. If he in turn slips up, then he gets a slap on the ear from the same person he hit earlier. And so on, counting and hitting, back and forth. At the start of the process, neither person is usually willing to slap the other one very hard. But by the time the game has gone a few rounds, ill-feeling and anger inevitably begin to build up, and the slaps get harder and heavier. By the end of it, the original friendship can be in tatters.

(xvi) *"Embracing the cassia blossom vase" (bao guihua tong)*. This is yet another means by which the toilet bucket - as in the case of the "cassia blossom perch" - gets pressed into service as an instrument of punishment. At night, after the guards have inspected the cells and counted the inmates, the person to be punished is told to go and wrap his arms around the "cassia blossom vase" and remain there motionless the whole night. If any of the other prisoners need to use the toilet during the night, the victim must stay in position and endure it all without complaint. (In the Changsha jails, hardly a night went by without someone receiving this punishment.)

(xvii) *"Blind man groping an elephant" (xiazi mo xiang)*. The aim of

88

this type of punishment is, as in the case of "learning to count," to try to break down any sense of friendship and solidarity among the prisoners. Unlike "learning to count," however, numerous prisoners are involved, rather than just two. The cell boss selects at least four prisoners, one of whom has to cover his eyes with a piece of cloth and play the "blind man." This involves groping at the other prisoners in turn and trying to guess their identities. If he guesses wrongly, the "blind man" will be given a slap around the ears by the person being groped, and he must then continue the routine with all the other prisoners until he manages to guess someone's name correctly. The latter person will then become the "blind man," and the game begins anew.

(xviii) *Eating red-cooked meat" (chi hongshao rou).* This is a form of beating in which the cell boss punches the prisoner repeatedly on the lower jaw. The name arises because the puncher, his fist resembling a slab of "red-cooked meat," slams the victim's upper and lower teeth together with each blow, as if he were "eating."

(xix) *"Playing dead" (ban siren).* A game used for punishment purposes. Two prisoners are placed back-to-back and ordered to bend forward low at the waist, their backs forming a kind of horizontal platform. A third prisoner is then lowered on to this platform and made to stiffen his whole body - just like a corpse lying in a mortuary. A large sheet is then placed over his entire body, covering the head and leaving only the feet exposed. If this "game" is continued for long enough, all three prisoners will eventually begin to feel extremely uncomfortable.

(xx) *"Learning the regulations" (xue jiangui).* Originally, this was a regular type of activity whereby cadres made the cell bosses responsible for teaching the other inmates the prison regulations. Gradually, however, it evolved into a type of punishment. It goes as follows. Several prisoners are ordered to read aloud in turn from a copy of the prison regulations, substituting the word "box" *(kuangkuang)* for any characters they do not understand. (Each character of the regulations is printed in a separate box on the page.) While each prisoner is reading, another one counts up the number of times he says "box." At the end, the prisoner is forced to give himself one hard slap on the face for every character he has failed to recognize. (Many common criminals are either illiterate or semi-literate, so the number is usually quite high.) After a brief lesson in how to read the characters in question, the prisoner is then made to recite the regulations all over again - followed by a further round of self-inflicted punishment for any mistakes. The process will be repeated over and over again until either the cell boss gets bored or the prisoner gets the text right.

The above catalogue of tortures and punishments includes only those most commonly encountered by prisoners in Hunan's Changsha No.1 and No.2 Jails. Numerous other kinds of torture and ill-treatment are widely employed by cadres and cell bosses both there and in the countless other prisons, labor camps and re-education centers throughout China.

To conclude, one other cruel kind of torture that is sometimes used by cadres in the Changsha No.1 Jail, namely "electric shackle treatment" *(dianliaokao)*, should also be mentioned. The existence of this type of torture, in which electric shocks are transmitted to the prisoner's body through shackles applied to the wrists and ankles, is a well-kept secret within the prison system. It is resorted to by prison officials, after all other punishments have failed to produce results, as a means of dealing with those prisoners who either create disturbances or who pretend to be crazy. It is sometimes also used against people who are in fact mentally ill. Ostensibly, this to done to "establish their true condition" (this would be culpable enough, were it true), but actually it is just a form of punishment treatment designed to stop such people from being "troublesome."

The torture proceeds as follows. The prisoner is shackled, hand and foot, to a specially designed board (one similar in shape to the "shackle board" described above), and a high-voltage alternating current is then administered via the shackles. Like the electric baton, the shock is of a low enough current that death cannot ensue, but the pain is unbearable, and it makes the prisoner want to die. The electric shocks are continued until the prisoner begs for mercy and guarantees that he will henceforth be entirely submissive.

In short, the range of abusive practices found in Chinese prisons and jails is diverse, complex and frightening. These practices should be condemned by all forces for justice and humanity throughout the world.

6. The Hunan Gulag

The territory of Hunan Province is home to one of the largest systems of prisons, labor-reform camps, labor re-education centers, jails, shelter-for-investigation centers and detention centers in the whole of China. *Appendix X*, below, lists details of 142 of the various custodial facilities that make up this vast, gray archipelago of state retribution. Forty-eight of them are prison, labor-reform camps or labor re-education centers where prisoners who have been sentenced either judicially by the courts or administratively by the police are sent to serve out their terms of imprisonment. These include, at a known minimum, seven large prisons, one of which is for women, and one smaller prison; 22 labor-reform camps including two for women; 16 labor re-education centers; and two juvenile detention centers. The remaining 94 units on the list are all either local jails, where prisoners charged and awaiting trial are kept, or else administrative holding and investigation centers of various sorts.

Prisons *(jianyu)* are high security units, and are used to incarcerate two types of sentenced criminals: those convicted of serious "common criminal" offenses who are serving sentences of around 10 years or more, and all those convicted of political offenses or so-called "counter-revolutionaries." Labor-reform camps *(laogai zhidui* or *laogai nongchang)* are often but not always located in the countryside, and generally hold criminals who have been sentenced to terms of less than 10 years. Juvenile offender centers *(shaonian guanjiaosuo)* are designed to hold all young criminals under the age of 18, except for those convicted on political charges. Labor re-education centers are for those sentenced directly by the police, without benefit of any trial.

Jails *(kanshousuo)*, shelter-for-investigation centers *(shourong shenchasuo)* and detention centers *(juliusuo)* are used to hold all those who have yet to be sentenced. In principle, jails are meant only for prisoners who have already been formally charged and are awaiting trial, while detention centers are for all those who have not yet been charged or who are destined for various forms of administrative detention. Shelter-for-investigation centers, which have no proper legal status, are meant to hold only those "who roam around from place to place committing crimes and whose identity is unclear." (In fact, they are used as a convenient

91

dumping ground for all those whom the authorities choose to arrest without first having obtained sufficient evidence of guilt.) In many parts of Hunan, however, these demarcatory guidelines do not apply, since many localities have only jails but no detention centers or shelter-for-investigation centers.

Prisons

The seven main prisons in Hunan are Yuanjiang Prison (Provincial No.1), Hengyang Prison (Provincial No.2), Lingling Prison (Provincial No.3), Huaihua Prison (Provincial No.4), Chenzhou Prison (Provincial No.5), Longxi Prison (Provincial No.6) and Changsha Prison. The two largest are Yuanjiang and Hengyang prisons, which hold more than 6,000 and 7,000 prisoners respectively. They are also the oldest, having already been in use at the time of the Guomindang regime. The populations of the other five prisons range from around 2,000 to 5,000.

Each prison is assigned a role in economic production, and publicly all are called factories. Provincial Nos. 1, 2 and 3 prisons are responsible for turning out automobile parts and accessories, for example, and the second is presented to the outside world only as the "Hunan Heavy Motor Vehicle Plant." Provincial Nos. 4, 5 and 6 prisons are mainly engaged in mining and quarrying activities. Longxi Prison, the place where I was sent after my trial and which thanks to its remote and barren location is known locally as "Siberia," is a marble quarry, producing partly for export. Changsha Prison is used mainly to hold female prisoners from all parts of the province, but it also accommodates a small number of adult male prisoners. It comprises several different factories, involved variously in garment making, handicraft production, engineering, machine-building and printing.

Conditions of detention in the prisons are better than those in the other types of facility, and the forced manual labor is usually less strenuous. Because of the high security regime in prisons, however, freedom of movement is even more restricted there than in the other units. Cells range from between 10 and 40 square meters in size, and the average number of inmates in a cell is usually around 20. A uniform daily schedule is operated in the prisons, stipulating the precise times at which inmates have to rise, wash, eat, work, join in political study sessions and go to bed. Any breach of the rules results in punishment.

As regards diet, prisoners generally have meat in their meals two to three times a week, although this varies between different prisons and brigades. The basic fare is just rice and plain vegetables, with scarcely a drop of edible oil to be found. The rice allowance is more or less sufficient, however, to stave off hunger pangs, and while new prisoners often feel hungry, they generally adjust to the diet after a few weeks inside.

Prisoners are each paid a government allowance of 2.30 *yuan* (less than US$0.50) per month, which has to be spent on toothpaste, toothbrush, face towel and soap. Throughout the year, only cold water is available for showers. Several hundred inmates have just one toilet room to share, so the facilities are always stinking and unsanitary.

Upon first arriving at the prison, newly convicted prisoners are put into "prison induction teams" *(rujiandui)* for a period of three months, so that they can be taught the prison regulations and subjected to preliminary disciplining. There is extensive "political study," the main purpose of which is impress upon new arrivals the need to obey the regulations without question. At the end of this time, prisoners are assigned to one of the various production teams to commence forced manual labor.

According to prison regulation, the daily working hours for a prisoner are restricted to a maximum of eight. But in practice, prisoners usually have to work at least ten hours, and some even have to work as much as 16 hours a day. This depends mainly on the type of labor to which one has been assigned and the daily quotas that have been fixed for the job. In general, those working in prison factories, performing such tasks as machinery assembly, find the labor considerably less strenuous than do those of their counterparts assigned to work in mining or quarrying.

In recent years, along with the improvements in living standards in society at large, some prisons have begun to provide basic amenities and even a few recreational facilities, for example a television room and a basketball court. Prisoners are usually only permitted to watch television once a week, but Sunday in the prisons is a rest day, and inmates are allowed to play poker or chess then. (To play these games at any other time is strictly forbidden.) Nowadays, there is generally a basketball court for each brigade, but it is mainly used for purposes of letting inmates take their daily exercise stroll at specified times. At all other times during the Sunday rest day, inmates have to remain in their cells. They are not permitted to make contact with, still less to visit, inmates in the other brigades, teams or cells.

Each prison has its own set of rules, some of which apply nationally, while others are drawn up by the local prison authorities themselves. Any violation of the rules results in immediate punishment, ranging from reprimands, use of shackles, short-term solitary confinement and placement in a "strict regime" unit within the prison, all the way through to long-term solitary confinement within the strict regime unit. The latter is used to punish prisoners who seriously violate prison rules, and specific measures include raising the prisoner's daily forced-labor production quota; making him remained seated and motionless, staring at the wall for many hours each day, so that he may "repent his sins"; placing him in prolonged solitary confinement; and a vague category referred to only as "punishment regime." This latter can range from such things as reduction of daily food rations and greatly raising the daily work quota, all the way up to gross physical punishment and torture. Prison cadres claim privately that they would find it impossible to operate and keep order within the prisons unless they had such severe punitive measures as this at their disposal.

Labor-Reform Camps

By comparison with the general regimen of the labor-reform camps, however, that found in the prisons appears relatively humane. Apart from such atypical labor-reform camps as the Changsha Match Factory (Provincial No.9 Labor-Reform Detachment), where administration is relatively orderly and civilized, life in the Hunan labor-reform camps and farms is often little more than a battle for survival.

As mentioned above, the 22 known labor-reform camps in Hunan (each of which is identified numerically) are used to hold prisoners sentenced to terms of less than 10 years. They do not generally take in either political prisoners or juvenile offenders. Most of the camps operate as agricultural farms, while a small number engage in manufacturing or mining. Some of the camps are enormous. Two of the largest, namely Jianxin Farm, located near Yueyang City, and Cendan Farm in Xiangyin

94

County, each have more than 20,000 inmates. In the Provincial New Life Coal Mine near Leiyang City, and in the Changsha Cement Factory near Pingtang, the camp populations range from 5,000 to 10,000. Most of the other labor-reform camps hold somewhere between 1,000 and 5,000 inmates.

The camps fall into two broad categories: agricultural farms, and factories or mines. The living conditions in the farms are the most harsh, whereas labor-reform camps organized as factories or mines are rather similar to the prisons. Just as in the prisons, for example, the latter operate production-related incentive schemes which allow prisoners to have their term of sentence progressively reduced. The adjustments are made on the basis of how many credit points a prisoner can obtain. Those who observe strict discipline and manage to finish their assigned production quotas on time are periodically awarded one credit point, equivalent to one four-and-a-half days' reduction of sentence. The system also works in reverse, however, and failure to meet the quota results in loss of the credit point and a corresponding increase in sentence.

Most of the labor-reform camps in Hunan, apart from a few which were already in existence in the 1950s, were set up during the early 1970s. These include Jianxin Farm, Bainihu Farm and the Pingtang Cement Factory. These camps were in a deplorable state in their early stages, but things have improved somewhat in recent years. At present, the government's subsistence allowance for a labor-reform camp prisoner stands at 29.50 *yuan*, just a little lower than that for a prison inmate. (They receive food and items of daily necessity to the value of just over 30 *yuan* per month.) Prisoners have to provide for any of their own daily sundry needs over and above this bare minimum, however, and most depend on their families for even the barest of luxuries.

Labor-reform camps are located in the countryside, where life is hard and the work is strenuous and unremitting. Take Jianxin Farm, for example, which has over 20,000 prisoners. The farm is divided into brigades *(dadui)*, which are in turn subdivided into squadrons *(zhongdui)* and then teams *(fendui)*. There are over 1,000 prisoners in a brigade, several hundred in a squadron, and several dozen in a team. At first sight, the farm looks just like a small town, complete with living quarters for over 100 cadres and officials, and there are also shops, a cinema, a market and a hospital. The farm has all the attributes and

95

facilities of a normal settlement - except that they are for the exclusive use of the labor camp staff alone.

The squadron forms the basic nucleus of camp life for the inmates. (The squadron in the farm is similar to the brigade in the prison.) All the members of a given squadron live together in an area surrounded by walls on all sides, and members of one squadron are not allowed to communicate with those of any other squadron. On the surface, life is much the same as in the prisons. The difference, however, lies in the far lower living standard and in the much more strenuous nature of the forced manual labor required on the farms. Prisoners in the farms have to work all the year round, moreover; and are only entitled to two or three days' rest altogether, during the Chinese New Year Festival. They have no Sundays off, and so the only other time they get a rest is when it rains heavily.

At busy times such as seed planting or harvesting, the work is unrelenting. The prisoners have to get up before dawn and begin work in the fields when it is still dark. They have their lunch in the fields as they work. (Special duty prisoners prepare lunch for the whole team in advance and bring it to the fields when they leave for work in the morning.) All prisoners have to work until nightfall before being allowed to return to their cells. Currently, prisoners engaged in farm work are each assigned a production quota, and failure to meet it normally results in punishment, such as a beating or being locked up in shackles. The guards, their truncheons in hands, stand behind the prisoners the whole time as they work in the fields, and beat any of them whom they consider to be slacking. The sight of one person treating another like an outright slave in this way is deeply offensive. When they return to the camp from the fields in the evenings, the prisoners all just fling themselves on to the sleeping platform immediately, fully clothed, and are asleep within minutes. None of them would even think of taking a shower before sleeping, and the stench of unwashed bodies all around them is the least of their worries.

The forced labor sites are usually located in areas near to the city suburbs. The cadres in charge mark out on the spot the boundary of the day's security zone, and any prisoner stepping outside the zone runs the risk of being shot. Few people, therefore, ever try to escape while working in the fields. However, there are times when prisoners do defy orders. One such moment is when a prisoner's hunger for food, stimulated by the sight of fresh vegetables on display right there in the fields, overcomes his fear of being discovered in the act of pulling them up, still covered in mud, and eating them. The prisoner will get a beating, but the taste of the fresh vegetable will often be considered worth it nonetheless.

Violence is rife in the camps, with both frequent fights breaking out among the prisoners themselves and extensive resort to force on the part of the cadres and guards. In Jianxin Farm, for example, prisoners who fail to complete their production quotas find themselves either being summoned after work to the so-called "education room" and used as human targets for martial arts practice by the guards, or else simply being visited in their cells and beaten up right there. As in the prisons, certain of the guards are known only by nicknames acknowledging their prowess in this field, for example "Killer Lei", "Desperado Tan" and "Three-Blows Wang" (a particularly violent individual who was known to have knocked a prisoner unconscious with only three blows.)

Self-maiming

Some prisoners in the Hunan labor camps try deliberately to maim and injure themselves, hoping that their self-inflicted disabilities will gain them a temporary respite from the miseries of camp life, the rigors of forced labor and the constant threat of physical violence. They even sometimes hope, although vainly, that becoming disabled will increase their chances of securing an early release from prison.

Cases of self-maiming occur quite frequently in the camps. The main aims of prisoners who injure themselves are, first, to secure a respite from the daily grind of forced labor, and second, to be released on bail to seek medical treatment (*qubao houshen*: a measure specified in China's criminal procedure law.) In addition, some prisoners use the opportunity of being sent to a hospital outside in order to escape and go on the run. There are several types of such self-imposed injury. One type involves injecting kerosene (often mixed in with rotten food) into the blood stream, via such parts of the body as the abdomen, legs or even the head. After a while, the affected part will begin to swell and fester, and the authorities usually have little choice but to allow the prisoner out on temporary bail for treatment.

97

Another method used by prisoners is to deliberately break their own limbs. This is done by placing the arm or leg between two heavy pieces of slate and then striking down hard on the slate with either a pick or a sledgehammer. When the slates splits into two, the prisoner's limb will often fracture as well, so rendering him incapable of performing manual labor. Other commonly used methods include swallowing harmful herbs or medicines which induce the symptoms of such serious contagious diseases as nephritis and hepatitis; swallowing small pieces of razor blade; slashing open the abdomen; and severing the leg tendon. Again, the prison authorities often have little choice in such cases but to grant the prisoner temporary bail. (Labor-reform units, especially those operating as farms, have only rudimentary on-site medical facilities and so cannot treat such conditions by themselves.)

Some prisoners did actually succeed in getting out of prison this way, although rarely for very long. The most gruesome instance of self-maiming that I came across in prison was that of a prisoner who used a twin-hook device, which he had specially designed for the purpose, to gouge out his own eyes. The injury was irreparable - but the attempt to secure release on bail backfired. For the prisoner in question was serving a life sentence, and the camp commander strictly adhered to a regulation which lays down that lifers are not eligible for release on bail.

Rather than respond humanely to what in some camps was fast becoming a near-epidemic of self-mutilation - by, for example, reducing the forced-labor quotas and starting to treat prisoners more fairly - the authorities instead decided to step up deterrence. In 1988, a directive was issued ordering that all requests by prisoners for release on bail to seek treatment for injuries which had been self-inflicted were to be turned down. In spite of this hardline attitude, however, the incidence of self-maiming in the camps has showed no signs of decrease. According to former labor-camp prisoners, hardly a day goes by without some such incident arising.

Strict regime units

Prisoners who regularly break camp rules are dealt with by committal to the "strict regime unit" *(yanguandui)*, a highly punitive regime where a host of imaginative abuses and indignities lie waiting in store. The strict regime unit at Jianxin, for example, is a veritable house of fun, being characterized by a series of punishment ordeals known collectively as "Playing the Three Games." The first one, called "Clinging Gecko," involves the prisoner having to kneel down on the ground, with his hands raised above head height and pressed against the wall, for several-hour-long periods. The strain on the muscles soon becomes excruciating, and eventually the prisoner will collapse on the ground in a state of shock.

The second "game," which is known as "Golden Chicken Standing on One Leg," entails the prisoner having one arm handcuffed to the foot on the opposite side and then having the other arm chained high up above head height. In this way, the prisoner is left to stand on only on leg, and when exhaustion sets in the leg buckles under him, thereby wrenching his arm socket.

The third delight is called the "Pillar Standing Feat," and involves the prisoner being made to stand atop a pillar of around one meter in height with his hands chained behind his back and fixed to the wall. After 24 hours of this ordeal, at most, even the strongest of prisoners become exhausted and unable to prevent themselves from nodding off or falling asleep. When this happens, the prisoner falls off the pillar, with his full body weight behind him, and again wrenches his arms.

Juvenile Offender Centers

In addition to the prisons and labor reform camps, there are two large Juvenile Offenders Institutes in Hunan. These institutes are part of the labor reform system. One is situated in Wangchengbo in the suburbs of Changsha, and the other is in Chenzhou City. They are called the Changsha Juvenile Offenders Institute and the Chenzhou Juvenile Offenders Institute. The former was set up quite recently, and the latter no more than 10 years ago.

Such centers hold in custody nearly all offenders under the age of 18 who have been given court sentences. (Two categories of juvenile offenders - namely political prisoners and women - are committed to prisons to serve out their terms.) There are about 5,000 prisoners in the Chenzhou Juvenile Offenders Institute and somewhat fewer in the Changsha unit. Both are engaged in matchbox production. ("Chenzhou matches" are manufactured by the former; "Changsha matches," sold throughout the country, however, are manufactured by the Hunan No.9 Labor Reform Camp, which is known outwardly as the Changsha Match Factory.) The Changsha Juvenile Offenders Institute also produces packing bags.

Supervision is even more rigid in these institutions than in the adult prisons and labor-reform camps, and young offenders are allowed less freedom of movement. Throughout the year, they are required to work indoors in prison factories located inside the institute compound; they are not allowed to work outdoors. Upon reaching the age of 18, juvenile offenders are transferred either to adult prisons or to labor-reform camps, depending upon their terms of sentence.

Labor Re-education centers

China's system of "re-education through labor" was originally learned and borrowed from the Soviet Union. It is a form of so-called "administrative detention" and is designed for those who "commit misdemeanors" which are "not serious enough to qualify for criminal sanction." In practice, it means that anyone who falls foul of the public security system can be locked up by it for up to three years without ever having had a trial. Until less than three years ago, there was not even any provision for appeal to the courts. (The current right of appeal, moreover, is largely a futile formality.)

There is little real difference between the living conditions for "labor-reform" criminals and those for "labor re-education personnel." Indeed, the two types of prisoners are often held in the same labor camp, although organized into different teams. One crucial difference is that if a person sentenced to a labor reform camp is subsequently found to have been sentenced by mistake, his case will be said to be a miscarriage of justice. It is a different story, however, for someone wrongly sentenced to labor re-education. The authorities will not acknowledge such a case as being a miscarriage of justice, on the specious grounds that "it wasn't even a criminal sanction anyway." In the eyes of the people in the street, they both amount to incarceration just the same.

In Hunan, there are 16 known labor re-education centers of diverse sizes. On average, there is one center in every district or in every city. The larger ones are the Changsha Xinkaipu Labor Re-education

Center (known publicly as the Hunan Switchgear Factory, a well known production enterprise), the Zhuzhou Lukou Labor Re-education Center, the Hengshan labor Re-education Center, and the Lengshuijiang Labor Re-education Center. Among them, the Changsha Xinkaipu Labor Re-education Center is the most well-known, being regarded nationally as a model labor re-education unit. Usually somewhat smaller than labor reform camps, their populations range from between 1,000 and 10,000. The largest, those at Changsha, Hengshan and Lengshuijiang, all have populations of over 5,000. Most have under 5,000.

Life in labor re-education centers is roughly the same as that in the labor reform camps. The one marked difference is that if those undergoing re-education have a "good performance" they can ask after certain intervals for parole for the purpose of home visits. Inmates in labor re-education centers are not described as prisoners. They are identified as "re-education personnel," since they belong to the category of so-called "contradictions among the people," namely "non antagonistic" ones. (Overtly political criteria such as these, of course, have no rightful place in a country's system of legal justice.) As for labor, production activities in labor re-education centers are mostly in machinery and other light industries, with a small number involved in mining. The Changsha Xinkaipu Labor Re-education Center, for example, is a factory producing various types of electrical switchgear. Several smaller-scale centers such as the Changqiao Labor Re-education Team and the Changsha Silk Factory are also local manufacturing enterprises. Persons in the labor re-education centers are divided into teams (publicly known as workshops.) There are engineers and technicians among these persons. The atmosphere in the centers is less tense and less dull as compared with labor reform camps, since prisoners are serving sentences of usually less than three years.

There are also at least two Women's Labor Re-education Centers in Hunan. They mostly hold women accused of engaging in prostitution or other petty crimes. In the Changsha Center, the population is more than 1,000. The Zhuzhou Center is by far the largest.

Jails and detention centers

The numerous pre-hearing custodial centers *(kanshou jiguan)* in Hunan Province are also worthy of mention here, since many pro-democracy activists were held in custody in them after the June 4 crackdown for periods ranging from a few months to well over one year, before finally being released. The various types include jails *(kanshousuo)*, shelter-for-investigation centers *(shourong shenchasuo)* and detention centers *(juliusuo)*. The larger cities, such as Changsha, Hengyang, Xiangtan, Zhuzhou, Yueyang and Shaoyang, are equipped with all three types of centers, whereas in the counties or smaller towns there is often only one jail, and no shelter-for-investigation center or detention center. But each county has at least one jail, the larger of which can hold several hundred or even a thousand or more prisoners, while the smaller ones only hold around a hundred.

Of the three types, jails are usually the most properly run - although all the pre-hearing holding centers in Hunan might best be described as "wrestling rings." The shelter-for-investigation centers and detention centers, however, can only be described as being like the proverbial "Palaces of the King of Hell" *(Yan Wang Dian.)* Almost all pro-democracy activists detained in 1989 were consigned to jails from the outset, with only a very few being detained in the other two types of holding centers. This mainly reflected the government's prejudgment of them all as being guilty, but it was also because jails are all guarded by the People's Armed Police, which is only true in a minority of the other two types of detention facility. The reason given by the authorities themselves for preferring the former in our case was that otherwise - so great being "the people's anger" toward us for having upset the tranquillity of the socialist idyll - they would be unable to protect us from being beaten up by the other prisoners.

Most of the various types of holding centers are grossly overcrowded. In the jails, detainees generally have less than one square meter of floor space each. The better-run ones have small exercise yards adjoining each cell, and prisoners are allowed out for short periods each day to walk around in them. The detention centers and shelter-for-investigation centers usually have no exercise yards, and prisoners remain in the cells 24 hours a day. In the two detention centers I know most about, namely the Changsha East District and the Changsha Suburban PSB detention centers, the cells are less than six square meters in area. At the height of the "crackdown on crime" campaign in mid-1990, 20 or more prisoners were commonly packed into a single cell, leaving an average of only 0.3 square meters of floor space for each prisoner. At

102

night, the lucky ones were jammed like sardines on to the sleeping platform, while others had to sleep under it (they were referred to in the local prison slang as "coal miners" *(wa mei)*. The rest simply had to stand around all night and await their turn to sleep during the daytime.

Throughout the pre-hearing detention network, the so-called "cell boss" system is rife. Sometimes there will only be one or two cell bosses per cell, but some cells may have up to five or six. When the cell door slams shut, their word is law, and they abuse and torment the other prisoners on a mere whim. For instance, when they feel like having a bit of fun, they just spit on the floor and order some hapless inmate to get down on his knees and suck it up, licking the spot clean afterwards. Almost no one would dare to refuse, so total is the cell bosses' power. They especially enjoy seeing the prisoners fight among themselves at their instigation.

The jail diet is grossly insufficient and of extremely poor quality. This is hardly surprising, given that the subsistence allocation for each prisoner is a mere 24.50 *yuan* per month. In addition, some jails and detention centers force the inmates to perform long hours of entirely unpaid manual labor in the cells. In Changsha No.1 Jail, where I was held, for example, we had to sit right there on the cell floor making matchboxes day after day, and we never received a single cent. (Prison labor, if properly administered, can be a quite acceptable practice in the case of sentenced criminals. But it is not so in the case of those held in jails and detention centers, since they have not yet even been tried and found guilty.)

On average, detainees are held in these various holding centers for periods of between three and six months before being put on trial. After conviction (only a tiny minority of defendants are ever acquitted by the courts), they are dispatched to either prisons or labor-reform camps to serve out their sentences. (In the case of labor re-education, the opinion of the local public security chief suffices to clinch the judgment; the authorities do not even bother with the formality of a trial.) Some detainees, notably major economic criminals and certain types of political prisoners, however, remain in the jails, shelter-for-investigation and detention centers for far longer, sometimes for as long as two to three years, if the authorities for any reason consider their cases to be "particularly complex."

103

The forced-labor production regime: Longxi Prison

I was incarcerated in Longxi Prison, western Hunan, from November 1990 until February 1991. Although the workforce there is made up entirely of prisoners, Longxi Prison is actually a large-scale marble quarrying plant, known to the outside world as the "Shaoyang Marble Factory." The following is a brief account, based on my own direct experience and observation, of the economic production, marketing and exporting activities of Longxi Prison.

Situated near Longxipu Township in Xinshao County, Shaoyang Municipality, the prison lies about 250 kilometers to the southwest of Changsha, the provincial capital, and about 50 kilometers from Shaoyang City. Far off in the mountains of Xinshao County, the location of Longxi Prison is without doubt the most remote and secluded of all the prisons in Hunan Province. The prison has approximately 2,000 inmates, around 70 of whom are political prisoners serving sentences ranging from two years' imprisonment to death with a two-year reprieve. The remainder are common criminals whose terms of imprisonment are generally in excess of 15 years.

The basic nucleus of prisoners' work and daily life in Longxi Prison is the brigade *(dadui)*. (A prison brigade has equivalent status to that of a section *[ke]* in the wider government administrative structure.) The prisoners are organized into six brigades, a prison induction team, a headquarters squadron *(zhishu zhongdui)*, a headquarters brigade *(zhishu dadui)* and a medical corps. Apart from Brigade No.6, which is responsible for mechanical and electrical work, all the brigades are directly involved in production activities.

The division of labor among the five production brigades, each of which comprises an average workforce of between 200 and 300 inmates, is as follows: Brigades No.4 and 5 engage in quarry operations and are called "field brigades" *(waigong dui)*. Brigades No. 1, 2 and 3 are responsible for processing the raw marble material into finished products. Prisoners assigned to the two field brigades work at marble quarries in the mountains, where core operations include rock blasting, marble cutting and transportation of the marble blocks back to the processing plant. The three brigades involved in raw-materials processing are mainly responsible for grinding and polishing the blocks of quarried marble and

104

then turning them into finished products. The production line is primitive, the only equipment being the basic stone-grinders and polishers.

Prisoners work under a strict system of production norms and must complete their daily quotas. Failure to do so means punishment. Poor performers generally have their sentences increased in accordance with a pre-set sliding scale. In more serious cases, however, offenders are either sent to the strict regime unit or placed in solitary confinement. Time spent undergoing either of these punishments is discounted, moreover, for purposes of calculating a prisoner's remaining length of sentence. Indeed, an extra day is added to the original prison term for each day of the punishment.

The most dangerous production task carried out by prisoners at the quarrying and mining sites is the laying of dynamite for blasting operations. Many prisoners suffer injuries or even permanent disability in the course of this. For prisoners with only minor injuries, the prison provides basic medical attention. But if a prisoner suffers serious injury or encripplement, he must simply resign himself to his fate. For in nine out of ten cases, the authorities will insist that the injuries were "self-inflicted," constituting an act of defiance and a deliberate attempt to evade productive labor, thereby disqualifying the victim from being allowed out on bail for medical treatment.

The finished marble products shipped from the prison comprise mainly goods for use by the building and construction industry, such as marble floor-slabs, wall tiles and decorative plaques. The prison also produces marble handicraft items such as office paper weights, table-lamp stands, vases, ashtrays, signature seals and pen stands. All these products sell extremely well in China, with demand outstripping supply in the local markets and prices varying wildly from one part of the country to another. One of the Longxi products, for example, a six-inch long, Chinese character-inscribed paper weight which sells for less than 1 *yuan* in the prison's sales office and in the nearby towns, sometimes fetches as much as 30 to 40 *yuan* in shops in the larger cities and in the special economic zones.

Like all other labor-reform units in China, Longxi Prison has in recent years tried to mimic the economic reforms that have been proceeding throughout the rest of society. The main innovation has been the so-called "production responsibility system," which stresses the free market, discourages state subsidies and gives performance-related rewards and penalties to individual workers - in this case, prisoners. In fact, despite the oft-repeated central government policy on labor-reform work of "reform first, production second," there is no doubt that production has nowadays become the primary activity at Longxi Prison. The prison's remoteness from the cities and central government departments, however, renders it less susceptible to any reformist political influences, and the leadership there remains hardline leftist in outlook. The economic reforms at Longxi and most other labor-reform units are little more than opportunist method of maximizing profits, and imply no movement whatever toward political reform or "liberalization."

Prisoners can even, in effect, buy their way out of prison early, thanks to a recently-introduced reform which encourages inmates to use their family members and business contacts outside the prison to secure sales contracts for the prison. The system works like this. If a given prisoner can manage to arrange outside sales of the prison's marble products bringing in a net profit of 8,000 *yuan*, then he will be awarded one so-called "minor merit" point, which in turn amounts to 20 "credit points." For each credit point gained, the prisoner's remaining sentence is reduced by a period of four and one half days. Hence, a "minor merit" wins the prisoner a three-month overall reduction of sentence. Significantly, however, an unwritten rule bars political prisoners from benefitting from this "flexible policy."

Exporting of prison-made goods

I was once present at a mass meeting of the inmates at Longxi Prison during which a prison cadre told us all to encourage our families to undertake sales activities on behalf of the prison. The official stressed in particular that foreign exports of the prison's goods were most ideal, since they yielded the highest profit. (Apparently, many overseas buyers are interested in obtaining marble building goods and handicraft items such as seals and paper weights.) The official even read aloud from a set of rules on the credits and awards that prisoners could earn through their prison-sales efforts and those of their families. Many prisoners then began asking their families and friends to seek buyers for the prison's goods, with a view to earning "minor merits" and getting out of prison

106

early.

I remember one prisoner, a cellmate of mine at one point, who managed to arrange such big overseas sales contracts through his family and friends that he eventually earned profits for the prison to the tune of several hundred thousand *yuan*. The man, whose name was Zeng Qinglin, had previously been an employee of an overseas Chinese import-export corporation based in Shenzhen, and he was serving a 10-year prison term for economic corruption offenses. His business background made it easy for him to fix the deals, but the sheer size of the profits created a problem for the prison leadership, since technically he had earned so much remission on his sentence that he would be due for release almost immediately. So a deal was struck, whereby the prison leadership privately assured Zeng that he would be granted parole once his term of imprisonment reached the fifth year. From then on, he became a highly privileged "guest" of the prison, surpassing all the other inmates in status and even enjoying better living conditions than some of the lower-level officials.

Goods produced by most of the other main prisons in Hunan are also available for export. Yuanjiang, Hengyang and Lingling Prisons, for example, produce vehicles and auto parts which are marketed in various South-East Asian countries. Products from the Changde Diesel Engine Plant are also available for export in small numbers.

While I was imprisoned in Guangdong No.1 Jail, I had to produce various types of handicraft products which, apparently, were mainly for sale overseas. (I was told this by a provincial foreign trade official who had been detained for trying to help pro-democracy activists escape the country.) Later on, during my time at the Changsha No.2 Jail, I had to make packing boxes for a Chinese medical product, a concoction made from snake gallbladder and juice of the pi-pa fruit, which was produced by the Hunan Pharmaceuticals Factory. Changsha No.2 Jail had been contracted to produce the packaging for this medicine, which was shipped for sale overseas in large quantities.

Two of the largest re-education facilities in Changsha, namely the Hunan Switchgear Factory (also known as the Xinkaipu Labor Re-education Center) and the Hunan Silk Factory (also known as the Changsha Women's Re-education Center), export large quantities of their

107

goods abroad. According to a "restricted-circulation" *(neibu)* volume published in Changsha in November 1989, the Hunan Switchgear Factory, whose workshops alone cover 125,000 square meters of floorspace, has since the 1960s been exporting a wide range of its high and low-voltage electrical appliances and products to various countries including Albania, Brazil, Thailand, Yemen and Hong Kong. More recently, the factory has added Tanzania, North Korea, Sri Lanka, Bangladesh and Pakistan to its ever-growing list of international customers. In 1986, according to the confidential volume, the Hunan Commission on Foreign Economic Relations and Trade (which is the provincial counterpart of MOFERT, Beijing's Ministry of Foreign Economic Relations and Trade) awarded the factory the glorious designation of "Advanced Unit in Exporting and Foreign Currency-Earning." The following year, it received the further accolade of "Advanced Unit in Completing Product Tasks for Foreign Aid Purposes."[36]

Similarly, the Hunan Silk Factory, a large production facility with workshops covering 74,500 square meters of floorspace, is said by the same internally published source to have been exporting a wide range of silk cloth products and garments to countries throughout Asia, Africa and Latin America ever since its foundation in 1958. "Since the early 1980s, moreover," continues the source, "the factory, in cooperation with [China's] foreign trade departments, has been exporting its pure-silk and silk-mixture quilt covers, its pure-silk jasmine satin cloth, its printed soft-silk fabric in satin weave and its silk floss taffeta to both the U.S.A. and Japan."

Try as they may, the authorities can offer no convincing denial of the clear fact that goods manufactured by prison labor in China are being exported. If one asks cadres of various Hunan labor-reform establishments at random for their views, they invariably take pride in the

---

[36] *Changsha Sishi Nian: 1949 to 1989* ("Forty Years in Changsha: 1948 to 1989"), compiled and published by the Changsha Municipal Bureau of Statistics, November 1989. The book carries the legend, "Internal Materials - File Carefully," and only 800 copies were printed, each of which carries a two-line form on the inside cover requiring recipient offices or organizations to enter their names and the identifying number of the copy issued to them.

fact that their products are able to find overseas markets. The Chinese government, for its part, does not consider its prison-goods export industry to be in any way reprehensible or a violation of human rights - regardless of the fact that thousands of political prisoners are among those currently being exploited in the Chinese *gulag* for this purpose - and it issues extensive disinformation on the topic as a means of deflecting the growing international criticism of its trade in forced-labor goods.

Forcible employment of time-served prisoners

From the early 1950s onward, the Chinese labor-reform authorities began to apply a policy known as the "forcible retention of time-served prisoners for in-camp employment" *(xingman shifang renyuan de qiangzhixing liuchang jiuye)* - or "forced in-camp employment" for short. Under this policy, millions of former prisoners have, over the past four decades throughout the country, been forced to remain behind after the expiration of their sentences as so-called "workers," usually for the rest of their lives, in the same prison or labor-camp enterprises in which they previously lived as prisoners.

Although blatantly unjust, the use of "forced in-camp employment" is widespread in Hunan Province. Government officials there argue that the policy facilitates the policy of "putting thought-reform in first place" and "allowing prisoners to reform themselves more thoroughly." Holding human rights in utter contempt, the authorities have broken up countless families and created untold numbers of domestic tragedies through this policy. The practice reached a high-point during the 1983 "campaign to crack down on serious crime," and in subsequent years large numbers of prisoners were forcibly retained as workers in prisons and labor camps, especially in northwestern China, after completing their sentences. Most were barred from ever recovering their original urban residency rights or returning to their homes.

After being released on parole in February 1991, I travelled around much of Hunan and was able to learn something about the "forced in-camp employment" situation there. Hunan Provincial No. 2 Prison, for example, is a factory producing heavy-duty trucks. Known outwardly as the "Hengyang Heavy Motor Vehicle Plant," it holds more than 7000 prisoners, organized into around ten different workshops

109

known as brigades *(dadui)*. There is also a small contingent of workers (i.e. non-prisoners) employed in the factory, a minority of whom are the children of prison cadres. The majority of them, however, are "time-served prisoners retained for in-camp employment." A small proportion of such people have remained voluntarily to work in the camp or prison enterprise after completing their sentences, but the great majority have had no say at all in the matter and are simply forced to stay on.

One prisoner I knew who had been forcibly retained as a worker was a man nicknamed "Springtime Pickpocket" *(chun pashou.)* He told me that in 1987 he had completed a 15-year sentence for robbery. As soon as his prison term had ended, however, the authorities canceled his Changsha urban residency permit *(hukou)* and forced him to stay on in the prison factory as a worker. Ostensibly a free citizen, his life remained, in fact, almost identical to that of the prisoners. His daily working hours and production quota were virtually the same as before, as was his daily rest entitlement. The only difference was that he now received a tiny monthly wage and was allowed to take care of his own domestic affairs. In addition, once in a while he was permitted to take a short holiday and go home to visit his family. His overall standard of living had hardly increased at all.

Certainly, his personal dignity was accorded no greater respect than before - the main reason being that, like other "forcibly retained personnel," he had to work in the factory alongside the prison cadres' offspring. Any one of the latter (even if he or she was completely illiterate) enjoyed an unrestricted right to exercise discipline and control over the "released labor-reform personnel." According to "Springtime Pickpocket," his only hope in life lay in somehow gaining personal favor with the prison cadres, so that one of them would eventually be kind enough to release him and allow him to return to Changsha. The great majority of "forcibly retained personnel" all cling to a similar hope. Despite being nominally free and equal citizens, therefore, they would never actually dare to demonstrate or lay claim to any such equality with the cadres.

In Longxi Prison, there was relatively little "forced in-camp employment." Because of its remote and isolated location, the marble plant's productivity was low and it usually ran at a loss. It thus had no great need of even the cheapest additional labor-power. This was also one

110

reason why Longxi had probably the most flexible parole practices of any of the major Hunan prisons. There were, however, a certain number of "forcibly retained personnel" kept in the prison, perhaps as part of a token effort by the cadres to show that they were implementing the "spirit" of the relevant central government documents.

Most of the other main facilities in Hunan Province, including Jianxin Farm, Yuanjiang Prison, the Hunan Diesel Engine Plant and Provincial No. 3 Prison, had larger numbers of "forcibly retained personnel." The average was around 100 persons per prison or labor camp, although some units held more than 200. Among these former prisoners, some undoubtedly were (as the authorities claimed) individuals who had resisted re-education and "failed to reform themselves well." Others were forcibly retained because they had highly-prized technical or professional skills; such people were usually the most wretched and miserable of all those forced to stay on after completion of sentence.

Naturally, these "forcibly retained personnel" feel a constant sense of resentment at the great injustice of their situation, and some do try to escape from time to time. But the authorities usually manage to recapture and bring them back again quite quickly. They rarely punish such people severely (for example by resentencing them), however, and instead usually just hold a criticism meeting within the prison or something similar. The real reason that so few "forcibly retained personnel" try to escape is, rather, because the only point in their doing so would be to return home - and they are all too well aware that if they were ever to return home, they would be caught and returned to the prison enterprise again almost immediately. Their unofficial life sentences would then merely become all the harder to bear.

*****

Tang Boqiao reached the United States in April 1992.

111

APPENDIX I

Data on Pro-Democracy Prisoners and Ex-Prisoners in Hunan Province

A. Currently Imprisoned

Yuanjiang Prison (Provincial No. 1)

▪ **Ah Fang** (nickname), 23 years old, originally a student at Changsha University. Home and workplace: the Changsha Nonferrous Metals Design Academy. During the 1989 Democracy Movement, he took part in the Students Autonomous Federation, but withdrew from its activities early on and so was not investigated by the authorities after June 4. In September and October 1989, he set up a private company together with a group of research staff from the Non-Ferrous Metals Design Academy and other institutes. At the end of 1989, the company was closed down by the authorities and branded a "counterrevolutionary organization." Ah Fang was arrested shortly afterwards, and in mid-1990 was tried by the Changsha Intermediate [People's] Court on charges of being "a member of a counterrevolutionary clique" and sentenced to five years' imprisonment. Initially held in Changsha No. 1 and No. 2 Detention Centers, he was later transferred to serve his sentence at Yuanjiang Prison. [5 YRS]

▪ **Chen Zhixiang**, 34 years old, originally a teacher at the Guangzhou Maritime Transport Academy. He was tried and sentenced on January 11, 1990 by the Guangzhou Intermediate Court to a prison term of ten years. (See *Appendix VIII.A*, below, for full text of the court's verdict on Chen.) During the 1989 Democracy Movement he allegedly organized student demonstrations in Guangzhou and wrote "reactionary articles" with an "extremely bad influence in institutions of higher education." He also had a "reactionary historical background." On June 7, 1989, Chen allegedly painted 20-meter long slogans on the walls along Yanjiang Road Central and Huanshi Road Central in Guangzhou, which according to the authorities, attacked "state, military and Party leaders" and called "for the overthrow of the people's democratic dictatorship." He was arrested shortly thereafter and was eventually convicted on a charge of "counterrevolutionary propaganda and incitement." While Chen is

113

reported to be currently held in Yuanjiang Prison, this cannot be confirmed. Other reports state that Chen is being held in Guangdong Province, although senior provincial officials there have consistently refused either to confirm this or to indicate in which prison or labor-reform camp Chen is currently being held. [10 YRS]

- **Fu Zhaoqin**, peasant from Taojiang County. During the 1989 Democracy Movement he actively participated in the student resistance movement and was accused by the government of "pretending to be a responsible person in the Students' Autonomous Federation, stirring up disturbances, disrupting public order, and humiliating public security cadres." He was arrested in mid-June and held in the Yiyang City Jail. He was subsequently sentenced to four years by a court in Yiyang City on a charge of disrupting social order. (According to the *Hunan Daily* of June 15, "during the period of chaos, the Yiyang City Public Security Bureau arrested a total of over 120 lawless elements who created chaos.") [4 YRS]

- **Gao Bingkun**, 37 years old, unemployed, resident of Changsha's Southern District. He was an active participant in the 1989 Democracy Movement. After June 4, he organized a mass lie-in on the railroad tracks and "caused the Number 48 train from Guangzhou to Beijing to stop for over 10 hours." He also shouted "reactionary slogans." On June 6, he was arrested and held in Changsha's No. 1 Jail. In early 1990 he was sentenced to four years by the Changsha Southern District [Basic-Level People's] Court on a charge of "disrupting traffic order." [4 YRS]

- **Huang Zhenghua**, 54 years old, originally a cadre from a government department in Nan County, Yiyang Prefecture, who had been assigned to work in Changsha. During the 1989 Democracy Movement, he made many public speeches in support of the student movement, and was later accused by the authorities of "inciting hostile feelings among the masses toward the government" and of "conspiring to form an underground organization." He was arrested in early 1990, and in October that year was tried by a district court in Changsha on a charge of "economic criminal activity" and sentenced to six years' imprisonment. [6 YRS]

- **Li Jian**, originally a worker at the Changsha Zhengyuan Engine Parts Factory, 25 years old. During the 1989 Democracy Movement he organized the Workers' Hunger Strike Team which held a hunger strike in front of the provincial government offices together with the students. After martial law was declared in Beijing, he took part in the founding of the Changsha Workers' Autonomous Federation and was its first chairman. On several occasions he organized strikes and demonstrations by the workers. He was arrested after June 4 and held in the Changsha No. 1 Jail. In April of

1990 he was sentenced to 3 years by the Changsha City Intermediate Court on a charge of being a member of a "counterrevolutionary group." A person named Li Jian also appears on a November 1991 Chinese government response to a State Department list of detainees, but the character for "Jian" is different. In response to an inquiry from the International Labor Organization, the Chinese government confirmed that Li was arrested around June 16, 1989 and was sentenced to three years for "disturbing the peace."   [3 YRS]

■ **Li Weihong**, a worker in the Hunan Fire Extinguishing Equipment General Factory, 26 years old. During the 1989 Democracy Movement he took part in demonstrations. On the evening of April 22, 100,000 people in Changsha took to the streets to demonstrate and shout slogans. They demanded the restoration of Hu Yaobang's good name. Li took the lead in shouting, "Down with the racketeering officials *(daoye)*!" Some radical youths ended up smashing some shops on May 1st Road, and there ensued a "chaotic" incident. Almost 40 shops were smashed and several dozen policemen were injured. That evening Li was arrested on his way home. Shortly after June 4, Li received a suspended death sentence from the Changsha City Intermediate Court on a charge of "hooliganism." (Twenty-seven others involved in the April 22 Incident were sentenced on the same day. In their November 1991 response to a State Department list, the Chinese

government confirmed that Li was sentenced.   [SUSP. DEATH]

■ **Li Xiaodong**, 25 years old, originally a worker at the Zhongnan Pharmaceutical Plant in Shaoyang City. During the 1989 Democracy Movement, Li took part in the Shaoyang Workers Autonomous Federation. On the evening of May 19, he led a group of workers to People's Square, the local government offices and elsewhere to demonstrate against the imposition of martial law in Beijing, shouting slogans which allegedly "incited the masses to break into the government headquarters." A clash with the police ensued, and Li was arrested the following day and imprisoned in the Shaoyang Jail. In October 1989, he was tried by the Shaoyang Intermediate Court on charges of "counterrevolutionary propaganda and incitement" and sentenced to 13 years' imprisonment.   [13 YRS]

■ **Li Xin**, originally a worker, subsequently resigned, 25 years old. His family lives on Kui'e North Road in Changsha. During the 1989 Democracy Movement he participated in the Changsha Workers' Autonomous Federation and was deputy head of the picket squad. He was arrested in June of 1989 and sentenced in December to a term of 3 years by the Changsha Northern District [Basic-Level People's] Court on a charge of "disturbing social order."   [3 YRS]

■ **Liao Zhijun**, 26 years old, a worker

at the Changsha Pump Factory. After the student movement was suppressed in Beijing, Liao on June 6 allegedly "blocked traffic in Dongfanghong Square and pretended to be a member of the Students' Autonomous Federation picket squad, inciting some of the masses who didn't understand the true situation to join in. He also forced passing drivers to shout slogans." He was arrested on the spot and held in Changsha's No. 1 Jail. In November 1989, he was sentenced to 10 years by the Changsha Southern District Court on a charge of "robbery." (The story of his arrest was carried in June in the *Hunan Daily*.) [10 YRS]

■ **Liu Chengwu**, 24 years old, a peasant from Huangtuhang Township, Suining County, Hunan. According to the authorities, "On May 18, 1989, he stirred up the blocking of vehicles in the square of the Changsha Railway Station. When public security cadres tried to get people to stop, he actually took pictures, trying to find some basis on which to stir up even more trouble. He was arrested on the spot." (See the report from mid-June in the *Hunan Daily*.) He was held in Changsha's No. 1 Jail, and at the end of the year sentenced to four years by the Changsha Eastern District Court on a charge of "disrupting social order." [4 YRS]

■ **Liu Jian'an**, teacher, 40 years old. Formerly a teacher at Changsha's No. 23 Middle School and a graduate of the History Department of Hunan Normal University. During the 1989 Democracy Movement he allegedly started listening to "enemy radio" in Taiwan and wrote 16 "counterrevolutionary letters to Guomindang secret agents", according to the *Hunan Daily*. He was also accused of publishing and distributing "reactionary books." Arrested in June 1989. On December 7, 1989, he was sentenced to 10 years in December by the Changsha Intermediate Court on a charge of "espionage." [10 YRS]

■ **Lu Zhaixing**, 27, originally a worker in the Changsha Embroidery Factory. He was an important figure in the Changsha Workers' Autonomous Federation. On several occasions he organized worker demonstrations and strikes by the workers of the Embroidery Factory. On June 14, he was arrested at home and held in the Changsha No. 1 Jail. In April of 1990 he was sentenced to three years by the Changsha Eastern District Court on a charge of "disrupting public order." [3 YRS]

■ **Mao Genhong**, 25 years old, originally a student at the Hunan College of Finance; active to a minor extent during the 1989 Democracy Movement. According to an internal government source, "After graduation, Mao Genhong, together with his younger brother Mao Genwei and others, in mid-1990 set up an underground organization which was broken up by the authorities at the end of 1990." Initially held in the Changsha No. 1 Jail, Mao was in mid-1991 tried on the charge of "forming a counterrevolutionary clique" by the Changsha Intermediate Court and sentenced to three years' imprisonment. He was sent first to Hunan No.3 Prison and then later transferred to Yuanjiang Prison. At least six other people, identities unknown, were detained and eventually tried in connection with the same case. The highest prison sentence imposed was five years. (The other sentences are not known.) [3 YRS]

- **Tang Changye**, 29, originally a worker, subsequently resigned. Wears thick glasses. During the 1989 Democracy Movement, he often printed handbills and posted big-character posters. Arrested in October 1989. Sentenced to three years in 1990 by the Changsha Eastern District Court on a charge of "disturbing social order." When he was being held in Cell 15 of the Changsha No. 1 Jail, he suffered a great deal of abuse from fellow prisoners. He was considered mentally ill by the cadres and convicts. [3 YRS]

- **Wang Changhuai**, worker, 26 years old. Formerly employed at the Changsha Automobile Factory. Served as Chief of Propaganda Section of Changsha's Workers' Autonomous Federation during the 1989 Democracy Movement. Surrendered to the government on June 15, 1989. Sentenced to three years on December 7, 1989 by the Changsha Intermediate [People's] Court on a charge of "counterrevolutionary propaganda and incitement." [3 YRS]

- **Wu Tongfan**, urban resident, 40 years old. His family lives in Fuzhong Alley, Nanyang Street, Changsha. During the 1989 Democracy Movement he had contacts with He Zhaohui, a leader of the Changsha Workers' Autonomous Federation, and others. He was accused of directing things from behind the scenes. He was sentenced (the period of imprisonment is unknown) in mid-1990 by the Changsha Intermediate Court on a charge of "counter-revolutionary propaganda and incitement." [? YRS]

- **Xia Changchun**, a worker in the passenger transport section of the Hong Kong Affairs Bureau, 24 years old. He was also arrested on the evening of April 22 and accused of "taking the lead in storming the municipal Public Security Bureau and stirring up chaos." He was held in the Changsha No. 2 Jail. In June, he was sentenced to 15 years by the Changsha City Intermediate Court on a charge of "hooliganism." [15 YRS]

- **Yang Xiong**, 25 years old, a resident of Changsha. During the 1989 Democracy Movement, Yang was involved in the Changsha Workers Autonomous Federation. For a time, he was responsible for the federation's picket squad and often organized and led members to go to local factories to urge the workers to go on strike. According to the authorities, "this inflicted upon the Changsha Woollen Mill and other factories economic losses of several hundred thousand *yuan*." On June 8, Yang was in overall

117

charge of the picket squad assigned to keep order at the mass mourning ceremony held that day at the Changsha Railway Station. He was arrested in mid-June, and in early 1990 was tried by the East District Court of Changsha on charges of "disrupting social order" and sentenced to three years' imprisonment. In response to inquiries from the International Labor Organization most recently in January 1992, the Chinese government confirmed the arrest but said he was sentenced to four years.

[3 YRS]

■ **Zhang Jie**, 25 years old, scientific researcher. A graduate of Hefei University, he was formerly employed at the Changsha Nonferrous Metals Design Academy. After the suppression of the 1989 Democracy Movement, he "established a secret underground organization under the cover of setting up a company" and was later arrested. Sentenced to five years in mid-1990 by the Changsha Intermediate Court on a charge of [being a member of a] "counter-revolutionary group." [5 YRS]

■ **Zhang Jingsheng**, 37 years old, worker at the Hunan Shaoguan Electrical Engineering Plant. Originally sentenced to four years in 1981 on a charge of counter-revolutionary propaganda and incitement because he had edited and distributed an underground publication during the Democracy Wall movement and supported a student protest movement at Hunan

Normal University. He was arrested again on May 4, 1989, after giving a speech at a mass pro-democracy meeting at the Changsha Martyrs' Park, calling, among other things, for the release of Democracy Wall activist Wei Jingsheng. Although freed several days later, he then joined the Workers' Autonomous Federation, and was re-arrested on May 28, 1989. In December 1989, he was sentenced to 13 years by the Changsha Intermediate People's Court on a charge of "counterrevolutionary propaganda and incitement." While in jail he wrote a large number of prison songs that are widely popular, and are sung by prisoners throughout Hunan, Hubei, Guangxi, Guizhou and other provinces. [13 YRS]

■ **Zhang Xudong**, worker, 32 years old. Formerly head of the Changsha Elevator Factory (a collective enterprise). His family lives in Chongsheng Alley in Changsha's North District. On May 20, 1989, founded Changsha's Workers' Autonomous Federation with Zhou Yong and others and was a member of its Standing Committee and its Vice Chairman. Several times he organized worker demonstrations and strikes. Arrested in June, 1989. During the entire time he was held at the Changsha No. 1 Jail he wore leg irons and handcuffs. This went on for ten months. (According to the usual practice, only a very small number of criminals who, in the authorities' view, "cannot be allowed to live" are subjected to this sort of treatment.) Sentenced to four years in mid-1990

118

by the Changsha Intermediate Court on a charge of "counterrevolutionary propaganda and incitement." The sentence was confirmed in a Chinese government response to an International Labor Organization inquiry in January 1992, but the government said Zhang was convicted for "disturbing the peace." [4 YRS]

■ **Zhao Weiguo**, 34 years old, originally a student at one of the universities in Beijing. Expelled from university in early 1987 because of his participation in the student movement of winter 1986-87, he returned to Changde, his hometown in Hunan, and together with eight other students who had also been expelled on account of their pro-democracy involvement, he established a small private business there. During the 1989 Democracy Movement, Zhao gave up his work with the company so that he could provide help to the students in his area. Later on, he travelled specially to Changsha in order to join the SAF and take part in directing and formulating plans for the student movement. In addition, he contributed almost 10,000 *yuan* to the cause. After June 4, 1989, Zhao became a major target of attack by the government, and was arrested in October 1989 and held in Changde City Jail. He was subsequently tried by the Changde Intermediate Court on charges of "counterrevolutionary propaganda and incitement" and sentenced to four years' imprisonment. [4 YRS]

(Two others were arrested at the same time as Zhao Weiguo. Both were originally students from universities in Beijing who had been expelled for their activities during the 1989 movement. One was later released, but nothing is known of the fate of the second.)

■ **Zhou Min**, worker, 26 years old. Formerly employed at the Changsha Nonferrous Metallurgical Design Academy. Participated in the founding of the Changsha Workers' Autonomous Federation during the 1989 Democracy Movement and was a member of its Standing Committee. Arrested in June 1989. Sentenced to six years in June 1990 by the Changsha Intermediate Court on a charge of "being the leader of a counterrevolutionary group." Sent in September to Yuanjiang Prison to serve his sentence. While held at the Changsha No. 1 Jail, he was frequently subject to corporal punishment and maltreatment. He has become mentally disturbed and his speech is incoherent. [6 YRS]

Hengyang Prison (Provincial No. 2)

■ **Cheng Cun**, 30, originally a reporter at the Yueyang bureau of the *News Pictorial (xinwen tupian bao)*. From the end of 1988 until June 4, he took part in several large demonstrations in Yueyang and, according to the authorities, contravened Party discipline by privately disseminating pictures of the

119

demonstrations, resulting in an "extremely bad influence." He was arrested after the suppression of the Democracy Movement. In early 1990 he was sentenced to five years by the Yueyang City Intermediate Court on a charge of "counterrevolutionary propaganda and incitement." [5 YRS]

▪ **Guo Yunqiao, Hu Min, Mao Yuejin, Wang Zhaobo, Huang Lixin, Huang Fan, Wan Yuewang, Pan Qiubao,** and **Yuan Shuzhu,** all workers or residents of Yueyang, all between 20 and 35 years old. During the 1989 Democracy Movement they organized the Yueyang Workers' Autonomous Federation and on several occasions organized demonstrations and strikes by the workers. After the June 4 crackdown in Beijing, they marched carrying wreaths and setting off firecrackers. Over 10,000 persons took part in the march. Prior to this they had lain down on the railroad tracks on Yueyang's Baling Railway Bridge to protest the violent acts of the government. When the demonstration reached the offices of the municipal government and the seat of the municipal [Party] committee, to the accompaniment of the shouts of the masses, they took down the sign saying "City Government" and trampled it underfoot, resulting in an "extremely odious influence." On June 9, they were all arrested on the street and held in the Yueyang Jail. In September they were all sentenced by the Yueyang City Intermediate Court on charges of "hooliganism." Guo Yunqiao was given a sentence of death, suspended for two years; Hu

Min and Mao Yuejin were given sentences of 15 years; Wang Zhaobo, Huang Lixin, Huang Fan, Wan Yuewang, Pan Qiubao, and Yuan Shuzhu were given sentences ranging from 7 to 15 years.
[SUSP. DEATH; 7-15 YRS]

▪ **He Aoqiu,** assistant professor in the Chinese department at the Yueyang Teachers' College, 55 years old. During the 1989 Democracy Movement he took part in student demonstrations and meetings and on several occasions made speeches at the meetings. He propagated democratic ideology and exposed the corrupt acts of the local government. He was arrested after June 4 and held in the Yueyang Jail. In March 1990, he was sentenced to three years by the Yueyang City Intermediate Court on a charge of "counterrevolutionary propaganda and incitement." [3 YRS]

▪ **Huang Yaru,** originally a professor in the department of political education at Yueyang Teachers' College, 47 years old. At the end of 1988 he planned to hold an "Academic Conference of the Politics of the Yin Zhenggao Affair," but was prevented from doing so. During the 1989 Democracy Movement he took part on several occasions in demonstrations by the Teachers' College students and wrote "reactionary articles." He was arrested in August, 1989. In March 1990, he was sentenced to five years by the Yueyang City Intermediate Court on a charge of "counterrevolutionary propaganda and incitement." [5 YRS]

- **Li Zimin**, 40 years old, originally a private businessman in Hengyang City, Hunan. He actively participated in the 1989 Democracy Movement and "stirred up trouble everywhere." He also allegedly sent coded intelligence messages to "the enemy" (Taiwan). He was arrested in June 1990. At the end of the year, he was sentenced to 15 years by the Hengyang City Intermediate Court on a charge of "espionage." [15 YRS]

- **Liu Weiguo**, 38 years old, originally a worker in Leiyang City, Hunan. During the 1989 Democracy Movement he allegedly joined a Taiwanese spy organization and "stirred up trouble everywhere," trying to storm the municipal government offices and sabotage his factory's production. In June 1990, he was arrested together with Wang Yusheng. At the end of the year he was sentenced to seven years by the Hengyang City Intermediate Court on a charge of "espionage." Wang's sentence is not known. [7 YRS]

- **Mei Shi**, 40, editor-in-chief of the *Yueyang Evening News* (the first editor of a Party organ in China to be hired for his professional qualifications). Stories about him had appeared several times in the press. During his period of tenure, he published several articles that were quite sharp in tone, exposing the corruption of the CCP. After martial law was declared in Beijing, he still published articles praising the righteous actions of the students. He was arrested after June 4 and held in the Yueyang Jail. In

April 1990 he was sentenced to four years by the Yueyang City Intermediate Court on a charge of "counterrevolutionary propaganda and incitement." [4 YRS]

- **Min Hexun**, approximately 29 years old, originally a teacher in the politics department of Yueyang Teachers Training College. Min supported the student demonstrations in 1989 and wrote a large number of "reactionary articles" urging workers to stage protest strikes. These were later said by the authorities to have "exerted an extremely bad influence." He was arrested in July 1989, and in early 1990 was tried by the Yueyang Intermediate Court on charges of "counterrevolutionary propaganda and incitement" and sentenced to three years' imprisonment. [3 YRS]

- **Qin Hubao**, originally a cadre in the Office of Discussion and Criticism (ODC) in Yueyang City. This was an office established single-handedly by Yin Zhenggao, the vice-mayor of Yueyang which existed solely for the purpose of criticizing cadres. (After it was closed down in late 1988, workers of seven factories demonstrated in protest.) Qin was involved in the same case as Yang Shaoyue, but had other "counterrevolutionary acts." During the 1989 Democracy Movement he went to Beijing and secretly sent back the No. 5, 1989 issue of *Reportage Literature (Baogao wenxue)*. He distributed copies widely in Changsha, Yueyang, and other cities. He was arrested in July of 1989. In December he was sentenced to 10 years by the Yueyang City Intermediate Court on a charge of "counterrevolutionary propaganda and incitement." [10 YRS]

■ **Teacher Mi** (name unknown), originally a teacher in the Chinese department at Yueyang Teachers' College. During the 1989 Democracy Movement he took an active part in student street demonstrations. On several occasions he organized student demonstrations, and often made speeches on campus and wrote "reactionary articles." He had connections with members of the provincial Students' Autonomous Federation. The day after June 4, he took part in a meeting to mourn those who had perished in Beijing. Shortly thereafter he was arrested. In early 1990 he was sentenced to three years by the Yueyang City Intermediate Court on a charge of "counterrevolutionary propaganda and incitement." [3 YRS]

■ **Teacher X** (name unknown), in his thirties, originally a teacher in the linguistics department at Changde Normal University and a graduate of the Chinese department at Hunan Normal University. He had long been involved in pro-democracy activities and joined in at the beginning of the 1989 Democracy Movement, organizing student demonstrations. He wrote a large number of "reactionary articles" and made speeches all over, stirring up the people to demand the restoration of their basic rights. After June 4, at the meeting held in front of the municipal government offices to mourn the perished of Beijing, he called upon the people to rise up to "resist the illegitimate CCP regime" and to carry on an uncompromising struggle. Shortly thereafter he was arrested. At the end of 1989 he was sentenced to 12 years by the Changde City Intermediate Court on a charge of "counterrevolutionary propaganda and incitement" and "being in secret contact with foreign countries" *(litong waiguo).* [12 YRS]

' **Wang Yusheng** (also seen as Wang Rusheng), an entrepreneur who was then 40, was arrested in June 1990 and accused of being a foreign spy. According to the authorities, he allegedly joined a Guomindang Military Intelligence Bureau in 1985 and returned to the mainland as a spy in October 1986. He was arrested together with Liu Weiguo (see separate entry). Both men "confessed" to the charges against them after authorities seized "incriminating espionage equipment", according to a Hunan Provincial Radio report. [?? YRS]

■ **Wu Weiguo**, 30, originally a cadre in the Yueyang Office of Discussion and Criticism. He was involved in the same case as Yang Shaoyue. He was arrested after June 4 and held in the Yueyang Jail. In December 1989, he was sentenced to five years by the Yueyang City Intermediate Court on a charge of "counterrevolutionary propaganda and incitement." [5 YRS]

• **Xie Yang,** 32 years old, originally the secretary of the Yueyang Communist Youth League. During the 1989 Democracy Movement he publicly declared his support for the patriotic acts of the students. He actively organized and participated in student demonstrations and wrote "reactionary articles." He also went to the Yueyang Teachers' College and other institutes of higher education and gave speeches. After June 4 he was arrested. In early 1990 he was sentenced to three years by the Yueyang City Intermediate Court on a charge of "counterrevolutionary propaganda and incitement."

[3 YRS]

• **Yang Shaoyue,** 36, originally head of the Yueyang City government Office of Discussion and Criticism. He was dismissed after the ODC was closed down in late 1988. During the 1989 Democracy Movement he supported the student movement and wrote "counterrevolutionary articles." In July 1989 he was arrested and held in the Yueyang No. 1 Jail. In December 1989 he was sentenced to five years by the Yueyang City Intermediate Court on a charge of "counterrevolutionary propaganda and incitement."

[5 YRS]

• **Zhang Jizhong,** 34, well-known reporter for the *Hunan Daily*. During the 1989 Democracy Movement he supported and participated in student demonstrations and made speeches., urging the broad masses to "overthrow bureaucratism." He was arrested after June 4 and held in the

Yueyang Jail. In December 1989, he was sentenced to three years by the Yueyang City Intermediate Court on a charge of "counterrevolutionary propaganda and incitement."

[3 YRS]

• **Zhu Fangming,** 28, a worker in the Hengyang City Flour Factory. He was a vice chairman of the Hengyang City Workers' Autonomous Federation and organized and took part in several demonstrations. He also took part in a sit-in in front of the municipal government offices. After the June 4 tragedy, he led the workers to the [offices of the] municipal government and the municipal Public Security Bureau to demand justice, and a clash with the police occurred. He was arrested shortly thereafter. (According to the Party press, this clash resulted in over 100 policemen being injured.) In December 1989, he was sentenced to life imprisonment by the Hengyang City Intermediate Court on a charge of "hooliganism." [LIFE]

Lingling Prison (Provincial No. 3)

• **Chen Yueming,** 24 years old, a resident of Changsha City, where he ran a motor vehicle spare-parts business. Chen was involved in secret underground pro-democracy work between 1989 and 1990, and was arrested in September 1990. Soon afterwards, he was tried by the Changsha Intermediate Court on a charge of "counterrevolutionary propaganda and incitement" and

123

sentenced to three years' imprisonment. [3 YRS]

- **Feng Ming**, in his twenties, a resident of Xiangtan City. Feng was arrested for alleged participation in an incident which occurred on May 22, 1989 in which a number of people "burst into the Pingzheng Road Police Station" (a local public security office located in Yuhu District, Xiangtan Municipality.) Feng was arrested on the spot. Later that year, he was tried by the Yuhu District Court of Xiangtan on common criminal charges and sentenced to three years' imprisonment. [3 YRS]

- **Gong Songlin**, in his twenties, a resident of Xiangtan City. During the 1989 Democracy Movement, he took part in numerous demonstrations and other protest activities, and was subsequently arrested for alleged participation in the "Pingzheng Road Police Station Incident" (see above: case of Feng Ming.) Soon after June 4, he was tried by the Yuhu District Court in Xiangtan on common criminal charges and sentenced to five years' imprisonment. [5 YRS]

- **Jiang Congzheng**, in his twenties, originally a worker at a Xiangtan factory. During the 1989 Democracy Movement, he took part in demonstrations and urged workers to go on strike. According to the authorities, he "sabotaged normal production activities in the factories," and after June 4 he "forcibly prevented workers from going on their shifts and insulted and

intimidated those who chose to do so." Arrested in mid-June, he was tried in early 1990 by a Xiangtan district court on the charge of "gathering a crowd to create disturbances" and sentenced to eight years' imprisonment. [8 YRS]

- **Liang Jianguo**, 26 years old, originally an employee of a guesthouse run by the Hunan Provincial People's Political Consultative Conference. An active participant in the 1989 Democracy Movement, in early 1990 Liang became involved in secret underground pro-democracy work. He was arrested in June 1990. Soon afterwards, he was tried by the East District Court of Changsha on common criminal charges and sentenced to six years' imprisonment. [6 YRS]

- **Liu Weihong**, 27 years old, originally a worker at a Changsha factory. During the 1989 Democracy Movement, he allegedly organized workers in his factory to "go on strike and create disturbances," and moreover "made impertinent remarks to the factory leaders." Arrested soon after June 4, 1989, he was brought to trial at the Changsha Intermediate Court in mid-1990 on a charge of "counterrevolutionary propaganda and incitement" and sentenced to four years' imprisonment. [4 YRS]

- **Peng Aiguo**, 20 years old, a resident of Xiangtan City. During the 1989 Democracy Movement, he was arrested for alleged participation in

124

the "Pingzheng Road Police Station Incident" (see above: case of Feng Ming.) He was tried soon after June 4, 1989 at the Yuhu District Court on a charge of "disturbing public order" and sentenced to six years' imprisonment. [6 YRS]

■ **Qin Dong**, 30 years old, journalist at a Hunan local newspaper and an enthusiastic participant in the 1989 Democracy Movement. Qin was arrested soon after June 4 and accused of having "written reactionary articles." Sometime in 1990, he was tried by Changsha Intermediate Court on a charge of "counter-revolutionary propaganda and incitement" and sentenced to four years' imprisonment. (NB: "Qin Dong" is a pen-name; the journalist's real name is not known.) [4 YRS]

■ **Wang Changhong**, age unknown, a resident of Changsha City and participant in the 1989 Democracy Movement. In early 1990, he established an underground pro-democracy group, and was arrested shortly thereafter on accusations of leaking state secrets. He was tried by the Changsha Intermediate Court in late 1990 on a charge of "forming a counterrevolutionary group" and sentenced to five years' imprisonment. Several other people were arrested and tried in connection with the same case, but no details are known of how they were sentenced. (A different man named Wang Changhong was sentenced in Beijing to 15 years for espionage in January 1990). [5 YRS]

■ **Wu Jianwei**, in his twenties, originally a worker at the Xiangtan Electrical Machinery Plant. During the 1989 Democracy Movement, he allegedly "took part in creating disturbances" and "shouted reactionary slogans." These actions were later said by the authorities to have "led to serious consequences." Arrested soon after June 4, 1989, Wu was tried at the end of that year by the Yuetang District Court, Xiangtan Municipality, on unknown criminal charges and sentenced to 14 years' imprisonment. [14 YRS]

■ **Yan Xuewu**, 26 years old, originally a worker at the Xiangtan Municipal Motor Vehicle Parts Factory. During the 1989 Democracy Movement, he was arrested for alleged participation in the "Pingzheng Road Police Station Incident" (see above: case of Feng Ming.) He was tried soon after June 4, 1989 at the Yuhu District Court on a charge of "disturbing public order" and sentenced to five years' imprisonment. [5 YRS]

■ **Yu Zhijian**, teacher, 27 years old. (Two others involved in the same case are **Yu Dongyue**, the fine arts editor of the *Liuyang News*, and **Lu Decheng**, aged 28, a worker in the Liuyang Public Motorbus Company.) He originally taught in the Tantou Wan Primary School in Dahu Town, Liuyang County, Hunan. During the 1989 Democracy Movement, he gave speeches in Liuyang, Changsha, and other places. On May 19 he went to Beijing with Yu Dongyue and Lu Decheng, and on May 23 the three men defaced the large portrait of Mao Zedong in Tiananmen Square by throwing ink and paint-filled eggs at it. (By defacing the portrait, they meant to denounce "Maoism" and the "proletarian dictatorship.") He was arrested on the spot. On August 11 of the same year he was sentenced to life imprisonment by the Beijing City Intermediate Court on a charge of "counterrevolutionary sabotage and incitement." (Yu Dongyue received a sentence of 20 years and Lu Decheng a sentence of 16 years.) He was later sent back to be held in Hunan Provincial No. 3 Prison. In prison he was put in solitary confinement for six months.   [LIFE; 16, 20 YRS]

■ **Zhong Donglin**, 25 years old, originally a worker at a factory in Shaoyang Municipality. Allegedly a participant in the "May 19" incident in Shaoyang during which some vehicles were set on fire, Zhong was arrested in July 1989. Later that year, he was tried by the Shaoyang Intermediate Court on a charge of arson and sentenced to ten years' imprisonment.
[10 YRS]

■ **Zhou Zhirong**, teacher, 32 years old. Originally a teacher at Xiangtan No. 2 Middle School and a graduate of the Geography Department of Hunan Normal University. During the 1989 Democracy Movement, he gave speeches on several occasions at public gatherings. After June 4, he put on a black woolen coat with the character "sadness" written on the front and the character "mourning" written on the back and conducted a

lone sit-in with his eyes closed in front of the Xiangtan municipal government offices. Afterwards he made a speech to an audience of several tens of thousands. In September, 1989 he went of his own accord to the Public Security Department to "surrender" (he does not acknowledge it as "surrender", since he is not guilty of a crime). In December 1989, he was sentenced to seven years by the Xiangtan City Intermediate Court on a charge of "counterrevolutionary propaganda and incitement." The sentence was later changed to five years. When at Longxi Prison, he was accused of organizing "counterrevolutionary meetings," and on the evening of February 12, 1991 was secretly transferred to the Provincial No. 3 Prison (Lingling Prison).   [5 YRS]

Longxi Prison
(Provincial No. 6)

■ **Cai Weixing**, worker, 25 years old. Originally employed at the Changsha Power Machinery Factory. He participated in demonstrations during the 1989 Democracy Movement and was arrested on April 22. His crime, according to the authorities, was "stirring up the masses to beat, smash, and loot." In December 1989, he was sentenced to four years by the Changsha Eastern District Court.
[4 YRS]

■ **Chen Gang**, worker, 25 years old. His family lives in Liberation Village at the Xiangtan Electrical Machinery

126

Factory. After June 4, he was arrested because he called for justice for his younger brother Chen Ding, a student at the Changsha Railway Academy who had been sentenced to one year on a charge of "counter-revolutionary propaganda and incitement" because he had exhorted workers to strike. At first his crime was said to be "counterrevolutionary propaganda and incitement," but when charges were laid seven days after his arrest, the crime had been changed to "assembling a mob for beating, smashing, and looting." When the public trial was held the next day, the crime had been changed again to "hooliganism." He was sentenced to death by the Xiangtan Intermediate Court. In May 1990 the sentence was changed to death with a 2-year suspension. [SUSP. DEATH]

■ **Chen Guangliang**, 48 years old, private doctor in Shaoyang City. Some years earlier, he had allegedly joined Liu Chunan's "spy organization" (see below: **Liu Chunan**) and engaged in intelligence collection. During the 1989 Democracy Movement, together with Liu and others, he "went all over the place stirring up chaos in a vain attempt to create even more chaos," according to the authorities. He was arrested together with Liu Chunan in December, 1989. In March 1990 he was sentenced to seven years by the Yueyang City Intermediate Court on a charge of "counterrevolutionary espionage." [7 YRS]

■ **Deng XX** (nickname: "Shorty"), 23 years old, a resident of Changsha and a small private businessman. Arrested on the evening of April 22, 1989 in connection with the so-called "beating, smashing, looting incident" which occurred there earlier the same day. In mid-June, Deng was tried by the Changsha City East District Court on a charge of robbery and sentenced to four years' imprisonment. [4 YRS]

■ **Ding Longhua**, in his thirties, a member of the standing committee of the Hengyang Workers Autonomous Federation. During the 1989 Democracy Movement, he made public speeches and organized strikes among the workers. After June 4, 1989, Ding organized a city-wide general strike jointly with the Hengyang Students Autonomous Federation. Arrested shortly thereafter, in February 1990 he was tried by the Hengyang City Intermediate Court on a charge of "counterrevolutionary propaganda and incitement" and sentenced to six years' imprisonment. [6 YRS]

■ **He Zhaohui**, worker, 24 years old. Originally employed at the Changsha Railway Passenger Transport Section. His family lives in Chenjia Wan in Chenzhou, Hunan. During the 1989 Democracy Movement, he organized strikes by railroad workers and posted slogans, big-character posters, etc. He was also a member of the Standing Committee of the Changsha Workers' Autonomous Federation. He was in the first group of people arrested in June, 1989. In June 1990, he was sentenced to four years by the

Changsha Eastern District Court on a charge of "disturbing social order." The sentence was confirmed in a Chinese government response to an International Labor Organization inquiry. [4 YRS]

■ **Hu Nianyou**, 28 years old, a resident of Guangzhou, Guangdong Province. During the later stages of the 1989 Democracy Movement, Hu went to Changsha and contacted the Workers Autonomous Federation there, and made contingency plans to assist leading members of that organization and of the Students Autonomous Federation to escape from China. In the course of a taxi journey between Changsha and Zhuzhou one day, he and Yao Guisheng and other leading members of the workers federation got into an argument with the taxi driver. After June 4, when the government issued its order for all members of both the autonomous federations to register themselves with the authorities, the taxi driver denounced Hu and the others to the police. Hu was arrested in Zhuzhou shortly afterwards, and in October 1989 he was tried by the Changsha Intermediate Court on charges of "robbery and injury" and sentenced to life imprisonment. [LIFE]

■ **Li Xiaoping**, 28 years old, originally a worker at a factory in Shaoyang. Li participated in the Shaoyang Workers Autonomous federation during the 1989 Democracy Movement, serving as deputy-chief of the organization's picket squad. He took part in many student demonstrations and petition groups, and on May 20 he led a crowd of citizens who pushed their way into the municipal Party Committee and government offices. He was arrested sometime later the following month. In early 1990, he was tried by the Shaoyang Intermediate Court on charges of "hooliganism" and sentenced to six years' imprisonment. [6 YRS]

■ **Liao Zhengxiong**, 24 years old, originally ran a small private business in Changsha city. Arrested in connection with the April 22, 1989 "beating, smashing, looting incident" in Changsha. Liao was tried by the Changsha City South District Court in mid-June, 1989 on a charge of robbery and sentenced to three years' imprisonment. [3 YRS]

■ **Liu Chunan**, 65 years old. He was a retired teacher from Shaoyang City. Some years earlier, he allegedly had joined a Taiwanese spy organization. "During the 1989 Democracy Movement he stirred up the wind and lit fires [apparently only metaphorically (tr.)], created chaos, and radioed information about the chaos to a Taiwanese spy organization." He was arrested in December 1989. In March 1990 he was sentenced to 15 years by the Yueyang City Intermediate Court on a charge of "counterrevolutionary espionage." (see also entry on Chen Guangliang] [15 YRS]

■ **Liu Hui**, 21 years old, an unemployed resident of Changsha

128

city. Arrested on the evening of April 22, 1989 in connection with the so-called "beating, smashing, looting incident" which occurred there earlier on the same day. In mid-June, Liu was tried by the Changsha City East District Court on a charge of robbery and sentenced to five years' imprisonment. [5 YRS]

■ **Liu Jian**, worker, 26 years old. He originally worked in the Xiangtan Electrical Machinery Factory. After June 4, because of his righteous indignation, he took part in the burning of expensive furnishings in the home of the head of the factory's public security section. After this he was arrested. In August of the same year, he was sentenced to life imprisonment by the Xiangtan City Intermediate Court on a charge of "hooliganism." He was sent together with Chen Gang to Longxi Prison for labor reform. (Of the 12 persons who participated in this incident, eight are known to have been arrested; of those, six are known to have been sentenced. The circumstances of the four not known to have been arrested are unknown.) [LIFE]

■ **Liu Xin**, middle school student, 15 years old. He was in grade 9 *(chu san)* of middle school in Shaoyang City, Hunan. On May 19, 1989, he went out on the streets with his elder sister's husband (the sister's husband was sentenced to life imprisonment; his name is not known) to watch the masses burning an imported car. Liu allegedly supplied some matches. He was arrested in June 1989. In September 1989, he was sentenced to 15 years by the Shaoyang City Intermediate Court on a charge of "arson." Liu, who is illiterate and of frail health, denies having supplied any matches during the incident, and insists he was merely a spectator. [15 YRS]

■ **Liu Zhihua**, 21 years old, originally a worker at the Xiangtan Electrical Machinery factory, and a supporter of the 1989 student movement. Liu was arrested soon after June 4, 1989 in connection with a public protest against the chief of the public security department of the Xiangtan Electric Machinery Factory, and was accused of inciting anti-government speeches. During the protest, more than 1000 angry workers had gone to the public security chief's home and carried some of his furniture and electrical goods out into the street and set fire to them. At the end of June 1989, Liu was tried by the Xiangtan City Intermediate Court on a charge of "hooliganism" and sentenced to life imprisonment. [LIFE]

■ **Lü Zijing**, 30 years old, originally the Shenzhen special representative of Shaoyang's Light Industrial Department. During the 1989 Democracy Movement, he returned on numerous occasions to Shaoyang, allegedly to "spread rumors from Hong Kong and Taiwan." On the evening of May 19, he took part in a large demonstration march around Shaoyang City by students and citizens in protest against Li Peng's imposition of martial law. That evening there occurred a violent clash between police and demonstrators, in which "a police vehicle was burned and several officers were injured." Lü was arrested in early August, after returning to Shaoyang from Shenzhen, and was detained in Shaoyang Jail. In March 1990, he was charged with the crime of "hooliganism" and sentenced to 13 years' imprisonment. He has submitted numerous petitions to the higher authorities, but these have all been rejected.   [13 YRS]

■ **Peng Shi**, 21 or 22 years old, originally a worker at the Xiangtan Electrical Machinery Factory, and a supporter of the 1989 student movement. After June 4, 1989, Peng took part, together with Chen Gang, Liu Zhihua, Liu Xin and others, in a public protest against the chief of the public security department of the Xiangtan Electric Machinery Factory. During this incident, more than 1000 angry workers went to the public security chief's home and carried some of his furniture and electrical goods out into the street and set fire to them. Peng Shi was arrested shortly afterwards and was charged with having led and participated in an arson attack. At the end of June 1989, he was tried by the Xiangtan City Intermediate Court on a charge of "hooliganism" and sentenced to life imprisonment.   [LIFE]

■ **Wu Hepeng, Zhu Zhengying, Liu Jiye** and six others arrested at the same time are workers or residents of Shaoyang City. They were held in the Shaoyang City Jail. During the 1989 Democracy Movement they all actively took part in student demonstrations and meetings. On May 19 the famous "May 19th Incident" took place in Shaoyang. Two imported cars and a police car were burned and three cars were overturned. All nine were present at the time, but only Wu Hepeng took part in the burning of the cars. The other eight were just watching or shouting slogans or helping others. That evening over 10,000 people stormed the Shaoyang municipal government offices, demanding that the city government declare its opposition to the declaration of martial law in Beijing. These nine Democracy Movement activists all took part. After June 4, the public security bureau arrested them all on the basis of videotaped materials. In September 1989, they were sentenced by the Yueyang City Intermediate Court on charges of "arson," "hooliganism," and "counter-revolutionary propaganda and incitement." Wu Heping received a suspended death sentence, Zhu Zhengying received a sentence of life imprisonment, Liu Jiye received a sentence of five years, and the other six all received sentences of upwards of five years. They are all undergoing reform through labor at Longxi Prison.

                [SUSP. DEATH; LIFE - 5 YRS]

■ **Xiong Xiaohua**, technician, 25 years old. Originally employed at Xiangtan Power Machinery Factory. He is a graduate of the Xiangtan

130

Mechanization Special School. His family lives near the Xiangtan Municipal People's Congress Building. During the 1989 Democracy Movement, he organized a group of former classmates to print and distribute propaganda materials, and during the Xiangtan May 29 Incident shouted slogans. He was arrested in July 1989. In November he was sentenced to 13 years by the Xiangtan City Intermediate Court on a charge of "hooliganism." [13 YRS]

▪ **Yang Xiaogang**, worker, 35 years old. His family lives at the [residential quarters of the] Changsha Science [and Technology] Federation. His father is the chairman of the Federation. During the 1989 Democracy Movement, he disseminated news from "enemy [broadcasting] stations" and spread "rumors." He was arrested in May 1989 on a charge of "assembling the masses for beating, smashing, and looting." In September 1989 he was sentenced to 3 years by the Changsha Eastern District Court. In December he was sent to reform through labor at the Longxi Prison. [3 YRS]

▪ **Yao Guisheng**, worker, 26 years old. His family lives in Changsha's South Gate. During the 1989 Democracy Movement he joined the Changsha Workers' Autonomous Federation. After June 4, he was getting ready with two people from Guangzhou (noted elsewhere) to hire a taxi to save Workers' Autonomous Federation leaders and get them out of Changsha. He got into a fight with the driver. Later he was arrested in Zhuzhou. In October 1989, he was sentenced to 15 years by the Changsha Intermediate Court on a charge of "robbery" and "assault." When he was in labor reform at Longxi Prison, he suffered inhuman treatment. He is now mentally ill. [15 YRS]

▪ **Zhang Song**, 24 years old, a resident of Changsha. Zhang was involved in demonstrations during the early part of the 1989 Democracy Movement, and was arrested on charges of "beating, smashing and looting" on the evening of April 22. He was tried in June 1989 on charges of "robbery" and sentenced to five years' imprisonment. [5 YRS]

▪ **Zhang Feilong**, 18 years old, originally a worker at a Shaoyang City factory, and a participant in many protest demonstrations and marches during the 1989 Democracy Movement. On May 19, upon hearing the news of the declaration of martial law in Beijing, a large crowd of Shaoyang residents surged toward the city center and gathered in People's Square to protest against the Li Peng government's attempt to suppress the student movement. The mood of the crowd was very angry and emotional, and several vehicles were set on fire and burned, including a government official's sedan car, a police vehicle and two imported trucks. Zhang Feilong was arrested in mid-June and accused of having participated in the incident. At the end of June, he was tried by the Shaoyang City

Intermediate Court on a charge of arson and sentenced to six years' imprisonment. [6 YRS]

• **Zhong Hua**, 24 years old, originally a student in the class of 1986 in the environmental engineering department of Hunan University. During the 1989 Democracy Movement he took part in the school's autonomous student union and was the head of its Picket Squad. At the end of May he organized a lie-in by the students on the railway tracks at Changsha Station to block the trains and thereby demonstrate opposition to the government. After June 4, he continued his studies at the university, but fell under suspicion after the Romanian Revolution and in March 1990 was secretly arrested. In July 1990 he was sentenced to three years by the Changsha City Western District Court on a charge of "disrupting traffic order." (Another Hunan University student in the same case, Yao Wei, was held for three months and then released without criminal prosecution.) [3 YRS]

• **Zhou Wenjie**, in his twenties, originally a worker in a Changsha factory. Arrested in connection with the April 22, 1989 "beating, smashing, looting incident" in Changsha. In mid-June 1989 he was tried by the Changsha City South District Court on a charge of robbery and sentenced to four years' imprisonment. [4 YRS]

Changsha Prison

• **Chen Bing**, originally a student in the entering class of 1986 in the Hunan Academy of Finance and Economics. He was a radical activist during the 1989 Democracy Movement and advocated no compromise with the government. He opposed all dialogue and links with the government. Later he took part in activities of the Workers' Autonomous Federation and was an important figure in it. After June 4 he was on the run for several months, but was arrested at the end of the year and held in Cell 22 of Changsha No. 1 Jail. I heard that he was later accused of acts of violence. He has not yet been released. His current circumstances are unknown. [? YRS]

• **Hou Liang'an**, democratic personage, 35 years old. He was originally the head of the Changsha Soccer Fans' Association and a member of the Changsha branch of the [Chinese People's] Political Consultative Conference (CPPCC). During the 1989 Democracy Movement, he contributed over 2,000 *yuan* to the students in the name of the Soccer Fans' Association, and on several occasions organized deliveries of food by members to students engaged in sit-ins. He was arrested at the end of 1990 on a charge of "extortion." He was held in Changsha's No. 1 Jail. He was sentenced to six months. After he got out of prison, he showed dissatisfaction [with his arrest and

132

sentencing] and petitioned the central and provincial governments. He was later arrested again and accused of establishing an underground organization. He is still being held, but the details of the handling of his case are not known. His influence among the people of Changsha was fairly large. When his father died, he was still in prison. The masses held for his father the grandest mourning ceremony ever held in Changsha in the past several years. Several tens of thousands took part. This was said to be killing two birds with one stone (i.e. both mourning his father and expressing support for Hou in a politically safe way.) [? YRS]

■ **Huang Haizhou**, 28 years old, originally employed at the Hunan People's Publishing House. During the 1989 Democracy Movement he organized a Publishing Industry League in Support of the Students and was a leading figure in it. On several occasions he wrote "reactionary articles" and organized demonstrations by League members. After June 4, he angrily denounced the Li Peng regime, and was arrested. He has been held all along in the Changsha No. 1 Jail. His current circumstances are unknown. [? YRS]

■ **Liu Fuyuan**, 35 years old, originally a small private businessman in Changsha City. During the 1989 Democracy Movement, he organized local residents to donate money to the students. In addition, he participated in the hunger strike and sit-down protest outside the provincial

government offices. After June 4, 1989, he allegedly "spread rumors" that "several thousand people were killed by the troops in Beijing." He then went to Thailand for almost a year, but was arrested in Changsha in mid-1990 upon his return. He was held in Cell 13 of the Changsha No. 1 Jail. Liu went on hunger strike many times in prison to protest at his treatment, and later developed a serious gall-stones condition. He is currently still in detention, and it is not known whether he has yet been brought to trial and sentenced. [? YRS]

■ **Liu Yi**, worker, 24 years old. He was originally employed at the Changsha Power Machinery Factory. During the 1989 Democracy Movement he joined the Changsha Workers' Autonomous Federation and served as its treasurer. He was arrested in June, 1989 and held in Cell 11 of the Changsha No. 1 Jail, next door to Tang Boqiao. He was released in December and arrested again in August, 1990 on a charge of posting "counterrevolutionary slogans." He has not yet been brought to trial. [? YRS]

■ **Yi Yuxin**, 36 years old, originally a cadre at the printing factory of Central-South Industrial University. After the suppression of the 1989 Democracy Movement he continued to engage in underground propaganda activities, printing and distributing propaganda materials. He was exposed and arrested at the end of 1989 and held in the Changsha

No. 1 Jail. His current circumstances are unknown. [? YRS]

Jianxin Labor Reform Camp

- **Teacher Liu** (name unknown), 37 years old. He was originally a teacher in the politics department of Yiyang Teachers' College. During the 1989 Democracy Movement he made speeches in Yiyang, Changsha, and other places and published "reactionary articles." He is an intellectual who took up activity in the Democracy Movement in 1980. He was arrested after June 4. In early 1990 he was sentenced to seven years by the Yiyang City Intermediate Court. He is currently serving his sentence at Jianxin Farm in Yueyang, Hunan. [7 YRS]

Pingtang Labor Reform Camp

- **Tao Sen**, 38 years old, originally a worker at the Changsha City Engine Factory. In his youth he was a student in the Chinese department of Hunan Normal University. In 1980, he had been an important figure in the student movement and the People's Congress elections at the school. In 1981 he was sentenced to five years on a charge of "counterrevolutionary propaganda and incitement." Late in the 1989 student movement he was secretly arrested by the authorities and held in the Changsha No. 1 Prison. In 1990 he was sentenced to five (possibly four) years by the Changsha Eastern District Court on a

charge of "economic fraud." He was earlier in the Provincial No. 1 Prison. It is said that he has now been transferred to the Changsha Pingtang Labor Reform Camp. [4/5 YRS]

- **Zhang Xiong**, worker, 24 years old. He originally worked at the Changsha Woolen Mill. His family lives on Liu Zheng Street in Changsha. During the 1989 Democracy Movement, he organized demonstrations and strikes by the mill workers. He also participated in the special picket squad of the Changsha Workers' Autonomous Federation. He was arrested in June 1989 on a charge of harboring Zhou Yong, former head of the Changsha WAF. (Zhou was later acquitted. Zhang's younger brother was also arrested at the same time but later released.) In November he was sentenced to five years by the Changsha Eastern District Court on a charge of "robbery." His former girlfriend reported to the authorities that a small tape player of the Walkman type in his possession might have been obtained from "beating, smashing, and looting". In June 1990, he was sent to undergo reform through labor at the Changsha's Pingtang Labor Reform Camp. [5 YRS]

Other Places of Detention

- **Dong Qi, He Jianming, Dai Dingxiang**, and **Liang Chao**, all workers or residents in Changsha. During the 1989 Democracy Movement they organized the

134

citizenry in support of the students. On the evening of May 20, they heard that the army had entered the city and was heading for Dongfanghong Square. They hurried to the Changsha Railway Station to discuss countermeasures with student leaders. When the public security cadres saw that they were not students, they came up to grill them. A dispute ensued and they were taken away by the public security cadres. During their interrogation at the public security bureau, it was discovered that they were all carrying small knives. (This is common and not evidence of criminal intent.) They were then arrested on a charge of carrying weapons and held in Changsha's No. 1 Jail. In October 1989, they were sentenced respectively to five years, four years, three years and three years by the Changsha Eastern District Court on a charge of "assembling a crowd to create a disturbance." They are currently serving their sentences at a labor reform camp.   [5-3 YRS]

■ **Gao Shuxiang**, around 40 years old, was formerly a cadre in the Hengyang Petroleum Company, where his wife still works. He later became manager of a collective enterprise involved in supplying labor-personnel services, and through his success in running the firm he gained a reputation as a pioneering figure in the economic reforms in Hengyang City. During the 1989 Democracy Movement, Gao went to Beijing, and was first arrested there shortly after June 4. He was then, one

month later, either released and returned voluntarily to Hengyang, or was escorted back there in custody. In any event, he was placed under arrest upon his return and charged with embezzling public funds from the company he ran. (The authorities had reportedly tried to pin charges of economic crime on him several times before.) The real reason for the arrest, however, is that the authorities reportedly suspect Gao of involvement in the pro-democracy movement, possibly in connection with provision of funds to the movement. During his interrogation by one Yang Zhanglong, an investigator in the Hengyang South District Procuracy, Gao is said to have been hit so hard that he has lost his hearing in one ear. He has not been given medical treatment, and he remains in incommunicado detention at Wanjiawan Jail, despite repeated rejections of the procuracy's charges by the local court.   [? YRS]

■ **Tang Zhijian**, 31, formerly a worker at the Hengyang Railway Maintenance Department, was arrested in March 1991 by the Hengyang Jiangdong Railway Police for having assisted the brothers Li Lin and Li Zhi (see p.151 for details) to flee China on a train in July 1989. He reportedly confessed, and after one week was freed after paying a fine of 1000 *yuan*. He was then made to sign further confessions, however, and was rearrested in May 1991 and taken to the Baishazhou Detention Center, where he still remains. Tang told Li Zhi, who was held two cells away in the same detention center in mid-1991, that he was being pressured to say that he had received money for helping the Li brothers escape in July 1989. The ostensible charge against Tang is that he had "stolen a tape-recorder on a train."   [? YRS]

(NB: Case information on Gao Shuxiang and Tang Zhijian supplied by Li Lin.)

■ **Wang Luxiang**, in his thirties, originally a producer at Chinese Central Television, and involved in making the controversial television series "River Elegy" *(He Shang)*. During the 1989 Democracy Movement he co-signed, together with other prominent individuals, the "May 16th Declaration" in support of the student movement. He was arrested not long after June 4 and held in a Beijing detention center. During 1990, the authorities announced that several hundred people detained since June 1989 had been released, and they provided a few names including that of Wang Luxiang. According to reliable sources, however, Wang was subsequently rearrested and is reportedly now being held in a prison somewhere in Lianyuan City, Hunan.
[? YRS]

■ **Yang Liu**, 20 years old, a peasant from Xiangyin County in Yueyang Municipality. During the 1989 Democracy Movement, he was working in Changsha as a carpenter and allegedly took part in an incident in which "people burst into a government office." Arrested soon after June 4, he was tried at the end of 1989 by the South District Court of Changsha on common criminal charges and sentenced to four years' imprisonment. He is now serving his sentence at the Mijiang Tea Farm labor-reform camp in Chaling County.   [4 YRS]

Place of Imprisonment Unknown

■ **Bu Yunhui**, 24 years old, a peasant in Group 6 (a village subdivision) of Tiepuling village, Yiyang County. During the 1989 Democracy Movement he took part in several demonstrations in Yiyang City and Changsha. After June 4, when he was lying down on the railroad tracks in Changsha station, he was threatened by public security cadres and, becoming angry, shouted slogans. He was arrested on the spot and held in Changsha's No. 1 Jail. In early 1990 he was sentenced to three years by the Changsha Eastern District Court on a charge of "disrupting traffic order." (The story of his arrest was carried in June in the *Hunan Daily*.)
[3 YRS]

■ **Hao Mingzhao**, originally a student in the entering class of 1985 in the geology department of Central-South Industrial University. He was the chairman of its [official] student union. In 1988, because he objected to the government's campaign against "bourgeois liberalization," he resolutely went off to Mt. Emei, changed his name, and became a monk. He was later brought back by his school. In mid-April, during the early part of the 1989 Democracy Movement, he was active in many places and planned demonstrations. He was one of the chief organizers of the "May 4th Joint Demonstration." From the time of the founding of the Students' Autonomous Federation he was a member of its Standing Committee. After June 4, he took part in the planning of the June 8 "Mourning Meeting" and made a speech at it. After the provincial government issued its "Registration Order" for the Students' Autonomous Federation, he turned himself in to the Public Security Bureau. He was expelled from his school and shortly thereafter secretly arrested. He was released after several months. He has now disappeared. (Possibly he has been jailed again.) [? YRS]

■ **He Jian**, in his thirties, a resident of Hangzhou, Zhejiang Province, where he worked in a state-owned company. During the 1989 Democracy Movement, he allegedly travelled around between several large cities in China and "incited local people to create disturbances." After June 4, 1989, he was arrested in Changsha, Hunan Province, and detained there for several months before being transferred to a detention facility in his native Zhejiang Province. His current circumstances are not known. [? YRS]

■ **Jiang Zhiqiang**, 37 years old, from Shaoyang City but original place of work unknown. During the 1989 Democracy Movement he engaged in extensive "incitement" of the local populace, advocating such things as the parliamentary political system and promoting theories against dictatorship. He also posted up a large number of "counter-revolutionary articles," and was involved in secret liaison activities in preparation for the eventual founding of a so-called "counterrevolutionary organization." Jiang was arrested in August 1989 and held in Shaoyang Jail. In early 1990 he was tried by the Shaoyang Intermediate Court on charges of "counterrevolutionary propaganda and incitement" and sentenced to 13 years' imprisonment. He was held thereafter for a while in Longxi Prison, but has since been transferred to another prison (location unknown.) [13 YRS]

■ **Li Shaojun**, originally a student in the entering class of 1985 in the physics department of Hunan Normal University. On the eve of the student movement he threw himself into activities for democracy. During the Democracy Movement he served as vice head of the Finance Department of the Students' Autonomous Federation. He took part in all the important actions [of the students] and was one of the chief organizers of the June 8 "Mourning Meeting." In August 1989 he was arrested in Hengyang and held in Cell 23 of the Changsha No. 1 Jail. He was released in December but arrested again in April 1990 at his uncle's home in Guangzhou. He was sent back to Changsha and held for over 2 months before being educated and released.

He has since been arrested again.
[? YRS]

- **Li Wangyang**, 36 years old, originally a worker at a Shaoyang factory. During the 1989 Democracy Movement, he helped organize the Shaoyang Workers Autonomous Federation, and served as its chairman. On many occasions, he organized strikes and demonstrations among the workers and gave speeches in Shaoyang's People's Square. He was a very influential figure locally. After June 4, he organized the population to carry out strikes at work and to boycott marketplaces. Arrested at the end of June, he was tried in early 1990 by the Shaoyang City Intermediate Court on charges of "counterrevolutionary propaganda and incitement" and sentenced to 13 years' imprisonment. He first underwent reform through labor at Longxi Prison, but was later transferred to another, unknown location. [13 YRS]

- **Liu Xingqi**, originally a worker at the Changsha Light Bulb Factory, 24 years old. He was a member of the Changsha Workers' Autonomous Federation. On several occasions he organized strikes and meetings and he took part in organizing the June 8 mass mourning meeting *(zhuidao hui)*. He was arrested shortly thereafter and held in the Changsha No. 1 Jail. According to a recent report submitted by the Chinese government to the *ILO*, Liu was eventually given a three-year sentence. [3 YRS]

- **Luo Ziren**, 25 years old, from Guizhou Province. He was originally a temporary [contract] worker at the Changsha Cigarette Factory. During the 1989 Democracy Movement he was a member of the Picket Squad of the Students' Autonomous Federation. He was responsible for the safety of the persons and documents of leaders of the Students' Autonomous Federation. Shortly after June 4, he was arrested at his home town in Guizhou. He was freed in 1990. In November 1991 he was arrested a second time for posting "reactionary handbills." It is not known where he is now held.
[? YRS]

- **Wen Quanfu**, 38 years old, originally the general manager of the Hunan Province Overseas Chinese Enterprise Company. He supported the students during the 1989 Democracy Movement, but this was later characterized by the authorities as "having encouraged reactionary ideas" within the company and "creating an extremely bad influence among the masses." He was thoroughly investigated after June 4, 1989 and was arrested in September of the same year and held in Changsha No. 1 Jail, in Cell 10. In early 1990, he was transferred to Changsha County Detention Center. There are alleged to be "complex political aspects" to his case, and it is unclear what has happened to him since then. He has definitely not been released, however. [? YRS]

- **Xu Yue**, 25 years old, employed in

138

the maintenance workshop of the Tianjin Nail Factory. During the 1989 Democracy Movement he took part in activities in Beijing and later joined the support group from Hong Kong stationed in Beijing where he was responsible for logistics. On June 4, he fled to Guangzhou via Changsha, and on June 8 returned to Changsha to take part in the mourning ceremony organized by the Students' Autonomous Federation. He also took a large number of photographs, which the authorities said he took "with the intention of carrying out additional reactionary propaganda all over the place." On June 13 he was arrested in a hotel in Changsha and held in Changsha's No. 1 Jail. He was transferred out of there in August and his current circumstances are unknown. (The news of his arrest was carried in the *Hunan Daily* of June 17.)   [? YRS]

■ **Yang Rong, Wang Hong** and **Tang Yixin**, originally all young employees of the Hunan Province Electrical Battery Plant. During the 1989 Democracy Movement they were all active in the Changsha Workers Autonomous Federation, organizing many factory strikes. Arrested after June 4, they were held for several months at the Changsha No. 1 Jail and then released as innocent. After gaining their freedom, Yang Rong and the other two continued to carry out underground pro-democracy activities, including publishing a journal and a newspaper. In mid-April 1990, they were all rearrested after posting up a slogan banner in

public. The government accused them of engaging in counter-revolutionary propaganda activities and of suspected formation of a "counterrevolutionary organization." Their case is still under investigation, but the authorities have apparently instructed that they be given a long sentence.   [? YRS]

■ **Zeng Chaohui**, 22 years old, a student at Hengyang Industrial College, class of '87. During the 1989 Democracy Movement he helped organize the Hengyang Students Autonomous Federation and served as its chairman. He took part in organizing many street demonstrations and gatherings, and led a group of students in holding a sit-in protest outside the city government offices which lasted more than 10 days. Zeng was arrested in July the same year, and in early 1990 was tried by the Hengyang Intermediate Court on charges of "counterrevolutionary propaganda and incitement" and sentenced to three years' imprisonment. He was held for a while in Longxi Prison, but his present whereabouts are unclear. (Two other students from the Hengyang Industrial College were also arrested, but their names and present circumstances are not known.)   [3 YRS]

■ **Zheng Yaping**, originally a graduate student in the computer science department (Department No. 9) of the National Defense Science and Technology University. Before the 1989 Democracy Movement he had

139

established his own company and engaged in propaganda on democratic ideology. During the Democracy Movement he did not publicly participate in the Students' Autonomous Federation or other organizations. (Discipline is extremely strict at the school because it is the highest educational institution of the Commission on National Defense Science and Industry and is considered of a military nature.) After June 4, he was active for a while in the Students' Autonomous Federation. In the same year he was secretly detained by the military court. His subsequent circumstances are unknown. [? YRS]

■ **Zheng Yuhua**, teacher, 37 years old. He operated his own private school and had a fairly high understanding of political theory. During the 1989 Democracy Movement, he continually gave advice to the Standing Committee of Hunan's Students' Autonomous Federation. He also organized a think tank. He was arrested in July, 1989. At first he was held in Changsha's No. 1 Jail. Since his transfer out of there in December, his whereabouts are unknown. His family members also have no news of him. [? YRS]

■ **Zhou Peiqi**, 29 years old, graduate of Central-South Industrial University. He was originally a technician with the Central-South No. 5 Construction Company. Before the 1989 Democracy Movement he had already been involved in the work of publicizing democratic thinking and

had taken part in a secret organization. When the Democracy Movement began, he threw himself into it. After May 4, he was in charge of the cash raised by the "Provincial Provisional Committee of Schools of Higher Education." Toward the end of May, he withdrew from the activities of the student organizations. Together with Chen Le (*alias* Liu Zhongtao) and others, he planned to set up a "Democracy Movement Lecture Center," but this came to nothing because of the bloody suppression of the students on June 4. He was arrested at the end of July 1989, and has not yet been tried. His whereabouts are unknown. [? YRS]

Beijing

■ **Wu Yun**, 23 years old, a student in a Beijing institute of higher education. He was an active participant in the 1989 Democracy Movement. "From June 3 to June 4, he blocked military vehicles in Beijing, beat PLA soldiers with pop bottles, and stole an army helmet." On June 4, he fled to Guangzhou through Changsha, and on June 8 returned to Changsha to take part in a mourning ceremony organized by the Students' Autonomous Federation. On June 13 he was arrested in a hotel. "On his person at the time was a large quantity of reactionary handbills and propaganda materials." He was held in Changsha's No. 1 Jail and later transferred to Beijing. His current whereabouts are unknown. (News of his arrest was carried in the Hunan Daily of June

140

17.) [? YRS]

■ **Xiong Gang**, 23 years old. He was originally a student in the Chinese department of Yuncheng Teacher's College in Shanxi and comes from Hanshou County in Hunan. During the 1989 Democracy Movement he went to Beijing and became the general director of the Federation of Students in Higher Education from Outside Beijing. He went all over spreading reactionary speech. After June 4, he fled back home and was shortly afterwards arrested by the local public security bureau. After being held for several days in Changsha's No. 1 Jail, he was transferred to Beijing, where his circumstances remain unclear. (The report of his arrest was carried in the *Hunan Daily* in June, 1989.)

[? YRS]

Shanghai

■ **Li Dianyuan**, 26 years old. He was originally a graduate student at Shanghai's Communications University and a Standing Committee member of the Shanghai Students' Autonomous Federation. At the end of May 1989, he went to Changsha and got in touch with the Hunan Students' Autonomous Federation, assisted in its work, and helped organize the June 8th mourning ceremony in Changsha. He was later arrested at his home in Shaoyang. He was first held for several months in Changsha's No. 1 Jail and later transferred to Shanghai. In June 1990

he was sentenced to three years by the Shanghai Intermediate Court on a charge of "counterrevolutionary propaganda and incitement." He is currently serving his sentence.

[3 YRS]

B. Executed

■ **Chen XX**, age and occupation unknown, a resident of Lian County in Guangdong Province, was arrested together with Yao Guisheng and Hu Nianyou (see above) sometime in mid-June 1989. The three men were accused of having attempted to help WAF members escape from Changsha after the June 4 crackdown. Chen was tried by the Changsha Intermediate Court, in either September or October 1989, and sentenced to death. He was executed on December 26, 1989.

C. Died in Prison

■ **Li Maoqiu**, 53 years old, originally a high-level engineer at the Changsha Non-Ferrous Metals Design Academy. In 1986, he went off salary from his unit, while retaining his affiliation. Li began his own breeding business. By the beginning of 1989 he had almost 10,000,000 yuan in assets, including a chicken farm, a dog farm, a salted goods shop, and a roasted snack shop.

141

During the 1989 Democracy Movement he contributed 10,000 yuan to the students. He had no other words or acts. He had, however, "historical problems." His mother's father and his father-in-law had both been students at the Whampoa Military Academy and during the War of Liberation (*i.e.*, the 1945-49 civil war) had been high-ranking Guomindang generals. Not long after June 4, he was arrested. Because no excuse could be found, in mid-1990 he was accused of "economic crime" (fraud). [The government] said that 8,000,000 yuan of his assets had been obtained by fraud and confiscated it all. What with his sadness and anger, in November 1990 Li "exploded to death" in prison. The cause of his death is unclear; the authorities said that he died from a rupturing of the blood vessels of the heart.

D. Re-education through Labor

■ **Boss Wu** (name unknown), about 40, originally the owner of the Wusepan ("Five-Colored Dish") Restaurant on May 1st Road East. The restaurant is situated about 100 meters away from the main entrance to the provincial government offices. During the 1989 Democracy Movement Wu and his family were moved by the righteous actions of the students. They put up a sign which said, "Students eat free." From the time martial law was declared in

Beijing until they were forcibly closed down by the government in early June, they provided almost 60,000 yuan worth of free food to the students. Everyone in Changsha knew about it. After June 4, the government played a trick. On the one hand, they published a notice in the newspapers cancelling the restaurant's business license and wrote a criticism, making it look as if the sanction would only go that far. On the other hand, they secretly arrested Wu and held him for a long time. In 1990 he was sentenced to three years of re-education through labor by the Changsha Eastern District Public Security Bureau. He is currently held in the Changsha Xinkaipu Labor Re-education Center.   [3 YRS]

■ **Chen Tianlai,** 24 years old, unemployed, high school graduate, resident of Dongan County in Hunan. During the 1989 Democracy Movement he "infiltrated the ranks of the students" and took to the streets to create disturbances. Moreover, he spread "rumors" and "superstitions" all over the place. He was later arrested. In November 1989 he was sent to three years of re-education through labor by the Lingling Prefecture Public Security Bureau.   [3 YRS]

■ **Deng Liming,** worker, 29 years old. He originally worked in Shaoyang City, Hunan. During the 1989 Democracy Movement he "created disturbances" in Shaoyang City. He disseminated "reactionary speech," posted big-character posters, and stirred up the masses to "wreck." He

142

was arrested in July 1989, and in December was sent to 3 years of re-education through labor by the Shaoyang City Public Security Bureau. [3 YRS]

- **Deng Yuanguo**, 32 years old, originally a teacher at the Huaihua No. 1 Middle School. During the 1989 Democracy Movement he appealed publicly on behalf of the student cause, and was placed under "shelter and investigation" for a period after the June 4 suppression. In 1990, following the failure of the August 19 coup in the Soviet Union, Deng made statements calling for the Soviet Communist Party to step down from power, and was promptly arrested a second time. Soon afterwards, he was sentenced to two years' re-education through labor. [2 YRS]

- **Duan Ping**, 32 years old, from Yongzhou City, Hunan; originally a teacher in Qiyang No.1 Middle School. During the 1989 Democracy Movement he allegedly made secret link-ups and stirred up "disturbances." He was sent to two years of re-education through labor. He was released this year. Upon his release, Duan opened an electronic game parlor. After the failure of the coup in the Soviet Union, he was arrested again, apparently for having made statements welcoming the coup's failure. He was again sent to the Xinkaipu Labor Re-education Center for three years of re-education through labor. [2+3 YRS]

- **Fu Guangrong**, unemployed youth (*shehui qingnian*), 27 years old, resident of Zhuzhou City, Hunan. During the 1989 Democracy Movement he spread "rumors" all over the place and directed the students to "create disturbances." He also helped the students hide. After his activities were exposed he was arrested. In early 1990 he was sent to 3 years of re-education through labor by the Zhuzhou City Public Security Bureau. [3 YRS]

- **Hu Junda**, teacher, 35 years old. He was originally a lecturer at the Xiangtan Electrical Machinery Specialized School. During the 1989 Democracy Movement, he wrote "counterrevolutionary articles," encouraged the students to create disturbances, and stirred up the workers to go on strike. After June 4, he fled to Shenzhen, and swam into Hong Kong from Shekou. Later he returned voluntarily to the mainland and was arrested. After being locked up in the Xiangtan Jail for 10 months, he was sent to three years of re-education through labor by the Xiangtan City Public Security Bureau. [3 YRS]

- **Jiang Fengshan**, teacher, 37 years old. He originally taught in the philosophy department of Xiangtan University. During the 1989 Democracy Movement he gave public speeches on several occasions. He supported the students in "creating a disturbance" and after June 4 stirred up the workers to go on strike and block traffic. He was arrested in July

1989 and held in the Xiangtan City Jail. In early 1990 he was sent to three years of re-education through labor by the Xiangtan City Public Security Bureau.   [3 YRS]

▪ **Liu Jianwei**, 30 years old, originally a worker in the Vehicle Section of the Passenger Transport Department of Changsha's Railway Bureau. During the 1989 Democracy Movement he took part in the Changsha Workers' Autonomous Federation. In mid-June of 1989 he secretly got several leaders of the provincial Students' Autonomous Federation out of the city on trains. He was arrested in September 1989. In early 1990 he was sentenced to three years of re-education through labor by the Changsha Railway Public Security Bureau. He is being held in the Changsha City Xinkaipu Labor Re-education Center.)   [3 YRS]

▪ **Long Xiaohu**, 30 years old, cadre. He originally worked in the Hunan Provincial Foreign Affairs Office and is a graduate of People's University. (He is said to be the grandson of the Guomindang governor-general of Yunnan, Long Yun.) During the 1989 Democracy Movement he did liaison work for the students. After June 4, he left China legally. In May 1990 he returned to China at the invitation of the PRC Asian Games Committee in order to attend the opening ceremonies of the Asian Games, having received an invitation from the State Physical Education Commission. He was then accused of hiding four blank passports and

almost HK$100,000 for the purpose of "rescuing student leaders." He was arrested on the evening of June 3 and held at the public security branch station in Changsha's Eastern District. He was later secretly sent to 2 years of re-education through labor. [2 YRS]

▪ **Ma Heping**, 29 years old, unemployed youth, resident of Hengyang City. During the 1989 Democracy Movement he allegedly "created disturbances" in many places, "sneaked into" the ranks of the students to take part in demonstrations and "cursed" the public security authorities. He was arrested in June, 1989, and in November was sent to three years of re-education through labor by the Hengyang City Public Security Bureau.   [3 YRS]

▪ **Peng Liangkun**, 25 years old, worker. He originally worked in a large factory in Xiangxiang County, Hunan. During the 1989 Democracy Movement he went to many places, according to the authorities, to "stir up the wind and light a fire," wishing to "bring chaos" to society. He also disseminated news from "enemy stations" (i.e. VoA and BBC.) He was arrested after June 4, and in November 1989 was sent to three years of re-education through labor by the Xiangxiang County Public Security Bureau.   [3 YRS]

▪ **Qian Lizhu** (the surname may be incorrect,) 26 years old, peasant, resident of Yueyang City, Hunan. During the 1989 Democracy

144

Movement he came to the city allegedly to "create rumors," attacked the Party and the government, and took part in "making disturbances." He was arrested after June 4. In October 1989, he was sent to three years of re-education through labor by the Yueyang City Public Security Bureau. [3 YRS]

▪ **Wu Changgui**, worker, 30 years old. During the 1989 Democracy Movement he helped organize the Xiangtan Workers' Autonomous Federation and was a member of its Standing Committee. On several occasions he organized demonstrations, sit-ins, and strikes by the workers. He was arrested in June, 1989, and in early 1990 was sent to 3 years of re-education through labor by the Xiangtan City Public Security Bureau. [3 YRS]

▪ **Wu Wei, Deng Jun, Xiong Jianjun,** and **Fu Guanghui,** all workers in the Changde City Water Supply Plant, all between 20 and 30 years old. During the 1989 Democracy Movement they organized a "Workers' Autonomous Organization" and agitated for strikes, leading to a brief shutoff of Changde's water supply. All four were arrested after June 4. In November 1989 they were sent variously to two to three years of re-education through labor by the Changde City Public Security Bureau. They may now be free, but Asia Watch has no confirmation of their release. [2-3 YRS]

▪ **Xia Kuanqun,** cadre, 34 years old. He was originally employed in a government organ in Changde City. During the 1989 Democracy Movement he got the cadres in his unit to go out into the streets to support the students. He also donated several hundred *yuan* to the students. He was later ferreted out during investigations. In November, 1989 he was sent to three years of re-education through labor by the Changde City Public Security Bureau. [3 YRS]

▪ **Xiao Shenhe,** 32 years old, a peasant from Ningxiang County, Hunan. He was quite active in the 1989 Democracy Movement and on several occasions took part in demonstrations and meetings. He also planned to set up an "Anti-Corruption Action Group." He was arrested after June 4 and held in the Changsha County Jail. At the end of 1989 he was sent to three years of re-education through labor at the Changsha City Xinkaipu Labor Re-education Center. [3 YRS]

▪ **Zhong Minghui,** 30 years old, teacher. He originally taught in a middle school in Jinshi City, Changde Prefecture, Hunan. During the 1989 Democracy Movement he wrote "reactionary articles" and spread "rumors," creating a very "bad influence." He was detained after June 4, and at the end of 1989 was sent to three years of re-education through labor by the Jinshi City Public Security Bureau. [3 YRS]

145

E. Psychiatric Incarceration

- **Peng Yuzhang**, professor, over 70 years old. Originally a professor at Hunan University; since retired. During the 1989 Democracy Movement he firmly supported the students from beginning to end. He took part in sit-ins and hunger strikes and moved many of the masses. Arrested in June, 1989. Held in Cell 24 of Changsha No. 1 Jail. He protested and all day long would shout demands that he be released. As a result he was punished by being placed on the "shackle board" *(menbanliao)* for several months. (See Chapter 5 for explanation.) After this he was released on the grounds of "mental illness." (I heard this directly from a cadre.) Only after I got out of jail did I learn that he had been locked up in a "mental hospital." His family is not permitted to visit him.

- See also: **Tang Changye, Yao Guisheng, Zhou Min**, above.

F. Released

Confirmed Releases

Cai Feng, originally a student in the entering class of 1986 in Central-South Industrial University, possibly in the physics department. He attended the "Conference on the 70th Anniversary of the May 4 Movement" held by "China Youth" magazine. His speech was very radical. He advocated "immediately taking to the streets," before the student movement had broken out. During the Democracy Movement, he was active mainly in his school's autonomous student union. He was not arrested immediately after June 4, but only in early 1990, after a "counter-revolutionary student organization" in which he had participated was broken up [by the police]. He was released after being held for several months. (Some other important members received prison sentences; their cases are related elsewhere.)

Cai Jinxuan, originally a worker at the Changsha Textile Mill, 24 years old. He was a member of the Changsha Workers' Autonomous Federation. On several occasions he organized worker strikes and printed propaganda materials. On June 15 he surrendered and was held in the Changsha No. 1 Jail. He was released in April 1990.

Chen Ding, originally a student in the entering class of 1987 at the Changsha Railway Academy. He was an active participant in the 1989 Democracy Movement. After June 4, he returned home and with a group of his fellow students mobilized the workers at a local factory, the Xiangtan Electrical Machinery Factory (a large provincial factory with several tens of thousands of employees) to go on strike in opposition to the government's violence. His arm was broken by a group of factory security men led by the factory's security section chief. After this the factory's workers spontaneously went to the home of the security section chief, carried off expensive furnishings, and burned them. This was a very serious matter, and as a result he, his elder brother Chen Gang, and six or seven workers were arrested. Seven days later he was indicted by the Xiangtan City Intermediate [People's] Procuracy on a charge of "counter-revolutionary propaganda and incitement." Trial was held the next day and he was sentenced to one year. His elder brother Chen Gang received a death sentence, later changed to a suspended death sentence. The other workers (see entry under Peng Shi for names) received sentences ranging from five years to life. After being released in mid-1990, Chen Ding returned to his school to continue his studies. (After June 4, his school expelled over 20 students, but later allowed them all back.)

Chen Guangke, in his forties, originally a cadre at one of the Hunan daily newspaper offices. During the 1989 Democracy

147

Movement, he enthusiastically participated in protest activities and wrote several articles for his newspaper in support of the student movement. He was arrested after June 4, held for almost a year and then released in mid-1990.

Chen Guojin, 22 years old, originally a student at Loudi Teachers Training College. During the 1989 Democracy Movement, Chen was an office-holder in the college's Students Autonomous Federation, and organized many student demonstrations and petitioning activities. He also carried out liaison work with students from other provinces. After June 4, he convened a large mourning ceremony on the college campus for the dead of Beijing and gave a speech in which he condemned the communist government. He was arrested shortly afterwards, detained in Loudi Jail and then released in May 1990.

Chen Le (also known as Liu Zhongtao), originally an auditor in the history department at Hunan Normal University and a worker at the Hunan Rubber Factory. On the eve of the 1989 Democracy Movement he took part in the activities of the "Democracy Salon." On May 4, he took part in organizing the Provisional Committee with representatives of various schools. Later he was relieved of his post because his status was "not genuine" (i.e. he was not a real student.) After the Students' Autonomous Federation was established he served as special

assistant to the chairman. (The Students' Autonomous Federation had 2 chairmen; each had a special assistant.) After June 4, he planned the establishment of a "Democracy Movement Lecture Center." In August 1989, the affair was exposed and he was arrested and held in Cell 17 of the Changsha No. 1 Jail. While he in he went on a hunger strike. He was released in early 1990.

Chen Shuai, 26 years old, originally a worker at Changsha's No. 1 Xinhua Factory. After the Beijing students began their hunger strike, Chen and several other local workers organized the Changsha Workers Autonomous Federation. He early on served as spokesman for the federation and played a prominent role in its work. Subsequently, he withdrew from any public activities. He was arrested after June 4, and in 1990 was tried by the Changsha Intermediate Court on charges of "counterrevolutionary propaganda and incitement" and sentenced to two years' imprisonment. Now released.

Dai Shangqi, 35 years old, originally a teacher at Shaoyang Teachers Training College. He joined the 1989 Democracy Movement during its early stages, supporting the just protest actions of the students. After the students in Beijing began their hunger strike, Dai led a group of students to hold a sit-in before the main gate of the Shaoyang government offices. He also wrote a large number of so-called "reactionary articles" asserting that the government had forfeited its own legal status through its actions; these articles were provocative and very influential. He was arrested and imprisoned after June 4. In 1990 he was tried by the Shaoyang Intermediate Court on charges of "counterrevolutionary propaganda and incitement" and sentenced to three years of "criminal control" (guanzhi).

Deng Keming, temporary worker, 21 years old, Sichuanese. He formerly worked at the Changsha Measuring Instruments Factory and other units. During the 1989 Democracy Movement he was an active participant. He was arrested the evening of the April 22 Incident. In July of the same year he was sentenced to two years by the Changsha Eastern District [Basic-Level People's] Court on a charge of "beating, smashing, and looting." He was later sent to Longxi Prison to undergo labor reform. While laboring in prison, his wrist was broken. He has now been released. He currently wanders from place to place.

Fan Zhong, originally a student in the entering class of 1986 in Central-South Industrial University. Before the 1989 Democracy Movement he was the chairman of his school's student union and the vice chairman of the Hunan Students' Union (all government-approved posts). Midway through the student movement he began to change his views and participated in the founding of the Hunan Students' Autonomous Federation, taking a leading role.

After the reorganization of the Students' Autonomous Federation he was a general director along with Tang Boqiao. He was in charge of the sit-in in front of the provincial government offices. After June 4 he took part in organizing the June 8th mourning meeting, but because of traffic problems was unable to attend it. On June 29 he was arrested and held in Cell 6 of the Changsha No. 1 Jail. He suffered a great deal in prison, and on several occasions was manacled to the "shackle board" (menbanliao) for several months. He was also subject to electric shocks. He was later accused of the crime of "disrupting social order." He was held until December of 1991, when he was "exempted from criminal sanctions" and released by the Changsha City Western District Court.

Gong Yanming, 38 years old, originally general manager of the Yinhai Company, a subsidiary of Hunan Province General Import-Export Corporation. During the 1989 Democracy Movement, he supported the righteous protest actions of the students, and encouraged cadres and officials of his company to take to the streets and participate in protest demonstrations. Placed under investigation after June 4, he was arrested in July 1989. The authorities accused him of economic impropriety, and he was later charged with the crime of corruption. He was released as innocent, however, at the end of 1990. In May 1991, an extraordinary article appeared in China Youth Daily (Zhongguo Qingnian Bao) asserting that

149

"political scores" should not be settled against people under the guise of accusing them of "economic offenses," and appealing against the injustice done to Gong Yanming.

He Nan, 34 years old, originally a cadre in a Changsha municipal construction firm. During the 1989 Democracy Movement, according to the authorities, he "spread rumors all over the place," and later on he "reproduced and distributed videotapes which had been made overseas and smuggled into China concerning the June 4 incident." Arrested in late 1989, He Nan was "released on bail for medical treatment" in August 1990 after developing kidney stones.

Hu Hao, originally a student in the entering class of 1985 in Hunan Medical University. During the 1989 Democracy Movement he was a member of the Standing Committee of the Students' Autonomous Federation and director of its secretariat. He took part in all the important activities of the student movement. After June 4 he escaped to the countryside and was later arrested and held in Cell 19 of the Changsha No. 1 Jail. He was released in early 1990.

Hu Xuedong, 26 years old, originally a student at the Central-South Industrial University During the 1989 Democracy Movement, Hu was responsible for secret liaison work in the Hunan SAF. Although not investigated or detained for some time after the June 1989 crackdown, he was denounced and exposed by someone to the authorities in March 1990. He was subsequently arrested and detained in Changsha No. 1 Jail for nine months, before being released as innocent in December 1990.

Huang Zheng, 23 years old, originally a cadre at a provincial import-export corporation. Huang was arrested in early 1990 for alleged "political offenses" believed to be related to the pro-democracy movement (although details are not known), and detained in Changsha Municipal No.1 Jail. Sometime in 1991 he became ill and was "released on bail for medical treatment." His case has not yet been formally concluded, however, and like other pro-democracy prisoners allowed out for medical treatment he could be redetained and brought to trial at any time.

Lei Shaojun, teacher, 30 years old. He originally taught in the department of social sciences of Central-South Industrial University. He was "the most popular teacher in 1988" (CSIU). After the suppression of the 1989 Democracy Movement, Lei announced at a meeting at the school to mourn "the perished of Beijing" that he was resigning from the Party. He was arrested in December, 1989, and detained in secret. In June, 1990, he was sentenced to two years of control (*guanzhi*) by the Changsha Intermediate Court on a charge of "counterrevolutionary propaganda and incitement." Since then he has been at the school subject to control and supervision (jianguan).

Li Jie, 27, originally a worker in Dept. 416 of the Ministry of Aeronautics. He was a member of the Changsha Workers' Autonomous Federation. He took part in hunger strikes and sit-ins, and on several occasions organized demonstrations and strikes. After June 4 he surrendered and was held in the Changsha No. 1 Jail. He was released in June 1990.

Li Lin and Li Zhi, two brothers who were involved in the 1989 Democracy Movement in Hunan Province, were released from prison in Hengyang City on July 15, 1991 following a campaign of international pressure on their behalf. Both men had fled to Hong Kong in July 1989 to evade arrest; Li Lin found work there as a motor mechanic, and Li Zhi, his younger brother, worked in a cosmetics firm. In February 1991, however, following public statements by Chinese leaders guaranteeing safety for pro-democracy activists who had gone overseas, the two returned openly to China. They were arrested almost immediately and placed in incommunicado detention. Li Lin, formerly a steel worker in Hengyang City and a member of the Hengyang Workers Autonomous federation in May-June 1989, had publicly renounced his Party membership following the June 4 massacre in Beijing. Li Zhi, a rock musician, had

been active in the pro-democracy protests in Changsha, the provincial capital. Following news of their secret arrests in February 1991, President Jimmy Carter wrote to the Chinese leadership requesting the brothers' release, and Hong Kong businessman and human-rights activist John Kamm lobbied vigorously to the same end within the Chinese governmental and judicial elite. On July 9, 1991, the Lis were brought to trial and sentenced to five-and-one-half months' imprisonment - backdated to February 15, the date of their arrests - on charges of "illegally crossing the border." Shortly after their release, they were allowed to return to Hong Kong, and they now live in the United States. Li Lin's wife and young child remain in China.

Li Yuhua, 21 years old, originally a student in the Chinese department at Changde Teachers' College. During the 1989 Democracy Movement he was vice chairman of the Changde Autonomous Union of [Students in] Institutions of Higher Education. On several occasions he organized student demonstrations and he conducted a sit-in for almost 20 days in front of the municipal government offices. On June 5 he organized a traffic blockage by students and city residents, "creating great economic losses." He was arrested in July 1989. In January 1990 he was sentenced to two years' imprisonment by the Changde City Intermediate Court on a charge of "counterrevolutionary propaganda and incitement." In April he was sent to Longxi Prison in Hunan to serve his sentence. He has since been released.

Liu Mianli, 32 years old, originally a teacher at the Loudi Teachers Training College. During the 1989 Democracy Movement, Liu wrote so-called "reactionary articles," gave numerous public speeches and called upon the students to take a confrontational stance toward the government. In his view, this was the only way to "win back justice." Several days after June 4, he took to the streets with some students and shouted out slogans such as "Down with Li Peng," creating a great stir. Arrested in July 1989, he was held for more than two years in Loudi Jail. He was only recently released.

Liu Jianhua, originally a student in the entering class of 1985 in the agricultural machinery department of the Hunan Agricultural Academy. On the eve of the student movement he was admitted to the graduate school of Fudan University. During the 1989 Democracy Movement he was the chairman of his school's autonomous student union. On several occasions he organized demonstrations in which students from campuses several dozens of *li* away [one *li* is about a third of a mile] in the suburbs marched to the provincial government offices. He was fairly influential among students at his school. His school was responsible for arranging the set-up of the June 8 "Mourning Meeting." He was arrested in September 1989 and held in the

Changsha No. 1 Jail and the Changsha County Jail. He was released in early 1990 and at that time expelled from his school. His student status has since been restored (as is the case with all students expelled from that school).

Long Jianhua, originally a student in the entering class of 1986 in the foreign languages department of Hunan Normal University. He took part in the early activities of the Democracy Salon and was in the front line from start to finish in the 1989 Democracy Movement. He took an important part in the planning of the May 4 Joint Demonstration, the organization of the Joint Action Provisional Committee of [Hunan] Institutions of Higher Education, and the establishment of the Hunan Students' Autonomous Federation. He was also the vice chairman of the school's autonomous student union. He wrote a large number of posters, banners, and other propaganda materials. After June 4 he fled back to his native place in the Xiangxi Autonomous Prefecture, Hunan, and was arrested there in mid-September. He was held in Cell 3 of the Changsha No. 1 Jail and released as innocent in December 1990. He returned to his school to continue his studies. In March 1990 he was arrested again because he had made up his bed to look like a coffin and had hung form it a portrait of Hu Yaobang edged in black silk. After six months he was released after being educated. He is currently teaching at a middle school in a village in

Xiangxi.

Long Xianping, teacher (female), 35 years old. Originally a teacher at Xiangtan University. During the 1989 Democracy Movement she gave several speeches, and after June 4 she organized mourning activities by the students at Xiangtan University. She was arrested in September 1989 and sentenced to three years in mid-1990 by the Xiangtan City Intermediate Court on a charge of "counter-revolutionary propaganda and incitement." She was released after serving two years in Changsha Prison (this prison holds mostly female prisoners).

Lu Shengqun, 37 years old, originally a sales and marketing official at the Hunan Province Light Industrial Institute. He played no important political role during the 1989 Democracy Movement, but after June 4 he helped leaders of the Hunan SAF, including Tang Boqiao, escape to Guangzhou and other places; in addition, he found a place for Tang Boqiao to hide temporarily. He was arrested in early July 1989, and held for several months before being released.

Manager Zhang (given name not known), in his forties, originally a manager of the Changsha Municipal Heavy Machinery Plant. During the 1989 Democracy Movement, Zhang supported the idea of the students and workers staging strike activities, and, according to the authorities, he "on several occasions gave banquets for students and local residents who

had come to the factory to make disturbances, which had an extremely bad effect." Arrested soon after June 4, 1989, he was detained for several months and then released. He is presently unemployed.

Mao Genwei, 22 years old, occupation unknown. He was arrested at the end of 1990 on suspicion of involvement in the underground group allegedly set up by his brother, Mao Genhong (who was later sentenced to three years' imprisonment) and others, and was detained for almost a year at the Changsha No. 1 Jail. In mid-1991, he was put on trial but then exempted by the court from criminal punishment and released.

Mao Yongke (female), in her thirties, originally a teacher at a school in Xiangtan. A Christian, she was arrested sometime prior to the 1989 Democracy Movement (probably in 1987) on charges of "using religion as a cloak for political activities" (i.e. pro-democracy activities.) She was sentenced to four years' imprisonment and held in Changsha No. 1 Jail. She was recently released. She has a daughter and is currently unemployed.

Mo Lihua, teacher (female), 34 years old. Originally a teacher at Shaoyang Teacher's College in Hunan. During the 1989 Democracy Movement, she supported the student demonstrations. After June 4, she made a speech at a mass meeting in the Shaoyang People's Square. The

153

response was unprecedented in warmth; she became a well known figure in Shaoyang. On June 14, she was arrested. On December 24, she was sentenced to three years by the Shaoyang City Intermediate Court on a charge of "counterrevolutionary propaganda and incitement" and was sent to Changsha Prison. She has since been released.

Pan Mingdong, private businessman, 40 years old. He was formerly a boxing coach with the provincial Physical Education Commission. He has been in prison several times for political reasons. During the 1989 Democracy Movement, he expressed sympathy for the righteous actions of the students and gave them assistance. He was arrested in October 1989 on a charge of "drafting a declaration of Hunan self-government." He was later sent to two years of re-education through labor because the accusation lacked an evidentiary basis. He was held in Changsha's Xinkaipu Labor Re-education Center.

Tang Hua, in his thirties, originally the deputy editor of *Young People*, a magazine published by the Hunan Provincial Communist Youth League. During the 1989 Democracy Movement, he often sought out the student leaders and helped them to work out strategies for the movement. He was later accused by the authorities of "spreading rumors" during the movement "to attack the Party and government" and of having published articles in *Young People*

magazine "championing democracy and science." Arrested after June 4, 1989, he was held and investigated for more than one and a half years before eventually being released.

Tan Li, student (female), 20 years old. She was in the entering class of 1986 in the foreign languages department of Hunan Normal University. During the 1989 Democracy Movement, together with another female student named Zhang Xiaoyan, Tan Li wrote and posted on a wall on campus a big-character poster. Because the poster said "Down with the Communist Party," she was arrested in November 1989 after being thoroughly investigated. (Zhang was locked up in the same cell as Tan for almost a year before being excused from criminal sanction.) In June 1990 she was sentenced to one year by the Changsha Intermediate Court on a charge of "counter-revolutionary propaganda and incitement." She was then sent to Changsha Prison and has now been released.

Tan Liliang, teacher, 28 years old, graduate of the education department of Hunan Normal University. While at university he was named a "model 3-good student" four years in a row, a major honor when only one student per department is so named. (The "3 goods" are virtue, *(de)*, knowledge *(zhi)*, and physical fitness *(ti)*.) Tan taught at Hunan's Loudi Teachers' College. During the 1989 Democracy Movement he organized class boycotts and demonstrations by the students.

154

He also planned a "long-term resistance struggle" with Hunan Normal University students who had come to make link-ups. He was arrested in July, 1989. In early 1990, he was sentenced to two years by the Loudi Prefecture Intermediate Court on a charge of "counterrevolutionary propaganda and incitement." He was then sent to Longxi Prison for reform through labor, and has since been released.

Tang Boqiao, originally a student from the entering class of 1986 in the politics department at Hunan Normal University. On the eve of the 1989 Democracy Movement he helped organize a "Democracy Salon." Its activities were first within Hunan Normal University, but it later extended to all institutions of higher education in Changsha. After the outbreak of the 1989 student movement, he took part in late April in the Committee to Prepare Demonstrations and Meetings in Commemoration of the 70th Anniversary of the May 4 Movement. Its key members were from Hunan Normal University, Hunan University, and Central-South Industrial University. After the demonstration and rally on May 4, together with representatives from institutions of higher education in Changsha, he founded the Joint Action Provisional Committee of Hunan Institutions of Higher Education and served as provisional chairman. On May 14 he went to Beijing to observe and participate in the Beijing student movement,

returning on the evening of May 19. On May 22 he took part in the reorganization of the Students' Autonomous Federation and served as chairman. On May 24 he directed a city-wide protest demonstration. On May 28 he drafted a "pledge of loyalty" for the students. That evening the Students' Autonomous Federation declared that the students would return to their campuses and held a collective oath-taking ceremony. On June 8, Tang and Zhang Lixin presided over a meeting of 140,000 persons to mourn the dead of Beijing. On June 27, 28 and 29, Hunan television repeatedly broadcast a province-wide "wanted notice" for him. In the early morning of July 13, he was arrested in Jiangmen City in Guangdong. On July 17, 1990, he was tried by the Changsha City Intermediate Court and sentenced to three years' imprisonment, with subsequent deprivation of political rights for two years, on a charge of "counterrevolutionary propaganda and incitement." In November 1989, he was sent to Hunan's Longxi Prison to undergo reform through labor. He was paroled on February 12, 1991. He subsequently escaped abroad, and was admitted to the United States as a political refugee in April 1992.

Tang Zhibin, 30 years old, originally a reporter for *Young People*, the journal of the provincial Communist Youth League. During the 1989 Democracy Movement, he joined with the students to take part in demonstrations and sit-down protests. According to the authorities,

155

he was "appointed as an adviser" by the students and "his ideology went into reverse." Tang was arrested at the end of 1989, and released in mid-1990. He was sacked from his official post, however, and is now unemployed.

Wang Jisheng, student, 22 years old. He originally studied in the Yueyang Engineering Academy. During the 1989 Democracy Movement he organized the Yueyang Students' Autonomous Federation and served as a member of its Standing Committee. On several occasions he organized student street demonstrations. He also held a sit-in in front of the offices of the Yueyang city government. He was arrested in July, 1989. In November 1989, he was sentenced to one year by the Yueyang City Intermediate Court on a charge of "disrupting social order." In 1990, having served his sentence, he was released from Longxi Prison.

Wang Yongfa, 38 years old, teacher, university graduate. He originally taught at the No. 1 Middle School of Lanshan County, Lingling Prefecture, Hunan. During the 1989 Democracy Movement, he distributed handbills and organized street demonstrations by the students. He was arrested in October 1989. Although declared innocent and ordered to be freed by the court at his trial in February 1990, Wang was nonetheless sent to undergo two to three years' re-education through labor by the Lanshan County Public Security Bureau. (See Appendix VIII.D) He was freed in February 1992. [3 YRS]

Wei Nan, originally a self-financed student in the construction department of Hunan University. He had been expelled from Beijing University at the time of the 1987 student movement. During the 1989 Democracy Movement he was a leader of the Hunan University autonomous student union. In general he had relatively few public activities. He was arrested after June 4 and held in the Changsha No. 1 Jail. He was released in December and arrested again in April 1990. He was held almost three months. He is now a student at Changsha's Communications Academy.

Wu Fangli, 21 years old, originally a student at Hunan's Xiangtan University. He became actively involved in the student protest movement only during its later stages, becoming head of the college's student propaganda section. He often led the students in street demonstrations, giving speeches and going around factories urging the workers to go on strike. After June 4, Wu went to the Xiangtan Iron and Steel Plant and other large-scale local enterprises to provide accurate news about the massacre in Beijing and called upon the workers to stage a total strike. He was arrested later that month and held until the end 1989, when he was released.

Wu Xinghua, around 50 years old, originally a senior journalist at the

156

Hunan branch office of *Xinhua* (New China) News Agency. During the 1989 Democracy Movement, according to the authorities, "Wu wavered in his political stance, and after the suppression of the counter-revolutionary rebellion he came out in clear opposition to the Party, with extremely adverse consequences." He was secretly arrested in July 1989 and detained for over a year. Eventually he was "released on bail for medical treatment."

Xiao Feng, 55 years old, originally general manager of the Hunan Province General Import-Export Corporation. After June 4, 1989, he was accused of having "donated company funds to the students" during the Democracy Movement and of subsequently helping the students to conceal the money. He was suspended from work and placed under investigation, then arrested in early 1990. Later that year, he was released on bail for medical treatment, and is currently unemployed.

Xie Changfa, cadre, 35 years old. He formerly worked in succession at the Changsha Steel Factory, the Changsha city government, and as a township head in Liuyang County. During the 1989 Democracy Movement he gave speeches on several occasions in Liuyang, Ningxiang, Wangcheng, Changsha, and other places. One speech in particular that he delivered in Liuyang County had a "particularly bad influence." He was arrested in

July 1989 and held in Cell 13 of the Changsha No. 1 Jail. In early 1990 he was sent to two years of re-education through labor by the Changsha City Public Security Bureau.

Yang Chang, 24 years old, a resident of Guangzhou, Guangdong Province, and originally a student at Jinan University. During the 1989 Democracy Movement, he carried out liaison activities between the students autonomous associations of various colleges and universities in the interior of China, including those in Changsha. After June 4, 1989 he was extremely active in helping students escape arrest and go into hiding, and he was himself arrested in August that year. Held first in Guangzhou and then in Changsha, he was released in mid-1990.

Yi Gai, originally a student in the music department at Hunan Normal University. In 1988 he served as the head of the "Hunan Cultural Delegation to Express Greetings to the Laoshan Front Line." During the 1989 Democracy Movement he served as head of the Students' Autonomous Federation Liaison Department, being responsible for liaison between the autonomous student unions of the various schools. It was also known as the "Internal Liaison Department." He also wrote a "Report of an Investigation into the Hunan Student Movement." [*Hunan xueyun kaocha baogao*]: the title deliberately mimics the wording of Mao's famous "Report of an Investigation into the Hunan Peasant Movement."] When he was

157

serving in the army he had been jailed for eight months by a military court for political reasons. He was arrested after June 4 and held in the Changsha No. 1 Jail. This time, too, he was held for eight months. He was released in March 1990, and has now become an unemployed vagabond.

Yu Chaohui, originally a student in the entering class of 1985 in the department of general medicine of Hunan Medical University. He was a fairly frequent participant during the latter part of the 1989 Democracy Movement and served as special assistant to the chairman of the Students' Autonomous Federation. On June 14 he fled with Tang Boqiao and others to Guangzhou, Xinhui County [in Guangdong], and other places. He was later arrested after returning to Changsha and held in Cell 27 of the Changsha No. 1 Jail. Because he "informed and established merit" while in jail, he was released in November 1989.

Yue Weipeng, originally a student in the entering class of 1985 in the Chinese department of Hunan Hydraulic Power Normal University. He took part in the later period of the activities of the Democracy Salon, and on May 4 took part in the founding of the Provisional Committee. After the founding of the Students' Autonomous Federation he was a member of its Standing Committee. He was a leader of the student movement at his school. He was arrested after June 4 and held in Cell 24 of the Changsha No. 1 Jail.

He was released in December 1989 and assigned to be a teacher in a remote county in Gansu.

Zeng Ming, teacher, 29 years old. He originally taught at Central-South Industrial University. During the 1989 Democracy Movement, he connected up secretly with the students. After June 4, he angrily denounced the government and demanded that Li Peng be punished. He fell under government suspicion after the Romanian Revolution and was arrested in December 1989. In May 1990, he was sentenced to half a year by the Changsha Intermediate Court on a charge of "counter-revolutionary propaganda and incitement." He has already been released.

Zhang Lixin, 25 years old. He was originally a student at Beijing Normal University and the leader of a Beijing Students' Autonomous Federation propaganda team that went to the south. He was also a member of the Standing Committee of the Beijing Students' Autonomous Federation and the leader of its picket squad. In early June, 1989, he went from Shanghai to Changsha and got in touch with the Hunan Students' Autonomous Federation. On June 8, together with Tang Boqiao, a leader of the Hunan Students' Autonomous Federation, he presided over a mourning ceremony held at the Changsha Railway Station. At the end of June he was arrested at a friend's house in Xiangtan City. Also arrested at the same time were 3 Beijing

University students. He was held at the Changsha No. 1 Jail and later transferred to Beijing. In mid-1990 he was released.

Zhang Xiaoyan, 21 years old, originally a student in the foreign languages department of Hunan Normal University. During the 1989 Democracy Movement she took part in her department's (unofficial) Democratic Propaganda Team. On several occasions she gave speeches both on and off the campus. She also wrote "reactionary articles and wall posters." She was arrested in late 1989 and held in the Changsha No. 1 Prison. In June 1990 she was exempted from criminal sanctions on a charge of "counterrevolutionary propaganda and incitement" by the Changsha City Intermediate Court.

Zhou Liwu, teacher, 27 years old, graduate of the philosophy department of Xiangtan University. He taught at the Hunan No. 2 School of Light Industry. During the 1989 Democracy Movement he wrote "reactionary articles" and planned student demonstrations. He also made speeches in public attacking the Party and the government. He was arrested after June 4. In early 1990 he was sentenced to 2 years by the Changsha Intermediate Court on a charge of "counterrevolutionary propaganda and incitement" and was sent to Longxi Prison to undergo labor reform. He never admitted any guilt.

Zhou Shuilong, 39 years old, originally a worker at the Changsha North Station of the Changsha Branch of the Railway Bureau. During the 1989 Democracy Movement he joined the Changsha Workers' Autonomous Federation and served as vice head of the Picket Squad. On several occasions he organized demonstrations and strikes and posted up numerous handbills. He was arrested in mid-August 1989. At the end of 1989 he was sentenced to two years of re-education through labor by the Changsha Railway Public Security Bureau, and was sent to serve his sentence at the Changsha City Xinkaipu Labor Re-education Center.

Zhou Yong, 30 years old, originally a worker at the Changsha No. 2 Ventilator Equipment Plant. During the 1989 Democracy Movement, he organized the Changsha Workers Autonomous Federation and served as its chairman. He led the workers to carry out hunger strikes, sit-in protests and demonstration marches, and frequently sent members of the workers federation to visit the various factories in the city and mobilize workers to go on strike. During a several-day period after June 4, several dozen factories in the Changsha area came out on strike. "In the Changsha Cigarette Factory alone, this caused more than 1 million *yuan* in economic losses." Arrested in mid-June, 1989, Zhou was released in early 1990 for having "performed meritorious service."

Presumed Released after Prison Terms

He Bowei, 22 years old, a student in the Chinese department at Hunan Normal University. During the 1989 Democracy Movement he threw himself into the student movement and organized a Dare-to-Die squad at his school, swearing to carry the democracy movement through to the end. The Dare-to-Die squad later changed its name to the Blood Song squad, and He served as the squad leader. The activities of the Blood Song squad among the students had a very great influence. He was arrested in July 1989. In April 1990, he was sentenced to two years by the Changsha Western District [Basic-Level People's] Court on a charge of "disrupting social order."

Xiao Ming, teacher, 35 years old. He originally taught in the philosophy department of Xiangtan University. During the 1989 Democracy Movement, he wrote a great number of "reactionary articles" and stirred up the students to go out into the streets to demonstrate. After June 4 he also gave several speeches "viciously attacking the Party and the government" and was arrested in July. In mid-1990 he was sentenced to 2 years by the Xiangtan City Intermediate Court on a charge of "counterrevolutionary propaganda and incitement." He was later sent to labor reform at Yuanjiang Prison.

Zhang Xiaojun, teacher, 24 years old. He was formerly the Secretary of the Young Communist League at Taoyuan County Teacher's College in Hunan. During the 1989 Democracy Movement, he organized student demonstrations and turned a deaf ear to the government's calls to desist. He was arrested in October 1989. In April 1990, he was sentenced to 2 years by the Changde City Intermediate Court on a charge of "counterrevolutionary propaganda and incitement." In July he was sent to Longxi Prison for reform through labor.

Presumed Released after Re-education

Chen Xiangping, cadre, 31 years old. He originally worked in a department of the Changde city government in Hunan. During the 1989 Democracy Movement his steadfastness wavered, his thinking went over to the other side, and he showed dissatisfaction with the Party. He was later investigated. In November 1989 he was sent to two years of re-education through labor by the Changde City Public Security Bureau.

Fan Yuntie, peasant, 32 years old, resident of Jinshi City, Hunan. During the 1989 Democracy Movement he "infiltrated the ranks of the students" and created opportunities to "make disturbances." After June 4 he also hid "reactionary elements." In November 1989, after his arrest, he was sent to two years of re-education through labor by the

160

Jinshi City Public Security Bureau.

Liang Wang, worker, 24 years old. He was originally employed at the Changsha Woolen Mill. He was exceptionally active during the 1989 Democracy Movement. He made link-ups, stirred up strikes, and got together with the students to "make disturbances." He was later arrested, but because of lack of evidence was sent to two years of re-education through labor by the Changsha City Public Security Bureau.

Liu Wei, 25 years old, originally a worker at a Changsha municipal factory. During the 1989 Democracy Movement, he joined the Changsha Workers Autonomous Federation and served as a member of its picket squad. He participated in several protest demonstrations and marches, and encouraged the workers to go on strike. Arrested in July 1989, he was sent by the Changsha public security bureau in November of the same year to two years of re-education through labor.

Qing X, teacher, 30 years old, graduate of technical college. Originally taught at the No. 1 Middle School of Yongzhou City in Lingling, Hunan. With Zheng Jinhe (see below), he committed serious political errors during the 1989 Democracy Movement. He wrote "articles of counterrevolutionary propaganda" and organized street demonstrations by the students. He was arrested in September 1989. In December, he was sent to two years of re-education

through labor by the Yongzhou City Public Security Bureau.

Xiao Huidu, teacher, graduate of Hunan Normal University, 34 years old. He formerly taught at the No. 1 Middle School of Huaihua County, Hunan. During the 1989 Democracy Movement, he connected up with students from outside the area and helped the students "make chaos" [dongluan]. In addition, he wrote "reactionary slogans." In October 1989 he was arrested, and in early 1990 he was sent to 2 years of re-education through labor by the Huaihua City Public Security Bureau.

Xiong Xiangwen, worker, 28 years old. He was originally employed in a factory in Linli County. During the 1989 Democracy Movement he stirred up the workers to go on strike and disseminated all kinds of "rumors" and "reactionary speech," "trying to create chaos." He was arrested after June 4, and in November 1989 was sent to two and one-half years of re-education through labor by the Changde City Public Security Bureau.

Yan Fangbo, student, 17 years old. He formerly attended middle school in Longshan County in the Xiangxi Autonomous Prefecture, Hunan. During the 1989 Democracy Movement he organized street demonstrations by middle school students and had contacts with Hunan Normal University students who came to Longshan County to make link-ups. He also posted "reactionary slogans." He was arrested fairly late in

161

1989. In early 1990 he was sent to two years of re-education through labor by the Xiangxi Autonomous Prefecture Public Security Bureau.

Zhang Guohan, unemployed youth, 32 years old. He is a resident of Changsha and lives on Shuyuan Road in Changsha's Southern District. During the 1989 Democracy Movement he actively supported the students and collected money on their behalf. He also got the individual businessmen *(geti hu)* to make contributions to the students. After June 4 he continued to have contacts with student leaders. He was arrested in August, 1989. In December he was sent to two years of re-education through labor by the Changsha City Public Security Bureau.

Zhang Ronghe, student, 17 years old. He originally attended middle school in Linfeng County, Changde, Hunan. During the 1989 Democracy Movement he posted big-character posters and disseminated reactionary speech. He also organized street demonstrations by students. He was arrested after June 4. At the end of 1989 he was sent to two years of re-education through labor by the Linfeng County Public Security Bureau.

Zhao Muyu, teacher, 28 years old. He originally taught in the No. 1 Middle School of Jinshi City, Changde Prefecture, Hunan. During the 1989 Democracy Movement he stirred up the students to go out into the streets and demonstrate and wrote articles attacking the government. He was arrested after June 4 and in December 1989 was sent to two years of re-education through labor by the Jinshi City Public Security Bureau.

Zheng Jinhe, teacher, university graduate. He was formerly the Communist Youth League Committee Secretary at the No. 1 Middle School of Yongzhou City, Lingling Prefecture, Hunan. He was influential in his work with youth. During the 1989 Democracy Movement, he took the side of the students and secretly supported them in joint demonstrations with the Lingling Teacher's College. He was subsequently arrested, and in December 1989 was sent to two years of re-education through labor by the Yongzhou City Public Security Bureau on the grounds of "counter-revolutionary error."

***

162

APPENDIX II

GLOSSARY OF CHINESE NAMES
(WITH OCCUPATION + CURRENT STATUS)

NAME		OCCUPATION	STATUS
Ah Fang	阿 方	Worker	5 yrs
Boss Wu	吴老板	Businessman	3 yrs [*]
Bu Yunhui	卜云辉	Peasant	3 yrs
Cai Feng	蔡 峰	Student	X [R]
Cai Jinxuan	蔡瑾璇	Worker	X [R]
Cai Weixing	蔡卫星	Worker	4 yrs
Chen XX	陈某某	Worker	Executed
Chen Bing	陈 兵	Student	? yrs
Chen Ding	陈 锭	Student	1 yr [R]
Chen Gang	陈 钢	Worker	Death w/r
Chen Guangke	陈光科	Cadre	X [R]
Chen Guangliang	陈光亮	Doctor	7 yrs
Chen GuoJin	陈国金	Student	X [R]
Chen Le	陈 乐	Worker	X [R]
Chen Shuai	陈 帅	Worker	2 yrs [R]
Chen Tianlai	陈田莱	Unemployed	3 yrs [*]
Chen Xiangping	陈湘平	Cadre	2 yrs [*] [R]

KEY:
"yrs"	=	length of prison/labor-reform sentence
"yrs [*]"	=	length of re-education through labor sentence
"?"	=	length of sentence not known
"X"	=	detained without trial
"death w/r"	=	death sentence with two-year reprieve
"(F)"	=	female
"[R]"	=	released

163

Name	Chinese	Occupation	Sentence
Chen Yueming	陈月明	Businessman	3 yrs
Chen Zhixiang	陈志祥	Teacher	10 yrs
Cheng Cun	城 村	Journalist	5 yrs
Dai Dingxiang	戴定湘	Worker	3 yrs
Dai Shangqi	戴商起	Teacher	X [R]
Deng Jun	邓 军	Worker	2-3 yrs (?)
Deng Keming	邓克明	worker	2 yrs [R]
Deng Liming	邓黎明	Worker	3 yrs
Deng XX	邓某某	Businessman	4 yrs
Deng Yuanguo	邓园国	Teacher	2 yrs [*]
Ding Longhua	丁龙华	Worker	6 yrs
Dong Qi	董 奇	Worker	5 yrs
Duan Ping	段 平	Teacher	2 + 3 yrs [*]
Fan Yuntie	范运铁	Peasant	2 yrs [*] [R]
Fan Zhong	范 中	Student	X [R]
Feng Ming	冯 明	Worker	3 yrs
Fu Guanghui	付光辉	Worker	2-3 yrs [*]
Fu Guangrong	付光荣	Unemployed	3 yrs [*]
Fu Zhaoqin	付兆钦	Peasant	4 yrs
Gao Bingkun	高炳坤	Worker	4 yrs
Gong Songlin	龚松林	Worker	5 yrs
Gong Yanming	龚雁鸣	Manager	X [R]
Guo Yunqiao	郭云桥	Worker	Death w/r
Hao Mingzhao	郝铭钊	Student	? yrs
He Aoqiu	合敖秋	Professor	3 yrs
He Bowei	何博伟	Student	2 yrs [R]
He Jian	何 健	Worker	? yrs
He Jianming	何俭明	Worker	4 yrs
He Nan	何 南	Cadre	X [R]
He Zhaohui	何朝辉	Worker	4 yrs
Hou Liang'an	侯亮安	Intellectual	? yrs
Hu Hao	胡 浩	Student	X [R]
Hu Junda	胡俊达	Teacher	3 yrs [*]
Hu Min	胡 敏	Worker	15 yrs
Hu Nianyou	胡年有	Worker	Life
Wu Xinghua	吴兴华	Journalist	X [R]

164

Hu Xuedong	胡学栋	Student	X [R]
Huang Fan	黄 凡	Worker	7-15 yrs
Huang Haizhou	黄海舟	Journalist [?]	? yrs
Huang Lixin	黄立新	Worker	7-15 yrs
Huang Yaru	黄雅如	Professor	5 yrs
Huang Zheng	黄 峥	Cadre	X [R]
Huang Zhenghua	黄正华	Cadre	6 yrs
Jiang Congzheng	蒋从政	Worker	8 yrs
Jiang Fengshan	蒋风山	Teacher	3 yrs [*]
Jiang Zhiqiang	蒋志强	Worker	13 yrs
Lei Shaojun	雷少军	Professor	X [R]
Li Dianyuan	李典元	Student	3 yrs
Li Jian	李 枧	Worker	3 yrs
Li Jie	李 杰	Worker	X [R]
Li Maoqiu	李茂秋	Engineer	Died in prison
Li Shaojun	李少军	Student	? yrs
Li Wangyang	李旺阳	Worker	13 yrs
Li Weihong	李卫红	Worker	Death w/r
Li Xiaodong	李小东	Worker	13 yrs
Li Xiaoping	李小平	Worker	6 yrs
Li Xin	李 新	Worker	3 yrs
Li Yuhua	李玉华	Student	2 yrs [*]
Li Zimin	李子民	Businessman	15 yrs
Liang Chao	梁 超	Worker	3 yrs
Liang Jianguo	梁建国	Worker	6 yrs
Liang Wang	梁 王	Worker	2 yrs [*] [R]
Liao Zhengxiong	廖正雄	Businessman	3 yrs
Liao Zhijun	廖志军	Worker	18 yrs
Liu Chengwu	刘成武	Peasant	4 yrs
Liu Chunan	刘楚南	Teacher	15 yrs
Liu Fuyuan	刘福元	Businessman	? yrs
Liu Hui	刘 晖	Unemployed	5 yrs
Liu Jian	刘 健	Worker	Life
Liu Jian'an	刘建安	Teacher	18 yrs
Liu Jianhua	刘建华	Student	X [R]
Liu Jianwei	刘建伟	Worker	3 yrs

Liu Jiye	刘继业	Worker	5 yrs
Liu Mianli	刘面立	Teacher	X [R]
Liu Wei	刘伟	Worker	2 yrs [*] [R]
Liu Weiguo	刘伟国	Worker	7 yrs
Liu Weihong	刘卫红	Worker	4 yrs
Liu Xin	刘新	High-school student	15 yrs
Liu Xingqi	柳星期	Worker	X [R]
Liu Yi	柳毅	Worker	7 yrs
Liu Zhihua	刘志华	Worker	Life
Long Jianhua	龙遑华	Student	X [R]
Long Xianping	龙献萍	Teacher (F)	2-3 yrs [R]
Long Xiaohu	龙小虎	Cadre	2 yrs [*]
Lu Decheng	鲁德成	Worker	16 yrs
Lu Shengqun	卢胜群	Salesperson	X [R]
Lu Zhaixing	卢摘星	Worker	3 yrs
Lü Zijing	吕自晶	Cadre	13 yrs
Luo Ziren	罗子任	Worker	7 yrs
Ma Heping	马和平	Unemployed	3 yrs [*]
Manager Zhang	张厂长	Manager	X [R]
Mao Genhong	毛限红	Student	3 yrs
Mao Genwei	毛限卫	Worker	X [R]
Mao Yongke	毛永科	Teacher (F)	4 yrs [R]
Mao Yuejin	毛岳津	Worker	15 yrs
Mei Shi	梅实	Editor	4 yrs
Min Hexun	闵和迅	Teacher	3 yrs
Mo Lihua	莫莉花	Teacher (F)	3 yrs [R]
Pan Mingdong	潘明栋	Businessman	2 yrs [*] [R]
Pan Qiubao	潘秋宝	Worker	7-15 yrs
Peng Aiguo	彭爱国	Worker	6 yrs
Peng Liangkun	彭良坤	Worker	3 yrs [*]
Peng Shi	彭实	Worker	Life
Peng Yuzhang	彭玉璋	Professor	X [R]
Qian Lizhu	千里柱[?]	Peasant	3 yrs [*]
Qin Dong	秦冬	Journalist	4 yrs
Qin Hubao	秦护保	Cadre	10 yrs
Qing X	卿某	Teacher	2 yrs [*] [R]

Tan Li	潭 丽	Student (F)	1 yr [R]
Tan Liliang	谭力量	Teacher	2 yrs [R]
Tang Boqiao	唐柏桥	Student	3 yrs [R]
Tang Changye	唐长业	Worker	3 yrs
Tang Hua	唐 华	Editor	X [R]
Tang Yixin	汤一心	Worker	? yrs
Tang Zhibin	唐致彬	Journalist	X [R]
Tao Sen	陶 森	Worker	4-5 yrs
Teacher Liu	刘老师	Teacher	7 yrs
Teacher Mi	米老师	Teacher	3 yrs
Teacher X	某老师	Teacher	12 yrs
Wan Yuewang	万岳望	Worker	7-15 yrs
Wang Changhong	王长宏	Worker	5 yrs
Wang Changhuai	王长淮	Worker	3 yrs
Wang Hong	王 虹	Worker	? yrs
Wang Jisheng	王吉生	Student	1 yr [R]
Wang Luxiang	王鲁湘	TV producer	? yrs
Wang Rusheng	王如生	Worker	? yrs
Wang Yongfa	王勇法	Teacher	3 yrs [*] [R]
Wang Zhaobo	王兆波	Worker	7-15 yrs
Wei Nan	魏 楠	Student	X [R]
Wen Quanfu	文全福	Manager	? yrs
Wu Changgui	巫长贵	Worker	3 yrs [*]
Wu Fangli	吴芳丽	Student	X [R]
Wu Hepeng	吴鹤鹏	Worker	Death w/r
Wu Jianwei	伍建伟	Worker	14 yrs
Wu Tongfan	吴同凡	Worker	? yrs
Wu Wei	吴 伟	Worker	2-3 yrs [*]
Wu Weiguo	吴卫国	Cadre	5 yrs
Wu Yun	武 云	Student	? yrs
Xia Changchun	夏长春	Worker	15 yrs
Xia Kuanqun	夏宽群	Cadre	3 yrs [*]
Xiao Feng	肖 峰	Manager	X [R]
Xiao Huidu	肖会渡	Teacher	2 yrs [*] [R]
Xiao Ming	肖 明	Professor	2 yrs [R]
Xiao Shenhe	肖申和	Peasant	3 yrs [*]

167

Xie Changfa	谢长发	Cadre	2 yrs [*] [R]
Xie Yang	谢 阳	Cadre	3 yrs
Xiong Gang	熊 刚	Student	? yrs
Xiong JianJun	熊建军	Worker	2-3 yrs [*]
Xiong Xiangwen	熊湘文	Worker	2.5 yrs [*] [R]
Xiong Xiaohua	熊晓华	Technician	13 yrs
Xu Yue	徐 岳	Worker	? yrs
Yan Fangbo	严方波	Student	2 yrs [*] [R]
Yan Xuewu	言学武	Worker	5 yrs
Yang Chang	杨 昌	Worker	X [R]
Yang Liu	杨 柳	Peasant	4 yrs
Yang Rong	杨 荣	Worker	? yrs
Yang Shaoyue	杨绍岳	Cadre	5 yrs
Yang Xiaogang	杨晓刚	Worker	3 yrs
Yang Xiong	杨 雄	Worker	3 yrs
Yao Guisheng	姚桂生	Worker	15 yrs
Yao Wei	姚 为	Student	X [R]
Yi Gai	易 改	Student	X [R]
Yi Yuxin	易于新	Cadre	? yrs
Yin Zhenggao	殷正高	Official	Sacked
Yu Chaohui	虞朝晖	Student	X [R]
Yu Dongyue	俞东岳	Editor	20 yrs
Yu ZhiJian	余志坚	Teacher	Life
Yuan Shuzhu	袁树柱	Worker	7-15 yrs
Yue Weipeng	岳维鹏	Student	X [R]
Zeng Chaohui	曾朝晖	Student	3 yrs
Zeng Ming	曾 明	Professor	8.5 yrs [R]
Zhang Guohan	张国汉	Unemployed	2 yrs [*] [R]
Zhang Jie	张 捷	Scientist	5 yrs
Zhang Jingsheng	张京生	Worker	13 yrs
Zhang Jizhong	张继忠	Journalist	3 yrs
Zhang Lixin	张立新	Student	X [R]
Zhang Ronghe	张荣和	Student	2 yrs [*] [R]
Zhang Song	张 硕	Worker	5 yrs
Zhang XiaoJun	张晓军	Professor	2 yrs [R]
Zhang Xiaoyan	张小燕	Student (F)	X [R]

Zhang Xiong	张 雄	Worker	5 yrs
Zhang Xudong	张旭东	Worker	4 yrs
Zhang Fei long	张飞龙	Worker	6 yrs
Zhao Muyu	赵牧羽	Teacher	2 yrs [*] [R]
Zhao Weiguo	赵卫国	Businessman	4 yrs
Zheng Jinhe	郑进和	Teacher	2 yrs [*] [R]
Zheng Yaping	郑亚平	Student	? yrs
Zheng Yuhua	郑玉华	Teacher	X yrs
Zhong Donglin	钟冬林	[?]	[?]
Zhong Hua	钟 华	Student	3 yrs
Zhong Minghui	钟明辉	Teacher	3 yrs [*]
Zhou Liwu	周礼武	Teacher	2 yrs [R]
Zhou Min	周 敏	Worker	6 yrs
Zhou Peiqi	周沛旗	Technician	? yrs
Zhou Shuilong	周水龙	Worker	2 yrs [*] [R]
Zhou Wenjie	周文杰	Worker	4 yrs
Zhou Yong	周 勇	Worker	X [R]
Zhou Zhirong	周志荣	Teacher	5 yrs
Zhu Fangming	朱芳鸣	Worker	Life
Zhu Zhengying	朱正英	Worker	Life
Gao Shuxiang	高树祥	Businessman	X
Li Lin	李 林	Worker	5.5 mths. [R]
Li Zhi	李 智	Musician	5.5 mths. [R]
Tang Zhijian	汤之健	Worker	X

APPENDIX III

Lists of Key Members of the Hunan SAF and Hunan WAF

A. Hunan Students' Autonomous Federation

Name	Institution	Position in SAF	Current status
Chen Kehao	Hunan University	Vice General Director of Sit-Ins	Expelled from university
Chen Le (Liu Zhongtao)	Hunan Normal University	Special assistant to chairman	Detained several months; now released
Fan Zhong	Central-South Industrial University	Co-chairman; General Director of Sit-Ins	Detained 1½ years; now released
Hao Mingzhao	Central-South Industrial University	Standing Committee member	Arrested in 1990; current status unknown
He Bowei	Hunan Normal University	Head of school Dare-to-Die Squad	Sentenced to 2 years
Hu Hao	Hunan Medical University	Standing Committee member	Detained several months; now released

Li Shaojun	Hunan Normal University	Head of Finance Department	Detained 3 times; still in detention
Li Wei	Hunan University	Vice Chairman of school Autonomous Student Union (ASU)	Punished administratively by university
Li Zheng	Hunan College of Finance and Economics	Standing Committee member	Expelled from university
Liu Chaohui	Hunan Normal University	Representative of school ASU	Punished administratively by university
Liu Jianhua	Hunan University of Agriculture	Chairman of school ASU	Detained for several months; now released
Liu Wei	Changsha Railway College	Standing Committee member	In France
Long Jianhua	Hunan Normal University	Standing Committee member	Detained twice for a total of 7 months
Lu Siqing	Central-South Industrial University	Standing Committee member	Surrendered; expelled from university
Shen Yong	Hunan University	Representative of school ASU	Punished administratively by university
Shui Li	Hunan University	Standing Committee member	Punished administratively by university

171

Tang Bing	Hunan College of Finance and Economics	Head of school picket squad	Sentenced to unknown term
Tang Boqiao	Hunan Normal University	Chairman	Sentenced to 3 years, then paroled; escaped and now in U.S.
Wei Nan	Hunan University	Vice Chairman of school ASU	Detained twice for a total of several months; released
Xia Siqing	Hunan Normal University	Representative of school ASU	Punished administratively by university
Yi Gai	Hunan Normal University	Head of Liaison Department	Detained; current status unknown
Yu Chaohui	Hunan Medical University	Special assistant	Detained several months; released
Yuan Ningwu	Central-South Industrial University	Head of Propaganda Department	Punished administratively by university
Yue Weipeng	Hunan Hydraulic Normal University	Standing Committee member	Detained 5 months; now released
Zhang Guangsheng	Central-South Industrial University	Head of Planning Department	Punished administratively by university
Zheng Yan	Hunan Normal University	Representative of school ASU	Punished administratively by university

172

Zhong Hua	Hunan University	Head of school picket squad	Sentenced to 3 years
Zhu Jianwen	Hunan Normal University	Standing Committee member	Punished administratively by university

B. Workers Autonomous Federations

Name	Work Unit	Role in WAF	Current status
Changsha WAF:			
Cai Jinxuan	Changsha Textile Mill	Standing Committee member	Held for eight months; now released
Chen Bing	Student, Hunan College of Finance and Economics	Activist	Still in detention; not known if tried
Chen Shuai	Changsha No.1 Xinhua Factory	Spokesman	Sentenced to 2 years; now released
Chen XX	Resident of Lian County, Guangdong Province [?]	Assisted escape network	Sentenced to death and executed
He Zhaohui	Changsha Railway Passenger Transport Section	Vice Chairman	Sentenced to 4 years
Hu Nianyou	Resident of Lian County, Guangdong Province [?]	Assisted escape network	Sentenced to life imprisonment
Li Jian	Dongyuan Engine Parts Factory	General director	Sentenced to unknown term
Li Jie	Dept. 416, Ministry of Aeronautics	Standing Committee member	Held for one year, now released

174

Li Xin	Resigned from original unit	Vice Head of Picket Squad	Sentenced to 3 years
Liu Jianwei	Passenger Vehicle Section, Changsha Railway Bureau	Activist	Sentenced to 3 years' labor re-education
Liu Wei	A Changsha factory	Picket	2 years' labor re-education; now released
Liu Xingqi	Changsha Light Bulb Factory	Standing Committee member	Held for six months, then released
Liu Yi	Changsha Engine Factory	Head of Finance Department	Sentenced to unknown term
Lu Zhaixing	Changsha Embroidery Factory	Standing Committee member	Sentenced to 3 years
Pan Mingdong	Private businessman (restaurant owner)	Standing Committee member	Sentenced to 2 years of re-education through labor
Peng Yuzhang	Hunan University teacher	Advisor	Sent to mental hospital
Tang Yixin	Hunan Electrical Battery Plant	Activist	Not yet sentenced
Wang Changhuai	Changsha Automobile Factory	Standing Committee member	Sentenced to 3 years
Wang Hong	Hunan Electrical Battery Plant	Activist	Not yet sentenced

Wu Tongfan	Resigned from original unit	Advisor	Sentenced to unknown term
Yang Rong	Hunan Electrical Battery Plant	Activist	Not yet sentenced
Yao Guisheng	Hunan Woolen Mill (detached from unit at no salary)	Head of Picket Squad	Sentenced to 15 years
Zhang Jingsheng	Changsha Shaoguang Machinery Factory	Standing Committee member	Sentenced to 13 years
Zhang Xiong	Hunan Woolen Mill	Head of Special Picket Squad	Sentenced to 5 years
Zhang Xudong	Changsha Hongqiang Electrical Machine Factory	Vice Chairman	Sentenced to 4 years
Zheng Yuhua	Detached from unit at no salary	Advisor	Still in detention; not yet sentenced
Zhou Min	Changsha Non-Ferrous Metals Design Academy	Vice Chairman	Sentenced to 6 years
Zhou Shuilong	Changsha North Station, Changsha Railway Bureau	Vice Head of Picket Squad	2 years' labor-re-education; now released
Zhou Yong	Changsha No.2 Fan Factory	Chairman	Released

Shaoyang WAF:

Li Wangyang	Shaoyang factory	Chairman, Shaoyang WAF	Sentenced to 13 years
Li Xiaodong	Zhongnan Pharmaceutical Plant, Shaoyang City	Activist	Sentenced to 13 years
Li Xiaoping	Shaoyang factory	Vice Head of Picket Squad	Sentenced to 6 years

Xiangtan WAF:

| Wu Changgui | Xiangtan factory | Standing Committee member | Sentenced to 3 years' labor re-education |

Hengyang WAF:

Ding Longhua	Hengyang factory	Standing Committee member	Sentenced to 6 years
Li Lin	Hengyang steel worker	Activist	Escaped, then returned to China and was arrested; freed July 1991, lives in USA
Zhu Fangming	Hengyang Flour Factory	Vice Chairman	Sentenced to life imprisonment

Yueyang WAF:

NB: Nine members of the Yueyang WAF are known to have been arrested and heavily sentenced, but none of the factory affiliations or WAF positions of the nine are known. Their names and prison terms (most of which are only approximately known) are as follows:

Guo Yunqiao:	death with reprieve	**Hu Min**:	15 years
Huang Fan:	7-15 years	**Huang Lixin**:	7-15 years
Mao Yuejin:	15 years	**Pan Qiubao**:	7-15 years
Wan Yuewang:	7-15 years	**Wang Zhaobo**:	7-15 years
Yuan Shuzhu:	7-15 years		

APPENDIX IV

Tang Boqiao: From Student Leader to "Counterrevolutionary"[37]

Flight from Changsha

On June 4, 1989, the sound of gunfire on Tiananmen Square shattered the nation's illusions. As the terrifying crackdown unfolded, the students fled in fear and trepidation in all directions. After co-hosting the "Oath-Taking Rally in Memory of the Martyrs in Beijing" in Changsha,[38] I myself escaped to Guangdong Province on June 14 and went into hiding in Guangzhou, Xinhui, Foshan, and Jiangmen. Thanks to the generous help and protection I received from many different people, I remained safe for many days.

As the head of Hunan's student pro-democracy movement, however, I felt I could not put my own safety first and so gave up any thoughts of escaping abroad. On July 4, I decided to "enter the jaws of the tiger" and go back to Hunan in order to distribute among other pro-democracy fugitives some of the donations that I had received from people overseas to help me escape. The remainder I would keep behind as a reserve fund for the future democratic movement.

I discovered, however, there was no way I could enter Changsha as copies of an arrest warrant for me had been posted up on the entrances and exits of all the railway stations in Hunan Province, and passengers getting on and off the trains all had to go through security

---

[37] An earlier version of this autobiographical account appeared in the Hong Kong monthly *Kaifang* in October 1991, pp. 60-65.

[38] Zhang Lixin, head of the Beijing Students Autonomous Federation delegation touring southern China, and I hosted this rally, which was held at Changsha railway station on June 8 with 140,000 people (including overseas media) in attendance.

checks. So I left the train at Hengyang, one stop before Changsha, and got on another train back to Guangzhou. During the journey (in an incident that was as suspense-filled as the movies), I just managed to evade detection by public security officers who came on to the train to carry out a search.

Upon arrival back in Guangzhou, I went to Xinhui that night and hid out in the home of a peasant family (relatives of a friend of mine), not leaving the house for several days. At about 11 p.m. on July 11, just as I was going upstairs to sleep, I suddenly heard knocks on the door and a middle-aged man came in and said something to my host in a loud, gutteral voice before quickly leaving. Running up the stairs, my host told me in poor Mandarin: "Pack your stuff and leave here with me now. That village cadre just told me that the public security men are here to get you." My heart missed a beat and I had a premonition that I would not be able to get away this time. I hardly remember anything of our departure from the village apart from the ghostly howls and barking of dogs. That night, the peasant, whom I will never forget for the rest of my life, and I trudged along in the wilds, breathless with anxiety, for nearly 40 kilometers.

The trap closes

The next day, we took refuge at someone's home in Jiangmen City. The nerve-wracking escape of the previous night had exhausted me and I fell into a deep sleep right there in the sitting room. In the early hours of July 13, I was suddenly awakened by the clatter of loud knocking on the front foor, and before I had time to react, a swarm of heavily armed public security personnel and officers of the People's Armed Police swarmed into the room like a pack of mad dogs. "This is Tang Boqiao," snapped one of them. I made a futile attempt to defend myself, asking "Why are you arresting me?", but the next thing I felt was a series of hard objects clamping down on my throat, and my whole body, upside down, being hoisted into the air. Fists and cudgels (probably electric batons) rained down on me, and I felt as if I was dying.

As they pushed me out of the house and I looked around me, I felt a sense of deep and tragic solemnity welling up within me. There before me stood a vast array of over 100 military police, all armed to the teeth, and a row of police cars glowing with a steely, cold light. The

180

police were all scurrying around as if in some rapid-deployment military exercise against an enemy army - and at that moment, I realized with great clarity my own value and the strength of democracy. We had made the butchers of the people frightened!

I was taken to the Jiangmen City No. 1 Jail in Guangdong Province, where, for the first few days, I came down with a high fever of 39.6°C. My internal organs had been badly injured in the beating and I could neither eat nor sleep for days and I passed a lot of blood in my stool. (I have still not fully recovered even today.) Because I was a "criminal awaiting trial," the cadres informed me that I was not entitled to any medical expenses and so no treatment could be given to me - not even medicine. I could do nothing but clench my teeth and try to get through the suffering on my own. My fellow inmates were outraged at this injustice.

A few days later, a four-member security team set up specially by the Hunan and Changsha public security departments came to Jiangmen and took me back to Changsha. En route, I was kept in the Guangdong Provincial No. 1 Jail in Guangzhou City for a week, and again I was given no medical treatment.

On the train journey back to Changsha, two incidents impressed me in particular. One was that the security forces lied to the train crew, telling them that we were all cadres from the Changsha municipal Party committee. We were put in the train's special soft-berth compartment, a privilege normally enjoyed only by cadres at or above the level of provincial bureau chief. My police escorts warned me not to greet any acquaintances on the way and to report to them if I happened to see any.

The second such incident was that upon our arrival at Changsha Station, a whole crowd of pot-bellied government VIPs were there "cordially awaiting" us. No one was allowed to watch us or take pictures, and some Hong Kong businessmen from the same train who tried to do so were roughly pushed aside. A Toyota Corolla Supersaloon raced up to the platform, and in a matter of minutes, I was bundled into the car and driven out of the station through an underground passageway direct to the Changsha City No. 1 Jail.

It was clear from these two incidents just how nervous the

181

security forces accompanying me felt about their own role, and how much fear they had toward the general public. I also got some insight into the overall efficiency of their repressive operations. All the high-ranking government cadres turned out to watch me being sent into custody, as if to make the point that I really was some kind of "arch criminal".

The interrogations

Once inside the jail, I found that almost all the prisoners there already knew my name and were familiar with the details of my case. Apparently, the jail commandant had earlier briefed them on my background and instructed them to actively inform the jail authorities of any "counterrevolutionary statements" I might make and to keep a close eye on my behavior so as to prevent me from attempting to escape or commit suicide. While I knew that any such happenings would have created headaches for the authorities, I had never expected that the government would be quite so worried about us "turmoil elements."

The came the endless interrogation sessions. According to law, interrogations are meant to be carried out humanely. But in rule-by-man China, where - especially since the June 4 incident - the law counts for little, my experience was anything but humane.

I was interrogated by three cadres of section-chief level from the pre-trial investigation division of the Changsha City public security bureau. All three were Party officials who had made it through the Cultural Revolution and had picked up some special tricks and techniques for dealing with political prisoners. After establishing that I was a "diehard element" who would not bow to simple coercion, they then started using some of their "brilliant tricks" on me instead.

The first thing they tried was the so-called "interrogation by shifts" technique, in which one is kept under constant questioning for many hours per day. This grueling ordeal lasted from morning till night and continued for at least four months. Sometimes, the interrogations lasted as long 20 hours a day. The aim was to break down my resistance and get me so exhausted that I would finally answer whatever questions they put to me. At one stage, for example, they tried to make me admit that I had contacted Wang Dan, the Beijing student leader, by cipher telegram. The charge was based on two things: that I had been in Beijing

182

during the mass student hunger strike there; and someone had informed against me. The interrogators grilled me on this matter for over ten hours a day for more than 20 days, but got nothing from me.

They even grilled me on my alleged relationships with a whole bunch of people of whom I had absolutely no knowledge, including senior Party and government officials, certain foreigners and also some leading members of the Hong Kong Alliance in Support of the Patriotic Democratic Movement in China. They also questioned me about my "contacts" with Liang Heng, a former student from my own college who had left China for the United States 10 years earlier and whom I had never even met. They made up endless ludicrous stories about my supposed nefarious activities with all these people. During the four months of my interrogation, five volumes of case records were compiled, each of over 400 pages and full of sheer rubbish.

The second technique they employed was to plant a spy in my cell - something I was entirely unprepared for. The person assigned to this task was a serious and well-educated looking man in his 40s, who introduced himself to me as being a former adviser to the Changsha City Worker's Autonomous Federation. Within a few days of joining our cell, he managed to insinuate himself into my trust and confidence, and I revealed to him many of my secret thoughts and also some confidential information about the movement, including details of the large sum of money that I'd been given to help me escape. As I later discovered, all this information went straight into the hands of the public security authorities, and once they had got what they needed the man was conveniently "released." Some time afterwards, he reappeared in another cell where Chen Yi, the main suspect in Changsha's biggest murder case of 1989, was being held. The stooge quickly became Chen's "good friend," and one month later the case was cracked and Chen was tried and executed.

Gang beatings

They also tried simple thug tactics to extort a confession from me. Their main method was to instigate the other prisoners in my cell to gang up on me, and since I would not easily submit to this I often ended up being attacked by all of them at once. Although several of my cellmates supported me, they never dared to stand up and protect me, for

183

fear of offending the cadres. On one occasion, in which seven or eight of the toughest inmates - two of whom were murderers famed throughout Changsha - all suddenly turned on me, I was so badly beaten up that I could scarcely move for a whole week. Even to this day, I shudder to recall the incident. When I complained to the authorities about the beatings, their response was merely to transfer me to an adjoining cell and instruct the prisoners there to continue my "treatment." In order not to go against my conscience, I endured all the torture without confessing anything. I fell ill again several times, and they continued to refuse me medical help on the grounds that I had not yet repented my crimes.

On December 29, 1989, I was formally placed under arrest. (Prior to then I had been held as a mere "detainee" and the process of interrogation had gone by the fine-sounding name of "performing one's duty as a citizen.") The charges levelled against me were "counter-revolutionary propaganda and incitement" and "treason and defection to the enemy" - the grounds for the latter charge being that I had had contact with a few college students from Hong Kong and had at one point considered "fleeing the country." Upon hearing the word "treason," I felt overwhelmed with anger and shouted, "Get out, you bunch of gangsters and crooks! You won't get away with this!" Surprisingly enough, they stayed quite calm and simply noted down what I had said - as evidence of my "bad attitude" - and then left. That night, however, war broke out in my cell, as the other inmates suddenly fell upon me all at once. The blows that rained down on my body, however, elicited only one response from me: "Cowardly beasts!"

For the next six months, no one paid much attention to me, and my life revolved around the daily ritual of making match-boxes (all the prisoners had to do this), eating and sleeping. There were usually around 20 other prisoners in my cell, although the number rose to more than 30 during the 1990 "anti-crime campaign." Since the cell was about 18 square meters in area, this meant less than one square meter per person at the best of times. At night, one had to lie on one's side on the communal sleeping platform, jammed up against the other prisoners, so everybody became infected with skin diseases. The monthly subsistence allowance from the government was only 24 *yuan* per prisoner, and each meal consisted of some sour-pickle soup with a little winter melon, pumpkin, and seaweed thrown in. The reward for a full day's work was either two cigarettes, or - if one failed to complete the day's quota (which

184

was often the case since the quotas were set so high) - a dose of the electric baton.

Because I was not "obedient" and was thought to be "up to instigation" in prison, they kept transferring me to different cells in the hope each time that the new "cell boss" would be able to subdue me and deter me from "speaking wild thoughts." The result was that I suffered more than I might otherwise have done, but many more people got to know the true face of the government.

My "public" trial

Finally, after I'd spent more than a year in detention (far longer than the legally permissable limit), my case was brought to trial. On that day - July 17, 1990 - I was pronounced to be a sinner against the people and a "counterrevolutionary" (fortunately, the charge of "traitor to the motherland" had been dropped) and was sentenced to three year's imprisonment.

What happened then is still fresh in my memory. As I was escorted into the Changsha Intermediate Courthouse, I saw three judges, two procurators, and a lawyer sitting there primly on the rostrum. My own appointed lawyer had failed to turn up, but when I raised a protest about this it was ignored. (The hearing, according to the rules of due process, should have been invalidated on this ground alone.) The audience consisted only of my two sisters (one of whom worked in the public security bureau) and some of their colleagues. Even they had only learned of the trial through "internal" sources and had had to rush to the courthouse at the last minute. None of my fellow students from Hunan Normal University who had promised to come and testify on my behalf were allowed to attend the hearing.

Once the judges and procurators had finished their routine questions and answers, they asked me whether I had anything to say. I asked them why they had not let my fellow students come as visitors and witnesses. They looked puzzled and replied, "Let your campus-mates come? Why, that would never do!" After a brief adjournment, the chief judge announced the sentence: three years in prison, with two years' subsequent deprivation of political rights. The entire hearing had taken less than two hours.

185

Afterwards, a kind-hearted cadre quietly told me that the hearing was just a facade, since my guilt and the length of my sentence had been pre-determined by the higher-level authorities a full month before. This was why the court had refused to admit any of my fellow-students to the trial; moreover, they had deliberately postponed the hearing until after the start of the college summer vacation. Before leaving, the cadre also told me, "Don't expect too much or you'll only suffer more." I vowed silently to my campus mates, "See you all in 1992!"

Life under the "proletarian dictatorship"

From then on I was formally a convict, no different from countless murderers, robbers, rapists and thieves. (The Chinese government does not admit that it holds any political prisoners.) The authorities then removed their hypocritical mask and began to exercise "proletarian dictatorship" over me. For the first two months, I was held in the Changsha No. 2 Jail and given intensive "ideological education for criminals." In early November, 1990, I was shuttled between several other jails and then sent to Longxi Prison to undergo labor-reform. Because the winter there brings a piercing cold wind, the local cadres call this prison "Siberia" *(Xiboliya)*. Publicly, it is known as the "Shaoyang Marble Factory," since it specializes in the production of marble goods, including for export.

Upon arrival, I was placed in a "prison induction team" to learn the regulations and undergo preliminary disciplining. Because I was the last of the "1989 counterrevolutionary criminals" to be sent to Longxi, however, I was effectively exempted from the special "political study classes" that all the others had had to go through. (This was the only good thing that had happened to me since my initial detention over a year before.)

There were two things that I found particularly intolerable about prison life. One was that we were forced each day to sing three songs in chorus: "Without the Communist Party, There Would be No New China", Socialism is Good" and "Learn from the Good Example of Lei Fang". The warden would then shout out three questions, to which we had to shout out the answers in unison:

Q: "Who are you?"   A: "Criminals!"

Q: "Where are you?"   A: "In prison!"
Q: "Why are you here?" A: "To reform ourselves through labor!"

At the beginning I tried to act dumb, but I soon found out it wasn't worth trying to resist them on this. From then on, I used to sing the songs as loudly as I could, and I answered all the questions with a yell. Each time I would clench my teeth in hatred.

The second ordeal was the daily parade drill, or "military training" as they called it. This was purely and simply an opportunity for the wardens to play around with us and humiliate us. Because I often used to show resistance, I ended up being put into fetters and handcuffs and being placed in solitary confinement. (Somehow, I found that such punishment only helped me to maintain my mental equilibrium better.)

At one point, I was assigned to be a teacher in the prison's education section - probably the best "job" that could be hoped for. But before I could give my first class, I was thrown into the "strict regime" unit - a prison-within-the-prison. The reason for this was that I had apparently participated in organizing a "counterrevolutionary rally." (Actually, it had been little more than a chat between a group of 17 of the political prisoners.) Seven of us were accused of having instigated and led the "rally" and were consigned to the strict regime unit as punishment. The incident caused quite a stir among the other prisoners and received close attention from the higher-level authorities.

For the first three days of this punishment, we had to sit motionless for an average of 10 hours per day performing so-called "introspection." This is actually one of the most oppressive forms of ill-treatment imaginable. One is made to sit on a tiny stool less than 20 cm in height on a raised platform of about 90 square cm, with back held bolt-upright, both feet flat on the floor and hands placed neatly on one's lap. Throughout, one has to look directly at the wall just ahead, and if for any reason such as a momentary lapse of attention one happens to slouch forward slightly or bend one's head, one will be hit by the guard with an iron rod or handcuffed to the door. At night, one is locked up alone in a small room less than two square meters in area, in which the only bed is a cement slab of about 30 cm in width.

The time when we were given this punishment was the coldest

187

part of winter, and we were unable to get any sleep at all. After three days, we could stand it no more and decided to go on a collective hunger strike as a means of protest. On the seventh day, miraculously enough, we were all "rehabilitated" by the authorities and sent back to the normal cells. (I still have a letter I wrote to the prison governor during the hunger strike - luckily for me, I never actually sent it.)

Released on parole

To my astonishment, almost the first thing that greeted me after I was released from the strict regime unit was an official "notice of parole." This was an unprecedented event in Longxi Prison history, and I was at a complete loss as to what the reason for it might have been. Only later did I discover that the prison authorities had had little choice but to issue the release order, since an internal document had just been issued by the central authorities requiring the local judicial authorities to review cases of certain relatively prominent pro-democracy figures who had been sentenced too heavily.[39] This clearly was largely due to the strong international and domestic pressure then being put on the Chinese government over the human rights issue. Another factor in my case was that certain enlightened figures in the higher levels of the Hunan provincial government apparently disagreed with the hardliners' policy and had intervened on my behalf.

During the 18 months I was behind bars, I was imprisoned in altogether 16 cells of seven jails and prisons in five different places. I was interrogated by agents of at least 10 different public security or screening organs, including security personnel from Beijing, Shanghai, Wuhan, Chongqing, Guangzhou, Yueyang, Hengyang, Changsha, Jiangmen and

---

[39] The main reason for this appears to have been the relatively lenient sentence of four years' imprisonment handed down to Beijing student leader Wang Dan in January 1991. While this sentence was intended to appease international pressure over the human rights violations, it also left the problem of glaring discrepancies between the Wang Dan sentence and the much higher sentences given to many other leading pro-democracy figures in other parts of the country, particularly workers. There is no evidence to suggest that this readjustment policy lasted for more than a few weeks, however, and the only beneficiaries of it seem to have been a few student leaders, including myself.

188

Xinhui. According to information disclosed to me by an internal source, my case cost the goverment more than 140,000 *yuan*. The Ministry of State Security alone sent its personnel to Hong Kong for investigation purposes at least twice. Dozens of people were involved as suspects in my case, including my relatives, my father's colleagues, the cadres of the provincial public security department, a few leaders of my university and also people from the various households that had given shelter to me while I was on the run. When I reflect on this, all sorts of emotions well up in my mind.

Just prior to my release, I was summoned before the prison authorities and told, "Remember, you are only on parole, and you can be sent back here at any time if your performance is poor!" In addition, they said, I was on no account to leave my hometown, have any contact with other "turmoil elements" or make any inflammatory remarks (so-called "counterrevolutionary instigation") when talking to people. I had been looking forward to having a few drinks together with two other released "counterrevolutionaries" after getting out. Now, I had to drop this plan.

The news of my father's death

One rainy day just before Chinese New Year's Eve, in February 1991, I appeared before my family again at last, shaven-headed and drenched from head to foot. How they both cried and smiled at me, with a mixture of sorrow and happiness! My mother, however, looked ten years older than before, and my sisters also showed signs of deep sadness. Then came the news: I had lost my beloved father! The day after he received his copy of the arrest warrant for me, with its twin charges of "counterrevolution" and "treason", he had been knocked down and killed in a traffic accident - the copy of the arrest warrant still in his pocket at the time. I was the only man left in my family, and I was devastated.

My father was only 54 years old when he died. He worked diligently for China in the field of education all his life. He underwent innumerable hardships and scored remarkable achievements. A man of strong integrity, he was much respected by the people in my town. But he left the world in despair. This was a story that could move Heaven itself to tears. I vowed then that I would record all the stories of suffering I had learned in prison, in everlasting memory of my dad.

189

On hearing the news of my release, all the neighbors came over. They took my hands and said tearfully: "You've suffered...", "You're back at long last...", "It's all right now..." and "Heaven is just..!" They then related to me many touching incidents that had occurred while I was away. For example, a former county magistrate had come to my home, with the help of a walking stick, soon after I was arrested and had said to my father, "Your son is an excellent student and always won the "three outstandings" award (*san hao*: academics, sports and ethics) for our locality. He must be feeling very sad now. You should comfort him and cook something nice for him whenever you can to keep up his health. You just tell him, "Your Uncle X says you are a good young man!" After the June 4 massacre, the people of my hometown heard a rumor that I had been killed in Tiananmen Square, so they held a memorial meeting for me. On the Festival of the Dead in 1990, moreover, some leading provincial cadres, who did not leave their names, rolled up in their sedan cars to pay their respects at my father's grave. All these touching stories gave me much comfort, and I was deeply grateful to my folks. They understood me.

A conflict between filial duty and loyalty to the cause

Once I realized that my own "parole" and the releases or reduced sentences of some other democratic activists, especially the students, had been a result of the people's silent resistance, my own convictions grew stronger. I quietly took an oath: I would share weal and woe with the nation throughout my life and dedicate all that I had to my motherland and the people who supported me.

Soon after the Spring Festival, I paid a brief visit to where my father's soul rested and then started on my journey. I left home and went to Changsha, where I immediately reestablished contacts with my former comrades and restarted pro-democracy activities, using the several hundred *yuan* that my mother had been saving up month after month through her own thrift and plain living.

My student status and urban residency rights had been cancelled by the government, and I could expect no help from them in finding a job. On several occasions, I tried to start up a business partnership with some private enterprises, only to encounter groundless interference and obstruction from the government. The authorities clearly intended to

190

keep me in a state of limbo, wretched and impotent, while all the time telling the people how "very lenient" they had been with us students!

After four months of extensive travel and liaison, some new prospects began to open up. During this time, I returned home only once. I visited my father's grave and stayed with my mother for only three days. I knew that she was still as anxious over me as she had been in 1989. She had only one wish: that I would stay with her, right there at home by her side. For more than a year when I was in prison, she had travelled hundreds of kilometers every month just to visit me - though she was never actually permitted to see me. One time, the bus she was on turned over and two of her ribs were broken, leaving her bedridden for over a month. What a parental heart! Seeing her face growing thinner day by day, I could only say this silently in my heart: "I'm sorry, my good mother. Your son cannot be loyal to his cause and filial to you at the same time." Wiping away my tears, I left home, with head bent low.

The government continued to regard me as a constant scourge and took a series of measures to monitor and threaten me. They knew wherever I went almost immediately and approached all those with whom I had contact, including my former girlfriend, warning them not to have anything to do with me as I was a "very dangerous person." Public security officials went to my home and told my mother that they were going to make me "repeat" what I had gone through before. I knew they had no evidence against me and that it was nothing more than a bluff. But on the second anniversary of the June 4 crackdown, when a series of wall posters appeared in Changsha and a small protest rally was staged, the authorities became convinced that I was the mastermind, and a secret order was issued for my re-arrest. (An internal source alerted me to this.)

I had no choice but to go into exile. It had been more than two years since the last time I had had to flee. After hiding out for a month in a friend's place in one of the cities, I realized I had very little time left before the net closed in on me. So I made my bid for freedom, and on July 28 I finally got out of the country. I was left with one lasting regret, however: that I had finally became worthy of the charge of "treason". Yes, I had betrayed that country held in the grip of the communist party dictatorship, and I deserved the name of "traitor to the country."

Two years earlier, my comrades abroad had strongly urged me

191

to flee the country. But I carried an unswerving sentiment for the land that had given birth to me and brought me up, and I did not have the heart to leave behind all those relatives, friends, and compatriots with whom I had a shared destiny. I did not see clearly, moreover, the true face of the government, and I believed in the idea of letting fate take its course. I became, as a result, a "criminal guilty of counterrevolution."

Today, however, I have a deeper appreciation of the peril facing China and of the sufferings undergone by its people, and I have a stronger love than ever for that profoundly nurturing land. I abandoned my country simply because I had no choice. As I look now at the colorful world on this side, I can only sigh at the striking contrast and try to strengthen my resolve.

APPENDIX V

In Mourning for the Perished of the Nation

[Oration delivered at the June 8, 1989
Mass Mourning Meeting in Changsha]

Was it the indignant, still-beckoning spirit of Qu Yuan from more than two thousand years ago that took you away? Was it the heroic spirits of seventy years ago that called to you? Was it the loving heart of your numberless predecessors before the Monument to the People's Heroes that moved you so? You have suddenly gone, suddenly gone. You have left behind only a river of fresh blood, you have left behind only a deep love, and a deep hate. You have gone. Spirits of Beijing, where do you rest? Oh where do you rest? The mountains and rivers weep, the sad wind whirls. Before the evil gun muzzles, before the ugly face of fascism, before my people in suffering, and before the calm, smiling face on your death mask, I can do no more than make this offering to your spirits with vibrant, leonine nerve.

You are gone! Today, two thousand years ago, Qu Yuan, his heart afire with loyal ardor, leapt into the pitiless Miluo River: "I submit to the crystal-clear depths - Oh Death, come now!" Today, two thousand years later, you, our loyal brothers and sisters, fell under the guns of the so-called "people's own soldiers," you fell under the tanks of "the most cherished ones."

Yes, you are gone! The tears in your eyes, the blood flowing now from your chests, all have become a river, a downpour. June 4: no Chinese of true heart will ever forget this day. June 4, June 4, 1989: every common man and woman who seeks freedom, democracy, and peace will forever remember. June 4: China's national day of everlasting

193

shame. China's eternal day of national disaster![40]

In Tiananmen Square, revered by all the people of China, three thousand lives were wiped out in a single night. In but a few short days, a myriad beating hearts were smashed into stillness. In those few days, the souls of all the people of China were ripped and torn into shreds, and the nerves of the people of the whole world were stretched and broken. Three thousand living, breathing, vibrant people who a few days before had flesh and blood and ideals and feelings were erased in a single night.

A myriad different lives, a myriad different stories, reduced in an instant to the [government's] single trite judgment: "suppressed thugs." But did they need tanks to crush them - those thugs? Did they need to engulf them in flames? Did they need to unleash dumdum bullets - banned worldwide - on the thugs? They called you thugs, and now your eyes cannot close in peaceful death. Your innocent, pained, and indignant eyes turn skyward and cry: "Oh Heaven! We are not thugs!"

You were the sons and daughters of loving parents, you were the students of proud teachers. You were brothers, sisters, friends, sometimes even enemies. But how many dreams you still had to dream! How many poems you still had to discover! You would have been fathers and mothers, you who still had so many new roads to travel down.

On that day, when you knelt before the Great Hall of the People, you became the sufferers who, wide awake, smashed their way out of the iron cell. You loved life; and so you knelt, seeking basic rights and honesty in the name of the nation and the state. How could you who had made so many poems accept the label of "chaos" for your acts? In past days you had been vibrant and active on your green campuses, painting in the broad brushstrokes of a life based upon ideals. Strolling among the flowers under the moon, you poured out all your most tender feelings. How beautiful it was!

---

[40] The original text says "June 3" here and elsewhere, since it was late that night that the killing began. In the period immediately after the massacre, it was symbolized in China by the date "June 3" and only later came to be known as the "June 4" massacre.

194

Then later, you cried out - with the voice of the whole people you cried out, and took to the streets with demonstrations, sit-ins, and hunger strikes. How could you who had dreamed so many dreams have imagined that unarmed and defenseless, struggling with only a loving heart and your own life for the right to a beautiful life, you would be so cruelly cut down and slaughtered by the fascist government? What was your crime? Oh what was your crime?

You have gone! The smile on your death mask is still before us. We bend our ears to listen, but we will never hear your voices again. We reach out to touch your face but can touch you no more. We call out "Brother," we call out "Sister," but you will never hear us again, Oh never again. We reach out to touch you, we stubbornly try to take your hand. But we cannot touch even a handful of your ashes.

You have gone, you youth have gone forever. You had time still to love, but you had no more time to live. So that those who lived on might live better, so that those who loved on might love better, you rose up from your place of kneeling, and embarked upon the road of no return. And then suddenly you fell, cut down from your proud place of standing. Although your heads were torn from your bodies, your souls could not be killed. China weeps now, mourning for its broken backbone. You are gone forever, and a generation of heroic outcries are lost to the nation.

The Goddess of Democracy has fallen. But you, who were cut down in your prime and yet shall live always in our hearts, you are the eternal Goddesses of Democracy. You shall always be in our dreams, in our memories. You shall live eternally in history. Fearless and proud, you died standing up, you died standing up. Look now: those who escaped with their lives from the bloody rain and the fetid wind have already stood forward. They are your brothers, fathers, teachers, friends -- in their own hearts, they have stood up.

Who has ever seen thugs with such thick glasses! Who has ever seen such a "People's Government" and a "People's Army," where the gun-wielders outnumber the pen-wielders. Those who knelt before have now, finally, stood up. No more do they weep, no more do they hope in vain, no more do they hesitate. No more do they worry only about themselves and their families. You will be proud of us! Your blood was not shed in

195

vain! Your tears did not flow in vain!

The salt of your blood adds a bitter strength to the life of the era. And the sun of life from your blood, the scarlet banner, now lights up the flames of love and hate. We, the living Descendants of the Yellow Emperor,[41] citizens for freedom and peace, have burst forth to exchange our warm blood for freedom, to wash away the dust with our warm tears, to make today's outcry remembered tomorrow, to show to the world the wounds of history! As long as the truth is in our hearts, we do not fear to shed our blood. We hereby vow: we shall never be deflected from our goal!

Hang Li Peng! Send Li, Deng [Xiaoping] and Yang [Shangkun] to the sacrificial altar!

Pray for the souls of Beijing, for the perished of the nation!

Rest in peace, Oh brave souls!

---

[41] A rhetorical term for the Chinese people.

APPENDIX VI

Hunan Daily on Arrests and Trials of Workers

Counterrevolutionary criminals Zhang Jingsheng, Liu Jian'an and Wang Changhuai are Sentenced to Prison Terms[42]

This paper learned that on December 8, the Intermediate People's Court of the City of Changsha called a special mass rally to pronounce judgment on and punish counterrevolutionary criminals. At that rally, the court publicly convicted three criminals who engaged in counterrevolutionary activities during the turmoil of last spring and summer. In accordance with the law, the court sentenced counterrevolutionary criminal Zhang Jingsheng to a fixed term of thirteen years' imprisonment, with three years' subsequent deprivation of political rights; it sentenced counterrevolutionary criminal Liu Jian'an to a fixed term of ten years' imprisonment, with two years' subsequent deprivation of political rights. Counterrevolutionary criminal Wang Changhuai was sentenced to a fixed term of three years' imprisonment, with one year's subsequent deprivation of political rights.

Zhang Jingsheng, pen-name Han Xing, male, 35, was formerly a casual worker of the Hunan Shaoguang Electrical Factory. He was sentenced to a fixed term of four years' imprisonment, with three years'

---

[42] "The City of Changsha publicly convicts criminals who engaged in counterrevolutionary activities during the turmoil," *Hunan Daily*, December [?], 1989. (Taken from undated press clipping.) Note that the article describes three cases, two of which - Zhang Jingsheng and Wang Changhuai - are related while the third, that of Liu Jian'an, bears no relation whatever to the other two. The paragraph on Liu, who is alleged to have been a spy, was even inserted between those on Zhang and Wang - for no other apparent reason than that the *Hunan Daily*, which had so little damning to write about Zhang and Wang, felt it needed to tar them "by association" with the spy case.

subsequent deprivation of political rights on charges of counterrevolutionary propaganda and incitement. He was released after serving his term. But he was unrepentant, and remained hostile to the people. On May 4 of this year, he made speeches to student demonstrators at Hunan University and the Hunan Martyrs' Park, clamoring for "democracy," "freedom" and a "multi-party system." He also complained and called for redress on behalf of the counterrevolutionary Wei Jingsheng. On May 21, he joined, on his own initiative, the illegal organization, the Workers Autonomous Federation. He incited the workers to go on strike and the students to boycott classes. What was especially abominable was that, after the counterrevolutionary rebellion broke out in Beijing, he wrote an extremely reactionary "Urgent Appeal," which was mimeographed by the Workers Autonomous Federation and hundreds of copies were distributed throughout the city. In that "appeal," he wildly pledged to fight the people's government in a bloody battle to the death. His counterrevolutionary bluster was extremely arrogant. As Zhang was a counterrevolutionary recidivist, he was sentenced severely according to law to a long prison term.

Liu Jian'an, male, 38, was formerly a teacher at Changsha's No. 25 Middle School. From May 1989 on, he secretly tuned in to broadcasts by enemy radio stations. He covertly planned to establish contacts with enemy secret services. Between July 2 and 14, he sent sixteen letters to Guomindang (Nationalist) secret services in Taiwan, Hong Kong and Japan, trying to establish a liaison. He used such aliases as Li Shiji, Li Ji and a dozen others, and mailed the letters from Changsha, Yiyang, Yueyang and Wuhan. In those letters, he described himself and his status to enemy secret services and applied to join them. He indicated his counterrevolutionary determination and vainly tried to establish secret organizations to conduct underground activities. He also wrote items for broadcast by the *Voice of Free China*, and organized the publication of reactionary manuscripts. He asked enemy secret services to send agents to get in touch with him, specifying the places and methods for rendezvous, and asked for assignment.

Wang Changhuai, alias Huang Feng, male, 25, was formerly a worker at the Changsha Automobile Engine Plant. On May 22 of this year, Wang joined the illegal Workers Autonomous Federation and became its chief of organization, standing committee member, and chief of propaganda successively. During that time, he was in charge of the federation's seal, banner, letters of recommendation and membership cards. He designed the organization chart for the Workers Autonomous Federation. When the counterrevolutionary rebellion broke out in Beijing, Wang became extraordinarily active, running around on sinister errands. He himself wrote a call to strike, mimeographed it and distributed, posted and broadcast it throughout the city. He also signed the "Urgent Appeal" written by Zhang Jingsheng, and mimeographed and distributed it all over the city. That appeal viciously attacked the party and government, fabricated rumors to mislead the people, and called on the people to get organized and go on strike. On June 15, 1989, awed by the power of government policy and the law, he went to the Public Security Bureau of his own accord and gave himself up. He was given lenient sentence according to law.

APPENDIX VII

Declaration of Hunan Autonomy[43]

Hunan Should Lead the Way and
Practice Patriotic Self-Government

Hunan is bounded on the north by water and hemmed in on three other sides by mountains. Hengshan, the Mountain of the South, sits astride the alluvial plain drained by the Xiang River, which flows right through the province. Like a "magic gourd," it collects all that is best in China.

As the sayings go, "Lake Dongting, measuring 800 *li* all around, is rich in fish and rice." "When the harvests are in from Hunan and Hubei, the whole country is well-fed." Hunan is known throughout the world for its rich resources.

Hunan controls the approaches to both the north and the south. It can respond to both the east and the west. It can attack and advance, or retreat and defend.

When we advance by cutting off supplies, Guangdong has to submit. When we move east down the Yangtze, we capture Shanghai, and Hubei, Jiangxi and Fujian will come to us. Divide our troops, we launch our northern expedition. Shandong and Shanxi will beat the drums and help us. Beijing and Tianjin will act from inside in coordination with our forces attacking from outside. We shall capture the bandit chieftain at one fell swoop. Then, we shall pacify the northwest, the southwest, the northeast, Tibet and Inner Mongolia, unifying the country with ourselves at the center.

---

[43] This document was drafted by a radical group in Hunan, comprised partly of PLA officers, and was printed up as a flyer and distributed around the province shortly after the crackdown began.

Retreat and we evacuate Changsha to lure the enemy in. We then break the dikes to drown the enemy. With small detachments in the mountains of Liuyang and Pingjiang in eastern Hunan, we will wage guerrilla warfare to tie the enemy down, and wait for our main force from the high mountains in western Hunan to come from the direction of Changde to surround the enemy. Then, our crack troops in Shaoyang and Hengyang will rush out, attacking the enemy from both the north and the south like bolting the door and beating the dog. The powerful invading enemy can only surrender or be annihilated.

The people of Hunan, being the offspring of centuries of intermarriage between northerners and southerners, are genetically advantaged and possess very high intelligence. In addition, the geographic environment gives the people of Hunan the advanced knowledge of the big cities as well as the toughness and determination of the mountain people. The legend of "outstanding personality from the land of wonders" and "only Hunan produces exceptional talent" is not just bragging.

Historical evidence abounds. The Mongols of the Yuan Dynasty ran rampant all over Eurasia. But when they advanced on Changsha, Hunan Province, "people heard the northerners sing: the walls of Tanzhou is iron-clad." The brutes of the Eight Banners of the Manchus could not have entered Changsha had they not bribed the traitors to hand over the city. The Japanese invaders were arrogant. But they had to enter and leave Changsha no less than seven times and lost 40,000 crack troops of the Guandong Army. And finally they surrendered in Hunan. Everyone knows what happened to the Taiping Heavenly Kingdom and the Communist Party.

Today, the reactionary dictatorial rulers face retribution for a life of crime. The people will triumph!

It is fitting that the banner of "democracy and rule of law" will first fly high over Hunan.

Preparatory Committee for Patriotic
Self-Governance by the People of Hunan

June 8, 1989

APPENDIX VIII

Court Verdicts and Re-Education Decisions

A. Case of Chen Zhixiang[44]

Criminal Verdict
of the Intermediate People's Court
of Guangzhou Municipality, Guangdong Province

Guangzhou/Court/Criminal No.262 (89)

Public Prosecutor:
Lan Jinping, Procurator acting on behalf of Guangzhou Municipal People's Procuratorate

Defendant:
Chen Zhixiang, male, 26, Han nationality, born in Nantong City, Jiangsu Province. Education: college graduate, former teacher at Guangzhou Maritime College. Residence: Room 205, 15 Pangui Street, New Port Road, Guangzhou. Taken into custody on July 4, 1989 and arrested on August 12, 1989. [The defendant is] currently in custody.

Defender:
Zheng Jinghao, Attorney, Guangzhou Municipal Legal Affairs Office.

Guangzhou People's Procuratorate brought an indictment in this

---

[44] Chen Zhixiang is currently reported to be held in Yuanjiang Prison, but Asia Watch cannot definitely confirm this. He may in fact be held in Guangdong Province, immediately to the south of Hunan. For further details, see p.113.

court against the defendant Chen Zhixiang who was charged with conducting counterrevolutionary propaganda and incitement. This court formed a collegial panel in accordance with law and on December 4, 1989 opened a court session and conducted a public hearing of the case. The public prosecutor appeared in court to support the prosecution. The defender appeared in court to defend the accused.

This court has, in the course of the public hearing, ascertained that the defendant, Chen Zhixiang, following the suppression of the counterrevolutionary rebellion in Beijing, carried with him paint and a brush on June 7, 1989 to the construction site of the former "Sails of the Pearl River" on Yanjiangzhong Road, Guangzhou and wrote on the wall there a reactionary slogan measuring more than 20 meters in length. It read: "Avenge the young people who died in Beijing. Hang the executioners Deng [Xiaoping], Yang [Shangkun] and Li [Peng] and execute the running-dog Chen[45] and all the other accomplices." Around three o'clock in the afternoon of the same day, the defendant Chen Zhixiang went to the east side of the Guiyuan Hotel on Huanshizhong Road, Guangzhou, and wrote on the wall a reactionary slogan also more than 20 meters long, which read: "Wipe out the Four Pests on behalf of the people. Hang Deng, Yang and Li, who butchered the common people, and execute the running-dog Chen and all the other accomplices."

The above-mentioned facts have been attested to by witnesses' testimony and written evidence; verified by criminal science and various technical devices; and admitted to by the defendant. The evidence is complete and sufficient to prove the case.

In the opinion of this court, the defendant Chen Zhixiang, harboring a counterrevolutionary motive, openly wrote large-scale reactionary slogans at public thoroughfares, maliciously attacking and slandering Party, government and military leaders and attempting to incite the people to overthrow the political power of the people's democratic dictatorship. His actions constituted the crime of conducting counterrevolutionary propaganda and incitement. The way in which the crime was committed was vile, and the crime itself is serious and must be

---

[45] This is probably a reference to Chen Xitong, the hardline-leftist Mayor of Beijing.

punished severely according to law. Taking the law of the land seriously in order to protect the political power of the people's democratic dictatorship and the socialist system, the trial panel of this court made a decision on December 24 after discussions and, in accordance with Articles 102 and 52 of the Criminal Law of the People's Republic of China, renders the following verdict:

The defendant Chen Zhixiang committed the crime of conducting counterrevolutionary propaganda and incitement and is hereby sentenced to a fixed-term period of 10 years' imprisonment (the period of imprisonment to be calculated starting from the date of this judgment's execution, and with a one-day reduction of sentence for each day spent in custody prior to execution of the judgment, that is, the imprisonment shall end on July 3, 1999), with three years' subsequent deprivation of political rights.

If the defendant does not submit to this judgment, he may, within a 10-day period starting from the day following receipt of the judgment, lodge with this court a petition, plus one duplicate copy, as an appeal to the Guangdong Provincial High People's Court.

The First Criminal Panel of the
Guangzhou Intermediate People's Court

Chief Judge: Li Jiangpei
Judge: Yang Liangan
Acting Judge: Deng Ganhua

[Seal of the Guangzhou Intermediate People's Court]

January 3, 1990
Clerk: Chen Weimin

APPENDIX VIII.B

Case of Tang Boqiao

Indictment
of the Changsha People's Procuratorate
(Hunan Province)
Chang/Proc./Crim.Ind. (1990) No.8

Defendant: **Tang Boqiao**, male, 22, Han nationality, born in the municipality of Lengshuitan, Hunan Province, college educated, a student of section two of the class of '86, the department of political science, Hunan Normal University.

Residence: school for the children of employees of the factory producing equipment for hydro-electric power plants in the municipality of Lengshuitan.

He was taken in on July 13, 1989 for the case in question and was officially arrested by the Public Security Bureau of Changsha on July 29.

Investigation of the case of defendant Tang Boqiao engaging in counterrevolutionary propaganda and incitement was concluded by the Changsha Public Security Bureau. The case was forwarded to this procuratorate for indictment on January 18, 1990. Later, however, it was returned to the Public Security Bureau on March 3, 1990 for further investigation. That was completed by the Changsha Public Security Bureau on April 10, and was forwarded again to this procuratorate for examination and indictment. Our examination shows that:

Defendant Tang Boqiao was chief leader of the illegal organization, Hunan Students Autonomous Federation. From May 1989 on, he organized and participated in illegal rallies and demonstrations on many occasions. After the quelling of the counterrevolutionary rebellion in Beijing, defendant Tang Boqiao attended, in the evening of June 7, a meeting called by Fan Zhong, Zhang Lixin and others. At that meeting, they plotted to hold a memorial meeting on June 8 for the counterrevolutionary thugs suppressed in Beijing. Defendant Tang Boqiao instructed Li XX, a student in the department of Chinese of Hunan Normal University, to draft a "memorial speech." That speech invented the story of our martial law troops having massacred students, workers and citizens and of having killed thousands of them. It was most pernicious. On June 8 of the same year, defendant Tang Boqiao co-chaired, with Zhang Lixin, the "memorial meeting" held on the square in front of the Changsha railway station. Liu Wei, Lu Siqing, Zhou Ming and Zhang Lixin (all prosecuted in separate cases) spoke at the meeting. They venomously attacked the party and government and incited antagonism. On June 12, 1989, the People's Government of the City of Changsha issued a public notice outlawing the Hunan Students Autonomous Federation and the Changsha Workers Autonomous Federation. Defendant Tang Boqiao refused to register with the authorities. On June 15, together with Yu Zhaohui and others, he absconded to Guangzhou and Xinghua and made telephone contacts with people outside the country. They accepted 92,500 *yuan* and HK$4,500.00, as well as a book of secret codes for communication sent from Hong Kong. Tang Boqiao passed out his calling cards, bearing the title of Executive Director of the Hunan Students Autonomous Federation, and copies of the memorial speech delivered at the "June 8" memorial meeting, to people outside the country. At the same time, defendant Tang Boqiao absconded to Muzhou township in Xinghui County, attempting to cross the border at Zhuhai and sneak into Macao.

The above-mentioned facts of his crime are attested to by witnesses' testimony, criminal scientific technique as well as by photographs, telephone receipts and evidence of confiscated booty. The defendant also admitted as much in his recorded confessions. The facts are clear and the evidence solid, complete and sufficient to prove the case.

In the opinion of the procuratorate, defendant Tang Boqiao planned and organized illegal demonstrations and presided over the "June 8" memorial meeting. His activities violated Article 102 of the *Criminal Code of the People's Republic of China* and constituted the crime of counterrevolutionary propaganda and incitement. In order to consolidate China's political power of the people's democratic dictatorship, defend the socialist system and punish counterrevolutionary crimes, and in accordance with Article 100 of the *Criminal Procedure Law of the People's Republic of China*, we indict the defendant and request that your court judge him according to law.

To the Intermediate People's Court,
the City of Changsha, Hunan Province

Luo Jingjian,
Procurator acting on behalf of
the Procuratorate of the City
of Changsha [Seal]
April 17, 1990

N.B.

1. The defendant Tang Boqiao is being held at the No.1 Jail of the Changsha Public Security Bureau.
2. Enclosed are case materials in three books and four volumes; and
3. Two books and two volumes of diaries as evidence.

Certificate of Release

(91) No.70

Tang Boqiao, male, 22, of Hunan Normal University, was sentenced on August 9, 1990 on charges of counterrevolutionary propaganda and incitement by the Intermediate People's Court of the City of Changsha to a fixed term of three years' imprisonment with two years' subsequent deprivation of political rights (from February 12, 1991 to February 11, 1993). This is to certify that he is being released on parole.

Longxi Prison
February 12, 1991

(This copy to be issued to the released individual.)

APPENDIX VIII.C

Case of Mo Lihua

Verdict
on the Criminal Case of Mo Lihua
Returned by
the Intermediate People's Court of the City of Shaoyang
Hunan Province
(1989 Crim-Pre.No.150)

Prosecutors:
Lu Kuiquan, prosecutor, People's Procuratorate of the City of Shaoyang

Wang Jianjun, acting prosecutor, People's Procuratorate of the City of Shaoyang

Defendant:
Pen name: **Mo Li**
Mo Lihua, female, 35, born in Shaodong County, Han nationality, was formerly a teacher of the department of education, Shaoyang Normal College.

Residence: Building No.6-1-1, staff dormitory, Shaoyang Normal College.

Taken in on June 14, 1989 on charges of counterrevolutionary propaganda and incitement. Formally arrested on September 10 of the same year. She is being held in the jailhouse of the Shaoyang City Public Security Bureau.
Defense attorney:

Chen Qiuming, attorney, No.1 Law Office of the City of Shaoyang.

On November 25, 1989, the People's Procuratorate of the City of Shaoyang, Hunan Province, in its (1989) Criminal Indictment No. 108,

209

brought before this court the suit against defendant Mo Lihua on charges of counterrevolutionary propaganda and incitement. This court organized a collegiate bench of judges according to law and held a public trial. It has been ascertained that:

Defendant Mo Lihua, together with Huang XX and Zhou X, students of Shaoyang Normal College, left Shaoyang on May 26, 1989 for Beijing to find out about the disturbances there. They collected some information about those disturbances. After they returned to Shaoyang, Mo addressed an audience of more than eighty people in the evening of June 3, in the training section classroom of Shaoyang Normal College. She talked about ten major issues in "Understanding the Beijing Student Movement." She attacked and slandered Li Peng as "creating disturbances and threatening the people with army troops," claiming that "the people will have instant peace the moment Li Peng is removed." She also clamored for "establishing democratic politics - the parliamentary system and a political design institute in China," etc. In the evening of June 6, Mo again addressed all teaching staff and students of Shaoyang Normal College through the college's public address system. She repeated those reactionary remarks mentioned above.

In the night of June 3 and early morning of June 4, the counterrevolutionary rebellion was suppressed in Beijing. Defendant Mo Lihua spoke at the "memorial meeting" held in the evening of June 4 at Shaoyang Normal College by Li XX and a few others to honor the handful of thugs. She also spoke at the People's Square of Shaoyang in the evening of June 5. She viciously attacked and slandered the suppression of the counterrevolutionary rebellion by our party and government as a "bloody suppression of the people by a fascist government." She arrogantly clamored for the building of a "still taller and still more beautiful goddess of democracy" to honor the handful of counterrevolutionary thugs. She called for overthrowing the Central People's Government as a memorial ceremony for the "courageous spirits" of the thugs, and so on and so forth.

The above facts have been attested to by witnesses, oral and written testimonies and recorded depositions. The defendant's confessions are also on record. The facts are clear-cut and the evidence is solid and sufficient to prove the case.

In the opinion of this court, defendant Mo Lihua made public speeches at a time when our party and state won a decisive victory in curbing the disturbances and suppressing the rebellion, voicing grievances on behalf of and praising the counterrevolutionary thugs in Beijing. She attached party and state leaders and viciously attacked the decision and measures taken by the Central Committee of the Party and the State Council to put an end to the disturbance and suppress the rebellion. She incited the masses to rise up and oppose the authorities in a vain attempt to achieve her objectives of overthrowing the political power of the dictatorship of the proletariat and the socialist system. Her activities constitute the crime of counterrevolutionary propaganda and incitement. In accordance with Articles 102 and 152 of the *Criminal Law of the People's Republic of China*, this court renders the verdict as follows:

Defendant Mo Lihua committed the crime of counterrevolutionary propaganda and incitement, and is sentenced to a fixed term of three years' imprisonment, with a one year subsequent deprivation of political rights.

This prison term begins with the execution of the sentence; one day in custody before the execution of the sentence will be counted for one day in prison.

If the defendant refuses to accept the verdict, she may, within ten days from the second day after receiving this verdict, submit her appeal and two copies thereof to this court, to appeal to the Higher People's Court of Hunan Province.

The First Criminal Trial Court of the
Intermediate People's Court of the City
of Shaoyang, Hunan Province (Seal)

Judge: Zhou Houhui
Acting judge: Xu Zhongyi
Acting judge: Xu Hong
December 24, 1989
Clerk of the court: Shen Zhiyong

Document of Shaoyang City Personnel Bureau
Shao/Personnel (1991) No.07

Written reply
Concerning punishing Mo Lihua by
discharging her from public employment

Shaoyang Normal College:

Your report asking for instructions concerning discharging Mo Lihua from public employment has been received.

Mo Lihua was sentenced to a fixed term of three years imprisonment by the Intermediate People's Court of the City of Shaoyang on December 24, 1989 (verdict Crim-Pre. No.150) on charges of conducting counterrevolutionary propaganda and incitement during the disturbances of 1989. In accordance with the spirit of Document No.160 of 1982 issued by the Ministry of Labor and Personnel, and after deliberations, Mo Lihua shall be punished by discharging her from public employment.

Personnel Bureau of the City of Shaoyang
April 5, 1991

Report to: the Personnel Office of Hunan Province
Send to: the Office of the City Committee of the Party,
Office of the City Government, Organization Department
of the City Committee of the Party, City Discipline
Committee
Issue to: Mo Lihua

APPENDIX VIII.D

Case of Wang Yongfa

[NB: In the following case, the defendant was sent to undergo re-education through labor despite a clear verdict of not guilty and an order of immediate release having been issued by the court. (Asia Watch)]

Lingling Sub-Procuratorate of the
Hunan Province People's Procuratorate

Decision Not to Prosecute
Hunan Proc/Ling Sub-proc/No Ind. (1990) No.01

Defendant: **Wang Yongfa**, male, 37, Han nationality, born in Lanshan County, Hunan Province, college educated, teacher of political studies, member of the Chinese Communist Party.

Residence: dormitory of the No. 1 Middle School, Lanshan County.

Taken into custody on October 23 (?), 1989 by the Public Security Bureau of Lanshan County on charges of counterrevolutionary propaganda and incitement. Arrested on January 7, 1990 by the Public Security Bureau of Lanshan County with the approval of the People's Procuratorate of Lanshan County given on December 26, 1989.

Investigations into the case of defendant Wang Yongfa, charged with counterrevolutionary propaganda and incitement, were completed by the Lanshan County Public Security Bureau, and the case was forwarded to the Lanshan County People's Procuratorate on January 8, 1990 for examination and indictment. Having examined the case, the Lanshan County People's Procuratorate, in accordance with Article 15 of the *Criminal Procedure Law of the People's Republic of China*, submitted the

213

case to this sub-procuratorate on January 13 for examination and indictment. It has been ascertained that:

In early June 1989, when the counterrevolutionary rebellion was being crushed in Beijing, defendant Wang Yongfa tuned in to enemy radio broadcasts and believed the rumors he heard. In the morning of June 5, when Wang Yongfa was making preparations for his class in the teaching and research group office, the chief political instructor, Fan Yucai, remarked: "The TV reported the killing of a People's Liberation Army man by the thugs. It was horrible." Wang retorted: "You are looking at it in a one-sided way. You only saw the death of one PLA man. Do you know that up to one thousand students and workers also died?" Later, he spread the story that "thousands of students and workers were either killed or injured. Hordes of PLA men rushed the students and machine-gunned them down." When he was criticized by other teachers, he added: "The Central TV has no credibility." Then, in the afternoon of June 6, when defendant Wang Yongfa was lecturing on political studies for classes of 38 and 39, he was asked by students to talk about the situation. He spread the rumor to students in those two classes that "the martial law troops in Beijing got into a fight with the students and citizens. Many died on both sides. The PLA suppressed the students and citizens. They used machine guns, tanks and armored cars to suppress groups of students and citizens." He added that Wang Dan was bayoneted to death by PLA men. He also said, "On Tiananmen Square, three college co-eds knelt before PLA men, imploring the latter not to shoot them. Yet the PLA men opened fire, killing two of them; the third was seriously hurt and was interviewed by a VOA reporter in the hospital." At the same time, he recited for the students some doggerel and made provocative statements. All this confused the students and was most pernicious.

The above-mentioned facts are attested to by the witnesses' testimony, by the written evidence and the recorded partial confessions of the defendant. They are sufficient for passing a judgement.

In the firm opinion of this sub-procuratorate, defendant Wang Yongfa has long neglected the remolding of his world outlook. He tuned in to enemy broadcasts during the counterrevolutionary rebellion and publicly spread sayings of incitement, causing confusion among teachers and students. His activities were of a serious nature. But the remarks defendant Wang Yongfa made during the quelling of the counterrevolutionary rebellion were mainly rumors he had heard, believed and spread. They constituted a serious political mistake. In accordance with Article 10 of the *Criminal Code of the People's Republic of China* and Section 1 of Article 11 and Article 204 of the *Code of Criminal Procedure of the People's Republic of China*, and after deliberations by the procuratorate committee of this sub-procuratorate, Wang Yongfa is not to be indicted and is hereby released.

Chief procurator: Li Shengqing
           [signature]

[Seal of the Lingling Sub-
Procuratorate of the Hunan
Province People's Procuratorate]
February 20, 1990

Certificate of Release
from Re-education Through Labor

This is to certify that:

Wang Yongfa, male, 39, of the No. 1 Middle School of Lanshan County, Hunan Province, was committed for re-education through labor on October 27, 1989.[46] Due to shortening of his term by exactly one month, he is being released from re-education through labor.

(Official seal of the Administration of
Re-education Through Labor, Xinkaipu,
Hunan Province)
February [?], 1992

Notes:

1. The holder of this certificate should go to the public security and food authorities of his domicile to register for residence and food rations.

2. (illegible)

Food to be supplied up to the end of February [?]: (illegible)

---

[46] This is incorrect. In fact, Wang was held in a detention center from the time of his initial arrest in October 1989 until February 20, 1990, when the procuracy formally decided not to prosecute him. He was only then - and quite in violation of the procuracy's decision, which also stated that he was "hereby released" - transferred to a labor re-education camp to serve out a 2½-year term of re-education. The document's mention of October 27, 1989 as the date of first committal for re-education is thus a cosmetic sleight-of-hand, albeit one which defers to the rule that time spent in pre-hearing detention should be deducted from the eventual length of sentence.

216

APPENDIX VIII.E

Case of Xie Changfa

People's Government of the City of Changsha
Administrative Committee on Re-education Through Labor

Decision on Re-education Through Labor

Chang/Re-ed/Labor (1990) No. 180

Xie Changfa, alias Fang Feiyu, male, 38, Han nationality, born in Pingtang Township, Wangcheng County, college educated, currently employed as a technician at the Changsha Steel Mill. Residence: No.501, the Huobashan Dormitory of the Refrigerated Warehouse for Foreign Trade of Hunan Province, the City of Changsha.

During the period of the disturbances at the end of spring and beginning of summer, 1989, Xie actively took part in those disturbances and engaged in counterrevolutionary propaganda and incitement activities. On June 4, Xie sneaked into the No.1 and No.4 Middle Schools of Liuyang County and made speeches to more than 100 students of those two schools. "I hope you students will actively participate in this movement and strive to become vanguards of democracy." he said. He added, "I have a mother and a loving wife and child. But I would not hesitate to give everything I have...for the revolution." Incited by Xie, some students wrote slogans and posters and planned to take to the streets the following day. On June 6, Xie wrote an "Appeal to All the Policemen and Fellow Citizens," and gave it to Fan Zhong, a leader of the Hunan Students Autonomous Federation, to be broadcast. Early in the morning of June 9, Xie made a speech in front of the provincial government compound. He proposed to those present to form a Citizen's Dare-to-Die Corps to "protect the students and the democratic movement..." He then took paper and pen from He Kede and called on those present to sign up. On that same day, Xie left Changsha for Liuyang, carrying with him ten copies of the reactionary journal, *Da Gong Bao*, [with the lead story] entitled "The bloody suppression continues in

Beijing; The number of dead and injured exceeds 10,000; The Public Indignant," and gave them to Jiang Shiruo, Tan Shaocheng and Wei Qiusheng, all township cadres. On June 10, Xie gave five copies of *Da Gong Bao* to Xiao Yu, Liu Jiangming, Deng Xihua and Liu Boming, all students of the No. 4 Middle School of Liuyang County. On June 11, he gave five copies of *Da Gong Bao* to Xun Chunling, Li Chunlan and Yao Zuoping and asked them to distribute the journal among their fellow students.

As described above, Xie Changfa travelled to and from Liuyang and Changsha, making speeches, writing reactionary articles and distributing reactionary journals during the disturbances. His activities constituted the crime of counterrevolutionary propaganda and incitement. In accordance with the *Provisional Regulations Governing Re-education Through Labor* transmitted by the State Council, it is hereby decided that Xie Changfa is to be taken in for re-education through labor for two years.

[Official Seal of the Administrative Committee on Re-education Through Labor, the City of Changsha]

March 23, 1990

Record of Search

December 20, 1990

Luo Haijiao, a member of the Sub Office of the Public Security Bureau of the City of Changsha, Hunan Province, with search warrant No.24 issued by the Public Security Bureau of the City of Changsha on December 9, 1989, and with Kong Songbo as witness, searched the body, residence and other relevant places of **Xie Changfa**, a resident in the local government of the Township of Guandu.

In the course of the search (give brief description of the search):

[BLANK SPACE]

The opinion of the party searched on the search was as follows:

[BLANK SPACE]

A copy of this search record (together with a list of confiscated items) has been issued to [BLANK SPACE] for his record.

The searched party: Xie Changfa (signed)
The witness: Kong Songbo (signed)
The searcher: Luo Haijiao (signed)

APPENDIX VIII.F

Case of Zhou Shuilong

[NB: In the following case, the defendant was unlawfully sentenced to re-education through labor by order of an office of the Public Security Bureau. According to official regulations, such sentences may only be imposed by so-called Labor Re-education Administrative Committees. (Asia Watch)][47]

Sub-Office of the Public Security Department
Guangzhou Railway Bureau

Decision on Re-education Through Labor
Chang/Rail/Public/Sub/RL (89)No. 16

Zhou Shuilong, male, 39, Han nationality, born in Hengshan County, Hunan Province, finished junior-middle school, currently employed as boilerman at Changsha North Station of the Changsha Railway Sub-Bureau

Residence: B4, Guangu Lane, Shuyuan Road, South District, the City of Changsha.

---

[47] The *Labor Re-education Administrative Committees* (LRACs) are supposed to be tripartite bodies comprising representatives of the Civil Affairs, Labor and Personnel, and Public Security ministries. Set up in the early 1980s, the ostensible purpose of the LRACs was to take away from the public security authorities the sole power to impose punishments of labor re-education, in order to reduce the latter's blatant misuse of this power. The reform failed, however, and public security officials have continued to impose labor re-education sentences entirely on their own authority. According to official press accounts, the LRACs meet only "once per year" and are "little more than old folks' homes".

Taken into custody for investigation by this Sub-Office on August 17, 1989 on charges of stirring up trouble and disturbing public order.

It has been ascertained that Zhou Shuilong violated the law, and the facts are as follows:

In mid-May 1989, he joined the Workers Autonomous Federation on the recommendation of He Zhaohui, vice-chairman of that illegal organization in Changsha. In late May, he became deputy leader of the Workers Autonomous Federation pickets, and received a card bearing the number "Changsha Workers Autonomous Federation Picket No. G0027." He assisted the illegal organization Hunan Students Autonomous Federation and served as picket for students staging a sit-down protest in the provincial government compound.

In the afternoon of May 24, the Hunan Students Autonomous Federation and the Workers Autonomous Federation organized an illegal demonstration. Zhou Shuilong served as a picket, carrying an iron rod about two feet long.

One morning toward the end of May, some members of the Hunan Students Autonomous Federation gave speeches at the Changsha Automobile Electrical Appliances Plant and clashed with the plant administration. Zhou Shuilong, holding a banner of the Autonomous Federation of Changsha Railway Workers, followed Zhou Yong, a leader of the Workers Autonomous Federation, and others, to give support to the members of the Hunan Students Autonomous Federation.

In the morning of June 4, Zhou Shuilong took part in blocking the crossroad at May First Road, disrupting railway and May First Road traffic.

On June 8, the Hunan Students Autonomous Federation and the Workers Autonomous Federation organized and convened a "memorial meeting" to honor the thugs killed during the suppression of the rebellion in Beijing. Zhou Shuilong was responsible for moving the wreaths from the provincial government compound to the memorial meeting held on the square in front of the Changsha Railway Station. He also served as a picket.

Between mid-May and early June, Zhou Shuilong, together with members of the Hunan Students Autonomous Federation, posted hundreds of illegal posters, "proclaiming strikes" and "appealing to compatriots," at the Changsha Cigarette Factory, the meatpacking plant, the aluminum plant, the Hunan Switchgear Factory, the machine tool plant and on the main thoroughfares in the South District of Changsha.

What was still more serious was that on June 7, Zhou Shuilong, together with Zhang Zhihui and others from the Jingwanzi team of Red Star Village of Yuhuating Township on the outskirts of Changsha, went to post "strike notices" at the Changsha Cigarette Factory. They clashed with the economic police of the factory who had tried to stop them. Zhou falsely accused the policemen of beating up people, and declared he would call in reinforcements to block the factory entrance. Early the following morning, Zhang Xudong, Commander-in-Chief of the Workers Autonomous Federation, sent people to block the gate of the Changsha Cigarette Factory. Zhou Shuilong arrived there later and incited the people gathered there, causing a day-long work stoppage which resulted in losses to the tune of 1,231,031.38 *yuan*.

In accordance with Section 4 of Article 10 of the *Provisional Regulations Governing Re-education Through Labor* of the Ministry of Public Security, transmitted by the State Council on January 21, 1982, it is decided that Zhou Shuilong is to be re-educated through labor for two years, beginning on August 17, 1989 and ending August 16, 1991.

(Official seal of the sub-office of the Public Security Department of Guangshou Railway Bureau)

December 19, 1989

APPENDIX IX

Prison Songs by Zhang Jingsheng

It's Not that I Want to Leave You

孤 独 的 我 一 人 不 知 走 向 走 向 何
As solitary and lonely I stare at an empty future,

方 漫 长 的 人 生 道 路 何 处 是 好
The road of life stretching endlessly ahead, no refuge in

宿 我 怀 着 一 颗 破 碎 的 心 站 在 了 十 字
sight, I hold my shattered heart at a crossroads.

路

秋 天 的 沙 啊 遮 住 了 我 的 双 眼
As autumn sandbirds fill the sky and obscure the horizon,

少 年 的 壮 志 失 去 了 我 哭 断 了
I shed bitter tears for the lost proud confidence of my

肠 得 不 到 亲 人 的 温 暖 我 离 开 了 故
youth, The loving warmth of family and home is now a thing of the

224

past, And all roads lead only to my old familiar prison cell.

In lonely anguish, I wander lost at this bleak crossroads,

The sun's evening rays lighting up the land all around,

For my heart is filled only with cold and emptiness,

And an endless pitch- dark

night.

Song of Changqiao Prison

長橋之歌

年青的我呀 被抓进了牢房 親人呀親
When I was young, I was thrown into prison, But don't grieve for

人 你不要悲 伤 如今的 社 会
me, my dearest one. For society's just that

就 是 这 样 有痛苦 有 烦惱
way nowadays, Nothing but pain and

还 有 悲 伤
trouble and sadness.

我站 在牢房 里手捧着三兩 米 还有 一 碗
I stand here in my cell, a ball of rice in my hand, and a bowl of

当 43 湯 这就是 長橋 的生 活
want-to-go-home soup. That's all there is to life in Chang qiao,

情切切 泪汪 汪 只当下悔 恨
An aching heart and tears of remorse.

天空的小 鸟在 自由地飞 翔 飞回了我
Little bird flying so high in the sky, You spiral

那 美丽的家 乡 带去我 深情
so gaily and free. Carry my thoughts on

亲切的问 候 祝福我爹 娘
back to my hometown, And bring health and good luck

身体健 康
to my loved ones.

LIST OF 142 PRISONS, LABOR CAMPS, RE-EDUCATION CENTERS AND JAILS IN HUNAN PROVINCE

INTERNAL NAME [+ NOS. HELD]	EXTERNAL NAME [+ PRODUCTS]	LOCATION [+ SOURCE REFS.]

A. PRISONS

1. 省第一监狱
YUANJIANG PRISON
(Provincial No.1)
[>6000]

[?]
[Automobile parts]

沅江市南咀新沅路
YuanJiang City,
Nanzui, Xinyuan Road
[B125/C79/D131]
Zip: 413104

2. 省第二监狱
HENGYANG PRISON
(Provincial No.2)
[>7000]

湖南重型汽车制造厂
Hunan Heavy Motor
Vehicle Factory
[Automobiles]

衡阳市同心路
Hengyang City,
Tongxin Road
[A313/B300/E140]
Tel: 23161

3. 省第三监狱
LINGLING PRISON
(Provincial No.3)
[4000]

省劳动汽车配件厂
Provincial Laodong
Vehicle Parts Factory
[Automobile parts]

零陵地区永州市
何家坪 Lingling
Prefecture, Yongzhou
City, HeJiaping
[A604/B413] Tel: 2692
Zip: 425000

KEY:
"A" = Hunan Province Telephone Directory 〈湖南省电话号簿〉, Hunan 1990
"B" = Hunan Province Zipcode Manual 〈湖南省邮政编码实用手册〉, Changsha 1990
"C" = Atlas of Hunan Province 〈湖南省地图册〉, Hunan 1990
"D" = Zipcode Atlas of China 〈中国邮政编码图集〉, Harbin 1989
"E" = China Urban Zipcode Atlas 〈中国城市邮政编码地图集〉, Harbin 1991

4. 省第四监狱
HUAIHUA PRISON
(Provincial No.4)
[>2000]

[?]

怀化市
Huaihua City

5. 省第五监狱
CHENZHOU PRISON
(Provincial No.5)
[4000]

[?]
Prison has "office"
listed at Wulidui,
Yanquan Road, Chenzhou
Tel: 22379 Zip: 423000

郴州地区
Chenzhou Prefecture
[A364/B383/E142]
[See also Item 47, below]

6. 省第六监狱
LONGXI PRISON
(Provincial No.6)
[>2000]

新邵县大理石加工厂
Xinshao Marble Factory
[Marble products]

邵阳市新邵县
Shaoyang Municipality,
Xinshao County
[B372/C88]

7. 长沙监狱
CHANGSHA PRISON
[3000: women]

a) 新生印刷被服厂
New Life Cotton Quilt
Printing Factory
b) 长沙新民工艺厂
Changsha Xinmin Handi-
crafts Factory

长沙市香樟路
Changsha Municipality,
Xiangzhang Road
[A4/C12/E130]
Tel: 31733

8. 桃源监狱
TAOYUAN PRISON

[?]

常德市桃源县
Changde Municipality,
Taoyuan County
[A423] Tel: 2964

B. LABOR-REFORM CAMPS

9. 建新劳改农场
JIANXIN LABOR-REFORM
FARM
[>20,000]

建新农场 Jianxin Farm.
(Sales arm is Jianxin
Trading Co. [建新贸易
公司], Tel: 24674. Farm
office at Mahao [马壕],
Yueyang, Tel: 22299.)
[Agricultural products]

岳阳市毛斯铺
Yueyang Municipality,
Maosi Pu
[A568/B151/C21+23]
Tel: 23708, 23847
Zip: 414000

10. 涔澹劳改农场 CENDAN LABOR-REFORM FARM [>20,000]	涔澹农场 Cendan Farm [Agricultural products]	津市竹田湖 Jin Municipality, south of Zhutian Lake [A439/C66] Tel: 2223, 3254, 2794
11. 临湘劳改农场 LINXIANG LABOR-REFORM FARM [<10,000]	临湘农场 Linxiang Farm [Agricultural products]	岳阳市临湘县 Yueyang Municipality, Linxiang County
12. 华容劳改农场 HUARONG LABOR-REFORM FARM [>5000]	华容农场 Huarong Farm [Agricultural products]	岳阳市华容县 Yueyang Municipality, Huarong County
13. 白泥湖劳改农场 BAINIHI LABOR-REFORM FARM	省白泥湖园艺场 Provincial Bainihu horticultural Centre	湘阴县白泥湖 Xiangyin County, Bainihu [A579/C25] Tel: 938
14. 罗家洲劳改农场 LUOJIAZHOU LABOR- REFORM FARM [1000]	罗家洲农场 LuoJiazhou Farm [Vegetables]	长沙市 Changsha City (suburbs) [B44]
15. 咪江劳改茶场 MIJIANG LABOR-REFORM TEA FARM	咪江茶场 MiJiang Tea Farm [Tea]	茶陵县咪晒坪 Chaling County, Mishaiping [A282/C34] Tel: 2655-6, 2667, 2678
16. 省第三劳改支队 PROVINCIAL NO.3 LABOR- REFORM DETACHMENT [>5000]	省新生煤矿 Provincial New Life Coal Mine [Coal]	耒阳市伍家村 Leiyang Municipality, MuJia Village [A337-8/B324/C49] Tel: 2101, 2363

17. 湘潭劳改大队
XIANGTAN LABOR-REFORM
BRIGADE (part of Prov-
incial No.4 or 6 Labor-
Reform Detachment)
[3000]

[?]
[Manganese mining]
(Has transportation
station at Jianshe
Bei Lu. Tel: 21896

湘潭市中路铺
Xiangtan Municipality,
Zhonglu Pu
[A195]
Tel: 21896 [转]

18. 常德市劳改支队
CHANGDE LABOR-REFORM
DETACHMENT (Provincial
No.4 or 6)
[5000]

湖南柴油机厂
Hunan Diesel Engine
Factory
[Diesel engines]

常德市樟木桥
Changde Municipality,
Zhangmuqiao
[A485/B186/C65]
Tel: 22568 Zip: 415127

19. 常德市劳劲管教支队
CHANGDE MUNICIPAL LABOR-
DISCIPLINARY TEAM

[?]

常德市万金障
Changde Municipality,
WanJinzhang

20. 怀化地区第一劳改队
HUAIHUA PREFECTURE
NO.1 LABOR-REFORM TEAM
(part of Provincial
No.8 Labor-Reform
Detachment) [>2000]

怀化毛织厂 [?]
Huaihua Woolen Mill
[Clothing]

怀化地区锦屏
Huaihua Prefecture,
Jinping
[A628]
Tel: 22988

21. 省第九劳改支队
PROVINCIAL NO.9
LABOR-REFORM
DETACHMENT
[>3000]

a) 省长沙火柴厂
Changsha Match Factory
b) 省长沙汽车摩托车修配厂
Changsha Car and Motor-
Cycle Repair Plant

长沙市左家塘赤岗北路
Changsha Municipality,
ZuoJiatang, Chigang N. Rd.
[A123]
Tel: 34151, 34161, 33354

22. 衡山劳改支队
HENGSHAN LABOR-REFORM
DETACHMENT
[>3000]

衡山钨矿
Hengshan Tungsten Mine
[Tungsten wire]

衡阳市衡山县
Hengyang Municipality,
Hengshan County

23. 郴州劳改支队
CHENZHOU LABOR-REFORM
DETACHMENT

郴州市郴县
Chenzhou Municipality,
Chen County

231

24. 零陵劳改支队
LINGLING LABOR-REFORM
DETACHMENT
[>8000]

东安农场
Dong'an Farm
[Agricultural products]

零陵地区东安县
Lingling Prefecture,
Dong'an County

25. 邵阳劳改支队
SHAOYANG LABOR-REFORM
DETACHMENT

湖南省群力煤矿
Hunan Province Qunli
Coal Mine
[Coal]

邵东县砂石乡
Shaoyang Municipality,
Shaodong County, Shashi
[A549/C89]]
Tel: 830, 853

26. 坪塘劳改支队
PINGTANG LABOR-REFORM
DETACHMENT
[3000]

长沙市水泥厂
Changsha Cement Factory
[Cement]

望城县坪塘镇
Wangcheng County,
Pingtang Town
[B56/C13]
Tel: 810326   Zip: 410208

27. 暮云劳改队
MUYUN LABOR-REFORM
TEAM
[>1000]

暮云农场
Muyun Farm
[Agricultural products]

长沙市
Changsha Municipality
[C13]

28. 虹桥劳改队
HONGQIAO LABOR-REFORM
TEAM

[?]

岳阳市平江县虹桥乡
Yueyang Municipality,
PingJiang County,
Hongqiao Township [C28]

29. [?]

醴陵煤矿
Liling Coal Mine
[Coal]

醴陵市
Liling Municipality

30. [?]

矿山新生锑矿
Kuang Shan Antimony
Mine *(New Life)*
[Antimony]

冷水江市矿山
LengshuiJiang
Municipality, Kuang Shan
[B249/C85] Zip: 417501

C. LABOR RE-EDUCATION CENTERS

31. 长沙妇教所
CHANGSHA WOMEN'S
RE-EDUCATION CENTER
[>1000]

湖南绸厂 Hunan Silk
Factory. (Sales: Zhen
Xiang Trading Services
[振湘贸易服务部] Tel:
44478) [Silk products]

长沙市东风路
Changsha Municipality,
Dongfeng Road
[A118/E138]
Tel: 24011, 26236, 82536

32. 株洲妇教所
ZHUZHOU WOMEN'S
RE-EDUCATION CENTER
[>1000]

[?]

株洲市
Zhuzhou Municipality

33. 长沙新开铺劳教所
CHANGSHA XINKAIPU
LABOR RE-EDUCATION
CENTER
[5000]

湖南开关厂
Hunan Switch Factory
[Electrical switches]

长沙市新开铺路
Changsha Municipality,
Xinkaipu Road
[A105/B24/C12/E138]
Tel: 32411, 32433, 52521

34. 渌口劳教所
LUKOU LABOR RE-
EDUCATION CENTER
[5000]

[?]
[Light industrial
goods]

株洲县渌口镇
Zhouzhou County, Lukou
Town

35. 益阳劳教所
YIYANG DISTRICT LABOR
RE-EDUCATION CENTER
[4000]

[?]
[Machinery]

益阳地区长春乡
Yiyang Municipality,
Changchun Township
[A450/C77]
Tel: 22232

36. 冷水江劳教所
LENGSHUIJIANG LABOR
RE-EDUCATION CENTER
[>5000]

[?]

冷水江市
Lengshuijiang Municipality
(See also Item 30, above)
[C85]

233

37. 衡山劳教所 　　[?]　　　　　　　衡山县
HENGSHAN LABOR RE-　　　　　　　　Hengshan County
EDUCATION CENTER
[5000]

38. 长桥园艺场劳教所　长桥园艺场　　　长沙市区长桥
CHANGQIAO HORTICULTURAL　Changqiao Horticultural　Changsha City, Changqiao
FARM LABOR RE-EDUCATION　Farm　　　　　　[A151/C13]
CENTER　　　　　　　　[Vegetables and plants]　Tel: 23060
[<1000]

39. 怀化地区第一劳教所　[?]　　　　　　怀化地区西冲村
HUAIHUA DISTRICT NO.1　　　　　　　　Huaihua Prefecture,
LABOR RE-EDUCATION　　　　　　　　Xichong Village
CENTER　　　　　　　　　　　　　[A628] Tel: 23158

40. 湘潭市劳教所　　[?]　　　　　　　湘潭市九华乡
XIANGTAN MUNICIPAL　(Located near Item 27,　Xiangtan Municipality,
LABOR RE-EDUCATION　above.)　　　　　Jiuhua Township
CENTER　　　　　　　　　　　　　[A195/C40] Tel: 22421

41. 娄底劳教所　　[?]　　　　　　　娄底地区关家脑
LOUDI LABOR RE-EDUCATION　　　　　　Loudi Prefecture,
CENTER　　　　　　　　　　　　　GuanJia'nao
　　　　　　　　　　　　　　　　[A495] Tel: 2257

42. 邵阳司法局劳教所　[?]　　　　　　邵阳市资江桥下
SHAOYANG JUSTICE BUREAU　　　　　　Shaoyang Municipality,
LABOR RE-EDUCATION　　　　　　　　ZiJiang Qiaoxia
CENTER　　　　　　　　　　　　　[A524/C86] Tel: 2452

43. 邵阳司法局劳教队　[?]　　　　　　邵阳市白田大队
SHAOYANG JUSTICE BUREAU　　　　　　Shaoyang Municipality,
LABOR RE-EDUCATION TEAM　　　　　　Baitian Brigade
　　　　　　　　　　　　　　　　[A524] Tel: 2306

234

44. 零陵地区劳教所　　[?]

LINGLING DISTRICT LABOR
RE-EDUCATION CENTER

零陵地区长茅坪

Lingling Prefecture,
Changmaoping
[A601] Tel: 3224

45. 常德市劳教所　　[?]

CHANGDE MUNICIPAL LABOR
RE-EDUCATION CENTER

常德市南湖坪

Changde Municipality,
Nanhuping
[A398] Tel: 23957, 24221

46. 白马垅劳教所　　[?]

BAIMALONG LABOR
RE-EDUCATION CENTER

[Electric stoves
and furnaces]

[?]

D. JUVENILE DETENTION CENTERS

47. 湖南省少年犯管教所

HUMAN PROVINCE JUVENILE
OFFENDERS DISCIPLINARY
CENTER
[5000]

[Matches and other
handicraft products]

郴州市燕泉路

Chenxhou Municipality,
Yanquan Road
[A348/B373]
Tel: 25717

48. 省第二少年犯管教所

PROVINCIAL NO.2 JUVENILE
OFFENDERS DISCIPLINARY
CENTER
[3000]

[Matches, packaging]

长沙市望城坡

Changsha Municipality,
Wangchengpo
[A4]
Tel: 83313

E. LOCAL JAILS AND DETENTION CENTERS

CHANGSHA

49. 长沙市第一看守所
Changsha Municipal No.1 Jail

长沙市左家塘赤岗北路 [A15]
Changsha City, Chigang North Rd.
Tel: 34327 (Pre-trial investigations)
Tel: 35714 (Reception Center)

50. 长沙市第二看守所
Changsha Municipal No.2 Jail

长沙市螺丝塘 [D48]
Changsha City, Luositang

51. 长沙市长桥收容审查所 [FN†]
Changqiao Shelter and Investigation
Center

长沙县长桥 [A15]
Changsha County, Changqiao
Tel: 48954, 48626, 48941

52. 长沙市郊区拘留所
Changsha Suburban Detention Center

长沙市郊区人民路 [A15]
Changsha (suburbs), People's Rd.
Tel: 35963

53. 浏阳县看守所
Liuyang County Jail

浏阳县百宜坑 [A183]
Liuyang County, Baiyikeng

54. 浏阳县治安拘留所
Liuyang County Public-Order
Detention Center

浏阳县唐家洲 [A183]
Liuyang County, TangJiashou

XIANGTAN

55. 湘潭市拘留所
Xiangtan Municipal Detention Center

湘潭市 [A195]
Xiangtan City

56. 湘潭市审查站
Xiangtan Municipal Investigation
Station

湘潭市三角坪 [A195]
Xiangtan City, SanJiaoping

236

57. 株洲市收审队
Zhuzhou Shelter and Investigation Team

株洲市 [A228]
Zhuzhou City   Tel: 21741

58. 株洲市看守所
Zhuzhou Municipal Jail

株洲市 [A228]
Zhuzhou City

59. 株洲市拘留所
Zhuzhou Municipal Detention Center

株洲市 [A228]
Zhuzhou City

60. 株洲县看守所
Zhuzhou County Jail

株洲县 [A260]
Zhuzhou County

61. 株洲县拘留所
Zhuzhou County Detention Center

株洲县 [A260]
Zhuzhou County

62. 醴陵市看守所
Liling Municipal Jail

醴陵市五华庙 [A265]
Liling Municipality, Wuhua Temple

63. 攸县看守所
You County Jail

株洲市攸县 [A276]
Zhuzhou Municipality, You County

64. 茶陵县看守所
Chaling County Jail

株洲市茶陵县潘冲 [A280]
Zhuzhou Municipality, Chaling County,
Panchong

65. 茶陵县行政拘留所
Chaling County Administrative
Detention Center

株洲市茶陵县 [A280]
Zhuzhou Municipality, Chaling County

66. 酃县看守所
Ling County Jail

株洲市酃县 [A285]
Zhuzhou Municipality, Ling County

237

67. 衡阳市看守所
Hengyang Municipal Jail

衡阳市王家湾 [A292]
Hengyang Municipality, WangJiawan

68. 衡阳市白沙洲拘留所
Baishazhou Detention Center

衡阳市白沙洲 [A292]
Hengyang Municipality, Baishazhou

69. 衡阳市收审所
Hengyang Shelter and Investigation
Center

衡阳市白沙洲 [A292]
Hengyang Municipality, Baishazhou
Tel: 22943

70. 衡阳县看守所
Hengyang County Jail

衡阳县东阳乡 [A294]
Hengyang County, Dongyang Township

71. 衡阳县行政拘留所
Hengyang County Administrative
Detention Center

衡阳市衡阳县 [A328]
Hengyang Municipality, Hengyang County

72. 衡山县看守所
Hengshan County Jail

衡阳市衡山县南郊 [A330]
Hengshan County, NanJiao

73. 衡山县拘留所
Hengshan County Detention Center

衡阳市衡山县螺头山水库 [A330]
Hengshan County, Luotoushan Reservoir

74. 南岳区看守所
Nanyue District Jail

衡阳市南岳区长衡路 [A333]
Hengyang Municipality, Nanyue District,
Changheng Road

75. 耒阳市看守所
Leiyang Municipal Jail

耒阳市 [A335]
Leiyang Municipality

76. 耒阳市行政拘留所
Leiyang Administrative Detention
Center

耒阳市 [A335]
Leiyang Municipality

77. 祁东县看守所
Qidong County Jail

衡阳市祁东县石门 [A338]
Hengyang City, Qidong County, Shimen

238

78. 衡东县看守所
Hengdong County Jail

衡阳市衡东县交通东路 [A342]
Hengdong County, Jiaotong East Road

79. 郴州市收审站
Chenzhou Shelter and Investigation
Station

郴州市人民东路 [A348]
Chenzhou Municipality, People's East Rd.
Tel: 23848

80. 郴州市治安拘留所
Chenzhou Public-Order Detention Center

郴州市 [A348]
Chenzhou Municipality

81. 郴州市看守所
Chenzhou Municipal Jail

郴州市 [A348]
Chenzhou Municipality

82. 桂东县看守所
Guidong County Jail

郴州地区桂东县 [A378]
Chenzhou Prefecture, Guidong County

83. 嘉禾县看守所
Jiahe County Jail

郴州地区嘉禾县东头桥 [A372]
Chenzhou Prefecture, Jiahe County,
Dongtouqiao

84. 资兴市看守所
Zixing Municipal Jail

郴州地区资兴市邝家冲 [A375]
Chenzhou Prefecture, Zixing
Municipality, KuangJiaohong

85. 宜章县收容所
Yizhang County Shelter Center

郴州地区宜章县 [A381]
Chenzhou Prefecture, Yizhang County

86. 宜章县看守所
Yizhang County Jail

郴州地区宜章县 [A381]
Chenzhou Prefecture, Yizhang County

87. 常德市收容审查站
Changde Municipal Shelter and

常德市万金障 [A389]
Changde Municipality, WanJinzhang

239

Investigation Center   Tel: 24369

88. 武陵区拘役所   常德市武陵区滨湖东路 [A389]
Wuling District Detention and   Changde Municipality, Wuling District,
Labor Center   Binhu East Road

89. 武陵区拘留所   常德市武陵区 [A389]
Wuling District Detention Center   Changde Municipality, Wuling District

90. 常德市看守所   常德市东堤 [A390]
Changde Municipal Jail   Changde Municipality, Dongdi

91. 鼎城区看守所   常德市武陵镇 [A390]
Dingcheng District Jail   Changde Municipality, Wuling Town

92. 桃源县看守所   常德市桃源县千梯山 [A423]
Taoyuan County Jail   Changde Municipality, Taoyuan County,
                                             Qianti Shan

93. 桃源县拘留所   常德市桃源县千梯山 [A423]
Taoyuan County Detention Center   Changde Municipality, Taoyuan County,
                                             Qianti Shan

94. 澧县看守所   常德市澧县 [A442]
Li County Jail   Changde Municipality, Li County

95. 澧县拘留所   常德市澧县 [A442]
Li County Detention Center   Changde Municipality, Li County

YIYANG

96. 益阳县看守所   益阳地区益阳县 [A452]
Yiyang County Jail   Yiyang Prefecture, Yiyang County

97. 桃江县看守所   益阳地区桃江县桃花东路 [A474]
TaoJiang County Jail   Yiyang Prefecture, TaoJiang County,
                                             Taohua East Road

98. 娄底地区收审所
Loudi Shelter and Investigation Center

娄底地区豹兰山 [A495]
Loudi Prefecture, Baolan Shan
Tel: 3629

99. 娄底地区看守所
Loudi Prefectural Jail

娄底地区关家脑 [A495]
Loudi Prefecture, GuanJia'nao

100. 娄底地区拘留所
Loudi Prefectural Detention Center

娄底地区关家脑 [A495]
Loudi Prefecture, GuanJia'nao

101. 涟源市看守所
Lianyuan Municipal Jail

娄底地区涟源市 [A502]
Loudi Prefecture, Lianyuan Municipality

102. 冷水江市治安拘留所
LengshuiJiang Municipal Public-
Order Jail

娄底地区冷水江市 [A507]
Loudi Prefecture, LengshuiJiang Munic.

103. 冷水江市看守所
LengshuiJiang Municipal Jail

娄底地区冷水江市中连乡诚意村 [A507]
LengshuiJiang Municipality, Zhenglian
Township, Chengyi Village

104. 新化县拘留所
Xinhua County Detention Center

冷水江市新化县枫林乡 [A513]
LengshuiJiang Municipality, Xinhua
County, Fenglin Township

105. 新化县看守所
Xinhua County Jail

冷水江市新化县上渡乡 [A513]
LengshuiJiang Municipality, Xinhua
County, Shangdu Township

106. 邵阳市看守所
Shaoyang Municipal Jail

邵阳市戴家坪 [A523]
Shaoyang Municipality, DaiJiaping

107. 邵阳市收审所
Shaoyang Municipal Shelter and
Investigation Center

邵阳市三里桥 [A523]
Shaoyang Municipality, Sanliqiao
Tel: 2797

108. 洞口县拘留所
Dongkou County Detention Center

邵阳市洞口县 [A543]
Shaoyang Municipality, Dongkou County

109. 城步县拘留所
Chengbu County Detention Center

邵阳市城步苗族自治县新田路 [A545]
Shaoyang Municipality, Chengbu Miao
Autonomous County, Xintian Road

YUEYANG

110. 岳阳市收审一所
Yueyang Municipal No.1 Shelter
and Investigation Center

岳阳市花板桥 [A553]
Yueyang Municipality, Huabanqiao
Tel: 24235

111. 岳阳市收审二所
Yueyang Municipal No.2 Shelter
and Investigation Center

岳阳市湖滨 [A553]
Yueyang Municipality, Hubin
Tel: 24530

112. 岳阳市看守所
Yueyang Municipal Jail

岳阳市岳城 [A553]
Yueyang Municipality, Yuecheng

113. 岳阳市治安拘留所
Yueyang Municipal Public-Order
Detention Center

岳阳市 [A553]
Yueyang Municipality

114. 汨罗市行政拘留所
Miluo Municipal Administrative
Detention Center

汨罗市 [A570]
Miluo Municipality

115. 平江县看守所
PingJiang County Jail

岳阳市平江县 [A589]
Yueyang Municipality, PingJiang County

116. 岳阳县看守所
Yueyang County Jail

岳阳市岳阳县 [A591]
Yueyang Municipality, Yueyang County

117. 临湘县治安拘留所
Linxiang County Administrative
Detention Center

岳阳市临湘县南正街 [A593]
Yueyang Municipality, Linxiang County,
Nanzheng Street

LINGLING

118. 永州市拘留所
Yongzhou Municipal Detention Center

零陵地区永州市太平路 [A601]
Lingling Prefecture, Yongzhou
Municipality, Taiping Road

119. 永州市看守所
Yongzhou Municipal Jail

永州市麻元村 [A601]
Yongzhou Municipality, Mayuan Village

120. 祁阳县看守所
Qiyang County Jail

零陵地区祁阳县交山村 [A609]
Lingling Prefecture, Qiyang County,
Jiaoshan Village

121. 祁阳县行政拘留所
Qiyang County Administrative
Detention Center

零陵地区祁阳县 [A609]
Lingling Prefecture, Qiyang County

122. 东安县看守所
Dong'an County Jail

零陵地区东安县 [A611]
Lingling Prefecture, Dong'an County

123. 东安县拘役所
Dong'an County Detention and Labor
Center

零陵地区东安县 [A611]
Lingling Prefecture, Dong'an County

124. 双牌县看守所
Shuangpai County Jail

零陵地区双牌县迎宾路 [A614]
Lingling Prefecture, Shuangpai County,
Yingbin Road

125. 蓝山县看守所
Lanshan County Jail

零陵地区蓝山县环城路 [A619]
Lingling Prefecture, Lanshan County,
Huancheng Road

243

126. 新田县看守所 零陵地区新田县 [A621]
Xintian County Jail Lingling Prefecture, Xintian County

HUAIHUA

127. 怀化地区收审所 怀化市 [A628]
Huaihua Prefecture Shelter and Huaihua Municipality
Investigation Center Tel: 22715

128. 怀化市行政拘留所 怀化市 [A628]
Huaihua Municipal Administrative Huaihua Municipality
Detention Center

129. 黔阳县看守所 怀化地区黔阳县白虎脑 [A642]
Qianyang County Jail Huaihua Prefecture, Qianyang County,
Baihunao

130. 大庸市看守所 大庸市凤湾 [A655]
Dayong Municipal Jail Dayong Municipality, Fengwan

131. 桑植县看守所 大庸市桑植县尚家坪 [A660]
Sangzhi County Jail Dayong Municipality, Sangzhi County,
ShangJiaping

132. 桑植县拘留所 大庸市桑植县尚家坪 [A660]
Sangzhi County Detention Center Sangzhi County, ShangJiaping

133. 慈利县看守所 大庸市慈利县打鼓台 [A663]
Cili County Jail Dayong Municipality, Cili County,
Dagutai

134. 慈利县拘留所 大庸市慈利县打鼓台 [A663]
Cili County Detention Center Cili County, Dagutai

244

XIANGXI

135. 湘西自治州收审所
Xiangxi Autonomous Prefecture
Shelter and Investigation Center

湘西土家族苗族自治州吉首市 [A673]
Xiangxi TuJia and Miao Autonomous
Prefecture, Jishou Municipality
Tel: 3345

136. 湘西自治州看守所
Xiangxi Autonomous Prefecture Jail

吉首市 [A673]
Jishou Municipality

137. 湘西自治州行政拘留所
Xiangxi Autonomous Prefecture
Administrative Detention Center

吉首市光明路 [A673]
Jishou Municipality, Guangming Road

138. 保靖县看守所
BaoJing County Jail

湘西土家族苗族自治州保靖县 [A684]
Xiangxi TuJia and Miao Autonomous
Prefecture, BaoJing County

139. 保靖县拘留所
BaoJing County Detention Center

保靖县 [A684]
BaoJing County

140. 永顺县拘留所
Yongshun County Detention Center

湘西土家族苗族自治州永顺县 [A686]
Xiangxi TuJia and Miao Autonomous
Prefecture, Yongshun County

141. 龙山县看守所
Longshan County Jail

湘西土家族苗族自治州龙山县 [A690]
Xiangxi TuJia and Miao Autonomous
Prefecture, Longshan County

142. 古丈县看守所
Guzhang County Jail

湘西土家族苗族自治州古丈县柑子坪 [A693]
Xiangxi TuJia and Miao Autonomous
Prefecture, Guzhang County, Ganziping

APPENDIX XI

MAPS

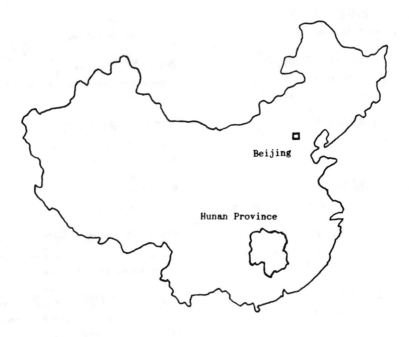

Beijing

Hunan Province

CHINA

247

CHANGSHA CITY

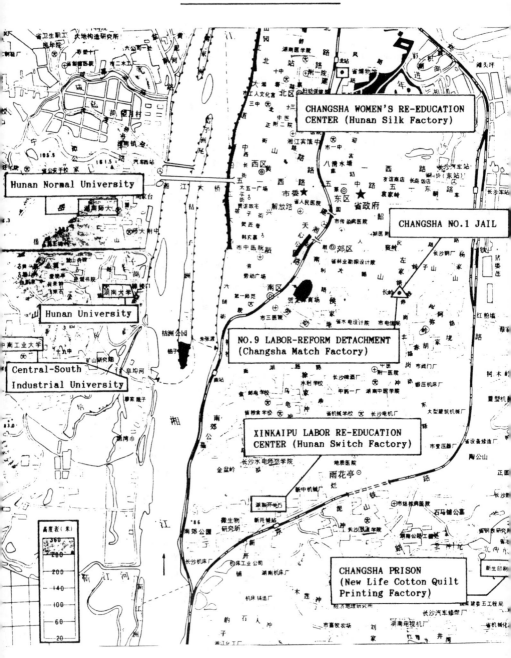

CHANGSHA WOMEN'S RE-EDUCATION CENTER (Hunan Silk Factory)

Hunan Normal University

CHANGSHA NO.1 JAIL

Hunan University

NO.9 LABOR-REFORM DETACHMENT (Changsha Match Factory)

Central-South Industrial University

XINKAIPU LABOR RE-EDUCATION CENTER (Hunan Switch Factory)

CHANGSHA PRISON (New Life Cotton Quilt Printing Factory)

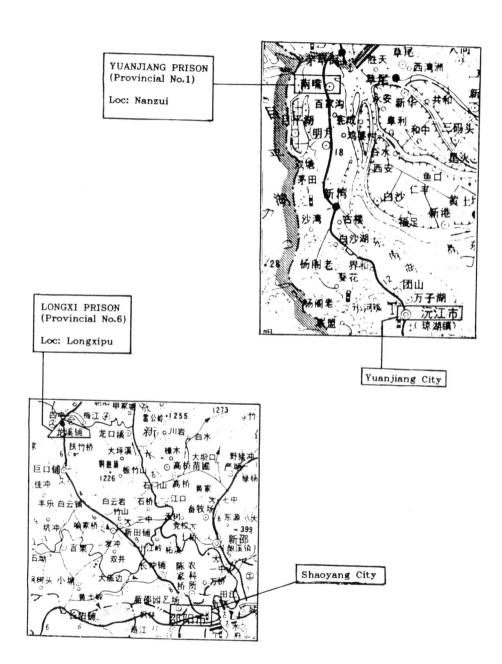

YUANJIANG PRISON
(Provincial No.1)

Loc: Nanzui

LONGXI PRISON
(Provincial No.6)

Loc: Longxipu

Yuanjiang City

Shaoyang City

249

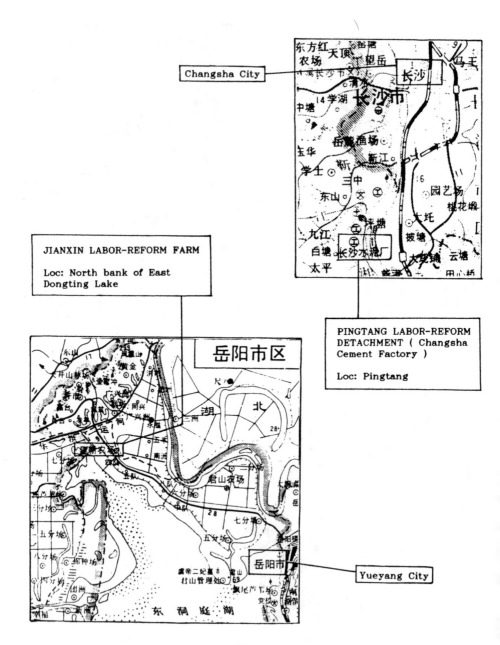

Changsha City

东方红农场 天顶 望岳 长沙 马王
万寿长沙市 长沙市 青
14学湖
中塘
岳麓师场
玉华
学士 靳江 新江
三中 6
东山 园艺场
桃花嫁
九江 平塘 大圻
白塘 长沙水泥厂 披塘
太平 大兒铺 云塘
田心桥

JIANXIN LABOR-REFORM FARM

Loc: North bank of East
Dongting Lake

PINGTANG LABOR-REFORM
DETACHMENT (Changsha
Cement Factory)

Loc: Pingtang

岳阳市区

东山 17
凤凰山
镀金
天井山林场 中 湖
同兴 北
运 三洲 湖
建新农场 28
七分场 新湖
君山农场
六分场
岳
28
七分场
五分场
五分场
八分场 育种场
树洲 虞帝二妃墓古 君
君山管理处 69
岳阳市
八分场 Yueyang City
华洲
东 洞 庭 湖

250

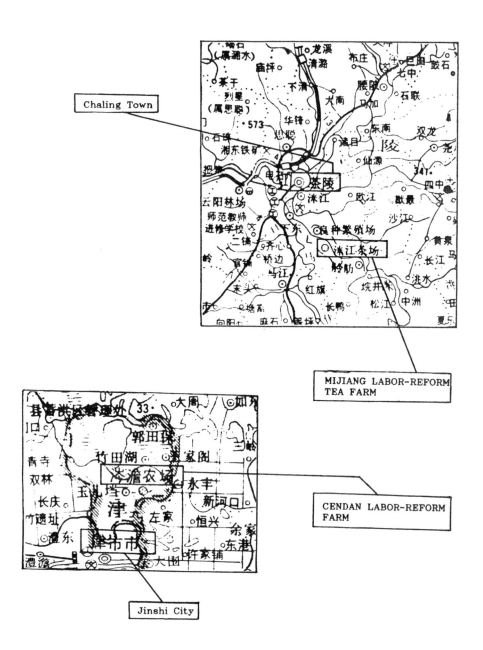

Chaling Town

MIJIANG LABOR-REFORM
TEA FARM

CENDAN LABOR-REFORM
FARM

Jinshi City

251

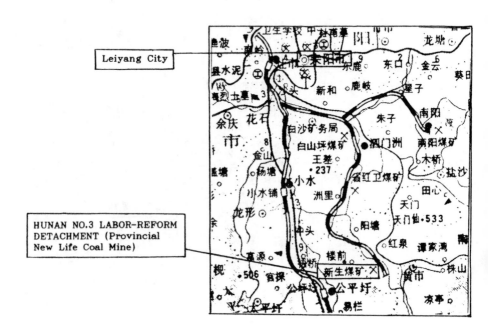

Leiyang City

HUNAN NO.3 LABOR–REFORM
DETACHMENT (Provincial
New Life Coal Mine)

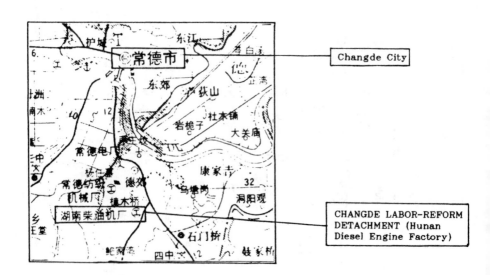

Changde City

CHANGDE LABOR–REFORM
DETACHMENT (Hunan
Diesel Engine Factory)

252

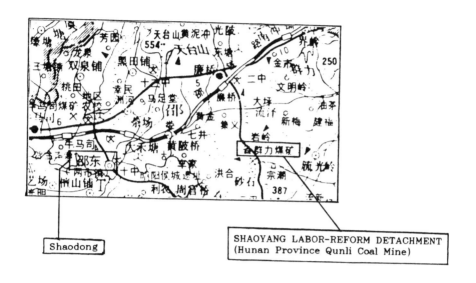

Shaodong

SHAOYANG LABOR-REFORM DETACHMENT
(Hunan Province Qunli Coal Mine)

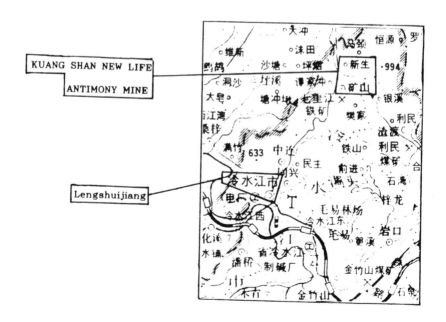

KUANG SHAN NEW LIFE
ANTIMONY MINE

Lengshuijiang

253

Index